CREEK COUNTRY SAGA
Book Six

Finding Pretty Wolf

Drawn by the Frost Moon

APRIL W GARDNER

BigSpringPress

Drawn by the Frost Moon: Finding Pretty Wolf
©2020 by April W Gardner

Cover design: Roseanna White Designs and Michelle Massaro
Cover Model: Mariah Henry
Big Spring Press logo: Karen Gardner

Scripture quotations taken from the King James Version.

All rights reserved. No part of this book may be reproduced or transmitted in any form or by any means, electronic or mechanical, including photocopying, recording, or by an information storage and retrieval system—except by a reviewer who may quote brief passages in a review to be printed in a magazine, newspaper, or on the Web—without permission in writing from the publisher.

Disclaimer: This work of fiction is the product of the author's imagination and was written for entertainment purposes. In no way is it meant to accurately portray any actual figures' actions or characters.

Library of Congress Control Number: 2020923847
ISBN-13: 978-1-945831-21-8

Published by Big Spring Press
San Antonio, Texas

Printed in the United States of America.

To the Shepherd of my soul.
For the still waters He faithfully leads me to.

The Lord is my shepherd; I shall not want.
He maketh me to lie down in green pastures:
he leadeth me beside the still waters.
Yea, though I walk through the valley
of the shadow of death,
I will fear no evil: for thou art with me.

Selections from Psalm 23

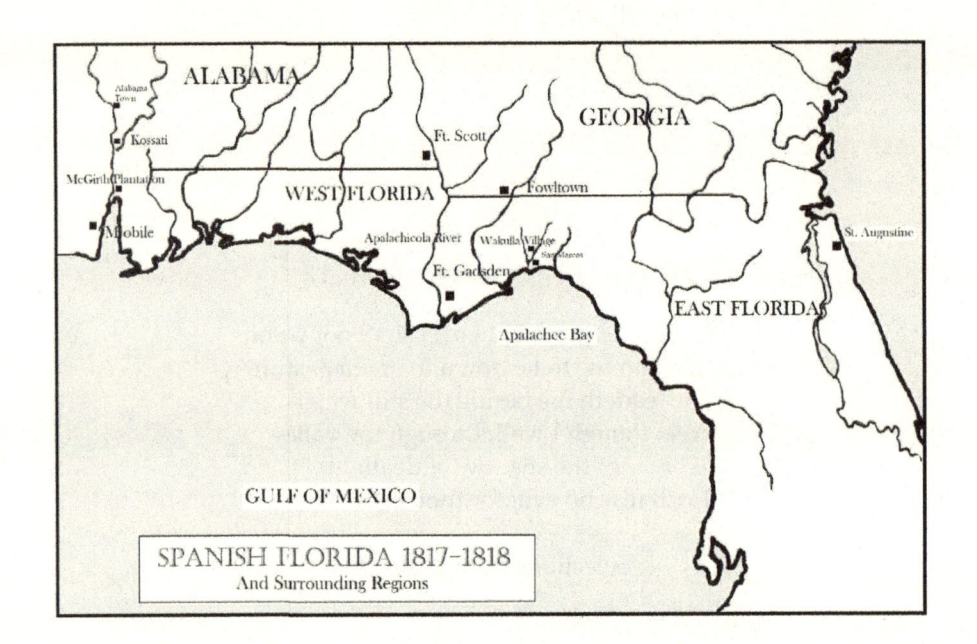

SPANISH FLORIDA 1817–1818
And Surrounding Regions

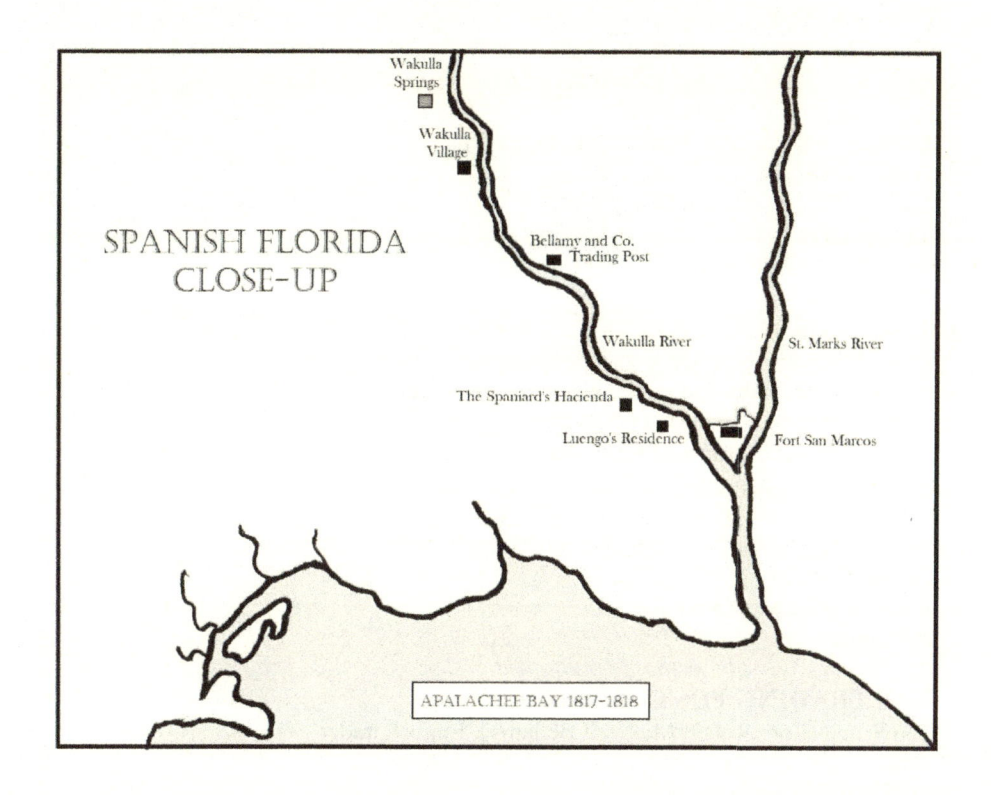

Cast of Characters

THE NATIVES
Wolf Clan
Pretty Wolf (Polly Francis), daughter of Chief Crazy Medicine
Tall Bull, uncle of Pretty Wolf
Big Warrior Totka Hadjo, mentor to Strong Bear
Noonday, wife of Crazy Medicine
Runs Like Deer, sister of Pretty Wolf
Rabbit Clan
Strong Bear (True Seeker)
Winter Hawk
Beaver Clan
Senior Warrior Fierce Mink, sister of Water Moccasin
Great Warrior Water Moccasin, war chief of Wakulla
Sunflower, Wakulla's head clan mother
Miscellaneous Clans and Characters
Kills Many, husband of Runs Like Deer (Alligator)
Flint
Micco Crazy Medicine (Josiah Francis)(Cougar), chief of Wakulla
Birdie (Turtle)
Screaming Buttons (Snake)
Big Voice

THE TRADING POST
Iron Wood (Lord Robert Maxwell Bellamy), English trader
Shem, ward
Korsan the Silent, accountant
Melon, compound matron
Rox (Lieutenant Harry Roxworth)

THE BRITISH AND SPANISH
Iron Wood (Robert Maxwell Bellamy), trader
Capitán Antonio Luengo, commandant of Fort San Marcos

THE AMERICANS
General Andrew Jackson, Old Sharp Knife
William Hambly, captive planter
Captain Marcus Buck, medicine maker
Sergeant Jerome Barkton, guard
Colonel Stoneham, commander of Fort Gadsden

Introduction

Welcome back to Wakulla, my friend!

The bulk of this book takes place in the days following Tall Bull and Mink's departure from Wakulla at the end of book 5, *Love the War Woman*. For those new to the series, *Finding Pretty Wolf* can be read alone, but it intertwines closely with the timeline and plot of *Bitter Eyes No More*, and *Love the War Woman,* the previous installments in the series.

For fuller enjoyment, you might consider reading *Bitter Eyes* and *War Woman* before *Pretty Wolf*.

If you like deeper reading experiences, you'll appreciate the glossary at the end of the book. **Boldface** words are those listed and defined.

Disclaimer: *Finding Pretty Wolf* is an artist's rendering of certain events in the life of Milly Francis. This work of fiction was written for entertainment purposes. In no way is it meant to accurately portray the actions or character of any historical figure. For a true summary of Milly's life, please see the Author's Notes at the end of this novel.

Enjoy!

~April W Gardner

Chapter I

Horse's Flat Foot, *last battle of the Creek War*
Little Spring Month (March) 1814

Polly Francis, a woman of white name and red skin, a daughter of Wakulla's chief, knew something of duty, honor, and contractual obligation. Happily, it was not obligation that bound her to the People. And it was not the betrothal agreement that pinned her to the shady side of a pine, devouring her in kisses. Never mind that they stood on the cusp of a war-ending battle, their enemy almost within sight.

At eighteen **winters**, Polly was allowed the occasional wild indiscretion.

Her betrothed topped her by ten years, yet he too had been trembling when their mouths first clashed, desperate and frenzied. He quivered still as his movements slowed and gentled into worshipful caresses.

Eyes closed, she savored him, her scant moan letting him know she approved. Of him, of this stolen moment—even though his war paint sat tart on her tongue, its red and black stark against his pale English skin.

A champion of their struggling cause, Robert Maxwell Bellamy had retired his British naval uniform and clothed himself in warrior's attire for the war's duration. Over the moons, his dedication had been so unbending, he'd earned himself the warrior's name Iron Wood. He already had the greatest reward: a pledge of marriage to the chief's daughter.

"Polly Francis," he whispered gruffly in the English they always spoke, "you are the very spark in my soul, and I cannot lose you."

"Never." She steered her chin to retake his mouth, but he gave a reluctant exhale.

"Forgive me, darling, but we've played with danger long enough. It's time for you to go." He dropped a soft kiss on the tip of her nose. "Barricade yourself in the lodge. Do not leave for anything." Iron Wood's eyelashes, a thick, black fringe on both lids, made his ice-pale blue orbs shine large and handsome. Today, they drilled her with a glossy sheen of fear. An unusual sighting.

He put a small distance between their bodies, red paint cracking on his pinched brow. "The Americans would make a prize of war out of you. If they learned who you are... Dear God, I dare not imagine how they might use you to achieve their ends."

Polly studied the tiny lines crowing out from the edges of his constricted eyes and gave a meager shake of the head, her touch lowering instinctively to her abdomen. "I am perfectly safe here, far from the fighting, and my father has yet to emerge. I will not leave him to—"

"Josiah Francis," he interrupted, using her father's birth name, "is warrior enough to pray in the river without his daughter standing as a lookout. I want you behind closed doors at once."

She bristled. "You wish me to *hide*? Truly? Me. The ***micco's*** daughter." She was Wolf **Clan**, not meant to be tucked away like prey.

"I would have you survive!" He rested his forehead against hers. "Stay *off* the killing field. There are plenty of other women to be ammunition runners. And keep out of sight. Before the end, I'll find you."

"Yes, you *will* because if you die on me," she fairly growled at him, "I'll leave your bones to bleach in the sun and your **ghost** to wander itself dizzy."

Both his eyebrows flicked up. Then he burbled a deep, masculine laugh. "Put that way, I hardly have any choice in the matter, do I?"

"Swear it to me, Iron Wood. Wipe off that smile and swear it like you mean it."

"I do." He punctuated the promise with a perfunctory mash of his lips to hers. "On every bloody star in the sky, I swear to live forever. Just for you." Grinning unabashedly, he retired a few slow strides, eyes gobbling her up as if she were a feast before a fast.

The cold spring breeze whistled through the pine needles. It rustled Polly's tattered skirt and toyed with Iron Wood's **breechcloth**, the swaddling fabric that hung, front and back, in a broad strip over his belt and down to his knees. It flapped lazily, and she could do nothing to stop the slow, silky smile from creeping up her lips.

Once her dragging sight met his, he vested her with one of his white man's winks. Teeth on full, cheeky display, he turned about and powered through the underbrush, long-knife coming neatly into his clutch. "To the *talwa*, dear heart," he called behind him, meaning the battlefield village, Tohopeka. "Now!"

His urgency coaxed her about, the thatch rooftops of Tohopeka scantly visible through the thickets. Then, from behind, **Water Spirit** chanted a beckoning tune. She jettisoned a huffy breath and, having made Iron Wood no promise, went to her father at the river instead.

The **Che-lo-kee**, their ancient enemy, had arrived.

In the time since ignoring Iron Wood and leaving her father, his burdensome, nerve-shattering prophecy still bleeding her ears, the sun had burned a substantial trail across the **Upper World**.

Bare feet swifting silently over the forest floor, Polly aimed for a child toddling through the forest that enclosed Tohopeka. At full speed, she dipped left and snagged the girl's arm. With her next stride, she hauled the small body up and flat against her chest. A glimpse of the child's dirty face brought forth the name Cricket.

Iron Wood would be furious she'd thrown his warning to the **west** wind and abandoned her shelter. Assuming he lived long enough to learn of it. Fear whipped about her, clogged her lungs as viciously as the smoke blackening the sky above the blazing talwa.

A shout stopped her short and ripped her head around to confront the destruction in the clearing. Every structure burned, a flaming pyre of their cause. Che-lo-kee warriors swarmed like a pack of dogs biting at the heels of women and children, herding them into the square.

Angry, unshed tears corrupted the scene. Polly had never been more grateful her sister, Runs Like Deer, and their mother were far off in another land. Her father had sent them to **the Floridas** to request sanctuary among the British as a fallback. One they would be using. If they survived.

Allies to that cunning dog, General Jackson, or **Old Sharp Knife**, the Che-lo-kees had done the unthinkable and crossed the swollen Tallapoosa River. Polly might admire the feat if her own battle fury weren't blinding her to all reason.

Battle? Laughable. At Tohopeka, there'd been only surround, charge, and scatter. The solitary blessing in this shameful fall—the Che-lo-kees were following white rules of war regarding innocents.

Another barked order. This one a command to come.

Did they mean her?

Fists clenched in the child's tunic, Polly squinted watering eyes to see through the gray haze trapped under the thick, leafy canopy above. A scan of the situation revealed not a head was turned her way. She'd made an entirely successful escape. Entirely useless.

The soles of her feet itched to fly, but there was nowhere to run. The treacherous river at their rear and flanks, the one they'd believed themselves so secure behind, had become the bars to their cage. There was only here, where she stood. Infested ground. In the span it took to load a musket, the land they'd staked as their own, wept over, prayed over, stomped dances over, had been lost to them.

Gone.

Polly felt her ribs crushing under the horror of it. And what of the engagement raging at the bulwark? Over the hours since the **Bluecoat** soldiers arrived, few reports trickled in. Not unexpected, seeing none of the **Defiance** men would leave the field. Hadn't they vowed as much? Stand or bleed and die.

As to the women and young, they had been assured safety—a forest, a field, and a timber-and-clay breastwork manned by a thousand painted males between them and the Bluecoats. Those warriors, the last ramshackle, hunger-thinned defenders of their ancient ways, had sworn even cannon fire would not penetrate their wall. They were secure behind it.

Lies. Fantasies. The naïve hopes of the desperate.

The noises reaching the talwa were telling. The canons ceased firing some time ago, those bone-rattling booms replaced by the *crack* of small arms and trill of the battle cry. Now, even the musket fire had dwindled from a drenching storm to a pitter-patter shower. A terrifyingly pathetic display of resistance. Polly was not delusional enough to imagine the soldiers to be the ones on the defensive.

Not after her father's sober warning.

After leaving him, Pretty Wolf made a war mask from the ash of burned lightwood. She was no war woman, but according to her father, a fight awaited her just the same. A fight that would not find her unprepared. Dagger strapped to her waist, the one accompanying her father's ominous prophecy, she would not go down easily.

The conflict at the bulwark would be close-contact, now. Hatchet to sword. Skin to skin. A sharing of sweat and blood, screams and agony, death and death, and yet more death.

And her father? Iron Wood?

Fear for them became a choking bitterness at the back of her throat, and Polly could not swallow it down.

Cricket squirmed in her arms, twisting to see behind them. In the same instant, a sharp beam of light cut into her side vision. Slamming that eyelid shut, she veered from the nuisance, then cautiously glanced back.

There was a boy. Rather, a brave, paint and perspiration smeared across him. He crouched behind thick shrubs, only his head and hand visible. In it, a piece of… Was that a signaling mirror? *Ehi*, yes. And he was signaling…her?

What could he want? And what was he thinking hiding there? Setting himself up to snipe the Che-lo-kees? Foolish boy! Scowling at him, she gave her head a firm shake. He should come out. Wash off that paint, join the children, and be spared.

She waved him in, intending to tell him as much. Hoping his fledgling warrior's pride would not prevent him from saving himself.

Vehemently, he shook his head and replicated her scooping motion, urging her to him. Polly's throat rumbled a growl. Was he too frightened to come out? Must she hold his hand?

She looked back toward the dying talwa, but same as before, the warriors had no interest in the surrounding woodland. A sign they had already infiltrated and secured it. Fortunately, inside this sector of shadowed woods, all was yet still.

Skin tingling, Polly darted her sight from trunk to bush across her horizon and around. Soldiers might spare the cowering brave, but the Che-lo-kees would not. War paint on a male was an invitation to tangle. Or to slaughter.

Growing furious, she took off toward the brave. As she went, she secured Cricket to her hip. Ten long strides had her squatting at his side.

He was looking off, putting on a good show of careful surveillance. Even so, his features were vaguely familiar; she'd seen him about.

"Have you lost all sanity, boy?" she hissed. "Put that mirror away!"

Something cracked behind her. A flintlock? Both their heads whipped around, but the forest was empty.

The boy continued panning, all the while heaving for breath, as if he'd run a hard, desperate distance. Sweat ran down his neck and over the rabbit tattoo on his bony chest. "Aren't you a…firebolt."

"Says the rabbit kitten who doesn't know when to stop playing warrior."

That swung his head back to her, and their eyes clicked.

His brows jogged up his forehead. As he canted in for a closer look, his thick eyelids spread wide. She knew what the boy saw, what entranced him— flecks of bright blue on dark hazel irises. A curiosity wherever she went. But they hadn't the time for this childish fascination. The enemy swarmed a mere arrow's shot away.

Her mouth was opening to say so when he drew back and seemed to regather his senses. His somber eyes suddenly told a different tale, a dire one, supported by the breath he still could not catch. "Iron Wood sent me."

Her teeth snapped shut.

"He's wounded and cannot come for you as promised."

Iron Wood. Wounded.

"Is-is it bad?" How her voice remained steady above her thrashing heart, she did not know.

"Bullet to the thigh. Prophet Francis bids him escape." Naturally. Because Iron Wood was critical to their future. "But your man, he will not leave unless you're with him. I swore I'd find you. Follow me." Without warning, he clawed onto her upper arm and, with surprising strength, yanked her upright with him. There was no need of force. Polly would follow this child into the worst of the fray if it meant convincing Iron Wood to make his escape.

They sailed through the underbrush, Cricket clinging to Polly like sticky weed. The distant clamor of war, the flash of the sun through the treetops—they were little more than a blur in her subconscious. All she knew was Iron Wood and bright red blood pumping through a powder-blackened puncture of flesh and muscle.

The boy more than kept pace with Polly's longer legs. Cutting around obstacles, leaping others, tearing through creepers and prickly vines, he fearlessly led. No hesitation, no deviations. Straight toward the swampy cove her father had shown her several **sleeps** earlier.

Nearing the spot, the brave slowed to a maddening crawl, ear cocking this way and that. Polly joined him, tuning her senses to danger. The river coursed around a rocky bend, its splash and gurgle to their right obliterating any auditory evidence of enemy presence. Nearby foliage did not appear disturbed.

Satisfied, the boy picked up his pace, soon reaching a fallen long-leaf pine propped high off the ground by its branches. He pushed a flowering shrub aside, enough to allow Polly to duck under the tree. Toes squelching into boggy soil, she pushed through the greenery and into an inlet sheltered on three sides. A ring of boulders, cypress stumps, and the fallen pine acted as decent coverage.

Finding Pretty Wolf

A single dugout waited empty at the water's edge. Beside it, on a dry hump of ground, Iron Wood sat propped against a cypress knee, one leg bloodied and bound up tight, the other sunk in silty water. At his sides were two warriors Polly recognized from her father's council fires.

Mink, a war woman renowned for fierceness in battle and on the stickball field. And Water Moccasin, Mink's brother and the warrior who taught Mink every twang of the bowstring and lunge of the knife. There were no two others Polly would rather have guarding her betrothed's flanks.

"Polly!" Bloody fingers outstretched, Iron Wood beckoned. Even across the distance, she noted the quake of his limbs, the wobble of his head as he struggled to keep it upright.

Polly stared, heart pounding away in her clogging throat. She hadn't known a white man could be so…white. Lips washed of all color, he sweated a river to match the Tallapoosa.

"Polly, dear heart?" His blinks fell sluggish, confused, mere beats from not lifting again. "Is it you?"

A brusque nudge from behind snapped Polly back into herself. She trapped a cry of pity behind clenched teeth and splashed a hurried trail through the shallows. "I'm here, I'm here!"

"Finally." Mink directed her glowering brow at Polly's guide. "Thought you were done for, boy." The war woman wasted no time squeezing her small but sturdy frame behind Iron Wood. She hooked her hands in the pits of his arms.

Polly jogged onto the scene, but Water Moccasin reached for Iron Wood's legs, blocking her access to him. He and Mink heaved, and Iron Wood groaned as he left the ground.

Polly bit back reproach at their rough handling and grasped for banter. "Quiet, you overgrown baby," she scratched out in English. "One would think they were sawing your leg off."

"Doesn't hurt a bit." The slur was worsening.

She cracked a watery smile. "Shall I have them saw next at your lying tongue?"

Lids shut, he stuck it out at her in offering.

A single laugh sobbed from her while she tried not to look at his leg. The amount of blood soaking his trousers staggered her. High on his thigh, the wound was too near that vital artery. Could he survive this?

Cricket bounced, and Polly patted the little bottom perched on her forearm. She followed close to the warriors as they hustled toward the dugout, Iron Wood's limp form swinging between them.

The vessel was narrow, room enough for two, certainly not three. Either Mink or her brother would be swimming alongside. How would they ever manage to get the craft beyond the soldiers? Dozens were likely camped along the river, rifles primed to pick off any who fled.

Cover, we need cover. Polly cast about for something that would suit. "That plank there," she said to the messenger brave, gesturing wildly. "Fetch it, will you? Be quick!"

Reading her mind, Mink abandoned her brother, who was arranging a groaning Iron Wood on his side in the dugout, and traipsed over to help the boy. Together, they freed a plank of half-rotted wood from beneath several others, then laid it over the dugout, covering Iron Wood's vital parts.

"How is that? Comfortable?" Polly stroked the damp hair back from his face. "Stable enough?"

"Mmm, fine," he garbled through pressed, death-white lips.

Hand on Iron Wood's shoulder, she looked to Mink. "My father?"

Water Moccasin averted his gaze and bent for a paddle, but Mink met the inquiry head-on. "Shot."

Polly's stomach turned. "Dead?"

"Shot many times."

"So, he is dead?"

"Three, four wounds, maybe more."

"Is. He. Dead." Polly gritted the words between her teeth. Why was this such a troublesome question?

Mink stared at her, face an unreadable slate of stone. "I cannot say. He fell."

"They could be flesh wounds." And her father was resilient.

"Who is that you have?" Iron Wood's voice was a mere rasp.

"Cricket."

"I can…take her." He patted the gap between his body and the wall of the dugout.

Polly considered the girl who squealed and made grasping motions at Iron Wood. She couldn't be much beyond two winters in age and already an orphan, the war having taken her father. Illness, her mother.

There was a risk in exposing her to the line of fire. But the dugout walls were impenetrable, and they couldn't leave her alone there at the river's edge. The brave would surely wish to head straight back into the glory of warfare, and Polly had her own plans. Plans that did not include a girl two-winters young.

"All right, Cricket. You can go." Refusing herself another morbid thought, Polly released the child to wiggle beneath the plank covering him. In moments, Cricket was nestling against Iron Wood's side. Half-conscious, he curled his body around her. "But you must lie very, very still," Polly said. "His leg hurts. Do not bump it, and if you raise your head, the ride will be over."

In answer, Cricket squirmed close to Iron Wood and babbled in his ear.

"I'll...keep her down."

"Of course, and you, Mr. Bellamy,"—she caught a leafy vine Mink flung overtop the plank—"no English heroics. Lay there and rest. On top of Cricket if she doesn't stop wiggling." Polly tried for a laugh, but it came out slightly manic.

Mink sank thigh-deep in the water, grabbed the vine from under the dugout, and wrapped it again—a shoddy tie-down and perhaps a hope they would pass for floating debris.

"Look at you. So scared for me." A smile quivered across his blood-spattered visage. "Such a pretty face...shouldn't have to worry so."

"Save your honeyed words for later and hold on." Polly pressed her mouth to his and held back tears at its icy touch. "Hold tight to life, Iron Wood. Hold fast. Do not leave me."

"Can't," he breathed through near-immobile lips. "You are my spark, and...you are here. I will...live." On that promise, his eyelids slid shut; his body slumped into unconsciousness.

"Done," Water Moccasin announced over the knot he tied into the vine's ends. "We must move."

Polly nodded, gaze pasted to the pulse fluttering in Iron Wood's throat.

"Get in the dugout, Polly." Mink. Adamant. Knowing.

"No." Polly took a step back. "I cannot leave my father to bleed out. If there is a chance to help him, I must take it." Her mother would expect it of her, demand it.

"Micco Crazy Medicine ordered us to—"

"Was I included in that order?"

Mink's nostrils blew wide. "Not specifically, but you are—"

"Then you and your brother will take my betrothed to safety. As the micco ordered."

Mink glared at her, and Polly returned it, their eyes in vicious combat. The battle of wills raged on in silence until, at last, the strict line of Mink's mouth softened. She tipped her chin sideways, head lowering in what surely could not be a bow of admiration. "Very well, Polly."

"Where did you last see him?"

"He went down on the far eastern side of the wall. Wait until the end. If he is going to live through his wounds, he will do so whether you arrive before the bullets have stopped flying or after. Do not risk your life needlessly, or he will lift my scalp. Then I will lift yours." Her lips peeled back in a ferocious baring of the teeth, then she reeled about and shoved the vessel into the water. "Have a care for your life, daughter of Francis. And when you see him, tell him I have his Englishman safe with me, and we will meet in the Point. Meaning the Floridas. "Where we discussed."

"I will. Keep him alive. And Mink?" When the woman glanced back, Polly sent her a look replete with promise. "If he begins his spirit journey, it will be me you answer to."

Mink grinned. "Understood, little she-wolf."

Water Moccasin chuckled, then stunned Polly with a brisk embrace. "For the People," he began. She finished with him. "No fences. No fetters." He withdrew and knuckled her under the chin. "Take care, sister."

Then he and Mink were shoving off, neither boarding but sinking up to their noses in the water, guiding the craft into the river's exuberant flow. With them went the steady rhythm of Polly's pulse, leaving her with an erratic version that lightened her head and jellied her legs.

"Don't watch."

Polly startled at the brave's voice then at the sweaty clasp of his palm to hers. When had he appeared at her shoulder? Of its own volition, her body leaned, seeking contact.

Without faltering, he took on the slight weight.

"Will he…will he make it, do you think?" she whispered, not wanting to hear the question, much less the answer.

For too long a stretch, he didn't reply, which was reply in itself. At least, he wouldn't lie to spare her feelings. Even so, she felt rocked to her core.

The brave let her lean on him and track the dugout as it rocked and hurdled through the swells. Too soon, he gave her an urging tug. "Come, look away.

Look to your father." He peered up at her then and frowned, swiped a finger along her cheekbone. Cool wet streaked across her skin. The tender gesture only made the silent tears fall harder.

For many sawing breaths, she stood there, eyes unable to break from the place they'd last seen the dugout. Warm water lapped at her ankles, and she begged Water Spirit to ferry Iron Wood past the soldiers without further harm. To guide him into safer waters and, one day, against all odds, back to her again.

"Polly."

Her lashes, weighted with droplets, lowered and lifted. Once. Twice. Then she dragged her sight to the boy and, for the first time, truly saw him.

Two tattered braids hung over his collarbones, bare of feathers, beads, or bands. Attired in only skin and breechcloth, his boyish frame was on full gangly display. Elbows, knees, ears, hip bones: he was all knobs and protrusions, and everywhere on him were angles. Where his neck met his shoulder. Where his ribs banked down along his sides. Where his cheekbones slanted high.

His jaw, though, hewn broad and sharp, was more man than boy. A queer contrast to his reed-thin neck. Every **Red Stick** on Horse's Flat Foot, especially the children, wore the face of hunger, but what had this one's mother been feeding him? Water and air?

On his person: a braided-leather bracelet dwarfing his bony wrist and the tattoo of a rabbit leaping over his heart. Apart from his sharp eyes and ragged fingernails, he carried no weapons. Had he lost them in battle? Assuming he'd *been* in battle—there were no scrapes or bruises to prove it. Only dirt and sweat and the war-paint illusion of manhood. A musket loader, then. Or munitions mule. Whatever had occupied him while the punishing sun arced the sky, it hadn't been sitting on his haunches with the children. Where he belonged.

He stood at least a hand shorter than Polly and was aged perhaps fourteen winters, fifteen at most. Far too young for this level of violence and slaughter. But his eyes... Earth-brown, fathomless. Steady. Arrow quick and just as piercing—eyes of such caliber missed nothing and spoke of an age well beyond his years. He clutched her gaze with his own, held it steady. In his, she found only light and strength.

Felt it enter her like a physical force. Her ribs expanded. Her shoulder blades pulled together. Her chin lifted a degree.

"Well done, Polly Francis. Look to living," he said on a sage nod as if he were an elder, a beloved man, instead of an errand boy. As if she were a girl awaiting her first bleed instead of micco's daughter and likely mother to Iron Wood's child.

The boy's sight flitted to her abdomen, where her hand had, entirely on its own, floated up to cradle her flat womb. His head tipped right, her arm fell away, and his eyes jerked back to hers. Indeed, those razor orbs of his missed nothing.

He coaxed her around and set his jaw, gaze drilling toward the field of combat. What had he seen out there to flare his nostrils with such determination?

"Living might be a stretch," she murmured wearily, "even for a child's hope." And she should know, having lost both her hope and her childhood three moons past on the gore-mottled banks of Holy Ground. "I'll content myself with surviving, **maddo**."

"Stop that," he clipped at once, swinging his attention back to her, his intensity rather intimidating for one so short and scrawny. "We will *live*. Together."

Together? No, they would not. She would scrub that paint off his face and send him trotting back to the women and children, while she made her way alone to the bulwark and, and...

The notion of entering that killing field alone stalled her brain, then cramped her bowels.

"Do not think you will go without me, Polly Francis." His voice was iron now. "Where you step, I will follow, and that is the end of it."

Well. If he was going to make a fuss about it, how could she argue? It was his death, his choice. And she had her English. Should the Bluecoats confront them, she would explain his childish eagerness for a warrior's honor.

"Well?" he demanded.

She almost smiled, both at the war paint smudging his whiskerless chin and at the bizarre loyalty fastening him to her side. Her attention rested on the creature inked into his flesh. Solid indigo, it leaped across his left breast. "What are you called, little rabbit kit?"

"True Seeker."

An intriguing name. "What is it you seek?"

"As of today, you. And whatever it is *you* seek."

Her brow pinched at the oddity of his attachment, but she wouldn't refuse the help or the company. Including that of a boy two missed meals from toppling over. Anchoring to his unflinching gaze, she curled her fingers tighter about his. Toes imprinting into **Earth Mother's** soft, spirit-buoying flesh, she tilted her head in a nod. "All right, then, Kit. Together."

Chapter 2

Spanish Territory, Bellamy and Co. Trading Post
Big Harvest Month (August) 1817

"'Where you step, I will follow, and that is the end of it,' he said." Pretty Wolf tapped a stick of chalk against her small blackboard, in part wishing she were still that girl, Polly, with her simple, unassuming name and her unmarred body. In part hating every recollection of her innocence and her astonishing stupidity. "'Together,' I told him. 'We go together.'" The one intelligent decision she'd made that nightmare day.

With a mental shake, she compelled herself from the memory and from the boy in it—much as she'd done a year later when she'd kissed his sleeping brow then run out on him. A full nine seasons had passed since she'd last seen him—two years and three months by the whites' calendar—and the hole in her middle was no less empty. But reminiscing did one no favors, which was why she'd never relayed the details of that day—or any of them after, really—to anyone.

Until now.

"Child?"

She dragged her eyes up from her lettering attempts on the board and rested them on her writing instructor.

Korsan the Silent—aged about as many winters as her father—had recently given in to her begging to teach her letter writing.

"When the spirits believe something to be important," her micco-father was known to say, *"they teach us themselves."*

Korsan, it would seem, disagreed. His price for the risk involved? The recounting of memories. Specifically, *that* day.

Her teacher sat opposite her, the clutter of his desk sprawled between them. His Ottoman heritage granted his skin a year-round bronze, a darker hue than her own warm beige. True to his name, he waited in patient silence, letting her set her own pace.

"They were no idle words either," she murmured in English, the language he felt most comfortable in. "Every step I took during the *long away*, True Seeker dutifully echoed."

At times, he walked behind. Other times, he strode at her side, carrying her weight, literal and figurative, on his stick-shoulders. And sometimes, predominately toward the end when she hadn't the will to rise from her pallet, his feet stepped nowhere at all but curled protectively around hers—along with his arms and any other part of himself he could drape over her lethargic form. Anything to hold her together.

"This True Seeker..." Though accented, Korsan's English was impeccable. "Do you yearn for him?"

Asking if she missed her friend was akin to asking a gallows man if he missed the ground beneath his swinging feet.

With a soft cloth, she scrubbed at the board's sloppy contents. "Every day," she admitted, voice encumbered with feeling. Her attention lifted from the smeared letters to Korsan's chicory-brown eyes peering at her through the smudged glass of his spectacles.

"You must unencumber yourself, child, of what came before and live here, *now*. It is the will of Allah."

No! was her immediate reaction, a spark of panic with it. Confused at herself, she mashed her lips together and made no remark.

Korsan dipped his ink pen in the pot and waited for a black drop to fall from the nib. "You forgot to recount the prophecy."

An unattractive snort rumbled her sinuses. "I *forgot* how to form the B letter. I do not forget the prophecy." Ever.

"Then you shall recount it," he said, slipping into his standard haughty air. "Begin where you disobeyed my master's instructions to go to the village."

Disobeyed? A frown overtook her. She did not *obey* Iron Wood. Neither did she relish dwelling in the realm of her failures.

The scratch of nib against parchment filled a considerable space of silence. "Or return the chalk to the tray and come back tomorrow for another attempt." He gave one of his superior sniffs.

One way or another, the man would have his story. And it wasn't as if the prophecy itself was an unknown. Only the *after*. Shoulders falling, she began a looping string of Ls on her board while she retraced her steps to that ghastly day...

At the Tallapoosa's slippery brink, Polly glanced back like a child making sure her parent hadn't caught her being naughty. In this case, it was Iron Wood's notice she wished to avoid. But she'd made him no promises to hide in Tohopeka, and she *did* plan to go. Eventually.

Satisfied she'd arrived unseen, she chose a patch of dirt on which to settle her rump—all the better to bond with Earth Mother. To touch soil, the spirit's skin. To feel stone, her bones. Water could be considered her blood, but Polly would leave such to her father, who had an affinity for that particular spirit.

She untied a leather hair thong from her belt. Footprints led from his discarded moccasins into the river. The water slapped almost violently against the bank, stretching its confines and daring any would-be invader to try its strength. Even with the Bluecoats bearing down, she felt safe.

Dividing her humid, unkempt tresses into three sections, she began braiding and counting. At twelve, her fingers were threading sleepily through the familiar motions. At twenty-seven, the water broke over her father's head. A proud smile eased over her as she worked the thong around the braid's tail and watched the legend emerge from his prayers with Water Spirit.

He rose steady and straight like an oak trunk breaking ground in a spirit world where natural laws held no sway. Eyes closed, arms held out at his sides, he splayed his fingers over the choppy surface and let the river dance about him, through him, down him.

Josiah Francis, Hillis Hadjo, Crazy Medicine—all the names of her father.

He'd never been subject to the river but in harmony with its moods and courses. As if he were a current in his own right, twining around obstacles and flowing along an inexorable path. As if his lungs were gills, his fingers were webbed, and his blood were silty river water instead of the red stuff their foes wished to spill.

Her father angled his face to the midday sun, the expansive inflating of his ribs the only indication he'd been deprived of air longer than any ordinary human should. But throughout the confederacy, no one disputed that Crazy Medicine—micco, prophet, rebel—was anything but ordinary.

Water Spirit *spoke* to him. Oh, for such a gift!

She well remembered cranking her neck back to gaze up at him from her niggling four-winters' height and dreaming of the day Water Spirit might deem *her* worthy to receive a vision powerful enough to blind her. For a period of ten **sleeps**, she'd led her father about by the hand. The day he recovered his sight, he began preaching of founding a strictly Red Stick talwa, and from that dream, Holy Ground was born.

"Holy Ground," she muttered, stroking her silver-set moonstone ring. "Talwa of blood and ash." Realizing she was trapped again between Bluecoats and a river, Polly loosed a cynical laugh.

The noise brought her father's lashes up from his prayers. At the sight of her, they flared wide, then he grinned and pushed toward shore, his breechcloth dragging behind. "Why I continue to be surprised that my little **miccohokti** is always exactly where she needs, I do not know." He hauled himself onto the grass so that he stood over her, water spitting onto her upturned face.

"Tell that to Iron Wood." She swiped droplets from the bridge of her nose. "And hear how he contradicts you."

"He would never." Her father began wringing the river from his silver-threaded hair. "Does the rabbit taunt the wolf? Iron Wood never forgets I am micco, and he is white."

Polly blinked at him. Iron Wood was no defenseless rabbit. And what had the color of his skin to do with anything? Both her parents were half-bloods. Polly herself could pass for a sun-browned settler or a Spaniard. She twisted at the waist, fronting her father with pinned-back shoulders. "He is also the ship that will sail you to his King George."

Ire flashed hot across the micco's face.

Swift as her next breath, Polly shielded herself with lowered lashes. "Forgive me. I misspoke."

"So you did." On a stout exhale, Crazy Medicine plucked up his deerskin hunting shirt. "But…he is your chosen, and duty demands you defend him." He shoved his arms into the garment, then reached for his leggings, looking up while bent double to cut her a look. "Even against Water Spirit's prophet and your micco." A backhanded acceptance of apology, but she would take it, for an apology from Crazy Medicine came along as often as a three-legged cock.

"Maddo, Micco."

While he strapped on his bandoleer, then his weapon's belt, then his moccasins and sash, his thoughts seemed pulled elsewhere.

She fidgeted with the shredded ends of the dingy purple ribbon that laced her blouse. "Where do your thoughts take you, Father?"

He stilled, his feathered turban cocked midway to its seat. "To what I've been shown." His line of sight stretched out before him, seemingly to the willow leaned precariously over the opposite shore. She knew the look and became stone-still. A few bats of his lashes, then he spoke, soft and deliberate. "For us here behind the wall, it is victory or death. There is no between. No compromise."

"None, Father." Did he fear her resolve had somehow been shaken, jeopardized? "No concession is worth so much as the ink in Old Sharp Knife's treaty quill." She spouted his own words back at him, which brought his eyes her way. They were a set of lances, thrilling her blood with their battle-ready edge.

"Old, mad Jackson has written my death song. He vows to sing it himself while burning our talwas like sacred fires to his white god. Farmers, cattlemen, trappers, they come at his urging and will not be content until they own every hill, doe, and corn plant in **Muscogee** country." The same anger-goading, blood-rushing story the warriors rehearsed before every engagement.

His passion drove her to her feet.

"But I make my own vow, Daughter, and it is this: I will not see Grandmother Sun rise on the day these terrible things come to pass," he declared, voice rising by degrees, body vibrating with a decade of fury. "I say that after eleven bloody moons of battle and flight, it is here we will stand. There is no surrender, no retreat. Whether on this ground or in the Point for those who've not joined us today, we will stand, war clubs raised, until there is none left to do so!"

He descended fast to his haunches. The fringe of his yellow sash mingled with the tall grasses as his long, brown fingers wrapped about the hilt of the silver dagger resting on the ground beside his hatchet. Soundlessly, he slid the work of art from its sheath, his breaths steadying. Sunlight caught in its glassy polish and ran to the tip of its silver, hand-length blade. He turned the weapon this way and that, examining every nook and curve of its antler handle.

Solemnly, he stood, took her hand in his, and laid the dagger in her palm. "You are to have this."

Jaw hung, she stared at him. "But it's your—"

"I know what it is." He curled her fingers about the stiff leather casing and presented her a wry smile. "Seeing I crafted it myself." After receiving the rank of big warrior.

Finding Pretty Wolf

An accomplished silversmith, Crazy Medicine celebrated victory somewhat differently than most. A broach for Runs Like Deer upon her first visit to the **moon lodge**. A tobacco box for himself when he returned from a campaign with Major Beasley's hair in his fist. A pair of teardrop earbobs for her mother, Noonday, when she became clan mother.

Silver for every notable occasion. That is, until he'd destroyed the forge in her sixteenth summer, slaughtered their livestock, and announced he was a prophet. They soon withdrew from Alabama Town to plant a settlement stocked with warriors who would follow his teachings to reject all things white.

Polly spun her ring, her last trinket from that peaceful season, and the only piece he'd allowed her to keep. From a ring to…what? Giving her the symbol of his leadership and cunning in battle? What did he mean by this? "Why? Why *this*? Why me?"

"When the time comes, little miccohokti, you will know." The words traveled on a pained whisper, as if having bloodied themselves on the way out, and Polly's stomach coiled with dread.

She tiptoed into her next question. "What exactly did Water Spirit show you?"

His lips bowed earthward, warbling the rows of horizontal lines inked into the skin beneath the eyes he locked on her. "The People's adversary, a bleeding head, and you."

Her brain seized. Her field of vision narrowed to the blade in her possession.

The adversary's head…by her hand?

"M-me?" At the weak sound of her own voice, shame heated her cheeks. Surely, Water Spirit expected better of her than shrinking like a lost little girl.

Eyes grave, her father dipped a lone nod, and the knots in her middle screwed so tight they stirred up acid. The knife reclined between her open hands, looking so innocent and beautiful. On its surface, a strip of her face reflected back—her glossy lower lip hanging separately from its trembling partner.

Pretty Wolf was a born fighter, but her usual weapons consisted of debate, savvy, even humor. Knives? Bleeding heads?

Spirits shield her, but she didn't want this. Not the dagger, not the rare insecurity shading her father's countenance, and indeed not the prophecy.

Fingers shaking, she secured the sheathed blade to her waist sash. "Anything else you wish to tell me, Father?"

Leaking a long breath, he aligned a flat hand with the side of her face and crooked a sad smile. "Only that you are the pride of a micco's people and the joy of a father's heart, and I miss you already."

Chapter 3

"Did your father see what lay ahead?" Korsan's question stopped the path of Pretty Wolf's chalk on her writing board. "Had Water Spirit warned him of…?"

"My long away?" Separated from her entire clan, trapped on the wrong side of the border, powerless against an enemy bent on herding her people like cattle.

Eyelids falling, he bowed his head in deference of those harrowing days.

Had her father known?

Though no stranger to the question, Pretty Wolf let her sight meander while she searched for an answer that would satisfy. Something to appease both Korsan's curiosity and her own burning need to know. Anything to prove Crazy Medicine hadn't foreseen, hadn't had the power to prevent…everything.

Had he known five bullets would pierce his hide before he crawled into the river? Or that one would pierce hers? What of all the rest?

Fingers resting on the empty place in her womb, she let her eyes skim the towers of books bracketing Korsan's workspace then shift to his lodge's single window. Grandmother Sun was a diffuse glow in its oiled-parchment covering. **Wind Spirit** whistled through the smoke vent in the center of the thatched roof, and Pretty Wolf wished there were a message in the breeze.

But the spirits hadn't bothered to speak to Polly, the girl she'd once been, or to Pretty Wolf, the drowned-rat woman who'd crawled out of Polly's broken soul.

The spirits being of no assistance, Pretty Wolf lifted clueless shoulders and set the blackboard on the desk.

Concern twisted the sea-weathered creases of Korsan's face. His elbows splayed wide on the desk's surface, one set of brown fingers touching the blue-glass amulet at his neck—a subconscious gesture to ward against the evil eye. He arched one bushy black brow at her in question, but she was finished with the past.

A corner of her mouth lifted. "Just thinking of Melon and those caterpillar eyebrows of yours."

At that, those very caterpillars crashed together over his gourd-like nose. "Can you even properly appreciate her figure from under there?"

He huffed. "Impudent child of seven monkeys." He began shuffling papers together, his abrupt movements knocking the inkwell.

She steadied it, barely keeping a handle on hysterics. "You know, Korsan, if you would let me weed them, her eyes might take a second helping of you."

His chest puffed up. "An Ottoman of such excellent bearing and of such large renown as myself is capable of wooing a woman from under a plague mask."

"Better to take *this* woman's advice while Sunflower still likes you. She can be fickle."

Though Korsan stuck to no clan, Sunflower, their head clanswoman, had made clear he was welcome to take a Muscogee wife. Or two. Males were in short supply, and the quicker they spread their seed, the quicker the People would strengthen themselves against the enemy.

Korsan straightened in his seat and adjusted the broad cuffs of his full, ballooning sleeves to cover the P branded on his wrist. His gourd nose made an impressive snort. "Grooming counsel from you? The woman whose foot would recognize neither shoe nor moccasin if it were crammed inside one?"

Pretty Wolf let loose her laugh. When his countenance went decidedly prickly, she leapt for a subject change. "Tell me, oh renowned one, what sort of respect will *I* have if I cannot properly read or write?" And the time to do so was short. Chances were high that once her father returned from England, he would learn of these sessions.

Crazy Medicine had shed many of his extremist views and come to understand their survival depended on accepting some white conventions, but in this, he would not bend. That he also intended her to board a ship as a qualified representative of the People had no bearing on his logic. But then, her father was his own breed of sanity.

Two years ago, he crossed the Great Waters on a mission of advocacy for the Defiance—the Red Sticks who'd refused to sign surrender during the late war. Due back, his ship could sail onto their horizon any day. Meanwhile, she trained to replace him as emissary.

She railed on. "Or if I cannot count shillings and groats and crowns? Or tell a knight from a squire or a mile from a furlong or a minuet from a country dance?" So much to learn before her voyage, her lessons with Korsan and Toño, the Spanish fort's commander, only a shallow dip into the barrel.

Korsan stared at her, fingers laced before him, placidly waiting out her rant.

"They already believe us to be simpleminded. How will I possibly change their views if I only confirm their opinion with my clumsy learning?" She swept a hand, indicating her sloppy markings. "For example." Her backbone dug into the chair-back as she slumped with a heaved sigh.

"Yes, your penmanship *is* quite atrocious," Korsan said, matter-of-fact, gaze lifting to a point over her head. "As is your endless whining. Your father and your betrothed undoubtedly have your best interests at heart."

"Undoubtedly." Iron Wood's voice sounded at her ear.

The chalk flew from Pretty Wolf's fingers, a squeak from her throat. "Spirits spare me, Iron Wood, you are wicked." She flattened the board to her chest, heart skittering guiltily. These lessons were secret. Even from him.

"Yes." Chuckling, he reached across the desk to where the chalk landed. The move draped him over her and brushed their cheeks. A slight tilt of his head effectively skimmed his lips across her jaw. "I am that." He placed the chalk in her trembling hand.

Last spring, Iron Wood had covertly begun teaching her to read. A word here and there, their shapes hastily memorized and added to her meager list. Writing was another matter entirely. He would protect his woman from every danger, including her father's oft-times irrational rules.

Korsan stood, joined his palms at breast level, and bowed over them. "My master." The man adhered to their mock master/slave roles as religiously as he did his prayers. In Spanish territory where so-called holy men tortured those of other spiritual beliefs, a Muslim pirate lived safest as a British lord's property. "*Khosh amadid.* Welcome to my humble dwelling."

"We'll speak of this later, you and I," Iron Wood replied, his mood a thin vein of warning.

The pirate showed them the top of his yellow turban. "As you wish."

Iron Wood planted both hands on the table's surface before Pretty Wolf, his head alongside hers, angled in, his words low and calm and meant for Korsan. "A string of hunters has pulled in. I'll follow shortly."

Korsan left like a breeze through the doorway.

When they were alone, Iron Wood wiggled the board from her grasp and gave it a critical *hmm*.

"I've been making a wreck of letters. As you can see."

"As I can see." Iron Wood hovered so near, the lavender and mint scent of his soap filled her up with fondness.

Why, then, did she stiffen and pull away from contact? Before she knew it was happening, it was done. An unconscious, self-preserving reaction. She did not understand herself. Not at all.

The breath leaving Iron Wood was slight, but at such proximity, there was no mistaking the hurt pushing it from his lungs. His head tipped a fraction for a study of her.

Let him scrutinize. Determine her value. With all her holes and tattered edges, he might finally realize he'd made the poorest deal of a lifetime. He hadn't given up on her yet, but at some point, he'd find himself grateful she hadn't signed their binding pledge.

Pretty Wolf flushed and slid beads back and forth on Korsan's abacus until Iron Wood's study of her slid off, exhausted. He had yet to voice it, but he didn't understand her either. Not any longer.

The old floodwaters poured down her throat, and she felt herself drowning. She made a failed attempt at swallowing, her chin jerking with the effort. "Where did I go wrong, Iron Wood?" The question sounded strangled, the possible interpretations of it so varied, she couldn't guess which he'd go with.

Which wrong. Which time.

Instead, he made another thoughtful hum, then tapped the blackboard. "Here and here. You've formed these backward." Wrapping his hand around hers, he gripped the chalk through her fingertips and began a slow, precise formation. He would not prevent her from learning?

The chalk squeaked along the slate for several letters, relaxing Pretty Wolf's body by degrees until a whispered, "Forgive me," hushed out.

How many more times would she have to say it?

Still writing, Iron Wood bent farther, his left arm slipping low about her ribs, his head coming to rest against hers. He set them on a gentle side-to-side sway, a strange music-less dance that soon had tears dripping from her chin.

One for each secret, another for each day she'd kept them from him, and countless more for the stifling floodwaters she could not vomit up. Black, fathomless, cyclonic. And she hated herself for it. For all of it. For how her secrets and her discomfort had become like a second heartbeat. For how she could no more rip it out than she could the actual blood-and-muscle organ.

Over the next half-minute, she and Iron Wood didn't speak. Simply created. Letter after letter. Four in all, strung together. When the full word peered up at her in white-on-black, she scrunched her nose. "I don't know it."

Iron Wood set the chalk aside and nuzzled against the soft plane behind her ear. "Soul," he said, voice low and rough. "You are my very soul."

Her chest hitched. Spirits forgive her, she did not deserve this man.

His arms flexed, tightening hard then abruptly releasing as running footfalls pattered outside.

Shem erupted through the doorway and slammed to a stop, the whites of his eyes prominent against his beautiful, midnight skin.

Pretty Wolf came to her feet, and Iron Wood snapped to attention. "What is it, lad? Something the matter?"

Covered in dust and spider webs, Shem's tight, black curls had the look of a duster. Sweat beaded over his dirt-crusted face. The boy was ceaseless mischief.

Shem bobbed one knobby shoulder. "Don't know for sure, Mastuh Bellamy, suh. Some chief I ain't seen before come callin'." His unique slave speak challenged Pretty Wolf's ears, but the apprehension splattered across his face was unmistakable, and it bled into Iron Wood's tenor.

"His name?"

"Stout Feather, suh. He be from—"

"Fowltown. Bloody bad." Muttering apologies for his language, Iron Wood stalked to the door and yanked his felt tricorn from a wall peg.

"Fat Warrior's Second," Pretty Wolf said grimly.

Fat Warrior being the Fowltown micco and another name for *pock on many a backside*. Backsides both white and red. The most zealous member of the Defiance, Fat Warrior recognized neither the treaty nor its new boundary.

She asked, "What could he want of *you*?"

At the door, Iron Wood settled the tricorn over his shorn hair, skewing its hawk feather. "I suppose I'm about to find out. Sit tight, Polly," he commanded, using her childhood name as was his custom when they spoke his language, which was almost always. "I'll pop back shortly."

"No." Determined strides carried her to him where a quick tweak of her fingers straightened his feather. She peered straight into his eyes, her tall stature being level with his white-man's frame. "You will not put me on a shelf. I am going." She dug a cocked elbow into his side until he surrendered the space before the entry, chagrin spelled out on his face.

Shem tried to scramble out of her way, but she caught his arm and looped hers through it. "We should tell Iron Wood that Muscogee women are not meant only for beds and shelves."

The boy stumbled to keep up as she tromped down the little path slicing through the copse sheltering Korsan's lodge from the trading post.

Iron Wood came up on her left and fell into lockstep with her, blustering out on a lungful of frustration. "Very well, you may come."

"Maddo, my love. I believe I will."

"The Rule, Polly."

Though his reminder was a gentle murmur, irritation scratched up her back.

The Rule stipulated only clansmen could touch her—Iron Wood being the single, unvoiced exception. Apart from saving her from harm, no masculine touch was too innocent to break Crazy Medicine's final order before he sailed: *Touch my daughter before my return and lose every feather.* A stripping of rank, every warrior's most chilling fear.

No one cleared a path through a crowded square more skillfully than Pretty Wolf, and it galled. The Rule set her apart and enhanced the aura of mystery and awe surrounding her apparent resurrection from the field of battle.

And how exactly did she survive? the whispers went.

My young companion, True Seeker, was there. Her complete report. *He saved me, stayed with me.* It was all they needed to know. All she could handle reliving.

Petulance screwed up Pretty Wolf's face. "Shem is but a boy."

Said boy presented her a dark look.

"I quite agree, mate." Iron Wood *tsk*ed in her direction. "Darling, look how tall he's grown on Melon's cooking. He's two turkey legs shy a man. Tall Bull would concur, and you wouldn't want Shem on the receiving end of *his* displeasure, would you?"

"Holy Moses, no, suh," Shem jumped in. "Don't want that chief after my hide for touching the lost daughter." A fierce shake of his head flung sweat off his chin.

Pretty Wolf flinched. At the sweat. At the appellation that would not go away. Discreetly wiping the droplets from her neck, she slipped her arm free of the boy's.

"And to the birds with the *sirs* and *masters*." Iron Wood tipped Shem a chummy grin. "We've talked about this, boyo. Bellamy or Iron Wood will do."

"You always be *suh* to me, suh."

A few moons past, on a crisp spring morning, the runaway had appeared out of the mist, bare feet cut and blistered, whip wounds festering. He'd collapsed at Iron Wood's feet, and there he'd stayed, his expression never losing its worshipful awe.

Iron Wood *did* inspire awe.

Presently, he fell silent, his sight already reaching toward the impending encounter. Each subsequent stride shed his leisurely, long-legged stroll for a tighter, crisper step. His back straightened; his shoulders pulled into a resolute setting.

An appreciative smile eased over Pretty Wolf. With his sea-frolic blue eyes, just-try-me bearing, and love-me smile, the man was unarguably one of Creator's finest achievements. Tentatively, she reached out.

Iron Wood extended his hand, meeting her halfway, and snuggled hers into the crook of his elbow. His attentiveness, his eagerness…two more stabs of guilt.

She shuttered herself against them; this was not the time.

The distant jangle of harnesses and braying of mules lured Shem into a gallop and guided Iron Wood and Pretty Wolf onto the trading grounds. Pretty Wolf's few possessions were split between her mother's compound in Wakulla and Bellamy and Co. Trading Post. She spent the greater half of each day at the post, organizing, hosting, talking down foolish trades, then stepping back for Iron Wood to soothe frayed tempers with his charm.

Today, it rivaled the activity of a kicked ant mound. Traders scurried to unpack their goods, and Korsan and Rox helped by unloading a pack mule tethered to the hitching post by the store.

The whitewashed store dominated the compound's square. Its length was twice that of the other structures, including a two-level storehouse and a lodge for Shem and Rox, Iron Wood's wards. A second lodge belonged to Melon, the resident cook and stand-in mother of all, except for perhaps Korsan, who might eat an entire unclean pig before putting the words *Melon* and *mother* into the same thought.

Pretty Wolf tilted her nose to the wind. She raised her voice and switched to her mother tongue. "Melon, is that corn stew I smell?"

The woman stood in the open-air cookhouse. As pleasingly plump as the bright indigo dumplings she was dropping into her pot, she glanced over her shoulder. The grin she shot Pretty Wolf shone so beautifully it was easy to understand how a man not her husband had risked a beating to fill her first with ***tafia***, that vile drink, then with himself.

Pretty Wolf never asked what became of her scoundrel husband, but his clan made their intent of **vengeance** on Melon publicly clear. That she retained her nose was thanks only to Iron Wood, who'd hidden her in his wagon and whisked her away.

"We should kennel you with the hounds, sister. Put that wolf nose to proper use." Melon tinkled a laugh that twisted Korsan about, his grasp missing the bulky pack Lieutenant Roxworth, or Rox as they'd taken to calling their slow-minded friend, was pushing off a mule toward him. The bundle thumped to Korsan's feet, and the skittish mule sidestepped. Into Rox.

The bulging satchel that hung crosswise on Rox's big body swung out and towed him down. His backside hit the dirt with a dust-billowing *thump,* and his forehead clocked the hitching post.

While Rox scratched at the dirt, bellowing in his childish way and raking his spilled rock collection back into his satchel, blood waterfalled down his face. Within moments, Melon had traversed the yard and was ushering the moaning fellow, satchel hugged to his chest, toward her lodge. The awkward lilt of his stride, the slight limp of his head to the side—all normal enough, but concern still flickered through Pretty Wolf.

"He'll be all right," Iron Wood assured, a light hand to her lower back.

"Ho!" The hail came from the stately figure standing across the courtyard by the storehouse. Micco Tall Bull. Sunlight caught his silver chieftain's headband and made plain the striking lines of his handsome face.

Pretty Wolf's cheeks split into a grin. "***Pawa!***"

Chapter 4

Picking up her skirt, Pretty Wolf launched into a trot. Stout Feather stood beside Tall Bull but was a mere blip on her notice.

"Niece." Micco Tall Bull, arm outstretched, mirrored her expression. "My eyes do not hold you often enough."

Her pouncing embrace exploded a laugh from his mouth. "Spare me a little air for living!"

This only made her chortle and squeeze harder.

"Iron Wood, my white brother," Tall Bull eked out like a death rattle. "Tend to our guest. My ghost will join you shortly."

But Stout Feather and Iron Wood were moving across the yard to the storehouse's loft and didn't hear.

"Your death blood is on your own hands," Pretty Wolf declared, still hung from Tall Bull's neck. "For being so sweet and cuddlesome."

"Our secret."

A secret Pretty Wolf and the war orphans were in on, Cricket especially.

He smacked a kiss to her cheek and set her down.

In her father's absence, Tall Bull stood in as micco, and because he was the only male of Pretty Wolf's clan, he claimed the title **pawa**, or maternal uncle. Thus, the Rule did not apply, making Pretty Wolf the envy of many an unwed female.

As tall and territorial as his name declared, Tall Bull was the ideal sketch of a micco, and he wore leadership like a sacred **medicine bundle**. He had everything—looks, rank, confidence, an untouchable warrior's reputation. Everything except a woman.

Leaping Waters, the love of his childhood, adulthood, and every day between, had met a tragic end, and Tall Bull refused to let her soul travel westward where peace resided. The unwashed widower's hair cropped to his chin, as well as the skulls in his once-fiery eyes, sang a continual mourning song. Fatigue smeared like gray paint under those skull's eyes—in part for grief, but mostly for the People he struggled to feed.

A situation with which Pretty Wolf was uncommonly familiar. During her long away, she'd carried the mule's share of the load, providing meat for their talwa of two. Her guilt in abandoning True Seeker revolved heavily around the state of his belly. How much had he suffered before he'd learned to keep meat on the spit?

Tall Bull draped an arm over her shoulders; she slipped one around his lean waist. They'd both been through enough, lost enough, to know better than to hoard affection. He guided her toward the store. "And how is my favorite niece?"

He had no qualms voicing his preferences. Tall Bull, whose nighest friend was a steely war woman, held little respect for the mousy Runs Like Deer, but Pretty Wolf loved her elder sister with a mother's aggression.

"Runs Like Deer is much improved, maddo." Pretty Wolf smirked at Tall Bull's tapered side-eye. "She's moved on from vomiting to eating everything in sight. With the way she is pestered, the child is a male, little doubt." Pretty Wolf had resolved her sister would carry the due time, then love and nurture her baby against all odds.

Her steps halted in the long evening shadows cast by the store's rear wall. She shrugged out of her pawa's hold and faced him, arms folded. "What brings Stout Feather?"

Tall Bull ran a slow hand down his face, all but groaning with exhaustion. "He wishes to make *yatika* of your betrothed."

"Yatika?" As Pretty Wolf processed the idea of Iron Wood as such, she shook her head. "Iron Wood is no orator."

"Stout Feather wants Iron Wood's plume and parchment, not a pretty speech. The words will belong to Stout Feather. A plea on behalf of his youngest brother. The fool brave has got himself caught by Bluecoats. Stout Feather swears his brother is innocent of theft and believes a smartly written explanation will untangle the mess."

An English letter. In Lord Robert Bellamy's elegant hand. Because Stout Feather, whose neck was due a good stretching by the Bluecoats, could not go within ten **sights** of any fort.

Revulsion thinned Pretty Wolf's lips. How convenient the skill of making letters had suddenly become to those who took pleasure in scorning it. And at whose expense? "It is a selfish, risky thing Stout Feather does, putting Iron Wood between his brother and the Bluecoats. Why did you even bring him?"

Tall Bull grunted, his frame lengthening at the challenge she thrust at him. "I have peace to keep, woman. And it is Iron Wood's choice to make."

"Choice," she bit back, batting at a fog of biting flies. "To Iron Wood, helping the weak is no *choice*."

"Such as yourself?" Tall Bull canted his head at her.

She wiggled her toes into Earth Mother and felt it ground her, but it was too late. Her eyes were already brimming, and pity was already entering his gentled tones.

"My beautiful, wounded niece." He brushed loose hair from her forehead. "So tortured. The sleeps given us with those we love are far too few to spend them alone, as this war has proved. Perhaps it is time you surrender yourself to your Iron Wood."

Anger burned across her skin. Who was *he* to lecture on grief? Unable to voice that defense without revealing her own loss, she spun and stalked around the building. Entering, she left him to catch the door flinging back in her wake.

Korsan was stationed beside a cluster of Miccosukee hunters gathered around a stack of hides, bickering with him over their value. Best of luck to them.

The fabric of her skirt whipped between her legs as she hurried past the group. She rounded the counter and busied herself organizing the pouches of seed-beads in their container.

Tall Bull quietly joined her and hefted a bead bag in his palm a few times. He cast about a surreptitious glance before angling near. "Sunflower tells me you've got some…a shipment in from Augustine." The earthy scent of *assee*, the tea he perpetually drank, wafted off his breath.

She gave him an appraising look, gaze drifting to the bag in his palm. "What of it?" Hand out, she wagged her fingers in a give-me motion, to which he raised an impudent eyebrow.

"Any, eh, writing ink come in?"

"Ink?"

"For…Iron Wood. The missive." His attempt at a stalwart tone could not have been less convincing.

"You're lying," she laughed, pitch shooting high.

Several heads turned. Tall Bull's lowered like his namesake's, horns locking in for the charge. "Fine," he growled out. "I've come for ribbons."

"At last, the truth emerges. But *ribbons*?" Had a female finally caught his eye?

He scratched at the base of his skull, knotting up his grimy hair. "I would like to, have to find—" Another growl. "Just get them out." A hilarious flush deepened the color of his cheeks.

"Certainly, Micco." Biting back a grin, she grabbed a wooden box from the shelf behind her and plopped it before him. "Ribbons. Who do you have in mind for them?"

"No one yet." He glared down at the colorful assortment, his big hands splayed flat on the counter on either side of the box. "Sunflower does not accept my excuses to dodge the blood moon binding ceremonies. I must wed. She counsels me to court with gifts, starting with—"

"Tall Bull!" boomed a masculine voice. "We will talk, you and I."

They turned to the form filling the doorway, its stance a war cry. Nothing new for Kills Many, whose life was a perpetual fight. For honor, for revenge, for a seat in the micco's booth. Pretty Wolf reviled the day her mother agreed to his union with Wolf Clan. Why Runs Like Deer did not divorce him was a mystery never to be unraveled.

The man prowled through the store, sights set on Tall Bull. The model of Muscogee allegiance, his head-to-toe buckskin clothing cried *Defiance*. Paleface manufactures never touched Kills Many's skin. Unless one counted his musket and ammunition. Those, he heartily approved. As evidenced by the inked lines slashed across his forearms, one for each scalp taken. A ladder of indigo halfway to each elbow.

"Kills Many, you bring me endless delight," Tall Bull drawled, not masking his disdain for his third in command. He leaned a nonchalant elbow against the counter.

Pretty Wolf made a fist around one of the spoons and imagined using it to dig out his ego. She'd be at it until her gray years.

"You have done the unthinkable," Kills Many hissed, conscious at least of their audience, "and I demand an explanation!"

"What, no greeting for your wife's sister?" Tall Bull waved a lazy hand Pretty Wolf's direction.

Kills Many's nostrils blew fat as he spared her not a flit of his hard-as-steel eyes. "Distractions will not save you my wrath or that of the People. You are a disgrace of a micco, and a sham of a Red Stick. May the spirits hasten the day Micco Crazy Medicine returns to slice you down."

Pretty Wolf slammed the spoon back down with its companions. "My father will do no such—"

Tall Bull's raised hand cut her off, then lowered to deliberately push his bulk off the counter. His shirt sleeve was rolled high to his silver armband, the display of bulging muscles no chance exhibit. "Say what you will of me, Kills

Many," he said, his languid speech impossible to mistake for weakness, "but I will not cower in shame for doing what I must to feed our children. You cannot understand because you do not sit on the micco's bench. Crazy Medicine knows as well as I when the fires lick at our faces, and the ground crumbles beneath our feet, you will always trample the innocents to save your own scalp."

"To save our ancient traditions! Whereas you, *you* have all but abandoned them. Taken up with the English and Spanish, adopted their ways, pleaded charity of them like a beggar." Kills Many trembled with the violence of his fury.

"We *are* beggars, brother! Broken and doing everything within our means to mend from the war."

"There will be no mending done here, *brother*." He spewed the word as though it were a contagion. "We must cut ties with all but our own. Depend only on ourselves, as did our ancestors before us. This land has beat us down, bled us to within a breath of the **darkening land**, and it is not finished. Neither is that cur Jackson. Even now, he swivels his pale-eyed sights this way. We must go south and go *now*." He pounded the flat of his fist on the counter, and the spoons bounced.

Pretty Wolf blinked at him. He'd lived in Wolf compound these two winters, but she'd had no inkling her sister's husband could speak so compellingly.

Tall Bull showed no wavering. "Until we have grown in numbers and strength, until Earth Spirit blesses with a decent harvest, we cannot leave—"

"We can, and we *must*. Our sun is set here. Darkness steals over us. That you cannot see this is proof you haven't the mind of a micco. We should have migrated last spring. Deep into the Point, where Bluecoat cannons sink in the grassy waters. Yet here we wallow. Camped outside Spanish gates, groveling for crumbs of pity. And when they do not come, what does our micco do? He smokes the pipe and brokers deals with that viper, the Spaniard!"

Kills Many was correct to compare Don Diego with a venomous snake. He served them well by keeping the vermin in check, but one never knew when a deadly strike would come or from which direction. Treacherous, heartless—only two of the descriptors she'd applied to the Spaniard in recent months.

She cupped her throat with a clammy palm and told herself to trust her pawa.

Tall Bull's hands curled and uncurled at his sides as he stared over Kills Many's shoulder, his mouth a remorseless line.

Like an alligator scenting blood in the water, Kills Many pressed his advantage, his tone laden with threat. "Undo this, Tall Bull. Undo it swiftly. Return us to the **order of things**, or I will do it for you. And you will not like my ways." On that pleasant omen, Kills Many stormed out, the scorched-temper reek of his threat lingering between them.

They stood unspeaking until Korsan snapped his fingers and brought the hunters' attention back to the hides. Their heated chatter resumed, and Tall Bull hunched forward, propping the heels of both hands against the counter's edge. "You will remove the judgment from your eyes, Pretty Wolf. I acted under Sunflower's guidance and will not belittle our head clan mother by apologizing for it."

Pretty Wolf's chin tucked itself out of his sight. "Forgive me, Pawa," she whispered even as she half-wondered if Sunflower's judgment was slipping. Bargaining with the Spaniard? Unthinkable.

He nodded, gaze fixed on the countertop. Frown lines scored his handsome face, and she ached for him. Never mind his claims of confidence in Sunflower, in himself, the man agonized with doubt.

The same slithered through Pretty Wolf, feeding her floodwaters.

Was it true? Was Old Sharp Knife gathering forces to invade?

No, no, no.

The deluge suffused her heart, swelling it painfully. She gripped the front of her blouse and willed the cold sweat accumulating at her hairline to stop. Just stop.

A set of pale blue eyes flashed through her mind, and they did not belong to Iron Wood. Musket fire split her ear with a single phantom *crack!* She flinched, lashes beating fast, and thought her heart might bruise her ribs with its lurch.

Coward. Coward!

Breathing methodically through her nose, she told herself how safe they were in Spanish country. How Jackson cared little to pursue their insignificant band of rebels. How their paths would never intersect and how he would never recognize her anyway.

The lies worked well enough to steady her voice when she finally asked, "What deal was made with the Spaniard?"

Tall Bull lifted baleful eyes to her. "In exchange for labor from four of our warriors, the Spaniard will send meat from…the ring."

The ring. He could only mean… "The bullfighting ring?"

Breath soughed from him on a groan. "Ehi, that ring."

Where men played with capes and danced with bulls. Where horses were gored on horns. Where bulls were tortured before receiving a sword to the heart. All to the tune of standing applause.

There could not be a less sacred method of taking life. With every kill, Creator must cry in agony. And Tall Bull had linked *their* warriors with the ritual? She had no reply. Only a parted mouth and a stone in her throat.

"He needs workers at his cow pens and stables. Milking, currying, mucking stalls. Whatever else." He flicked a disgusted hand as if to brush it all away.

For a Red Stick, the subject of subsisting on livestock versus the hunt was never a comfortable one. Not because they were ignorant of the process—some had owned cattle before the war—but because to return to such a way of life was to discredit every battle fought, dishonor every life lost.

Shoulders to hips, a shudder rocked her.

Tall Bull made a pained expression, then hurried forward with, "It is no small payment, Pretty Wolf. We receive the last two bulls killed in the season. By English measurement, one thousand and six hundred pounds of flesh, bone, sinew, hide." Roughly, the equivalent of twenty white-tailed bucks.

Pretty Wolf exhaled through tightly rounded lips. "I see the allure." As much as she hated to admit it. "So. We have meat. Good. What of corn?"

"That…I don't know."

"Seek the spirits."

"Wise counsel, Niece." His smile read as forced. "Sunflower and I worry for whoever should volunteer at the ring, for their standing with Grandfather Moon. During the blood moon, he might hold this against them."

Pretty Wolf rounded the counter and aimed for her pawa. Smiling thinly, he raised his arm in invitation.

She pressed her face to his hard chest and let his smoke-and-assee scent enter her with a different sort of embrace. "Our warriors simply need to balance out their work for the Spaniard with their work for the People. Leave them to me. In fact,"—she patted his chest—"leave it *all* to me. You have enough to worry yourself with."

Old Sharp Knife's looming presence being at the top of the dung-pile of troubles.

A chill skittered down her spine. This time, Tall Bull was there to press a kiss to her temple and rub the gooseflesh from her arm.

If only he could reach the icy fear crusting over her heart.

Chapter 5

Kossati*, Creek Country*

Pebbles like teeth cut into Strong Bear's knees through his travel leggings, and the straps holding his supply kit on his back burrowed uncomfortably into his armpits. Even so, he couldn't make himself rise. Not with Flint straddling his thighs and clinging possessively to the loose hair at his nape.

The boy freed one chubby hand to pinch Strong Bear's nose as if he were milking one of Copper Woman's goats. "How you know you find her? Pophecy say?"

"A prophecy, no." Strong Bear sounded like he suffered a head cold. "A peace. Felt here." He thumped a finger against his breastbone.

"What it feel like?" Flint lifted his thick fan of black lashes and wrung Strong Bear with his beautiful, trusting eyes.

A miniature quiver filled with tiny, useless arrows jutted up from behind Flint's shoulder—his means of protecting Copper Woman and her "belly baby," as if her imposing Totka Hadjo were not warrior enough for the task. It amused her no end, but Strong Bear added to the quiver regularly, and Totka gave the child watch over her during her daily afternoon rests. Never once had Flint strayed from his post, and it swelled Strong Bear's heart so that it throbbed painfully against his ribs.

Bundling the child closer, he breathed in the scent of sweaty little boy and locked it away tight for pulling out and savoring again in the lonely nights on the trail.

Throat cluttered with emotion, Strong Bear said, "Peace feels like when you snuggle under your bearskins and the wind is calm and the fire is warm. Willow Woman's blue dumplings fill your tummy. She kisses your head, and you know she loves you, and life is safe and good. Creator is safe and good. That is what peace feels like, little scout, and that is what I want for Polly."

Lips turned down in mien of serious contemplation, Flint nodded gravely. "Find her, Bear." The pinch at Strong Bear's scalp lessened then vanished as Flint released him and slid off his thighs.

"I will, and you will practice your shooting." Strong Bear removed the slingshot from his belt. To Flint's giggle and nod, he shoved it into the little quiver. Then, he wrapped his hands about the boy's ribs to hold him in place. Not ready yet to let go.

This would not be the first time they'd been parted, but it was the most significant. He harked back to when he'd been called True Seeker. Specifically, when Willow Woman and her kin rambled into Alabama Town's Rabbit compound. If it could be called that with its scant inhabitants. He'd never laid eyes on them before—her, the boy on her hip, or the one clutched to their frail grandmother's hand—but she stuck to his clan. She was Rabbit. She had come home.

The babe sleeping in the cradleboard on her back was an altogether different story. Chin glistening with drool. Stubby fingers tangled in Willow's hair. The baby's lashes had blinked open, locked onto him, and... Strong Bear hadn't known love could be instant.

By first nightfall, Willow was *aunt*, Mahila was *grandmother*, and the three boys in need of a pawa were his renewed *purpose*. But little Flint...

Flint was his heart.

In a single inhale, True Seeker had gone from wet-eyed brave, grieving the woman who'd run from him, to straight-backed pawa, rationing out his stores. What choice had he been given? None. It was feed his clan or die in the attempt. The latter, he almost made true.

Moon after moon, winter after summer, Strong Bear had worked and waited. Prayed and waited. Nurtured and loved those in his care, anticipating one person more, the prettiest, in the compound. And waited.

Path Maker, his Creator and Savior, had never spoken through a vision or with voice or tongue, but the day White Warrior McIntosh's runner came through with a request for warrior volunteers to fight Crazy Medicine in the Point, Strong Bear *heard*. Like a warm wind pushing at his back, Creator said *go*.

With the prompt came peace, a firm knowing: The road was given him. The woman was given him. The time had come to fetch Polly home.

Reluctantly, Strong Bear let Flint go, ashamed a child of under three winters had more strength for it than himself, a man of eighteen. As he stood, he gripped the straps at his shoulders. He turned in place and, taking Flint's small hand, swept his gaze over the vast panorama afforded by the hillock under their feet.

He saw none of it. Only the southerly trail winding into the chest-high autumn grasses and disappearing into the sea of pines. "The day has come, Flint. I go to the enemy to fetch Polly home." Strong Bear did not believe in coddling the hearts of the young. He'd been weaned on the blood of war. Knowledge of the threat to Strong Bear's life would strengthen the boy's spiritual backbone.

For that reason, he said, "In the peace of our beloved Jesus Creator, you will not fear for me. As you wait for our return, you will watch for us here at every dawn, and you will stand as strong as the stone for which you were named. You will make your mother proud. And I will go straight as an arrow to the Point with you in my heart."

At that, Flint grinned and shot an invisible arrow into the south, the land that stole the woman they loved best: Strong Bear because his bones had formed around her name, her breath, her voice; Flint because Strong Bear made it so. Through vividly recounted tales, Polly had grown so large in his little head, so magnificent, that when Strong Bear felt Creator's nudge, Flint all but dressed him in his travel attire, rolled his blanket, and shoved him out the lodge.

Even now, as Strong Bear powered through the grasses, legs eager to haul his leaking eyes out of sight, Flint stood jumping and waving on his hill, trilling like a bystander at a stickball tournament rallying his favorite shooter. Trilling that carried Strong Bear along until the pines muffled the sound then silenced it altogether.

Chapter 6

Spanish Territory, Bellamy and Co. Trading Post

Sludge covered Pretty Wolf and pasted her lashes together. Sucking at her body, it pulled her down, down where floodwaters ruled. Where they toyed with their victims before drinking the spirit from their blood.

A dream, just a dream.

Then it was raining, the downpour stinging her scalp, covering her face in a suffocating wash. Mouth agape, she gulped at nothing but Water.

The spirit took on life and shoved into her nose, her mouth, pressed icy fingers into her eyeballs, and muffled her hearing as if intent on invading every orifice. Intent on her end.

No, not my end. His.

This was *his* death she was experiencing, and she could do nothing to halt it. Not now, now then.

She couldn't even silence the cry, that pitiful mewl.

In an instant, the water drained away, replaced by a rifle staring her down. A flash of red flame from its muzzle. A puff of smoke from its pan.

Then pain. Sharp and searing.

Clutching her abdomen, she coiled inward and screamed.

"Polly! Wake *up*!" Dark and distorted, a form loomed above her.

Her gaze darted about her night-blackened surroundings, landed on a carved wood headboard, then swung in an arc across a curtained wall. *Trading post.*

"Iron Wood?"

"Yes, darling. It's me." He hauled her up and wrapped her in an unrelenting embrace. Lungs pumping, she panted into his neck as he stroked her back in long, tender ministrations. "It was a bad one, love. You fought, and you wouldn't wake, and—" He shot off a distasteful word he'd once banned from her mouth. "I almost slapped you. Would have, too, if—" Another expletive, this one uttered in brokenness. "You can't continue in this fashion. *We* can't. The nightmares. Flinching at the notion of touch. Your silence."

How right he was. She could not go on like this, a sweaty, quivering version of her former self. Bound to pain and secrets. Even now, the past formed an ugly ball of confessions that forced its way forward. She choked it back, chest lurching with the effort. Confessing would fix nothing. Space though...

With the sun, she'd leave for the cow pens. Assuming she could unstick Iron Wood's tentacles long enough to mount her horse.

Breath soughed from him. "You aren't happy."

The statement sent her back four winters.

There'd been a series of traders interested in forging bonds with the Defiance through marriage. *This* trader's short and brazenly confident bid for her was the only one she recalled.

"Send the other men away," Lieutenant Robert Bellamy said with a flippant wave of his fair-skinned hand. He'd worn the blue frock of his navy as well as two titles: lieutenant and lord. The former, he resigned two moons later. The latter would own him for the span of his life. *"You waste your time, my good sir. Your daughter won't have them."*

Her mother snorted, and her father's warrior eyes made a sudden appearance. But Polly laughed—exactly what Bellamy intended if the sun shining in his grin was anything to go by.

"You know this how?" Crazy Medicine challenged. An excellent question, given the Englishman had done no more than trade gazes with her from across the council lodge.

He ignored her father in favor of locking eyes again with Polly. "Tell me any one of them will give you even the thinnest sliver of happiness."

"I cannot, but neither can I say you will."

"True, but no other will work himself weary trying."

And that was that. Because, above all else, after all the running and the conflicts and the losses, she'd wished for happiness.

She was still wishing.

Iron Wood's hold tightened, and in the still room, his swallow was an audible click. "Talk to me, Polly. I can't help if I'm not privy to the torments you carry. I beg you, *talk* to me." The plea trembled its way out of his shaking body, uprooting her heart.

The man didn't know what he asked. What he'd been begging her to share since the day she'd stumbled into Wakulla.

Finding Pretty Wolf

Fourteen moons, eight sleeps. The time it had taken her to reunite with them in the Point. The last twenty-eight of those days, nothing but hard travel. Famished, trail-torn, absent the greater portion of her spirit, she'd been a walking ghost. Until her mother embraced her and joyously announced Polly had risen from the battlefield and come home.

By the next moon, she'd been fattened, purified, and made new. Renamed. Pretty Wolf.

Pretty, because she was. A reflecting glass showed her features to be balanced and delicately etched. A straight, fine nose topped a triangular mouth. Standing in bold contrast to her light russet skin: dark hair, dark eyebrows, bright eyes. Proud Indian eyes, Iron Wood called them, for their mildly slanted set.

Wolf, because true to her clan totem, she bared her teeth at fear. So the clan mothers said. During the long away, Polly had scouted and stalked prey to feed the one in her care, and when the opportunity presented, she'd run for days to reunite with her pack.

She was still running. Every day, running.

It was the month of the Big Harvest moon, and though unseasonably cool due to mystifying red-tinted cloud cover, heat suffused her in waves. "I'm leaving. For the cow pens." She'd decided she would be the fourth volunteer stipulated in the contract. Incredibly, she looked forward to whatever challenges the task presented. The night was young enough that Screaming Buttons might still be awake.

"What? *Now?*"

She'd meant to leave at dawn but, "I won't find sleep again." She pushed the blanket off her lower half, and the reek of summer and fear lifted off her sweat-dampened skin. She scrunched her nose. "I should bathe first." Bathe and pray Water Spirit to release her from the madness of regret.

His chilly fingers tucked wild tufts of hair behind her ear. "Don't go. It's dark."

"Balada knows the path." The mare would thrill at the nighttime adventure.

He rose from his crouch and stood before her in nothing but his thigh-length shirt and his white legs. Shadows washed him in blacks and grays, vanishing half his features and distorting the remainder. In place of his sky-blue eyes, a set of fathomless black caves. Instead of his amiable smile, a twist of lines more at home on a tie snake from the deep than on the gentle man she loved. "I don't like it. And we should… We should discuss…things." By *we*, he meant *she*.

"I'm going." The ticking crackled as she crawled from the bed, ignoring Iron Wood's testy outbreath. At the water basin, she stood and tracked his sounds: the pad of his footfalls, the tumble of wood in the hearth, the rushing crackle of flame. In short order, the space was awash in flickering light.

Iron Wood had no lodge, only a Spanish bed that he'd stationed it in a partially draped-off corner of the store, close to the fireplace. A tall trunk presided over the foot of the bed. It contained records of business as well as personal effects, such as his neatly folded seaman's uniform. By the curtain's edge nearest the hearth sat the hip bath he'd ordered for her and beside the bed, a small table on which rested his feathered tri-cornered hat.

Scooping cupped hands into the filled basin, she lowered her face for a rinsing, then became snared on her dim reflection in the pool. Nausea churned. Fingers parting, she let the water trickle free and hunched, gripping the stand.

"Steady on, love." Coming alongside her, Iron Wood dipped a cloth into the basin and wrung it out. Taking her chin lightly between fingers and thumb, he bathed her temple to chin with a slow, soothing caress. A pause as he seemed to debate.

Then his lips landed lightly and followed the trail of the cloth. Its languid, purposeful trek crossed over her mouth, and her eyes flung open.

"Iron Wood…" She swallowed roughly. "Did you put your mark on Stout Feather's paper last evening?"

Firelight glinted hot in the pale eyes he leveled on her. A flash only. "Korsan stopped me on my way in for the night." There was a quiet, no-yield cast to his voice. "Did he show you the hides the Miccosukees brought in?"

Molars clamped, she flipped her lashes down to spare him the full dose of her hurt.

He wasn't going to share this burden with her. For the same reason, he glazed over his dealings with the Spaniard, or pushed calming herbal teas at her, or assigned Blue Shoes or some other warrior to dog her heels whenever her path required she leave the bounds of Wakulla or the post.

To protect her fragile self from undue strain and unseen dangers.

Or was this passive revenge for her own silence? If so, as piqued as she was, she would cast no blame. He couldn't know her silence was a mercy.

Whatever his reason, it closed about her throat like a slow-squeezing fist, severing any response she might have made. She scarcely noticed the cool rag against her clammy skin as she turned her back to the water basin and set her sight upon her satchel. Two items left to pack. In the few minutes it would take to dig them up, she could be gone.

Patiently, Iron Wood shifted with her, all the while buzzing on about the deerskins as only a trader could. "Trimmed and well-dressed, each one. Fair in size. Weighing in at over three chalks some of them and— What... Pretty Wolf what are you doing?" The washrag dangled from his fingers, and a question scored his brow.

She was at the bedside, reaching for the trunk's latches. "I already said. Going to the cow pens." Her voice was a slight, weak noise, and it disgusted her.

"Excuses," he snapped as sternly as ever she'd heard. "Confide in me!"

At his command, the confession hurdled back up her throat. A gagged cry stopped it short. "Leave me be!" Launching back into motion, she yanked her wrap from the chairback with such force the chair keeled over.

Iron Wood shot forward and took her by the upper arm, catching her in half-kneel before the trunk, pulling her back up. The orbs of his eyes were large and vibrant with moisture as they plumbed her own. A collection of stuttering heartbeats passed before he spoke, voice raw. "Come back to me."

"I *did* come back to you, Iron Wood. A moon of sleeps traveling to do just that. Hungry and alone. To return to you." *Not entirely true,* her conscience accused. *You came back for family, for Father.* For his prophecy and the hope its fulfillment might fix her. Undo her wrongs.

The prospect of Iron Wood at the end of her journey had been unthinkable. She'd convinced herself his bullet wound was too grave to survive. And if he'd recovered, he would have believed her lost and boarded the first vessel back to his homeland. But no. The undefeatable, the honorable Lord Robert Maxwell Bellamy had stayed and fulfilled his end of the betrothal contract, even while believing her dead.

His head bent forward for an aggrieved wag. "Some part of you was left there at Horseshoe Bend or in Alabama Town or, or...somewhere between. You're lost, Polly, but you needn't be."

"No one is lost." She knew exactly where the missing piece of her soul could be found. On that mud-slicked bank of the Coosa. In Water Spirit's embrace.

"Keep lying to yourself, and you'll never heal." He trembled with the intensity of his conviction. "You are gone, Polly!"

"I am here and perfectly—"

"Yes, yes, you are perfectly well. Lies! Admit it or not, my dearest heart," he firmly maintained, not a hint of mockery in the endearment, "some vital part of you has broken off and become lost. So lost that at times I wonder if you even recall its existence. *Her* existence. Polly Francis. Do you remember her?" He gave no pause, hands rising to clamp her shoulders. "I remember that bright and pure girl, and I won't let her go!"

Stubborn, noble man. And stupid, stupid! For attempting to raise the dead. For refusing to let her go, though her spirit had climbed halfway into the grave.

"I understand it must be difficult to voice," he went on, gentler now, "but we'll take it apart slowly. Bit by bit. Then you and I, with whatever tools necessary, we'll put it back together." Put *her* back together, he meant. In his collection of broken people, she alone had not succumbed to his repairs. How it must madden him.

"Enough. *Enough*. There is no *putting back together*. Have me as I am, Iron Wood," she said, voice as dead as her threat was alive, "or do not have me at all."

Eyes flaring with shock, Iron Wood worked his jaw, but no sound emerged.

She ripped from his grasp and flung open the trunk lid. "I'm going." She plunged her arm into its innards. Her exuberant rummaging unsettled the raised lid. It would have slammed down on her arm if Iron Wood, standing stiff-legged beside her, hadn't employed his snake's reflexes.

"You're *not*," he graveled.

She barely contained the snarl pushing to escape as she yanked a pair of breeches free of the trunk's stew, then dug for the time-stained shirt she knew to be buried there. "Let us not fight, Iron Wood." The shirt's ruffled sleeve peeked out from under a hatbox, and she grabbed it.

"You are not"—he snatched the article from her hands—"leaving. No lady of mine will be seen mucking about with cattle and strange men, and she will most certainly *not* be wearing breeches!"

Pretty Wolf threw up her arms, having no time for such barbarism. "You are neither my micco nor my clan mother. And as to the breeches," she continued, voice crisp, unrelenting, "they will cover my legs when I ride. As you would, I am sure, prefer."

Iron Wood bristled. If the man could, he'd wrap her in layers of felt and secure her in the trunk until every manner of evil in **This World** became acquainted with the full length of his bowie knife.

Starting with the cow pens contract and her decision to be the fourth volunteer.

Ironically, apart from Sunflower, the only person to support Pretty Wolf's decision had been her fainthearted sister. In Wolf compound—while she'd packed and Kills Many fumed about Tall Bull—Runs Like Deer quietly helped gather the last few personal items. The things she kept in her mother's lodge for the nights she stayed over.

"Never mind my husband," she'd whispered as she tucked a quill brush into Pretty Wolf's satchel. *"You are the one destined to save the People, and it burns him up inside."*

Pretty Wolf playfully rolled her eyes. *"Have you inherited the gift of prophecy?"* She took the bag from Runs Like Deer and nudged her toward a chair. *"And what have I told you about lifting heavy things?"*

Without protest, Runs Like Dear sat, one hand cradling her heavily rounded womb. "One needs no word from the spirits to see you for what you are, Sister."

"Is that so?" *Her light laugh fell short the mark of humor.* "What am I then?" *Besides failure decked in a skirt.*

Runs Like Deer pulled back enough to lock their eyes. Hers filled to the brim with sincerity as she whispered, "Our light on the dark path. You will guide us home."

Home? They were already home.

On the other side of the curtain divider, the store clock gonged away. With each chime, Iron Wood's countenance grew firmer.

She crammed the set of clothes into her bag and shoved past him.

"Polly, I'm— Wait. Polly!" He followed close as she whisked through the store. "Polly, *stop*. This is Tall Bull's problem. Let *him* herd cattle. It isn't safe, and the store needs you here."

She laughed at that. "Yes, I am certain the ribbon box will feel the loss of my tidying efforts. The spools will all unravel in their grief."

This. Over the cow pens! Bless the spirits, how he'd blow if she spilled her secrets. She rounded a stack of hides, and the floor slats vibrated under her anger.

"Come now, dearest, satire is unbecoming a lady. As is stomping off in a fit of temper!"

At that, her inner wolf snapped. "I am not a *lady* but a daughter of the People." And too long had she put embroidery and dance lessons and *ribbon sorting* above them. Too long had she denied herself the pleasure of being one spirit with the tribe, of dedicating her days, her sweat and blood to its betterment.

At the top porch stair, she glanced rearward. Iron Wood pulled to a fast stop within touching distance of her back. "My body is strong, Iron Wood, as is my spirit, and my heart leads me true."

He took possession of her wrist, and his gaze dusted over her face. "Your heart is known to be a foolishly impulsive thing, Polly. It has already paid a dear price. I, no, *we* have paid the price! One day, the cost might be too high to bear." The jagged, tear-torn edges of his voice severed all the wrong threads.

Her heart must be a burdensome thing to love. It was a great wonder he so fiercely clung to it. She plucked at his clamp on her until he let her pry his fingers open.

Blinding herself to the desperation contorting his features, she chuffed a humorless laugh. "If you still think me that naive girl, you know me less than I thought." She dropped a heel to the next tread down. "Do not follow, Iron Wood. When my foolishness lifts, perhaps my impulsive heart will lead me back to you."

Chapter 7

"*Ali, señorita.* That one there." The stable boy lifted his lit palm-sized oil lamp to indicate a dark door, the only one to punctuate this side of the Spaniard's stables. "The spare tack room. Want this?"

"Gracias, Tito." She smiled, swung down from her mare, and took the lamp he offered. "See you tomorrow."

"*Hasta mañana*, Lobita." Having flashed her his crooked canine, he trotted off with Balada, the mare's cream coat a beacon in the moonlight.

Pretty Wolf pushed off toward her men. *My men.* Until this ordeal had passed. Hers to tend and protect and oversee. Tall Bull had given her all the authority of a clan mother, and she'd have to make certain her men knew it.

She flung the door open and caught two of them mid-scramble. Kicking Knife, blanket in a tangle about his ankles, stood before her in a suit of umber skin, plus breechcloth. On the floor, Screaming Buttons stilled in tableau, looking as if he'd been grappling for a nearby hatchet.

In his gray years, Kicking Knife was sedate and introspective, and she knew little of him apart from his widower's status. Screaming Buttons was his contrary. A mid-ranking warrior, aged thirty or so, he boasted an overlarge forehead and a long, venturesome history with Pretty Wolf.

It began at Horse's Flat Foot.

Same as her father, Screaming Buttons escaped the slaughter by hurling himself into the river. Although, unlike her father, Buttons injuries amounted only to scratches, and he swam across with minimal trouble. And while Crazy Medicine's men found and hied him away to safety, Screaming Buttons was being apprehended and shuffled in with the captive women and children.

His fate intersected with hers and True Seeker's when the Bluecoats released the survivors with strict instructions to reestablish themselves at their pre-war talwas. Polly had desperately wished to travel to the Floridas to reunite with her mother and sister, but even if the soldier escorts hadn't been forcing them north, she never would have had the stamina.

Foolishness had earned her a wound, so memory of their travel was a foggy veil. She did recall Screaming Buttons sidling up and throwing an arm around her as she stumbled along in blinding pain. Between him and True

Seeker and her own staunch determination, she somehow managed not to die of sheer agony.

Their paths diverged from Screaming Buttons' at the Ockchoy crossroad a day south of Alabama Town. During the long away, he visited every few moons. Stayed the night on occasion. Brought news, meat, the odd tool. Friendship. Their only friend for most of it.

In the end, he'd migrated south with her again. Ockchoy to Negro Fort. Their shared journey of fear, hunger, and uncut trails had made the man a brother in every sense but clan.

He'd always attired himself in a profusion of rattlesnake tails: ears, neck, hair, the tops of his moccasins. Snake Clan to his marrow, he rattled out his name with every casual movement. Such as now with the relieved shake of his head. "It is only you."

"Only myself."

"Daughter of prophecy." He lowered his chin in respectful greeting, and she fought to keep a smart *enough with the prophecy!* behind her closed-lipped smile. With Screaming Buttons, protest was futile. Everything to him was prophecy, omen, or spirit-spoken.

"You are come." Kicking Knife's ending pitch swept a little high, presenting more as a question than their traditional greeting.

She forced her residual irritation into a level vocal cadence. "I am, maddo."

"It is well, sister." He relaxed his stance, and Screaming Buttons abandoned his blade to gain his feet. Neither man moved to revise his state of undress. But then, neither knew they'd be sharing their **couch** with the micco's hands-off daughter. Eyes large, they quietly awaited the explanation of her arrival.

She stood at the tack room's entrance and, jaw set hard, swept the lamp in an arc to take in the five-pace by five-pace excuse for a bunkhouse. Shadows scampered off the saddle stands lining one wall, then off the bridles dangling from hooks above them. Cluttering the remainder of the walls: harness racks, empty blanket bars, cabinets, and shelves. Not a breath of space to be found. Save for a meager patch on the dirt floor. There, spread thin, lay a carpet of flattened hay, the missing horse blankets stretched atop it.

"*This* is our lodgings?" Pretty Wolf shook her head at the scrap of floor space before her, stepped inside the room, and mentally braced for a back-aching night. On a protracted exhale, she tossed her satchel to the side.

"In all its marvel," Kicking Knife said, dry as kindling, then lifted his sight to the whisper of tread behind her.

An over-the-shoulder glance filled her vision with a sour face wearing an impressive nose wrinkle—the funny looking one that always accompanied Big Voice's foul moods. In training to become the talwa's yatika, he behaved as if entitled to cast his opinion about. The man ruined many a scene like a roach in the **sofkee** pot. "Did you say *our*?"

Pretty Wolf jetted air from her nose. "I did." She toe-nudged her bag under a saddle rack and set the lamp on a shelf. "Catch." She tossed her bedroll to Big Voice. "You may stretch it out next to Buttons."

"Ehm, Pretty Wolf, you are...staying?" Screaming Buttons was scratching his head, looking as if she'd announced she had grown bat wings and would be sleeping upside down in the rafters.

"Why so appalled, Buttons?" She unpeeled the woolen wrap from her shoulders. "Afraid I'll bite you in my sleep?"

"You mean bite me *again*?" He rubbed his arm as though it pained him still.

"Such grudges you hold." She clicked a reproachful tongue. "Can I be blamed for vivid dreams? The badger felt *quite* real. You should have let me scream."

Screaming Buttons harrumphed, but that was humor there, barely contained behind his false scowl.

Humor, banter, Big Voice was having none of it. A snarl ruined his otherwise handsome set of lips. "Why are you here?"

Blame for that went to her overactive conscience. She'd been offered her own quarters, but she couldn't sleep warm and comfortable while her men shivered on the ground. Tall Bull had told her the men were in cold, tight quarters, but her imagination had clearly failed her. Should Iron Wood learn she'd transferred her bedding to this over-snug place, even her fearsome micco pawa would not be able to subdue the Englishman's fury.

"We needed a fourth." Folding her wrap, she jounced a shoulder as though the decision hadn't jostled her insides about. Or possibly delivered a death blow to her tenuous bond with their resident trader. "Being as no other stepped forward, I did so myself. I expect you all agree we have no other choice and will make me welcome." She moved her eyes from man to man.

All gave firm nods, though Screaming Buttons stared in abhorrence at the bedroll Big Voice was whipping out. His throat jerked with a swallow.

Pretty Wolf's deft fingers ran through her braid, unraveling it. "Sunflower and Tall Bull are aware of the arrangement," she mumbled around the hair tie between her teeth. Their head clan mother's opinion was the only one that truly mattered, but Pretty Wolf knew the path these warriors' thoughts wandered. "They've given me authority here, but you are trusted men. There will be leniency with the Rule while at the cow pens."

With a pointed foot, Screaming Buttons poked at the rumpled end of Pretty Wolf's blanket. "It isn't the Rule that concerns me."

Kicking Knife dumped himself back down on his blanket, stretched, and groaned out, "Off he goes again with his fears."

"We'll be up all night hearing it." Big Voice stalked to the straw and sank to his rear, then began yanking at his legging ties.

Rattling to wake the dead, Screaming Buttons shoved at his shoulder. "Training to be yatika doesn't entitle you to voice every opinion. And fear is not always unwise."

Pretty Wolf hardly wanted to ask. "Fear of what exactly?"

"Are you mad, woman?" Big Voice's interjection sounded closer to menace than contribution. "Don't ask."

"Fine with me." She dropped her shawl on the satchel, hoping the subject went with it.

Kicking Knife decided to be helpful anyway. "He fears watchful spirits and avenging ghosts of the bulls."

Pretty Wolf sympathized but couldn't allow for even the smallest doubt. "The spirits understand we work for the good of the People. Think of Blue Feather instead," she suggested.

"Ehi, at the **Frost Moon** dance, she'll be yours, and then"—Kicking Knife slapped his friend on the chest—"you will put to good use that lodge you built her."

Flat on his back, Screaming Buttons folded his hands under his head, his splayed legs and jutting elbows consuming an inordinate amount of their limited space. Closing his eyes, he sighed like a girl.

Kicking Knife propped up on one elbow. "And you, Pretty Wolf?"

"What about me?" She blew out the lamp and picked her way through the inky dark to her place beside Screaming Buttons. On the way, her little toe stubbed hard against his calf. "Ack, my toe! Move over, you greedy lug."

Hay rustled and crunched as they shuffled to make room for her.

"Will you live always in the store," Kicking Knife persisted, "or will Iron Wood build you a lodge?"

The question knocked the strength from Pretty Wolf's knees. She stumbled to them, and just that swiftly, she was in the past, the ebony night offering a blank canvas on which to paint another setting from another time…

Alabama Town
Mulberry Month (May) 1814

Beneath Polly's unshod feet, Earth Mother's ocher flesh burned warm from the heat of her anger.

Behind her, a wall of pine and thickets, her childhood playground.

Flanking her, the desecrated ground that was Wolf Clan square.

Before her, the blackened remains of a lodge. Timbers jutted up from its earthen foundation like the broken ribs of a long-dead carcass. Inside, a ring of stones sat half-buried in mounds of ash. The skeleton of her mother's fire pit.

Cinders blew into Polly's eyes and invaded her nostrils with their biting tang. Tears flooded and ran. From the irritation? From the grief welling in her chest?

Neglectful of the drip from her chin, she looked straight through the structure's remnants to the silent talwa sweeping down the hill and away behind it. With grave intention, she settled her watery gaze on the charred hulls of Beaver compound and let the grief of it seep into her bloodstream. After, she moved her sight to the black shapes that were once Turtle's quarters. From there, on to Snake and Bear where a sob broke from her.

A solitary lodge had miraculously escaped the Bluecoats' destruction: Rabbit Clan. Its whitewashed walls and perfectly laid bark-shingle roof stroked the tattered seams of her spirit, and she found her thumb doing the same on the back of the hand cradled within hers.

A head tipped to rest on her shoulder.

True Seeker.

The boy always had some part of himself on her. Most often, clasped hands. As if, should he let go, he might lose her. Or stumble along the way.

Polly didn't mind. Indeed, she encouraged it. Loss was a brutal reality. Something they'd both experienced in the multiples of hundreds.

True Seeker was it. The last. All the rest had either walked the spirit path or hacked out a new life in the Point. Entirely inaccessible to her. She'd sooner stitch the youth to her side than lose him.

Ignoring the ache branching from the scabbed-over wound on her chest, she wrapped her arm around him and pulled him tight into her side. Together, they stood and wept and watched tiny gray cyclones whip up in the center of her old family lodge.

Together.

Over two moons had passed since he'd thrown his body over hers and vowed he would not leave her. Sworn they would go on together.

And so they had…

Frightening nights of fever.

Infuriating days of captivity.

Frustrating moons of healing.

Blistering leagues of travel.

After they'd left their camp at the battle site, they'd hobbled into Alabama Town, her childhood home, only to find it abandoned. Two years earlier, the majority of the talwa had migrated to Holy Ground, her father's vision of a traditionalist haven. The sacred fire had journeyed with them, leaving only a cold square ground and a few elderly who hadn't life enough to travel. Now, even those were gone. The elderly taken away by clan or death, the square a scorched monument to the Red Sticks' ruination.

Not a chicken or dog remained.

True Seeker's thin arm looped about her waist and tightened. His chest wall expanded deep and even, and his eyes were dry, focused. Determined. "We are strong, Polly. We'll hunt. We'll survive."

"Hunt with what? Your slingshot and my wounded arm?"

"Ehi."

"We should have gone to the Point, gone south to my family." South: the cardinal direction associated with warmth, peace, happiness—all these things more needful now than ever. "Much summer remains. We could still go." Their old argument.

"No more of that. We stay." So saying, whether intentionally or otherwise, he turned his face in the direction of tomorrow's sunrise, much the way a chieftain does to show he watched over the interests of the talwa.

"Have we a new Alabama Town micco?" She jabbed a finger into his side.

He didn't budge. "I gave my word to keep you safe. Simple as that. And your clan will know to look for you here."

"Even if they knew I am alive, they would not come. No Red Stick will. The land between here and there swarms with Bluecoats."

"Exactly. And I shudder to think what games they might play with a woman as beautiful as yourself. We stay, and that is the end of it."

Though he kept his sight dead ahead, Polly stared at him. He'd never spoken with such authority. Or so bluntly. "I'd have you to protect me." A new tactic. She jostled him playfully, and the bone of his shoulder dug into her armpit. "Unless you're saying you are too frightened of them to try?"

"I am frightened. But not for myself." He settled a hand, warm and tender, on her taut womb.

A hummed exhale escaped her. The boy was right, of course—a nettlesome habit of his, that of being right. As weak as she was, a rushed cross-country trek would risk the child.

How life still grew within her after such a wound, she could not fathom. Every morning she feared it would be the one her body rejected the pregnancy. And every night when they huddled together—a malnourished brave and a wounded mother against a wide, hateful world—and she allowed herself to cry into True Seeker's chest, she was shocked all over again to feel the butterfly flutterings of life deep inside.

Ehi, above all else, the child. Their future.

Even so, the temptation to put the morning sun on her left cheek and take the trail... It was a potent lure.

"Rabbit's summer lodge still stands," True Seeker finally said and ticked his chin that direction. "We have shelter. We have each other."

"We have winter before us and no stores laid by. No seed. No weapons or tools." She struggled to speak calmly, to keep from shrieking the counterarguments. "No woman to help me birth this little one."

"You carry the baby. Let me carry the worry. When the time nears, I'll find a woman to catch the child as it comes. Or I'll do it myself."

Catch her baby? The brave was in earnest.

"But that is many moons off. Meanwhile, I will be strong as a bear for you," he said, making a pitiful muscle.

She resisted snickering. "Not strong as a rabbit?"

"Gentle as a rabbit, but strong as the bear. And *you* will be fearless as a wolf."

Clacking her teeth, she growled wolfishly through a grin.

The knot on the bridge of his newly broken nose shifted with his responding grin. "Each day its own trouble, ehi, Wolf? Today, we clean the square and light the sacred fire."

"And now you are **beloved man**?" She tutted in mock disapproval. "Micco, birthing assistant, and elder rolled into one. Quite an accomplishment for a boy of twelve winters."

At this, his neck snapped around, making whips of his braids. "Twelve!" He snorted disdainfully. "I've seen my fourteenth."

One of her eyebrows climbed north as she counted the ribs laddering down his narrow chest. She'd been teasing with the twelve. "All right, then, Kit. Fourteen. Forgive me. Regardless, you haven't the rank to light the fire."

"**Fire Spirit** would understand."

"You'd be a fool to risk it. Just as you're a fool to think we can winter here alone."

"Perhaps." His head lowered, but he wasn't cowed. No, he was drawing in the dirt, scratching out a picture with one filthy toe. "But Creator gave this land to his Muscogee children. It is the dust and blood of our ancestors. I'll not leave it again." His fingers sought hers to weave through them and clamp down.

"All others have."

"True. They are scattered like little birds before an eagle, but just as we have done, they'll gather themselves and return. Meanwhile, the talwa is ours alone to breathe life into. My fight is here now, Polly Francis. As yours should be." The lines of his drawing came together to form a crude lodge. Another set of them became a stick figure. "There is nothing in the Point but more of the same. War. Hunger and death. The baby brought you *here*. Honor his wishes and stay." Two more stick people emerged from the earth.

A considerably shorter one beside the first. Female, by the skirt and long hair. Next to her, a tiny, stump-legged figure.

Smiling, Polly slanted her head at the trio. "We are backward, Kit."

"Today, perhaps. But this"—he tapped his big toe under the largest figure— "is me tomorrow."

"How swiftly you grow." She laughed and ruffled his hair before he could duck his head away. "Is that a chimney on Rabbit's lodge?"

"This is not Rabbit's. It is yours."

"But I have no lodge."

He angled his body to peer up into her eyes and said with all the solemnity of a chanting **medicine maker**, "You will after I build you one."

Creek Country

Strong Bear perched on his calves in his storm-pummeled campsite and frowned at the handsome beading on his new moccasins, now crusted red-brown with muck. And at the birds, twittering with heedless joy. Then at the impossible knot in his bedroll twine. The first night on the trail to Spanish Florida could, indeed, have gone more smoothly.

In case the unceasing sting of rain hadn't been misery enough, the howling wind blew the oil-cloth tarp off his supplies and soaked his spare clothes. At least his parched corn and treasured papers, relocated to the warm place beside his heart, had been spared. Thankfully, his pocket watch was still ticking along despite the moisture fogging the inside of its glass covering. The twine, however, might be a lost cause, its massive tangle not dissimilar to the state of his thoughts.

Roiling inside him: excitement over this long-awaited journey, apprehension over the battle he'd have to wage to reach its end, worry over Flint and regret over the necessity of leaving him.

And love. Blinding, driving love. Love so compelling he was answering the Bluecoats' call to arms against the Red Stick Defiance as an excuse to get as near to her as possible. How his Wolf might react to him arriving as the conquering force... Well, he would deal with that complication when it mattered.

First, he must put this trail behind him.

Firming his jaw, he flexed his thighs and shoved upright. Letting the garbled strand dangle from his fingers, he set his sights southeast. Toward Polly Francis, the Wolf who'd branded on him. The woman who called his newly declared enemy *father*.

But all his eyes could see was the scaly orange-brown of myriad pine trunks. The bowels of the woodland stretched far, gloomy with the unknown. Endless sights lay between him and Polly. And that was only if he could find her.

No, not *if*.

"One day, I will come for you!" The shriek still rattled his throat, and he felt himself spinning as he'd done that day when his desperate gaze had

scoured the woods, and he'd cursed his atrocious tracking skills. *"Do you hear me, Polly? I'll find you!"*

He would.

The hollow behind his sternum, the one she'd created when she'd fled, flared bright and aching. He rubbed the spot and let his head fall back to keep the water in his eyes from overspilling.

Above, violet and bronze smeared the cloudless dawn, and a crescent daytime moon roosted pale and slender atop the swaying pines. Since he'd last seen Polly, he'd counted many such moons. Twenty-seven, in fact. Double the number he'd planned—each one a lesson in frustration and patience—but life and the care of loved ones tended to alter one's intentions.

Meanwhile, he'd filled his gut with good food and pounded out his vexation at the forge with Totka. And he'd grown. Up and out and up some more. Until Copper Woman tossed her hands in the air and despaired of making clothes and moccasins to fit his ever-broadening frame.

Would Polly even recognize him?

At times, he still could not comprehend that she had left. That after all they'd endured together, she'd even been able.

"My mother, Kit, I just need my mother and father," she wept that last night when he once again tried to speak reason to her. Her crazy prophet-father was the last person she needed.

"You deceive yourself. In truth, you go seeking confirmation of the Englishman's death."

"And if I do?" she snarled, all Wolf hackles.

"Then you waste your time, and only grief will welcome you. We both know he could not have survived his wound. If you had a doubt, you would not have pricked ink into your skin. Your head is not right!"

Strong Bear hadn't known Polly's delicate nostrils could widen so, or her breast heave with such indignation—not toward him—and he knew he'd erred.

"In that case, I shall go for my clan, for the prophecy, and for purpose. *I need it. There is nothing for me here, True Seeker."*

A slap could not have stung more. He reared back.

She blinked and promptly amended, *"For us."* Not promptly enough to stop the gouge to his heart.

The following morning, he'd stretched and turned over to find their pallet cold and empty.

"Coward!" The first word out of his mouth when he'd realized she left not only their blankets but him, shouted it so viciously it stripped his throat. Instant remorse swept in. Polly, the woman who'd assailed the Bluecoats' high chief, was no coward. She was simply broken, out of her mind with grief, unable to rationalize that time would heal. And they *did* have purpose. To rebuild.

He'd torn up his feet tracking her, but following sign had never been his strong suit and leaving none had always been hers. How many times during that hunt and since had he chided himself for not arguing further that last night? For not tying her to himself while she slept? Instead, she slunk away, and he'd endured years of regret. Each worse than the last.

There were mornings he still woke from vivid dreams and reached for her only to find searing hurt and loss where she should be. Each time, after his eyes had dried, the power of Creator Jesus granted him the emollient of forgiveness.

Polly had only done what she must to survive, and she was waiting for him. He knew it because he'd commanded it. Shouted it right along with his vow to find her.

And he *would*.

He fixed his gaze on the horizon and began a mental calculation of how much the water-logged earth and the swollen creeks might slow his progress.

The wind shifted and brought in the faint, unmistakable scent of man—sweat and tobacco and processed hides. An instant later, the birds went silent. Prickles crawled up Strong Bear's spine, and he stretched out his awareness. Hand going to the knife sheathed at his hip, his head began a slow rotate, his much swifter eyes skimming every shrub and shadow.

There.

His gaze latched to an unnatural outline barely visible through the foliage of an inkberry shrub. Gray on darker gray. His heart stuttered out of cadence, then dropped to a calculating thrum. Who might be stalking him? Muscles coiling, he slipped the knife from its case, and flipped it in his grip, the cold steel of the blade reassuring against his fingertips.

The man's form tilted left, a shift of weight to one crouched leg, and Strong Bear's shoulders plunged. His heart backed down from his throat. "Totka Hadjo. That fouled-up leg of yours keeps giving you away."

The smart remark earned him a harrumph.

Rising tall and lean, Big Warrior Totka Hadjo stepped from behind the inkberry. The silver of his armbands winked in the morning sun. His shin-high moccasins parted the lower branches as he advanced, a smirk shimmying his mouth to the side. "Well done, little brother. You are less terrible at that every time."

On impulse, Strong Bear stamped a foot forward, his throwing arm going with it. The knife spun out from his grasp and twanged eye-level into the pine an arm's reach from Totka's ear.

Totka's upper body lurched away from the impact. A wicked grin split his face. "Who taught you to throw so well?"

"A smelly lurking Wolf. And before you comment," he said, with a finger jab at Totka, "I do not mean the she-wolf of my dreams." Although, she'd done a fair bit of teaching as well.

"No, no." The senior warrior waved off the correction and began wrangling the blade from the trunk. "This Wolf is happy to take the credit, insult to my cleanliness or not. And I would never dare insult—" A grunt and vicious yank freed the weapon. "—the *she-wolf of your dreams*."

Strong Bear's smile shriveled, fingers curling into a ball against his will. "If you've come to stop me from going to her, you may as well turn around now."

Totka scoffed and bent behind the shrub. When he straightened, it was with a travel pack and bedroll slung over his shoulder. The barrel of his handsome rifle jutted up over his shoulder.

Fist falling open, Strong Bear felt the blood slow in his vessels. "What are you doing with that?"

"What does it look like?" Totka groused and kicked at Strong Bear's drenched bedding. "Coming along to watch your fool back."

Brow in a tight wad, Strong Bear gaped at his mentor. "But Copper Woman. The-the baby!"

The man wasn't known for leaving for the forge without two, three, four checks to ascertain his pregnant woman had every need met, every comfort at her disposal. Yet he would accompany Strong Bear to *the Point*? The gaping went on.

Head down, Totka scratched at the back of his neck and muttered something unintelligible.

"What?"

"I said she kicked me out!"

Strong Bear rolled back on his heels, the sharp arch of his eyebrows question enough.

"She said I was…brooding over the nest and…" The rest disintegrated again into grumbles.

"And *what*, what did she say?" This, Strong Bear could not miss. It might piece together the confusing bits of the verbal brawl between Flint and Totka that he'd walked in on.

The man heaved a gruff exhale. "And squawking and flapping about like a nervous mother chicken." He hung his head, too dejected to further guard his pride.

That didn't stop a snort from bursting out of Strong Bear's nose. Or the next from shoving insistently at the back of his throat. He felt his face grow hot with the effort to hold it in.

Every feature torqued with a fierce scowl, Totka glared. A dare to ridicule him, to snicker, to whisper one mocking word.

Opening his mouth, Strong Bear tipped his head back and blared laughter to the skies. Hoots and cackles wracked him hard until he was wiping tears from his eyes. When he cleared them, it was to the guilt-nipping vision of Totka, shoulders slumped, partway turned from him and facing Kossati, Strong Bear's talwa for the last fourteen moons.

Alabama Town had never recovered, so he'd taken up Totka's offer to join him and Copper Woman in Kossati—the best decision he'd made in his short manhood, especially where it concerned Flint. Strong Bear enjoyed his stand-in fatherhood, but no boy could ask for better than Totka Hadjo as mentor.

Strong Bear shuffled up to his old friend and clapped him on the back. "Squawks or not, you make a good husband. One day, I hope to be half as good to my Polly."

Groaning, Totka rolled his eyes and trudged off down the trail, grumbling, "Polly, Polly, Polly."

Indeed.

Polly.

Grinning like a lovesick fool, Strong Bear crashed to his knees to give his bedding a sloppy roll.

Polly.

His heart relinquished happy, tripping thuds as he crammed his supplies into his kit.

Polly.

On that invigorating chant, he lurched to his feet, pointed his moccasins south, and began to jog.

Chapter 8

San Marcos de Apalachee, Spanish Territory
Big Winter Month (December) 1817
Four months after arrival at the cow pens

Had Pretty Wolf known she was about to collide with her past, she would have greeted the day differently. Risen with a prayer, perhaps. Or scrubbed off the stench of cattle. She'd undoubtedly have combed her snarly, hay-speckled hair and checked her teeth for last night's pork. Any one of those would have given her a crisper edge of confidence.

As it was, when the horse in the adjacent stall began a stamping demand for his morning oats, she wiped the drool from her cheek and winced at a painful throb in her shoulder. She rotated the joint while repeating to herself why she chose to be in this heartless tack room-turned-bunkhouse, why she spent her night sleeping on the ground and her days covered in animal waste. All at the risk of angering any number of spirits.

A slow drag of pre-dawn air chilled her airways and prompted a toe-pointing stretch. At least here, away from Iron Wood's patrol, she could break the Rule. And she wouldn't apologize for it, wouldn't regret it, even if Screaming Buttons was, at present, snoring sour breath down the back of her neck.

Her nose crinkled up.

Four moons into this assignment, the man was an old moccasin: familiar and faithful but wearing thin and starting to smell. Regardless, he was a dear soul. And apart from Iron Wood, there wasn't another fellow she'd countenance sleeping beside. Well, not in the Point. Unlike the dour Big Voice or the reserved Kicking Knife, Screaming Buttons wore smiles as comfortably as he did his hide, and he never skimped on duty.

None did. Every day, she and her men toiled and sweated alongside one another. Slept and played, argued and ate at each other's sides. Twenty sleeps more of this, according to their arrangement, then they'd carry home their reward.

She shivered and resisted the urge to scoot farther into Screaming Buttons' bubble of warmth. Blue Feather, the woman he'd wed at last moon's turkey dance, wouldn't appreciate it if Pretty Wolf shortened the careful gap she kept between herself and Screaming Buttons.

And Iron Wood… He would make the spirits' wrath seem like kitten scratches.

Pretty Wolf had yet to tell him exactly how close, quite literally, she and these good men had become during this assignment. On that thought, Pretty Wolf edged a hair closer to the drafty wall an arm's stretch from her frosty nose. Their shared horse blanket offered little defense against the unusually frigid Big Winter month weather. Despite being crammed together, their bodies did shoddy work maintaining a bearable temperature.

When she'd gone to the Spaniard furious over such mean shelter, he'd replied, *"It is all we have, princesa."* Princess, he'd crowned her upon first meeting, much to her exasperation.

She was no royalty. Merely the daughter of the Point's most notable micco. Notable for his ruthless tactics against the whites, for his miraculous survival in battle, and for his dogged pursuit of a renewed alliance with the British.

That pursuit continued.

The day of last Frost Moon, her father returned from England, his two-year mission, complete and, as it turned out, an epic failure. Which he intended for her to right. Her, her immaculate English, and her immaculate Englishman.

All these things made her *princesa* to the Spanish, but she was nothing without her men.

So, she stayed. And froze the tip of her nose.

As the cow pens began to stir, Spanish voices trickled through the door Kicking Knife—Big Voice with him—had left open when he'd limped out on his broken big toe. Bowl in hand, he would breakfast at the eating hall one last time. It killed Pretty Wolf to send Kicking Knife home, but she wouldn't ask any more labor of him. The lovely task of finding a replacement went onto the day's list of chores. Right after shoveling manure and right between pleading and groveling.

How very ready she was to call this contract worked and done. Of course, that would mean mending the tears in her betrothal.

Eyelids falling closed, she brought Iron Wood's face up before her, then let herself long for his wit and masculine grace, if not his controlling nature and his probing of her soul.

During her last lesson with Toño, he'd given her a stern, fatherly talk. *"'Put off falsehood and speak truthfully,'"* he'd quoted, taking a wild, bewilderingly accurate shot at the cause of her unrest. *"Talk to him. The time has come to repair the rift with Señor Bellamy, mi hija. Your soul will thank you."*

Wisdom. Shocking, that, since his guidance had been Jesus talk from the Ancient Words, a book he'd read from aloud several times. Eerily, instinctively, she'd felt at once the thing was worth its weight in parchment.

She'd lowered her head, lips trembling. *"Sí, soon."* More a wish than an outright lie.

Beside her, Screaming Buttons snorted with the resonance of a boar and kneed the back of her thigh. Hard. Hissing out her pain, she drove a cocked arm back and into his ribs.

In the next instant, he was up. Knife in hand. Fighter's stance broad and steady. Eyes wide and keen. All with hardly a wisp of sound.

Pretty Wolf flopped onto her back, pulled the blanket over her eyes, and pinned it there with an arm. "It was Big Voice. He went that way," she scratched out, not bothering to point.

Screaming Buttons growled good-naturedly. "I will skin the tattoos from his chest. Or...no. I suddenly have a tremendous urge to make water. In his mug. Where is it?" His kicking about ripped the blanket off her face.

"Be still for once." Scrunching her sleep-swollen eyes, she yanked the blanket back up. "And can you not silence those earbobs of yours? They're far too merry for this miserable cold."

He rattled about in the demi-light of dawn, raining down vows of vengeance on Big Voice, which was acceptable to her. Big Voice was no man's favorite fellow.

"Are you sleeping on it, woman?" Screaming Buttons hooked a hand about her calf, lifted her lower half clean off the ground, and gave her a shaking.

She squealed. More laugh than indignation. Blood rushed to the top of her skull. Just in time, she clapped an arm about her middle to stay the slide of her upended sleeping shirt and thanked every spirit that she'd donned Iron Wood's old trousers for warmth.

"All right, all right!" She clawed onehanded at the straw like a digging dog, her torso twisting midair. "I did it!"

Screaming Buttons dropped her.

Grunting, she rearranged her limbs into a more dignified reclining pose.

"This World must be living its last if lies are being shaken out of the talwa's flawless daughter."

Flawless. It took everything within her not to scoff. Or duck her head, face flaming.

Either of those responses would only confuse Screaming Buttons. He might be teasing her, but sadly, his use of the term was genuine. However, he would not be so glib with her high standing in the tribe if he knew how wrong he was.

Between his brief, seasonal visits to Alabama Town during her long away, he'd missed much. Most notably, her gradually rounding belly, for which she was deeply grateful.

On the pretense of working crust from the corners of her eyes, Pretty Wolf squashed a prickle of unwanted moisture. "Worry not, brother. This World is not ending. The threat of destruction came and went with the Bluecoat war vessel." She turned over, giving him her back as if those six, long-as-the-winter days weren't the most frighteningly precarious of Wakulla's existence.

Relegated to the cow pens, Pretty Wolf had missed most of the excitement, her father's untimely return from England during those days further distracting her. But she had attended the lavish celebration at the Spaniard's hacienda, an eye-glittering affair conducted in honor of the Bluecoat medicine maker who'd saved his daughter's life and whom she'd chanced to meet. Marcus Buck. A decent enough man. As Bluecoats went.

A shiver snaked through Screaming Buttons' voice when he said, "From the first moment of that warship's unlikely appearance, I owned a strong sense of foreboding." He *always* owned a strong sense of foreboding.

"And yet," she said through a yawn, "the paleface sailors came and went, as harmless as a flock of robins."

"More lies, little sister? Keep telling them if it closes your eyes at night."

She would. As did they all.

The rumors of Bluecoat advancement were increasing but contradictory. Their destination, their target, and even their numbers changed with each scout's report.

"Go on, woman, get up and get it done before noon." He bopped her ankle with his toes. "We cannot give Rivas fuel to burn the contract."

Before she could catch it, a small cringe tightened her face. Screaming Buttons was not wrong. She must find an immediate replacement for Kicking Knife.

Don Diego was master of every man and blade of grass within three sights, and his contract clearly stipulated four men from Wakulla. Four. Not three. If she could find no willing male, what would she do? Recruit Cricket from the orphan's lodge? Melon from the cookhouse?

"I'm up, I'm up." She climbed to her feet and stretched high, yawning until her jaw cracked. "What do you think my odds are with Kills Many?" Part jest, that question. Part last resort.

Screaming Buttons looked at her like she had hay for brains. "He is with the war party."

Smacking a palm to her brow, she groaned. She *did* have hay brains. For not recalling that half her troubles were thanks to the war party being gone.

Her zealous father—back not twenty sleeps—had mixed his red paint and left with his warriors to pick a fight with bigger dogs to their north and to their west. Pale-faced, blue-coated dogs who made treaties with handshakes and ink, then unmade them with betrayals and blood. Dogs whose snarls and growls Pretty Wolf swore she could hear these many sights away in Spanish Florida.

She ran a hand down her face. "It escaped my memory they were gone." It was easy to forget that talwa life carried on outside these cow pens. She'd had few reprieves, the latest being the Frost Moon marital dance at which she'd conveniently made herself too busy to set foot in the square—much to her mother's horror and Iron Wood's humiliation. Some things could not be helped.

And her Pawa Tall Bull? For all his dread talk of ribbons and pushy clan mothers, the night of the dance had ended with him unwed as well. A tragic account of male stupidity and love lost.

"Besides," Screaming Buttons continued, pulling her from the Frost Moon. "Kills Many is too selfish to dare sleep in such close quarters with you. He wouldn't risk banishment." The promised result of his next infraction of the Rule.

"At least he'll finally get blood vengeance through combat." When a bullet found his sister during the attack on Fowltown, he'd lost all reason. He was convinced he'd find it again in spilled blood. Any white man's would do.

"I wouldn't be so sure," Screaming Buttons said dryly. "Unless he can get close enough to feel warm blood between his fingers, he won't be satisfied."

"He'd *better* come home done with that business. Runs Like Deer can't afford the strain of his obsessions. Not with the baby due in so few sleeps." Pretty Wolf snatched up their blanket and stalked to the entry. "I'm airing this. It's sour." As was her mood, and it was destined to worsen. She flung the blanket over the top of the open door, and Screaming Buttons appeared at her side to assist.

"The spirits tell us we should not be here, aiding this cruel sport." He waved vaguely in the direction of the bullfighting arena.

Pretty Wolf would not deny the truth of that, but there was no need to give it earth in which to set down roots. She lifted her gaze to the bullring presiding over the compound, its red-tiled rim scarcely visible over the stables. Falling back on the assurances Toño gave her when she felt particularly distraught, she said, "The bulls are born fighters, Buttons. They would rather face their executioners, horns down and charging than standing helplessly to have their throats slit. No matter the pain it brings."

"They would rather be free to live as Creator purposed."

She swiveled to the man. "Enough. Before I start believing you'd have us watch the flesh shrivel on our children's bones."

Nostrils distended, he met her head-on, giving her a clear view of the hurt warbling his pursed mouth, and she knew she'd gone too far.

An invisible fist clamped about her throat, but she pushed through it and thrust beseeching eyes up at him. "My tongue slipped its leash. Forgive me, brother."

His features softened with a hint of pity, and he reached out and cupped her cheek. "Our tireless leader. Too young for the weight she carries every—" The thud of trotting hooves severed his speech.

In tandem, they looked behind her.

Iron Wood, astride his black-maned gray, rounded the far end of the stables.

Screaming Buttons took a crisp step back from her. "Why is he here?" he asked, somewhat piqued. "Is there not a mule train due at the post this morning?"

"There is." The talwa had been abuzz with it for days. She walked out to meet her betrothed, Screaming Buttons trailing. As he drew rein at her right, her mouth bowed up. "Iron Wood."

Chapter 9

Eyes never leaving her, Iron Wood removed his hat. As always, it was primly brushed, its hawk feather perfectly preened. His snug frock coat boasted four silver buttons buffed to glittering in the sun, and its indigo color highlighted the blue in his eyes. Breathtaking, assessing eyes.

They passed over her, from her rumpled hair, over her sleep shirt and his trousers, to her dusty bare feet, where they stuck. A frown formed. *She'll catch her death of cold*, she could practically hear him thinking.

She stood still for him; he wouldn't be at ease until he'd assured himself she was whole and well.

At last, he dipped a gallant nod. "Hello, dear heart." The English greeting was soft as goose down. "Are you all right?"

Her forehead pressed down. Why wouldn't she be? "I am."

By his rigid aspect, he was not.

English lord by blood, naval officer by discipline, Red Stick by vow, Iron Wood could be a formidable enemy. Never hers, but she didn't envy those who experienced the rare instances his charming nature was thrust aside in favor of his more combative one.

His gaze tightened on Screaming Buttons. "He'll soon be counting a tidy sum of regret if he doesn't heed the Rule."

Pretty Wolf heaved a long-suffering sigh. "Put away your teeth, Iron Wood. I am the wolf, not you."

"Iron can have teeth too," he said, then showed his canines. "Don't pretend you haven't seen mine."

Oh, she had. The engagement at Horse's Flat Foot was not so distant a memory as to be even remotely hazy. For her, though, he had only tenderness. "Hush, now, my love, while I scare this bloke straight." He peered down the trim line of his nose at Screaming Buttons, his eyes two chips of pale blue flint as he shifted into her mother tongue. "The micco might have gone away, but his orders have not. What reason will you give him for breaking this one?"

"Apologies, Iron Wood." Sweat glistened around Screaming Buttons' mouth, but his spine did not bend. "The lost daughter grew anxious. In offering strength, I forgot myself."

Pretty Wolf bit her tongue at the byname. Clearly, she was *right here*. Aggravation heated her skin. She settled a hand on Iron Wood's thigh. When his eyes flashed to hers, she said lowly for him alone, "And *you* forget to trust me. I can handle myself with the men."

Tension bled from his body, and that irresistible charm of his crept across his lips. He glimpsed downward at their contact and winked. The wink was a complex gesture, having various uses and meanings. The implication of this one, however, was simple enough to grasp.

Old, familiar, wholly irrational needles of panic prickled along her skin. He'd obviously interpreted her touch as an invitation to be accepted later. She tried to slip away, but he wrapped gentle fingers around her wrist and bound her to him. "Sorry, Polly, sorry. Blast, I shouldn't have done that." His attention flicked behind her and back, now laden with strain.

Not her desire at all to humiliate him in front of another male. Yet here she was.

"The time has come, mi hija. To repair the rift with Señor Bellamy." The realization that Toño's *soon* should perhaps be *today* torqued her stomach into knots. Palming her middle, she studied the stitching on Iron Wood's saddle as if the solution to overcoming her queer anxieties lay hidden between the threads. *Later, I'll tell him.*

Smoothing down her disheveled hair, he raised his voice to include the man behind her. "Now, what trouble has the two of you so tense?"

"The spirits warn us with an ill omen," Screaming Buttons announced without apology. "Kicking Knife is lame, and Pretty Wolf despairs of a replacement."

Fingers snug about her wrist, Iron Wood—grinning like a raccoon with his paw in a fish weir—held her firm against his leg. "I do not hold to spirits and portents. Regardless, I'll admit the timing of this omen of yours is exceptionally convenient." His focus came back to her. "A small number of the war party returned last night. Among them, a few wounded and—"

"Captives?" she cut in, her tenor hopeful. His raccoon's grin now made perfect sense, and her own challenged it for breadth. She'd sent Tall Bull off with a bid for captives. If he could contrive to catch a few. For every able-bodied slave they brought in, one of her men could go home.

At her girlish delight, Iron Wood discharged a laugh. "Precisely, my dear. You're done here at last."

Pretty Wolf had no plans to leave the cow pens, but this was not the time to enlighten Iron Wood about her notions of personal sacrifice.

He switched to English. "Three captives in all. Your father snared his traitorous English supplier—God spare him. The two others are warriors fighting for McIntosh. Melon tells me at least one holds particular promise as a replacement."

"Excellent. I'll get Balada, so we can be off." Her sight flicked to her mare's stable box then to Screaming Buttons. "Have Kicking Knife stay on until we've returned with the slaves." At her friend's agreement, she began for their quarters.

A short while later, the ruffled hem of her full, midnight blue skirt swept the dirt as she stepped out of the tack room empty-handed. Flashing Iron Wood a disarming smile, she whisked the door closed behind her and prayed he hadn't glimpsed the single bed of straw inside.

He was striding toward her, scanning her person. "Your satchel?" Knowing Iron Wood, he wanted her ties to the cow pens severed at once.

"I am eager to see my choice of slaves." Pinning her woolen wrap at her collarbones, she brushed past.

"Polly."

The grated warning in his voice stopped her flat. Without turning, she waited.

"You intend to stay, don't you."

Not a question. Good. If he could be blunt, so could she.

"Yes." Tart. Unequivocal.

Silence. Then, "We shall see."

Minutes later, Pretty Wolf flung open the stall where she kept her little Spanish horse, Balada. The mare swung her head up from the hay bin, her blue eyes wide and eager. At Pretty Wolf's, "Come, girl," she tossed her mane and followed puppy-like into the yard.

At Balada's side, Pretty Wolf drew the body of her skirt between her thighs and up into her waistband. Ignoring Iron Wood's offer of assistance, she vaulted in a single leap onto the mare's saddleless back—her father to thank for her long, well-powered legs.

While Iron Wood slipped a coin to Tito, the stable boy, she spurred Balada forward. Neck arching proudly, the mare took off. Tuned to hoof-fall behind her, Pretty Wolf held the mare in check, so Iron Would could catch up. At his side, she repaid his knitted brows with a bright baring of her teeth. He responded in kind, but from there, a stubborn, uncomfortable silence ensued. They maintained it for the better part of their trek down the Wakulla trail, Iron Wood riding at her left and fore, ever scanning the terrain. So diligent. So faithful.

Her heart pinched. The man made it exceedingly difficult to stay peeved. Remorse finally won out over pride. Pretty Wolf cleared her throat. "If this is a contest over which of us can last longest without speaking, I assure you, I will win."

After a startled glance, he chuckled and reined back to bring his horse level with hers. "I've missed you, Polly. So terribly. Please, blame my overbearing behavior on my prodigious love for you." Apology outlined the melancholy smile he formed for her. "It is simply that I fear for your safety and wellbeing."

"Yes, too much fear," she stated, eyebrows cutting low.

"Darling, you're practically my wife, and with your uncle gone, your safety is my responsibility. Did he not make it so?" Iron Wood steered so close their knees brushed. "These are troublous times; there's no such thing as *too much*."

She blew out her cheeks and elbowed aside her disagreement. As well as her disquiet at his mention of their future. From her perspective, their relationship teetered on the brink of a high, deadly cliff. She veered from it. "Have you seen them yet, the captives?"

Iron Wood eagerly locked on to the neutral topic. "Haven't had a chance. Fog caught Melon in Wakulla last night. She stayed over. Arrived back at the trading post this morning with a message from Sunflower that I'm to fetch you to Beaver compound directly."

They broke from a mixed copse of palm and pine and entered a straight, clear stretch of sandy ground. She nudged Balada into a lengthened stride. The mare took to it with spirit, and muscle rippled beneath her cream-colored coat. Iron Wood clicked his tongue twice and kept pace.

"Spirits be good, we will find the slaves are in one piece." Pretty Wolf elevated her voice over the pound of hooves.

Iron Wood secured his tricorne against the thieving wind. "I highly doubt Sunflower would call you for men too broken to withstand sturdy labor. We'll examine them thoroughly and proceed from there. At least one has to be worth his muscle."

She pulled her mount to an abrupt walk. "You plan to stay?"

A few beats later, Iron Wood did as well, stopping just ahead, not speaking until she'd sidled up. "I'd never leave you alone to such as this." *Such as this* being unknown men. He may as well say it.

She tamped down irritation. "What of the string coming in? Korsan will work himself into a sweaty fluster over those twenty mules and their packs. You know his pirate ways slip through when he is pressed. Take me to Sunflower, then go. I have no need of you." *Great spirits, Pretty Wolf.* She hadn't meant it to sound so dismissive. So cold.

He shifted in his saddle, his gaze on the horizon, his nostrils sprawling.

"Iron Wood, I did not mean—"

"No, no." A flat smile pushed across his face. "I forgot. I'm supposed to disregard the memory of finger marks on your arms and trust you can *handle* yourself with volatile, unpredictable men." His knuckles went white around the reins, causing the gray to prance in place. The animal had scarcely calmed before Iron Wood barked "eyah!" and lurched into a gallop.

Sighing, Pretty Wolf held Balada in place and let the man ride out his hurt. His protective nature needed no encouragement to thrive. Unfortunately, Kills Many's tantrum last moon, when he'd manhandled her for accusing him of mistreating her mother, had given it just that.

Kills Many had paid for his attack with every feather he'd earned from brave up, but Pretty Wolf had paid by losing the ongoing argument that she didn't need a personal guard. Since that day, an armed warrior had hovered nearby. If not Iron Wood at the store, then one of her men at the cow pens. She was never alone. And she was never touched.

The Rule felt more oppressive than ever.

At the talwa's perimeter, Iron Wood pulled rein and slowed for her. They said no more until they'd crossed Wakulla's bustling square, navigated its grid-pattern lanes, and turned onto the path leading to Beaver compound.

Longing for sweeter ground between them, she cleared her throat. "How is everyone at the post?"

Iron Wood plucked up her peace offering. "Yesterday, Shem tried to use Melon's fabric basket for a stepstool. Shoved his foot straight through. His leg was scratched all to tatters as payment, or Korsan would have let Melon cuff him about the ears."

That got a chuckle out of Pretty Wolf. For a few luxuriously neglectful moments, she forgot about everything broken between herself and Iron Wood and basked in the familiarity of their shared life. "Brave man, Korsan, standing between Melon and her target."

Iron Wood's shoulder bobbed. "He knew she'd regret it once she'd cooled, and a fellow will risk any amount of displeasure for the woman he loves. Even if she doesn't return it." He didn't look at her when he said it, but really, there was no need. She received his talk precisely as he'd meant her to.

Her smarting conscience had her averting her sight to the approaching compound. Still a distance out, she finger-combed her tangled hair before whipping it into a loose braid she draped over her chest.

"Lovely, my dear," Iron Wood said through a smile that grooved his face too rigidly to not be forged by worry. "You've made it so you'll be in need of a good kissing before I leave."

The muscles between her shoulders pulled tight, but…she could give him that, a farewell kiss. "Whatever makes you feel better about leaving me with them."

"Are you up for a challenge, my pretty little wolf?"

Lashes flittering at the abrupt switch, she tried to recall if he'd ever come so close to using her new name. "Always," she chimed, a challenging boast of her own. She arched an expectant brow.

Several moments trundled past as he gnawed at his lip. "Before the night's through," he said, voice treading atiptoe, "you'll share…whatever formidable memory had you panicking at my touch."

Her heart slammed her sternum, then lurched into her throat, closing it right off. Heat flashed through her chest in the same instant that a chill raced over her limbs.

"Allow me to clarify," he rushed on. "I'll admit when it comes to women, I'm not the sharpest quill in the tin, but I do know that whatever has you flinching at every touch stems from…something dark. *That* is what I want. This pain you live in, your secrets…" He wiped a hand across the back of his neck. "It kills me, Polly, *kills* me."

Indeed, the slow death of his jolly disposition—today, every day—rested fully on her shoulders; they sagged under the knowledge it had only just begun. Spirits shield him once he was exposed to the murky floodwaters slapping at the tattered edges of her soul.

"The time has come…your soul will thank you."

Heat built in her eyes and converted to a film of tears.

"Polly, I know—"

Arm raised, she showed him a silencing palm and took a moment to hobble together her scraps of courage. *One word. It's all he wants.* It came out like a croak. "Maybe." Not exactly the one she'd had poised on her tongue.

"Maybe?" Hope warbled his pitch. "I mean,"—he cleared his throat—"are you in earnest?" Eyes round and glowing, he gazed at her as if she held the final ingredient to his happiness.

How tragic was it that the mere *hope* of her confiding in him could bring out such brightness? Tragic indeed. More so that such knowledge didn't stop dread from thickening in her veins.

Strands of Balada's mane bit into her tightly clenched fists. "Yes," she managed again, this time more steadily. "I am in earnest."

He took this in with a lengthy dip of a nod and let the rustle of palm leaves and the creak of saddle leather fill her ears.

"But be warned, Iron Wood. Once you know the darkness," she confessed, pushing past the thorny ball of terror obstructing her courage, "you will not love me the same. If at all."

"Impossible," he retorted and blessed her with a gentle smile and gentler tone. "There's not a thing in the world that could shake my devotion."

Pretty Wolf's curving mouth did its best with her wavering belief in his assertion. Head bowed, she twirled her moonstone ring around her finger and thought of the words she would use later to earn his forgiveness. *I would give everything to go back to that forest. To undo it all. I would wipe out every step I took between you and the end of that battle. I would do as you asked and—*

No, her heart denied. *You would not.*

Did she *ever* do as he asked? Certainly. When his desires coincided with her own.

Guilt burned hot in her gut, but she thrust out a stiff breath and set her sights toward Beaver Clan's parcel of land.

Chapter 10

Pretty Wolf cast her sight down the lane she and Iron Wood rode. It ended where the corners of Beaver Clan's storehouse and summer lodge met. Through the gap, Sunflower's courtyard fire burned cheerily in welcome. A tea kettle and a pot could be seen hanging from a crossbar over the flames.

Outside the compound, two warriors stood with their hands bound before them. Three others loosely surrounded the captives, these armed and wearing familiar, if haggard, faces. Behind the defeated warriors, stretched patches of winter-shriveled stalks of bean and corn, the stripped garden standing as poignant imagery of the People's plight.

As for the captive's plight… Unless Pretty Wolf intervened, they would become the bodily targets of every stone-wielding woman in Wakulla. Immediate execution was the other possibility—should any clan be owed blood vengeance for a slain member.

Facing those options, the captives' loyalty to White Warrior McIntosh's red war club would surely not hold. At war's end, the half-breed had received a blue uniform, complete with shoulder tassels, and a general's rank. Those of red birth who lifted the hatchet at his side were deemed the most despicable of traitors. Even so, what reasonable Muscogee would choose fealty to him over working for her?

Looking ahead to the figures, she attempted to pick out detail. "They are both of good age, and that one on the right has a sturdy frame for labor," she observed. "Any English opinions on them, Iron Wood?"

With a thinking cock of his head, he narrowed his eyes at the duo. "They seem uninjured. Capable. Whether they are of the correct disposition to follow orders should be easy enough to discern through a brief interview. The sturdy one, for instance, hasn't stopped glaring at us since we turned onto the lane. It sets my teeth on edge."

True, the lesser warrior hung his head, dejected, while his companion's gaze was level and pointed their direction. Whether he was glaring though—or whether his features matched his striking physique—was impossible to tell from this distance.

Both boasted the typical, lofty stature and toned musculature of Muscogee males, but the larger fellow rose half a head taller than all the others, guards included. Now that she'd drawn closer, she realized *sturdy* was a miserly description for his measure. He stood like a boulder, solid and unmoving. Layers of clothing weren't the cause of his width either. No, that was pure brawn filling out his long-shirt and thick woolen vest.

Uncertainty bent her mouth. When pitted against someone near her own weight, Pretty Wolf could hold her own. This warrior, however, could swallow her frame inside his own. In a physical confrontation, he would mash her into puree without shedding a drop of sweat.

If she accepted him as a slave, she'd need to be convinced his vow was spirits-take-him genuine. Otherwise, she and he might end up in a power struggle...or worse.

"Ignore that one," Iron Wood said. "We wouldn't want him to think himself worthy of your attention. Look elsewhere."

She would like to, but if she shied away now, the captives would never respect her. To that end, she replenished her lungs and, as they passed, greeted each Wakulla warrior by name. Nodded kindly. Welcomed every man home. Played the part of micco's daughter, taking to the task with pleasure.

These were fine warriors, all. Loyal men with stout hearts, and they'd brought replacements for the cow pens. Far better to put the enemy in the path of the spirits' displeasure rather than her men. Even the grumbleton, Big Voice.

On the far side of the compound, Sunflower stepped from the shadows of her open-air cookhouse and shaded her eyes. When Pretty Wolf left her mother's womb, it was Sunflower who wrapped her in deerskin and prayed the spirits' blessings over her. The old woman might be Beaver by birth, but Pretty Wolf was certain there was a Wolf's heart in her.

Arm high, Pretty Wolf hailed her. Sunflower repaid the gesture, then turned in the storehouse's direction to signal to someone out of sight.

Their path had brought them even with the captives, so Pretty Wolf took the opportunity for a cursory assessment. Head lowered and stationary, the smaller man observed her from beneath his lashes, his expression dull.

She offered a nod, and his eyelids fell farther, his chin pulling in sharply.

"At least one of them knows his place." Iron Wood dimmed his volume. "Don't look directly, but the big chap's still tracking your every move. Polly,

I don't like him. He looks in dire need of the gauntlet. A few projectiles should bring him down a notch or two."

Attune now, her side vision picked up the slow, bold turn of the larger man's head as it maintained alignment with their progress. His sight probed her in the side like a hot poker, daring her to turn and meet him eye to eye.

She aimed her chin up and looked in the opposite direction.

The man was chattel. Better he accept his groveling rank before he became insolent and earned himself entry to the gauntlet. She needed his body unbroken.

A familiar form rounded the storehouse, and her agitation vanished. "Winter Hawk! You are a dear sight."

Musket clutched to his side, the brave came clomping up, all big feet and mischief-eyed. "As are you, Pretty Wolf." He flashed Iron Wood a cheeky grin.

The Englishman returned it, relaxing into the saddle and folding his arms. "One battle and the brave thinks he is grown enough to cross hatchets with me."

In his fourteenth winter, the featherless brave had spent recent months in the **warriors' house**, bemoaning their peaceful state. Too eager for death, in Pretty Wolf's opinion, but there was no helping it when a pure red stick heart beat in a male's chest. Like her father, Winter Hawk would always be most content when in action.

"Perhaps he is." Pretty Wolf stroked Balada's ivory neck and gave the brave an overt inspection. "Did the Bluecoats put any holes in you? Give a turn and let us see."

"Holes!" Winter Hawk snorted and thumped his chest. "Lead shot pings off this wall of iron."

Laughter burbled out of her. "What did I tell you, Iron Wood? Indestructible, this one."

"No holes in his tongue at least," Iron Wood conceded, eyes gleaming. "Find war to your liking then?"

"It was wild and lively and glorious. Until I crashed into Strong Bear." Winter Hawk jabbed a thumb at the captives, bravado giving way to brutal honesty even as his round face bulged with a careless grin. "And if I am still whole, it is only thanks to Micco Tall Bull. He saved me being torn limb from limb." Winter Hawk tipped back and laughed as if he were recounting an explosion of flatulence during a meal instead of a brush with death.

"I'll have to thank him," she replied, smiling. "My pawa, how is he?"

"He is well. The White Warrior's men burst from the mist like ghosts and caught us off our guard, but Fierce Mink arrived in good time. In the end, I sliced them all down."

"No surprise there." She gave him a proud smile that had him ducking his head and shuffling his feet. "Plump Dove will be impressed when I tell her."

The brave's head popped up. "Maddo, Pretty Wolf."

"You earned it," she said on a shoulder bounce. "Now, what can you tell me about my slaves? Did they give you trouble along the way?"

Behind her, there came a disgusted grunt from the persons in question. She felt their eyes on her like an itch between the shoulder blades, and it was a trial not to fidget.

"Depends on the trouble you mean. Mortar there"—he gestured in their direction—"suffered an illness that came and went over several sleeps. Strong Bear half-carried him at the fever's worst. Mortar has improved health since yesterday, but you wouldn't go wrong giving him a day before working him."

"Understood." She swung her leg over Balada's withers and hopped down. The mare shoved her muzzle over Pretty Wolf's shoulder, intent on sticking close.

Iron Wood moved in. "I'll take her, love."

She handed over the lead rope, then turned to skim the captives. Her gaze bumped over the tall one—Strong Bear, she deduced—as if he were nothing at all and came to rest on the other. "Mortar?"

The warrior lifted his eyes, and his true state struck her, starting with his lips, which were cracked and as white as the beads strung through his hair. Arms crossed over his chest, he stood hunched. He wore the usual leggings, shin-high winter moccasins, and long-shirt, but no head covering or outer garment.

A gust beat at Pretty Wolf's braid as it whizzed past to plaster Mortar's shirt against him. Sketched out in such a way, his gaunt torso said much about his state of health.

She pitched her chin toward the nearest guard, Thunder Feet. "For pity! Put a blanket on the man."

A frown marring his brow, Thunder Feet looked comfortable wrapped in his woolen **matchcoat.** He reached back to yank at the ties of the rolled blanket strapped across his shoulders.

"And cut him free," she added. "You'll act orderly for me, will you not, Mortar?"

In reply, the slave burst into a chesty cough, and Pretty Wolf winced. The man hadn't the stamina to run far anyway. Or to curry a horse. Or do much of anything.

Disappointment sank into her.

Leaning away from the cough, Thunder Feet severed the man's slave cords, then slapped the blanket against his torso.

"Maddo, Thunder Feet," Iron Wood said, returning from having tethered both mounts to the hitching post by the storehouse. Hands clasped at his lower back, he came to a stop at Pretty Wolf's side. "We'll see the blanket returned to you."

Mortar huddled under it. "Daughter of Crazy Medicine, allow me to—" He took one step forward before wobbling, but a set of bound hands flung out and hooked under his shoulder, taking part of his weight.

The other captive. Strong Bear. "Save your strength." His voice rumbled with concern. "She knows you're grateful. Is that not so, Pretty Wolf?"

At the audacious direct address, her eyes snapped up to his and became instantly ensnared. Not on the orbs' tight-lidded intensity, nor on their earth-brown depths, but on their cry of *see me! know me!*

See him? She did.

But his face was all wrong. The flesh too filled out. The cheekbones structured too densely, their breadth a clash against her memory. And that thick strip of muscle layered over each hinge of his jaw... None of it belonged.

The nose, however. *That* was not wrong. Broken and knotted below the bridge, it was perfectly right.

Know him? She did.

And it made her brain skid and crash. Made the mental wall she'd constructed around every longing for him shake with the impact. She palmed her flailing heart and stared at him for an erratic set of beats, for ten or a thousand. She lost track as she soaked up the upward twitch of his mouth.

Like a feather in a gale, memories rolled and flipped and careened through her head. Toes curled into the dirt, she braced for the rush of floodwaters, but they didn't rise. No, they receded.

Her eyes widened, heedless of the stinging wind, and moisture sprang up. But she didn't need clear vision to call up those bronze-splintered irises. To know that they sheltered under thick upper lids and a canopy of stubby black lashes, that they were too closely set to be handsome and too unabashedly direct to be anything but faithful and true.

True, true...

"*You cannot leave, Polly,*" he'd once said. "*Not really.*"

Her heart *ker-thudd*ed against her hand, against a single thought: *He has come.*

Unblinking and ever obstinate, he gripped her in his speaking gaze. "*Muscogee country is your flesh; the Coosa, your blood; and I, Polly, am the ink beneath your skin. You will never get me out.*"

Absolutely, horrifyingly insane, that's what he was. As well as **White Stick**, enemy, slave.

"*Fine, Polly! Go. Run if you must.*" The last words she'd heard from him—True Seeker opening his hands and releasing her to her foolishness. "*But you will wait for me. One day, I will come for you. Do you hear me, Polly? I'll find you!*"

That shrieked promise, desperate and hoarse with the pain of abandonment, still resonated through her. Probably still vibrated the oak that had sheltered her from his sight.

Well, he wasn't shrieking anymore—doubtful the bulge of that corded neck could even produce such a pitch any longer. No, those were calm, fearless, nigh on smug eyes he showed her, and though his lips were closed and faintly bowed, she heard:

Found you.

Found you.

The thought, as unreal as the dream of *them*, gained substance and rang merrily through Strong Bear's bones. And Pretty Wolf, that exquisite thing, looked rung like a bell. Her shaky posture and blinking stare made giddy laughter erupt inside his mind.

What, had she believed all these years that he hadn't meant what he said, that he wouldn't keep his promise? Or did she think he'd been spouting childish, fear-fueled nonsense?

Four days ago, Strong Bear and Totka were en route to General Jackson with news of the flatboat massacre when they'd become embroiled in a skirmish at Medicine Point. That day, they'd been torn from each other—Totka hidden and spared, Strong Bear overcome and taken captive.

His captors? Pretty Wolf's own warriors.

Upon learning that, he'd immediately presented his wrists. And while the slave cords were going on, while they were cutting off the blood to his fingers, he was biting back a smile.

Nothing could keep him from his Wolf. Nothing.

Not with Path Maker on his side.

Latched to her rounded gaze, he ticked up one corner of his mouth, stopping short of tutting. *You know me better than to be shocked, woman.* He would put the mild rebuke to voice if he knew whether she wanted their history concealed. How she would manage such a thing, he couldn't guess, but he would leave the decision to her.

He was, after all, only a slave.

Her slave.

Hers.

The fact curled up and settled cozily inside. Did rabbits purr? Because a contented hum was rumbling deep in his spirit.

Strong Bear had known Wakulla was the end of his endless hunt. Known her name was no longer Polly but Pretty Wolf. Known her betrothed Englishman had indeed miraculously survived his wound. All this confirmed but days ago by Strong Bear's old acquaintance, Marcus Buck, when their paths collided on that war-ravaged bank of the upper Apalachicola.

What he hadn't known—but *should* have, given he worshiped a loving Creator—was whether his captivity would earn him a violent end or whether Pretty Wolf would have the power to intervene should the war widows decide to tie him to the **slave pole** and apply firebrands to his tender places.

Yet here he stood, his first morning in the talwa, whole and hale, slave to the woman herself. Which was hardly a change in status. He'd been enslaved to her from first glimpse. Slathered with war ash and cradling a lost child to her breast, she'd looked fierce and determined enough to challenge every Chelo-kee on the peninsula. In that moment, gangly boy or not, Strong Bear had been owned, heart and body. Rather like he felt himself now.

Willingly owned.

Ehi, he was wholly hers. The difficulty would be in making her *his*.

For that, several obstacles stood between them: the Defiance that enslaved him and her crazy chieftain father. But her betrothed, the suspected British agent, Robert Bellamy—the man currently glaring flaming arrows at him—made the other hindrances appear tame. Or perhaps it was Pretty Wolf's fixation with the man that was the truest, most daunting hurdle to overcome.

Bellamy narrowed his stunning blues to slits before slinking an arm around Pretty Wolf's waist and casually resting a hand on the hilt of his sizable knife.

Again, laughter knocked at the back of Strong Bear's teeth, begging for permission to fly. If the Englishman wanted the Wolf, Strong Bear was not the one to contend with; Bellamy would have to go up against Path Maker's will. And a bowie knife, no matter how impressive the size, wouldn't quite do the job.

Just the same, Strong Bear spared his rival a smirking glance.

Challenge accepted.

Chapter 11

Pretty Wolf's lashes were still beating, and she had yet to rip her eyes away from True—

Strong Bear. His name was Strong Bear.

Delight cavorted through her flesh. That name. It had to have been precisely, perfectly chosen.

"Strong as the bear." The words left her on so scant a breath that none seemed to hear.

Fixed on her mouth, Strong Bear thrust his gaze up and filled it with beautiful secrets as her eyes filled with *him*.

Over a white, travel-stained shirt sat a snuggly fitted fur-lined vest, spruce blue in color. If he had any adornments, they'd been stripped from him, along with his weapons. The usual sash, belt, and their sundry pouches encircled his hips, though the various loops hung limp, deprived of their weapons. A length of blue stroud covered his loins, and wool of the thickest quality protected his stout legs. Moccasins, also fur-lined, rose to shin height and boasted what must have been a hide's worth of beadwork. Somewhere in Muscogee country, there was a woman who'd calloused her needle fingers loving him.

A feeling of loss twinged Pretty Wolf's heart, then vanished. Because he had come.

The other captive, Mortar, was speaking again. To Iron Wood. "…work would you have us do?" But she couldn't focus on him because that single thought would not let her go.

He has truly, finally come. Spirits preserve him, was he keg-deep in the tafia? Perhaps, in his captivity, he'd succumbed to insanity. That must be it because he stared intently at her, his big frame coiled as though on the verge of rushing her. To do what? Snatch her up and charge through her warriors? Haul her back to Alabama Town?

He'd once threatened to do just that should she think to rejoin the Defiance. At the time, she poked at his undernourished muscles and laughed.

She wasn't laughing anymore.

If he acted on that fire glinting in his eyes—a genuinely True Seeker brand of defiance—he'd be on the **four-day spirit journey** before he could say *firebolt*.

The beat of her lashes still wouldn't slow. Neither would her heart. It buzzed like a fat beetle in her throat.

Iron Wood's arm came around her. His voice sounded. Conversing with the other captive.

Strong Bear's clutch on the fellow dropped away; his study of her did not. Rather, it expanded.

In double-time to the downward roam of his eyes, heat climbed her body. It reached her cheeks with a tingle of awareness that spread when the folds of Strong Bear's mouth bent in a slow, approving curve.

She choked on her next inhale.

In her periphery, she sensed Iron Wood turning to her, his tongue back to English. "Mortar doesn't seem up to snuff, I regret to say."

"M-mortar?"

Winter Hawk stepped in to cut away the binding on Strong Bear's wrists. Over the brave's head, Strong Bear maintained connection with her.

"Polly, what is it?" Iron Wood's voice puffed at her ear. "Didn't I tell you to pay that bloke no mind? Darling?"

Chest rising and crashing, she peeled her gaze from Strong Bear to do more blinking at Iron Wood.

Worry circled his face as he drew her around. With cautious movements, he lifted a hand to brace her cheek. "Is that devil frightening you? I'll have him carted off, all right?"

He didn't recognize Strong Bear. Little surprise there. He'd been delirious with pain when he'd demanded an oath that tied True Seeker to her life.

His thumb stroked under her eye and bending, head tilting left, shortened the distance between their mouths. "You're safe," he said, voice intimate and gruff. "I won't let him near you."

A second before contact, her brain caught up, and she jolted. But he drew her hip to hip against him and bowed over her. She angled away before he caught her lips, and hot breath spilled over her ear with his anguished, "Polly, please."

She stilled.

Finding Pretty Wolf

What was she doing? *Running again, you coward.* But she wasn't. Her responses were reflexive. Instinct driven. A hurtful, misshapen instinct that made as much sense to her as the combinations of his English alphabet letters.

Iron Wood hovered, not sparing her the full panorama of his misting eyes. Every feature tightened with the effort of restraint. Just the same, she saw it there, behind his twitching muscles, the torment. *"This pain you live in, your secrets...it kills me, Polly, kills me."*

Or perhaps it was the shame of rejection driving the knife home. Either way, remorse rang deep.

Sunlight hit his eyes, constricting his pupils. Their blue burst into a vibrant azure, and Pretty Wolf recalled her promise. At her shaky forgive-me smile, he dumped breath from his lungs and drew her in.

Her eyelids fluttered closed.

An age had passed since they'd shared intimacies, but when she allowed it, her body remembered him to be a gentle and generous lover. Even if her mind rejected the notion of a repeat.

Chilled and firm, his mouth covered hers and melded. But he'd scarcely touched her when the fingers at her cheek fell away. Their brief scramble at hip level preceded a set of metallic clicks, distinct in their intent.

Her eyes flew open, her head jutting back.

Still in possession of her, Iron Wood—eyes blazing, jaw muscle protruding—swiveled his neck to look down the arm he extended at shoulder height. The pistol he gripped bore center-chest on Strong Bear.

Her friend stood poised mid-stride, three steps closer than before.

With a garbled shout, she slapped Iron Wood's arm down. It gave way with unexpected ease, the muzzle now directed about Strong Bear's ankles. Only then did she notice his pointer finger wrapped about the handle, not the trigger. Small comfort next to Iron Wood's unusual volatility.

Apart from the hands white-knuckled at his sides, Strong Bear showed no alarm at having a pistol drawn on him. His unrelenting eyes belonged only to her. *"Pucase,"* Strong Bear said, voice quiet and deliberate, "does this man distress you?"

Her mouth fell ajar. Pucase, was she? Master? As ridiculous as it sounded coming from him, she supposed the title to be appropriate. In the strictest sense. But call her what he will, they both knew Strong Bear had no master.

"She is perfectly well," Iron Wood bit out. "Mind your place, slave."

Strong Bear's gaze never flickered from hers, but there was a telling tic in his left nostril. He quirked a brow at her.

Off to the side, Winter Hawk, musket butt jammed to his shoulder, held steady aim on Strong Bear. She flagged him off while edging back from Iron Wood. "All is well, maddo."

Again the tic, right before Strong Bear's clenched hands eased open and went rigidly straight. "Your reaction said otherwise, but forgive me, I've been told I'm no good at reading sign."

"A convenient mistake, ehi, Iron Wood?" Cackling, Sunflower hobbled to join them. The elder had a majestic face, craggy as the hills, a tale of the People inscribed in every groove and whisker. Her baggy lips bent with mirth. "Another male to see to your Polly's good care and safety. Ehi, convenient. You should thank him."

"Thank him!" Iron Wood huffed.

Sunflower made reproachful clicking noises at him. "Stow that fireclub." She flapped her hands, and behind the chickadee-yellow fabric of her caped dress, her sagging, unbound bosom echoed the motion. "Before you blow a vent in the slave's moccasin."

The flick of his thumb uncocked the weapon. On a grunt, he nudged it home behind his belt.

"Beloved." Pretty Wolf went to the **winter woman** and kissed the furrowed flesh of her cheek. "You remembered the slaves I asked for."

The elder crossed her arms over layers of shell and glass-bead necklaces. "It is my teeth I have lost, girl, not my head." The evidence flashed through her wide smile. "What fine pickings our warriors bring us, eh?" She divided her filmy gaze between the captives. "That one maybe not so much. But Birdie's fine fish stew will cure him. Plenty for all. Come share my fire." One gnarled finger aimed at Iron Wood. "Except you, English."

At her address, he whipped the hat from his head. "Pardon?"

"Go to your place of trade and come back to me tomorrow with news of goods." Cradling a hip, she winced as she tottered off. "Have a bowl for the road if you must."

Iron Wood snagged Pretty Wolf's arm before she could follow. "I will not leave Polly with these strangers alone."

Sunflower stopped and slowly turned, her map of wrinkles deepening.

Thunder Feet and the remaining guards, minus Winter Hawk, cast nervous glances at her and scurried off to investigate the pot.

"Which one worries you, English?" Sunflower said. "The one with fever wetting his brow or the one who would challenge an armed white man at the thought she is distressed by him?"

Iron Wood's expression crashed. His eyes darted to Strong Bear—whose countenance was a mask of nothingness—then off to some faraway place. Fire could not redden his pale skin more.

The weight of his shame stuck like sludge in Pretty Wolf's gut. With a brazenly pointed look to her elder, she elevated both her chin and her voice. "Let every man know, whatever distress there be, it is my own doing. And it is no concern of *any* other." Including Sunflower.

The whiskers on Sunflower's chin rippled into either a suppressed smile or a scowl. With the old woman, there was never any knowing.

Strong Bear's reaction was less vague, but then, she'd always read him like tracks in flattened sand. A thin line formed between his pinching brows as he lowered his head and stared at Pretty Wolf through the tops of his eyes: a challenge.

Any other, save Strong Bear, she amended.

Still gazing into the distance, Iron Wood missed, or ignored, it all.

Taking his hand, she spun him on the spot, putting his back to Winter Hawk's wide-open ears and Strong Bear's level stare. Though stiff, her betrothed didn't resist. She braced his scorching cheeks and tipped his face to hers. Inhaling the lovely notes of his floral scent, she brushed her lips against his. "The mule train comes soon. Korsan needs you."

Sluggishly, his focus returned. He peered long into her eyes, lips turning down. "But you do not."

"I do," she hurried out, heat building behind her eyelids. "You are my world, Iron Wood." Until the cow pens, he'd comprised every part of it. He would again soon. Then, with the next incoming vessel, it would be just them afloat on the Great Waters, the mysterious England climbing up the horizon.

"But *you*, Polly, are my soul." His confession emerged raw, bare. "My very soul. Living without you is a misery not to be borne."

There it was, their imbalance. It shredded her.

With some effort, she conjured an understanding smile and lowered a hand to squeeze his. "I know, and I'm sorry for it."

Her reassurance began dispelling the fog of doubt that grooved his features. Nodding, he trailed the backs of his fingers down her cheek. "Then I'm glad I had your tub and satchel brought home."

Brought home…what?

Fire singed her veins. Stepping back, she clenched down hard on her teeth and put into a look everything she would not say in another's courtyard. But he'd already turned, was already replacing his hat and striding for his horse.

No matter. She knew where to find him.

Him and her bathing tub.

Chapter 12

Veins a network of ice, Pretty Wolf stared at the place Iron Wood last occupied—the end of the lane where the slanted palm overshadowed the way, its fronds undulating under the wind's ministrations.

She squeezed a knotted muscle on the back of her neck, and her stomach soured at the confrontation to come. One good thing to result from Iron Wood's meddling and control was that it made her too angry to even contemplate that *maybe* talk they'd discussed. Anything directed at him in the next few days would be nothing but vitriol.

When she finally peeled off that putrid bandage, it could be with nothing less than abject humility.

"When you have done brooding about your English," Sunflower said from over Pretty Wolf's shoulder, "you may cease pretending you are a stranger to your new slave."

Pretty Wolf twisted abruptly at the waist to take in the elder's pleased-with-herself expression.

"You know?" Pretty Wolf demanded in the same instant that Winter Hawk exclaimed, "You know him?"

Behind them both, Strong Bear watched her unabashedly, subdued happiness sitting on his lips. Settling in, he crossed his arms. The motion broadened his upper half, accentuating his trim lower half and swelling already uncommonly swollen muscles. This wasn't the build of the average young warrior. That was to say, sleek and fit, strong enough to draw a bowstring to the lips and hold indefinitely. This—the slabs of muscle tautening Strong Bear's shirt—resulted from a meat-and-fat rich diet combined with strenuous daily labor.

What *had* he been doing these years they'd been apart?

Her gaze trailed up his chest and snared on a four-string reed choker. From its center dangled a silver emblem. Two crossed sticks, the horizontal one a third the size of the vertical. A cruder, wooden version of the same stood atop the Black Robe's sacred lodge in the villa.

Her lips bunched. She'd left True Seeker in an almost empty talwa with only Grandmother Sun for company. When had he been exposed to the spiritual beliefs of the palefaces? Who'd come along to teach him? Pretty Wolf had missed much.

Jealousy needled. Toward whoever had spent those days with him. Toward *him* for having been able to educate himself, for having the freedom to explore other beliefs and practices. To choose them for himself if he so desired. And clearly, he did.

With her next thought, the jealousy yielded to a rush of more noble feelings. True Seeker had unabashedly made his own way through this new world of theirs, and for that, she felt pride.

She spread her toes out then in, gathering Mother between them, her loyalty unshaken. Still, to have the opportunity to learn whatever she wanted, unimpeded… What a gift. One she'd purposefully forsaken in her pursuit of family. But should she not be allowed to have both?

Freedom and family.

Strong Bear had kept his freedom, but had he found family? She glanced at his moccasins. Was that who'd beaded his footwear, who'd given him that adornment on his neck?

Rather brazen of him to wear it in their talwa. The Black Robe was a despicable man who taught love and lived hate, but Pretty Wolf was not so small-minded as to believe he represented every Spaniard—or Muscogee—who wore the cross. Toño could be named a pure-hearted example of one who practiced the goodness taught in the Ancient Words. Even so, Strong Bear had surely been informed of the potential repercussions of bringing the cross into her father's domain.

The object of her fixation quivered as Strong Bear cleared his throat. Her gaze darted up. *Caught you*, his expression teased, and a warm wave began to climb her throat.

Sunflower, who'd been saying who-knew-what to who-knew-whom, turned to Strong Bear and, bless her, stole his attention by grabbing his cheeks in both twisted hands. "The moment I laid these old eyes on him, I knew Strong Bear for the nephew of Lame Deer." She administered a set of smacks to his jaw. "My, but you are the reflection in his mirror."

"Grandmother Sunflower," Strong Bear said, using the term of respect for all winter women. His eyes crinkled as he took her hands in his. "The Great Maker of my path and of all things shines on you, for only his strength could bring you this far." His voice was a mill, grinding deep with affection and making Pretty Wolf wonder if Sunflower had caught his fall from the womb as well. "The road to Wakulla could not have been an easy one."

It most certainly was not, every footfall a different form of pain. By the end, even the most hale stumbled along the path.

After the treaty—the not-signing of it—the Defiance repaired to the Apalachicola River and its Black Fort, an abandoned British stronghold sheltering escaped Georgia slaves. There she found her clan, but shortly after, so did the Bluecoats. Or they would have, had the People not thrown their meager belongings onto their backs and flown, pushed hard to get ahead of the marching boots and rolling cannons.

The fort did not survive. Not one stone of it, the runaways in it blown to tatters. But the People escaped and found sanctuary in the Point. Reluctant hosts, the Spanish had fallen on lean, uncertain seasons themselves, but there the People had settled, and there they would stand. In Wakulla.

At least, Pretty Wolf would. She'd run her last.

"Work these old bones, and they won't kink, I always say." Sunflower cackled and wrinkles folded over her eyes, hiding all but the white lashes. "How well it suites my heart to sit a child of Alabama Town Rabbit at my fire. And you are welcome indeed, dear man, for providing for our lost daughter during her long away."

"I'm not lost," Pretty Wolf inserted, but Sunflower went on, jowls shaking to the beat of her gushing.

While Strong Bear focused on the elder, Pretty Wolf took advantage to catalog him more thoroughly.

He was an intriguing combination of youth and manhood. His build and strong features were without question those of a mature male, but that powerful jaw was as smooth as the sole of a newborn's foot. Upper lip, chin, neck—nothing but clean, sleek ocher, Creator's fondest color for his red children. Neither whisker nor blemish could be seen, and there was a glaring absence of scars and ink.

What warrior, wearing no less than three feathers, had gotten that far on the battlefield without scars? The knot on his nose being the exception—herself to blame for that one.

And what of his hair? Even Winter Hawk, who must be a full four seasons younger, had **roached** his scalp in the fashion of warriors—all hair shaved apart from an upright crest bisecting his head. Strong Bear wore his uncut and unbound. His feathers clung to a beaded tuft at his temple; the rest fell about his shoulders, absent its typical kettle-black sheen. Natty strings of it puddled on his crossed arms. Nothing a handful of soap nuts and a stiff porcupine-quill brush couldn't repair.

That was the sum of Strong Bear, the man-boy who boasted paleface beliefs and outfitted himself in finery too abundant for one so young. Hadn't he yet to reach sixteen winters? *More*, that well-formed body declared. Seventeen then? Why could she not remember how many seasons separated them?

She flung her hearing open in time to register him breezily shrugging off Sunflower's gratitude.

"Little enough *providing* done, Grandmother. Pretty Wolf cares for herself." Wearing a small knowing smile, he raised his eyes to her.

Thankfully, she'd finished ogling him.

"None will argue that." With the bob of the elder's silver head, a strand shook loose from the bun pinned at her crown. Pretty Wolf reached to tuck it back in while Sunflower went on. "Then I thank you for allowing her return to us."

"I allowed her nothing," he spouted. "The woman does what she wants. I seek only to serve."

This amused Sunflower no end, her shoulders rocking now along with her head. "Ah, True Seeker. That old name befitted you so. As does the new, I see." She pinched various muscle-bound spots on his body—arm, breast, thigh—then grunted her approval. "Pretty Wolf, greet the man properly, then bring him to my pot. Before you take him away, we must fill this belly."

She poked him there, and he sucked in his gut. A titter escaped him, his lack of shame over the silly sound only enhancing his likability.

She threw her gaze elsewhere—Balada's rump would do. If only Strong Bear had become a scar-faced scoundrel. Then maybe she would feel more at ease about the upcoming nights. Nights spent in a breath-frosting, single-blanket, one-pallet lodge.

The sudden quiver in her heart could mean many things, but she ruled on anxiety. This wouldn't be the first time she'd slept beside Strong Bear, nor the fifty-first. But that was…then.

She groaned within. This was not good. Chances were great Strong Bear would revert to his old ways. That of inserting himself between her and Screaming Buttons. To say nothing of burrowing his nose into her hair while he slept. Then Iron Wood would peel the hide from his body and trade it at the store for a cup of salt to throw on his wounds. She hated the thought of Strong Bear out in the cold, but there was nothing for it but to try and scrounge up another blanket and wish him good sleep elsewhere.

"Come, Winter Hawk. You too." Sunflower flapped a hand at Mortar and began a shuffle toward the courtyard. "If you want food and rest, bring yourself with me."

Hunched and coughing anew, Mortar obliged.

Winter Hawk obliged himself by staying put. He swung his head between them. "So then..." One cheek bunched in a sly smile worthy of the talwa's most skilled gossip. "How is it you know one another?"

Pretty Wolf answered, "From our childhood talwa." Then, as though an afterthought, "He is still a baby in my eyes. I once wiped his backside when he soiled himself." A small stretch of the truth.

A frog couldn't bulge its eyes any better than Winter Hawk, but Strong Bear tipped back his head and laughed rich and long.

"*That*," he said, coming down for breath, "is your proper greeting? Tales and insults?" He turned to Winter Hawk. "I'd seen my fourteenth winter before we met, and I assure you, I was not still soiling myself." Laughing tears glistened at the corners of his eyes, and she desperately wanted to laugh along with him, but that would hardly be "pucase" of her.

"Four, fourteen." Pretty Wolf gave an unconcerned shrug. "And, ehi. It's all the greeting you'll get."

He returned her a charming grin. "It will do. For now."

What did he expect would happen later? He behaved as though he, a White Stick despiser of their heritage and sacred traditions, did not stand in the camp of his enemies. As though there were not a hundred threats looming over his every breath.

Fear for him scorched a cold trail through her heart. He did not belong here. With her. With the Defiance. Why else would she have slipped away in the night? Because her father would crush his white-leaning, peace-praying spirit, then start on his body—that emblem at his neck, all the evidence required.

She blinked slowly—to make believe he didn't affect her—then rotated away to look again at the hitching post. "Why have you come, Strong Bear?"

"What a question, Pucase," he replied glibly at her back. "You phrase it as if I bound myself in slave cords and threw myself at your micco."

"Did you not?" She pivoted back, heat racing through her blood and tightly balled fists. "Dress yourself in slave speak if you like, but I know what lies underneath—the mind of a keen strategist. You made yourself captive because you could not come in as the White Stick, McIntosh follower that you are."

"A spy?" Winter Hawk's grip went to the musket strap on his shoulder.

Strong Bear snorted. "I do not *follow* the red general, nor will I ever."

"Thank spirits for that," Winter Hawk breathed. "I'd be loath to put you down." His interjections slid past them.

"Then who *do* you follow?" she challenged.

Of late, there were treaty-toting White Sticks, and there were tradition-abiding Red. To reject the one was to adhere to the other. Middle ground did not exist, and she would pass out from fits of hysteria if he now claimed allegiance to the Red Stick Defiance. Strong Bear would always be White to the marrow.

"Really, Pretty Wolf." The tilt of his mouth somehow managed to mix hurt and swagger in one down-tick. "That hardly requires voicing."

"Yet voice it you will."

Expression blank, he said nothing, and tension stretched taut between them, a drawn bowstring.

Sunflower called from the direction of the fire.

Winter Hawk plucked at the fringe of his sash.

Aggravation mounting, Pretty Wolf locked down in a battle of the eyes, stepping so close his scent invaded her: sweat from the road blended with a strong note of pine. "Before we take one step outside this compound," she demanded, "I *will* hear your loyalties spoken plainly. Who do you follow?"

Their eyes brawled, their breaths—hers ragged, his irritatingly even—clashed, and the silence grew, each moment more heavily laden with memories and unspoken feeling than the last. So much feeling it frightened her.

Afflicted with the same, Strong Bear didn't blink away the shimmering thread that accumulated on his lower lids. His mouth opened and hung for moment before he scratched out, "You, Wolf. I follow you."

Chapter 13

The truth of Strong Bear's declaration inscribed every line of his face, each a story in dedication, pursuit, promise. Pretty Wolf swallowed with an audible *click*. Her eyes put down the hatchet and began a searching trail of his altered features.

She missed the boy she'd once shared a life with. Shared a love with. Brotherly, granted, but love just the same. Profound, unerring love. Sprouted from calamity, rooted in adversity, watered daily with faithfulness and unconditional friendship, her love for him would never be shaken.

It had been beautiful then; it was beautiful now.

As was *he*. Handsome, no. Not in the sense of balanced, finely crafted features, but in the familiar, sturdy cast of their people.

Their people. Did they share a people anymore? The notion they did not gave her such an ache in the heart that she touched the place.

Strong Bear's gaze broke for a downward flick, then lifted again with a smile that eased the twinge in her chest.

"I think…" Winter Hawk leaned in for a whisper-shout. "That is warrior speak for *I want to build you a lodge*."

"It is not," Pretty Wolf huffed, as Strong Bear stated, "Already done."

"Already— What?" Winter Hawk gave his head a slight shake. "When did you build her a lodge?"

Pretty Wolf rolled her eyes, fondly recalling True Seeker's construction efforts. "Ehi, he did try."

Thoughts whirring behind his faraway gaze, Winter Hawk seemed not to hear. Then suddenly, "True Seeker!" He slapped a hand to his forehead, the exclamation drawing the attention of Sunflower and Mortar from their position by the fire. "You are the daring brave, True Seeker!"

Strong Bear rendered a light, deprecating laugh, and Sunflower crowed, "You have only this moment realized it, boy?"

Pretty Wolf would never hear its end now. She sighed and drooped almost as proficiently as Mortar.

The captive had seated himself at one of the four benches outlining the fire. A steaming bowl rested on his thigh, but his limbs were boneless, his body bowed in. Sunflower touched his shoulder, and he rose to shuffle after her, the dish clutched two-handed against his chest. Pretty Wolf watched until Sunflower ducked her gray head into her small, thatched dwelling and disappeared into the shadows, Mortar on her heels.

"True Seeker,"—Winter Hawk was still squawking, Strong Bear still chuckling—"the boy who played husband to the lost daughter has rejoined us at last."

Horrified, Pretty Wolf sucked air. "Husb— I never said such a thing!"

"Calm yourself, firebolt." Strong Bear's large hand settled on her shoulder; she shook it off. "I take no offense you thought of me in such a way."

A laugh trumpeted from Winter Hawk. "Firebolt! What a fitting name. May I use it?"

"Only if you want a nose to match mine."

"Bah! I can fend off that one's swings."

"Pretty Wolf would not be the one swinging." Strong Bear's smile had something of his namesake in it, but Winter Hawk only beamed at him with sappy-eyed worship. As if having his nose reshaped by the renowned True Seeker would be the ultimate honor.

The brave pounded his heart twice and extended his arm to Strong Bear. "On behalf of every Wakulla boy who has dreamed of being True Seeker to the micco's lost daughter, I welcome you among us."

Strong Bear shook the proffered arm and showed his teeth in another bear's grin. "Maddo, brother. You may tell your fellow braves I will be stopping by later to castrate them."

"Castrate, ehi, of course. I'll pass it along." The vigorous pumping of the arms now included Winter Hawk's bouncing head. "I've cast my eye on Plump Dove, so this one is all yours. But I offer myself should you need extra muscle wrestling her from Iron Wood. I like him well enough, but we are Rabbit, you and I. Clan before all, eh?"

Fury heated Pretty Wolf in an instant, and much like the lightning she epitomized, she exploded. "Stop this! Stop this now!" She tore between them, ripping apart their ridiculous camaraderie, then glared first at one, then at the other. "There will be no *wrestling* and no more talk of, of...husbands!" She jabbed her pointer into Winter Hawk's sternum. "You just want to roll around in the dirt with the boys, throwing your fists, and *you*—" Another jab, this one for Strong Bear.

He leaned back and raised his hands to fend off impending assault. "Hold there, now. I've no intention of wrestling you from anyone." Sounds of disappointment rumbled from Winter Hawk, but Strong Bear paid him no heed as he clutched the symbol at his throat and let his eyelids slip down. His mouth twitched with brief, unvoiced words before his lashes lifted again. "I have something to tell you. It is most important, but take us away from listening ears." He still pinched that bit of silver, clinging to it like a lifeline.

So the cross was it then, his *something*.

The worry she'd nurtured since first recognizing him vined through her. Strong Bear's spiritual path was his own, and by the brilliance of his eyes, it gave him happiness, which gave *her* happiness. But he could not flaunt it in open daylight. In Wakulla, of all places, in front of the loose-tongued Winter Hawk, of all people.

"I see your spirit journey has taken a happy turn, but you shouldn't have come. Your sacred symbol cannot be for me, Kit." Though she *did* have a quiverful of questions—they'd been accruing since she began lessons with Toño. "And for you, in this talwa, it will bring only trouble, if not death." Palm up, she waggled her fingers in a give-me gesture. "It will be safe in my keeping."

"You misunderstand." His arm swung down to his side. "This has nothing to do with the cross."

Her fingers quieted. Then what could it be? Certainly nothing worth his life. For he'd indeed risked it by coming south.

"Perhaps not, Strong Bear, but..." Winter Hawk rubbed his chin and hummed, a decent imitation of her father on his council bench. "She is likely correct. Micco Crazy Medicine will not tolerate it, and I would be loath to put—"

"—me down." Strong Bear cut across him, tone drab. "You've mentioned it, but I've sworn no fealty to the Defiance or its tenets. I may wear whatever sacred object I wish."

At that, Pretty Wolf snorted. "You're a slave. Your wishes go no further than the puff of breath that formed them. Take off the choker, White Stick." The finger-waggle restarted, and the cross disappeared again inside his clasp. "Think," she snipped. "It is for your protection."

"A higher power than yourself guards my life."

She dared not ask which, but she could practically see the name *Jesus* hovering in his voice box. And it stung her flesh with pins of fear.

Her hand flinched with the urge to smack down over his mouth and muzzle his crazy talk, or to simply smack him. How could he not see the gravity of the matter? Feeling backed into a corner, she lowered her arm and stepped away. "Very well. Keep it on." She shifted to Winter Hawk and starched the cast of her voice. "You will pack provender for ten days and escort Strong Bear out of Wakulla. Give him the food and free him. For his own wellbeing."

She prayed Strong Bear wouldn't force her hand because, sweet spirits above, she did not want him to go.

"Free him? But—"

"She bluffs, Winter Hawk," Strong Bear said, though it was herself his gaze burned. He planted his legs wide and linked his arms at his breast. "I'm not leaving."

She sighed her exasperation. "You wear the cross and speak of lodges with the micco's betrothed daughter. You are not welcome here." An outright lie. She could no more *not welcome* him than she could the flow of her own blood.

"Girl, what did I tell you about feeding that man?" Sunflower's crackling voice carried over.

Pretty Wolf shoved around and stalked across the yard to the old woman. "Strong Bear cannot stay, Grandmother. We must send him back. He wears a—"

"Psht!" Sunflower poked a long spoon in her pot. "You have said enough for one morning. Time you practiced silence. Serve your slave stew before hunger tips him over." Her rheumy sight lifted over Pretty Wolf's head. "Never mind our feisty Pretty Wolf. You are come to us for a purpose, and you will stay."

No! her mind screamed, but her tongue was delighted to observe Sunflower's orders. Strong Bear had proven to have sway over the floodwaters, and the notion of having him always near to quell them sent relief sighing through her.

"Maddo, Grandmother," Strong Bear said from behind, his bold hand coming to settle again on her shoulder.

"The Rule, Strong Bear." Winter Hawk cast a look of warning over his shoulder from where he had moved to wring his hands over the fire.

"What rule?"

"No male is to touch the micco's daughter. Other than clan."

"You cannot be serious."

On a forceful outbreath, Pretty Wolf said, "Quite serious."

Strong Bear scoffed a laugh. "As if you were plagued with the dangerous spots?" The mirth in his eyes dimmed as his gaze caught hers, no doubt seeing what it cost her. As always, her soul stood naked before him.

"Ehi." Winter Hawk nodded. "Much like that. As punishment, warriors are deprived of honor feathers. But a slave…" A line formed across his brow.

"Shut your yap, boy. Strong Bear and that rule live in different lands." Sunflower snapped her fingers. "Make yourself of use and dig about the storehouse for the summer lodge door flap." As he trooped off to obey, Sunflower patted Strong Bear's arm. "Have you taken the vow of loyalty to the Defiance?"

"I cannot. I am under another already."

"A man can be under two oaths at once."

"Not if the interests of the second endanger the first."

Sunflower bunched her wrinkled lips. "To whom did you give this first vow?"

"To the trader, Iron Wood."

This swung Pretty Wolf's head up and around to show Strong Bear her knitted brows. He fashioned her a tender smile.

"The nature of the vow?" Sunflower persisted.

His fixed gaze went the tiniest bit melancholy, his smile slipping. "May I have a moment to ask counsel of our elder, Pucase?"

Pretty Wolf's head tipped left in question, but at the return of his reassuring smile, she gave him a short nod. "I'll look in on Mortar."

In the summer lodge, she found the man laid out flat on the couch and snoring. She took his empty bowl from its precarious perch on his chest and pulled the blanket to his chin. She checked his brow—mildly fevered—and left to collect more firewood from the stack beside the cookhouse.

From the corner of her vision, she made out Strong Bear and Sunflower seated on a bench, heads bowed close. Pretty Wolf had every intention of giving them privacy, but her mettlesome eyes would have none of it.

Sunflower was clutching the front of her blouse, her face shaped by shock or grief or… What could he be telling her?

Telling her… Strong Bear was telling her! Had already told her, judging by Sunflower's soft wail and the shaking hand that couldn't contain it.

Strong Bear braced his arms on his splayed knees and drove every finger into his hair. A wounded cry strangled in Pretty Wolf's throat, and Strong Bear wrenched upright.

Skirts hiked, she reeled about and powered across the yard to Balada where she crushed her face against the mare's warm neck. The pungent scent of horseflesh filled her nostrils and sorely tempted her to swing up and ride away. To put Wakulla and the cow pens, Iron Wood and his demands, responsibilities and old heartaches at her back and gallop away. To the Point's end and beyond.

Experience reminded her, however, that running accomplished nothing. Did her bones not still moan with the despair of Alabama Town? They'd moaned there; they moaned here; they would moan at the farthest reaches of the land.

Her one consolation: Sunflower was one to keep a woman's confidence.

Balada whickered and bumped her muzzle against Pretty Wolf's head. Blindly, she reached out and scratched the creature under the forelock.

Strong Bear would be arriving at any moment. To him, privacy was a ridiculous word. In times of sadness, he invaded her space and trespassed her heart, never resting until she was right again. True Seeker, the remedy to every ailment of the heart.

Until one day, there had come a sadness that all his crowding and plundering and diligence could not repair. And he'd agonized. With her and for her... For his own failing. Still, he'd hovered, coaxed, comforted. As he would now.

He didn't.

Neither in that moment nor in any other over the next half-hour of time.

In the interim, Pretty Wolf collected herself, fed Balada a handful of grain, watched Winter Hawk grump at the door flap that wouldn't stay hung, and wandered out to the decomposing cornfield. She drew letters in the dirt with her big toe as she mentally composed a response to Sunflower's inevitable interrogation.

Birdie arrived leading a mule and two-wheeled cart. Inside, the third captive. Hambly, the English supplier accused of treachery. His bloodied condition came as no great shock, but he lived, and for that, Pretty Wolf was grateful. Birdie waved a greeting as she passed into the courtyard, then aided the man from the cart and into the summer lodge. Between Birdie's and Sunflower's ministrations, he would recover in short order.

Finding Pretty Wolf

Earth gritted between Pretty Wolf's toes. Yearning closer contact, she crouched and scooped up a handful.

Shuffling footfalls approached. Rising, she stared out across the shriveled cornstalks and pressed the fist of earth to her heart, then shut her eyes to better sense its soothing properties.

Feeble arms wrapped about her from behind. "What a grief you've borne these many moons, dear one. Why did you say nothing?"

"The grief was mine to tell." The words trembled out of her, and she clung harder to her tiny portion of Mother. "*Mine*."

"Strong Bear did not know. He could not imagine you would bury the pain so deep for so long. He has a heart that throbs warmly for you, child, and it is troubled. As is mine."

Guilt tore at Pretty Wolf's throat and thickened it into an ache. Head hanging, she conceded that for all her mental preparations, she was not ready. Her heart would not open to Sunflower, never mind her mouth.

Chin leveling with the horizon, she loosened her fist. Dirt trickled away. "We have other concerns."

Sunflower gave her a sigh and a squeeze before rounding to her side. "Which concerns?"

In a few brief lines, Pretty Wolf related how the last day had unfolded. The angry cow. The broken toe. Screaming Buttons' superstitious fears and her own theory that the spirits had no part in it.

Sunflower tapped her lips and hummed. After an extended pause, she nodded. "If this is work of the spirits, it is not punishment but a sign that Kicking Knife must get off his feet for once. He is up in years but labors as a youth."

The ache in Pretty Wolf's windpipe relaxed with her light laugh. "Yes, beloved."

The elder released a lungful of rasping humor. "And then there is this one."

"This one?" Pretty Wolf looked to her, expectant. What she did not expect was to find Strong Bear stationed immediately behind them, countenance grave, tracks of salt dried on his cheeks. Her eyes flashed open wide.

Mouth twitching, he reached out and picked a stub of hay from her braid. "I arrived with Sunflower."

Pitiful and wistful, a smile curved her lips. "Your stealth is much improved, White Stick."

He shrugged. "I had good teachers."

More than one? Well, she supposed the twigs could be considered teachers. Once, after he'd crackled foliage underfoot and frightened off game, she'd smacked his bare toes with a stick and told him to walk on a bed of them until he could do so soundlessly.

Sunflower tapped the deer-antler handle of the knife newly hitched at his belt. "Our Strong Bear is rearmed."

Arm a captive warrior? Did the elder trust him so thoroughly? Whatever the case, Pretty Wolf would not bring attention to the supposed folly. She preferred him protected. Instead, she knuckled him lightly on the shoulder. "Too grown for your sling shot, eh, Kit?"

"Never. I loaned it out."

"I regret you lost your musket." Sunflower went on in a rambling manner. "But the knife will serve well enough for your purpose."

Pretty Wolf launched an eyebrow her way. "What purpose?" Shoveling manure was hardly dangerous business.

"Guarding you, of course." An impish chortle bared Sunflower's half-rack of teeth. "Did you not hear? There is rumor Bluecoats are afoot."

Chapter 14

Strong Bear was shaking.

Distress trembled his innards. Breath left him in tattered rushes, and the arm reaching for the mare's lead rope shook like that of a feeble old man.

He unwrapped the line from the post, braced an elbow against the horse's neck, and gripped his forehead.

Steady yourself! She could not see him this way.

Out of sight of the women, he knotted his fingers in the horse's mane and hung on. The last hour had been one of the most trying of his existence—the culmination of over two years of waiting, preparing, seeking. And pining. So much pining.

Emotions pounded through him so chaotically he could scarcely get a grip on one before the next moved in for assault.

Confusion. About her choices.

Frustration. At himself, her clan, Bellamy.

Hurt. For the woman she believed herself to be.

Love. For the woman she was and, Christ permitting, would be.

He even dedicated a few bone-rattling shakes to anger. At life. For hurling itself against her again and again. Travail seemed to have chosen her for its darling, and every slice at her cut him in equal measure. Coming south was supposed to have been restorative. She'd sworn it would be.

Yet here he was, finding her these long seasons later, as buried in grief as ever. Right off, he'd seen hints of it—in the shadows skittering about her eyes, in her fickle interactions with Bellamy.

Sunflower's concise, too-full history filled in the rest.

"Well, I am come now," he murmured to the jittery mare. His position as slave to the woman was no mere happy throw of the dice. Unless it was Creator Jesus whose hand had thrown it. "We will rest in that, ehi?" With a stroke to the little horse's quivering shoulder, he guided her toward the woman who owned him.

She was giving Winter Hawk's arm a couple of approving smacks.

A gaggle of braves of varying ages, two of which were the perfect head-pat height, came clamoring around the bend beyond the old corn patch. The tallest, a peer to Winter Hawk, announced their presence with a drawn-out yipping hail.

Winter Hawk, who might've been confused for Coyote Clan instead of Rabbit, returned a masterful yelp. Then he tapped a fist to his chest and raised the arm to Strong Bear before jogging down the talwa trail. Hopefully, to tell his fellow braves to keep Pretty Wolf out of their fantasies.

A muscle twanged in Strong Bear's jaw at the reminder. Of that and of the absurd rule which, in addition to heaping loneliness on her wounded soul, could only serve to increase her desirability—as perceived rarity often did. The youths were no competition, he realized, but when it came to this woman, his protective streak refused to heel.

"Do you wish to ride, Pucase?" he asked when he'd reached her, voice subdued in deference to the bleak revelations of the last hour. He still wasn't certain of her mood toward him.

Earlier, when she hadn't known he was behind her, anger had honed the edges of her accusation. He deserved it for his foolish wag of the tongue. Moments after, she'd donned a wan smile for him.

Generally, her firebolt ire flared fast and hot but was gone in a puff of smoke.

"No," was her curt, though not-unkind, reply.

He glanced back at the lodge, reluctant to leave his fellow captive. "What of Mortar?"

"He'll be coaxed to health and given to a needy clan." She flicked a finger toward the mare. "Wind the lead around her neck and release her. She'll follow." Saying no more, Pretty Wolf clasped her hands at her lower back and set off on a lane leading out from behind the winter lodge.

He stared after her. Even speckled with hay and manure, even barefoot and ratty-haired, even demanding and half-angry—especially demanding and half-angry—she was lovely. So lovely it constricted his ribs.

A breath. Space. He desperately needed both.

To that end, he looped the rope as instructed and, guiding the mare by her halter, placed her between himself and Pretty Wolf. He let the woman set the pace at a crisp, march. Her face pointed straight ahead into the pines and thickets, toward whatever had her jaw ruminating.

Food was scarce, he'd been warned, but compared to the gaunt woman his memory served him, this one suffered no hunger. The soft lines of her face and her perfectly rounded body had never looked better, more touchable.

Groaning inwardly, he fisted the mare's halter and examined the sandy white ground as it passed beneath his feet.

Every so often, she'd stop, poke around in the dirt, then straighten and carry on. When they crossed a pathetic little stream, her hunt finally produced a stone. She turned it over in her palm, studying every facet, before tucking it into a drawstring pouch hanging from the sash about her waist. "Done. Let's go."

He bent at the waist. "Yes, Pucase."

On a purse of the lips, she passed him a drab look but made no comment.

A smile broke free, but he nabbed his lip between his teeth before it could get out of hand. To the mare, he made kissing sounds, and she walked on with him. They fell into step behind Pretty Wolf.

He itched to ask where exactly these cow pens were, what changed the Defiance's stance on raising cattle, and so much else. Allowable questions, but by the straining cords of her neck, she didn't seem in the mood.

Topics not allowable: all the ones he'd come to Wakulla to address. Sunflower's decree. The elder absolutely forbade it. So strongly, she'd threatened to transfer his servitude to Pretty Wolf's mother should he violate her command.

"Protect her. Love her." These were his complete orders. In other words, carry on. He had no complaint with that, but his rehearsed words, the ones he'd traveled countless leagues to speak, were lodged in his throat like a fishbone.

"What if she herself broaches it?" he'd prodded, wanting clear guidance. He understood how imperative it was that Pretty Wolf not become distracted. Sunflower described the cow pens contract as essential to the health of Wakulla's helpless ones. Strong Bear would not jeopardize it.

"Follow her lead," was Sunflower's advice, and Strong Bear suspected that had been the elder's method—indeed, the entire talwa's—since Pretty Wolf's return. Be patient. Tread lightly. Wait her out.

Strong Bear puffed a snort. How could they know their own daughter so little?

Pretty Wolf's commanding presence made *following* a simple choice for most, but what served the woman best was a sturdy push. Did anyone ever truly challenge her? On anything? No, they walked on toes around her inner wreckage, giving such a wide berth that males weren't permitted to so much as lay a finger on her.

For that alone, Strong Bear's respect for Sunflower hovered somewhere around his knees. If she had any wisdom about her at all, she would snatch Pretty Wolf into a crushing embrace and not let her go until she'd bled out in tears and disgorged the whole mess of it.

Skittish, cowardly lot of them.

Strong Bear suffered no such ailment. He would hold her fast to him and make her face herself, then he'd love her all the way back to Muscogee country. At the proper time, of course, which could not come soon enough for his liking. His muscles already vibrated with fatigue from clamping down against the urge to grab her and run.

A branch of white pine dipped low across his path. In passing, he ripped off a twig and tucked a few of its needle tufts into his pouch, leaving one out to crunch on. One grind of his molars washed his tongue in the wild citrus flavor he'd come to enjoy. A few more cooled his airways and cleared his thinking. Perhaps he should offer a tuft to Pretty Wolf…

A study of her stride from behind told him much about her mood. The line of her shoulders sat too squarely on the line of her spine, which fell too straightly to her hips, which rolled too stiffly above her tramping bare feet to color her anything other than war-path red.

"It's hard to think back here," he said, exaggerating the lift of his volume, "with those feet of yours slapping down so loudly." The tease produced a laugh from her, albeit a brief and slightly bitter one. "How do you expect to attack him with any success when he's surely heard you coming from a sight away?"

She swung her head back, mouth bent with confusion. "Who?"

"Whoever smeared that manure on the seat of your skirt. You are putting off quite the noxious draft. I'd be angry too."

The laugh she gave this time squinted her eyes, but Strong Bear didn't release his own full smile until her stride limbered and her arms were swinging freely at her sides. She didn't bother to check her skirt or scold *him* for checking. She simply walked on, carrying a now-placid bearing into a teeming compound. After a detour to the paddock to release Balada—the name she affectionately murmured to the blue-eyed animal—they strode into a hive of activity set to the discordant music of belled harnesses and braying mules.

In the shade of sprawling oaks, a dozen or so traders—Miccosukees, by their colorfully striped mantels—stood near their goods: pottery, bowls of pearls, blankets strewn with conch shells, clay pipes, baskets, and bundles of deerskins, that ever-dwindling commodity.

Atop the yard's largest structure, a British flag snapped in the wind. The blue letters painted on the building's whitewashed side read "Bellamy and Co. Trading Post."

"Bellamy," Strong Bear muttered under his breath. Swallowing bitterness, he reminded himself of who the man was rumored to be—trader of illegal arms and Buck's quarry—and what Strong Bear had come to do. And, Creator help him, it galled.

Across the way was the Englishman himself, bedecked in a ruffled shirt, thigh-hugging breeches, and pasty skin. He stood with his back to them, a pallet of wooden dishes at his feet, engaging in lively barter with a tub-bellied Miccosukee. If Pretty Wolf looked Bellamy's direction, her head didn't follow; it remained pointed at the cookhouse occupying the space between a smokehouse and a corncrib. The plump back end of a tobacco-brown skirt backed out of the smokehouse's opening, and a squat, round-faced woman emerged. Basket on her hip, she hustled down the ladder's three rungs.

At the base, she caught sight of them and smirked. "Look who's finally returned. The pretty ghost herself. I would have thought you dead, except Iron Wood isn't in mourning garb. Broods as if he is though."

"That I believe," Pretty Wolf said, tone plum-tart, and leaned down to kiss the other's sweaty cheek.

The woman eyed him over Pretty Wolf's shoulder. "Whom have you brought me?" She turned for the cookhouse.

Pretty Wolf took up at her side and playfully punched the other woman. "You cannot have him. Korsan would be heartbroken you asked."

"How would I know? Korsan does no asking himself." Mouth a strict line, the woman dropped her empty basket into the collection hanging from the cookhouse's four open-air posts. Red coals flickered in the shelter's low-flamed pit. A raised slab of wood served as a work counter on one side, and another held teetering stacks of bowls, mismatched spoons, tin cups, and a dripping puncheon. She took down a bowl while looking at Strong Bear askance. "He is yours then?"

"Mine."

Strong Bear's chest inflated at her instant, dare-dispute-me reply. Ehi, he was hers, and soon, she would be his.

"The spirits have brought me the most unusual help." With her back to him, Pretty Wolf bent low at the waist to sniff the bubbling contents of the iron skillet balanced on the coals, oblivious to the picture she presented him. Pulse kicking up, Strong Bear diligently counted exploding bubbles until she'd straightened and turned, her cheeks rosy with a most becoming flush. "My old friend, True Seeker, is now my new slave, Strong Bear." She glanced at him while giving a side-nod toward her companion. "This is Melon."

He offered his host a respectful inclination of the head.

She returned a perfunctory nod, then dished up from the skillet and passed him the filled bowl.

"Maddo." Sweetly scented corn pudding steam warmed his nose.

"Don't burn your mouth." Lips jutted, she sized him up and down, smacked his upper arm twice hard and sidestepped for a rear view, stopping short of pulling out his lip to check his teeth. She clicked her tongue at Pretty Wolf. "You said he was a boy."

"He was. He is. Look at all that hair." Pretty Wolf brandished a spoon at him.

He snatched it from her, jetting affront from his nostrils. In Alabama Town, she'd called him a boy. He'd allowed it because it had been true. Then.

His body might have taken longer than average to realize it, but manhood found him the morning Willow Woman and the boys wandered in. Pretty Wolf hadn't witnessed those man-molding days, the ones he wouldn't trade for all the corn pudding in Muscogee country.

He stirred the contents of his bowl and arranged his limbs in an authoritative stance—legs firmly rooted, elbows held slightly out from his sides to expand his width.

The upward crawl of his lips had, of course, nothing to do with the jog of Pretty Wolf's eyes over his build or with the pink erupting on her cheeks. "In the wisdom of the Muscogee Falcon," he said, "ceremonies do not make a man. Neither does a shaved scalp." The scalp bit was his own wisdom, but saying so would only complicate the argument. "I'm a man full grown."

"Sixteen winters is hardly grown," said the woman, too childish herself to reveal her interest by flat out asking his age. She'd never gotten it right. Maybe now that he owned a noteworthy spread of muscles—which she *did* note— she would finally see their gap in age wasn't so gapped at all.

Fingering his beaded strand of hair, he crooked his smile. "Eighteen."

"Chh. Fifteen."

"Who taught you to haggle, woman? You're going the wrong way."

Melon barked a laugh. "Where this one lacks in haggling, she abounds in denial."

Sticking out her tongue at them, Pretty Wolf grabbed another bowl and, skirt swishing, sashayed back to the fire. Mercy find him, that figure of hers…

Loaded with pudding, Strong Bear's spoon almost became lost on the way to his hanging jaw.

Melon snapped her fingers before his nose.

Blinking, he shoveled in the bite. Heat scorched his tongue and palate. He hissed in a breath, eyes instantly watering, and scarcely caught himself from spitting the boiling-hot mouthful all over Melon.

The woman shook her head at him. "Dumb as a buck in rut. But I like you. Consider my fire your fire."

Wincing, he gulped and waited out the blazing trail in his gullet. "Maddo, Melon," he finally wheezed. "I'm pleased to have come."

"Words never to be said again by a captive." She thumped his chest with a hooked forefinger. "But then you are no ordinary captive, hmm?"

"Where has Rox hidden himself?" asked Pretty Wolf, ignoring them as her eyes roamed the bustling yard.

"Under his blanket." Patience thinly limned Melon's tone. "He claims to have fallen and banged his elbow, so naturally, he cannot walk. No trouble eating, though. This is the second batch of pudding."

"I'll get him up." Pretty Wolf strode from the cookhouse. "Come, slave. And bring an extra spoon."

After sharing a roll of the eyes with Melon, he did.

Chapter 15

Pretty Wolf ducked into one of the compound's lodges, and Strong Bear followed. His vision adjusted to the dark interior in time to see her on the right, settling on the edge of a bunked couch. At its head, a musket stood upright against the wall. Shelves and hooks lined the rear of the structure with a trestle table and bench occupying the space on the left. Storage baskets stuffed the rafters.

It took several blinks to convince Strong Bear the lack of light wasn't to blame for confusing his sight. Melon's banter had sketched their charge as a fractious child, but it was a broad, red-coated back that reclined on that couch. And no mistaking, the incoherent grunting of the large figure pitched deep with manhood.

"If that is how you feel," Pretty Wolf said, breezily, "I will eat the corn pudding myself."

The man launched to sitting, and a lopsided grin split sloppily shaved cheeks. "Pah-ee!" He flung his arms about her in a clumsy, grasping hug that nearly knocked the bowl to the floor.

Laughing, she held the dish out of the way but otherwise returned the embrace. "I missed you too, friend."

An order to *get off her!* shot up Strong Bear's throat, but he caught it before firing off. The man, *Rox* she'd called him, had to be a simpleton, unaware he breeched courtesy. Breeched the *Rule*. Nothing else explained the saliva stringing from the corner of his flaccid lips and into her hair.

An interminable quarter-minute later, Pretty Wolf nudged him off her and stretched behind him for his blanket. "Melon tells me you are invalid."

Her English, Strong Bear marveled. Over the seasons, it had become crisp and precise and so lightly accented he might mistake her for British-born.

"Ess," Rox slurred. "Faah."

"So I heard." She balled up the blanket, propped it against the wall, and patted it as she extended the bowl. "Settle back and eat. Pudding is known for returning strength to bumped elbows."

On a whine, Rox pushed the dish back toward her and pointed to his so-called injury, his forearm and hand lying limp and useless across his threadbare jacket. A haggard British uniform? Ehi, those embossed brass buttons could belong only on a military coat.

"Ah, poor friend. Here." Pretty Wolf swooped the utensil through the pudding and blew at the steam rising from the heaping spoonful. She then hovered it before Rox's sloppy smile.

The man slurped the contents down and leaned back on a sigh. Strong Bear took it back—the sly fellow knew precisely what he was doing. Undoubtedly, so did Pretty Wolf. He looked forward to watching her move the game pieces.

"I've brought you something to make you feel better," she sing-songed, "and I don't mean the pudding."

Rox's high-pitched, garbled reply and kicking leg screamed his approval.

"Maybe," she drawled teasingly while portioning out another bite. Had she actually understood the man, or was she contriving conversation?

Rox clapped, his smile growing as broad as the dead side of his face would allow. Green eyes sparkling, he loosed a goose-honk of a laugh.

Pretty Wolf said, "You think you know me so well."

Fascinated with the exchange, Strong Bear lounged against the far wall and, ankles crossed, dug into his cooled pudding.

The move seemed to have alerted Rox to his presence. In the next second, he had one big hand—from his *wounded* arm—folded around the barrel of the musket. He tightened his good eye at Strong Bear.

What dim-brain put a musket within this fellow's reach? Casually, Strong Bear drifted a hand closer to his knife's handle.

"He's harmless," Pretty Wolf said, whether to Strong Bear or Rox was unclear. She used the spoon to scrape a clump of mashed corn off the man's drooping lip.

In reply to his mouthful of distorted sounds, she said, "That's Strong Bear, a boy from my old village."

Grunting, Rox released the weapon, sat back, and uttered a perfectly intelligible, "No boy, Pah-ee."

"He is a boy. Trust me."

Smile out in full force, Strong Bear shoveled down more of the sweet concoction. *Boy* his man-sized foot. Her denial was charming, and with every instance, she only gave herself away.

"Man," he countered, just so he could hear her shoot right back with, "Boy."

While opening his mouth for another bite, Rox bounced a thinking gaze between Strong Bear and Pretty Wolf, appearing not at all sold on her bid for trust. At last, he cradled his elbow again and blared, "Coor." Masticated food sprayed onto her sleeve. "Coor woo."

"*Again?*" She moaned like the sick.

"Coor woo!"

"All right. **Corn Woman** it is." She finger-picked the slimy bits off her sleeve, making no fuss, and Strong Bear loved her a little more for it. "A short telling only. Soon, I must take the boy Strong Bear for his nap. Else, later, he will be in a foul temper."

Rox quirked his single well-behaved brow at Strong Bear; Strong Bear quirked his back.

When Pretty Wolf looked behind her to smirk at him, he lifted his dish to chin level, on the pretense of taking another bite. It couldn't be helped that the motion swelled his muscles so handsomely.

She took note precisely as she had earlier, her visual sweep slow and thorough. Complimentary. Somewhere along the way, her lips parted and held—the perfect kissing posture.

Strong Bear had always applauded his memory for its perfect storage of her lips, called on it frequently to perform, but either it had let him down over the years, or her steadier diet had done her mouth as good a service as it had her figure.

Stay put, he schooled his eyes. *Do not drop*. They didn't fight him, there being plenty to peruse right where they hovered: the peak of her upper lip, full and markedly scooped in the center; the lower thin in contrast but not wanting. Never wanting.

It took the sharp snapping of her teeth to sever his focus.

He gave a little jolt. When their eyes reconnected, it wasn't desire or even embarrassment he read on her, but…warning.

The corn fermented in his mouth. He forced it down his gullet and bowed his head. Guilt or apology. Either would do.

He'd overstepped. More than once since they'd reunited.

The woman was entangled with another.

Robert Maxwell Bellamy. Iron Wood. Lord Control, high and mighty.

Strong Bear's fingers curled hard into the bowl. From his side vision, he watched her turn her face forward again, then released the breath he'd bound up.

Path Maker had gone before Strong Bear's every step to Wakulla, making level the way, protecting his hair in battle, using the enemy as an escort to his safety. And still, the waiting was not ended.

He must guard his eyes. Bind his hands if necessary. Corral that unceasing, torturous *want*.

Because the woman was not his. Yet.

"Corn Woman is the offspring of Earth Mother," she began.

Strong Bear rested his head against the wall, closed his eyes, and let her storytelling voice coat his skin, seep into it, saturate his blood. His lungs depleted on a protracted exhale, the sigh of a long-deprived man drinking his fill.

"She was born of the earth plants and of the dew and of warmth. 'I am love,' Corn Woman said. 'I am strength-giver. I am nourisher.' In time, she appeared to the people as old and dirty, and they despised her for it. So, she found a group of orphans and lived with them. The children said, 'We are hungry and will die,' but the nourisher had nothing to give them." For dramatic effect, Pretty Wolf made scraping noises with her utensil against the dish's empty bottom. "Corn Woman wept and said, 'I will make food to fill your little bellies.'"

Many dark nights in Alabama Town had been filled with the recounting of sacred myths such as this one. Since that time, Strong Bear had learned other ancient stories.

Between his rubbing fingers, the cherished symbol felt cool and silky. Solid. Certain.

Contentment shifted his mouth. Soon, he would share the new stories, and she would listen. He knew it like he knew the exact shape of her curiosity. Never mind her protest over his cross. He'd seen the flash of intrigue. And hadn't his many prayers been met with a sense of peace?

She would listen.

The myth of Corn Woman went on until she paused so Rox could join her in a slurred recitation of the ending. "She lives on, and in undying love, she renews herself time and again."

They exchanged smiles, hers sweet, his awry. Then Rox dropped his jaw and belched.

The lodge erupted in peals of laughter, Strong Bear with them. When the hilarity died down, she dabbed at her eyes. "Are you healed enough for your gift?"

It was promptly decided he was. So, she loosened her pouch's drawstring and extracted...the rock. One would have thought it a gold nugget with the way Rox hooted and clapped and carried on.

She and the man spent the following minutes, heads bent together, extolling the stone's every virtue. Its smoothness, its roundness, its whiteness. Strong Bear scratched his jaw, unsure which dumbfounded him most—Rox's uncommon fascination or Pretty Wolf's exploiting of it.

When they'd exhausted the rock's list of noble qualities, Rox dragged a bulging shoulder bag from the corner of the couch, flipped it open, and carefully set the stone on top of what could be no less than a hundred others.

Pretty Wolf held the flap down while Rox's clumsy fingers struggled with the ties. "Right then. Your stomach is happy. Your elbow is happy. Shem is not. How long are you going to leave your young friend to handle all those mules alone?"

Rox's entire body deflated, but without another mutilated word, he stood. Hefting the bag onto his back, he shuffled out, his sluggish foot scoring a dashed trail into the dirt.

"Lieutenant Harold Roxworth." Pretty Wolf's belated introduction. "Bullet to the skull. The conflict at Orleans." With that, she reverted to their more fluid native tongue. "When it was certain he would heal no more and would forever be a child, his father disowned him. But Iron Wood loved his friend and became a pawa to him."

Something uncomfortable slithered eel-like through Strong Bear's innards. It took him the time Pretty Wolf spent folding the blanket to identify the emotion as admiration. A pucker soured his mouth. "Don't give me a reason to like the trader."

She laid the blanket at the foot of the couch and collected the dirty dishes, including the one sitting at his feet. When she straightened, she wore a warped smile. "Better to like him than not since you are bound to him by oath."

He shook his head. "Sunflower transferred the oath to herself."

The cocky slid out of her smile. "Can she do that?"

"I would love to watch Bellamy try to take it back from her."

A devious squint winged up one of her eyebrows. "We could make an official match of it. What do you say, Kit?"

At the old tease-turned-endearment, his heart warmed. "We do it. And we invite the talwa."

"Charge entry."

"One river stone per person."

The laugh that burst out of her rippled over him like silk. Bowls stacked and hugged to her belly, she ducked her willowy frame through the doorway and into the sun. "Come on, White Stick, before you give me a reason to like you."

Right behind her, he batted the braid hanging down her back. "Too late. You already love me."

Chapter 16

Pretty Wolf cast Strong Bear a broad smile over her shoulder, no contradiction to be seen on her anywhere.

Rightly so. Their love was as long and as solid as the trail between home and Wakulla and back again. Unending sights of solid ground beneath his moccasins—her bare feet—stretching behind and far into their future.

Encouraged, he grinned back, and a dancing laugh rode from that luscious mouth of hers.

Still smiling, she cut across the compound courtyard, Strong Bear trailing like a proper slave. They rounded the store to its front, where Bellamy haggled with a basket seller.

The Englishman broke briefly to swing his attention their way, expression brightening. Ignoring him, Pretty Wolf climbed a set of stairs to a porch that shaded the store's entrance. Several Miccosukees lounged against the railing. One stretched out on the wooden slats, hands folded on his chest, a winter-lazy fly circling his unfastened mouth.

Inside, several lanterns provided light for the windowless interior, its cozy, golden-moon glow mismatched with the hoard of scents colliding inside Strong Bear's nostrils. Among them, the musk of deer hides and the moist earth of potatoes. Stirred into those were hints of tobacco and coffee, grain and sugar, and undergirding it all, wafting about the place with the swagger of a **medal chief**, was the unmistakable tang of black powder.

The last stopped Strong Bear's tracks just past the entry's threshold. By his nose alone, he'd accuse Bellamy and Co. of being in violation of the late war's peace accord: the proclamation that England must not aid America's enemies in their cause. Should he be caught, Bellamy would be destined for shackles. The hanging rope could be taken off the flag waving from his roof's ridge.

Marcus Buck's warning resurfaced. Before they'd parted ways on that river, Strong Bear's Bluecoat friend had taken him aside and, aware of his goal, laid out his suspicions regarding the Englishman's illegal activities. Here sat the evidence that he'd been correct.

This was an armory.

And Pretty Wolf was knee-deep in it. Did Bellamy even care he'd embroiled his betrothed in his corruption? Coals kindled low in Strong Bear's center, bunching his hands into fists.

You're here now, he reminded himself. *To get her out.* He rolled his neck, cracking the joints to release tension.

To his left, a turbaned fellow, whose brown-skinned heritage Strong Bear couldn't place, manned a counter. Traders milled about the stocked shelves lining the opposite wall or sat idly on crates and kegs—of powder?—gnawing on jerky.

Hung from a line, panels of dark fabric stretched across the store's far end to section off an area. Between there and Strong Bear, sacks, piles, and barrels populated the floor so thoroughly there was hardly a square of space to set one's foot. Pretty Wolf navigated it with feline adroitness, while Strong Bear squeezed in on himself and bumbled after her.

Her destination was a basket on the ground near the curtain. Filled with straw, it appeared to house an assortment of soaps. As she lowered to her knees before it, she gestured to a chair set before a small desk. "Wait there."

Never one to complain over an opportunity to gaze at her, he sat. Views didn't come more beautiful than any Pretty Wolf occupied, no matter all he could see was her bowed back as she dug through the container. It was those black-bottomed toes of hers peeking out from the hem of her skirt that slammed him.

He'd found her.

She was here.

They were together.

Together.

Whatever the future held, they had now. This time. Whether days or mere hours, it was theirs. Because he'd *found* her. With not a month—a week?—to spare.

Emotion plugged his throat, and it took everything in him to not fling himself at her, cover her with his body, and snarl at any who objected. To stay himself, he braced an elbow on the table's surface. It skidded on shifting papers.

Curious, he pitched himself over the pile and scanned the topmost sheet. Among a hundred others, a single word snagged his eye. Then clenched his lungs. His gaze jumped to the beginning. At every skimmed line, he thanked Copper Woman for the lessons.

Finding Pretty Wolf

One other time, Strong Bear had been given occasion to peruse a similar parchment—Totka had shown him. This one was crafted similarly with text at the top and three inked lines at the bottom stretching out beside three printed names.

The first line underscored a non-letter mark beside the name Josiah Francis. The next held the slanted signature of Robert Bellamy. The last signature line lay glaringly, gorgeously blank. The name beside it: Polly Francis.

"We decided this bloke wouldn't make a good slave." Bellamy stalked past, his frost-blue eyes giving Strong Bear no quarter.

"Sunflower decided he would." Polly continued her rummaging.

Bellamy went to stand at her heels. "She'll eventually see the error of that," he muttered and propped a hand on his hip. "But it makes no difference to me, now you're not at the stables anymore." He glanced Strong Bear's direction, then jolted and strode over to snatch the contract off the desk. "Your slave is a snoop."

Pretty Wolf sat back on her thighs and pushed off them to stand. "My slave does not read. Hold this for me." She tossed Strong Bear a bar of soap.

"You can't know that." Bellamy rolled the parchment and tucked it under his arm.

"I can." Something beyond Strong Bear summoned her eyes. They slitted before sliding back to Bellamy. "About my returned bathing tub."

Strong Bear skimmed his thumb over the soap's waxy surface and glanced back at the tin-plated hip bath. He frowned. Still not bathing in the river, then.

"What about it?" Bellamy said, brow dipping. "You're here now."

On a huffed mumble, she tramped to the curtain and slipped through the panels into a dark space.

"Darling?" Bellamy said, setting Strong Bear's teeth to gritting. The merchant took off after her and vanished as she had. His voice, though lowered, carried through the barrier. "You can't possibly be considering staying at the stables. With *him*."

"I can, and I will."

"But the slave makes four workers and—"

"Kicking Knife is lame. He goes home. I stay."

"Lamed on the same day a slave arrives? Quite convenient for your tactics of avoidance, Polly."

131

"How perceptive you are," she snapped. "Yes, I paid the cow well to stomp on his foot."

Silence. The curtain fairly rippled with the force of it.

It wasn't difficult to imagine the flinty mien fronting Bellamy just then—the jutted jaw, the fiery hazel eyes, the rising steam. Pity bubbled in Strong Bear's middle. No…that was the corn pudding.

He settled back in the chair and kicked up his feet, ankles crossed on the desk. He scrounged about in his accessories pouch, fingertips gliding past the sleek gold of his watch and the crinkle of paper until he came out with his birch twig. He inserted the mashed end into his mouth and, as the chilling stillness continued, began on his front tooth, cleaning it of grime.

He was moving on to the next by the time Bellamy ventured a low, "You belong here, and I will not apologize."

"Apology or not, I will be staying there," she said, each word slow and pinched.

"Please, Polly, try to understand. You shouldn't have to work at that filthy place to begin with, and I—"

"Stop. *Stop*. You've said it all before. It excuses nothing. Move."

"No."

Strong Bear's eyebrows jumped high. The twig froze on a molar as he waited for Pretty Wolf to release a firebolt. He could practically feel the warning crackles through the fabric.

The Englishman should be backing away now or taking cover. "You said we would talk tonight," he persisted, whether foolishly or bravely was yet to be determined.

"That was before you decided to control me! I did not— I *will* not—" Frustration growled out of her. Several beats passed, then, "When I've cooled enough to speak reasonably, we will talk."

"Please, Polly, don't leave like this."

Why did he dishonor her by using her old name? And why did she not slap him for it?

"Move," she seethed as through clamped teeth.

"You needn't go." He was pleading now. "I'll have Shem take your slave to the cow pens."

"The only thing Shem will be taking to the cow pens is my tub." She batted her way through the curtain panels, face aflame and eyes spitting sparks. A whirl of skirts sent her back around to face off with Bellamy, who'd barreled out after her. Some part of her swinging appendages knocked into a stack of vermilion bags. One flew off and burst open at Bellamy's feet. Red powder exploded onto his boots and breeches.

He came to a fast halt but otherwise ignored the wreckage. "You aren't seriously going back there!"

Chin hoisted, she drew her length up to its fullest, and Strong Bear's chest filled with pride, as if he'd crafted that lovely spine himself. She said, "I *am*."

"You are *not*."

Scarcely containing a grin, Strong Bear hopped his gaze between the combatants. The twig's nub squeaked along the last of his lower molars. He sucked the tooth and, satisfied with his work, shifted the tool and began on the top set.

"Strong Bear," she said in their language, not breaking her glare, "on our way out, take a dish from the stack on the shelf by the counter. The cow pens provides daily rations but no bowl."

He dropped his feet to the ground, scattering papers, and lazily stretched his way to standing. "Ehi, Pucase."

"Polly," Bellamy warned, low and challenging. He gripped the panels hanging on either side of him as if to tear them both off the line.

Crisply, she turned to leave, and Bellamy grabbed her elbow. She yanked free and twisted back, voice severed to a hiss. "Do not touch me! And do not come for me. I will not be happy to see you."

Nothing feline about her, she plunged through the store, not checking to see whether Strong Bear followed.

He lingered, waited for Bellamy's agonized gaze to shift from Pretty Wolf to him and turn stony. Strong Bear used his English to say, "One cannot reason with a dead woman."

Bellamy's nose wrinkled. "What are you on about, man?"

"Polly is dead. As is True Seeker." His tongue flicked at the stick nestled in the corner of his lips while he paused to watch recognition blink across Bellamy's face. "I am Strong Bear now, but my vow remains."

With that, he launched into the words Bellamy had made him swear on that gory field, the ones Strong Bear had lived by since. "Where she steps, I follow. If she stumbles, I break her fall. If another strikes at her, I take the blow. Her safety is all things to me. *She* is all things to me." A direct recitation apart from the final line, a fact he revealed in the name of fairness and honesty.

Every man deserved a fighting chance, and a fight it would be. Strong Bear, however, would not be the one in combat. He had a mighty Creator for that, as well as a firm peace. Still, he wouldn't tread warily around his purpose here. The red hatchet had been delivered, war declared.

The Englishman blanched—ehi, there it was, the understanding—and at last, the burbling in Strong Bear's gut became genuine pity.

Such a quantity of pity that as Strong Bear turned away, he spoke the last of his gibe to himself. *Be at ease, Bellamy. Pretty Wolf is in good hands.*

Chapter 17

Firebolt didn't quite suit Pretty Wolf in this instance. *Burning wick*, perhaps. A lengthy, greased wick coated in black powder.

Slightly ahead of Strong Bear, she stormed over the compact, white sand, deaf to her horse's capers. The little Spanish mare trotted dog-like behind, her hoof beats alternating between sprightly and silent, the occasional tuft of grass on the byway to blame for the latter.

Strong Bear clicked his tongue in Balada's direction. There came another loud rip of grass before she pranced forward again, green poking from between her maneuvering lips.

The creature must be sister to that firebrand Wind Chaser. Thought of the mare led to thoughts of its owner, Copper Woman, her figure outlined with a rotund child-filled belly. Which ferried him into images of other little ones and…

Home.

Overhead, palm leaves rustled, and he imagined it into the whistle of his beloved long-leaf pines. He tightened his fist, and the wind-up screw of his pocket watch pressed comfortably into his palm. The golden casing sat warm and familiar against his skin as his feet made tracks toward the unknown.

"With its every tick," Grandmother Mahila once said, her toothless grin and ageless wisdom much missed commodities in their lodge, *"remember that in a world of mixed people and warring spirits, all things are possible."*

With God, he added on a heavenward plea for guidance…and constraint. A thing he much needed at present.

Shouldering Pretty Wolf's pack, into which he'd shoved the soap and bowl, he kept a liberal arm's length between them. He had yet to properly greet her, and he couldn't trust himself not to tackle her with enveloping arms she wouldn't find her way out of until next moon.

It helped she was presently engaged in a remarkable stamping fit. Arms slicing the air, feet pounding the earth, the woman sparked so furiously, the dry forest should shudder in fear.

Strong Bear shuddered for an entirely different reason.

Sparking, steaming, spitting flame, she was a vision no matter her temper. Her features were simply incapable of organizing themselves into ugliness. This look—nostrils and eyes contracted, lips bunched—was one of his favorites. More than once, he'd riled her up for the sole purpose of instigating this exact expression. Now, he ached over the distress it illustrated.

He cleared his throat. "Will we be stomping the whole way to…?" He looked ahead. "Where does this path lead?"

"Don Diego's cow pens and, ehi, we will." She kept her eyes pinned to the horizon, her voice as straight and sharp as a long-knife.

"Bellamy deserves a full-dress war stomp, certainly, and I'm pleased to join you. But these sand spurs I've picked up are a torment. The gauntlet could not do a man worse."

"Perhaps then," she whipped back, "I should have left you to the widows." There, that upward tick at the fold of her mouth. The cave-in he'd been teasing for.

"Better even, we could stop, so I can pluck the little terrors out of my feet."

"You are the only *little terror* within sight. Little terror, little bellyacher, little kit."

His eyes flicked sideward at her. If she insisted on refusing to acknowledge he'd changed, he might begin to worry she would only ever see him as True Seeker.

She waved toward his feet and went right on blithely hacking him down. "The hide on those moccasins is too new for you to be bothered by a burr. And if you were, you'd be hobbling and whining like a kicked pup."

He grinned broadly enough for her to hear it when he fired back. "You confuse me with True Seeker." Who, on their arduous trek to Alabama Town, had used complaining as a means to prompt the same out of her.

Back then, pallid and weak, the hole in her shoulder festering less than the one in her heart, she'd trudged sight after sight in stoic silence. Brooding. It had taken True Seeker's exaggerated griping to spawn any release of emotion.

"I no longer whine," he said, matter-of-fact. "I merely complain in a high pitch."

She stopped. Twisted to face him and transformed herself with ringing laughter. "Spirits shield me from your terrible wit."

He grinned. "You've missed me." When he got no response beyond a cryptic smile that settled sweetly in his belly, he nodded ahead. "Is it far to these cows?"

"Three sights." Long and languid now, her stride resumed, and he congratulated himself on both his success and his intimate knowledge of her inner workings.

Pretty Wolf was an exquisite piece. Though complex and finely tuned, her cogs and springs and wheels were easily thrown out of cadence. Simple trouble for a man who owned the tools to realign her gears.

"An entire three sights?" He loosed a deep bellyacher's groan. "But I've just come off a two-day captive's march."

"I never had a slave complain so much in high pitch." Above her hips, her long braid resumed its sea-grass sway, undulating in the gentle current of her stroll.

Warmth poured through him, making him work for an unaffected tone. "You never had a slave before me. If you had, your face wouldn't make such a look of glee every time you order me about."

"The glee is purely for you, White Stick. Ordering anyone else about wouldn't bring me half the pleasure." She glanced back, gaze alighting on the watch chain swinging between his fingers, and extended an upturned hand.

He placed the timepiece in it, voice warming with affection. "And it is my pleasure to bring you happiness in whatever form. You have far too little of it."

"That isn't true." She lifted the glittering instrument to eye level, childlike wonder lighting her up. "Wakulla is a happy place. The happiest since childhood." She rotated the watch to view it from all sides.

Regardless of her endearing curiosity, he frowned, stung. "We found happiness together, you and I."

A cup over a candle, his declaration extinguished her glow. Gaze drifting into the distance, she no longer saw the watch, them, or their sweet days. Every beautiful memory suffocated by *one*.

She was twisting her ring now, a habit he'd always interpreted as mining strength from her father's belief in her. Sunflower's admonition hit him keenly just as Pretty Wolf's nostrils began to quiver, her prelude to tears.

He hastily added, "That is, until the time you left out the acorn bread. From there, it was all disaster and woe."

Her lashes beat several times before the seams of her mouth gave way to quiet amusement. She said nothing, but he hoped she was reliving that midnight scene: the raccoon that invited himself into their bark shelter then got tangled up in the netting that held their food above ground. The creature snarled and hissed. Polly hollered and flailed. True Seeker rolled onto his back and laughed until his stomach cramped. Before Polly was through, the shelter had fallen around them and caught flame in the fire pit.

When he'd said *disaster*, he meant *delight* because they'd spent the remainder of that night cuddling against the biting wind. Though she wouldn't recall it being quite as delightful as he.

A fond chuckle shook his chest, but whatever reliving she had done, it was over. She slanted his watch to catch the sun, then squinted at the inscription etched into the gold backing.

He reached across and opened the lid. The face read 10:32. "Tell me about this happy place, Wakulla."

"Wakulla," Pretty Wolf cheerfully replied, "is always yellow sunshine, clear springs, and blue skies." She smiled at the magic in her palm; he smiled at the magic in her smile.

He squinted up at the sky, now blessedly absent its red tint. "Did the cold season not reach this far south?" He looked back and clucked his tongue at the loitering mare who nickered and kicked out her foreleg in a playful hop.

"It did, and it was a trial of body and mind." She was a bird, head cocked at the tiny, revolving sticks, fingernail pecking at the softly domed glass. When she glanced up, her eyes were round and glossed with hope. "But the clouds have gone. The heat will soon return. The corn with it since Fierce Mink secured us maize from her white grandfather. And now, you and I will secure us beef."

Noble occupation. So far, he much approved this stint of slavery. "What of the Spanish?"

"They are good and generous neighbors, though they have had little to give. Capitán Luengo, the commander of the fort, made it plainly known he is my Spanish pawa. His spirit is kind, and there isn't a storm fierce enough to blow away his smile." The watch enthralled her. She hadn't asked what it was, so this mustn't be her first exposure to a keeper of time. Even so, she scarcely looked away.

"What of your clan?" Strong Bear took her by the elbow, guided her around a stump in the path, and then raised her wrist to set the device against her ear.

A tiny gasp parted her lips as wonder unfurled across her. A full minute of ticks must have passed before her mouth eased closed, then popped open again for a blurted, "What?"

He laughed. "I asked after your clan."

"Oh..." She fingered the delicate chain, laddering her way to its toggle. "Wolf is small in number. We are only my mother, my sister, and I, plus Tall Bull. He is pawa to Runs Like Deer and myself."

Strong Bear's feet scraped to a stop. "Micco Tall Bull you say?" What were the odds her adoptive pawa would be cousin to his mentor? He almost burst out laughing at the irony and at the bug-eyed expression that would leap to Totka's face when he learned of it.

Several steps beyond him, Pretty Wolf paused to look back. "Ehi, he is war micco."

"Cropped, ragged hair? Has a little war woman hooked to his side?"

"That would be Fierce Mink." She gave a contemplative nod. "You know my pawa?"

Strong Bear flattened his tone. "He tried to kill me."

An open-mouthed laugh stuttered from her. "When was this?"

"Medicine Point. My capture."

"Don't tell me you beat him in a brawl." She snapped the watch closed.

Quirking a wry smile, he stalked up to her and plucked the item from her grasp. "If by *beat* you mean fought off unconsciousness in a choke-hold until his cousin arrived to show him the hot end of a rifle muzzle, then ehi,"—he rapped his chest—"I beat him." When her face scrunched with saucy amusement, his pride kicked back. "Tall Bull proved a formidable opponent. Against him, I stood no chance."

"Few men do. It is said his bones are made of war clubs."

Strong Bear hummed agreement, having heard this before. "And his cousin's of stickball sticks."

"That is thrice now you've remarked on Big Warrior Totka Hadjo. How do you know him?"

"I was asked to carry a message to him on the battlefield." For starters.

"How did you persuade the great Muscogee Falcon to guard your back?" she asked, all sincerity. A most puzzling attitude.

He slipped the watch into his pouch and secured the drawstring. "You would call him great?"

"Is Totka not great?"

Actually, he was not.

Strong Bear wouldn't degrade the man with such a paltry word. Distinguished. Honorable. Dauntless. Those began to touch on the warrior's character. But Strong Bear didn't suppose Pretty Wolf cared to sit for a lengthy extolling of all that Totka had been and done, taught and tested, sacrificed and won.

As much as one man could love another inside the grounds of brotherhood, Strong Bear did Totka Hadjo. Perhaps more even than he had his own father. Because Totka did not give or do for blood or clan, but for the abundant goodness that made a home in him. And for Creator Jesus.

But Totka and his cousin, Tall Bull, were falcon and snake, predators eternally opposed, Red Sticks whose war clubs had always clashed, always swung for different causes. The bloodiest being that of women. One in particular. Strong Bear had listened to the telling of those hateful days, heard the decay of grief over a cousin turned enemy, and it had filled him up with sadness.

The same tugged at him now, along with awe at learning his own Pretty Wolf claimed the enemy cousin as pawa, that she admired him, that she admired *Totka*.

After a backward thrown summons for Balada, Strong Bear set out again, taking the lead. "With Tall Bull for a pawa, I'd think you would have heard only the *un*great."

"The opposite," she stated, matching her pace to his amble. "Tall Bull makes light of his cousin's misdeeds while making much of his own. He speaks nothing but cherries and dumplings of him. One would think the man's armpits incapable of stink."

"His wife certainly does," Strong Bear said in a dry vein. Despite having lived in the couple's Kossati compound for several seasons, he had yet to grow accustomed to their unapologetic, very public…handling.

"Totka Hadjo is wed?" Incredulity mixed with delight to steepen her pitch. "To whom?"

"His white captive, Copper Woman."

"He bound himself to his slave? The one from Mims' place?" Wonder beamed from her. "A story I'd wish to hear."

Indeed, it was quite the tale. One he intended to make his own. But in reverse. How better to emulate his mentor?

Strong Bear chuckled inwardly at the stupidity of such an aspiration, then outwardly as he realized it wouldn't be reversed at all. Totka was just as much the slave to Copper Woman as Strong Bear was to Pretty Wolf, minus the bit where he'd be hunted and tortured by her talwa should he run.

That sobered Strong Bear quick.

Pretty Wolf curved him an inquisitive brow.

The ground began a gradual incline, so he hefted the pack to adjust its strap more comfortably on his shoulder. "I can tell you their story, or... Can I tell you my own?"

"Yours. Most definitely yours." Prompt. Exuberant.

He grinned at her reply. "Where shall I begin?"

"On the day you stopped weeping lakes over my absence." There was a cheeky smirk on her that he didn't much appreciate.

"Not much of a story then, given that was this morning."

She laughed. "And I thought campfire smoke was to blame for your swollen, red eyes."

She didn't believe him.

Well, *lakes* was a stretch, but *weeping* was not. How many times had Flint climbed onto Strong Bear's couch and caught him blinking vigorously to fend off the sting of loneliness?

As they entered a deeply shaded hummock, Strong Bear told Pretty Wolf none of this, holding it close to his heart for the day he could tell her *all* of it. He did, however, rewind the watch to several mornings after she fled—to the morning Willow Woman, Grandmother Mahila, and the boys—Tadpole, Sun Chaser, Flint—walked into their compound.

As a consequence of the treaty, Willow had suddenly found her freshly built talwa on the wrong side of the new border. Alabama Town, thankfully, stood on the correct side, along with the rest of their **Tribal Township**: Pigeon Roost, Ockchoy, and Kossati.

He told Pretty Wolf of their hunger, their dreams, their determination to live.

Pretty Wolf absorbed every detail, interrupting every so often to beg finer points. Strong Bear supplied, keeping nothing in reserve, well aware of the spear his tale would be, and well prepared to clap a hand over the bleed...

Sun Chaser's sickness, worsened by hunger.

His death.

Willow's grief without end.

Her flight.

Pretty Wolf, who could not miss the kinship to her own tragedy, shed silent tears over the hummock's rich soil. Her face went pale, her arms went slack, but she didn't stumble, and she didn't tell him to stop.

So he didn't.

He related the account of Willow's journey south, which True Seeker had followed. Which led to her white father, McGirth. Who was also father to Copper Woman. Who sent True Seeker with a message for her Totka. Who was **yahola** to the warriors fighting at the Black Fort. The name of which extracted a sharp gasp from Pretty Wolf.

Swiping at straggler tears, she stopped and grasped his upper arm. "You were at Black Fort? *I* was at Black Fort." His eyelids stretched wide, but she didn't allow a breath of space for questions. "Were you part of that-that—"

"No. No, I arrived after."

Nodding, she inhaled a shaky breath and loosened her grip. "It's where Screaming Buttons and I came across my father and my— well, everyone. We were just finding our peace, building lodges and planting corn, when we received word the Bluecoats were on the warpath again. We took up our few movables and fled." She said this with a shrug and a dog-tired slouch.

Being shuffled about by her father, being chased by the Bluecoats—such was a matter of course for Pretty Wolf. An almost yearly affair. This year's, should Strong Bear's speculations on Jackson's plotting prove accurate, lay just around the bend.

Sorrow—at what awaited them, at his own uselessness—trundled through him. He held her damp gaze, his own gentling in solidarity as she found her words.

"It was but days later we heard. The fort, it… We *heard* it, Strong Bear," she said, voice cut jagged. "We felt the explosion through our feet. The treetops trembled, and the birds scattered. It was…" Her sight went distant for an extended time before she shook her head. "We didn't know what it was, not until we'd reached San Marcos."

Delayed panic numbed Strong Bear's lips. They resisted him, slightly slurring his speech. "Just days?"

"Days." Her fingers dug into his flesh, and he blanched from the memories. How diligently he'd worked to expunge that carnage, only to have its vivid gore flood him again at first mention. Even Horse's Flat Foot—its stacks of corpses, its ponds of blood—could not compare. And Pretty Wolf had missed it by *days*. He had missed *her* by days.

Her beautiful face, large-eyed and pale-cheeked, peered up at him, and gratitude filled his unvoiced prayer to Jesus. *Maddo, maddo.* He'd never stop saying it.

Even before he knew Jesus, knew to pray to the God-man for Pretty Wolf's safekeeping, the Savior had done just that. For him? Undoubtedly. At least in part. Path Maker knew that Strong Bear and Flint and all in their compound would not be whole until Pretty Wolf hung her matchcoat on their lodge poles. Rather, *her* lodge poles. The ones he'd erected for her. In Kossati because he wished to be near his mentor. Who, by Divine working, was Wolf. Same as the woman Strong Bear intended to wed.

He covered her hand with his and squeezed. Then he drew a roughened breath through his tight throat and took a leap. "I can read."

At the abrupt change in subject, the flesh between her brows furrowed, but only for a three-count. Clever woman, the wrinkles soon disappeared as clarity entered her eyes. "You read the marriage contract."

His chin lowered, lifted. "Your signature is absent." At her tiny flinch, he swallowed thickly and pressed on. "Why? Bellamy is torn up from the wait, and I needn't read letters to see it. Two winters, woman, and still you make him wait. Why?" An agonizing question, but he wouldn't shy from it or, he vowed to himself, from her.

If it were possible, he would queue these words behind her sealed teeth: *I waited for you.* So many times, he'd said the same to himself, to Totka, to Flint. To any who would hear, really. Said them. Prayed them. Dreamed them. And most recently, shouted them at the Bluecoat healer Marcus Buck. Above all, he *believed* them.

She waits for me.

"Why?" he pushed, hating the very sound of the word, but without a proper lay of the land, he could not do battle.

Her lashes dropped, her sight settling somewhere on his center. "I don't like you thinking ill of Iron Wood. His heart is good."

What sort of reply was that? More denial? Deflection, perhaps. What it wasn't, unfortunately, was delusion.

"So you have said, and…so I've glimpsed." Strong Bear felt quite unsavage for admitting it when everything within screamed at him to unearth

Bellamy's every flaw, then sit her down for an education on why the Englishman was the lesser applicant. Of course, for that, Strong Bear would have to actually apply, a move he would not make until he'd given her an education of another nature.

So much yet unsaid between them...

"Difficult not to see his heart when he wears it outside his chest." Strong Bear's non-savageness was fading, rivalry coming on like a poison, but he managed a wan smile. Even if his timbre was colored in a slightly acerbic envy-green. "You occupy the whole of it, I fear."

"Why do you fear that?" True bafflement tipped her head to the side.

Because, he longed to snap at her, *the man is not your people. Because he is not your equal. Because he is not* me.

Instead, he touched light fingers to the curve of her jaw, mellowed his tone, and countered, "Why do *you*?"

Chapter 18

Pretty Wolf's instinctive response was to deny. Fear of occupying Iron Wood's heart? What rubbish.

She broke from Strong Bear's piercing inquiry and moved back to mount Balada, elevating herself to pucase.

"Pretty Wolf." He stepped nearer, the pleading note in his voice irresistible to her gaze, though her down-glance at him wasn't as *down* as she'd expected. The horse was small, and he wasn't. Yet another reminder he was not True Seeker.

A fact she wasn't yet sure she enjoyed.

True Seeker had never let her flaws slide without making her confront them, but Strong Bear doing the same struck her harder, more profoundly, and she couldn't gauge why. Only that it set loose a mess of claw-footed beetles on her insides.

Averting her sight, she fidgeted atop her mount and hoped he thought her to be adjusting her seat. "I do not fear my betrothed," she returned with as much conviction as the beetles allowed. Tightening her thighs, she instructed Balada to set off, only to have Strong Bear take the horse's mane in a commanding fist.

"Then what *do* you fear?"

The potential answers could fill a river. And did. The same black river she was sunk in up to her chin, waves slapping at her face in their drive to drown her with their shadowy spirit-bleeding death. Whether she'd ever get a handhold on the one true answer, the reason she'd become a skittish cat hissing at her mate again and again, well… For that, she'd have to dive deep, and the fear of never coming back up was perhaps the greatest of them all.

Whatever it was, that reason, Strong Bear would not be hearing it. If ever she found courage enough to scour the depths and identify the trouble, Iron Wood would be the first to know. Rightly so.

She flicked Strong Bear's fist, the one restraining Balada. "Release my horse. Slave," she tacked on with enough tease to avoid a sting and, spirits willing, set them back on less-ruffled grounds.

Breathing out, eyes shut, he pinched the lump on his nose, the one with her name on it, as if he might squeeze her out of his life. Perhaps, better for him if he did.

As he finally eased back, she lost the courage to hold his gaze. To see the frustration setting his jaw slightly to the left or the hurt tugging his brows down. But she felt him against her skin like sand in the wind, penetrating every crevice, never to be entirely removed.

The beetles became frantic, their little claws pick-picking at her innards.

With a harder-than-necessary bump of her heels, she urged the mare into a walk.

Strong Bear took up at her left, his sleeve brushing her leg, but they didn't speak again. His attention remained firmly elsewhere: on the lush grazing grounds they entered, the patches of hoof-indented mud they circumvented, the massive bulls congregated at the stream, and the cluster of whitewashed buildings growing on the horizon.

Head on constant rotate, he took it all in, contentment sitting on his mouth.

The same entered her, along with a fillip of excitement at the prospect of sharing this snippet of her life with him. A grin appropriated her then, a thing that had his instant focus.

With his chummy smile, he said: *I know, I understand, I agree. This is good. We are good.*

She drew wind into her airways and stretched her ribs to straining—the freest breath she'd drawn in a long while. No flood to be seen anywhere. Her breath eased back out on a sigh that tapered off with an outstretch of her hand.

Strong Bear encased her fingers in his warm ones, briefly, long enough for her to note the change in their size and texture. Looking off, he released her, and she was left cold and lightly puzzled.

Then again, she'd be peeved, too, if he'd turned a deaf ear to such a question as she had.

The pasture ended at the cow pens, which consisted of a long row of stalls, each opening into a corral on one side. Beside it, a paddock, and beside that, a heaping cart whose steam filled her nostrils with a pungent, far-too-familiar odor.

The overseer, Jesús Rivas, leaned against the fence, one booted foot propped on the lowest rail. Broad leather chaps swooped down from his knee. He wore all gray: short-coat, breeches, round hat, the brim of which he touched as a grin stretched his brown cheeks. *"Buenas, señorita."* His eyes roamed her liberally.

"Señor Rivas." Face impassive, she dipped her head, at once conscious of the length of skin exposed by her hiked skirt.

Strong Bear sidled closer and wrapped his hand around her ankle in a blatantly possessive move, his cold gaze on Rivas.

The overseer's boot dropped to the ground, his hand to the coiled whip at his waist. "The snake-man warrior explained your absence, princesa. This is the slave you went to retrieve?" He jerked his chin at Strong Bear. "He's a bold one."

Resigned to seeing this through and counseling herself not to kick Strong Bear in the kidney, Pretty Wolf halted her mare and replied in the melodic language of the Spanish. "He's a longtime friend. Charged with my safety. As you can see, he is devoted to duty and will serve you well."

Rivas, stance rigid, kept a sizing eye on Strong Bear. "What skills has he?"

Pretty Wolf considered this, then considered some more, her lower lip rolling between her teeth at her inability to fashion a quick reply.

True Seeker had been useless at tracking, unless it was to follow the aroma of her bubbling pot; somewhat helpful at skinning, when he didn't pull too hard and tear the pelt; decent at fashioning tools, not taking into account the three bows he'd carved and cracked; downright awful at laying snares, except for catching raccoons in netting.

Oh! He made the net. Repaired it too.

Now that she thought on it, he was also a proper shot with a sling. Pretty Wolf didn't suppose either skill was the type Rivas might value. She switched to **Muskogee**. "Strong Bear, what can you do?"

His eyes narrowed on Rivas. "Quite a bit, actually. If I get the whip off him first. If not—"

Her leg jerked out. With a loud crack, her pinky toe crumpled against his immovable frame. She grimaced to withhold a hiss of pain. When he slanted a concerned look at her foot, she huffed. "I meant skill, labor, craft. Rivas, the chief of these pens, the one you've glared a hole through, wishes to know what you *do*."

"A hole is less than he deserves for the wicked thoughts his eyes were speaking."

"And what are *my* thoughts speaking?" She affected a low-lashed glare and stuffed it with vexation.

"Iron work," he blurted, raising a staying hand. "I'm apprenticed to a Kossati *blacksmith*." His use of the English term set her a few beats behind him. "...can shoe a horse in one half of an hour," he was saying, "and my sledgehammer swing is strong and certain. My skill is humble but adequate for an assistant." His low tone matched his claim to humility, but he said *sledgehammer* and *shoe a horse* the way she said *ribbons* and *barter for hides*. There was no masking his love of the craft, and it staggered her.

Strong Bear can work iron. He can shoe a horse. And work iron. Her lashes did their compulsive beating routine while her brain tried to fit itself around Strong Bear hefting a heavy hammer. That explained the muscled shoulders.

She pivoted her gaze to Rivas and, in a gush of words, apprised the overseer of Strong Bear's skill. Proudly. He had found a trade, a coin-garnering trade, and even she, daughter of a staunchly nativistic prophet, could not be more pleased for him.

The overseer clapped his gloved hands together. "*Excelente*. Send him to the forge."

"Sí, *jefe*," she said to Rivas, who tapped his hat to be done with her before turning back to his men. To Strong Bear, she said, "He sends you to the forge."

"And you?"

"Me?"

"Where will you be? I'm never to leave your side. Sunflower's orders."

She cut her gaze to him. "Ever?"

"Until the contract with the Spanish is complete, or she says otherwise."

Never leaving her side seemed a trifle excessive for the circumstances—and might also create some awkward situations—but she wouldn't put it past their chary clan mother to make such a demand of him. If it meant protecting the talwa's golden, "lost" daughter.

Strong Bear said, "Is it a problem?"

"A problem?" Only if Iron Wood caught scent of it. He already disapproved of Strong Bear on principle of...being a *big chap*? Having the wrong disposition? Glaring? He'd accused Strong Bear of all three. She could see now that he'd misinterpreted Strong Bear's intense focus as being fury and vengeance versus affection, surprise, longing, all the feelings that had assaulted *her* minutes later. Whatever their cause or interpretation, Iron Wood instinctively rejected them.

Knowing she would spend the last days of their contract working alongside Strong Bear must be cutting Iron Wood to ribbons. Once he learned of Sunflower's order, he would be in fine, fretful form.

Strong Bear stared at her. "Rabbit droppings."

"Rab— What?"

"Just checking you could still speak beyond repeating me." Amusement faded from him as he drew in close, a hand resting behind her on Balada's pale rump. A set of tiny lines grooved into the flesh above his nose as he studied her. "Bother shadows your face. What puts it there?" He had his **knower's** voice on, blowing it across her on pine-scented breath.

Inhaling, she willed the blood to stay in her constricting heart and out of her cheeks. "No bother. And you'll be working within sight of me."

Though he arched a skeptical eyebrow, he pushed off the horse and said, "Within sight is acceptable, I suppose."

A press of Pretty Wolf's heels invited Balada to step on and, spirits please, leave behind the nagging concern that these days with Strong Bear would result in less help than trouble. The urge to talk it out with him came over her strongly, but she bit it back. Better to deposit him at the forge directly and sweat out her worries with endless shovelfuls of manure.

Strong Bear wedged his thumbs under the shoulder strap of his satchel and stuck to her like chickweed as they advanced through the hustling yard.

"The arena." She pointed ahead to the towering circular structure linked to the paddock by an extended brick passageway. The distant hum of an animated crowd reminded her that the cows' testing was scheduled for that afternoon.

"What goes on there?"

"Fights. Man against bull." Constructed of solid coquina, the arena's thick walls rose to a height above five rods, its mass hiding the rest of the Spaniard's holdings on the structure's opposite side.

As they approached, Strong Bear tilted his chin up to take it all in. His arching brow painted him impressed. "Does the bull ever win?"

"Sometimes. It is a bloody affair either way, and I—"

"Señorita Francis!" Tito, dressed in the ratty, besmirched attire of a stable boy, hopped manure patties on his way to reach her. "Your horse, please. I will brush and grain her if you wish."

Before Pretty Wolf could answer, a flash of light lured her gaze to the arena's exterior stairway. Sunlight cast itself off the regalia of a familiar rotund figure waddling up to the viewing booth atop the wall.

Tickled at this chance meeting, Pretty Wolf lifted her arm and hailed, *"Tío!"*

Capitán Antonio Luengo, Toño for short, begged she call him tío. He stopped and twisted back to cap eyes on her. The immediate sparkle on his fleshy face emulated the gleam of the war metals adorning his blue, red-trimmed uniform coat. Since blood had little say in ties of the heart, she had no qualms calling him *uncle*.

"Ala!" he called down. "See here who the cows have brought in with them. None but my favorite Loba Bonita." He smacked his knees and ripped out a laugh that was all bouncing belly as if the Spanish version of her name were the greatest of jokes.

She nudged Balada to the base of the stairs. "How are all at Los Robles?" Her responsibilities at the cow pens had halted her every-third-day lessons in his home, and she'd missed him.

"*Bien, claro*. All are well but feeling the loss of you." As he descended, he sucked in his gut so others going up might get by on the narrow passage.

He scurried the rest of the way down, and she dismounted to receive an air kiss at each cheek. Toño: loyal respecter of the Rule. "Fourteen days remain on the contract," she said. "May I come see you on the fifteenth?" She adjusted his hat so that its crimson cockade sat in line with his long nose and double chin.

"Come the fifteenth, come the sixteenth. Come to stay! Always a joy to see the Muscogee princess." His eyes crinkled with affection before they shifted to Strong Bear, who'd stepped back with the horse and was smiling down at Tito. Spanish rattled off the boy's tongue at head-spinning speed.

"Who is your brave young friend?" Toño inquired.

Young, she could see. "What about him says bravery?"

"The broken nose. One could argue it says stupidity if it weren't paired with the cross and your father."

That knotted nose had nothing of stupidity about it. She would kiss it if the act wouldn't send any signal other than fondness and gratitude. "You're right. He is brave. This is True Seeker."

Toño leaned back, mouth falling open. "Your Alabama Town True Seeker?"

"The same." Pretty Wolf beamed, wholly uninterested in bridling her pleasure. "Now called Strong Bear. He's come to help me here." As if he'd gotten himself captured just to milk a cow.

"*Bueno!*"

The exclamation pulled Strong Bear's notice from Tito, while the boy pulled at the satchel. He relinquished it and met Pretty Wolf's eyes with a humorous glint in his own.

"A fine specimen, your friend," Toño gushed on. "You must be overjoyed to have him returned to you."

"I am," she replied, Toño being, perhaps, the only person to whom she could openly admit it.

"Come here, *hombre*. Let me welcome you." Grinning, he opened his arms wide and gathered up Strong Bear in a full-body, back-slapping embrace.

Over the man's shoulder, Strong Bear blew out his cheeks, feigning strangulation.

She coughed over a laugh. "This is Antonio Luengo, the commander I told you of."

Strong Bear spoke the expected words of appreciation and honor, Pretty Wolf rendering them into Spanish, then backstepped a safe distance.

Toño said, "Have your warriors met him yet?"

"We have just arrived, but we're going to them now."

"No, no, bring them here. They are men. They will enjoy the event." He snapped fingers at the waiting stable boy. "Take Lobita's horse and summon her *indios*. Show them up." He shifted back to Pretty Wolf. "And now, the trials! Come, come. Join me," Toño urged with an overhead flail of an arm that knocked his shako askew again. "They begin shortly. Bring your Bear with you. We will bulge his *indio* eyes with a fine show, no?" Toño chortled and rotated his pudgy frame to repeat his panting climb.

Mildly curious to know what transpired behind that wall, she handed off Balada's care and trudged up the stairs after him, saying to Strong Bear, "Toño has invited us to join him in watching a cow testing of some sort. I cannot promise you won't be appalled by it, but the man is impossible to refuse."

"It cannot be as appalling as sand spurs in the moccasins." Grinning, he made himself that very thing on her skirt, sticking to her as they ascended. At the summit, she stopped short. Strong Bear bumped into her from one stair down, then caught her forward tip with a swift handhold of the back of her blouse.

In contrast to the heat along her spine, a crisp breeze penetrated her clothing and stung her cheeks. They'd come out at the open-topped spectator's box, a raised platform abutting the ring's upper lip. Filled to swelling, its half-walls were reduced to slivers of white visible between the vaqueros and soldiers propped against them.

Directly below lay the bullring—a stunning sight in itself—but it was the countryside that stilled the wind in her lungs. Strong Bear's position on the last step brought him level with her and placed his low murmur of awe right at her ear as they paused to take in the view.

The plaza's far rim underlined three fenced pastures presided over by cows and their calves, yearling bulls, and a herd of the magnificent Arabian horses Korsan salivated over. Those green expanses bled into row upon brown row of harvested fields. The plowed ground adjoined the gardens encompassing La Conchita, Don Diego's red-roofed hacienda. Beyond, barely visible from her vantage point, orange groves and a mixed forest of pine and palm carried the Spaniard's lands clear to the river.

"Beautiful," Strong Bear murmured, erupting a tingling ear-to-jaw line of gooseflesh in the path his breath took across her skin. "I've never been this high. Seen so far."

She leaned away and craned her neck toward the crowd. "High enough to see where Toño went?" The mass of bodies had absorbed the shorter man. "Can you spot him from up there?"

He stepped up to her level, pushing her forward into the crush. Two men hustled past into the box, jostling her, and Strong bear yanked her close. Reflexively, she clamped onto his hand for stability, the one fastened to her ribs. She abruptly released him. "Apologies."

"For?"

"Holding your hand. Old habit." During the long away, she would have been dead a dozen times over—body or soul, pick the day—if she hadn't been clinging to one part or another of him.

"I don't recall complaining." He smirked as he circled her to take lead, deftly stealing her fingers to re-thread through his. "Stay close."

His command, his hold, both felt natural, intrinsic to who they were. Comfortable and comforting. An inalterable state of being that would make Iron Wood weep, that made her own eyes sting.

Confused, racked by guilt, she wiggled free. "The Rule, Strong Bear."

He halted, rounded back, and leaned into her space. "I am *above* the Rule," he said, forceful, implacable, disdain thick in his voice.

Her nostrils flared. "If my father hears you—"

"I answer to Sunflower and my Creator-given conscience. Not your father." As if in defiance, he snaked an arm around her waist and drew her aside. Just then, three jocose vaqueros bustled past, bumping her shoulder.

What was it Sunflower had said? Something about Strong Bear and the Rule living in different lands. Grudgingly, she conceded that gave him a vast amount of liberty.

He bent close. To be heard, or possibly to make his presence larger before her. "My orders are to protect you however I see fit, and if I feel touching you is needful to guide you through a mob of excitable men, I won't hesitate. And I won't apologize. And *you* will say no more of this ridiculous rule. Is this clear?"

Her lips fell open.

"Good." He stole her hand and, turning, placed it at the sash hugging his hip. He waited until she grabbed on, then softened his features and said, "Together."

Chapter 19

Slightly stunned, Pretty Wolf huddled at Strong Bear's back, not unhappy to shelter in his wake as he forged into the gathering, men parting on either side like water curling away from a prow. In a few strides, they reached the front wall where he swiped a few men aside and took the place next to Toño. The commander's rank provided him prime viewing as well as a nice buffer of space around his person. Nodding to him, Strong Bear dragged Pretty Wolf around himself and stationed her at his front.

"There you are." The commander rubbed his hands together. "Only a few minutes more."

Hip bones locked against the waist-high wall, Pretty Wolf stood stiff, hyper-aware of the other wall at her back. Sometimes, Strong Bear was True Seeker and True Seeker was Strong Bear, and other times, such as now, Strong Bear was a formidable, brain-blinking stranger.

Shaking off the awkwardness, she bent to take in the full arena below. Three men, berry-pink capes draped over folded arms, leaned against the whitewashed ring. "That *color*," she said in Muskogee. "Have you ever seen such a bright pink?"

Moving to her side, Strong Bear lowered to prop on his forearms and peered down. "I have. Every time you get riled."

"You mean every time you rile me." Fending off amusement, she lobbed him an irritable look, her braid swinging out over the dirt far below.

"Someone has to keep the great daughter of prophecy humble on her perch." Lips twisting, he flipped her braid over her other shoulder.

"Atención," someone announced. "The trials commence!"

"It begins." She straightened.

Strong Bear rose with her as if hooked on by a string. When the crowd stirred, vying for better viewing, he made a barrier of himself by placing his body flat against her left side.

Toño posted himself at her opposite flank.

At the bristly sensation of a sidelong look, she jerked her eyes right and found him scrutinizing every point of contact between herself and Strong Bear. The long, oiled whiskers on his upper lip drew down.

Then Strong Bear swayed forward and back, absorbing the impact of some exuberant fellow in the impatient crowd.

Toño's mustache shifted back, his gaze lifting to hers, grave and resolute. "What does Señor Bellamy have to say about this intimate friendship?"

A sweeter, more benevolent man one could not find anywhere in all of Spanish territory, but Antonio Luengo could cut to the soul of a matter with a rapier's thrusting blow.

Buying time to concoct a reply, Pretty Wolf nipped at her lips and looked out over the arena. Several seating tiers rose on stalks outside the wall to wrap around one half of the circular structure. They sat as empty as her brain. There was no help for it but to meet Toño's strike thrust for thrust. "In this, Iron Wood's opinion cannot matter."

He turned away, his disapproval descending on her like a black cloud. But there would be no ducking her head. Pretty Wolf had done—was *doing*—nothing wrong, and Strong Bear was merely following orders. "One of my men is lame, and I must have four workers, or we lose our winter meat. While I can prevent it, my people will not go hungry."

Tension filled Strong Bear's body and radiated into her. Had he learned Spanish along with English letters, or was it merely her agitation that had him on alert?

Below, a wooden panel on the arena's wall began sliding to the side on its rails, a dark passageway revealed behind it. The crowd instantly settled.

A cow emerged from the tunnel at a mad charge. Horns high, head on a jerky swivel, she galloped freely, the men having hidden behind the protective barriers punctuating the ring at even distances—all but the horseman. He hugged the far side and kept his blindfolded mount perfectly still and out of the cow's interest.

"Were no other captives brought in?" Toño asked.

"One other. He's feverish. Strong Bear stays, Tío." She stressed the last word while studying the cow's heaving sides. "How do they test the cow?"

Toño donned an unhappy smile but backed off and better positioned himself to watch the creature. "They will let her run a while. Then do a bit of cape work. They judge her agility and reaction time while taking an accounting of her energy and character. A tame cow, say a milker, will roll over after a knockdown and resign herself to what's coming, but a superior female from this breed will show resilience."

"For what purpose? Do the females fight as well?"

"No, no. Only select males have the honor of fighting for their lives before slaughter. But from where do you think the bulls get their spirit and courage?"

The massive beast darted across the plaza and ran headlong into a panel. The tips of her horns buried into the wood before she tore away, spraying splinters, and backed up to cock her head at some other perceived offense across the way.

Pretty Wolf's lips bowed up with an unexpected swelling of pride. "Their mothers give it to them."

"They do."

She nodded at this, thinking of how Sunflower would appreciate such knowledge of female power. "And from their fathers?"

"From their sires, they receive muscle and good looks." Toño waggled his black eyebrows.

Pretty Wolf grinned. "This one certainly has spirit."

"She does that, but they've also separated her from her calf to stir her up."

A dart to the heart, the words dashed away her smile. The rough coquina edges of the wall's upper surface dug into her palms as she blinked through the rush of waters compressing her lungs.

"What's upset you?" Strong Bear murmured, his body curving around her.

With her deliberate inhale, her ribs slowly expanded, waters retreating. "I'm all right."

For five ticks of her chaotic heart, his lungs stood full and motionless. They restarted with a rough exhale. "I shouldn't toss the commander to the bulls, then?" The crowd's hush made his undertones, the ones puffing against her hair, that much more...intimate.

Spirits help her. Toño was right.

She forced a chuckle up her throat. "No tossing necessary."

Without warning, Toño twisted to her, giving the ring his back. His gaze flitted about her face, unable to land, his speech picking up speed. "As your devoted uncle, I must speak frankly, and you must listen. No, you must *hear*. This Bear friend is a fine man, I'm sure, and will make a good worker, but he is too forward. Stands too near."

Toño wasn't wrong there; Strong Bear couldn't stand any closer without merging their skin. Though her inner beetles perked up their pestiferous little heads, she brushed away Toño's concern with a flip of her hand. "True Seeker always wore integrity like armor. I expect Strong Bear to be the same. And he is on orders to both work the cow pens and to protect me. Orders that rank higher than my betrothed's sensibilities. It was a spirit-blessed wind that brought Strong Bear to me, and I won't send him away because Iron Wood scowls in his direction." Even if having him—and his cross—so nigh to her father terrified the strength from her joints.

"Señor Bellamy scowls in every man's direction." Toño's droll line was intended as a calming draught, she knew. It might have worked but for the thrown-on, "Pity you, child."

"I do not want pity," she clipped, blocking out Strong Bear's increasing heat. "I want trust. I want my father, my clan mother, my *village* to believe I can protect myself, and I want Iron Wood to let go the belief that contact with men sets me to quaking."

"The way it does with him," Toño finished quite accurately, sadness tinging his eyes. More of that pity she couldn't stomach.

She turned aside her head, using interest in the ranting cow to hide the turbulence that surely beamed from her features. The poor beast was furious and out for blood, charging, skidding, pivoting at every noise of threat, nostrils flared, ribs heaving, hooves rutting the earth, horns driving, impaling the barriers again and again.

"Ay, chica," Toño said lowly beside her, "how weary your legs must be. The running cannot go on."

Toño didn't know what it was she ran from, only that her legs had been churning since she arrived in Wakulla.

Her eyelids trembled shut. *Weary, so weary.* "Once he knows, he will hate me," she said more to herself than him.

"The *Santa Biblia* tells us not to worry about anything, to instead pray about everything, to tell God all our needs."

Her lids flipped open. When Toño imparted some tidbit from the Ancient Words, she listened.

"I would challenge you, Lobita, to do this and to speak your heart to Señor Bellamy before week's end."

Two challenges in one morning? Plus Kit's arrival. What were the spirits trying to tell her?

Toño went on. "Find your courage, child. Dig it up from wherever you've buried it and *speak* to him. Your time for dallying has run out. This young man"—he gave a pointed nod in Strong Bear's direction—"might have done your señor a great service before, but don't fool yourself to think his presence here will be tolerated for long."

Mouth bobbing, she stared at him, at the anxiety tightening his brown eyes, her brain still picking apart the implication that Iron Wood might consider her friend to be…what? Too forward, too close—she could see that. But an actual contender? That was a more difficult notion to swallow. Especially when laid beside the betrothal contract and Iron Wood's essential connection to the People's survival. Never mind her own heart on the matter.

Strong Bear might have brought with him muscles and talk of lodges, but reality was an engraved stone and not so easily altered by flirtations. If that was what they were.

Exasperated, she entwined her arms over her breasts. "What are you saying, Tío?"

"When backed into a corner, even good men do grievous things."

Such as move bathing tubs. Her arms unfolded and fell to her sides. Iron Wood *did* tend to be overprotective of her, of them.

"Will you take up the challenge, Lobita?" He crowded her, placing his urgent words right before her, where she could not miss them. Strong Bear rumbled a low growl of warning that reverberated through her, but Toño ventured on. "Speak to him this Sunday, not a day later. I *defy* you to do it."

Sunday. Three days.

She should. Really should.

But the thought of agreeing was a stomach-disturbing malaise. A desperate longing overcame her to turn on the spot and muffle a scream in Strong Bear's chest. Palming her belly, she took a moment to breathe and squinted through a dust cloud as she turned her face to the arena.

Toño's "cape work" seemed to be in play. Head lowered, the cow charged the teasing fabric held out at a fighter's side. Her massive body brushed his to a chorus of *olé!*, and exhilaration rushed Pretty Wolf's veins. She resisted joining in the applause, head too filled with round after round of *Sunday, Sunday*. Groaning, she scrubbed a hand over her face, then hastily dropped it as Strong Bear changed positions from behind to beside.

"Quite an act," Strong Bear said, but he wasn't looking at the plaza.

Pretty Wolf formed a stiff smile as the soles of her feet picked up vibrations from the cow's charge.

The beast was thundering toward the mounted pikeman. In the face of her rage, the horseman held steady center-ring. At the last instant, he swiveled his horse in a tight, stationary circle and artfully avoided a gutting.

Pretty Wolf flattened a hand over her heart, its beat matching that of the beast's hooves.

Not halting, the cow spun and stormed across to a cape bearer, while behind her, the horseman kicked his mount into a sprint and followed. He adjusted his blunted lance with a few skillful moves and, without slowing, slammed it into the cow's hip. Her rear legs went out from under her, and her massive body spilled across the ring, billowing dust.

Strong Bear flinched, and Pretty Wolf peeked through one eye, the other closed in a grimace.

Toño broke protocol to lay a hand on her back. "To such a large animal, it is more shock than harm. For the honor of calving a fighting bull, this trial is a pittance. Now, let us see what mettle this one has."

Pretty Wolf nodded, her shoulders lowering from accumulated tension.

"I am come," said a Muskogee voice behind her. A glance back revealed the gaunt, triangular face of Screaming Buttons. "Only myself. Big Voice and Kicking Knife are..." The explanation trailed off as his sweeping gaze crossed over Strong Bear. And came back. He blinked, then broke into a hearty chortle. "Ho, there! It cannot be True Seeker. But it is! Look at that nose."

Strong Bear laughed with him, though he rubbed the old break self-consciously. "Strong Bear now, my friend. The most blessed slave to walk the Point." Taking Pretty Wolf about the waist, he worked her around to swap their positions.

"It is well, brother." The men clasped arms for a shake that ended on a bump of the chests, a brief touching of hearts that had Pretty Wolf grinning along.

Together again, the three of them.

Screaming Buttons slapped the thick of Strong Bear's arm. "You are all grown, complete with a warrior's name."

Strong Bear slid her a smirk. She returned him the big-eyed smile of the clueless, and he rolled his eyes back to Screaming Buttons.

While the two reacquainted, she turned back to the ring.

Knocked down again, the cow made a frantic scramble to rise and orient herself. Her keen, black eyes were learning, taking in every menace. At the flicker of another cape, she was off, barreling toward it. The goadsman pursued and repeated.

Strike, spill, charge.

Again. Again.

The cow met each tumble with yet another rush of fury. Until, finally, on the horseman's fourth approach, she reeled, dropped her horns, and drove straight for the horse's chest.

Pretty Wolf's breath suspended.

On a shout, the pikeman skittered his mount sideways, earning a bloody scratch across the horse's rump.

The crowd roared. Even Strong Bear, beside her again, applauded the save.

Over the cheers, she shouted to Toño, "Exceptional courage." Man, horse, cow.

His head bobbed. "High scores for that one."

The large panel slid aside. The cow darted for it, and Pretty Wolf was almost sad to see her go. As the creature's tail disappeared into the black of the tunnel, Pretty Wolf roused her own courage. "Sunday."

Toño swung toward her. "Eh?"

She ran sweaty hands down her front. "Challenge accepted. I will talk to him."

The folds of Toño's brow shifted to form an impressed arch.

"What?" She curled her mouth up on one side. "Did you think me a milk cow?"

Chapter 20

"What is *this*?" Strong Bear waved disgustedly at the dark, empty horse stall. It stank of not-Wolf.

"The sleeping place I was to show you." Beside him, Screaming Buttons rattled a shrug. "Now that's done, we can go to bed. Come. We lodge in the spare tack room. It's tight but better than outdoors." He padded down the wide outdoor alley that ran between two rows of stables, Strong Bear matching his languid stride.

"So, Sunflower appointed you as Pretty Wolf's guard?" Screaming Buttons' question boomed through the evening stillness of the Spanish-owned cow pens, and a horse whickered in annoyance.

The same threaded through Strong Bear's stilted smile. "She did." And if Buttons wanted to argue it, Strong Bear wouldn't spurn the opportunity to name all the reasons he was the proper choice to oversee her guardianship.

Guardianship....

Did she need it? Like the wolf needed extra teeth.

Did he mind it? Like the bear minded growling.

Before Buttons could think to mock the notion, Strong Bear continued. "I am certain it's only an excuse to keep us close. Unless there's a danger to her I'm unaware of?"

The mere mention spurted blood hotly through his heart and snapped his gaze to attention. It combed the grounds and delved into the shadows. Several caped Spaniards wandered the premises, heads down and boots shuffling through the dusk. They looked eager for their couches rather than any nefarious business.

"There's no threat." Screaming Buttons smacked Strong Bear's hand off his sheathed knife. "No, your thinking aligns with Sunflower's ways. Nothing against Iron Wood, I believe, for he's a likeable fellow, but Sunflower never favored him for Pretty Wolf. Noonday the same. And for all Pretty Wolf's talk of wedding the man, she has remained *un*wed these many seasons."

Because she waits for me. Whether she realized it or not.

Smug satisfaction worked Strong Bear's mouth into a half-cocked smile. Oblivious, Screaming Buttons rattled on. "The women, no matter their preferences for the lost daughter, would not go against our micco's wishes, and Crazy Medicine wishes the talwa permanently joined to the English trader."

"Then why create a false guard position for me? Why throw gunpower into the fire by making me a fixture in her life?" Strong Bear's earliest memories included several of Sunflower during **township stomp dances**. He'd always thought fondly of her and believed the sentiment returned—her welcome to Wakulla affirmed it. But he wouldn't say that *he*, a cross-wearing White Stick, was worthy enough for their beloved Pretty Wolf.

They rounded the rear of the structure. Buttons pointed at a door a short distance down, and they angled toward it. "Perhaps, in her old age, Sunflower has decided to cease pandering to the micco and dote instead on the micco's daughter."

"Whatever the cause," Strong Bear said, "it works in my favor."

That swiveled Screaming Buttons' head. "You've come to win her away then?"

Strong Bear opened his eyes wide and innocent. "How do you mean? I am only a worthless slave."

Screaming Buttons shook his head, his shoulders bouncing with silent laughter. The amusement faded when he neared the closed door. Stopping before it, he grabbed the latch and went still. Chin tucked, he stayed just so for several heavy breaths before he spoke, voice solemn. "I've been eaten up with regret for the pain I caused you, brother, but…for her, for the prophecy, I would do it again."

Old anger simmered to life, but Strong Bear stamped out every spark.

The man before him had been a relentless friend to them both for more seasons than Strong Bear had toes. After the Bluecoats had finally released the Horse's Flat Foot survivors, Screaming Buttons, in his greater age and experience, had guided them home. Over the next year, he'd extended flawless friendship. Until he plotted with Polly and left. Buttons had always believed her nightmares were the prophecy calling her home, and no man—not even her devout True Seeker—could stand against the spirits' wishes.

As much as he hated the result, Strong Bear understood the man's devotion. Did his own adherence to Creator Jesus not equal it?

And so, swallowing his hurt and bitterness, he'd found forgiveness. Putting that exact sentiment into his voice, he cupped Buttons' tight shoulder and said, "She would have left regardless. I am only grateful you were there to protect her."

The bones beneath Strong Bear's fingers eased downward, the muscles unwinding. Buttons exhaled on a nod. "Maddo, brother." He cranked open the door and unveiled a brick-sized room, a sleeping woman, and the sliver of bed space beside her.

Lightning scattered through Strong Bear's veins, and he swallowed. For precisely two beats of his heart, he considered that lone, empty stall. Its solitude. Its shelter from temptation. On the third, he glanced at the room's other occupants—both males, both watching him, both far too near her—and growled, "I sleep by the woman."

Something jostled Pretty Wolf, easing her to half-waking. She lay there unmoving, mourning the loss of her dream—a delicious cocoon of sunshine and ocean waves whooshing rhythmically in her ears. The musty scent of hay penetrated her nose, and darkness covered her eyelids.

Night, tack room, cow pens.

Strangely, the sun's warmth didn't shatter along with her dream, and that hypnotic tide kept rolling in. No complaint from her. Neck to hips, belly to throat, a velvety heat seeped through her skin, the coziest she'd felt, the sweetest she'd slept, in so long.

Coherent thought warbled, faded…

She sighed, licked dry lips, and snuggled down into the hay, leaned back into the fire's glow. Except there was nowhere to go. Neither back nor up, as a wiggle-test confirmed. Her mind gained traction on reality.

Something, no some*one*, a large someone, had her in a full-body grasp.

Gradually, her senses began registering other details: an alien weight pressing on her ribs, the sibilant cadence of breath at her ear, a heavy leg twined with her own, flesh on flesh.

Her eyes flung open.

This was bad. Quite bad.

Hadn't she known there would be a night Screaming Buttons forgot himself and confused her for his wife? Blue Feather would absolutely spill her beads over this.

Maybe if Pretty Wolf slipped free without waking him…

She'd not gone farther than a short twist of the torso when the arm bracing her jerked taut about the ribs. A grunt tickled the hair at her nape.

"Buttons?" She loosed the tentative whisper into the stillness and rapped the firm muscle of his upper arm. Teeth gritted, she shoved to the rear of her mind that his forearm grazed her bust and his broad hand nestled her throat. Long fingers wrapped around the back of her neck, their palm a hot slab against her rapidly increasing pulse. "Buttons, wake." Another several raps. "Buttons, you must—"

The arm contracted and pulled her shoulder blades flat against his chest, a seemingly reflexive move. When he nosed into her hair, she abandoned discretion and snapped, "Wake up!" She drove her heel into his knee.

A disgruntled *guh,* then the band of bone and muscle relented.

Three night-gray forms bolted to sitting, one of them hers, the farthest rattling like a viper, the last jerking up with a musket already in hand. None of them the man beside her.

No, *he* merely heaved over onto his back and graveled out, "Was that necessary, woman?" It was then the rattle of snake buttons sank in. Rather, their exact location did.

She scrambled to her feet. The patch on her neck where the hand had lain flared into a scorching burn. "Kit!"

"Wolf."

The burn spiked inward, licked up her veins in an angry sizzle. "What do you think you're doing?" And why was he even in the tack room? Beside her!

When she'd skipped the evening meal, she'd left Screaming Buttons with clear instructions to show Strong Bear to one of the unused stalls. Exhausted from catching up on her daily chores, she'd then slogged into their quarters and crashed to the hay. She fell asleep within moments, a prayer of thanks on her lips. With Screaming and Strong Bear at her side, the remaining days of labor would pass like a spring-scented breeze.

Provided each stayed in his proper place.

"Sleeping," he slurred. "What else?"

"What else! You cannot be here. Move," she demanded, and because she could, she kicked him again, toes sharp against his thigh.

Quick as a mantis, he snatched her about the ankle and held fast. "Happy now you've got that out?"

"No!"

"What has he done?" Screaming Buttons rubbed his face, muffling a yawn.

She pointed an accusing finger at Strong Bear. "He was holding me."

"Was I? Old habit." The excuse, *her* excuse turned on its head, rode from him on an audible shrug.

"Terrible habit." She growled and dislodged her ankle, too flustered to care what the others might infer—or imagine—from the divulged "holding."

Strong Bear flung an arm over his eyes. "All right."

"Clearly, he agrees," Screaming Buttons deadpanned.

Big Voice, who bedded at their feet, lowered the musket and, huffing, rearranged himself on the pallet. "Quiet children, the grown people are trying to sleep."

She pinned her arms over her chest and glared at Strong Bear, pointedly waiting for him to transport his bulk elsewhere.

Abdomen curling, he sat up and draped his arms over his up-drawn knees. "It wasn't a terrible habit before."

"I wasn't betrothed before!"

There passed a weighty pause as he looked at her, chin tipped to the side. "Ehi. You were."

"You were." Screaming Buttons, such a kindly helper.

No valid response on her tongue, she snapped her mouth shut to contain another growl and took an alternate approach. "You're in Buttons' spot."

"He put me here."

"Buttons!"

"What?" he retorted. "Blue Feather would prefer it this way, as would I. Besides, this is True Seeker. He's no stranger. What is the trouble?"

"Ehi, Pretty Wolf, what is the trouble?" Strong Bear yanked twice on the hem of her long sleeping shirt. "Myself, Screaming Buttons. What difference does it make?" He formed the questions with a grain of daring far too playful for a middle-of-the-night spat.

Must she really explain this to him? Could she explain it to herself? Never mind the explanations, what of the Rule? Just now, he'd broken it twelve times over. And this was no crowded bullring. He couldn't plead *protection* here.

"Buttons stays put when he sleeps," she defended. "He doesn't curl himself around me or nuzzle my hair like a suckling kit. Or wrap his hand around my throat!"

"Suckling kit?" Big Voice boomed a laugh while Screaming Buttons shoved Strong Bear in the shoulder. "You beast, you grabbed her throat?"

"How upright you act, brother." Big Voice was coming down from laughter. "As if you haven't dreamed of strangling her a time or two yourself."

Buttons blinked innocent eyes. "Never."

"There was no strangling. No dreams of it either." Strong Bear's voice firmed. "Apologies, Pretty Wolf. I won't do it again."

Big Voice snorted. "He'll do it again."

Head hanging back, she cast her eyes to the shadowy rafters and beseeched patience of the spirits. "You cannot make that promise, Strong Bear. Big Voice is right. You will do it again."

"If I do, you may kick me again." Easing back down, Strong Bear arranged himself on his side—the side facing *her* side—and laid his head on the bulge of his upper arm. "Big Voice has had a laugh at me. Screaming Buttons has lost the fear of his wife's jealousy. And *you* have the hope of landing me another bruise. See? Everyone is happy." A massive yawn warped his voice. He held the blanket open in invitation. "Lay down, firebolt."

Of its own volition, her foot flew into his shin, and she grinned deviously at his grunt. "You're right. Kicking you does make me happy."

Invitation revoked, he tucked the blanket up under his chin. "Has anyone warned Iron Wood about this one?"

"He is plenty warned," Big Voice drawled. "Is he not, little miccohokti?"

She scarcely refrained from a childish stamp of the foot. "Move, Strong Bear. Buttons, switch with him."

Screaming Buttons flipped over, gracing her with the back of his head and a string of incoherent mutterings.

"Buttons, please, you—"

"Enough, woman." Big Voice cut her off. "The slave is only doing the clan mothers' bidding, and you are spoiling everyone's rest."

Pretty Wolf dropped to her knees by Strong Bear's shoulders. She grabbed a fistful of his hair and pulled his head up to hiss a heated whisper into his ear. "Why are you doing this to me? My Englishman will not understand Sunflower's order, and it is already bad enough between us!" Distress crackled her voice.

Maintaining her grasp on him, she withdrew the space of a few hands to glare into the black pits of his eyes.

Too calm for her aggressive treatment, he gazed back, his breaths a regular cascade over her face, warm, piney, soothing in their caress. An irritating tonic. Echoing her posture, his forearm lifted from the straw to catch her by the hair at her temple. Only, his fingers weren't grasping or pinching but weaving and coaxing, tugging her down again.

"I will switch with Buttons," he said in a secretive hush, lips moving against the shell of her ear, "if you'll do one thing." At her tiny, eager nod, he said, "Admit to me the true reason you are uneasy sleeping at my side."

She swallowed. "And…what would that be?"

Against her, his cheek bunched, his tone sheathed in a swaggering smile. "Admit I'm a man."

Chapter 21

She refused to admit it. Just as well. She would eventually, and tonight, it worked in Strong Bear's favor.

He hadn't meant to snuggle into her, but some habits—old habits, terrible habits, the best of habits—were impossible to break. She'd be kicking him again at some point. Not tonight. Doubtful he'd catch another wink. He couldn't risk pushing his luck on that front, not with the woman still sparking beside him. Every few minutes, there came another nosey snort, another muttered word or testy movement, but none of her tosses were substantial enough for their bodies to come near to brushing. No, she was practically kissing the wall, as close as she lay to it.

His chest, his abdomen and thighs, his calf, even the toes he'd somehow hooked around her ankle still felt the impression of her. So as not to frighten the sensation away, he lay motionless, focused on each part, committing the feel of her to memory. How she could turn her back to it, not sense deep in her core the rightness of it, he couldn't comprehend.

The whole arrangement—the stables, the hay, the single small sleeping space shared by so many bodies, a female among them—was laughable. Infuriatingly so, beautifully so…he hadn't decided which.

On entering that night, it had taken some doing to wrangle his anger down to a level where he could recognize it wasn't their fault they'd been crammed into a pipe bowl. It took a bit longer to admit it was more bitterness and envy boiling his blood than anger, which make him feel like a brute. Only then was he able to release the compulsion to drive his fist into her bunkmates' faces. He'd calmed remarkably once he claimed the spot beside her unchallenged.

Unchallenged, that was, until she woke in a tizzy and in one blow kicked the stuffing out of both him and of his sweetest memories. It stung but, despite his indifference at her anger, it was right. Their once-natural, innocent touches now lived in prohibited territory. Too bad that, for now, it left his arms empty and his back covered in gooseflesh.

"Blanket thief," he muttered, expecting no reply if she was asleep, no pity if she wasn't.

To his surprise, she exhaled long and shimmied backward.

He wasted no time shimmying forward, readjusting the blanket to drape fully down his back. The warmth along his front increased with her nearness and melted off the remaining prickles in his spirit. Finally, he allowed himself to settle in and close his eyes, keeping a tight leash on his hands—and arms and legs. And thoughts.

There were two other bodies within thumping distance, but hers was the only one in the room, hers the only respiration he heard, tuned his heartbeat to. He curled his fingers tight to slay the urge to reel her into his chest, this time deliberately. It helped that the journey and the day's emotional intensity hit him hard of a sudden. His muscles, protesting the long absence from rigorous labor, burned from working the iron, shoeing five horses until past sundown. The aches and fatigue dragged him under despite his whirring brain.

Next thing he knew, a mourning dove was cooing, and Screaming Buttons was heaving himself upright, bumping Strong Bear twice in the process.

Strong Bear's eyes flashed open to account for his limbs. All in their rightful places. Pretty Wolf lay a few hand widths away in the exact position he'd last seen her. Her ribs rose and fell in the slow rhythm of sleep.

At Strong Bear's feet, Big Voice groaned, stretched, and ripped wind.

In passing, Screaming Buttons walloped his head with one of his moccasins. "There's a woman here, pig."

"Pretty Wolf still sleeps," Big Voice mumbled, "and she isn't a woman who cares."

Strong Bear hated that he was right, that he knew such things about her. He was also relieved to know Pretty Wolf was not too far removed from Polly, the young woman who'd made wagers of gaseous explosions: weakest one earned its perpetrator fire-tending duty that night.

"Pretty Wolf does not still sleep," she slurred adorably, worming down under the blanket, covered to her nose.

Strong Bear propped up on his elbow and, aiming for his accessories belt coiled at the wall's base, stretched over her. Using her as a bolster, he fished about inside the pouch for a tuft of pine, his weight expressing a little grunt from Pretty Wolf.

One full-glower eye squinted open at him.

He grinned down. "Good morning, Pucase."

"Slave."

Still tinkering in his pouches, he widened his grin when he caught her eyes tracing the rippling cords of his forearm. Male satisfaction stirred within.

The glower deepened, as did the color of her cheeks. "You smell of sweaty armpits and rotten teeth."

His laughter jostled her. Staying put, he jammed a needle tuft between his molars. After a few quick crunches, he blew his breath in her face. "One of those is true." Her scrunched nose brought on another chuckle, then a pointed sniff. "At least I don't smell like a cow's crusty hind end."

Hand to her hip, he shoved up, paying no heed to her grumble of denial or objection at being momentarily crushed. On his feet, he turned to find the tack room vacant, which suited him fine. Screaming Buttons was a true brother, but the other male was a mouthful of lemon juice.

Reaching over his shoulder, he grabbed a fistful of the shirt on his back and pulled it over his head. He tossed it onto a blanket peg and rotated in place, casting about the confines for bathing supplies; the hip bath didn't count.

Iron Wood, in a feeble attempt at appeasement, had promised to have the tub delivered this morning, but Pretty Wolf had pointed her nose to the sky, strapped the awkward basin to Balada's back—much to the mare's annoyance—and brought it herself.

"What do you look for?" She'd rolled to her back, her sleep-swollen eyes fast on him.

"The soap. I'm **going to water**." Strong Bear had particular plans to carry out there.

She pointed at a shelf and yawned. "I'm going to sleep. It is early."

Skipping out on the river then. As he'd suspected. He forced a teasing tone. "Plenty of time to scrub between the toes then."

"Don't forget your pits." Her mouth swooped lazily to one side.

Strong Bear's muscles clenched as he stared at her, riveted. How could a woman speak of stinky underarms and look sensual doing it?

She lay sprawled on the blanket, one arm flung over her head, the other draped across her chest. As her mouth relaxed back into drowsy neutrality, her long, dark lashes fluttered shut, sleep reclaiming her.

His lips twitched with the urge to brush against those lashes to learn whether they felt as soft as they appeared. In on the idea, his tongue slid out to lay down moisture, the temptation to taste her too compelling to risk casual touch. So, he dropped to his haunches, grabbed the blanket's edge, and without warning, rolled her up like tobacco in a palm leaf.

She squealed and went into instant fight. But all her undulating was useless against the tight trundling. "What are you doing!"

"Not touching you." *Not tasting you, not dragging your stubborn rear end back to Muscogee country and tying you to our lodge poles.* "Was that not what you wanted?" A scoop, a heft, then the wriggling bundle of woman was draped over his shoulder, her ratty braid hanging out of the blanket. "The cows shouldn't have to be subjected to your stench." He tugged her braid like a bell pull, eliciting a growl of halfhearted rage. "You're going to bathe. You can nap on the way."

She went still. "Bathe…where?"

And there it was. The old, misguided avoidance. But one could not simply renounce life-giving rivers.

"Where do you think?" He set his face that direction, his strides long and determined, unyielding as they ate up the ground of opportunity to sway his course.

He wouldn't.

"I won't do it! Put me down, you flea-bitten jackrabbit!"

"Ho, no reason to attack the clan."

"I'll attack whatever and whomever I want! Release me!"

"Soon enough."

Men stopped in the yard, their astonished expressions hastening his pace. He smiled and nodded as if lugging trundled-up women were a daily Indian affair.

"The tub. I have a tub!" She writhed, but a slight contracting of his muscles locked her down. Her efforts, as well as her weight, were inconsequential; her fighting spirit was another matter. She bucked enough to break her back.

With much effort, he refrained from smacking her on the rump. Just. "You can't cleanse properly in a tub. The river is better."

"The river is *not* better," she seethed. "The river is…is…"

The embodiment of your grief. The hurdle to healing that you trip over again and again. An affliction of the mind in dire need of banishing.

He ground his teeth in silence since his words were on severe restriction, per his vow to Sunflower. His actions, however, had the run of the field.

"Stop this, Kit!" She wriggled like a worm in a bird beak, her speech bouncing with his near-trotting steps. "You know what the river is to me."

"The river is the river, Pretty Wolf. Nothing more. Nothing less." Its rushing grew loud in his ear, and the ground softened beneath his bare feet, sloped down toward an azalea-lined bank. He aimed for a break in the bushes where the water lapped at a sandy beach.

The sound must have registered with Pretty Wolf because her shrieking and threatening disintegrated into blubbering and pleading, even if her striving remained vicious.

"Please, please, let me go. I don't want— I won't do this!" Her jagged breaths and brisk words were drowned in the sloppy noises of tear-fall. "Don't make me, True Seeker, I beg you."

At his old name, his steps faltered, indecision a snare in the path. But wasn't that the core of this rot? Pretty Wolf trapped in the past? Casting blame about like grapeshot.

March resuming, re-firming, he shouldered through the narrow gap in the head-high shrubbery and blinked hard at the sun's myriad reflections off the water's silvery surface. "My name is Strong Bear, and we are nearly three years downriver of—" He snapped his jaw closed, a quiet growl rumbling through his teeth. "The river is not your enemy, woman. It is not deserving of this hate."

If she was going to blame a spirit, it should be Earth. The slippery stones had taken her down, broken her ankle, deserted her on that bank. What did the river do but embrace her death-blue child at their bidding and carry him away?

He sloshed to his hips in the frigid water and swung her down into his arms. Crushing her shuddering body to him, he laid his jaw against the curve of her head and whispered a prayer that she might begin to heal. Or at least not hate him. "Fearless as the wolf," he began their mantra, but all she gave in return was a limp-bodied wail that bled his heart and about did him in.

Nearly three years of this. Three! At that brutal reminder, he unrolled her straight into the current.

Limbs wild, she belly-flopped and sank beneath the swells. He'd scarcely wadded up the blanket and lobbed it to shore before her feet were under her, her body whipping upright for a mad gulp of air. Spluttering, she stood unsteadily and flailed for him, blinded by the hair and water streaming over her scrunched-up face.

"Right here." He reached for her, guilt a barb in his chest. Both for her distress and his lack of foresight into how her clothing's thin fabric would cling.

She dug nails into his forearm and pierced him with a gaze so furious and flustering, he didn't see the swing coming. Her fist exploded pain across his teeth. His head wrenched to the side. He wrenched it right back, legs spreading, planting for another assault. She was welcome to go at him all she pleased—fair redress for this stunt—but he truly would be a suckling kit before he let her take him down.

Arms slack at his sides, he held her livid gaze, her water-logged lashes narrowed. She could skewer him with those eyes, loosen a tooth with that pale-knuckled fist trembling at the water's surface, but as he took her in—her grief, her fears, her drowned-pup condition—all he could feel was pride. With a finger, he drew a line across her brow to clear hair from her eyes. "Look at you. Standing tall and fierce in the river."

She blinked. Air exploded from her parted lips, spraying water. Then slowly, her shoulders collapsed, and her fists sank beneath the curls and eddies. A shiver wracked her as she looked at the crystal water coursing around her. Head hung, she took a few deep breaths, then raised cupped hands and stared at the glistening puddle she held.

He asked, "What do you see there that is so awful?"

Another few moments of study. "Myself." When she lifted her face, red rimmed her hazel irises.

Love, that beautiful, cruel hammer, socked him hard in the gut, and it was all he could do not to gather her in and stroke away every terrible memory, every shard of self-reproach and loathing.

A weighted breath leaked out of her, then resolve came over her like a wave, flattening her mouth. She plunged. Straight down. Water closed in over her, and Strong Bear laughed out loud. "Don't forget your pits, firebolt."

She rose, a wobbly smile ascending with her. "Turn around."

"So you can run off without scrubbing?"

"So I can undress."

She may as well have punched him again. Heat swamped him, pounded a path straight to his throbbing jaw. Any moment now, steam would be lifting off the river's surface. To hide how thoroughly her innocuous statement unraveled him, he raised a cocky eyebrow and did as she said.

It wasn't as if he hadn't seen her before. But for both their sakes, he could perpetuate the charade that her naked body was a mystery to him, that he hadn't been the one who clothed her when the bullet wound rendered her incapable, or the one who swabbed the torn and bleeding apex of her legs when she was too weak to do it herself, or the one who bound her aching, milk-laden breasts when grief robbed her of the ability to rise from her mat.

Or that her pale yellow sleep shirt wasn't concealing much to begin with.

A few splashes sounded behind him before a lump of fabric slapped down across his shoulder.

"Straighten that out for me. The sleeves are stuck inside."

He dragged the sodden garment off him. "At once, Pucase."

"Finally. Behavior fitting a slave. I'll be ringing your jaw more often."

Grinning, he rubbed the aching lump. "Does your slave get an opinion on that?"

"Naturally. Right or left. You may choose the side."

A laugh took him. "Such generosity." He began wrangling the dripping sleeves. "What are the day's plans?"

"For you, whatever the forge master demands, I suppose. For me, the usual excitement. Feeding and milking, mucking, saddling. Finished with my shirt?"

He flung it back. "Do you never go home?"

"Some. Mostly the store. My father's been away, so I'm back to leaching writing lessons off Iron Wood's accountant." Still jamming an arm through a sticky sleeve, she came around him, a devious plot written in her features. "Want to ambush him with me this evening?"

He crooked a wily grin. "I am your eager slave."

Chapter 22

"Find your own cover." Pretty Wolf jabbed an elbow into Strong Bear's solid abdomen. "This tree doesn't begin to hide your fat gut."

Skirt wrapped about her legs, she hunkered behind a pine slightly broader than herself, which meant half his body was at risk of exposure. Arm raised, he supported his weight against the trunk, his gaze straying from the path ahead, keeping a watch.

Pretty Wolf aimed to avoid Iron Wood until the following day, so she'd sent Melon into the store to fetch Korsan back to his lodge in the wood. If she knew her friend at all, the woman would use the request to her advantage.

"Blame my lack of stealth on my wilderness mentor who taught me no better." With an impatient exhale, Strong Bear squirmed, raining bark down on her.

And he wondered why he rarely brought home meat.

She made a face and spat woody bits off her lips. "The Muscogee Falcon *isn't* great, after all, eh?"

"I meant *you*, woman." He pinched her waist; she smacked at him. "Vicious wolf."

"Big, dumb bear."

He growled and nipped at her ear.

"Chh!" She palmed his face off her. "They come."

Low voices filtered through the trees moments before Korsan's yellow turban flashed through the foliage, Melon's faded red blouse beside it, their dark skin blending into the dusk. Dampened laughter reached Pretty Wolf next. Masculine. Resonant and...provocative?

Their ambling figures had scantly appeared on the path when Melon nabbed a fistful of Korsan's shirtfront and, giggling as she backed up, dragged him into the brush. He stumbled after her, not a speck of resistance about him.

Eyebrows spiked high, Pretty Wolf peered back at Strong Bear.

He tilted a sardonic smile. "Happy captives all over Wakulla."

"Undoubtedly happy." She clapped quiet, gleeful hands. "We'll wait in his lodge."

By the time Korsan arrived, Pretty Wolf had boiled water for tea and set herself up in her usual chair, bare feet propped on his desk. Strong Bear had chosen to remain outdoors, leery of entering a stranger's domain without his say so.

There came no murmurs of introduction from the yard before Korsan thrust himself through the flapless doorway. His glare might have menaced her if his turban weren't cockeyed, his sash sloppily tied, or his mouth a brilliant, kiss-puffed red.

"My compliments." She raised her steaming tea in salute, then gestured to the stash of dried fruit she'd raided and laid out. "You must have worked up a tremendous hunger."

He brushed a slow hand down his tunic and planted a self-congratulatory expression on his face. "I am quite sated, thank you."

"Was it the trimmed eyebrows?"

"Eyebrows," he jeered and straightened his headpiece. "It was inevitable the woman fall victim to my many charms."

Cup to her lips, Pretty Wolf barely staved off a chortle. "And you do have *many*."

He bowed his head in gracious acknowledgment, then faced her fully, hands clasped behind him. "I'm told your slave-guard is the young brave True Seeker."

"He is." She still quivered with the joy—and fear—of it.

"He gave me the eagle eye just now, before stepping aside so I may enter my own abode."

Pretty Wolf sighed. "He has always been wholeheartedly…" Attached. Fixated. Single-minded. "…devoted."

"Hmm." Korsan's chicory eyes slanted behind his square spectacles. "We shall see. Summon him inside. If you wish to use my chalk and board, it will cost you both."

Nothing she hadn't expected. In fact, she'd been anticipating it, eager for Korsan's opinion of Strong Bear and nervous he wouldn't adore her friend as much as she did. Strong Bear's silent challenge in the yard might have been the undoing of that possibility. Or its clinching. Who knew a sea rover's mind?

"Everything at a price with you, pirate." She re-crossed her ankles on the desk and raised a smirk. "Did you charge Melon as well? A doubloon for every kiss?"

He shot slit-eyed arrogance down his nose. "If I had, she would've gladly borne the dues. It is a high honor to share passions with an Ottoman of such magnificence."

This time, she let free her big, blustery laugh. Thudding her feet to the ground, she called for Strong Bear.

The introductions were curt, each male silently evaluating the other. Strong Bear eyeballed the pink-fleshed P on blatant display, and Korsan seemed to assess Strong Bear for where he might fall on the scale of magnificence. Or possibly insignificance.

Pretty Wolf ignored the stand-off and took up the chalk. "Strong Bear, this is Iron Wood's accountant, Korsan the Silent. A formidable pirate if his tales hold any water. Korsan, you have before you my dearest friend in all three worlds. Hurt him in any way,"—she brandished her chalk at him—"and I'll whiten the black from your eyes."

With a snort, Korsan broke off glaring to point a strict finger at her blackboard. "Uppercase Bs. Slanted lines, steady curves." He circled the desk to station himself in his kingly armchair across from her. "Keep that lazy monkey's wrist off the table and resume your memory of the battle. You left off at the slave here vowing to stay with you."

The bare mention of that conflict had Pretty Wolf's floodwaters churning. Her fingertips paled around the dusty writing instrument.

Strong Bear's powerful presence moved in behind her, bolstering.

She'd given him due notice of Korsan's payment, and he'd taken it in his typical easy stride, merely curious as to the strange arrangement but pleased she was speaking of those days. If only with her writing instructor.

"Before we left the inlet, I told True Seeker I wouldn't accept his company if he did not dunk in the river and cleanse himself of war paint." She lobbed a small smile back at Strong Bear, and he chuckled lowly, the sound defined by melancholy.

"I'd forgotten that."

Their gazes knitted, their smiles sad and lingering. Pretty Wolf continued. "He drew himself up and said straight to my face..."

"Just as I accept you in your snot-smeared ash, you will accept me in my paint, and when we are through, you will cling to my neck and offer me thanks for my company."

Korsan paused in shuffling his ledgers. An almost approving expression gentled his sea-leathered face. "And did she?"

Strong Bear blinked woeful eyes down at her, his volume muted. "She did. Before the sun took to her couch that same day."

Leaned over his interlocked fingers, Korsan asked, "What happened, child, on that field?"

Drawing an embattling breath, she turned her face down to the chalkboard and squeaked out her first slanted line. And then told him…

From the inlet where they'd watched the dugout slip away, she and True Seeker had flown through the woods, uncaring they might be heard despite the battle clamor. Despite it having dimmed to the occasional spattering of musket shot. The forest was empty, every man focused on either climbing or defending the bulwark that, by the minute, was less Red Stick and more Bluecoat.

"In those moments, my thoughts were a single arrow pointed Father's direction." Pretty Wolf tilted her ring, so the pale blue streak shimmered within the opalescent stone. "As you know, I never found him."

Her first glimpse of the field had told her how far-fetched that idea had been. "When we emerged from the trees, I took three steps before my knees gave way. Then my stomach emptied itself." The splatter of bile on dried pine needles would forever be branded on her. Its sour odor combined with the metallic reek of blood strong enough in her memory to churn her stomach even now.

She lifted her mug, the liquid's sting on her tongue an anchor to hold her in the present.

"A shocking sight, I am certain," Korsan stated, now studiously annotating spirits-knew-what in his jotter.

"One thousand warriors." Lips wobbling, she labored to maintain a brave, level tone, even as a maelstrom tore through her.

"Or more," Strong Bear joined in, hoarse. His large hand slid over her shoulder. "They were strewn across the ground, the length of the wall. Piled atop one another like a child's stick-fort kicked down by the wind and trampled. Bone. Flesh. Innards. Exposed as they should not be. No death was neatly met."

Her eyes squeezed shut to block the vision, to keep it from fully claiming her. "That morning, the thousand had been alive, unconquerable. Then everyone was simply…gone."

Korsan raised his lashes to her, to the hand on her shoulder, his gaze unreadable.

Finding Pretty Wolf

"They were broken, Korsan." As was her voice. As was she. "To a man, they were broken and split open, left to bleed out as if they were cattle at slaughter. And the blood..." A shudder wracked her frame, and her lips clamped shut. She lifted the chalk to the board, numbly forming another B.

B for blood. It filled her vision. Puddles, ponds, downhill streams. The ground bogged with it.

As they wandered aimlessly across the field checking faces, liquid seeped into the indents left by their treads. Despair pressed down on them. In time, Grandmother Sun's weakening rays glowed ruddy on the faces of the Bluecoat soldiers calmly scaling the wall, confident in their ownership of the day. Just as Polly did, they waded through the dead to find the dying. To end them.

True Seeker stuck to her like a freckle, his only weapon the daggers of his eyes, which he hurled at every paleface who took a second glance their way.

Clutched to each other, with Polly keening unabashedly, their image of grieving innocents served them well. The soldiers took notice—though perhaps not of the knife in Polly's fisted hand—and allowed them to go where they willed.

Fools, the lot of them.

"There was a pocket left," Strong Bear interjected. "The last resistance."

Through tight lips, Pretty Wolf blew out a breath toward the lodge's thatching, focused on Strong Bear's stroking thumb, and let him take over.

"They'd holed themselves up at a well-defended angle of the barricade. Hidden under brush, they could not escape. The cover shielded them excellently, but General Jackson himself set about to bring them from their burrow." The echoes of the general's voice were needle stings in her ears.

Touching the blue eye-bead at his throat, Korsan muttered, "With the will of Allah. May we survive the White Devil." He vehemently maintained Jackson would come for them, cannons blazing.

"Through a Muscogee interpreter," Strong Bear continued, "Old Sharp Knife offered promises of life and humane treatment if they would put down the fight and give themselves up."

Pretty Wolf picked the story back up. "Their reply was a musket blast that blew the speaker from his horse. He fell dead." Her eyelid ticked. "I laughed." That cackle's deranged notes played again in her head, as did the deafening return fire.

Eyes downcast, unseeing, she wondered, not for the first time or the thousandth, how much her father had foreseen. If he'd known Old Sharp Knife and Polly's fates would align.

Pretty Wolf worked a swallow through her thick-as-tar throat. "The general sought cover behind a stout oak. Which put him...directly in my path." She lifted her gaze in time to see Korsan's eyes spring up from his work. His neat brows crashed together, and her mouth slanted into a nasty smile.

"What did you do," Korsan breathed, less question than horrified statement.

Strong Bear's fingers dug into her, but he didn't halt the telling.

"Father's prophecy came at me in force, and I knew what must be done."

Polly's vision had blackened at the edges until all she'd seen was the paleface chief, that beast who'd heartlessly mangled their warriors, denied the People their land, and torn their lives apart with his own hands. She'd heard only the wind, its direction and speed. Felt only the spring of her muscles as she burst into a run.

"I recall little between realizing I held power over his life and flinging my father's dagger." There was also the bone-cracking impact of failure and despair.

"Regrettably," she sighed, "my aim is not as good as yours. The blade knocked Jackson's bicorne off his gray head and kept going. The brute barely flinched. Just turned his eyes on me." Sharp blue, those eyes. Cold. Stormy. Altogether terrifying. "They froze me, and I knew I was done." By the half-dozen rifles swiveling her way, she'd known it.

Korsan's lips bled white. He trained a blistering gaze on Strong Bear. "Why did you not stop her?"

Strong Bear huffed a humorless laugh. "Stop Pretty Wolf?"

Her frame deflated, her eyes dropping to her slate. Apparently, while recounting, she'd filled the board with a butchered scrawl of letters. "True Seeker, he... I acted so quickly that he did not see what I'd done, didn't know the details until days later. And I am glad for it. Else he would have thrown himself over me. Taken the musket ball in my stead."

"Fool of a girl!" Korsan's palm smacked the table. So hard it wobbled his tower of ledgers. "Have you trained in the skills of a warrior or the arts of an assassin? To *Duzakh* with the prophecy! Is it not enough the White Devil lusts after your father's neck? No, no. You must offer him yours as well. Wrapped neatly, handed to him in the form of an accursed blood sacrifice!"

She peered up at Korsan, lashes beating slowly, unmoved by his wrath. He'd said nothing she didn't already know. Her attempt on Sharp Knife's life was as foolish as tying an arrow to a bow, and her poor thinking had cost her dearly.

Nostrils blowing round, Korsan met her glare for glare. "You do realize when the White Devil comes, he will have double reason to slaughter your family."

Though Pretty Wolf shivered, she refused to be ensnared by fear. There was no call for it.

Korsan's attention jerked to Strong Bear. "You must take her away."

"Make it possible, and we are gone," he shot back, a keen look of accord passing between the males. "I would take her tonight if I could." His thumb pressed hard into the base of her skull, his fingers into her collarbone right over the numb flesh of her scar.

She shoved his hand away, then scrubbed erasing fingers over the board. "You worry for nothing. Both of you. My face was disfigured with a war mask. Black ash. The general could not have known me. And not for lack of study. Once I was taken down, he came rather near and…"

With her next heartbeat, she was there again. On that acreage of desecrated meadow. Panting through multiple forms of pain. The moans and death rattles of the wounded on every side, her own restrained only by her dying pride.

General Jackson stalked to where her life spurted from between True Seeker's clamping fingers. For a long, agonizing minute, he peered down his aquiline nose at her from his shockingly lofty height. Assessing. Judging. Deciding her fate.

True Seeker, snarling at any who neared—Sharp Knife included—was stretched half atop her, one leg twined tightly about hers as if to say, "You take one, you take both." As though his scrawny body would be any deterrent to the hundred and more soldiers gathering for a glimpse of the girl crazy enough to attack their highest chief.

The boy's eyes were flint-hard, and blood streamed from a broken nose, compliments of his brawl with the first Bluecoat to dare touch her. The fellow, who now stood off a distance, leery-eyed, hadn't come out unscathed. His lip bled, freshly split, and his cheekbone shone with a bright red spot.

Urgently, True Seeker whispered assurances: she would live, he would not leave her, they would go on together. Together, he stressed.

She listened with half an ear, gritted her teeth against the hot poker of pain digging under her collar bone, and affixed half-lidded eyes to Old Sharp Knife.

"The girl threw the knife, you say, not the brave?" he asked, looking her dead in the eye. Someone answered in the affirmative, and one of his gray eyebrows jogged up. "A noble attempt, young lady." His tone was a stomach-turning mixture of admiration and taunting. "But you missed."

She collected saliva in her mouth and lobbed it onto his boot. The one wet with the blood of her people. Baring her teeth at him, she ground Muskogee between them. "I would be pleased to try again."

More voices, more questions, all muffled by the roaring inside her head, then he smirked. "Plucky little thing, I'll give her that." In her pain, the world smeared and ran together, but then Sharp Knife barked, "Absolutely not, Captain. She's had punishment enough. Patch her up. If she survives, put her with the rest of the captives." She surrendered to unconsciousness, then. Right after realizing he didn't know that he looked upon the daughter of his most excellent enemy.

Whether he would recognize her face now—cleaned of ash and blood spatters—as belonging to the girl who'd nearly staked his eye with a dagger was a tale she could not yet tell.

To hide the sudden shaking of her hands, she tucked them under her thighs and organized a proper retort. "Old Sharp Knife never connected me to my father. Nor will he. He will never see me again, for should he invade, we…we will beat him from our coast," she blustered.

Korsan blew through his nose. "This from the girl who waded through the gore of Horse's Flat Foot."

"One who cannot form a proper B to save her scalp." Strong Bear bent over her for a closer look at her new lettering, his features twisted as if in pain. He shared another look with Korsan, this one puckish.

Humor flitted about the pirate's mouth. "You should see her Fs."

A flick of her wrist pinged her chalk off Korsan's forehead and into his tea with a splash.

Strong Bear laughed. "At least her aim has improved."

"So it has." Korsan's whiskers ruffled with a smile before he leveled her a dry look. Weaving his fingers together, he rested them before him. The return of his placid posture contrasted sharply with his uncompromising eyes. "Now then, my young assassin, I lay a choice before you. By high sun tomorrow, you will recount this misadventure to Iron Wood. Or I will. Allah *akhbar*."

Chapter 23

A trickle of sweat broke free of Pretty Wolf's hairline and slid toward her eye. She swiped a sleeved forearm over her brow and, with a few last scoots of her rake, finished distributing the clean hay across the floor of the stall. On a cleansing inhale, she arched her spine backward and groaned at the cracks and pops.

"Feel better?" Screaming Buttons stood smiling in the tall, slat-sided hay wagon parked in the alley, ready with another fork-load of hay.

"Not even close." Being done at the cow pens meant being hitched to a task far less pleasant than cattle droppings.

Sunday had arrived.

Cankerworms of worry writhed in her gut. As the spirits lived, she would protect Iron Wood from hurt. As much as the truth allowed. Undeniably, today's was a darksome path.

She waved off the next lift of Screaming Buttons' burgeoning pitchfork. "We've finished."

"Finally." He shook the dried grasses from the tines and hopped down. "Strong Bear and Big Voice are several horse boxes behind."

The other half of their mucking team worked the line of stalls on the opposite side of the desolate alley. This morning, the cow pens were deserted, every Spaniard taking the day of rest required of their god-man creator. Toño once shared how he believed the world was created and how that creator became a man who walked among people and did marvelous things. His were pretty stories he believed as truths because they'd been written down by those who'd witnessed the events. Each one inscribed in the Ancient Words. One day, if she scrounged up enough ability, she might be able to read the stories for herself. Another reason to stay persistent with her studies—whenever her father's absence allowed.

"We are all exhausted and slowing down." Pretty Wolf beat foul-smelling dust from her skirt, then sneezed, quite ready to be done with the place. Once she and her men were done milking, mucking, and graining, they'd be engaging in rest as well. Minus the ritualistic worship and prayers.

Unfortunately, the day also set in motion her promise to Toño.

At the thought, her floodwaters pitched an impressive fit, sloshing bile. Once Iron Wood knew all, Earth Mother herself would not be able to hold him up as he crumbled. Hand to her midsection, Pretty Wolf fought a serious urge to spew. At least her stomach was vacant. Her throat had mutinied over the morning gruel, so she'd scraped the mush into Strong Bear's bowl and watched him disappear it in one inhale. The male could eat. And he could soothe and hush.

She might have expected his arrival in her life to be a perpetual reliving of her darkest days, but no. His presence close at her back had gotten her through last night without sneaking out and spiriting away to some remote, inaccessible swamp in the Point. Sleep never came, but his steady inbreath-outbreath stood as reminder that no matter the day's outcome, he would be there at the end of it. He would stand at her back.

Their devotion to one another was like the grass that covered the vast prairies—infinite, perpetual—and there was little about her Strong Bear didn't know. Mistakes, flaws, weaknesses. Nothing was hidden from him. Or his affection.

Today, the same would be revealed to Iron Wood, but whether her betrothed remained at her side... She tried to balance her speculations, but in every scenario she conjured, he rejected her.

And why wouldn't he? *She* would reject her, were the situations reversed.

Her stomach took another fractious turn. A dose of Strong Bear would not go amiss. She tossed the rake into the wagon bed and guided the mule to where he shoveled manure into a pushcart. Beside him, Big Voice reclined against his upright rake, a snarl bunching the flesh on the bridge of his nose.

"Big Voice appears to be having a fine morning," she muttered to Screaming Buttons beside her.

"He's likely been as useful to Strong Bear as a drum with a hole."

"You've both earned your rest. Go home. Strong Bear and I will finish here."

Neither man tarried, and she soon found herself working in amiable, tummy-calming silence with Strong Bear, him pitching hay from the stack, her spreading. After the last stall was freshened and the water trough filled, she stowed the buckets and tools in the shed and returned to find him stretched out on his back in the hay wagon, sunk into the yellow mound like an oversized chick in a nest. One arm bent as a prop for his head; the other held a sheet of paper above him. A twig protruded from between his lips.

She said, "Do you want a beating, slave? Reading is banned in Wakulla."

"We're not in Wakulla." Fully absorbed in his reading, he shuffled sideways, opening a space.

She climbed aboard and flopped down, raising a cloud of hay dust. "Have you not heard? I am princess of the talwa. Where I am, Wakulla is." Breathing in the sweet scent of warm grass, she snuggled down into the nest and rested her head on Strong Bear's crooked elbow, pulling his gaze from the parchment to her. She peered straight into his earth-brown eyes and flashed him her broadest, most winning smile. When he blinked at her stupidly, she executed a quick snatch.

"Ho, woman!" He strained to take the paper back, but she laughed and shooed him off, too easily for him to be putting any effort into it.

"For owning contraband, a hundred lashes of my ribbons. For your insolence, another twenty."

Rumbling pleasantly, he grinned and settled back down. "Mercy on your slave, Princess Firebolt."

"Hmm. I'll remove the charge of insolence if you…" She raised the page high between them.

He tipped his head into hers as, together, they looked up at it. "If I…?"

"Silence. I'm debating a sufficiently miserable substitute." Even rows of handwriting filled the yellowed parchment top to bottom, unending lines of beautiful script. She skimmed the words, her eyes pausing at those she recognized. A handful, perhaps. Too few. "If you help me read."

"Read, ey? You have an addled notion of *miserable*. Or might you be thinking of what your father will do to me when he discovers it?"

"Irrelevant. You are *my* slave and thus outside the bounds of my father's power." Her pointer tapped an eight-letter word from the first line. "This word. I've never seen it." There were many she'd never seen, but her pride squirreled that fact away.

Strong Bear craned his head to look at her as directly as their close positions allowed. A deep furrow formed between his eyes. "What will Crazy Medicine do to *you*?" A waft of pine scuttled across her nose, and the wagon rocked with the mule's restlessness.

Her arm thumped down on her stomach, which, she realized, had settled to a mild malaise. "Not harm me, if that's what worries you. He'll simply forbid it. In his opinion, if the spirits wanted us to learn to write, they would teach us."

A grunt pumped Strong Bear's ribs. "Then he will forever use orators and messengers."

"Ehi, and smoke signals."

"Encoded bead belts?" The stick he rubbed over his teeth distorted his speech.

"Flags and sign language. All effective means of communication," she said, unimpressed. "But pen and ink? A **witch's** concoction."

Thoughtful silence crowded the wagon bed as they stared into the filmy clouds in the cobalt expanse above. Strong Bear broke it with carefully subdued tones. "With respect to you, Pretty Wolf, your father has truly earned his name."

"Take care, White Stick," she warned, her tone not quite as careful or subdued. "I love him."

"And I love *you*," he flared right back. "When he hurts you, deprives you, stunts your growth, I cannot help but come to your defense."

Perfectly loyal reasoning. Her lungs emptied. "As I would come to yours."

"I know." His voice was the deep, mellow pluck of a bowstring.

He unhinged his elbow and corralled her to him in a single-arm hug she was fairly certain didn't fall into the category of "orders to protect." But the deprivation of physical touch stayed her scolding tongue and melted her into him. The point of his chin came to rest against her crown, his voice raining down softly. "He is my foe for more than one reason, Pretty Wolf."

Suddenly choked, she turned her face slightly away. Their enemy status was too disconcerting a thought to bear. Their friendship and future so nebulous and uncertain it shook her to her foundations. Strong Bear's embrace might console her in all the places she was most fragile and frightened, but this enemy speak…

"But I am *not*," she said.

He replaced his chin with a lingering press of his mouth against her hair and a warm breath of, "Never."

Wheels creaked. Hooves stutter-clopped.

Strong Bear's muscles tightened like drums as his head and back lifted a fraction. "Did you set the brake?"

"I can't remem—"

The wagon jerked and rocked backward, then abruptly forward, setting them in motion. The mule brayed high and jubilant.

Strong Bear rolled her as he unwound his arm to climb the slatted side and peer over. "The sassy beast decided she's done waiting."

Flat on her back, Pretty Wolf brushed hay off her face and uttered a small laugh. "Let her take us where she will."

Strong Bear dispensed her a shrewd look. "Someone is delaying the inevitable."

"Guilty."

The inevitable, as far as he knew, being her goal of repairing the rough patch from the tub-snatching incident, instead of humbling herself in a long-in-coming confession. A feat that, presently, seemed daunting and unattainable. If she couldn't even scratch up the courage to tell Strong Bear that this was *the day*, how would she find the courage to *make* it the day?

On a slow shake of the head, he eased into a roguish smile. Strong Bear might not be handsome, but with his unmarked copper skin aglow in the sunshine and his glossy midnight hair afloat in the breeze, he was no affliction on the eyes either.

Intrigued by the realization, she watched him fold his bulk back down beside her.

He laid on his side this time, his body spanning the length of the bed, large and imposing. His head settled on the heel of his hand, his unshorn hair falling around him in a thick black sheet. His eyes, curiously amused, came to rest on her, as did his piney breath when he spoke. "Any cliffs we should worry about falling over?"

Uncomfortable with the submissive posture—and the proximity of his strapping form—she wiggled into a mirror recline and laid the creased parchment between them. She returned to her faux study. "There's a bluff two miles north." Her body hummed and bumped with the passage of ground beneath them, the ride even enough to suggest the **four-legged** followed the Wakulla road.

Strong Bear's tooth buffing resumed. "Since when do you speak in miles instead of sights?"

There went their comfortable mood. But she'd known this was coming. She lobbed her braid over her shoulder. "Since Iron Wood and Toño have been preparing me for a journey across the Great Waters."

His lips parted; the twig plunked onto the parchment.

Affecting disgust, she flicked the damp cleaning tool off the page. It landed in the folds of his shirt. He left it.

Belligerence fell in a darkening wave across his visage. "Why?"

"Iron Wood hopes to present me to his king. I'm to advocate on behalf of the people and return with aid. We travel with the next vessel to leave our waters."

The tic of Strong Bear's nostril tempted another flick, but with his next exhale the fire in his eyes mellowed to an ardent, head-tipping consideration. "What preparations have you made?"

Thrown by his about-face, she flittered her lashes before shrugging. "Boring things. Walking pretty, sitting pretty, dancing pretty. Drinking tea and pouring tea and saying pretty things while I do it."

Strong Bear chuffed and shoved upright. He hooked an elbow around one upraised knee and forked brusque fingers into his hair, flipping his feather bunch about. "You need no lessons in *pretty*. Why would any wish to alter...this?" He swirled a hand through the air as if subsuming all that she was. "It goes against the laws of good sense. Men of every color and rank are charmed at the sight of you, Pretty Wolf. England's king would be no exception. If any man will not have you precisely as you are, he deserves none of you."

His intensity shackled their gazes. Those were possibly the comeliest words ever spoken to her, delivered with such energy that air deserted her lungs. Deserted, no. Simply fluctuated to smother her heart with...what? What *was* that unpleasant thing crushing her insides?

Heedless of her pooling eyes, she stared at her friend, looked straight into the seat of his zeal, and knew in her Indian heart he would follow her to the depths of the **Under World** and back.

It came to her then what that crushing thing was.

Longing.

For what—absolute acceptance, release from obligation, a reversal of time to *them*—she didn't care to explore.

Unspeaking, she listened to his agitated breaths gradually reduce to a peaceful stream.

"Shepherd," he finally grunted out.

"What?"

He swiveled his body to face her, the toes of one moccasined foot nudging under her calf. "The word you couldn't decipher." He tapped the parchment, the quality of his voice back to its standard congenial rumble. "Remember the rule of S and H. When they sit beside one another, they make a *shh* sound. But this H here, because it trails a P, makes no sound at all."

She pushed up on one hand. "What are you saying? That the letters follow rules?"

He gave her a tilt-headed look. "Of course."

Choler sizzled her cheeks. "This is new to me. I've been memorizing the shape of each word."

His eyebrows edged up his forehead as questions began inscribing across his features. Instead of asking them, he raked his nails along the base of his jaw. "All right. I'll help you read. The rules are many, but with them in hand, you can puzzle out most any word."

"Incredible." That such a key was available to her. That Iron Wood had kept it from her. That Strong Bear possessed it too. Crossing her legs beneath her, she sat up fully, then observed the page as though for the first time. Reading had always seemed an insurmountable exercise in memorization but now felt as though if she but stretched a bit more, it would brush her fingertips. "Read the rest."

The folds of his mouth spread wide. "The Lord is my shepherd, I shall not want. He maketh me to…" He went on, quoting more than reading, his earnest expression dedicated more to her than to the writing. The cadence of the words caressed her hearing in a familiar, melodious pattern, and oddly, the verbiage, too, struck her as recognizable.

"…the paths of righteousness for—"

"Wait." She touched his knee, an idea setting up lodge. "Are these the…sacred Ancient Words?"

"You know of them?" he asked with a gladness she didn't quite follow.

"I do. Toño quotes passages in Spanish. It is always good wisdom."

"It is." Strong Bear's vigorous nod set his silver cross to swinging. "For that reason, the Sacred Writings have been translated to many languages and spread across the world."

"Has it really?" As one, their heads bent over the sheet as if gazing down on a cherished babe. Her voice became a thoughtful hush. "Ehi, I can understand how, over time, such a thing would be inevitable." She ran a tracing fingernail over a line of ink, the movement drawing focus to the grime on her skin. She balled her fingers. It wouldn't do to sully the Words. "You copied some of them here?"

The shake of his head tickled the hairs of her scalp. "My letter writing is not so precise. This paper is from Fierce Mink. It's a collection of passages taken from different parts of the Writings. She gave it to me outside of Hambly's lodge before sending me on with Winter Hawk."

A shocked laugh blurted out of her. "No. Mink? She adheres to the stories of the man-creator Jesus?"

"I would assume so." He reached for her hand and uncurled her fingers. A lick of his thumb, then he was scrubbing at her stained flesh, heating it with friction. "She had two other papers with her and would only part with the one. She slipped it into my pouch when Tall Bull looked the other way." He examined her digit, satisfied, then helped himself to the next and frowned. "I haven't enough saliva for this."

She withdrew her hand, fear for Mink creeping across her heart. The war woman's friendship with Tall Bull had been precarious of late, especially since her marriage to Ten Cats. Her adherence to the Ancient Words could not be healthful for their relationship or for her place in the tribe. "I have said it before," Pretty Wolf murmured somberly. "Mink is very brave."

Cutting his eyes up to her, Strong Bear dared, "And you?" He dangled the parchment before her, as he might a grasshopper before a bass. "What are *you*?"

Today? A liar and a coward.

But what a question. He knew what she was, what she'd sworn to always be. Her backbone went arrow-straight. "Fearless as the wolf." *Wholly dedicated to our pack of two,* she finished silently, ashamed that in the end, she'd failed him.

"Strong as the bear," he fell in. "Standing tall and roaring at adversity."

They shared a warm smile. "Your warrior name," she said. "You requested it." Not usually done, but they lived in unusual times.

The slow dip of his chin and the devotion in his gaze said it all.

The clan mothers were responsible for Pretty Wolf's new name, but Strong Bear had chosen his purely out of dedication to their vow and, she knew, to her.

Again, that crush of longing, its cause clearer now: a yearning to the return of simpler times, when she was brazenly fearless and he was wishfully strong. When all they had was each other and a vow.

Finding Pretty Wolf

The cart dipped sharply and jounced her bones. Strong Bear tumbled back against the slats, and Pretty Wolf flailed for a grip on the wagon wall. She grabbed hold before pitching face-first into him. Clearly, they'd left the road.

Ears honing, she picked up the gurgle of water, the sound gaining in volume with each bump of the wagon wheels.

"The mule must want a drink." The words wobbled out of her, the hay not cushion enough for her bouncing tailbone.

"She could have gone to the trough we broke our backs filling." Strong Bear teetered to his feet. "Or perhaps she knew you could use a washing up before seeing Bellamy."

Pretty Wolf's stomach bottomed out, and it couldn't be blamed on the wagon's lurching stop. *Iron Wood.* For the last little while, she'd forgotten what lay ahead. Her innards were making up for it now, twisting almost painfully.

She stood and waded through the hay to reach Strong Bear at the wagon bed's front panel. She eyed the river dubiously. Bathing off her barn stench *would* be the polite gesture, but her mind still revolted at the sight, clinging stubbornly to its irrational grudge.

Yesterday's dip had been…restorative. In a way she hadn't foreseen. As she'd lain awake those long hours of the night, she'd debated whether it had been the work of spirit or man.

A snort jetted from her nose. *Man?*

She sliced a discreet sideways perusal at Strong Bear. He stood tall against the panel, forearms resting easily along the top, sight cast far to the squadron of aquatic birds lifting off the river. The curve of his jaw was sharp, the tendons leading from it distinct and thick and, yes, manly. And when he turned to catch her stare, his lashes hung low as he looked down at her from his loftier height.

A touch of a smile glazed her lips as a sigh of resignation passed through them. At some point, she was going to have to admit to herself that the young brave True Seeker, her dearest companion, had grown into a man.

He jerked his head sideways in the direction of the watery ribbon glistening through the trees. "How fearless did you say you are, Wolf?"

She harrumphed and thrust up her chin. "Watch and see."

Chapter 24

As Pretty Wolf strode into the store's empty courtyard, she questioned the value of her dip and scrub. Its usefulness in stalling this meeting had expired all too soon, and she reeked again already. Fear, a smelly emotion. And all too visible. Sweat cooled her brow and dampened the underarms of her blouse, and she couldn't convince her tight shoulders to stand down from their high-guard position.

At least her water-glossed hair hung down her back in an orderly plait, and the dirt was removed from under her nails.

Strong Bear enclosed his hand around hers, surely not failing to note the tacky dampness there, too. Once he'd slowed her to a stop, he bent, bringing close his thick-lidded, earthy brown eyes so that she couldn't miss their steadiness. Or the great strength of feeling in their depths, glowing like a banked fire. "There is such worry in you over this," he murmured, brows pinched. "Whatever comes of your talk here, I pray you have peace in knowing you are never alone."

Breath traveling rapidly through her open mouth, she nodded. "I know. We will always have the other to fall on."

Earth Mother could crumble beneath Pretty Wolf's feet, and Strong Bear would stay at her side, go down with her, cushion her landing.

"That is true." Fine lines forked out from the folds of his eyes. The expression yielded the full rack of his meticulously burnished teeth. "We'll always shield the other."

What did it mean she could not say the same of her betrothed?

Possibly, her own fears were to blame for her doubts. Through all the seasons and trials—the latter not being scant in number—Iron Wood had never given reason to believe so meanly of him, if even fleetingly. He deserved so much better than her lack of faith. Better than *her*.

"But I spoke of the Great Path Maker. No matter how rocky the way may seem, Pretty Wolf, he"—Strong Bear lifted a finger skyward—"will still be on it, reigning over This World in all wisdom and love."

A beautiful sentiment. "He leads me on the path of rightness?" she quoted, her curiosity about the Writings an allure, even now. Equally enticing? The confidence and peace Strong Bear had in his Path Maker. "I could use some rightness."

If possible, his smile expanded. "Righteousness. Ehi. For his name's sake."

"And mine, too, I should hope."

Strong Bear rocked back, laughter belting out of him. "And yours, too. For his glory. For *your* soul."

If it was help his man-god was offering, she would not reject it. *May he, in his wisdom and love, lead my path this hour*, she prayed, then released a nerve-quelling exhalation. With a little pat to Strong Bear's jaw, she pasted a smile on her wobbly lips and stepped back. "Wait for me by the dock?"

Before he could reply, she pivoted, it being imperative she get her feet moving toward the store.

"Pah-ee!" Rox appeared from the smokehouse. One boot scrape-hopping behind him, he nattered the whole way to her about Bemy this and Bemy that, then clobbered her in a hug.

She thumped affection into his back. "Bemy is why I've come," she said, using his name for Bellamy as well as her most sympathetic tones. "I heard he was sad, and I've come to…" *Break him further*. "Rox," she said, tapping the lumpy satchel strung about his neck. "I have need of a stone." Upside the head would be best.

A massive lopsided grin opened his jaw wide, and Pretty Wolf smiled at his simple joy.

"I want it big and dark in color. With many cracks." The perfect symbol of her day. "When you find it, you must throw it as far as you can into the river. Can you do that for me?"

His brows reached for his hairline, but he didn't question her. Just lumbered about and set off on his mission.

Satisfied she'd given him a suitably distracting task, she rounded the building and discovered Korsan and Melon working shoulder to shoulder on the porch.

On the table before the pair sat a bulging sack, Melon scooping out white granules, Korsan portioning the substance into palm-sized bundles. With a light smack on his wrist, Melon relieved him of the one he'd been tying off. Chattering instructions, she set to retying it. Hands behind his back, Korsan listened and watched, nodding along.

"And so, the teacher becomes the pupil," Pretty Wolf said, containing humor between drawn-in lips.

Melon looked up and waved, her round face bright with greeting. "Ah, there she is, our lost little sister."

Korsan's shoulders tugged back, his eyes landing on Pretty Wolf and closing to haughty slits.

"Iron Wood," Melon shouted toward the store's open door. "Your betrothed has come to repair what is broken between you!"

"Woman, you cannot know Pretty Wolf's mind." A ridiculously thin vein of rebuke threaded Korsan's tone.

"Bah! We women know many things more than a mere man can comprehend. Look at her."

Indeed, Pretty Wolf's neck, cheeks, even her ear-tips blazed hot. All humor vanquished at the stark reminder of her purpose.

Behind the couple, Iron Wood edged from the interior shadows and stalled in the doorway. Pallor clung to his skin, several days' grease to his hair. His mouth hung at the corners, and the untucked shirttails and unbuttoned vest suggested he'd been attempting sleep. The dark half-moons beneath his eyes suggested he'd found poor success.

Guilt slithered up her, thickened by the thought that this visit would likely not aid him in those endeavors. Pretty Wolf was rather skilled at distressing good men. What she wouldn't give for those green pastures and still waters the Writings tantalized her with, and that righteous path. Could Creator truly be a wise and loving being who guided one's steps through written words?

As Pretty Wolf gazed at her betrothed, she saw more clearly than ever how poor a guide of her own path she had been.

Iron Wood's bleached-blue eyes shifted to focus on a point behind her. They tapered, on Strong Bear was her guess, then came back to her. In them, a mixture of wariness and more than a touch of anxiety. "Hello, dear heart." His voice wavered. He cleared it. "Won't you come in? There's a pot on."

Would he have their talk overheard? She shook her head, her closed throat disabling speech, and his lips drained of the last of their color. He straightened, stiffened into his addressing-the-miccos posture, a self-protective donning of lordly armor.

She sighed with regret, but it might be more of a cruelty to relieve him. To give false hope. Better to tell all and let him decide whether the armor was merited.

Another tip of her head indicated he should follow. Trusting he would, she set upon the trail leading down to the water and the sitting-log they favored. Her peripheral vision caught Strong Bear. His sauntering trajectory would take him some twenty paces upriver. Out of earshot. Within sight.

In short order, Iron Wood caught up, his ensemble now semi-respectable, as a lord's standards went. Shirt hem inside the waist of his trousers. Vest fastened. Running tidying fingers through his light brown mane, he sidled up. "Polly, I'm ever so glad you've come." His mouth spread a trifle.

Unfortunately, she couldn't return the sentiment, so she simply settled her hand in the crook of his proffered elbow.

At the log, he swept out an arm, inviting her to sit first.

"Thank you." Compelled to please him, she employed white lady manners and lowered herself with as much dignity as a decaying cypress log allowed. Back straight, she clasped her hands primly in her lap and made certain her skirt hid her crossed ankles.

Iron Wood glimpsed the spot beside her. "With your leave?"

"By all means." She scooted to give room, hating this rigid formality yet unwilling to mislead him by behaving as if all were well.

Iron Wood bent his starched limbs and perched on the edge of the fat log, hands laid flat on his thighs. "Before you say anything, my love, permit me to express my sincerest regrets over my actions of three days past. It was never my intention to offend by presuming to collect your things, and I am deeply sorry for the wall it's erected between us. I offer my most humble apology."

Such a pretty one, too.

She scraped an arid tongue over her lips. "In truth, I've not thought much on the tub since that day."

"Oh?"

"My mind has been too consumed with"—her heart fluttered erratically, and she pressed fingers to it —"my own confession."

The O of his mouth went flat. "Yes, well... Korsan told me of your stunt at the Horseshoe. Your actions, rash and thoughtless as they were, did indeed displease me. As did the suffering you endured for it, my dear. But let us call it over and done, shall we?" With a tentative reach, he slid his hand over the twined set of hers, stilling the round and round twist of her ring.

Over and done. How simple it would be to take him up on it, to make her escape now, to let him believe her wrongs were as simple as throwing a dagger at a general. Acid scorched her ribs, the ease of such a plan clenching the muscles of her legs, urging them to shove off and leave Iron Wood in his ignorance.

Movement drew her attention to the figure skipping rocks across the river's surface. As if sensing himself in her thoughts, Strong Bear looked over and dipped a supportive nod. If she abandoned her efforts now, she wouldn't be able to bear his sore disappointment in her.

Inevitability crashed in, and tears fogged her vision. "Not *that* confession." A tiny lie. Wasn't it all one sticky web of shoddy judgment? If he never marked how the threads connected, she'd bless the spirits.

"Darling." Iron Wood, no less wooden than he'd been at the start, paid her a slow, cynical laugh. "How many confessions do you have?" His eyes cut suddenly upriver, and the smile melted off his face. "Polly?" The sudden vulnerability in his pitch wrecked her.

It would be barbaric to not squash *that* notion. Swallowing around the pulse pounding in her throat, she rushed to cure him of it. "Scars."

"Scars?"

"Yes. I've not wanted you to see them."

"You refer to the musket ball wound? Why, my dearest, surely, you cannot think such a mark would lessen my esteem. Not a bit of it! You will always be a handsome woman, no matter your blemishes. The degree of my regard should never be in question." He pulled slightly away, head tipping to the side. "Is *this* why you shy from me? Because of shame?"

"No," the word rasped through her painful throat. "And yes."

"Polly, you're positively shaking."

A glance at her lap told her that, indeed, she was. The whole of her racked with violent trembles, her fingers so numb she couldn't hold a button were she offered a reprieve from confession to do so. Breath high in her chest, she rattled as if this confession, too long contained, had every aim of shaking its way out of her.

"Steady on, darling. You'll swoon." Iron Wood reached to gather her to him, but she raised a barring arm. A chapfallen expression sagged him, but she didn't relent.

His embrace would dash her to pieces, delay the execution. Now that she'd arrived, she simply wanted it finished. Angling forward, she dug every fingernail into the disintegrating wood on either side of her. "The scars I've kept hidden are from…childbearing."

He jerked back, eyes flung wide, the irises a solid crystalline blue.

Her constricting chest labored to fill. "During my long away, I delivered a baby boy." Hot, fat tears dripped from her chin. Landed cold on her hard-balled fists. "He was s-small, too small. Silent and"—a jarring hiccup cut in—"blue." A horrid, odious shade. "I l-lost him."

A stone effigy, Iron Wood hadn't moved, hadn't flitted an eyelash. Shock dominated his mien. Hollowed it out. When it gave way to other emotions, which would they be? Grief? Fury?

"The father, pray?" he asked, his timbre as vacant as his expression. "Or will you continue to deny it?"

"What?" she rasped, but he merely gazed at her, waited for an answer as she sat there, a deluge of tears carving paths into her cheeks that would surely never heal. Even though his suspicion came as no surprise, she hadn't expected it to be his first words of reply.

Smothered by hurt, she barely got out, "Who else, Iron Wood, but you?"

He blinked, expelled a gust of breath. "Forgive me, if I've wounded your sensibilities, but I've long—"

"If? If!"

"Polly, listen." He reached to take her hands but in a wild, double-hand flurry she beat him off.

"It was *your* son I carried inside me, Robert Bellamy!" Somehow, she'd made it to her feet, was barely restraining herself from slapping his face red. "Your son I pushed bloody into This World. *Your* son I held dead in my arms!" Her voice fractured, and from the corner of her eye, she glimpsed Strong Bear nearing at a clip.

"Pretty Wolf?" Alarm rang in his voice.

She gave him her back, her rant still expending itself. "My mistakes are many, this is true, but unfaithfulness is not among them!"

"Not at all, my poor darling." Face scored by remorse, Iron Wood stroked her hair, her face, her quaking arms. Quite daring when bloodless fists were attached to the ends of them. "No, of course, you would never play me false."

Not ten paces behind him, Strong Bear had stopped cold. He stood flexed and swollen with readiness, his face a mask of agitation.

"However," Iron Wood continued in placating tones, "you are surely aware I have long suspected some blackguard took his foul liberties and left you too damaged or too overcome with denial to voice it. Do not be so severe on me, darling. I only meant to learn his name. So I might seek him out and relieve him of life." Encapsulating her face between his palms, Iron Wood formed a dismal smile. "But I see now how wide the mark I was."

Her shoulders came down. Almost in the same instant as Strong Bear's. He took a contra-stride, then several more.

"The child was mine," Iron Wood said on an introspective murmur.

As she nodded, lashes wet and heavy, a sob battered her chest.

Then he was matching her tear for tear, silent, the reality of her confession seeming finally to register. "A born son, you say?"

"Yes," she mouthed, her vocal cords in disrepair. A complication, as she was not yet finished confessing.

Iron Wood groaned, stricken. He released her and, knees buckling, sank to sitting. "We had a son." He hunched over and buried his face in his hands.

Weary beyond measure, Pretty Wolf released her limbs to the log. While the river gurgled, the birds chittered, and the sun glittered with callous indifference, she stroked his back and wondered if Strong Bear's Path Maker was somewhere about. Perhaps willing, in his "surely goodness and mercy," to walk this one for her.

She permitted Iron Wood long minutes of private grief before whispering, "There is more."

He looked up, his face streaked with shiny trails. Sniffing, he sat tall, as though readying himself for another blow.

"A moon or more before the baby was to arrive, I committed myself to reaching the Point. True Seeker gave his all to dissuade me." That she hadn't heeded him was a tragedy beyond description. That she didn't know how the birthing might have gone if she *had* heeded was a question that stole many a night's sleep. She glanced at him now, gleaning strength from the sight of him, even across the distance he'd widened in his retreat.

"Bright lad enforcing your confinement."

The concept of such control, such strict treatment of women ruffled Pretty Wolf's passions. But she had to concede that if she'd practiced confinement, even the last month, instead of believing herself invincible, her child might be alive. If she'd listened to the boy whose opinion she'd so badly respected…

"He did try." Fresh tears salted her lips. "You chose my protector well. Without fail, True Seeker was everything good and right to me."

Iron Wood snatched a glance at the grown version of the boy, nodding. "But?"

"But I…" She coughed the crackle from her voice. "Led him to believe I would check the snares, then I left. To find you."

Iron Wood's face shut down. "Go on."

Shame ducked her head, the memories powerful and almost too much to bear. "The rains had been plentiful, and the river was swollen." Its roaring, churning waters slapped anew at to her eardrums. She resisted covering them and clenched every muscle to keep from screaming obscenities at Water Spirit. "There was nothing for it but to cross or return home to deliver our baby without a woman's aid."

"You carry the baby. Let me carry the worry," True Seeker had said. *"When the time nears, I'll find a woman to catch the child as it comes. Or I'll do it myself."*

Why, *why* hadn't she given him more time to locate help? Why hadn't she trusted *him* to help her? In the end, he'd been everything she'd required. Her child though…

Another sob lashed her.

"Dear God, Polly," Iron Wood croaked through a shaky breath. He thrust both hands into his hair, elbows riveted to his knees, and became very still.

"The current was mighty, and I was big and clumsy. At the brink, I s-slipped on rocks." Water, Earth, they'd been in league to stop her, though it hadn't been Mother who'd swept her away. "The river carried me off," she said bitterly. "Kept me under. I took in water. Next I woke, I was tossed on the bank. In agony. My leg was broken, and my labor pains were far along. Rain was falling. Hard." Stinging and blinding. Same as her tears did now.

Iron Wood remained as he'd begun, his shoulders vibrating with contained emotion.

"True Seeker found me as I began to push and guided me through. The baby drew no breath, and no amount of coaxing could induce him."

And they had tried. Rubbed his freezing little body until her finger joints complained. Puffed breath after breath into his tiny mouth. Pleaded and wept and prayed to every spirit, then cursed them all. Cursed herself most.

A raven screamed as it lifted off a pine. Just below, Strong Bear paced several relentless strides up and down the bank, hand to his mouth, elbow sitting on his crossed arm.

Through it all, through every push and scream, every fearful cry, through the blood and gushing fluids, through the first moments of wonder and subsequent moments of terror: True Seeker.

His gaze caught and held hers. Whatever silent message he'd meant to convey blurred away with another flood.

Iron Wood drew himself erect on the log and swabbed his nose with a kerchief. The wet in his eyes magnified their color and blackened their thick fringe. "I understand now," he said, voice subdued and precise, "why you did not tell me."

Her heart stuttered. The reproach entering his eyes told her he was less understanding than she was *understood*. Her rash behavior killed their child, and he knew it. None had ever accused the man of being anything other than fox clever.

"I have lived these years," she eked out over the din of her chaotic pulse, "in much anguish and remorse, in fear of your hatred."

Did I fear wrongly? she would ask if she didn't also fear the answer.

"That day, at the Horseshoe Bend..." he began, speech laggard, a horde of thoughts visible in the play of emotions across his features, "...did you know?"

The temptation to lie was a battle-worthy force, but she resisted, done with running. She commanded her tongue to move but conjured only the strength of a whisper. "I...suspected."

"Yet you said nothing. You..." Forehead crumpling, eyes darting to the river and back, he seized two quick breaths before continuing. "You put me in a canoe and...stayed with the enemy." The accusation in his tone mounted. "Then confronted General Jackson and got our—" Consternation rearranged the landscape fo his face. "Got yourself shot."

"I know, I know!" The shake of her hands returned with zeal. She fluttered them uselessly about her. "You can say nothing I haven't said to myself a thousand times over already. If I hadn't...if I hadn't..."

"If you hadn't *what*, Polly?" he demanded, his composure down to a sputtering nub. "If you hadn't ignored my pleading to stay in the talwa and *survive*? If you hadn't left my side in order to search out your insane father?" he boomed. "If, for *once*, you hadn't been so blasted impulsive!"

"Forgive me, Iron Wood!" she bawled, crashing to her knees before him. She clung to his hands and dropped her forehead to his thigh, ribs jolting with every heave. Her abdomen ached from the power of it. "Please! If you refuse, I will not be able to go on! Send me away from you if you must, but I beg you, offer some crumb of forgiveness!"

"Send you away? Why would—?" His voice broke. "No." Then more firmly. "No. There's no occasion for that."

Perplexed, she lifted her head, sniffled. "Isn't there?" Occasion and then some. She deserved no better. Their son's wee bones said as much from his watery grave.

His response was some time in coming as he seemed to wrestle within himself, the strength of his own trauma not to be disdained. He caressed her hair, crown to braid tip, pulling the plait forward to fondle its haggard ends. "You are the spark of my soul, Pretty Wolf. To lose you is to lose life."

Her lungs suspended, her ears replaying the rare sound of her name coming from his throat. It could only mean he was sincere: she was vital to him, he would not reject her, they would move on. Her darkest fears of reaping his hatred began slowly to evaporate.

Stunted solely by his glaring omission of forgiveness.

But if she couldn't forgive herself, how could she expect him to? In truth, it wasn't a forgivable offense. Anyone who learned the story would agree. Except Strong Bear.

The weight of Iron Wood's hand settled on her head, as if in benediction. "I want only for you to change these impulsive tendencies of yours. They cost us too dear, my love."

The price: our child, she expected to hear next. She didn't.

A shudder ran through him. "And they petrify me. From one day to the following, I cannot predict your next escapade, or if it will take you from me by and by. We will survive this, but you *must* give over tossing your life at danger. You must think more sedately, live more sedately. With propriety."

She shook as his words sank into her.

Propriety... Sedately...

She saw herself upon a velveted chair, backbone an unyielding dowel. A corset's boning strangling her ribs. The world spinning around her in every brilliant hue while she practiced her posture. Unappealing expectations, but not unreasonable or unforeseen. She must embrace the duty of a lord's wife and make amends for her costly mistakes.

He hooked her under the chin. "Marry me, Polly. *Love* me. Work beside me. But for the sake of all that's holy, *think* before you act." His voice thickened, the fresh tears roosting on his lower lashes a dagger to her conscience. "Can you do that for me?"

"Yes," she whispered at once, though a tiny corner of her spirit pulverized under the concession.

Tenderness softened the curve of his mouth as he brought it to rest on her forehead. Two splashes cooled her skin. "Thank you, dear heart." He drew back, caressed away the wet, his bleak smile a grievous thing. "You will excuse me now. I've an uncommon desire to reflect alone."

So saying, he rose and left her sitting back on her heels and telling herself no sacrifice was too great for his approval and, perhaps, one day, his forgiveness.

Chapter 25

A muffled cry ripped through Strong Bear's dream, dissolving the phantasmal Pretty Wolf in his arms.

Disappointment bit him hard. Relief devoured it. He exhaled.

There was no explaining how his unconscious self had resisted pulling her in and cradling her, shushing away the memories that invaded her dreams and made her cry. Sometimes, they emerged as deep, racking sobs. Other times, heartrending little whines. Each time, they woke everyone but her.

Another snuffle roused him further, though sleep clung to his brain like sap. Interrupted rest did that to a man. To three men.

At his left, Screaming Buttons dumped a groaned breath. Near his feet, Big Voice tossed about, his motions abrupt and irritated. To his right, Pretty Wolf mewled. It cut off with a reflexive *ish-ish-ish* of an inhale that shuddered their shared blanket.

Strong Bear wiped crust from the corner of his mouth and wondered how many hours the short hand of his watch had counted off since he'd fallen asleep. Since he'd wondered if he'd get any more tonight. Wondered how many would be spent in prayer and how many in stomach-sickening worry and blame.

Shortsighted as he was, he hadn't predicted the confession. Possibly, neither had she. Possibly, she'd plotted it for days. He wouldn't know—since that afternoon, she'd been as tight as a clam about it. And it rubbed his fur backward. Twice, he'd attempted to draw her out of herself. But no. Pretty Wolf would not malign her betrothed; the strength of her loyalty rivaled that of her totem. Strong Bear wouldn't fault her for it if she would stop flogging herself with blame.

But if he'd *known*. If she'd warned him where the conversation might lead, he would have... He would have... The brutal truth was, he still wasn't sure how he might have proceeded.

But there was no putting those waters back into their broken dam. All that was left was to be there for her in the dark when anguish attacked on the sly.

Might this be the night her tears tapered off without intervention? There would come a point it did. It had before, in the days when her state of *lost* had nothing to do with where she stood on a map. In the days he could actually do something about it. Such as attach himself to her side, day and night. Quite literally.

Here, outside of prayer, he was powerless.

This might not be his first taste of what her deepest sorrows did to wreck her, but it was his first with his hands bound by slave cords. Slave cords, vow cords, honor cords. *Rule* cords. Enough cords to strangle any bear.

Nine nights of strangulation and adding. If her nighttime tears didn't give way soon, something was bound to break. The cords. His restraint. His mind.

Blinking dry eyes, he gazed at the back of her head. As was her pattern, she slept on her side, facing the wall. Stray hairs tickled his chin, and the curving line of her back brushed the arm he kept folded close to his chest as a barrier. So close. So very far.

Holding her would bandage the wound. Talking to her would seal its jagged seams, heal it to scar-pink. If he were permitted, he would do both. Corral her to him and spill every word in his heart. But he'd been refused, both by Sunflower and by her commitment to another man.

Strong Bear pressed a fist to his forehead and rehearsed that vital fact: *Pretty Wolf is not yet yours. She is Bellamy's. Self-centered maggot that he is.*

Since her catastrophic revelation, she'd been quiet, pensive, somber even. Diligent at her work, but so unlike herself in deportment that even Big Voice was looking upon her with brow-rumpling concern. That is, until night rolled around and she reverted to the grieving mother from Alabama Town. The one he knew so well. The one Buttons had chanced to witness on a random visit.

He'd shown up five or six days after the tragedy. By that point, Polly had crawled from her pallet and begun living again, if morosely. The nightmares, though, they'd persisted.

Concerned, oblivious to the reason behind her mood, Buttons had stayed on several nights and spelled True Seeker in his wakeful vigils. Now, here they were again, and there was some comfort in Buttons' presence, even if the man was clueless to the cause.

Strong Bear wasn't fully informed either. He hadn't been close enough to hear the bulk of the exchange by the river, but he'd not been blind to the bitter twist of Bellamy's features. Not deaf to the tone of her pleas in her louder, more urgent moments. The man had said something to her, something critical or judging. He might have amended it before it was all through, but the damage was done. Strong Bear saw it every time he looked at her. The hurt.

And she'd gone to her knees for that hurt.

The image of her there—hunched, convulsing, compelled to grovel for forgiveness... It steamed the blood in his veins. Pretty Wolf, the micco's daughter, the beat of Strong Bear's heart, should never be on her knees before any man, especially one who made staunch claims of devotion.

Only to Creator should that woman ever bend her knee, and He saw her, knew her pain, heard her questions. Creator understood she'd given her child to the river and now sought forgiveness and freedom from guilt. But had Bellamy offered even a modicum of comfort? An embrace? No, indeed, he'd left her in the dirt. Doubtful he'd offered forgiveness either.

Strong Bear had almost stormed over there and shoved himself between them as a shield, but a Whisper had touched his spirit: *"Bellamy can do nothing. My forgiveness covers all, comforts all. Teach her of Me."* It stopped him fast, but in perfect honesty, if Strong Bear had known Bellamy's response would have this effect on her, he'd have done it anyway and apologized later.

The sniffles became vocal. A muted keening.

Screaming Buttons jolted, perhaps having fallen asleep again. Growling, Big Voice thumped Strong Bear's foot.

He ignored the unsolicited advice, anger precluding every thought. Anger at Bellamy for stirring up these old wounds. At his stupid Rule and his stupid betrothal. At Sunflower, who'd shackled his tongue and coddled his woman.

Not your woman, fool. Not yet.

Soon. So long as the Bluecoats didn't send her fleeing into the depths of the Point. Strong Bear could not follow her there, would not. Up to now, he'd gone along with captivity, played the slavery charade. That would end the moment it took him farther from home. Pretty Wolf alone did not own his love and commitment.

Flint was standing on the rise, eyes south. That, Strong Bear knew.

One other was looking south: General Jackson.

A nobody warrior, Strong Bear wasn't abreast of the general's plan, only that the Bluecoats *were* coming, and these Florida forests and swamps could hide an army.

Another bleat. Another thump to the arch of his foot. This one stung.

Strong Bear sighed explosively, but he'd lost the battle. If he didn't act, Big Voice would. In an unwise fashion. Such as informing her of these midnight crying jags, a thing Strong Bear had rigorously forbidden. Pretty

Wolf couldn't control what she did while asleep, and her load of guilt already heaped so full she couldn't bear up.

He tilted slightly forward, enough to place his mouth at her ear. "Hush," he murmured soothingly. "Hush, Pretty Wolf."

After a little hitch, her lungs resumed a relaxed rhythm.

Eyelids falling heavily, Strong Bear hovered. Waited. Defied the almost overwhelming urge to put an end to it all and hold her. These wakeful nights enervated them all. And she'd felt so good against him that once. As if precisely fashioned for his body, its lines and crooks.

He fought waves of drowsiness that almost had him slumping over her and let another minute tick by before pulling back.

Pretty Wolf jerked. Moaned.

Strong Bear rolled to his back and flopped a hand over his face.

Up on an elbow, Screaming Buttons whispered, "It is the same as before. Could it be the prophecy?"

Shocked it took the man this long to broach the prophecy, Strong Bear sighed. "This is about Bellamy."

"They argued?"

"You could say that."

"What did he do to her?" Menace elongated the question.

"She's told me nothing."

"Truly? Hmm." He paused. "This cannot go on. You must speak with her about this crying."

"What good will that do?" Strong Bear snapped on a whisper, exasperated, taking it out on the wrong individual. "Forgive me, but she cannot control which dreams she catches."

"But you *can*, slave," Big Voice chimed in, not quietly. "You have a certain power over the woman. If you put an arm around her, she mightn't—"

"No."

"Then speak to Iron Wood." Big Voice brimmed with impossible solutions. "Drag him here. Clearly, he's wounded her. Make him apologize."

Strong Bear snorted. This went so much deeper than the trader. Whatever repairs Bellamy might make wouldn't be enough. Strong Bear did intend to speak to someone—he'd been on sharp lookout for an opportunity—but it wouldn't be Pretty Wolf or Bellamy.

"There'll be no dragging," Screaming Buttons said. "The Englishman is kindhearted. He must be unaware he's troubled her so."

Pretty Wolf's nasally sleep noises switched to groaning.

Big Voice took up his blanket and stormed out.

She was rocking now, and pain for her welled achingly in Strong Bear's throat. Wearily, he turned to his side and leaned over again, hand poised over her, temptation so potent his fingertips burned with it. He curled a fist. "Shh, Pretty Wolf. I'm here. Sleep easy now."

Again, she quieted, muttered nonsense. Sighed.

"I thought I knew the cause of it, but..." Screaming Buttons let the sentence dangle.

Strong Bear didn't bite. He hadn't prattled her secrets up north, and he wouldn't here either.

"I call her friend as well, Strong Bear. What in the name of every merciful spirit happened to her?"

His words brought to bear how long she'd wrestled this monster. Shaking his head, Strong Bear could barely speak through the stone in his throat. "Too much, Buttons. Too much."

She cried out, flailing.

It was Strong Bear who jolted this time. Without the excuse of disrupted sleep. His heart exploded in his chest. *Creator Jesus, do something! Or I will.*

"Big Voice was right," Screaming Buttons cautiously dared. "And...the only eyes around are ours."

If you put an arm around her...

Strong Bear crammed his eyes shut. "Do not tempt me."

"Just do it. A body cannot function on so little rest."

"Leave me be!" Strong Bear hissed.

"True Seeker?" Pretty Wolf mumbled, her tongue clumsy. Perhaps awake, probably asleep. Reaching back, she fumbled for him.

He met her hand, squeezed, and guided it back. "I am...Strong Bear." The clarification about strangled him, so potent was his desire to join her in the past. But the deception would only destroy.

A space of silence, then a soft, "Oh."

"Sleep, Wolf," he said on a bold caress of her hair. When she sighed and gave a little nod, he stroked again. Forehead to crown. Slow and gliding. The feel of her like tafia to a drunkard, making him sway on the spot.

Blessedly, her body soon sagged, and she relaxed back into slumber.

Stillness filled the room. Filled his spirit.

Indeterminate time trudged past before he uttered a heartfelt *maddo* to the Spirit residing within him. His arm fell languid to the hay. A dream was within sight when a hand clapped onto his arm from behind.

"It is good you've come, Strong Bear. You are an honorable man. More so than I. More so than many."

If only. "You cannot see the thoughts of my heart, Buttons." The lust. The envy. The ever-raging battle against himself.

"Perhaps not, but I see who is right for the woman. And who is not. Be patient, brother. In good time, she will see it too."

Patience, Strong Bear had; time, Strong Bear had not.

Chapter 26

The murmur of two male voices brought Pretty Wolf reluctantly into another day of tedious pretending. Unrested, she stifled a moan. If she burrowed down into the hay, might they forget she existed and go on about the day without her?

By the door, the muffled discourse continued, the sound of it triggering hazy memories of the night. Blips of wakefulness came back to her, one of them clearer than the rest.

A peculiar exchange faded back in, starting with the dream...

True Seeker was there. And Screaming Buttons. They stood over her, wearing matching expressions of concern. Drowning in heartache, she wept uncontrollably, her clothes drenched through with tear-fall. Or river water.

Raised voices startled her.

Dream had tangled with reality. Alabama Town with Wakulla. Confusion had her reaching for the wall of warmth at her back.

Strong Bear stroked her hair and recited his name.

She might've stopped him, kept up her pretense of fortitude, if the gesture hadn't been exactly the cure. It planted her firmly in the Point and reminded her she'd overcome a great deal. Survived years beyond her child's death. She could handle another day more. And another beyond that.

Strong Bear's voice spiked over Screaming Buttons'. Were they discussing her? She thought she heard her name. Staying still, she fabricated sleep but blocked them out, having no wish to overhear their worry about the wretched state of her. From these two, she'd heard it all before.

The click of the door latch perked her ears. Had they left? No, footfalls padded close and stepped on her blanket. Under the man's weight, the wool tugged at her sleep shirt. A knee joint creaked as he descended but didn't lay down. There came a brush of labor-roughened fingers to her brow, a whisk of hair from her face. A sweetly recognizable piney scent blew across her a moment before Strong Bear laid a kiss to her temple.

She blinked her lashes open and was met with a swirl of colorful beads on leather. Those handsome moccasins he prided himself in. Apparently, at some point in the night, she'd turned over to face him. Hopefully, she hadn't done anything inappropriate.

Down on one knee, he had a forearm laid across his raised thigh, his broad hand dangling there, thick veins snaking across its russet surface. He'd gathered his hair all to one side, and it hung dense and rod-straight over his white hunting shirt.

Once, when he'd been up to his elbows digging clay, Polly had braided that hair. Her fingers recalled it being heavy. How much heft would it have now that it reached mid-ribs? That day, after she'd finished tying off the end, he'd twisted back to rub his cheek on her prodigious middle. *"An itch,"* he'd claimed. *"Ah, let me,"* she'd laughed and swatted his face with his own braid.

He might have had an itch, but also, her rotund belly was his favorite pastime. Her unborn child, the endless recipient of his affections, his silly songs and loving rubs, his elaborations on a future brilliant with happiness. A future in Alabama Town.

Lovely dreams. Perfect dreams, really. Why could she see that now but not then? What a stubborn, foolhardy child Polly had been.

She met Strong Bear's gaze, and his finger returned to chase a tear over the bridge of her nose. It brought her focus to *his* nose, charmingly crooked as it was. Tenderness throbbed large in her chest. The sentiment must have been written on her because the look he returned her was its double.

His warmth soon fell prey to brow-lowering worry. Unwilling to drag him back into those dismal times, she'd told him little of her exchange with Iron Wood. But he'd seen enough to know. Both then and in the days since. Evidenced in the weariness tinting the flesh around his eyes and in the unseen weight rounding his shoulders.

He observed her patiently. Waiting for her to fully wake? To explain the leaking eyes? If she unloaded the rubble cluttering up her insides, he'd help her carry it. She was parting her lips to do so when he finally spoke.

"I must see Sunflower. Today."

Surprise deposited a swift *why* on her tongue, but she bit the word off. He'd respected her privacy; she would respect his. She swallowed and nodded. "All right. At day's end, we'll go." The three-sights walk to Wakulla would provide ample time for unloading.

"Maddo."

"It is nothing." She formed a lazy smile. "Happy slaves are productive slaves."

Their gazes lingered, his narrowing, beginning a dance with mischief. "When you sleep," he said, "your breaths wheeze a bit. And your lips gap."

She blinked. "Eh?"

"Ehi, like so." He wiggled a finger at her face.

Her teeth clicked as she snapped her mouth shut.

At the quizzical cock of her brow, a grin absconded with him. "A tip. For next time you feign sleep." He laughed and dodged her pinching fingers. "Up with you, slug." He slapped her calf and heaved to standing. "The river calls."

Did it? She wouldn't know, herself and the river not quite on speaking terms yet.

Besides, her pregnancy scars might no longer startle Iron Wood, but there was an entire talwa yet to shock. She'd prefer it didn't happen through the gossip vine, initiated by some woman or other who'd caught sight of her scarred stomach. There were better ways to reveal her shame.

The day trotted along moderately more cheerful than the handful of others before it. Grandmother Sun doused them with warmth, Wind Spirit's breeze cool against their heated skin. The horses pranced and swished their tails. The cows stood still for their milking. Big Voice grumbled not once, and the anticipation of a leisurely walk with Strong Bear kept gloomy thoughts at bay.

When that hour came, however, so did Shem, his toes caked in mud. "The suh, he be plumb broken, Missy Polly. Salty as barreled pork, he is. Ain't even cracked a smile. Korsan say you supposed to get yourself home and make him sweet again."

The news soured Pretty Wolf's fledgling contentment and *plumb broke* any desire to rehash her humiliating confession. So, she sent Shem back with the message that her evening was already spoken for, but she would come at first opportunity.

That unpleasant business sorted, she set off with Strong Bear and after a long mile of broody silence ordered he take out his parchment.

He did at once, unfolding it with care, and began where he always did. "The Lord is my shepherd…"

Hands clasped at her back, she kept her eyes on the trail, gaze bouncing from one scrubby patch of grass to the next, her whole focus on the comforting rumble of Strong Bear's reading voice. The now-familiar passage had a musical cadence, she decided, and certain phrases struck her more precisely than others—*leadeth me beside still waters, restoreth my soul*—not strictly for their curiously antiquated structure but for their inspiration. What might she give for calm waters in her soul? Instead of the riotous flood.

What *wouldn't* she give? Very little, she reckoned.

Strong Bear called that first section "song twenty-three," which meant there were twenty-two others before it. *Songs*. Exactly as she'd suspected.

He read other passages after the still-waters song. One exhorted the listener to strength of spirit. Another urged mercy and forgiveness. Several were of worship. All pointed to Creator, each powerful.

When he paused to clear his voice and snatch a breath between selections, she jumped in. "You may stop anytime, you know." He'd read the page through, front and back, several times now, and his voice was showing abuse, more graveled than usual.

"I'm always pleased to read for you." And perhaps pleased for a break, too, because he was already folding up the parchment. "As many times as you'd like until you're able to read them yourself."

Myself... That would be a beautiful day. "Those passages must have been read many times over the ages."

"Too many to count." Strong Bear plucked that nubby, nasty twig from one of his pouches and attacked his teeth.

"How old do you suppose they are?"

"Several thousands of years. Some more. Some less."

"Indeed? They really are quite ancient then. And," she drew out the word, wishing her father could hear this, "we would never have known of them had they not been preserved in ink." How many of the People's legends and histories had been lost for lack of a permanent recording system?

"Even without ink, Creator will always find a way to speak to his children."

"Speak how?"

The twig between his molars waggled up and down as he pondered the question. "The usual way. Through dreams and prophets. But if faithful servants are not to be found, he reveals himself through his creation." He swept an arm in a broad arc, indicating the spiky palmettos, the noisy palms, the cloud-speckled sky, and the V of brown pelicans gliding through it. "His most important message, though, was brought down by his son, Jesus, whose words and deeds on Earth are recorded in the Writings."

"His exact words?"

"His exact words."

Those words she would very much like to hear. How many times had she wished for her father's ability to hear the spirits, to know their wishes and thoughts? The ability had seemed as impossible as palming a star. And yet, wasn't that what Strong Bear was doing? Holding a spirit's words between his hands?

A sudden burning rose within her breast. "Are any of them there?" She jabbed a finger at his waist where the parchment lived. "Did he sing the still-waters song?"

"Another king wrote that, one named David who lived hundreds of winters before Creator Jesus. But they are of the same tribe, same bloodline."

"You never said Jesus was a king!" Although it did make sense. If a Great Being had to live for a time as a lowly man, he may as well make himself king.

"Because he wasn't, and...he was." Strong Bear absentmindedly touched his cross. "He lived as a worker of wood, died a criminal."

A poor life and dishonorable end. She frowned. "So, he was *not* a king."

"Certainly, he was. Is. He rose a king and rules the kingdom beyond the Upper World, called Heaven."

"A criminal king of the Upper World? Should we be concerned?" She shot her gaze over to Strong Bear and winked. Or tried. Both eyes ended up closing, but she was still pleased with her perfectly appropriate use of the wink.

"This is no game to me, Pretty Wolf."

No, indeed, as was immediately apparent in the low, serious nature of his tone. Regret cut through her like a winter wind.

"Forgive me. I tease only because you confuse me. And because it's better than crying," she finished more quietly.

She hadn't meant to be coy or manipulative, but by the instant compassion seen on his face, she realized her words had done just that. He hooked a meaty arm around her neck and hauled her in for strangle-hug. "Tears, teasing. Give me your worst, little she-wolf."

"Always do, chubby cub." Chuckling, she gave his ribs a light punch to shove him off. "So, explain then. What do you mean by *rose*?"

A proud grin formed on him. "From death, of course."

Ah, so Creator rewarded Jesus's sacrifice by restoring his life.

"You asked for his exact words, so listen again." He extracted the page, flipped it over, and read: "I am he that liveth, and was dead; and, behold, I am alive for evermore."

"Jesus said that?"

"He did. Spoken some time after he died. He gave the message to one of his most faithful men. John wrote it down for all who follow, so we may know the truth. So we may believe and our spirits may live with him in his country upon our own deaths."

"Why would we want to live under the rule of a lawbreaker?"

"He was never a lawbreaker. Then or now."

She squinted a skeptical eye. "Are you *trying* to befuddle me, Strong Bear?"

"No!" Looking a little horrified, he wagged his head. He dropped his gaze to his moccasins and rubbed at his jaw. "I never thought I could butcher something worse than I do venison."

A light chuckle escaped her, but she couldn't help observing his chagrin. "This *is* important to you."

He lifted his face to her. "Very much."

"Then it's important to me," she said, voice subdued and earnest. "Try again. Was he or was he not an offender of their laws?"

A brew of concentration and determination tightened Strong Bear's jaw. "Jesus broke no law, Pretty Wolf. Not once in his life. Those who hated him cast false accusations. What's more, he could have saved himself but chose a gruesome death instead. Having done no wrong, he made himself a blood sacrifice according to the laws of vengeance. As a result, much life came from his death."

He chose a terrible end when he, himself, was not guilty? Pretty Wolf was beginning to understand Strong Bear's esteem of this sacred myth.

Life from death. The notion looped through her mind, and strangely, she felt as if she already knew this story...

She asked, "Whose wrongs did his death appease?"

"Mine." He paused, shot her a glance from the side of his eye, and grimaced. "Yours."

Surprise jerked her head back. "What?"

Palms up in a gesture that pleaded patience, he hurried on. "All the world's wrongs. Every wrong ever committed. Murders, jealousies, lies. His blood was powerful enough to avenge every one of them. From the beginning of time until now."

Pretty Wolf couldn't comprehend a blood sacrifice of that magnitude. When a wrong was committed, no matter the gravity, restored balance was a must: a lost knife repaid with a tool of similar value, a destroyed hunting dog replaced with another of equal skill, a death recompensed with the execution of the accused or, as in the case of Fierce Mink, with a life substitute.

But one dog could not stand in payment for a lost hunting pack. One man's execution would never suffice as vengeance for a slain clan, never mind a talwa, or the wrongs of every man of all time.

If a single man's death was meant to balance such a mass of wrongs, he would have to be... he would have to be...

Not a man at all. But an exceedingly great spirit. The greatest of spirits.

Was it possible? Possible that a spirit more powerful than Water and Earth and every other could—*had*—already counterbalanced every misdeed? *Her* misdeeds?

Before her, the trail disappeared, replaced by the unseeing ice-blue eyes of her cold, dead son. The unforgivable wrong. Or...not?

Her heart thudded, lungs working to supply it more air. She blinked and cut her gaze to Strong Bear, her voice intense, a demand. "I have questions."

"I expect so." A soft, understanding smile twitched his lips. "But...we've arrived."

She followed the stretch of his arm to the desiccated corn patch outside Beaver compound. "So we have," she said, shoulders falling. "Later then."

Later, she would ask her questions. Later, she would get her answers. She couldn't yet say whether she would believe them, but Strong Bear believed, and that was almost enough for her.

Chapter 27

At Beaver compound, Strong Bear went directly to Sunflower's dwelling, Pretty Wolf to the draftier summer lodge to see after Hambly and Mortar. Flipping back the doorway cover, she ducked inside. A glance about the stifling interior revealed Hambly, their one-time ally, cross-legged before the fire pit. Behind him stretched the lodge's single usable couch, the others serving as storing shelves for Sunflower's sundry herb baskets.

Nowhere to be seen, Mortar was either given as slave to another clan, or he was dead. Hambly had the look of a man who believed he might soon be. He sat limp-armed and frowsy. Although he couldn't be aged more than forty winters, wrinkles heavily populated his forehead and cheeks. Every one of them drooped. A blanket haphazardly draped his stooped shoulders, and he peered dazedly into the fire, glum as rainclouds.

The drone of flies and crackle of flame commanded the silence.

Face scrunching at the lodge's rank odor, Pretty Wolf hooked the door flap on its jamb nail to allow a breeze. She approached, finger blocking her nostrils, and toed the edge of the blanket away from the coals. "It is unwise to tempt Fire Spirit, Englishman."

He startled, his posture straightening as though he'd not noticed her entry. The blanket slipped off and puddled behind him.

"Or do you call yourself American now?" She batted a buzzing pest from her nose.

"Who are you?" His voice sounded gruff with disuse or, feasibly, with hostility.

On an impertinent whim, she drew in her chin and curtsied. "You may call me Pretty Wolf. I am daughter of Chief Francis and betrothed of the English trader Robert Bellamy."

Such self-importance. Such farce.

Opposite Hambly, a comfortable distance from the oppressive heat, she lowered herself to her knees, tucking her skirt in around her as she perched on her heels.

"The lost daughter of Wakulla." Hambly either ignored her frown at the designation or did not see it through the fire's glare. "On the trail, that young

Winter Hawk fella busted at the britches with tales of your adventures. Yours and everybody else's," he finished on a satirical note. A gaunt smile plucked at his wrinkles. "That's good English you have there."

"I will pass your compliments along to my instructor." When she was speaking to him again. "My first sight of you was of a droopy man in a cart. Your health is improved." She couldn't speak quite as politely to his cleanliness, unfortunately.

Graying whiskers thickly carpeted his jaw and throat, and his loose shoulder-length hair would bless him for a comb. The heat did such good service to his stench, it begged the notion he was using it as a shield, though the flies were certainly not appalled. They zipped in circles between him and his untouched bowl of tripe soup.

"William Hambly," he said, "master of Spanish Bluff, captive of my old allies. But I suppose that's no secret to the chief's daughter."

She dipped her head in agreement. "I trust your treatment in Beaver compound has been favorable."

"So far, sure." His grim gaze drifted out the open doorway as if on watch for widows armed with pointy sticks. "Will your father…torture me?"

Pretty Wolf held the man's hazel gaze and refused him false hope. "Perhaps."

The protruding knot of his throat bobbed fitfully. "How?"

"Any number of ways." A cyclone might be more predictable than Crazy Medicine.

"To the death?"

He was dead before he was captured. "Is it true, William Hambly? Did you betray us?"

The man discharged a defeated breath, but instead of answering, he eyed her through tight lids. "Do you have a child, Miss Francis?"

"W-what?" The blood drained from her face, her thoughts stuttered, and her temper flared. "Why ask me *that*?" Such a random question.

"Because a parent behaves differently than someone who has no children to feed. Or someone who's suffered a child's passing."

She glared at him, head going light and lips numb, unable to keep the prickle in her eyes from multiplying.

"I see…" He lowered his gaze. "Sorry for your loss."

An embarrassing half-choked sound escaped her throat. How was her own mother ignorant to her most guarded secret, while with a few exchanged lines, this captive had revealed it with a sea otter's clam-cracking proficiency. "You...you cannot... No one knows!" For now. Might Iron Wood speak of it? To Korsan, perhaps? She hadn't asked him not to.

Perplexity reorganized Hambly's wrinkles, but he nodded. "I'm no gossip, Miss. Your secret's safe, and your grief..." He blinked, his eyes going remote. "I'm familiar." He spoke as if from that place, his voice distant and pain-filled. "We've buried three, me and my wife. All just days old."

Pretty Wolf's anger disintegrated. *Three.* The poor woman. How did she function?

"Daughter or son?" Hambly pried, but she allowed it. He saw, he felt, he understood. At least in part. Even her enemy could likely not be blamed for the deaths of any of his babies.

Throat an arid plain, she croaked, "S-son."

"What would you have done to protect him, Miss Francis? To save him?"

"Anything," came her immediate, burning reply. "There is nothing I would not have done."

"And if you'd been forced to choose between protecting a friend and protecting him, meaning his food and the roof above him."

"Him." The Defiance, Wolf Clan, even Iron Wood—all would've fallen under her trampling feet if it meant preserving her son. And didn't she understand the burden of feeding children? "Always him."

"Exactly!" Hambly canted sharply over his knees and lanced her with untamed eyes. "The war mixed everything up. Boundaries and borders moved and confused. My land got eaten up in the exchange and put me in a rough spot with the new flag.

"They threatened me, you know," he went on. "The soldiers. Said if I showed the slightest sympathy to your cause, they'd raze my house, my crops, my barns. They'd take my livestock and leave me with the shirt on my back. Since the soldiers are stationed closer than your warriors, well,"—he huffed a dry laugh—"it didn't take much brain to make the smart choice. If I'd kept my alliance with your people, I would've lost *everything*, Miss Francis. And my babies would have hungered, fallen ill..." Voices trailing, he cast his glazed expression into the fire. Recalling, perhaps, those children he'd already lost.

Was that what this betrayal amounted to? A man trapped by treaties and cornered into choosing family over far-off friends?

It could be argued, Pretty Wolf conceded, that a desecration of trust was not quite as severe when the alternative was to betray the most sacred of trusts. That of fatherhood.

Strong Bear's raised voice, firm and driving, penetrated the thick mood. Through the doorway, she saw him stalking out of Sunflower's lodge. He scanned the courtyard, tension as visible about him as the wind swirling through his loose locks.

Hoisting upright, she deserted Hambly and emerged into the blessedly fresh air. "I'm here."

His head whipped left. On sight of her, his features pinched, locking down on emotion.

"What's wrong, Kit?" Her legs propelled her across the lot.

Frustration ripped out of him in a growl. It halted her approach several paces out, but he devoured the gap, slung an arm about her, and drew her in. Her nose mashed into his collarbone, and her trapped arms crumpled between them. An unseemly chortle escaped her. "What's this?"

His hold on her only strengthened. Over his shoulder, she spotted Birdie straightening from where she bent over a rack of fish smoking over the coals. The black woman braced a hand on her lower back to watch the drama, her brow drawn in concern. Pretty Wolf understood the sentiment, if not the cause.

"Forgive me." The words puffed hotly against her ear.

"I'll consider it…after I can…breathe again."

His chest shuddered with a quiet laugh. He let her go, stepped back, and shed whatever had him vexed. More specifically, whatever Sunflower had said to vex him.

On a little growl of her own, Pretty Wolf assailed the elder's lodge with a dark look. "What happened in there?" By her reckoning, he'd requested something of Sunflower and been denied.

Raking fingers into his hair, he closed his eyes and shook his head. "It's…nothing."

She snorted softly. "Why do you lie to me?" His reticence stung, but then, of late, she hadn't been a font of sharing either. Since when did they not tell each other everything?

"No lie just…" He breathed out and, weary gaze roving her face, presented her a wretched smile. "Just waiting on my Path Maker."

"Waiting on him or on *her*?" Her sideways nod at the elder's lodge was more of a spasm.

The wry slide of his mouth said she'd struck this peg dead center. "She might say they are one and the same."

"She *might* be losing her wits."

"No…" He hung his head and shook it again. "What she says is not witless. Merely unwelcome."

"Trout be ready!" Birdie waved a long-handled fork high in the air before flourishing it at the rack. She could speak Muskogee but did so only when pressed. "That is, if you two's done with your sourpuss faces."

Pretty Wolf gave an acknowledging lift of the chin, then met Strong Bear's deeply contemplative gaze. Should she be worried? Seeking a distraction?

"Hungry?" she inquired.

"As a bear." A smile wavered on him, there and gone.

"Pudgy as one too." The backhanded bop of her knuckles against his solid abdomen said otherwise. "Come on then." She began toward the fire. "Have you met Birdie? Ah, and there is Korsan. He's a rare sight in Wakulla," she mused. Whatever lured the Muslim out of the protective nest of his British sanctuary was no slight matter.

Arms tucked behind him, Korsan marched into the compound. When his sight swung her direction, his steps stuttered then picked right up, his newly pressed scowl leading the way. The wind plastered his loose, brightly colored pantaloons against his trim form, and his hand snaked to rest on the hilt of his cutlass.

"Somebody in *trouble*." Birdie drew out the syllables in singsong fashion.

"Surely not myself," Pretty Wolf drawled.

"Always herself." Strong Bear muttered the aside to Birdie, winning himself a skeptical look.

"And you be?"

"Birdie, this is Strong Bear, my s-slave." Heat swamped Pretty Wolf's cheeks at the indelicacy of presenting her "chattel" to a runaway. "He's not… That is…" Was it safe to admit his slavery was a ruse?

"Mmhmm." Birdie dragged her critical tawny eyes over Strong Bear, feathers to feet. "'Spect it's a *terrible* cross to bear bein' stuck at the hip to this one." She jabbed her thumb at Pretty Wolf, humor simmering behind the slight curve of her broad mouth.

Strong Bear grinned at her. "My master is perfect in all her ways."

Birdie slapped her thigh and exploded in cackles. "You got 'im good and trained, girlie."

"Shame be on you!" Korsan scolded from ten paces out.

"On whom?" Pretty Wolf deflected, suspicion churning that the message Shem delivered hadn't been well received.

The Ottoman thrust himself into their midst, chin pitched imperiously. "The lot of you! Reveling like a squad of monkeys while my master languishes from illness of heart, may Allah smile upon him." He thinned his lids at Pretty Wolf, leaving unspoken the *for his betrothed certainly does not.*

Stance shifting, Strong Bear placed half his body in front Pretty Wolf. "Korsan the Silent should practice his silence."

How tempting it was to let her overeager sentinel deal with the ruffled pirate. But Iron Wood's drawn and weary aspect resurfaced, and guilt nipped. She sighed and nudged Strong Bear out of the way. "You've come for one of Sunflower's remedies, Korsan? A sleeping draught?"

Korsan's black, barely tamed eyebrows twitched.

"He come for a love potion." Humming guilelessly, Birdie forked a fat fillet off the rack. "And it ain't for your Mr. Bellamy."

"Did he?" Pretty Wolf inquired, to the splutter of Korsan's indignation.

"Yes'm." She extended the loaded fork to Strong Bear. "Sunflower been stewin' it all day. Don't reckon he gonna be doin' any sleeping with it though."

On a burst of laughter, Strong Bear gingerly pulled the hot flesh off the fork.

Korsan's face blazed dark. "An Ottoman of such allure as myself requires no potions! At the will of Allah, women clamor to my side. Fall at my feet!" He lifted a knobby, brown pointer. "As our own chief's daughter has seen with her two eyes."

"Yes." Pretty Wolf dropped a hand onto her cocked hip. "If my two monkey eyes can be trusted."

Korsan sniffed. "I desire you to come to the store to console my master."

Ah, there it was.

"She will come when she is—"

"No, Strong Bear." A pat to his arm brought his stiff shoulders down. "I'll go tonight." She'd put it off long enough. "After a bite of Birdie's good fish."

"I shall tell him to expect you. *Bedrood*." Retreating a stride, Korsan lowered into a shallow bow, then spun on his slippered heel and sauntered toward Sunflower's lodge. For his not-love potion, presumably.

Back to her innocent humming, Birdie served Pretty Wolf, indicated a courtyard bench, and went back to her smoking duties.

Steaming fillets held delicately on their fingertips, Pretty Wolf and Strong Bear picked at their fish, the enticing aroma reminding her stomach she'd been skipping meals. Meals, sleep, prayers. She swirled a toe through Mother's grainy flesh.

"She's a runaway?" Strong Bear asked quietly.

"Mmm. Adopted by clan Turtle, but she can most often be found here. Sunflower's only other clanswoman is the talwa's only war woman."

"Fierce Mink?"

"The very one. She lives in the warriors' house, and really," Pretty Wolf said on a light laugh, "no one wants her stirring a stew pot." She paused to nibble at her fish. "Mink's brother, **Great Warrior** Water Moccasin, arranged for Birdie's presence here in Beaver. To help Sunflower, he claims, but we all know it's only to keep her within wooing distance."

The man had the patience of the viper inked into his forearm. Comfortably coiled, perfectly motionless, he waited for her to relax in his presence and draw near. His strike and bite, however, would be nothing but gentle and sweet. Of this, Pretty Wolf had no doubt. When charming a skittish runaway, what other option was there for a male in love?

Strong Bear flashed a grin. "He made a wise move there, and you"—he tapped a foot beside the curving line she'd created—"made a letter."

Head cocked at it, she hummed. She hadn't meant to, but there it was.

"First lesson." He popped a pink flake into his mouth and switched to English. "S says sss, like for *snake* and *sat* and *stop*."

"And for...?" When he arched a mild brow at her, she swayed into him, bumping shoulders. "For Ssstrong Bear."

Another grin stretched his mouth. "And for Strong Bear."

"Your first lesson was too easy. You'll have to do better."

He leaned back on the bench, long legs stretching out before him, and boldly assessed her. When he spoke, his voice was subdued, a careful nearing. "What of Ṣ for *speak*? Will you *speak* about what happened with Bellamy, my fearless Wolf?"

231

Her smile dropped off, but before she could decide whether to reply, a chorus of trilling cries rang dimly from the talwa.

Pretty Wolf leaped up, lesson forgotten. "The war party!"

The earth stung her bare feet as she raced through the compound and across the talwa to where her father would stop first. Strides effortless, Strong Bear kept pace at her side.

The whoops carried on sporadically and worryingly sparse. Too few men had returned. Or too few held pride in their battle prowess.

Checking her pace, she entered Wolf compound at a slow jog. A bloom of perspiration coated Strong Bear's brow, but his breath came moderate and regular. His eyes shone clear. If he had any jitters over the imminent meeting with her father, he hid them well. Satisfied, her gaze left him to stretch across the square to the reunion—and the disagreement—taking place outside her mother's lodge.

Crazy Medicine had Noonday wrapped in his arms, lifting her moccasined toes above the dirt and almost entirely concealing her thin form. Red and billowing, her crimson skirt framed his buckskin leggings, and the curve of his neck muffled her shriek of joy.

Runs Like Deer stood off to the side, hands cupping the undercurve of her pregnant belly. She quietly pleaded with her husband, his stiff figure overshadowing her.

"Who is *he*?" Strong Bear's leg span stretched to carry him beyond Pretty Wolf, but she yanked him back.

"Kills Many. My sister's husband. He'll not harm her." Spoken as much to remind herself as to disable the casual grip Strong Bear had on his knife. As protective as a red fox, or a toad, Kills Many did love his wife and their unborn child. His one redeeming quality.

Strong Bear swung keen, hooded eyes to Pretty Wolf. "As he did *you*?"

Phantom pain throbbed in her arms at the spot of Kills Many's bruising clamp. A shiver traveled her spine. At the memory? Or at the protective menace in Strong Bear's aspect—that endearing quiver in his left nostril. She smiled at it. "We are known for our rows, he and I. Ignore him."

In timely distraction, Crazy Medicine laughed his great, booming laugh, the one that said he had his woman in his embrace and nothing else mattered. Which was hardly true, as illustrated by the battle still clinging to him. Dark red splotches marred his shirtsleeves, and the hem of his vest hung in tatters. Tangles gnarled the long tail of his hair—his turban upturned on the ground by his feet—and only one arrow jutted from the quiver on his back. War-gaunt, his body showed hipbone through his clothing, but he appeared intact.

The cincture around Pretty Wolf's chest released, and she took in air through her growing smile. The Bluecoats might have won this round, but they didn't have their greatest prize.

"Husband, wait." Runs Like Deer called after Kills Many who hustled away from her, his strident march passing so close to Pretty Wolf, he created his own wind.

She paid neither him nor his inflamed expression any heed as she rushed on. "Father, Father!"

She was rounding the fire pit when he deposited Noonday and swiveled to meet Pretty Wolf, his grin as wide as his arms. He scooped her up and enveloped her in his tobacco and wood-smoke scent, wrapping her in childhood recollections. Lap cuddles before an autumn fire while he relaxed. Lectures inside his forge while he worked.

Their height matched, as did their laughter. Loud and carefree. The arms about her had a lean strength, which felt slight in contrast with Strong Bear's.

Her thoughts skipped to him lurking somewhere off to her left, and her pulse skipped with them. But Crazy Medicine was setting her away from him now, pressing a kiss to her forehead, hording her attention. "My fierce little miccohokti," he murmured, eyes twinkling with fondness. "As beautiful as ever. You are hale, I see."

"And you are thin. Was the campaign so trying?"

"It was. But after, we ventured east to recruit Singing Falcon's band. The trail was long and hard."

By the dour turn of his voice, Pretty Wolf deduced the meeting didn't have a positive outcome. "He refused."

"He's too busy profiting from his raids to organize into a collective force." Her father's eyes darkened, but he immediately blinked it away and refocused on her. "And how is our intrepid Englishman?"

"He's perfectly well, Father. Did you bring home hair?" She leaned sideways, as though to check his belt for scalps.

Keen to her distraction, Crazy Medicine closed his eyes to slits. "Hmm. We'll discuss your betrothed later."

A telling concoction of indignation, fear, and shame flushed her cheeks hot. But the talk he demanded—and the disgorging of her soul—was inevitable. "Ehi, Father." She made a point of glancing about. "And Tall Bull?

Why is he not here?" Pray the spirits, he'd simply stopped in first at the warriors' house before coming to his home. "Is he...well?"

With startling swiftness, wrath eclipsed her father's features. "He is alive. By my good graces."

"What?" Noonday's pitch spiked with ready dispute. She stood to Pretty Wolf's left, her hands propped on her narrow hips. "What can *that* mean?"

Tall Bull was Wolf. Noonday's head clansman. Her daughters' beloved pawa. Micco or not, Crazy Medicine would surely not presume to pluck a hair of Tall Bull's head.

"Talk of *Tall Bull*," Crazy Medicine snarled, "and battle, will also wait for later." Confirmation they'd not been victorious.

"Ehi, Father," Pretty Wolf acquiesced, chin lowering, questions rising, railing at her. How badly had they lost? How many dead? Who?

But her father was right. They should discuss it later, beyond her sister's hearing. In addition to the delicacy of her condition, Runs Like Deer was a quiet soul, weak, and content to stay that way. A more apt name for her might have been Trembles Like Fawn. Even now, she stood apart from this bland demonstration of their father's temper.

Pretty Wolf went to her, kissed her cheek. "Sister."

"Sister," she replied, a timid smile turning her sweet mouth. Indian nose broad and flat, Scot's eyes weak—though a fetching green-flecked brown—Runs Like Deer carried her beauty within, but she had it in no puny sum. Beneath her breasts pumped a generous and kind heart. Where she got such a disposition, no one could guess, for Noonday was brusque and unrelenting, and Crazy Medicine was... Well, if he was generous, it was in doling out musket balls to his enemies. Very speedily. If he was kind, it was in aiming for their hearts instead of their entrails.

Crazy Medicine's current aim had found Strong Bear. Or rather, the silver pendant dancing and glinting cheekily in the sun. A sneer warped his lips. "What fool is this who enters my talwa bedecked in the symbol of that odious Spanish, the Black Robe?"

Pretty Wolf huffed in irritation. Hadn't she warned Strong Bear of this?

Posture tall and unafraid, Strong Bear fixed his adversary with a steady look, his deep voice every bit as staunch and stable. "I was once True Seeker, companion to your daughter during her long away. Now, I am Strong Bear. Willing slave to the same."

Crazy Medicine turned his confused expression on his wife.

Finding Pretty Wolf

"He is a White Stick now, Husband." As if that explained all. Perhaps Noonday didn't recall that the war party fought in two forces—led by Crazy Medicine and Tall Bull—the parties making simultaneous assaults on separate marks. Her father wouldn't have known the details of Tall Bull's band.

Pretty Wolf stepped to Strong Bear's side. "He was taken captive, Father, during the skirmish at Medicine Point. Tall Bull sent him to me, aware of our need at...for labor." A clumsy finish. But in her father's present state, reminder of Tall Bull's controversial contract with the Spaniard would only sink him further into whatever mire his mood had fallen.

"You've made yourself the enemy." Crazy Medicine raked a scathing gaze down Strong Bear's length. "What a disappointment you are. A blow to your noble lineage."

Pretty Wolf's head tugged back. "A warrior's value is not found in the color of his feather." Red or White, it did not make or erase his loyalty. His *noble* character was responsible for that. As proved by Strong Bear's response to her father's abuse.

It had set off his nose twitch, but otherwise, he did not react. He simply stood his ground, gaze level and lax—at least to those who didn't know him. Pretty Wolf easily whiffed the emotion blowing off his skin. Not the scorch of anger or the bitterness of scorn, but the metallic tang of the wounded. And why not, when *this* was the payment he received for all he'd done and been.

Her wolf hackles spiked. "If not for Strong Bear during—"

Low at her thigh, Strong Bear snatched her wrist in a silencing grasp he kept hidden in the folds of her skirt. In the oblique, categorical gaze he cast her, he said, *Maddo, but I fight my own battles.*

She gritted her teeth, but her father wasn't done snapping his. "Your pawa would hunt you down if he knew." His knife was suddenly in his hand, at Strong Bear's throat. With the tip, he flicked the pendant. "For this alone, White Stick, he would drain your blood into the earth."

Pretty Wolf's breath strangled in her throat. She tried to jerk forward, but Strong Bear's grip bore down, his elbow locked open, tethering her in place. Runs Like Deer covered her gaping mouth, but Noonday drawled, "Husband, really."

Her mother's casual rebuke, as if there were no real threat, restarted Pretty Wolf heart. As much as she wanted to trust her father, his blade's point was digging into Strong Bear's throat. A bead of blood bubbled up, and rage like shattering glass blew through her.

"Father," she ground out, her free fist balled hard at her side to keep from tearing at him. What could he be thinking? Was this a test? A display of dominance? Neither was acceptable. This was *True Seeker*. Hadn't he already proved himself loyal to Wolf Clan of Wakulla?

Unflinching, Strong Bear held her father's gaze while skimming a thumb across her inner wrist. It did nothing to appease her anxiety. Her body vibrated with it, demanded she attack, claws extended. A terrifying urge. In all her father's unpredictability and irrationality, she'd never felt an inkling of anything but love toward him.

A light touch settled on her back. Runs Like Deer, reminding her of clan, of family trust. And of the Rule. Her sister wriggled her fingers between Strong Bear's hold on Pretty Wolf until he squeezed and released.

While Runs Like Deer faded back behind their mother, Pretty Wolf forced her muscles to relax, her head to *think*. "Sunflower gave him to me. The man is mine, Micco. And you are *damaging* him." Clan law was a language Crazy Medicine spoke well, his code of honor being a twisted, unreliable thing. Too much damage to her slave, and he'd be required to restore balance.

"I suggest," Noonday said with a tap to her husband's arm, "you leave our daughter's slave be. Unless you have a replacement slave stowed somewhere?"

Crazy Medicine's soft snort eased the blade's tip back a fraction. Even though his glare had yet to leave the cross, Pretty Wolf's chest crashed with her tremendous exhale.

"Father..." Clearing her throat, Runs Like Deer took a meek step out from behind their mother, her voice gentle. "Blue Feather tells me Strong Bear labors at the Spaniard's forge. Being a fellow metalsmith, you might appreciate a male who crafts iron." Leave it to the peacemaker to call attention to their commonality. "And what of the forging tools you brought over the Great Waters? Haven't you need of a worker?"

Their father hummed contemplatively, and Pretty Wolf presented her sister a small, grateful smile.

"It's true," she added. "Strong Bear is exceptionally skilled with iron."

"Well-muscled for the labor, too. As you can see." Runs Like Deer nodded vigorously, leaning into her role. "With many years of work in his strong, young back."

"Hmm." That from Noonday, who stepped up to give his spine a good thumping, then grunted approval.

Strong Bear's expression went bland with strained patience, and Pretty Wolf fought off a nervous chortle. "He is true as a north wind, Father, and he holds to his vow." No reason to waste breath on his steadfast friendship or the fact she'd be heartbroken to see harm come to him.

Squinting, Crazy Medicine tipped his head at Strong Bear. "What is this vow she speaks of?"

"Where she steps, I follow," Strong Bear launched in. "If she stumbles, I break her fall. If another strikes at her, I take the blow. Her safety is all things to me." He spoke as if in perfect recitation—words she'd oddly never heard before. "The oath I made to Iron Wood at Horse's Flat Foot is unchanging. To me, there is no color of feather or faction. There is only Pretty Wolf."

The passion of his timbre hit her with force.

Pretty Wolf shrank inside herself, her sister's stare like the midday sun on her cheek. Her mother's like an incoming gale, the first gusts of it heard in her little gasp.

It was her own fault they didn't know how deep the currents ran between herself and Strong Bear. They couldn't fathom that his declaration might mean something other than a pledge of courtship.

Crazy Medicine discharged a curt laugh. "Careful not to choke on that oiled tongue, nephew of Lame Deer." A brisk yank of his knife severed the choker. It bumped down Strong Bear's chest and landed in a splatter of bone and reed. Eyes steadfast on Strong Bear, her father sneered and mashed the cross under his heel. He stepped back and turned to Pretty Wolf. "Iron Wood will not tolerate this one about the trade store. What will you do with him when your contract at the cow pens is ended?"

"That is an excellent observation, Husband." Noonday's agreement came out slowly, her tone more colluding than Pretty Wolf liked. She was, however, correct. They both were.

Foolishly, Pretty Wolf had not contemplated what would happen after the cow pens, caught up as she was in surviving each day.

"Sister." Runs Like Deer held out a thickly folded square of cloth, which Pretty Wolf took.

"Hold still," she murmured as she pressed the wad to Strong Bear's dripping wound, tongue clucking her disapproval.

The well-behaved slave, he stared placidly at some point behind her, not allowing her the apologetic glance she had prepared for him.

"The solution," her mother said, "is to make a concubine of him."

Pretty Wolf's head whisked sideways. Strong Bear's with it.

Noonday beamed. "Two men for the talwa's most esteemed daughter. One to give you status. One to give you children." She all but rubbed her hands in anticipation. "Don't look at me that way, Daughter. Look at *him*. And tell me he will not make a good mate, if only a second. You may lodge him here. I shall work him at the river. With those strong hands he'll wring the wet from the laundry so fast the women won't be able to dirty their clothes fast enough."

"Scrub clothes?" Her father belted out a laugh. "Like a woman!"

"Like a *slave*." Noonday huffed. "Pretty Wolf can visit him when her womb is ripe. If we are wise about it, all her children might be pure Muscogee."

Pretty Wolf stared at her parents, uncertain whether to bark at them for such terrible treatment of her precious Kit or break down in hysterics.

Clearly, Strong Bear had chosen the former. He stood so close, she saw his muscles lock tight as drums, the tic in his nostril going wild. Low between them, she returned the favor and snatched him by the wrist to dig in her nails in warning.

He glared down at her. *I dare you to reduce me to a stud bull.*

Her lips slinked upward in a tiny private smirk. *Dare accepted.*

"I see what you mean, Mother." Edging back, she rubbed her chin and looked him up and down. "He *would* produce stout, red children."

Strong Bear's nostril-twitch ceased, his eyes compensating with their abrupt flare.

Runs Like Deer tittered, and Crazy Medicine just shook his head.

Her mother clapped in glee. "Think of the strapping warrior sons he will give us!"

A devious glint came into Strong Bear's eyes. He returned Pretty Wolf's blatant perusal, lazy and head-to-toe. "I am your humble slave, Pucase. If it is red children you want,"—arms spread wide, he presented himself—"I am here to serve."

Pretty Wolf breathed in saliva and choked. She stood hacking and pounding her chest while Runs Like Deer burst out in uncharacteristic hilarity.

Her father dispensed a few manly smacks to her slave's shoulder, and Noonday nodded broadly. "There, see? He is willing. But what man wouldn't be delighted to have my most beautiful daughter?"

It was just as well Pretty Wolf was still coughing. She had no words.

Finding Pretty Wolf

"Chief, chief!" Birdie came tearing into the compound, her face shining with sweat. "It's that fool man again, causin' trouble!"

Chapter 28

Not waiting to hear more than "square" and "hurry," Pretty Wolf tore from the Wolf compound. Strong Bear cast her furtive glances as he jogged close to her side. Before they'd reach Wakulla's main thoroughfare, a storm was already blowing fiercely through her bones.

Someone shouted, "Pretty Wolf has arrived. Open a way!"

The warning in the cry might have been credited to her looming, hulking slave. But not even her miccofather, who lagged inexplicably behind, could be blamed for parting those gathered. No, this was the Rule. Once in a blood moon, it almost made up for all the misery it thrust upon Pretty Wolf.

Either that or the People were overly eager to see what came of the inevitable clash between herself and her sister's husband. This, however, would be no repeat of their last humiliating encounter.

A swivel of the head told her the micco had yet to make a reappearance. Several lanes back, he'd veered off without warning or explanation.

She fought a scowl. Whatever muck Kills Many was creating, he would never listen to her.

"Will you fight him, lost daughter?" came a random voice.

"Wait for your father, child."

"Where *is* our micco, Pretty Wolf?"

How I would like to know!

Winter Hawk shoved through the wall of bodies surrounding the slave pole, a frantic look marring his face. "Pretty Wolf, thank spirits. Kills Many has my captive!"

"Which one?" Strong Bear asked before she could respond, Winter Hawk's anxiety bleeding into his tone. "Is it Hambly?"

Popping out of the crowd, Winter Hawk's flock of young friends surrounded him like a micco's security band. Their eyes bulged large yet lacked their leader's battle-wisened alarm.

Strong Bear clapped a hand on Winter Hawk's shirt and dragged him along on his other side. "The rest of you, stay back." He rattled Winter Hawk's shoulder. "Speak."

"Ehi. The paleface, Hambly. Alligator approved him for blood vengeance. For Kills Many's sister, Cedar Berry."

"What?" Pretty Wolf blurted, tripping over her own toes.

Strong Bear snagged her elbow to keep her upright. Gasps sputtered around them, spawning immediate whisperings. Stupid Rule. She pinched her tongue between her teeth to keep from smarting off. They really should tend to their own affairs.

"For *Cedar Berry*," Winter Hawk reiterated unnecessarily.

Cedar Berry's death had been a harsh blow for Alligator Clan of both talwas, but slaying Hambly, a crop-raising settler, wouldn't restore proper balance. A Bluecoat took the woman's life; a Bluecoat's life should be taken as payment.

Pretty Wolf tossed up her arms in exasperated bewilderment. "Did Kills Many not bring home any Bluecoat scalps from the attack on the fort?"

"That matters little." The brave skittered around the back of Strong Bear and flanked her other side. "Not when Micco Tall Bull ordered the Hambly paleface to be kept alive. Alligator knows this, but since Tall Bull has run off to be with Mink, they've disregarded—"

Pretty Wolf slammed to a stop. "He did *what*?" What was Winter Hawk implying?

"Later, later." He swiped, eliminating that from discussion, though not quite from her churning mind. "They've disregarded his order and..."

Ran off with. He couldn't mean... Tall Bull's interest in ribbons came flooding back. Had they been for Mink? But she was wed to another! He would never. It was a lie. Or a misunderstanding. She craned her neck to see across the shifting sea of turbans and black-haired scalps, as though she might spot him this moment.

"Are you listening?"

Fingers snapped before her nose, and her lashes batted.

Strong Bear smacked Winter Hawk's hand away. "Give her space, boy."

"No..." Eyes closed, she rubbed her forehead. "He's right. I..." What had he been saying? She got her legs back in motion. "Why would Tall Bull care what happens to this slave?" Had her pawa suddenly sprouted paleface sympathies?

"How should I know?" Sweat ran down the side of Winter Hawk's scalp when he leaned down to speak into her eyes, voice thorny with rare frustration. "I'm a featherless warrior. You think the miccos tell me these things?"

Her head drew back, away from his intrusive nearness. "No, I don't suppose they do."

"That isn't *space*." Strong Bear stretched across her shoulders, seized Winter Hawk by the back of his collar, and yanked him behind her.

"All right, all right." The brave's grumbles floated up. "Let me go. Plump Dove is watching."

To the tune of myriad murmurs, the masses gave way before them, like wood splitting under an axe head. After hearing the cruel accusations about her pawa, she was feeling as sharp and ruthless as one.

At the end of the human path stood the slave pole. Attached to it, one bare-chested, soft-bellied white man, hands behind his back and a rope strung about his neck. The tether ran through an eye high on the pole and drew him up on his booted toes, painting his face a shocking purple-red. Shallow slashes crisscrossed his torso, blood shining in the dense mat of chest hair and dripping onto his trousers. Trembles wracked his body, but his knees held firm. And he hadn't soiled himself yet.

Kills Many circled the captive, knife held blade-backward in his fist. Every few strides, he lurched. Sometimes slicing flesh, sometimes stopping short, then hooting at Hambly's flinch.

"That son of a vulture." Pretty Wolf charged on and drew up short at the line of stones ringing the pole.

"Bartering fodder." Strong Bear spoke into her ear, his piney aroma zinging the back of her nose. "That is Hambly's purpose."

Her gaze snapped to him. "Tall Bull told you this?"

"Ho!" Kills Many shouted. "The micco's daughter arrives! We are honored." Leering, he used the flat of his blade to land several crisp smacks to Hambly's cheek. "Are we not, white dog?"

"Miss Francis!" Hambly strangled out, eyes protruding her direction. "I d-didn't kill his sister. I didn't kill anyone! P-please! This isn't—" He bleated and shied but couldn't avoid Kills Many's swiping kick. Feet flying out from under him, he swung, gagged, and gurgled, Kills Many watching as his boots scraped and scratched for traction.

Pretty Wolf's breath congealed. She clamped down on a rant of indignation and prayed the man to get his legs under him again, to get air into his lungs.

Kills Many prowled. Observed.

From the crowd, whoops mingled with snipes and shouts and clamors of affront. On the opposite side of the ring, Birdie bowed over, hands clapped over her face. Sunflower, disapproval twisting her age lines, stood beside the woman, an arm wrapped about her shaking shoulders.

At last, Hambly's boot tips halted his swing and leveraged him up. Air skidded down his throat in a horrendous wheeze just in time for Kills Many to whirl with a feral scream and slice. Hambly coughed out precious air as he cried out and writhed away.

Pretty Wolf shook and smoldered. Furious tears scorched her eyelids, but she blinked them into oblivion.

"Steady there, firebolt." The thrum of Strong Bear's voice was all that held her in place.

Teeth bared, she prayed strength to resist dashing into the circle. According to Winter Hawk, this spectacle had been deemed clan business. And she wasn't Alligator.

Smirking, Kills Many strutted around the pole, arms stretched wide, the blood on his knife glistening a ruby red. Sleeves rolled to his upper arms, he brandished the kill-tallies laddering his forearms.

Such swagger for a warrior boasting not a single feather in his hair. *Her* doing. Self-satisfaction nestled cozily inside, as though careful scheming had prompted his abuse instead of his infantile temper.

"Despicable dog indeed," Strong Bear observed darkly, volume sliced low.

Winter Hawk, in a dark voice not belonging in his throat, muttered, "Runs Like Deer deserves better than that carrion fodder."

She very much did. Pretty Wolf had known it from the start, had said as much to her mother, to Runs Like Deer herself. Her parents hadn't listened, and her sister could more easily lop off her own pinky than tell their father no. With Runs Like Deer paying the price, Pretty Wolf found no satisfaction in Crazy Medicine's prompt regret. Fortunately, the People were wise enough, forgiving enough, to not hold her husband's foolishness against her.

Currently, the fool shuffled a stomp dance, mimicking an alligator roar and looking every part the wild savage.

"Where is my father?" Pretty Wolf quietly snarled. Her appeal must go above clan to micco, and she *would* appeal. If for no other reason than that Hambly's coat was not blue. He was merely a father caught between two warring peoples and ensnared by a madman's unquenchable pursuit of vengeance.

"Shall I fetch him?" Strong Bear offered, but Kills Many was whirling back to his quarry, blade poised high for another strike.

"Enough!" Tolerance fractured, she stepped one foot into the ring. "You'll stay that blade, Kills Many. Until Micco Crazy Medicine has come, not one more drop of blood."

Beating apathetic lashes at her, he lowered the weapon and sank straight into a mocking bow. "Certainly, sister of my wife." His reply came too easily, too smugly to give her any hope this would end peaceably. "But I promise you that before the colors of evening push down on the sun, another kill will mark my skin." The blunt side of his blade passed over the inside of his forearm to indicate where.

Hambly's garbled lament drove a shuddered breath out of her.

"You *must* preserve his life, Pretty Wolf." Strong Bear's breath blew soft at her ear, his tone urgent. "For bartering purposes, it is the wisest move. Considering."

Eyes cutting over her shoulder, she frowned. "Considering what?"

He dropped a weighty look on her. "You *know* what."

She did?

"We do?" Winter Hawk interjected his head between theirs. "What do we know?"

Gaze fixed to hers, Strong Bear palmed the brave's face and pushed him back. "Save the paleface, Pretty Wolf." He slid thumb and forefinger down his white feather, and her stomach gave a dreadful flip.

A rock formed in it, and her fingers clenched, yearning for a solid fist of dirt to cling to. "Who are we meant to barter with, Strong Bear?" The Spanish? *Please, the Spanish.* "Tell me. What do you know?"

His mouth pulled into a flat, inert line.

She scoffed. "That's it? You'll say no more?"

He stared at her blankly, fiddling with the tip of that troublesome feather.

A lip-curving vision of herself ripping the adornment out and smacking him with it couldn't dim the suspicion that she *did* know what. Or halt another revolting turn of her stomach. Was the rumor of the marching Bluecoats no rumor at all? Were they coming? A thousand and one questions pelted her at once, but this was not the time.

"Report, Daughter." Crazy Medicine laid a commanding hand on her shoulder.

She spun to him, the Red Stick in her whooping that he sought her out for this. The wolf in her growling at his delay. "Where have you been?" She pushed the snarl discretely through a locked jaw.

A coal lit in his black eyes, but that might have been a ghost of approval molding his lips. "In conference with clan Alligator."

"And?"

The ends of her father's twig-thin mustache pointed sharply earthward. "Shining Moon deems this death a proper means of blood vengeance. Kills Many is within his rights."

Shining Moon was a malleable nitwit.

"Only because they weary of his antics!" Pretty Wolf hissed low between them. "You cannot approve of this, Father. Surely." By the dismay grooving his forehead, she saw he did not.

"Come, Daughter, you know clan law outplaces my power here. I cannot interfere." That was genuine regret, with perhaps a hint of disgust, snapping his syllables.

"Kills Many has only this day returned from *battle*." She thrust an arm toward the deranged warrior trilling now in his victim's ear. "He had to have gotten his belly-fill of white flesh."

"Ask him. Perhaps the impossible will happen, and he will listen to reason," her father said, dry as old bones and swept a granting arm toward the macabre scene.

For one indiscriminate moment, she gaped at her micco. Being vested the role of yatika was not what she'd expected coming into this, but there wasn't a chance in all three worlds she'd walk away from Hambly if it was in her power to intervene.

"Maddo, Micco." Dispensing a curt nod, she strolled into the circle, paused to cast a lengthy, encompassing look at her people, then stated the obvious in a clear, bold voice. "Micco, this *featherless warrior* intends to kill Winter Hawk's captive."

Springing a grin, Winter Hawk elbowed Strong Bear's ribs. Arms folded broadly over his chest, Strong Bear rolled him a bland expression. They seemed awfully blithe now. Indifferent? No... Confident. In her ability to defuse the situation. A subtle display of trust, but enough to bolster her spine.

"It's true, Micco." Kills Many, fodder of carrion, was now flipping and catching his knife by its point. "This slave's life was awarded me to do with as I wish. And I *wish* to watch him bleed." He stalked to Hambly, sneered in his face, and carved another line across his breast. "Before he dies."

Jaw clenched, Hambly bore the pain in courageous silence.

The crowds buzzed and rumbled. In approval? With bloodthirst? If she didn't hasten her yatika talk, Kills Many might feed off their goading and slide that steel across Hambly's bobbing throat.

She pressed forward. "The man's value as a bargaining tool to the People is greater than his value to your clan as blood payment."

"Do you so little trust your warriors that you believe we cannot defend our home?" Kills Many dared question her belief in those who'd thrown their lives at the war, who still fought it. "That our honor will be so far gone one day as to be reduced to beggary?"

The ensuing rumble was not so vague as the first had been. This time, apparent dissent rippled over the People. Nervous caution crinkled her father's eyes, making her pulse trip out several beats.

Strong Bear shifted where he stood. Their eyes collided. Faith beamed from his, the motion of his lips forming a single soundless word. *Fearless...*

So she was. Resolve settled firmly into her bones, and her mouth sloped into a defiant smirk. "As the wolf," she murmured, and Strong Bear winked.

"What say you now, woman?" Kills Many taunted.

Summoning the hackles of her totem, she faced Kills Many and jerked her chin high. "I say, do *you* so little care for the People you would destroy our last safeguard against our enemy? And for what? Vengeance you've already exacted on the battlefield?"

Kills Many's vulture strides didn't so much as hitch. "I didn't make any kills during battle. None that satisfied." His teeth flashed through his twisted smile.

A quiet growl rolled through her throat as she grappled for another argument. Something irresistibly persuasive. An offer of exchange? But what? She owned so little. "Let us trade. Hambly's life for... What do you want?"

"What do I want, what do I *want*?" he repeated, swiftly eliminating the distance between them. "What else but my feathers!" Spittle flew and dotted her chin and neck. "Every. Last. One."

Squinting with disgust, she fisted her skirt to keep from scrubbing at her face. "What sort of request is that? Feathers aren't mine to give, and you know it. They are earned."

"Then earn them for me!"

Earn them for him? What, through acts of cunning and bravery that were somehow credited to him? A laugh pealed out of her. "That-that... It isn't possible!" Or even reasonable. Hadn't her father said as much? Reasoning with the man was like chasing the wind.

At her floundering, Kills Many sniggered and backed off a step to crow at his audience. "Lineage above all! The paleface's life is forfeit."

Upheaval erupted, the people's mixed shouts rivaling the rage boiling through Pretty Wolf's flesh.

The paleface was *not* his. Not his to cut, not his to mock, and certainly not his to slaughter. William Hambly belonged to the People. Under no circumstance would his life serve this ignoble purpose! Not while Pretty Wolf had blood in her body to spare.

Roaring through her clamped jaw, she twirled about and threw herself at Hambly. He grunted, his back slamming into the pole. Arms flung about his chest, she locked her hands behind him and lifted enough to relieve his throat.

"Woman, what are you doing?" Kills Many growled, breath spilling over the back of her neck. Would he disdain the Rule and wrest her away? She prayed so. Because the only thing he had left to lose was his wife and child, and none in Wolf compound would bemoan his absence.

He disappointed her. Kept his distance.

So, she grappled Hambly, getting a firmer hold and a strong whiff of fear and blood, and shouted, "Your blade will have to pass through my body first." If Kills Many wanted cunning and bravery, he would get it. "The captive belongs to the People! And I will die before I let you have him."

Outcries thundered all about, nearly drowning Hambly's voice in her ear. "Miss Francis, you shouldn't—"

"Hold your tongue, Englishman. Back off, Strong Bear!" She didn't need her eyes pointed his direction to know he was moving in to do something foolish.

As predicted, his furious growl sounded not three rods off her right shoulder. Off the other, someone was chortling, a booming, delighted laugh that could belong to none other than her crazy father. The micco was well aware Kills Many would never scrape up enough courage to call her bluff.

Finding Pretty Wolf

From dead ahead, Iron Wood exploded through the mass of shuffling humanity. Shirt twisted and tearing against those restraining him, he darted his wild eyes between her and Kills Many. "Polly, what in heaven's name are you doing! Let your father deal with this. Come to me, darling." Arm out, he strained for her, begging with his whole body for her to stop this. "No more recklessness, remember? You promised me not ten days past!" His broken plea, and the awful truth of it, relaxed her muscles a fraction. Guilt stinging like a swarm of irate bees.

"Save the paleface, Pretty Wolf," Strong Bear had urged. *"It is the wisest move."* Was it though? Was *this* the wisest move? While he couldn't have predicted she'd taunt Kills Many with a deadly blow, he'd believed this man might be key to preserving the People. It was enough for her.

Delivering Iron Wood her most regretful look, she gave her head a tiny shake. He had every reason not to trust her impulses, but in this case, he must.

Fury washed his face red. "Polly! Release him. There is a knife pointed at your back!"

Hambly slumped and thunked his skull resignedly against her hair. "Do what you must, Miss Francis."

She interlocked her forearms against his sweat-soaked back and twined her lower leg around his. "I do, Englishman. I do."

Behind her rose a wordless, enraged shriek.

Her father's laughter doubled. "She has outdone you, Kills Many!" Crazy Medicine spouted. "So what will it be? Will you take my daughter's life, or will you seek your revenge elsewhere?"

Chapter 29

Pretty Wolf rose from her thin bedding on the ground, unable to catch even a glimpse of a dream. She moved to stand beside the guest lodge's sole couch. By the sleepy firelight, she bent over a snoring Hambly and laid a palm over his brow. Content that, for now, fever kept its distance, she stroked his coarse hair off his forehead and wondered how, in a half moon's time, she'd gone from no slaves to two.

Thank the spirits, they both slept, this one knocked unconscious by Sunflower's potent tonic. The other, by a solid day's labor at the forge and the heart-stopping actions of a pucase who didn't know the meaning of caution. Behind her, Strong Bear occupied the ground on the fire's opposite side. He'd not moved two rod lengths from her since Kills Many pelted her with a wordy tirade. Summarized, his vengeance was not satisfied, but it would be. Eventually.

Immediately after, Strong Bear had thrown her a grumbling glower, but his displeasure had nothing on Iron Wood's purple-faced censure. If not for her father's intervention, her betrothed might never have left Wakulla. She'd still be in his rib-splintering embrace. Possibly shackled to his ankle.

As it stood, she'd shooed him on home and stayed to nurse her new slave, which she'd acquired with her offer of sacrifice—no higher payment than one's life.

Worth every drop of sweat, every villager's horrified shock.

Hambly would live. He would labor. He would serve a great purpose. A greater one than softening the slave pole grounds with his blood. A purpose that served *all*. Whatever and whenever that might be.

For now, he slept. Recovered. Dreaming, hopefully, of his living children.

The chill night crept under the door flap and skillfully evaded the fire pit's anemic heat to reach her. It laid icy kisses up the skin of her unclothed legs and directed her thoughts to Strong Bear's lack of comfort. With less bedding than she, he'd lain down between her and the doorway, his knife unsheathed and within easy reach.

Kills Many's "eventually" might mean next moon with a different paleface; it might mean next morning with a sly attack. In all truth, his madness frightened Pretty Wolf, drove her into hiding. Sunflower and Crazy Medicine alone knew where she and her slaves had slinked off to for the night—Wakulla's seldom-used guest lodge located on the outskirts of Rabbit compound.

With the next whistle of wind, Pretty Wolf gently tugged the blanket higher up Hambly's bandaged chest, then glanced over her shoulder and froze.

Strong Bear's night-black eyes were fixed low on her, yet he hadn't clued in to her notice. He lay on his side, jaw propped in the heel of his upraised hand, fingers disappearing into his thick scalp. The loose raven curtain of his hair hung down his upraised arm, tickling the dirt at his elbow and rustling in the slight breeze. Twig working in his teeth, he casually perused her…feet?

Dirt darkened the gaps under her toenails. Was he judging her? Crafting a speech about her avoidance of the river?

She watched, perfectly still, avidly curious, as his gaze ambled up. And stumbled across hers. He startled. Then broke out in a grin that displayed the entire top row of those shiny teeth. "What? Can a concubine not admire his wife?"

It was her turn to startle. Admire? Discomfort wiggled through her belly as Toño's words of warning reentered her hearing. *But wait.* He'd called himself a concubine. A blatant untruth.

He teases, she told herself until the knot in her stomach unwound.

She straightened and bounced a nonchalant shoulder. "Fair point." In two steps, she'd strolled back to her pallet and folded her legs under her blanket.

"Sleep," she ordered. "You'll want to be rested for all those dirty garments you will scrub tomorrow."

Strong Bear's smile tumbled off. "I was in jest. The concubine bit, it was in jest."

She leveled him an implacable look. "You have no say in it, slave." The plan was to prolong his suffering, but at his first nostril tic, a laugh snorted out of her. "Gullible as ever."

"Pretty Wolf." Her name spilled out of him on a light growl, his features puckering into contrived fury.

Worming down, she yanked the blanket over her mouth to muffle her laughter. "Your eyes, Kit! I've never seen them so big."

"With reason!" On a harrumph, he flopped down onto his back. "You'd best pray Sunflower doesn't latch onto your mother's ridiculous notions and force the matter. Concubine. Bah!"

"Complaining again in high pitch?"

"This is no simple complaint." Fingers laced, he rammed them under his skull. "It is a refusal. I'll not do it, no matter what Sunflower orders. *That* is my say in it."

She stared at his strong profile, the stubborn set of his mouth, the beautiful crook in the line of his nose. He'd never hesitated to step in when and where she needed him. Her playacting a moment before might have thrown him off, but she'd made clear in the end it was just that, an act. So why the fierce protest? She was asking before she could think better of it. "Would it be so repulsive to be attached to me in that manner?"

"In that manner?" His tone sharpened with disdain. "Ehi. Most definitely. I am not meant for such, and no male wishes to be strongarmed into marriage."

She hummed. "Too true. And strongarmed or not, any woman would be honored to have you as husband."

Briskly, his head turned. He looked at her as if she'd just tripped over the laces of her own moccasins, then grunted.

"What was *that* for?" What had she done but compliment him?

In reply, another grunt, disobliging and irritating. He rolled his head to stare back up at the ceiling and folded his arms over his chest. A drawn-out, uncomfortable minute lumbered by. "A thought for a thought?"

She blinked at his unexpected proposition, but at least the whimsy was back in his voice. And their old game-not-game never failed to be entertaining. Excruciating, too. But if a woman couldn't handle either of those with her closest companion—even an uncooperative one—she may as well pack up her soul and begin the spirit journey.

Settling in, she tucked the covers under her armpits and crossed her forearms snuggly under her breasts to trap in heat. She began with the obligatory phrase. "Do you have a thought?"

"I do," he practically chirped. "In your compound earlier, you called me a man."

She masked a wince and stared busily up at the dusty rafters. It was to be excruciating right off, then. "So it would seem." Pretty Wolf had less than no desire to discuss how that classification had so sleekly ridden from her tongue. *The man is mine, Micco.* The label, the proprietary use of the wording. No desire whatsoever. "And," she elongated the word, "that is all *that* thought merits." She dropped her voice in growly mimicry of his voice. "Do *you* have a thought, Pretty Wolf? I do," she replied to her own question. "Maddo, Kit."

"Ey!" He laughed. "I sound nothing like that."

"Tall Bull would *never*," she went on, ignoring his feigned affront, "live with a married woman. Either someone is trying to smear his character, or Ten Cats is dead."

Strong Bear's silence compelled the turn of her head. His lips were set at a doubting slant, but when he spoke, it wasn't to voice it. "While we are on the topic of concubines, might this Ten Cats husband have gone with them?"

Tall Bull, the great and beautiful micco, lowering himself to second husband? She chucked out a humorless laugh. "It's more likely Tall Bull rang his neck like a wet rag. They are dog and cat, those two." With Tall Bull and Mink being vine and stake. Intricately woven. They'd spent the greater portion of their lives together, too few of those years in company of Pretty Wolf.

Far too few.

And it infuriated her, robbed again, as she was, of a loved one. A theft that had yet to fully register. Any moment, Tall Bull should strut in, smelling of assee and authority. But he wouldn't. Why? From the snarl she'd seen on her father's face, one or both of them—Tall Bull or Mink—had lost their place in his meager graces.

Her head shook in denial. "I refuse to believe my pawa would leave me for anything less than a threat to Mink's life." The only excuse she could stomach. Tears coated her eyes as the hurt of rejection wrestled the ache of loss.

Strong Bear hadn't uttered a peep against Tall Bull, but the micco's reputation—and Strong Bear's bond with his cousin—were accusation enough. He reached across to her, sympathy curving his lips as she entwined their fingers. "In my few moments with him, strained though they were, I learned Tall Bull is a brave warrior whose heart beats strongly of loyalty and love. If he has gone from you, it is not without dire cause."

Pretty Wolf swallowed thickly and nodded as that truth seeped in to curry away the sharpest edges of injury. Tall Bull loved her, but undoubtedly, he loved the war woman more. For Mink, he would abandon anything and everything. "Maddo, my friend."

Smiling, Strong Bear squeezed her fingers and released, then shuffled about under his blanket and withdrew his gilded timepiece. He flicked up the cover and tilted the inside toward the fire.

"What does it say?"

Arm outstretched, he presented it to her in his open palm. "You tell me."

She took it and studied the positions of its tiny, glinting blades. "Two and…" She counted in increments of five then one, as Iron Wood taught her. "Thirty-two."

"Two thirty-two." Warm approval lilted the correction.

"What time is dawn?"

"During this moon, five-thirty. Roughly."

"Three hours…" A yawn clobbered her. "Do you have a thought?"

"I do. Why does Bellamy use your old name?"

Her thumb paused in its idle stroke of the timepiece's velvety rear casing. She voiced a contemplative note. "Well…Polly is an English name. Iron Wood is English."

Strong Bear clucked his tongue. "But he's fluent in our language."

"Ehi, but he first knew me as Polly. Perhaps, he never adjusted to the changed name."

"Or perhaps,"—chin to chest, he peered at her from the tops of his eyes—"to the changed *Polly*."

No "perhaps" at all. Iron Wood longed for Polly's return, begged for it. In vain. The one trade her English merchant could not manage: Pretty Wolf for Polly. But if Pretty Wolf were Iron Wood, she'd wish for it too. Polly might have been a little delusional and a lot stubborn, but she was wholesome and unbroken.

Pretty Wolf sighed.

The fire crackled lazily. They'd reached the point in the silence where she should nod, agree with Strong Bear, but shame burned her cheeks and lodged in her voice box. If she'd listened to her betrothed, locked herself away, and played the common villager to the Bluecoats, if she'd slipped into the dugout with him, kept her dagger in its sheath, and stuck to her role as dutiful lover, if she'd not believed herself invincible, instead waited until after birthing to try for the Point, perhaps—

She snapped the watch shut. There was no perhaps. There was only persevere.

"Pretty Wolf?"

Cheeks blazing, she glanced away, ostensibly to check on Hambly. The man's jaw sagged heavily, still a victim of Sunflower's tonic.

"Forgive me," Strong Bear murmured. More silence. "Do you…have a thought?"

My gracious Kit. Pretty Wolf stroked her cheek with the soft side of his pouch-clock and watched Hambly's lips flap with his snores. "I do." Unhealthful thoughts. Worrisome thoughts. She turned back to find Strong Bear reclining again on his elbow, a moue of concern grooving lines into his brow.

"As I lay here thinking," she mused, "of all the foolish deeds Kills Many has carried out by order of his whim, I begin to understand Iron Wood's frustration with me."

Strong Bear scoffed so harshly, it set his feather bunch to swaying. "Even I, having witnessed him in action only the once, can see the man is a night-long thunderstorm to your single firebolt."

That acquired him a little smile that soon dissolved. "That may be so, but we are both rash and impulsive. Determined to have our way. I know his mind, Strong Bear, and I tell you, the paleface is not safe here. Kills Many will have his vengeance, and he will not wait long."

Hambly was Pretty Wolf's to protect. Earlier that night, he'd closed his eyes in sleep and entrusted his life to her safekeeping. What a tragedy to save him from the pole only to lose him to a sliced throat as he slept or to a stray arrow as he traipsed to the privy.

"Do you mean unsafe here in the guest lodge?" Strong Bear's hand slid nearer his weapon. "Or in Wakulla?"

"Pft. In the Point."

Fingers drumming the dirt, Strong Bear let his gaze wander, their game suspended while his mind churned behind his contracted eyes. "What of the fort?"

San Marcos? She pushed up on one arm in facsimile of his pose. "What of it?"

"Does it have cells? Might Toño confine him there for you?"

Locking him behind bars seemed somewhat extreme. Hambly snuffled loudly, as though in agreement.

Pretty Wolf twisted sharply at the waist to find his lids sealed. Smacking his tongue, he scrubbed clumsily at his nose with the back of his wrist. The hill of his flabby gut juddered. Where he'd moved the blanket, she could see dried, black-red blood striped across his white bandaging. A man couldn't look more vulnerable.

But the intensity of Strong Bear's questions reminded her that Hambly might not be the vulnerable one. Or at least, not for long. His vehemence at the slave pole came back to haunt her. *"Save the paleface, Pretty Wolf."*

Her innards kinked, and she flipped to her stomach. Up on two elbows now, she gripped her forehead in both hands. "How soon will our enemy arrive? What do you know? When? How?"

"I cannot say."

She slapped the dirt. "To the flames with your *cannot*! There are women and children at risk. You *can*, White Stick. You simply won't." The certainty of it launched her up to sitting on her hip. "Tell me something. Anything!" It was her firebolt anger that gritted out her demand, that hurled the watch at him.

With jackrabbit reflexes, he snatched it from the air, then slowly sat up and pinned her with irascible eyes. "I love you, woman. To protect you, I would offer my neck to the knife. But I *cannot* say. The Bluecoats tell me nothing. You ask the impossible." Blast his even tone. She wanted a fight! A vent for her frustration and fear. "Besides, any warrior, Red or White, worth his feathers can predict that Jackson's forces will not delay."

Her body felt suddenly made of lead. Shoulders flagging. Arms limp, useless ropes. The Defiance wasn't ready, its warriors so fresh from conflict that Pretty Wolf had yet to hear the tales. Had they even destroyed the fortifications they'd targeted? She'd been so preoccupied with Hambly, she'd found no opportunity to ask. Whatever they'd done, it had exhausted them and further depleted their slim numbers. Of all the times to attack, this was worst.

Therefore, the wisest. Depending on one's position.

The urge to pester Strong Bear for more became a physical pressure on her tongue—how many? what artillery? what route?—but she pushed it back. He had no more to give. The best she could do was prepare, protect those under her lodge poles. Starting with Hambly.

"At dawn," she said, fatigue coaxing her back to her pallet, "we take the paleface to Toño."

A commotion of excited voices in the yard cracked open Pretty Wolf's scratchy eyes. Through the doorway, pink was invading the indigo sky. "What's going on?" she garbled, lips and tongue so sluggish it wouldn't surprise her if she'd been dosed with Sunflower's draught.

Hambly lay on his back, snoring on, but Strong Bear was already on his feet, the tip of his knife sliding home in its sheath. "Stay here." He'd not yet reached the door when Winter Hawk exploded into the lodge.

The brave skidded into Strong Bear, the whites of his eyes a full, bright ring around his black irises. "There's a vessel! Moored along the coast. It flies a British flag!"

Pretty Wolf popped upright, her brain fog blown clear away. "They came?"

"They came!" Winter Hawk hiked his chin and trilled a sharp war cry.

At the screech, Hambly loosed a shout, all four limbs jumping straight up. He rolled and, tangling in his blanket, splatted face-first on the ground.

Scrunching an eye shut, Strong Bear leaned away from the boy. "At least we know your war trill works." He jutted his chin at Hambly, whose only visible part was the trembling rump he hadn't managed to wedge under the couch.

Winter Hawk hooted and drew an imaginary bow. "He left a broad target."

"On your feet, William Hambly." Pretty Wolf was already hunkering in the shadows, changing. In fits with her skirt, she looked for where to step in. "That was only our exuberant friend practicing his morning greeting." She kicked her legs through the waistband, then whipped it up over her hips.

They'd come through for them, the British. They'd actually done it! Defied the treaty and provided aid. And here the People had believed the monarchy to have despised their cause. Apparently, not. Spirits bless them, they'd decided to favor the Defiance after all. So soon, too. The supply ship must have left England mere weeks after her father. No, days. And well they did, with the Bluecoats breathing over the backs of their scalps.

As Hambly began a wiggling reemergence, Strong Bear strapped on his accessories belt. "Our plan for the paleface?"

"The same." She finished the knot of her skirt tie in time to catch the blouse Strong Bear tossed at her. "The ship, Winter Hawk. It's not in the harbor, you say?"

"Farther up, sheltering in a cove."

She knew the one he spoke of. "Clever." The Spanish should not be implicated that way. With her back to the men, she whipped off the borrowed sleep shirt. "My father?"

"Gone out to meet them with his Second."

Her voice muffled as she dove her head into her blouse. "That would be...Water Moccasin?" Beaver's head clansman should be next in the rise to leadership with Tall Bull and Mink galloping into the Point and Kills Many stripped of rank.

"Did you not hear?" Winter Hawk's voice cracked and shot into an upper register. He cleared it. "Water Moccasin went off with Mink."

Pretty Wolf rotated, her blouse's lower hem falling to her hips. "He left us too?"

Winter Hawk put his head to the side. "You are surprised?"

"Actually...no." Of course, Water Moccasin would tie his life to his sister's, no matter her offense. But what of Birdie? Had Pretty Wolf—no, the entire talwa—been mistaken about his affections for her? Or were those affections simply too far beneath the ones he fostered for his sister?

Clan above all.

The People's life-leading truth. Even so, with Water Moccasin's parting, Beaver Clan was grievously hewn down. His chipped smile, his unerring bow, his wise voice in council, all would be desperately missed.

Darkness loomed in her spirit. How many more would be taken from them before it was all over?

Scooting close, Winter Hawk leaned into Pretty Wolf for a conspiratorial, "What is the plan for him?"

She shook off skulking grief and rammed her blouse into her waistband, her head spinning. "Who?"

"Hambly."

He'd finally emerged wearing strands of cobwebs and gingerly touching his chest where fresh blood wept into his bandaging.

Strong Bear slapped a tuft of pine into Winter Hawk's hand. "The plan is to not kill him with your swamp breath. You're to stay with him until we leave. Be on watch for Kills Many." Turning to Hambly, he exchanged their mother tongue for English. "We take you now to the Spanish. For safekeeping." A hurrying motion ushered him toward the door. "Go. Ready yourself. We leave at once."

"Yes, yes. I do approve, Miss Francis." He scurried outside in the direction of the privy, Winter Hawk marching behind and issuing orders.

As she ran fingers through her gnarly tresses, a grin took possession of her. Hope, that bright and beautiful song of the soul, burst to life within her. If the British provided the items her father requested, the Defiance would have more powder and lead, cornmeal and muslin. For starters. Her father must be ecstatic. She certainly was.

Silent and somber, Strong Bear moved in beside her, tugged and yanked at her blouse, straightening, re-tucking as he went around the back. He mustn't be pleased to hear the British were breaking treaty with his Bluecoat allies, but Pretty Wolf couldn't find it in her to care. The People were desperate, and if what he'd shared last night about impending invasion held any truth...

She stepped away from his fussing. "Don't look so glum. This gives us a fighting chance!" Her voice arced with high spirits as she whisked herself into the sweet morning air. "To the fort with Hambly. After, the cow pens. I want our work complete by high sun, so we can come back this evening to stuff our ears with news. Hurry, you big lumbering bear!"

Hurry, as it turned out, couldn't be done with a wounded man in tow.

Stooped and sweating, Hambly sat astride Balada, bareback. His legs trembled in their weak grip of her flanks. Strong Bear, fisting the lead rope, guided the mare to keep her usual exuberance in check. Off his other shoulder, Pretty Wolf matched his moderate pace. Balada, ears sagging a bit to the sides, appeared as happy about it as Pretty Wolf.

The sun was already mounting the treetops, but they'd scarcely covered half the distance. Irritation blustered from her in a vocalized exhale.

Strong Bear cast her an amused glance. "Deep breaths, firebolt. The news isn't going anywhere."

"Perhaps not, but the day is. The sun moves twice as fast as our slug's pace. Look at it!" She flung an arm at the sky.

He pitched his sights across the sandy, scrub-scattered clearing in the palms. Brow twitching, he cocked an ear, then stopped. He gripped her hand and pulled her slightly behind him. "Someone comes. One horse. Shod. Galloping hard."

She heard it then, the *ba-ba-bum, ba-ba-bum* of driving hooves. Far into the verdant palm grove on the opposite side of the glade, a shadow streaked in flashes through the widely spaced trunks. The man, heels sunk deep in the stirrups, hovered expertly over his sprinting gray.

Pretty Wolf smiled and shimmied her fingers from Strong Bear's grasp. "It's only Iron Wood."

Behind, Hambly panted out, "Friend of foe?"

"My betrothed." In quite the hurry.

Finding Pretty Wolf

Grumbling, Strong Bear wrenched the corncob stopper from his water gourd and took a brusque swig. Water dribbled down his chin, but his eyes, acute and weighing, never left their swiftly nearing company. "Hambly. Off the horse. Find rest." He waved the gourd at a patch of shade beneath a palm just off the road.

"Believe I will." Hambly moaned, two thuds alerting to his clumsy dismount. Boots shuffling through the sand, he ambled off.

The gray's tread was thunder now, a vibration against the bottoms of Pretty Wolf's feet. Iron Wood spotted her and lifted a brief hand from the reins, but he wasn't slowing. No, he leaned farther into the gallop.

Unease needled over her calves and raced up to grip her around the back of her neck. Iron Wood's reckless speed soon brought his features into focus, but it was the flushed, sweaty, disheveled state of him that struck fear into her joints. On its heels, the vast, frantic blue of his eyes.

Her grip found Strong Bear's sleeve and flexed into it hard. "Strong Bear…"

Fingers against her hipbone, he prodded her away. "Mount up, Pretty Wolf."

She looked at him, but his hardened stare was not for her. Heart a hammer against her ribs, she ignored the order and lowered to scoop a handful of hot, white sand. Clinging firmly to Mother, she came erect, fine grains streaming like salt between her curled fingers.

From twenty rods out, Iron Wood shouted, "They're here! The bloody Americans, they're here!"

Pretty Wolf's stomach bottomed out, her head filling with air. Fingers going flaccid, she released Mother to the wind.

"Woman, I said get on that horse." Strong Bear's command was categorical.

This time, she listened. In a bound, she swung up. Strong Bear flung her the lead rope. He snatched Balada by the halter to steady her as Iron Wood brought his gray to a haunch-lowering, hoof-skidding halt beside them.

"Here *where*, Iron Wood?" Pretty Wolf clung to the horse's mane, Strong Bear at her side.

Breaths coming in short gasps, Iron Wood riveted to her, not sparing a flick of the eye for Strong Bear standing between them, or for the firm hold he had of her calf. "Everywhere. Fort San Marcos via the sea. The infantry by land." He gasped frantically for air, his words rolling out in a rush.

"Land? Which direction?"

"Foot soldiers from the north." His chin jerked, pointing. Toward Wakulla. "A frigate arrived ahead to negotiate surrender. Heavily armed. Fifty-six guns."

Her head wagged, trying to comprehend, categorize, calculate. "Toño has seen them? Is he in talks with—"

"Curse that man!" Iron Wood's voice erupted with fury, spittle flecking his lips. "Antonio Luengo has relinquished the fort, Polly. Just handed it over!"

"W-what? He wouldn't!"

"Oh, he *would*." Iron Wood spat a bitter laugh. "As of the last hour, Fort San Marcos and surrounding lands are under command of the blazing United States Marines." The bright flush began draining from his cheeks. "By God's mercy alone, I made it to the stables and out of town unnoticed." Both hands fisted into his hair and pulled, his tricorn absent, elbows splayed high. Fear and desperation poured off him, slamming into her.

The ramifications of the invasion and the rapid, uncontested shift of power began spreading out before her. The cause, the people she loved. *At the store, at the talwa—*

"My father," she gasped in the same moment Strong Bear blurted, "The British ship."

Iron Wood's head snapped to him. "What British ship?"

"In a shoreline cove," he replied. "Supplies from your king."

"Is this true?"

Pretty Wolf gave a vigorous nod. "It flies a British flag. Shelters in father's secret cove. What else could it be? He has gone to greet them."

Iron Wood's beautiful midnight lashes blinked rapidly as he took it all in. "Splendid. Yes, capital." Slivers of hope brightened his voice. "Go after him, Polly. Tell him to board that ship and to stay put. You do the same. Unless it's taking on water, you do not leave. I'll come as soon as I'm able."

Strong Bear's grip was hot and inflexible about her calf, tightening in support of Pretty Wolf's shaking head. "Wakulla, my mother—"

"There isn't time!" Iron Wood burst out, sweat tumbling over his brow. "The village will have to fend for itself."

"No!"

"Don't argue! I want you away from here. Safe! Soldiers were raiding the stables for mounts before I left. They'll be swarming the area within the hour. The main body descending from the north not long after."

"What of yourself! If they catch you, Iron Wood—"

"They won't!" Stretching, he reached for her, grasped her hand hard in his damp palm. "Listen. I'll be fine. Luengo swore to me he'd not give away the store's location. I'm going there now."

Good. He'd see to Shem and whatever else needed hiding, burning. "What of Birdie?" For either of her black friends, to be captured was to be clapped in shackles.

"I will hide Birdie myself," Strong Bear vowed, then tipped his head in a listening fashion. He dropped to a knee and pressed a flat palm to the earth. "Many horses. Riding fast."

"Iron Wood," she croaked. "Go." He could *not* be spotted.

Chest heaving, he stared at her, a thousand unspoken words warbling his bloodless lips. The horse beneath him fretted, stamped, and tossed her head against his white-knuckled fist on the reins. Pretty Wolf quite agreed.

"Go!" She flung his hand away, but he was undeterred. Reining forcefully, he maneuvered in and collapsed the space between their mounts.

Strong Bear grunted and leaped clear of prancing hooves.

On his taller mount, Iron Wood's thigh aligned with her waist. He hooked her by the back of the neck and leaned down. Yanking her to him, he kissed her hard on the mouth. "No mad risks, Polly. I love you." Another abrupt mash of the lips, then he reined the gray hard into an about-face and spurred into a sand-spitting gallop.

The pounding of dozens of hooves reached her senses. Pretty Wolf gulped through an arid throat and forced her mind off her betrothed. She looked to Strong Bear. He stood at her knee again, gripping it. Almost golden in the sun, his eyes teemed with love and surety. "I'm a swift runner, and my feather is white. Save your worry for those who need it. Yourself first. Get on that ship, and do not look back."

"But...will I see you again?" Barely contained emotion distorted her voice. "Strong Bear, I—"

"No." Binding their gazes, he touched fingertips to her hipbone. "Remember this..." She sucked in a startled breath, but his fingers pursued, pressing in, driving his point home. "You will always have me with you." Lead rope in hand, he hauled the mare around to face the coast. He returned to Pretty Wolf's side and hastily tied his watch pouch to her belt. Parchment crinkled within. "Apart from you, I cherish *this* above of all else." He rapped the pouch. "When you are safe and times are less fraught, come find us." Much the way Iron Wood had done, Strong Bear pulled her in. But instead of a meeting of the lips, he skated his cheek along hers and rasped another vow. "Whatever happens, Wolf, I am yours."

Before she could conjure a reply, he withdrew. "Be fearless. Be strong. Quickly now!" Stepping back, he smacked the mare's rump.

She was off then. Reeling. Galloping toward the cove. Eyes streaming in the biting wind.

It wasn't until the clearing was half a sight at her back that a man sprang to mind.

Hambly!

"Ho, Balada! Ho!"

The little mare whinnied a protest but dug in her hooves so abruptly Pretty Wolf had to clench her thighs hard to prevent flying over the animal's head. Craning her neck, she looked back, debating. Could she reach the paleface before the Bluecoats? Gag him, hide him. Use him as leverage. She'd hazarded so much for that man!

Time. There is no time!

She'd have to let him get away.

Balada came up slightly on her hind legs and performed a half-leap in the direction they'd been headed. A growled shout of rage scratched her throat on its way out as, fingers weaved through with mane, she gave the creature her head and directed every thought toward the cove. Toward her father.

Chapter 30

The muscles in Pretty Wolf's back ached from rowing. Grandmother Sun's rays beat upon the turquoise cove and sparkled blindingly off its glassy surface. Pretty Wolf squinted at the ship bobbing some thirty oar strokes ahead, the stinging salty spray no help.

A specimen of medium size, the vessel sat high in the water, its colorfully striped Union Jack—as Iron Wood called it—hung lifeless from the foremost of its two masts. Men scurried about the decks, a scattering of red coats among merchantmen in stocking caps. A fellow wearing a black frock stood at the rail and surveyed her approach. But Pretty Wolf cared only for the two brown-skinned Natives. They climbed the rope ladder hanging above the dugout floating astern.

Her father must have delayed his leave of Wakulla, else he would have already been aboard sitting down to brandy with the captain or opening chests and barrels to inspect the donations. Near the top rung, Crazy Medicine clapped arms with the Redcoat leaning over the railing. Grin plastered on his face, he let himself be hoisted. He slung a leg over and turned back to assist his Second, a short, two-feather warrior called Sun Bird.

Crazy Medicine stood proud in his paired crimson turban and shirt, and Pretty Wolf's lungs loosened. She ejected a freeing breath, even as she continued to strain at the oars. Only the spirits knew what fate awaited Wakulla, but her father was safe. The British, shackled by a treaty, might have been reluctant in their aid, but they'd never wished the Defiance ill. After all, they shared a mutual enemy.

A tasseled, bicorned officer strode crisply toward Crazy Medicine and stopped short for a bow. Mouth widening in a smile, he gestured midship invitingly.

"Father!" Pretty Wolf called in Muskogee, arm brandished high, but Crazy Medicine was lavishing the officer with his hearty micco's laugh and didn't turn.

Others did. Sun Bird looked back, surprise enlarging his eyes. The black-coated man cocked his head at her. Several sailors trotted to the rail to peer down, a Redcoat with them.

Twenty strokes to go. Backbone bowed, Pretty Wolf dug her paddles deep and propelled forward—her chosen vessel, the small, communal fishing boat kept anchored above the tide line. The bow sliced easily through gentle waves.

"Father, wait!"

"Halt there!"

Gunfire cracked. Twice. Fast. Wood splintered off the bow. Off her paddle.

Pretty Wolf's heart boomed. She ducked, alarm zinging down her extremities. Head between her raised knees, she screeched, her anger more potent than her confusion.

"Cease fire, cease fire!" a man shouted. "Can't you see that's an unarmed woman? Imbeciles!"

Heart on a rampage, she peeked over her knee, relieved to note she'd had the presence of mind to hang onto her paddles. In the still air, gunpowder smoke hung above the culprits—one in army red, the other in the plain breeches of a sailor. Thankfully, the muzzles of their rifles now pointed skyward.

"Miss?" The fellow in black strained over the rail, concern meshing his brows. "Miss, are you hit?"

She shook her head, more to clear her thoughts than to answer him. Apart from the shock of being unjustly targeted, something was off about him. His accent. It lacked Iron Wood's precise enunciation and rounded vowels, and his face…

A flash of movement to her left. Sun Bird leaping over the side, arms extended to pierce the water. An instant later, he vanished beneath the surface. Coming to help her?

"Forget him!" someone barked.

"Daughter!"

Her eyes snapped to the call.

Why was her father struggling? Two Redcoats barely arrested him by the elbows as he strained toward the rail. Face a mask of shock and horror, he gaped at her from above. "Flee, Daughter!"

Flee? "Father, why are they—?"

He heaved around and rammed his forehead into one of the soldiers. In payment, a rifle butt to the head that jerked it sideways. He slumped to his knees.

Finding Pretty Wolf

She shot to her feet. "What are you doing? Leave him alone! We are allies!"

Her demands were met with another wallop. One of the merchant sailors this time. She growled through her teeth. As he loomed over Crazy Medicine, poised in readiness, the soldiers beside him began unbuttoning their jackets. The ship buzzed with activity that, from her low position, she could catch only snatches of. The sails were being hoisted. The anchor creaked in its upward haul.

Stance wide in the canoe, knees flexing with the waves, she breathed hard through her mouth and tried to make sense of it all. Had she done this? Inadvertently ruined something? Perhaps, he was to have come alone. Regardless, she had to tell him. Tell *them*.

Mouth bracketed with cupped hands, she shouted, "This is a misunderstanding!"

"Miss Francis?"

She couldn't peel her eyes from the inert lump of her father, from the red jackets being tossed aside. One, two, they fluttered onto the deck. *Why do they—?*

"Miss Polly Francis?"

The use of her old name snapped her attention to Black Coat standing high above. Her proximity had brought him into sharper definition. His vestment, she could now make out, was of military cut and adornment, the lines of his face those of no stranger.

A stone plunged through her center, crashed her backside hard to the canoe's bench. "B-buck?" The name squeaked from her disbelieving throat. Then louder. "Marcus Buck?" Her brain was a doe caught in a quagmire, thrashing for footing that would not be found.

Buck was American, was he not? Ehi, a Bluecoat healer. So she'd been told. Then why… Why would he be on a British…?

Her eyes vaulted to the top of the foremost mast—barren. Then down. To a new flag shimmying up the ropes. Stripes. Stars.

Another red coat sailed high on a victory whoop.

"No, no, no," she rasped.

Pain lanced her. The pangs of betrayal.

No, of humiliation and loss. Friends and allies betrayed. These men, Buck included, were neither.

He leaned stiffly into the rail, gripping it as if to launch himself over. Even across the distance, she picked out the remorse living in his eyes, in the strict line of his mouth.

Her knuckles burned around the paddles. She would wield them against him were he within range. Were she not a useless blob of flesh floating on a slab of wood.

Blue frocks materialized. One soldier spoke to Buck, about Pretty Wolf it would seem, since both sets of eyes were locked on her. Buck gave a firm shake of the head, then a clipped order. The man retreated.

The American flag reached its peak just as a gust of wind swept in from the sea. The fabric lifted and spread its blood-red stripes in the sun. Below it, her father's dragging, bumping feet disappeared through a dark hatch.

"Marcus Buck," she spat, "you are a worm of the vilest sort!"

To Buck's credit, he held her killer gaze. "Turn back, Miss Francis. Rest assured, I'll give your father's wounds my utmost care."

Father...

Her chest hitched. Loss consumed her. Ravaged her heart and scattered her thoughts. Above it all, hovered a terrible sense of finality and doom.

The Defiance was finished.

Its throat sliced and bleeding out, the life fading from its eyes. Her lifelong flight from the Bluecoats had, at last, come to a neck-whipping stop.

Flotsam in a wreck, she drifted. Her mind. Her canoe. Aimless. Though several calls to action screamed at her.

Storm the ship.

Row out to the horizon and never look back.

Turn for Wakulla and whatever disaster was befalling her people. Her mother and sister, Sunflower and Birdie.

Strong Bear.

She plunged her right paddle into the water and heaved. The canoe spun. The ship and the watery horizon skimmed out of sight. Before her now: rocks, palms, white sand. And two figures. Big Voice, pacing. Screaming Buttons, hailing her wildly.

Both her paddles dove deep. "I'm coming!"

Chapter 31

Wakulla was the same tragic story told another way. It was Hillabee Town minus the slaughter of unarmed warriors. Holy Ground minus the miraculous escape. Tohopeka minus the flames and the bloody field strewn with the bodies of those who refused to surrender. Or it *would* be once Pretty Wolf reached the square and made it so.

As of that moment, Wakulla's lanes were pandemonium, battering at her ears. Bluecoats herding. Women screaming and running and hauling their little ones. Children stumbling. Wailing.

Warriors sheltered in every nook, popping off wild shots. Coming from every direction, clans poured into the square, propelled at gunpoint. Clothes rumpled. Faces wet.

Fright was a reek on the wind. An acrid coating on her tongue and a curdling churn in her stomach. These were her beloved people. *Hers.* And they were being treated like cattle. Before it was through, they'd be corralled and branded with destruction and defeat. With every resolute stride toward the square, Pretty Wolf swore to herself that all these things would be bearable if she could only prevent despair and death.

So far, she had not come across any bodies. No small relief there, but there was always time for slaying. Jaw set, she stalked down the center of the main thoroughfare. On either side, Screaming Buttons and Big Voice scanned for danger, twitching at every sudden movement, of which there were many.

When news of the warship blew into the cow pens, they'd taken wing, flown straight to her. Apparently, she'd streaked past them on her way to the cove. They'd followed her tracks. Never more grateful for their loyalty, she raised her voice above the clamor to any within range. "Stow your weapons! Give no excuse to attack!"

Screaming Buttons repeated the order, but none seemed to hear. If they did, their only response was to continue shrieking.

"Stand down!" she shouted futilely.

It went against every instinct, defied their Defiance blood, but to do otherwise was to invite slaughter. Stuffed to her gullet with death, Pretty Wolf would slay her pride and that of every Wakullan if it meant preserving even one life.

At the corner of Snake compound, a warrior crouched behind a handcart and squinted down the sights of his musket. He aimed beyond the intersection toward the Bluecoats patrolling the square ground's perimeter. The same grounds that teemed with his own people.

Two leaping steps had Pretty Wolf at his side, the back of his shirt bunched in her fist. She shook him hard. "Give me that!"

Before he could respond, Screaming Buttons tore the musket away. Spluttering, the man stumbled to his backside and gaped up at her in surprise. "P-Pretty Wolf, what is this?"

"It is your micco's daughter, saving your fool scalp. Get to the square!" Presenting him her back, she marched forward, eyes on constant rotation for Strong Bear.

Spirits, she needed him now. His strength. His sustaining presence. Was he safe? Had he been caught hiding Birdie? Nausea flared, but she staved it off.

At the end of the lane, she stopped by the communal cookhouse and took in the square. It stood directly ahead, visible through the break at the corners of the eastern and southern booths. A gap opened in the shifting crowd and revealed the sacred fire burning brightly. Relief slackened her shoulders.

"Remove your weapons, men." She pointed to the cookhouse's exterior wall. "Stack them there."

Who or what gave her the power to give orders, she could not say, but at the beach, her men had both immediately fallen behind her. Big Voice a mite reluctantly, as seen in the nose wrinkling above his sneer. His fingers whitened on his musket, but at her barked "now!" he released it to the ground and began unsheathing his knife.

Screaming Buttons hesitated, gaze darting toward the sacred fire. "The spirits will not be pleased if we do not defend them at all costs, if we lay down arms without a fight."

She passed him a soft-eyed look of understanding. "Your loyalty to the cause is noted and admired. The spirits see this, be assured. And I have no plan to leave our sacred fire undefended. Disarm, Buttons."

A resigned breath, then Screaming Buttons' hunting knife clattered to the pile Big Voice had begun.

"Maddo, brothers," she said above the chaos rippling over her eardrums. "Are you still my men?"

Big Voice replied, "We are."

"Good." She gripped Screaming Buttons' shoulder. "You know where the conch is stored?"

"In the micco's booth." With their sacred artifacts and ceremonial items, in a compartment at the back of the stall.

"Bring it. Meet me at the fire." She pushed him on his way. "Be quick. Be careful. And don't even think to touch the bow he keeps there," she threw on. Worried for him, she monitored his determined stride until the rattler buttons adorning his turban vanished in the masses.

She turned to Big Voice. "Stay with me?" Outright orders she would save for someone who better received them. One wouldn't know it by the multiplying nose wrinkles, but Big Voice didn't disappoint. At his jerked nod, she gripped his elbow. "When we pass the elders' booth, will you fetch Old Wild Dog's footrest?"

"I will, Pretty Wolf."

She took off again and went the opposite direction in the four-booth square. The people split before her, Bluecoats the same. Perhaps they saw the death written on her face and were wise to their distance. She swung by the elders' booth and slowed for Big Voice, who leaped like a buck up the tiers for the stool.

"Halt." Fingers bit into her arm. Midnight blue flashed at the side of her vision.

She let the soldier twist her about, gaze swiping over the rifle held low at his side, then over the red plume rising from his conical hat.

His shrewd gaze tracked Big Voice's scamper up and across the tiers. "You there!"

"Let me and my man do what we will, Sergeant." Her English, flawless.

The sergeant's head jutted back, sea-gray eyes mapping her features.

She stared straight into those confused orbs, voice unequivocal, strong to rise above the noise. "The People will listen to me. I can calm them."

On a grunt, his chin fell, his lower lip making an appearance from under a long, droopy mustache. "You even Indian, Miss?"

"I am Wolf, and I protect my own." She jerked, and he freed her. Snapping her fingers at Big Voice to follow, she proceeded to the square's center. To the fire.

Bluecoats were known to cast water on it—the height of disrespect—to quench a talwa's fight, to declare *you are no more*. That would not happen here. The Defiance had carried it with them from Alabama Town all those winters before, to Holy Ground, through the war, through every wilderness flight since. They would carry it on from here if Pretty Wolf had to make tinder of herself to rekindle the coals.

"Pretty Wolf!" a woman cried. "Pretty Wolf has come!"

The clamor rose all about, each despondent cry another boulder of responsibility on her shoulders.

"We are done for!"

"We are *not* done for," she rebuffed harshly.

The cries and pleas kept coming.

"Where is our micco?"

"The lost daughter has come!"

"What shall we do, Pretty Wolf?"

"You will calm yourselves!" Apart from that, she hadn't a clue. A long sit in a vision pit to make offerings of tobacco bundles and receive guidance of the spirits would come in rather helpful. Unfortunately, she had only the time it would take to reach the square's center.

They began to press in, grasp at her, the Rule trampled under their panicked feet. Her sleeve ripped, and Big Voice roared. "Stand back!" He cast them off, wrapped an arm around Pretty Wolf, and bullied their way to the fire.

The stool clattered to the ground. Big Voice scooped her up and planted her on it.

Screaming Buttons shoved through the bodies, white conch shell extended. "Take!"

Reaching, Big Voice nabbed it off him and thrust it at Pretty Wolf. She raised it to her lips, filled her lungs, and blasted out four short notes. *Peace.* Then one, protracted and mournful. *Come.*

A blanket falling from the sky, quiet descended and covered the square. High above, a hawk screamed a descending scale. Like a thousand pinpricks, she felt every eye of every color shift and penetrate her. In an instant, her throat was a barren waste, her tongue a bundle of cotton as she dragged it over her lips.

"Well done," Screaming Buttons said, volume discreet, but Pretty Wolf would not count her ears of corn before harvest. Instead, she calculated how long it would take for slaughter to break out should even one fractious warrior choose to attack that ring of blue.

Her warriors were bulls caged in a fighting plaza, edgy, horns swiveling in threat, and she was asking them to take the blows, to stay down. To be milk cows. It galled like acid in the gut, but she would not see a repeat of Hillabee. Refused to wade through another lake of blood.

The hot, gray breath of Fire Spirit warmed her feet, pushed itself up under her skirt and bolstered her back. *I am not extinguished*, he soothed. Screaming Buttons made himself a stanchion at her left. Big Voice, the bridge of his nose crinkled tight, took up her right.

The square continued to fill, but not a voice was heard, English or Muskogee. Only the shuffling of feet, the fussing of babies, the snuffling of noses. Her own eyes sat dry in her skull. Purposeful denial. They refused even a glance at the piteous state of the Defiance.

She rotated on her perch, using Screaming Buttons' shoulder for stability, then that of Big Voice. Skimming over heads, she cast her gaze long, to the wide-eyed stragglers and the Bluecoats hemming them in.

One of them, an officer by his fore-and-aft hat, maneuvered toward her with the lazy, sinuous moves of a panther. The masses repelled away. Claws retracted, he carried his long gun slung over his back. An umber-skinned, turbaned fellow strode in his wake, the shifty swivel of his head compensating for his brazen confidence.

Uncertain of their intent, she gave her chin a superior lift and projected her voice across the square, as clear as the conch shell blast. "A trap was laid. My own eyes are witness. The ship in the cove flies the flag of the Bluecoats." The silence tightened like buckskin stretched over a frame. Behind her, the fire cracked its encouragement. "Our micco is taken, and his Second has fled." The warrior was last seen fading into the bush going the wrong direction. For his sake, she hoped a Bluecoat cut him down. He wouldn't care for it as much if Pretty Wolf got her nails into him.

The crowd rippled, yielding a collective gasp, and from the back, a solitary wail rent the square.

Mother.

With Pretty Wolf's next inhale, a stone bloomed in her throat. Refusing it, she gulped hard and spoke over Noonday's grief. "From the north, a mighty force of our enemy has descended upon us." She waved broadly as if the crowd could not feel the ring of blue cinching them in. Three men thick on every side and increasing. "From the sea, a war vessel. We are vastly outnumbered. For reasons their own, the Spanish have chosen not to raise the hatchet. The commander has given the fort to our enemy."

An unstoppered keg, cries poured from the people. Anguish. Anger. Avowals of revenge.

Pretty Wolf's eyes smarted. She blinked frantically.

The officer interjected himself into her bubble of space before the fire, his traitorous Muskogee speaker hissing into his ear. His attention landed on her, singular and acute, like a curled finger hovering over a trigger. And still, no weapon occupied his hand.

He watched her, waited.

Beneath filmy veils of cloud cover, she raised her arm high, signaling quiet, and sustained it until the fire's voice could once again be heard. "Our long and bloody road has reached its end. Today, we lay down the club and the war paint, and we take up our courage and our pride."

Her voice built. Louder, fiercer, almost animal in its ruggedness. "We will wield them mercilessly, slaying fear and hatred," she bellowed, "until even our great foe cannot deny we are a stalwart, unconquerable people. Wakulla, hear me. Our sacred fire is yet lit. Our hearts yet earnestly throb within us." She pounded her chest, then paused for a firmer grasp on their hearing. "We have finished our fight, my beloved people, but we are not *finished*!"

No White Stick peacemaker's speech, her words spread like wildfire, igniting eyes and wicking up tears. Backbones straightened and heads nodded. The accompanying murmurs rose with just the right amount of volume and resolve.

"Please, Miss, allow me." At the corner of her eye, the officer shifted forward, palm up as if to help her down, relieve her of duty. She veered around to address the other half of the square. "In the absence of Micco Crazy Medicine, I offer myself as mouthpiece, emissary of the People with Yatika Big Voice as adviser. Do any object?"

Apart from Big Voice's stupefied chuff, silence greeted the proposition. Until it didn't.

"Come now!" came a scoffing cry. "Am I the only warrior with brain enough to see we'd be fools to send the micco's youngest child into a battle of tongues with the Sharp Knife?"

Pretty Wolf scanned until— There. Near the elders' booth. Her eyes sharpened on the featherless head. Her dear brother-by-marriage.

Disturbed murmurings surged across the square. Agreement, disapproval. Impossible to know, but it was all the encouragement Kills Many needed to continue. "The girl Pretty Wolf is so soon out of her spring years she still plaits her hair. She hasn't even a proper husband! My people, let us be reasonable. What experience, what *success* can she possibly have against our fiercest enemy?"

"Stay that lizard tongue, wretched husband of my eldest!" Noonday blazed a path through the throng, face distorted with a mother's wrath. "All here know well that Pretty Wolf holds a marriage contract with our esteemed Iron Wood, and if you had not stomped off yesterday like a petulant child, you would have seen me join her in marriage with her faithful slave Strong Bear. My daughter has not one husband but *two*! What other woman among us can boast the same?"

Boast? This was no boast. It was a falsehood! A mother's grand delusion.

"Close that stupid mouth, woman," Big Voice whispered. It took his quick yank on her skirt to realize he meant *her*.

Molars clicking together hard, she hissed back, "That isn't what happened. Strong Bear is not—"

"Psht! A worry for another day. Let her finish."

As he said, her mother's impassioned speech was still shooting out of her. "…because none will deny that no other is better groomed for the role than she. Has she not spent many moons studying, rehearsing even, to stand moccasin to oot with white men of power?"

Groomed. Willing. Terrified.

When Noonday challenged them again for protests, none were given. Save for Kills Many who clomped up the tiers of the elders' booth and disappeared into a shadowed corner.

Petulant child, indeed.

"So it shall be," Noonday said in conclusion. "Until the clan mothers proclaim otherwise. **A'ho**."

"A'ho," was the automatic response. Neither emphatic nor enthusiastic. A reserved acceptance.

No one moved. All faces pointed at her expectantly.

Sweat ran between her shoulder blades and breasts, and the fire could not be blamed for all of it. Numbness crept into her hands.

Big Voice leaned close. "My first piece of advice, Pretty Wolf—they need more than an emissary. Give them a miccohokti."

Her throat vibrated with a restrained growl. She'd rather give them her father! Her beaten, bloodied father.

"Quickly, woman." Screaming Buttons spoke low through stiff lips. "Or surrender the stand to that blue vermin behind you."

The ring weighed heavily on her finger, its etched silver biting into the bones of her fist. Exactly as it had when she'd clutched her dagger and envisioned it buried in Old Sharp Knife's eye.

But her dagger was tossed away. Her father captured. Her cause destroyed.

And Old Sharp Knife still had two good eyes with which to sneer at his latest conquest. With which to recognize her. What was it Korsan said? *"You do realize when the White Devil comes, he will have double reason to slaughter your family. Is it not enough that he lusts after your father's neck? No, no. You must offer him yours as well."*

She should assign another. But who besides herself? *Who?* And if herself, then *how*? By the spirit of the earth, she did not know.

Breaths sawing in and out of her nose, she blinked through the smoke and heat distorting the air. If she could just clear her vision, see the path ahead, make it lie down neat and certain and safe before them...

Path Maker... Wasn't that what Strong Bear called his god-man? *Path Maker, I call on you*, she inwardly cried, envisioning her prayer rising on the smoke. *Find me here. See me. Open the way, so I might lead these, your red children, righteously according to the Ancient Words. In all love and balance. To the still waters you promise.*

"Well," Big Voice broke into her supplication. "What do you wait for, Miccohokti? The Bluecoats grow restless."

Inhaling a stuttery breath, Pretty Wolf shook out her arms and instilled command in her voice. "Mothers! Autumn women and fledging braves! Gather your little ones and your elders and shelter in your compounds until you are released." She circled on the stool, stopping when her gaze aligned with the officer's. If he wished to halt her, he should do so now.

The translator mumbled his English rendition, and the Bluecoat's thin mouth arranged itself into the barest of upturns.

At the slight lowering of his chin, Pretty Wolf proceeded. "Warriors! Pile your weapons by the cookhouse, then return to me for instruction. Do this now."

Finding Pretty Wolf

When no one moved to obey, the officer made a vague gesture toward her feet. "Shall I give it a go?" Rifle strap crossing his chest, he stood heedless of his own safety. Or perhaps trusting her to secure it.

"Give him the stand." The speaker barked the needless translation, far too eager with the seed-fluff power he'd been granted.

Teeth gritted, she measured the distance between herself and him and wondered if his costly silver nose ring was outside the reach of her sidekick. Scrapping that bit of fantasy, she stepped off and thanked the spirits when her knees held.

The officer took her place, boosting himself long enough to holler, "Open a path, men! The warriors have been instructed to place their weapons in a designated spot and return. Do not interfere. Do not provoke them! Let the women, children, and elderly exit where they will. No hand is to be laid upon their persons, or you answer to me!" Shaven cheeks rosy with heat, he hopped back down, tugged the bottom of his coat, and clasped his hands at the small of his back. He smiled at her. "That should do it."

Indeed, the soldiers parted, and the square began to clear. Starting at the outer edges, the count thinned. The children were carted off to safety, their small noises dimming then winking out. The Bluecoats milled about the edges, but from Pretty Wolf's vantage, she saw none trailing the helpless ones.

Her shoulders began to lighten, her airways to loosen. Relaxing back down her throat, her heart settled into a more regular tempo. The closest to sensible it had come since those warning shots out on the water.

Not much of a reprieve, since other frantic thoughts were swooping in to abscond with her. About her father, what they might do to him. About Strong Bear, where he might be. About Iron Wood, how he might evade capture. And Birdie and Shem and, spirits help her, even Korsan. If they uncovered his past, would they execute him? Or was it only the British who stretched a pirate's neck?

Screaming Buttons—perhaps noticing the slight tremble of her lower lip—stole her hand and hid it in the shelter of her skirt folds for a brief squeeze.

The officer, a fine coating of perspiration on his freckled face, moved a cooler distance from the fire. The droopy-whiskered sergeant and the white-feathered translator stuck like lint to his uniform. They stood unspeaking, only listening to the clatter of musket falling on musket and observing the humble shuffle of the defeated.

To a warrior, they came back to her, not dignifying the Bluecoats' presence, though every man paused before her to pound a fist to his heart. In respect. In sympathy. In loyalty. She couldn't be sure, but each gesture did its work. Further engraved the small, wistful smile sitting on her lips. Reassured that they would survive. They would overcome.

One following another, they came. Twenty-five, eight-three, she counted. None with the face she most longed to see.

One hundred twenty-two all tallied. Such meager, pathetic numbers when stood beside Old Sharp Knife's powerful army. But who could measure the strength of a heart, of one's courage and resilience? If such were possible, there would be no measure. No comparison.

In orderly fashion, the warriors congregated according to feather and rank—Winter Hawk and his herd of braves cloistered like buffalo calves in their center. Gathered off to the side, they fastened their eyes upon her.

Something tapped her elbow, and her heart gave a small upbeat. When she looked to find Screaming Buttons on her left peering down, a water gourd on offer, disappointment slammed her. Why her mind had leaped first to Strong Bear, she couldn't reckon. Neither could she stop the unease rushing in.

Kit, Kit, Kit.

Screaming Buttons' lips moved, but the loud internal worrying fogged her hearing.

She shook her head. "What?"

"Drink, Miccohokti," he blared, his use of the title too liberal, too assuming, and far too public.

She scowled at the gourd. She would *not* indulge her thirst while her warriors were being rounded up to—

Her gaze snagged on the tiny, impish crinkles around Screaming Buttons' eyes, then darted to the two men currently paused before her. They stared at her, unblinking before lowering their heads for a murmured, "Miccohokti."

Too late. The appointment to talwa leader had caught. Without being cleared with the clan mothers. Same as her supposed binding to Strong Bear. But this was not the time to reverse them. Ceding a gracious nod, she brushed off the offer and cut her volume low. "Slick as a snake, you are, Buttons. Almost as slick as my mother."

"Maddo, Miccohokti."

Finding Pretty Wolf

Pinned now with her new title, like it or not, she raked the crowd for a certain face. When the last man had joined the formation, she gave in to selfishness and withdrew a space from their captors. "Have any here seen Strong Bear?" Her voice kinked hideously on his name, and she inwardly grimaced. In all her losses and speeches that day, this was where she broke? Shame flushed through her, her hot cheeks small payment for his whereabouts.

When none answered, she cleared her throat. "Anyone?"

"No, Miccohokti."

She didn't catch who spoke, but it was just as well because the officer's gaze was scorching the rear of her head. The urge to scour the talwa for Strong Bear came over her with tidal force, but she raised her head above it. She faced the Bluecoat, English on her tongue. "Thank you, sir, for your restraint and patience."

The officer startled, the tassels on his shoulders visibly jostling. He blinked three times fast, then yanked again at the bottom of his coat and dipped into a crisp bow. "Captain Justin Telly in your debt, Miss... My pardon. Your name, if I may be so bold?"

"*Bold,* sir, is invading and overrunning a village," she said sweetly. "As is rounding up its innocents like cattle. How unfortunate for us you did not seek permission for *that.*" To the crimson splotching his cheeks, she performed a neat, if shallow, curtsy. "Pretty Wolf Francis, your spoils of war." Although gratified at this second blow of shock widening his eyes, she maintained a neutral demeanor.

"Francis, you say?" He flattened an astounded palm against his chest. "As in—?"

"Josiah Francis, yes. Chief of Wakulla. My father."

Iron Wood would be livid she'd given away her identity, but this she-wolf would be a pelt around Jackson's shoulders before she denied her heritage. Besides, would it have stayed hidden long? The Bluecoat medicine maker named Buck might not reveal her family ties, if he was feeling generous, but eventually, the connection would come to light.

The folds of Telly's mouth kicked up in an aggravatingly jolly grin. "That explains a great deal. Your command of English, your composure."

My urge to slice you down where you stand.

A dwindling urge, truth told. Captain Telly had taken the walk of the fearless—unarmed through the ranks of his enemy—and he formed all his words with the quiet restraint of a White Stick elder. In another place, she might like him. In *this* place, she could at least respect him.

She manipulated her face into what she hoped was a fair representation of goodwill. "We are yours to command, Captain Justin Telly. What instruction shall I give my warriors?"

"Miss Francis." His tone warmed with unassuming kindness as he bowed his head again. "Your name and your beauty precede you. Neither were exaggerated. Please, allow me to extend my gratitude for your intervention here. Your judicious actions have surely prevented much bloodshed."

"If only I could say the same was afforded my father." The goodwill was slipping off her face. She buoyed it with a purse of the lips. "My warriors, sir?"

Captain Telly shifted as though he suddenly had a pebble in his boot. "Right. Pointless blather has never been my partiality either," he said on a short, stuttered laugh. He angled toward the body of warriors, every black eye pointed back. "I require assurance the village will remain docile. Toward that end, six warriors of your choosing shall be taken prisoner. The rest will proceed directly to their dwellings. Excepting yourself, as I understand you are to be emissary?"

"That is correct, sir."

"The general will be most delighted to receive—"

A dull thump cut him off. An arrow shaft. Buried in the side of his neck. Belatedly, her ears registered its faint incoming whistle.

Telly jolted and gurgled. His eyes flared and fixed to her with pleading horror. Red sprayed from his lips. The hot spatters pelted her face and neck.

Stunned, she batted blood-heavy lashes.

The sergeant swore and crashed to a knee. "Hostiles! Take cover!"

Bluecoats shouted. Scrambled. Like falling hail, myriad rifle cocks *click-click-click*ed.

Pretty Wolf's blood ran cold.

Telly blubbered, scrabbled at his torn throat. Panic flamed across his face as his fingers circled the embedded shaft. And yanked.

Before Pretty Wolf could cry "No!" the arrow was out. It clattered at their feet. She lurched forward and smacked her palm over the jagged hole. A torrent of warm, sticky red gushed around the seams, but her frantic eyes belonged only to her scattering warriors. "Down, down!" Salty fluid coated her shouting tongue. "On your faces, now!"

They dropped where they stood.

A shielding body slapped against hers from behind. Arms enwrapped her. Rattler buttons sang in her ear.

Gasping, drowning on his own fluids, Telly buckled.

Pretty Wolf lost her hold on the slippery wound but managed to loop him under the arms. She sagged with him to the ground, and Screaming Buttons stuck to her back like a sweaty shirt. She landed on one hip, crying, "Buttons, help!" as Telly's unbalanced bulk began tipping her to the side.

"I have you!" He thrust an arm around her and under the captain, adding to her strength. With the other, he upheld her in the awkward pose—legs bent beneath her, Telly seated on her lap, the entirety of his top half dead weight in their arms.

"The shooter?" Screaming Buttons breathed hard down her neck.

She plastered a hand to Telly's neck—little good it would do—and sliced her gaze in the direction of the arrow's flight. "Micco's booth. Top tier." The only possible site for this shot. And there was only one possible shooter.

Spirits slay that man!

"I see no one." Screaming Buttons' report matched her own.

Bluecoats swarmed, searching, several now stationed protectively around their superior, but Pretty Wolf suspected no more arrows would fly. The rogue warrior had made his point. All she could do was beg every spirit for the Bluecoats to show reason and not retaliate. Too viciously.

So far, their rifles, though at the ready and sweeping, remained silent.

The sergeant lowered to a crouch before them. Whiskers in full droop, he settled a hand on Telly's shoulder and met her eyes.

Though he surely could see the situation for himself, she gave a tiny shake of the head.

He returned a somber, agreeing nod.

She strained at Telly's weight. "Help me. Make him comfortable." They maneuvered the captain until his neck rested in the crook of her elbow.

Face a sheet of red-bespattered white, Telly worked his jaw, but his voice was a ruin. Shallow, liquid gasps fluttered his chest. His spirit journey hovered but breaths away.

"Hold on to your courage, Justin Telly," she urged.

His erratic eyes found hers and went soft. Resigned. Dimming. Hers washed and blurred. Dripping.

Perhaps he wore a blue coat. Perhaps his skin was pale, and his rifle balls were smelted with prayers to obliterate the Defiance, but he'd been gravely wronged. Shot on the sly by a people who'd promised surrender. A dastardly, cowardly act.

With sticky, dirt-gritted fingers, she stroked Telly's cheek, his hair, one last comfort. She sniffed to catch a drip in her nose. "Have you a woman at home, Captain?"

His lashes fluttered in what must have been a yes.

The sergeant supplied, "Flora."

"Flora." Pretty Wolf smiled at Telly and caught the tear tracking from the corner of his eye. "A beautiful name, yes? Put Flora's face in your mind now. She is holding you here, loving you. She prays you onto your new journey."

His bloody mouth wobbled, its attempt at a smile. Vision no longer tracking, he eased his head to the side. Blood poured over his teeth and onto her sleeve.

"How bravely you meet death, Justin Telly. Let your spirit free. But first, hear my vow: I will avenge this wrong. Do you understand me? I *will* avenge you." The words had no sooner finished cramping her throat than he went limp, the light leaving his green eyes.

Screaming Buttons squeezed her waist, and her lungs emptied. Body aching in every joint and sinew, she lifted damp, sticky lashes to find the sergeant staring at her intently, a deep notch sitting between his eyebrows. Some disturbing emotion brewed in the man, but she hadn't the energy to dissect it. "Your name."

Mustache undulating, he assessed her a moment longer. "Jerome Barkton."

"Take him, Sergeant Barkton."

Barkton grunted what she guessed to be some version of "yes, ma'am," then relieved her of Telly's body.

Groaning, she allowed Screaming Buttons to haul her up. His frown stretched the full width of his narrow face.

Big Voice produced a cloth, took her chin in a gentle grasp, and began wiping her mouth and chin of gore. "What do you need, Miccohokti?"

A pained sigh shivered out of her. What did she *not* need? "Fresh clothes. A message sent to my mother assuring her I am well. Someone to inquire after Iron Wood. Quietly. Birdie and Shem too."

Big Voice's ministrations moved along her jaw now. She let him and sought Screaming Buttons' eyes. There, she found his typical unquestioning loyalty. "And I need a Second."

His eyes grew. "What of your husband?"

"My…" Waving that off, she shook her head. "Strong Bear is not—"

"Enough." Big Voice shoved her hand back down. "You are Miccohokti. Buttons is Second. Strong Bear is your husband." When she opened her mouth to protest, he scrubbed at it with his cloth. "Quiet, woman. It is as it must be."

Chapter 32

Clothes stiff with dried blood, Pretty Wolf paced. From Big Voice sitting on the cot's edge, forearms on thighs, to Screaming Buttons installed before the barred door, arms knotted over his chest.

Four strides there, four back. The sacred number, that of balance and equality.

But there was nothing sacred or balanced or equal in what was transpiring in Spanish Florida. In Fort San Marcos. In that bleak sleeping chamber.

Four cold stone walls.

Four empty vessels—one pitcher, one basin, two cups.

Fours restless hours waiting for an audience with Old Sharp Knife.

Warm in her palm, Strong Bear's pocket clock ticked in time with her strides. The impulse struck her again to flip open its lid for another read of its gold blades. The long one couldn't have moved for than a space or two since last she checked. She clamped her fingers over the instrument, knuckles tight with grime.

"You will have to listen to the white chief, Pretty Wolf, truly listen," Big Voice droned, cramming a lifetime of yatika training into this short period. "Understand him. His desires and fears, his objectives and concerns. For he will not see through your eyes until he believes that you see through his. You must—"

"Bind my tongue. Do nothing rash," she said, tone drab. "You are beginning to sound like Iron Wood." The mention of him shot tingles of alarm down her limbs. She shook them out.

His mare was fleet of foot. He had to have gotten clear well before the Bluecoats appeared, and they would be preoccupied in securing Wakulla and the fort. The soldiers wouldn't expand their reach for at least a day. Plenty of time for Iron Wood to hide or burn anything condemning. Then run.

Spirits, please, may he run.

Above the clamor of courtyard activity came the scrape-and-clunk of the bar being removed from outside the door. Screaming Buttons faced it just as it swung out. Arms still crossed, he stared down at a shorter blue-clad form.

"Sergeant Barkton here for Miss Francis." His voice sounded gruff as if rarely used. Without uttering a word, the sergeant had escorted them to San Marcos, through the fort, and straight into this room. "The general calls. Just her."

Pretty Wolf touched Screaming Buttons on the back. "Maddo, brother. I'm summoned. Only myself." When he reluctantly stepped aside, she met Barkton's unreadable gaze. Arms folded before her, she planted her feet. "I must insist on water for my men. Enough to drink and wash up. All of them." The chosen six had been herded toward an outlying building before Pretty Wolf and her small party crossed the mote into the stone fortification.

Barkton jerked his chin at someone outside her view, and footfalls sounded as the unspoken order was carried out. He angled his body to indicate she should exit and raised a brow at her.

"Shall we, Sergeant?" Sliding the timepiece into its pouch, she strode into the sunlight that slashed down from the west. Its golden beams cut across the square courtyard and along the high wall opposite her chamber, setting aglow the stones' faded whitewash.

The door slammed behind her, and two soldiers took up sentry at her sides. Barkton bypassed them all and marched through the courtyard's busy center. The hustle and hum of an army going about its business came to a gradual stop as they noted her presence.

Her pulse went jagged.

This was not just any army. It was Old Sharp Knife's.

The body of men she'd spent a lifetime fleeing. Those who hunted her by day behind their cannons and by night behind her closed lids.

She stretched her backbone to its full length, adhered her gaze to the leather straps crisscrossing Barkton's back, and followed his trail of raised dust.

He led her to another chamber, this one three times the size. A long, paper-strewn table sat in the room's center. Six chairs ran its sides, an additional one on each end. The wrought iron fixture hanging above it gave the place a cozy glow that made her want to hurl something at it. Knock it into a violent swing and spill wax onto the parchments below.

A dark wood side table traced the left wall with rows of glasses and bottles with amber liquid lining its polished surface. They glinted in the candlelight. As did the self-satisfied smile of the man poised before them.

Finding Pretty Wolf

At their first meeting, she'd thought their great foe to be exceedingly tall. In the years since, she had attributed that perception to her back-in-the-mud position. She saw now that her first impression had not been far off the mark. The general's columnar height was exceeding indeed, rivaling that of Tall Bull. His musculature was a pale match, but what he lacked in width he made up for in austerity.

She'd always remembered Old Sharp Knife in the red shades of blood and paint and rage. Now, she saw him in gold, blue, and white. Gold buttons, trimmings, waist sash, tasseled shoulder ornaments. The ring on the large-knuckled hand that manacled a liquor glass. Blue metals and irises. Blue veins snaking under his aging skin. Impeccable white sleeve cuffs and ruffled cravat. And white hair—only the short waves swept forward over his brow. The rest, dark and cropped close to the skull.

All this underscored by black. Black boots and uniform coat. Black look. Black heart.

This was not Old Sharp Knife of Horse's Flat Foot. This was General Andrew Jackson.

Invader. Cunning deceiver. Ruthless conqueror.

Destroyer of dreams. Master of her father's shackles.

Fury tore across her skin. Above scorched cheeks, her eyes burned dry, and in that moment, she didn't care if he recognized her. Didn't care if the last breath she took was the one before she cracked his neck.

If only she'd saved her father's dagger for now, for *this*. She'd drive it between his ribs and thank the spirits her refugee life had served some purpose.

By the interest lighting Jackson up, he saw it, her fury, her fight for control.

Breathe, woman! Control, control.

In. Out. Four breaths.

Balance.

Showing him every fingerbreadth of her substantial height, she held herself with as much dignity as her deplorable, humiliating state allowed and met his blue gaze head-on.

Eyes so like Iron Wood's. Yet so vastly different. Where her beloved's pale blues were a spring sky, the petal of a cornflower, the lapping waves of the cove, Jackson's were ice and frost and a disorienting mist. Where Iron

Wood's lashes were thick and black and fanned gently, the general's were thin and colorless, blunt and unblinking.

For unending, unspeaking moments, those ice-chip eyes passed scrutiny over her, taking in every detail—ratted braid, blood-darkened clothes, unshod feet. Especially her feet. His smile showed teeth. "Well done, Sergeant. Help yourself to a tumbler. The island rum is sweet and fiery. Much like our guest, I hear."

"I'll pass, sir."

"Fine." Jackson waved his glass. "Come in. Close the door. We're in want of a chaperon."

Behind her, the door snicked. Booted soles rasped against the planked floor. One pace, two. They fell silent at her back. Barkton's breathing sounded deep and regular, irrationally safe, and Pretty Wolf resisted the urge to ease closer to him.

She was Wolf. She didn't recoil. Not even from a hissing viper.

This viper tipped his head, his eyes honing on her, circling her features. She kept them straight, her gaze unwavering and dagger sharp. Curiosity tightened the skin of his forehead.

Let him look, let him realize. Recall her face, her blade. Let him well consider his opponent.

"Have you found what you seek?" Miraculously, she kept her voice to courteous tenors.

"Forgive my bold perusal, but a gentleman can hardly be blamed for misplacing his manners now and again when he's subjected so routinely to savages." Glass raised to his thin mouth, he took a long, deliberate sip of the wicked drink. The flagrant study of her continued from over its rim.

If he wanted savagery from her, he would be disappointed. She'd sealed all that bone-blazing fury deep in her marrow, stored it up for when it would count most. For now, he'd receive only the stiff curve of her lips. "Your men *could* use a bath and shave. They reek of sea voyage and illegal invasion."

Surprise opened his face wide. He advanced to stand before her and furnished a tight bow, his coattails barely rustling with the gesture. "General Andrew Jackson."

She extended her filthy hand, palm down. "Pretty Wolf Francis, princess of Wakulla."

Fist to his mouth, as though to conceal a smile, he said, "Princess?"

More or less. Toño would confirm the more, while Miccohokti was less princess than chieftainess.

She arched a brow at him.

After a protracted moment in which he bestowed a skeptical look on her blood-encrusted knuckles, he slipped his fingers lightly under hers. "A true pleasure, Princess Pretty Wolf." He bowed and the gush of his breath over her skin felt too warm, too human, his smile too genuine.

She plucked her hand away before he made contact.

Coming up, he murmured, "I am at your service."

"Good." Finding her stride, Pretty Wolf looked off, unimpressed, and meandered past him to run a finger along the side table's glossed rim. "Because there are a few alarming matters you may rectify for me."

"I expected as much." Casually, he indicated the table. "May I offer you tea first?"

Eyes tight on him, she wheezed out a dry laugh. "Next, you will want me to pull out the calumet and tobacco and smoke friendship with you."

"Why, yes, I will."

"As long as the rivers run, that will never happen."

Chuckling, he wrangled a cork from a tall dark green bottle. "Careful, Princess. You're sounding rather like your father." He poured a few splashes into a glass and held it out.

"Thank you, sir." She flashed her Wolf's teeth and accepted the drink.

"You enjoyed an eventful morning, I understand. My naval officers report your presence in the cove." He paused to watch her take a sniff of the poison. Its fumes and decay-sweet aroma wrinkled her nose. "Please, permit me to apologize on behalf of my exuberant seamen and express how relieved I am you did not come to harm. The *civilized* do not put women and children in their sights." Disdain burnished the eyes that swung up to her.

Never mind understanding the man's desires and fears. If he alluded to savagery one more time, she would learn how much force was required to crack a glass over his skull.

The general blinked his stubby, gray lashes at her white-fingered grip on her cup. "My compliments, Miss Francis, for aiding in a swift and bloodless appropriation of the Red Stick village. Rather, I should say…*mostly* bloodless." He paused for a pointed glance at her stained clothes, but Pretty Wolf was not about to offer further apologies. Not to him. "Also, there's been a report from Sergeant…" He glanced to the stone-faced soldier by the door.

"Barkton," she filled in, prompting a twitch of the whiskers from the man himself and the hike of one wiry brow from his chief.

"Yes." Jackson circled a lazy finger in the sergeant's direction. "He reports you comforted Captain Telly in his last moments. That you swore reprisal, even, on his murderer."

With a recalcitrant look, she said, "A woman's vows of vengeance are intimate to her and not a matter for discussion." This topic must go away. Before Jackson got ideas of exacting his own vengeance. On one of her six in confinement.

Choosing them had been no painless task. If she'd been confident they would be treated humanely and released in good time, she would have sent elders and reserved her fittest men to care for the innocents. Instead, she'd chosen the most robust and prayed they wouldn't emerge from their cells as skeletons. The People desperately needed its strong men for whatever humiliation Old Sharp Knife plotted for them in that cunning, gray head of his.

She quickly redirected. "What of my offer to stand as liaison to my village?"

"I accept."

"Very well." She placed her untouched glass on the table and laced her fingers before her. "We shall begin with my father. Where have you put him?"

"Behind lock and key. Until five o'clock this evening."

"And at five o'clock?" Her thoughts strayed to the instrument sitting on her hip. Last she'd looked, it read 3:37.

Jackson tipped back his head, downed his rum, and thunked his glass down beside hers. "His execution."

Her shoulders jerked like a released bowstring. The man, the room, the feel of her legs dissolved to a blur. She swayed, ears ringing with *execution*.

Something gripped her elbow. Her head turned.

Sergeant Barkton. Worry gathered under the scraggly thatch brushing his brows.

She blinked at him, aware but not caring that Old Sharp Knife spoke. Thinking only that she should not be so stunned. That she was a proper child to have entertained the belief there might have been another outcome. Thinking next that she would not degrade herself by begging. A sly creature of the mud, Jackson had his snapping turtle jaws locked onto his most treasured prey. Short of a head severing, he would not let go.

Imaginings flickered through her mind: Jackson without a head. Jackson with a slit throat. Jackson with a dagger hilt for an eye.

Pretty Wolf refocused to find her gaze had drifted to the general's sword belt. Would it be her *father* missing a head that day? Beheading. Firing squad. The typical methods of exterminating a high-ranking enemy.

"My dear lady," Jackson said, tones placating. "You are pale. Please, get off your feet." A chair screeched across the floor.

She stared at it. "Has…" Bitterness erupted on the back of her tongue, and she swallowed convulsively. Tried again. Prayed the tremble from her voice. "Has the trial already been held?" Was that what had filled those four hours? His trial?

"Have a seat, now." The general's touch at her other elbow snapped her spirit back into place.

She gnashed her teeth and contorted away. "His *trial*, sir."

He sidestepped, something approaching hatred creeping into his eyes and grinding in his voice. "Rabid dogs do not receive trials. They are exterminated. Post haste."

Done with pretense and diplomacy, she let inner violence rankle in her body. Fists. Iron jaw. The breath that wheezed through her bared teeth.

Do not be rash, do not be rash!

"Daughters should never be subjected to such tragedy," he said. "But there's no help for it. Francis has long reigned terror over the region, bloodying soldier and settler alike. Today, that comes to a swift and just end." Satisfaction recast Jackson's features.

That alone plugged the flow of her rage. She bound up her lungs to slow her pounding heart, then loosened her hands and exhaled a lengthy breath, her self-restraint as fragile as a splinter. "I demand to see him."

Not meeting her lanced gaze, Jackson strode to the sideboard and poured himself another portion of drink. The stream tinkled against the glass. "Demands are hardly necessary, Miss Francis. Naturally, you may visit the prisoner." His icy blues swiveled from the rum to the sergeant. "Five minutes."

Chapter 33

The prison house was a squat building topped by red tiles and situated along the main thoroughfare of San Marcos village. To its left, the Black Robe's worship lodge. To its right, the metalsmith's shop, heat and clamor radiating from its open-air workspace.

Strong Bear surged to the top of Pretty Wolf's mind. She banished him, choosing instead to give the Black Robe a stony glare.

Bowing his head in pious repose, he lifted the wooden cross hanging about his neck and held it upright before him as he floated toward her. "Beg your heathen sire to repent, *mi hija,* before his soul is condemned to eternal flame."

"Back, priest." Barkton bodily blocked him, the command gritty and ominous.

"Thank you, Sergeant." Pretty Wolf's stride didn't falter, and her gaze didn't fall from Noonday.

Her mother slouched—frame and face—on a bench outside the prison house. She stared at nothing as the wind snatched determinedly at her time-thinned blouse. Pretty Wolf sank to her knees before her and collected her cold hand. "A blanket for my mother, Sergeant."

There came a scurry of murmurs and boots, but Pretty Wolf paid them no heed. Neither did her mother, who gave Pretty Wolf the same treatment.

Pretty Wolf looked within herself, felt about for pity and grief and the weakness that shook her jaw, then she wrangled them all into a far, far corner. There she left them, buried under a barbed mound of anger, and withdrew. Plate by iron plate, she cloaked herself in a shield until she felt nothing but those barbs. Saw nothing but the burden of duty.

To clan, to talwa. To her men.

Her teeth locked down. Her hands steadied. She used one to stroke Noonday's dry cheek. Stretching up, she laid a soft kiss on it. "You have seen Father?"

Noonday's lashes shivered closed. "No." The word was more wind than voice.

Pretty Wolf stroked again, detesting the sight of her strong mother fractured in this way. "I go to him now. Shall I tell him something from you?" She waited five breaths, ten, then took her mother's blank-faced silence as answer and pushed to her feet. "Luis." She addressed the Spanish soldier guarding the door. *"Llévame a mi padre."*

"Si, señorita." The man tossed Barkton a trade blanket and led the way inside.

"Stay with her." With a touch to Barkton's arm, she left Noonday to his care and entered the building.

The immediate area appeared to be a guard station. A cursory appraisal revealed a scratched table, two chairs, and a rack of muskets. Rings of keys hung on pegs along one wall. The guard's keys jangled as he worked one into a metal door on her right. A *clack-clack*. The squeal of hinges. Swinging open, the door created wind that carried malodorous fumes. Mold, excrement, decay.

Knuckles pressed to her nose, Pretty Wolf gave a little cough. *This* was where her father was spending his last hours? Her molars scraped, challenging the hinges with their squeak.

The guard stepped in, and as her vision adjusted to the dark interior, she took in the block of cells, five in each row divided by a corridor. Thick iron bars caged the front of each compartment.

"Pretty Wolf!"

Her pulse leaped. She knew that voice, spun to it. Found the crooked nose and thick-set eyes it belonged to.

Strong Bear stood at the nearest cell's bars, one broad hand wrapped around a rail, the other reaching through.

"Kit!" Her feet moved, and suddenly, she was pressed to his prison, the bars digging into her cheekbone and chest. One arm thrust itself through to hook him around the ribs.

His fingers snagged in the hair at her nape, and his breath puffed heat over her forehead. "There is blood! You are covered in—"

"Not mine."

His lungs released another gust. "Jesus help me, I feared for you."

"I am here, Strong Bear."

He clutched her harder, and she didn't protest. "And *I* am here."

No great puzzle how that had come to be. The Bluecoats must have mistaken him for a member of the Defiance. Pretty Wolf would set them straight. "Give me the day. I'll see you are freed."

"Fine. But we must speak." Urgency drove the insistence. "Soon. You and me and—"

"Polly?"

For the second time, her gaze then her body yanked toward a familiar voice. This time, no relief accompanied it. Only aching dread. Those inner barbs rotated within her and gouged deep. She unpeeled from Strong Bear.

"Iron Wood," she breathed, taking in his broken lip and torn shirt, the spots of blood and dirt marring its usually pristine white. "How...?"

He gripped the bars of the next cell down. Manacles hugged his wrists, a chain swinging heavily between them. His rounded eyes teemed with consternation. "You were supposed to be gone."

"As were you!" She grabbed both his hands, barely able to speak for the emotion welling in her throat. His gaze hooked to hers and reflected all their past, every tenderness and pain, every shared and shattered dream. Was it too late to make repairs?

No. Absolutely not.

He would be freed. They would go back to the days of Holy Ground when she first saw him, first loved him. They would begin anew.

But what did this mean, him being here? Had the Bluecoats discovered the store already? Had they caught him burning documents? Hiding weapons? The questions piled up on her tongue, but all she could get out was, "My father!"

Face crumpling, Iron Wood caressed her hair, scalp to braid tip. "Yes, dear heart. I know. It's simply barbaric. I am so very sorry. Go to him, love." He loosed her with a gentle shove. "We'll talk later."

"Yes. All right. Later." Later, she would have her answers. And her men. If it took falling on her face before Old Sharp Knife, she *would* have them.

The blue of Iron Wood's thickly fringed eyes shone luminous and stunning in that dank place. As she walked away, Pretty Wolf clung to that light until her neck protested and she was compelled to look forward.

The soldier led her past four cells more, her six warriors trapped in them. Upon murmurs of assurance and gratitude, she brushed their fingers, then faced the end of the corridor and a final door. This one constructed of solid iron with a small, barred opening at the top.

Another key. Another crank. Then Crazy Medicine occupied her vision.

He sat at a small table, hunched over a piece of parchment, scratching a feather pen hotly over its surface. A stubby taper candle lit the windowless room. It flickered on the table, its brass stand trembling from the force of her father's furious writing.

Writing! What was this? When had he taken up with letter and ink? He was wiser than to tempt the spirits so close to his four-day journey because such were his beliefs about written language. Had always been.

"Father?" She ventured forward, fussing with her ring, twisting it dizzy.

Without glancing up, he raised a silencing finger.

Mouth ajar, she watched as he dip-dip-dipped the feather's point into the ink bottle, a woodpecker in single-minded pursuit. Black dribbled across the paper's surface as he slung the quill back into position and resumed his business.

Twist, twist. The silver was heating against her skin when she forged ahead. "Father, please. They will be back for me shortly."

"Ehi, I know!" He scribbled out a few more lines before sitting back in his chair and giving the sheet a satisfied nod. He laid down the feather and folded the parchment in half without first sprinkling it with sand or blowing it dry.

She cringed as she imagined the smears of wet ink.

Standing, he brought it to her. "For your mother. They will not let me see her."

Emotions strummed her ribs, and Pretty Wolf wasn't sure what to do with them. Scream? Cry? Bang the door in protest and demand?

Large blotches bled through to the back of the parchment. To hide the tremble in her hands, she straightened the page's uneven fold. "Since when do you know letters?" Since when did he approve the *use* of them? And why was she wasting precious seconds asking about this?

According to the proud smile appropriating her father's features, he deemed it a fine question. "The spirits timed their teachings well. Just now, they have instructed me in the markings of the English."

She stared at him. At how handsomely he'd dressed for the meeting with the supposed British sea captain—and for his own death, it would seem. At the quality frock coat, gray in color, snug against his lean build. At the fringed buckskin leggings that Noonday had toiled over in his absence. At the lines tattooed horizontally under his eyes and the ruffled cravat blossoming under his chin. At the wonder glowing in his gray eyes and the shadows huddling around their thick Indian lids.

And she loved him. For all his crazy and all his **medicine**, she did. Not in spite of, she realized. But because of.

Would the People ever find a more faithful warrior-leader? One who adhered to his beliefs and his tribe, fought for them as avidly, as fiercely as he?

They would not. And Old Sharp Knife knew it. Counted on it.

Without Crazy Medicine, the Defiance would become a plucked flower withering under the sun, for he embodied all that they were. But would he get proper recognition at the place of his execution? Certainly not.

"Un minuto mas," the guard warned through the door.

Her father crossed to her, and she convulsed with a choked sob. Just one. The rest, she smothered against his neck as he clasped her tightly to him. Her breath came in fits and stutters as she drank in his wild scent. Tobacco and sweat and forge fire. The latter she surely conjured from sweeter times. Times that would never again be. Another sob lashed her.

Clamped to her shoulders, Crazy Medicine pushed her away and showed her a stern brow. "Lift your chin and wipe your nose. You are not a child. You are Wolf, a Francis, and the daughter of prophecy. The People will be lost without you."

The prophecy, eh? At least one of them still believed in it. Soon, there would be no one. Throat an achy lump, she sniffed and nodded. "I will not fail them."

"No, you will not." Not an order. A fact.

The certainty of his statement cranked her spine erect and determined her to repay him in kind. "Crazy Medicine, legend of the Defiance," she said in tone of yatika, "you are a beacon to the People, sacred keeper of the **Old Beloved Path**, the pride of a daughter's heart. And I miss you already." On the last, her voice crackled.

In a first showing of emotion, a thin line of moisture sprouted along his lower lids as he leaned in to press trembling lips to her forehead. "My pretty little Wolf."

Eyes slipping shut, she absorbed his scent one last time, pulled it in and savored, then let it out on a whispered, "May you fly swift and straight on the spirit road, Father."

The door shrieked. Her father's arms fell away.

Turning, she left. Her toe stubbed against the dirt and cracked. She felt no pain, no grief. Her iron carapace firmly back in place.

Dead quiet pervaded the corridor. Every man stood at his bars, watching. Most likely listening. She looked at no one until she'd arrived at Iron Wood's cage.

Shiny streaks trailed his cheeks. He didn't speak, but the slow batting of his ink-dipped eyelashes was rather vocal with compassion. Spirits above, she needed him out of there.

Feeling her purpose returning to her, she thumbed at the wet on his cheekbone. "I'll free you, Iron Wood. I swear it."

She would see him absolved of any wrongdoing, guilty though he was. In certain eyes, at any rate. The Bluecoats could not, *would* not come into this territory and continue to fling their might about as if they owned the Point. The Spanish Crown would not tolerate it, much less the English. Iron Wood was a man of privilege in his country. A titled lord. She must simply remind Jackson of this.

The general already had her father. He would *not* steal Iron Wood too.

Tipping his head, he kissed her palm sweetly, but that was not hope furrowing his brow.

"Expect me back soon after…" Her voice cut off, unable to form the rest.

Iron Wood ducked his head. In sympathy, she thought, until he murmured, "You should…look at that."

Breath soughed out of her, and she became aware of the hush and of her audience. The guard stood behind her, seeming unperturbed by her detour. Her six peered discreetly through their bars, but Strong Bear leaned against his, unapologetically spying from three paces away. He jerked his chin at the missive, urging her on.

Nodding, she angled it toward the light coming from the nearest window. Stiff with too much ink, the parchment resisted opening. Or perhaps that was her. In either case, she wished she hadn't. Wished she'd touched it to the first fire she came across and spent the rest of her life wondering. Instead of knowing that in the last moments of his life, her father had lost his sanity.

From top to bottom, nothing but black, messy scrawls and scratches. Not a legitimate alphabet letter to be seen anywhere.

Pretty Wolf's hand spasmed. The other swiftly joined it to crumple the page into a tight, angry ball. Humiliation whooshed hot up her neck.

What a fitting representation of her father and his cause! What a perfect summary of their existence. Refusal to reform. Desperation to live.

Meaningless hopes. Stamped out.

It gutted her.

Strength suddenly spent, she propped a shoulder against the bars and twined her fingers with Iron Wood's.

"Noonday doesn't need a letter. She has you," he soothed.

Pretty Wolf pulled his hand through the bars and brushed her lips across his knuckles. "I love you, Iron Wood," she rasped, feeling it more in that moment than she had in many moons. Voice lowered to the barest whisper, she said, "And…I want to make things well between us. Am I…too late?"

Gladness spread across his face, lighting up his eyes. "Not a bit."

His words freed a tight band constricting her ribs, her next inhale the fullest she'd drawn in an age.

"Señorita. Ya es hora."

"He's right," Iron Wood said, his loving gaze trawling her features. "Go to your mother. Be her strength. I'll see you…after."

Pretty Wolf sighed and shut her eyes to her surroundings, to her father's fate, and prayed it all away. When she opened them again, the letter was still in her fist, and her men were still in their cages.

But Noonday…

With a last peck to Iron Wood's knuckles, Pretty Wolf pushed off the bars and ghosted down the corridor. On her way past, Strong Bear lifted his head from its weary hang. He curved her a close-lipped smile and said nothing, but she heard him all the same.

Fearless as the wolf.

Chapter 34

Lower back pressed to the bars of his cell, Strong Bear sat with knees raised, elbows resting atop them. Pervasive cold seeped through his breechcloth, the ground's unforgiving surface bruising his sit bones. Fingers forked through his hair, he thumbed massaging circles into his temples.

Crazy Medicine's haunting death song filled every crevice of the jailhouse, of the mind. Added oppressive weight to air so thickly putrid it lodged like foul sludge in Strong Bear's throat. There was no swallowing it down.

Not until the micco was dead. Strong Bear might be quick to follow.

He curled a fist to inspect his swollen, bluing knuckles. Comfort rested in the fact that the soldier's nose looked worse. Striking him had not been the most prudent choice for a distraction, but when Strong Bear realized the band of riders would overtake Pretty Wolf in her flight to the cove, self-preservation hadn't been the first thought to tear through his brain. Prudence hadn't formed enough substance to even *become* a thought—until the cell door slammed behind him.

No matter the color of a warrior's feather, there was only one outcome for violence against a Bluecoat. A stretched neck.

A growl pushed between Strong Bear's teeth. One punch to the wrong nose, and here he was, caged next door to the infamous Iron Wood.

Even in this disaster of a predicament, Bellamy had the advantage. General Jackson would not be so brazen as to execute a British lord and risk strife between their countries, especially with their precarious truce so freshly penned. Most likely, he'd be exiled. Barreled and shipped back to England. A mere *tsk-tsk*, considering he'd have Pretty Wolf on his arm, leaving Strong Bear on this side of the Great Waters. Either in the ground or alive in pieces. He might say the former was preferable, were it not for Flint waiting on that rise.

Strong Bear thudded his skull back against the bars. Once, twice. They vibrated dully but offered neither answers nor a helping of faith.

Indeed, if Path Maker could open Heaven's door for one such as himself, He could open an iron cage. And still, gloom crawled over Strong Bear like flies on putrefying flesh. The decay in this instance being his confidence in the Voice. Creator *had* said *Go*, had He not? Strong Bear had been so sure, so *convinced* that the path unfurling before him included Pretty Wolf in his arms and a lifetime of secret nighttime kisses. Had he simply been a delusional boy projecting his heart's desires onto Creator's will?

Sitting in this dank cell, the micco's death song reverberating through him, all paths of escape barred off…it appeared he was not sent to win a wife. Merely to protect. And deliver life-altering news. A task not yet complete.

If he ran out of time, what would become of her? When Strong Bear began his journey to Creator, his sorrow would be past. But Pretty Wolf's would stretch out before her, and it rent him in two.

The one consolation: Bellamy and Pretty Wolf seemed at peace. Perfectly timed reconciliation. She would be relying on him more than ever once Strong Bear's path ended.

He craned his neck for another glance at his jail mate's murky quarters. Wherever the man had put himself, it wasn't near the bars. In the hours they'd shared imprisonment, he and Strong Bear hadn't exchanged more than a nod at his initial passing. Which suited Strong Bear fine—it was not yet time to speak to the Englishman.

An invisible clock ticked frantically in his ears. He clutched his head, positive he'd go mad if he didn't soon find a way out of there. Death songs, clocks… And those three gut-twisting words.

Though it had been Strong Bear whom Pretty Wolf had clutched like a lost lover, it was Bellamy to whom she had whispered.

"*I love you…*"

She'd tacked Bellamy's name to the end, but Strong Bear severed the memory there.

It wasn't as if she'd never used them on him before, those words. But never like *that*. Muted. Hoarse. Strung with intensity. Laden with intimacy. With memory and meaning.

Strong Bear's thumbs dropped to his ears and crushed them closed, a feeble attempt to mash out the echo of it. That was *not* a sound to be taken to the gallows as a final thought.

The death song took on a wild air. Its simple melody strained the micco's upper ranges, its lyrics a brazen taunt of his adversaries. Soldiers blooded. Scalps stolen. War dances stomped in victory.

Meanwhile, Bellamy made not a sound of complaint, no plea of innocence, but Strong Bear could imagine he must fear for his freedom. Particularly if they'd found the store. In its bowels sat all the evidence needed to support Buck's riverside accusations: breaker of treaties, inciter of violence, purveyor of arms to America's enemies.

A short while ago, a Bluecoat sergeant arrived to list the charges and inform Bellamy his trial would convene the following day. Standard procedure from what Strong Bear understood. And a great deal more than Crazy Medicine had been granted.

The door leading to the guard station rattled open. Light flooded the corridor and outlined a lean, ample-shouldered figure. A tri-cornered officer's cap crowned his head. A sword rested against his thigh, and a compact bag hung low at his knee.

Squinting, Strong Bear fought the daylight piercing his pupils to make out the white man's features. When he did, a charge of shock zinged down his limbs. He scrambled to his feet, a grin already absconding with him. "Marcus Buck, old hound, you sniffed me out." Strong Bear rammed his arm through the bars until the thick of it caught against the metal.

Buck's gaze whipped to him, his eyes flashing wide an instant before his mouth outshone the glare behind him. "Didn't even know I was looking." His bag slapped the dirt before he launched across the hall and clasped Strong Bear's forearm in a firm brother's greeting. "You big dunce, you got yourself captured by the wrong party."

The chant reached a mournful crescendo, and Strong Bear's burst of joy matured into solemn gratitude. He clasped Buck close, not letting him go, his volume lowered. "Captured by both if you can believe it, brother. The Red Sticks at Hambly's. Then the Bluecoats today, outside Wakulla."

Buck shook his head, humor spraying out in crinkles around his shining eyes. "Now, *that* is a particular talent. But..." He drew the word out and paused as though to savor what came next. "You found her. Your Pretty Wolf." A spirit of admiration warmed his tone, and Strong Bear's delight almost stormed back in.

Until he remembered it might all be for naught.

Conscious of shuffling movement in the adjoining cell, Strong Bear's reply emerged as a thick-throated, "I did." Voicing the fact to an old friend made it real in a way he hadn't experienced, and wonder swelled in his chest so that he could scarcely breathe.

Why, *why* would Creator so neatly give him the woman just to take him out of This World? This could not be the end. It could *not*. Didn't Buck's arrival suggest as much? His old friend would surely do everything in his officer's power to put Strong Bear on the opposite side of these bars.

Hope, that frighteningly fragile thing, began a slow sift back through his organs.

Buck unhooked himself and stepped back to give Strong Bear a medicine maker's tight-eyed scrutiny. "While staying attached to that pelt of yours, I'm thrilled to note."

For now. Air exploded from Strong Bear in a snort. "I do prefer it where it is." In emphasis, he scratched his scalp.

Buck flicked a finger at Strong Bear's head. "Change your mind about dying the feather?"

A quiet, self-conscience chuckle floated over Strong Bear's tongue as he remembered that, for all of half an hour, he'd intended to change his feather's color. He gave it an affectionate stroke. "No more of that for me, Buck. I am White to my death." He'd given up Red about the time Polly was blown flat to her back, a lead ball embedded between her bones. Their cause had been worth every loss until that instant.

He hadn't looked back since. Not even while threatening to dye his feather. He'd intended to playact a Red Stick so he could breach Wakulla's borders. He'd be a spy. He'd find his woman. She'd adore him despite his duplicity. In the moment, it had been a stroke of brilliance. A blazing fire of a notion that his wise mentor, Totka Hadjo, had promptly put out.

As Strong Bear looked back to that riverside foolishness, he again saw himself a naïve, eager brave bouncing on his feet, too energized with confidence to stand still. How quickly his captive's march to Wakulla had hewn away that naivety. Now, two iron bars warming beneath his grip, he felt himself aged, his feet aching and planted fast to the earth, his spine weighted with cares and fears. A generous portion of them directed at Pretty Wolf.

She'd entered the jail a shocking, tattered mess. Braid a string of knots. Eyebrows, jaw, ear streaked with crusted blood. Blouse so stained he couldn't recall its proper hue. Her eyes, though, they'd sparked and flared, their blue flecks capturing every stray beam. Defiantly shooting them back at any who dared meet her furious gaze. It was those eyes and the rigid set of her shoulders that kept the air flowing in and out of Strong Bear's lungs. The only time it snagged—during those three words.

Oh, how he wished them for himself! And yet he begrudged Bellamy nothing. Rejoiced, in fact, over Pretty Wolf's courage. A long time in coming, her healing was the next stride on Path Maker's trail. The steps along the way mattered far less than the beautiful promise at the end. If she could only come to love Jesus as Savior, every hardship—Strong Bear's included—would be inconsequential.

Buck nodded, his hum of approval bringing Strong Bear back from his musings. "Yet it's the U.S. Army," Buck observed wryly, "that has you locked up like a criminal. How'd you pull that off?"

"At the Hambly raid, I was snared like a pathetic rabbit." The vinegary twist of his lips, though halfhearted, was unavoidable. Defeat, even for a good cause, tasted bitter. "Fortunately, Totka's brother, Tall Bull, took pity and let me keep my hair. He packed me off to Wakulla with the captives to become a slave." Strong Bear could not disrespect Bellamy by gushing, so he finished with a straight tone. "The day I arrived, the Great Path Maker brought me before Pretty Wolf. She took me as her own."

With thoughtful deliberation, Buck folded his arms and rocked back on his heels. He shook his head in awe. "Incredible. You always did say you'd find her. I admit I had my doubts."

Strong Bear loosed all the gushing he couldn't speak and crammed it into a cheek-aching grin. "With Path Maker, all things are possible."

"Captain Buck, the time, sir." A soldier stood behind Buck, casting anxious glances at the steel door.

Strong Bear hadn't noticed him there. Hadn't noticed the quiet either.

Crazy Medicine's song had ended.

About now, Pretty Wolf would be coiled tight, a bowstring drawn to the lips, ready at the first provocation to fire.

And Strong Bear, a helpless rabbit again, could do nothing to prevent it. Or could he?

Buck's mouth swiveled down into a grimace. "Right. On it." He collected the black bag from where he'd dropped it. "The general is taking advantage of my recently accrued knowledge of the area and acquaintanceship with the locals. I'm to serve as a medic to the Creeks during the return march, starting with a pre-execution physical assessment. Detestable business." A quake ran jaggedly over him. He jetted a hand through the bars to clap Strong Bear about the neck. "Hold tight, Strong Bear, and I'll do what I can to have you out of here."

There it was, the promise Strong Bear anticipated. "I thank you for it."

"Wouldn't consider doing otherwise, old friend."

Before he could pull away, Strong Bear grabbed his sleeve. "During the execution, where will you be?"

"Where do you need me?" was his instant reply, the grip on Strong Bear's neck reaffixing.

"With Pretty Wolf. She will not be herself and might act carelessly. Without thought to her life."

"Possibly with violence." That was Bellamy.

Buck jerked his arm from between the bars and took a leaping leftward step. Jaw hung, he stared for a three-count, then snapped his molars shut and glared daggers into the cell.

Ah, Strong Bear had nearly forgotten. They shared history, those two. Less than amiable history, Buck perhaps being the reason Bellamy stood behind those bars.

Strong Bear smirked at the irony. Buck glared on.

Bellamy broke the silence. "You'll keep a watchful eye on my betrothed?"

"The way you kept a watch on my charge?"

Silence. Then, "You're a better man than this, Captain."

Stiff in body and voice, Buck spoke from between his teeth. "For Pretty Wolf's sake and for Strong Bear's, I will stand by."

"Thank you." The stillness that followed grew so dense Strong Bear heard Bellamy swallow. "And...Miss McGirth?"

Strong Bear couldn't reckon how Bellamy would know Copper Woman, so the man must mean the younger sister, Lillian, the Bitter Eyes. And were they ever bitter. Her eyes. Her voice. Her detestable rope. At a phantom burn, Strong Bear reflexively touched his throat, his lip curling into a snarl.

Buck, however, unwound those broad shoulders of his, then rolled them back in a proud bearing. "Miss McGirth is now Mrs. Buck."

"What?" Strong Bear said while Bellamy released a two-note, incredulous laugh.

"Upon my soul," the Englishman said. "Though how it comes as a surprise, I cannot say."

Strong Bear could. Totka had suspected Buck of deep feeling toward the bitter sister, but Strong Bear only his slapped his back and chortled. The only feeling Lillian McGirth could conjure in any man was disdain. Now, unable to help himself, Strong Bear looked at his friend crosswise and wondered at the condition of his head.

Bellamy was speaking again. "My sincerest wishes of happiness to you both, Captain Buck. Did she make her way home?"

"She's en route." By his glum tenor, this fact did not exactly please Buck.

"Splendid, splendid." Bellamy sounded more relieved by that news than was reasonable. "So then. Our deal?"

Buck heaved a great breath, then slowly gave a conceding bow. "As agreed, I will speak on your behalf."

"There's a good man." Clear as sunshine, Bellamy was beaming. "Didn't I tell you we'd be fast friends, old chap?"

Chapter 35

Crazy Medicine was three-hours dead. Three-hours hung.

Hung.

His body, dangling from the raised portcullis, presided over the fort's gateway, the breezes catching and lifting his hair as if he still galloped into battle.

Outside the fort, at the mouth of the lowered drawbridge, Pretty Wolf and her mother stood in observance on San Marcos's main way. Littering the ground around them were the remnants of Noonday's hair, the locks that hadn't blown away. *"A knife, Daughter."* The only words she'd spoken since her husband stopped moving and she became a widow. Now, jagged strands hung at her ashen jaw and fluttered across her dead eyes.

The villa sprawled on both sides of them, doors and windows closed on its places of business and trade—as silent as Earth Mother who lay frigid and stale beneath Pretty Wolf's numb soles, the spirit's usual hum of life conspicuously absent. While her spirit mother withheld comfort, Pretty Wolf bore the weight of her earthly mother, a slumping Noonday. If she loosened her grasp, Noonday would crumple, and Pretty Wolf wasn't confident she'd notice when her body hit the ground.

So, she held on. Would keep holding on. The sun's downing could not be much longer in coming.

Pretty Wolf blinked sluggish lashes and turned her stiff neck. Her sight skimmed past Barkton. Stuttered on Buck. Slitted accusingly then lifted to the sky. West. The path of souls. The territory of the darkening land. Somewhere along that route journeyed the spirit of Crazy Medicine. His days on This World were ended. Even if his execution was not.

Another blink to register the weakening sun. The orange globe still squatted a hand's width above the trees.

Her heart sank.

Hours remained—two, perhaps three—before they'd be allowed to remove her father's body.

A plaything of the wind, it swayed this way and that. His shadow traced a slow, unpredictable pattern in the fort's open gateway, and the tasseled end of his unraveling waist sash dragged the dirt.

Pretty Wolf's request for a head covering had been denied, and she hadn't the abdominal steel to look again at his bloated, discolored face. His leggings provided a better target for her vigil, more bearable since the wet patch had mostly dried.

Looped over the lifted portcullis, the rope squeaked where it rubbed the last rung, a soft *meep-meep* of a sound made loud by the villa's eerie hush. So different from the clamor Crazy Medicine raised when he realized a noose awaited him. A cruel and brutal death, hangings were meant to humiliate, to strip a warrior of courage and dignity.

"What?" He balked, legs locking. "You will slay me like a dog? Too much. Shoot me, shoot me! Where is General Jackson?"

"He's out at the encampment with the army. Now, move." The officer prodded him forward.

"Send for him!" A struggle. A loss. Of ground. Of carefully groomed composure. "I will die willingly if you will let me see the general!" he shouted as his turban was ripped from his head and replaced with the noose. "This is no chief's death! Fetch your general!"

They hadn't.

The rope was secured. The stool knocked out. Then the interminable frothing and thrashing. Before it was done, Old Sharp Knife had succeeded in a complete disgracing of his enemy. Down to the soiled breechcloth.

And it cracked Pretty Wolf to the bones. That they hadn't crumbled, that she remained upright, could only be attributed to the fury making mortar of her muscles.

A whimpering sound emanated from her mother, traveled through Pretty Wolf's ears down into her marrow, and stoked the coals of her rage.

Had it been only yesterday she'd thrown herself between a white man's chest and a Red Stick's knife? Only this morning that she'd wept over a slain Bluecoat? Sworn vengeance by her own hand? So much angst, so much risk. And for what?

For this. *This.*

Cramps seized her calf, a hot knifing pain, but she welcomed it. Ground her teeth and added a spasming jaw to the list of bodily aches. Those of the soul were hidden too well beneath her iron shell for her to sense much. Anger though... *That* she felt in every part of her. In the sizzle of her blood and in the burn of skin stretched tight over her straining joints.

Crazy Medicine had only ever wanted peace. Been willing to fight viciously for it, ehi, but he'd left his tribal talwa to create a sanctuary, one in which he could live the old ways without interference from naysayers. When confronted, he'd raised the hatchet, but he'd fled equally as much. To the black fort. To Wakulla. Lands far distant from his enemy. And yet, at every turn, he was hunted down, chased away, and now, destroyed.

Noonday juddered an exhale, and Pretty Wolf firmed her grip around her waist. Over the hours, her mother's keening had devolved into crying, then whimpering and moaning. Not for the first time, Pretty Wolf heaved a grateful prayer she'd rejected her Second's advice to have her sister brought in for the killing. No power in all Spanish Territory was great enough to compel her to further risk Runs Like Deer's unborn child. Shock and grief were damage enough on their own.

Per her demand, only she and her mother stood as the People's witnesses. She might've allowed Sun Bird, the micco's Second, but he'd vanished like a lizard in the sand. Big Voice and Screaming Buttons were yet to be released from the locked holding chamber, or she would've had one or both escort her mother home by now.

"Miss Francis, please. Won't you come away?" Marcus Buck. Bluecoat officer. Mulish medicine maker. Him, his black bag, and his pestering sweettalk.

None of the day's tragedies were his fault. By his own hand, he'd done nothing wrong, made no promise he had not kept. And yet she felt his presence across her like a whip of betrayal.

She'd set herself to ignoring this renewed pleading when he added, "One of your men has arrived with transportation."

The announcement pulled her attention to the old cart and jenny she hadn't heard roll in, then to Winter Hawk. Stricken and scrubbed of his usual glow, the brave bent his head in deference. "I am come to take you away. If you will allow."

Pretty Wolf stared at his scalp lock and the empty bead chain tied to it, and inordinate fear trembled up through her knees. Whatever feat of bravery would one day add a first feather to that chain, she dearly hoped it was not warfare. Getting a tangible sense of Earth beneath her feet, she prayed Winter

Hawk might find a road of peace. Instead of fleeings and slayings and hangings.

"Who is it?" Drought scratched Noonday's question, the words toneless.

"It is Winter Hawk, Mother." Pretty Wolf stroked her hair and paced her speech as she might for a confused child. "He's brought a cart to carry you home. It is time." A slightly skewed fact. Nothing her torpid mother would notice. "Runs Like Deer will be crying for you. Let Winter Hawk take you to her. I shall see to Father."

Taking that as invitation, Winter Hawk sidled up and carefully scooped Noonday's slight frame into his arms. She didn't protest. Simply tipped her head against his neck and closed her eyes. Winter Hawk swung her away from the scene and strode from Pretty Wolf's sight. Not a minute later, the squeal of an ungreased axle passed behind her, and Pretty Wolf felt a weight lift. Minuscule, but enough to fill her lungs with the crisp evening air.

"Will you drink?" Marcus Buck presented a cup.

She brushed it away, refusing it even a glance. The medicine maker could indeed try one's patience.

Rounding her, he took her mother's place at her side and cleared his throat. "Strong Bear and I are old friends." When her eyes pinged to him, they found he'd readied a wistful smile. "Thought you might not have known. Anyway"—his tongue flashed a sweeping pass—"I went to the general on his behalf but got nowhere. Apparently, while being detained, he went a little feral and broke a soldier's nose."

The news spiked her brows. Then somehow managed to tempt her mouth with a flash of humor. Whatever the provocation, Strong Bear would be celebrating that small vengeance. A nose for a nose.

Pretty Wolf had once called his broken nose fierce. *My ugly face wants no help there*, had been his prompt rebuttal. She'd grabbed him by the cheeks and planted a kiss right on the crook. A somewhat cheering memory.

Until Marcus Buck said, "He's now considered a hostile. Unless you don't mind him getting moldy in there," he said, hitching a thumb toward the prison, "he's going to require a prettier advocate than myself." Again, he extended the cup and held it, waiting.

Staring into its rippling center, she revisited the men in the cells, saw their big, trusting eyes pinned on her, and smelled the rot of their predicament. Iron Wood's case bulged large and imposing before her, but Strong Bear's… That, she could do something about. "I require my Second be released and brought to me."

"Which would that be?"

"Screaming Buttons, the warrior with the snake rattles."

"See to it, Sergeant."

Pretty Wolf watched astounded as Barkton launched into action. She called after him. "My speaker, as well."

A pause allowed the sergeant a glance to take in Buck's nod of assent. Then, boots clacking with purpose across the drawbridge, he gave her father wide birth and disappeared inside the fort.

If she had known the black-coated Buck would be so accommodating, she would have made her demands sooner. Her belly cinched uncomfortably, but she ignored it. Too late for regrets. Plenty of time for remedies. Clasping her arms behind her back, she parked inflexible eyes on him. "I also demand a respectful burial."

Buck's expression softened. "Leave it to me. Be certain, Miss Francis, I will do all in my power to see that he is treated with every dignity. You may hold me to it."

His compassionate, almost tender attention was too much. Fissures began spreading across her shield, so she plucked the cup from his hand and leveled sharp eyes on him. "Be certain, Marcus Buck. I will."

Chapter 36

The night bugs were silent. In observance, Pretty Wolf would like to think. In truth, it was the bitter cold. A northerly, rain-scented breeze cut through the monstrous oaks in Toño's expansive lawn, making sure to run icy fingers across Pretty Wolf's face as it shrilled through the house's covered porch.

Night might have fallen, but her worries were only rising. Birdie, had she escaped? Were the warriors making preparations as instructed? What of Shem and Runs Like Deer and—

Sergeant Barkton opened the front door, a gentle heat inviting her in, but when Pretty Wolf's foot touched the threshold, she paused and looked back. "Marcus Buck."

The medicine maker halted his descent of the porch steps and swiveled at the waist. He'd escorted her and Barkton to her mandatory lodging and was now returning to the villa. Light from the home's interior brushed across the dark stubble on Buck's jaw and highlighted the patient query on his arched brow. "Yes, Miss Francis?"

"Are you going now to check that my men are comfortable?"

A beat passed in which he appeared to be weighing her. "I can." Something about Buck's slow, tight delivery said he would find no pleasure in it. How unfortunate for him.

"I ask that you do. The weather is fierce, and they have no blankets or fire. While you are there, tell my betrothed to sleep easy. I am well."

Buck shifted on the stairs, one leg propped on a higher tread. A frown bent his somewhat thin mouth as he leaned into his raised knee and studied her. "On the last, I beg to differ."

Her chin jerked in. Why would he think her unwell? Had she not walked to Los Robles on her own power, head high? "Beg all you like, Marcus Buck. I am *truly* well." She laid a hand on the door frame and let it discretely take some of her weight. "That is all, sir. You may go."

Laughing lightly, Buck shoved off his knee, touched his hat, and backed down the stairs. "Yes, ma'am." The humor cut off when he shifted his stern captain's eyes to Sergeant Barkton. "The lady is weak from lack of nourishment. See that she eats, bathes, and sleeps. In that order." His tone allowed no room for argument. From either of them. "I entrust her care to you, Sergeant."

Pretty Wolf bristled like a porcupine. "I require no care from a Bluecoat. Be gone, Marcus Buck."

Barkton made a strangled noise in his throat, but Buck's grin returned in force. "Good night again, Miss Francis."

Skirt flaring, she spun and stalked into the house, refusing to acknowledge the lightheadedness that flashed white spots across her vision.

Over the next hour, she refused two other things—admitting that the hearty bowl of fish soup she'd gulped down eased a terrible pain in her stomach. And the offer of a bath. The night had grown late, and she would not be found soaking in a tub when Toño arrived from conference with Jackson. Her Spanish pawa had much to answer for regarding the surrender.

So, outfitted still in her soiled clothes, she sat at his dining table, forearms languishing on the polished oak, and waited. Her eyelids fought the weight of exhaustion, her body the same as it curved over a half-empty teacup. Brown liquid trembled in the white porcelain, tea-leaf sediment speckling the bottom. Its steam quit long ago—back before the mantle clock chimed ten. The drink was likely as cold as the gaping hole in her chest. Such a large, murky hole. And dug so quickly, so violently.

She stared straight ahead, helpless against the painful void.

And her dearest friend…

She palmed her hip, the sensation of Strong Bear's touch as fresh as if he'd pressed his fingers to the spot only moments before. *"Remember this. You will always have me with you."* The fervent rumble of that truth sifted back as strong and sure as when he uttered them, and a thread of strength began flowing into her. Nurturing her floundering spirit.

Though Strong Bear was Native and considered "hostile" by the Bluecoats, her fear for his life placed strangely low on her catalog of troubles—they'd gotten out of tougher scrapes. Even so, securing his prompt release would be her chief priority. For with Strong Bear at her back, she could tackle the remainder of the worries with considerably more fortitude.

Sergeant Barkton gave an inglorious snort where he snoozed in a plush armchair. Guarding Pretty Wolf was, apparently, fatiguing business. That, or he trusted she would not slip the knife from his boot, bury it in his throat, and make a dash for parts far removed from all things blue: coats, coves, frost-encrusted eyes.

Another gong echoed through the room, startling away her faint smirk. Barkton didn't stir, but she straightened and rolled her shoulders in a stretch while catching a glimpse of the timepiece on the mantel. The clock's long hand now pointed directly south. Another thirty minutes gone, and Toño was still unseen. Yet another person responsible for the cavern behind her ribs.

Toño had been present at the hanging, after which he'd offered her and her mother a generous bow, then excused himself to attend pressing matters. Naturally, a commander would be detained, clearing whatever debris resulted of a fort being overtaken. But Pretty Wolf's matters were pressing as well, her questions cluttering every thought.

The most imperative: how could she intervene for Iron Wood? If he was convicted, what would be his punishment? Banishment to his homeland? Not an altogether terrible consequence; they'd already intended to leave.

Secondary to all that: what was to become of the People? Would the general allow them to stay in the Point now that the micco was in the ground and the warriors had been unarmed?

As an advocate to the People, she must learn these things, must return to the talwa with *something*. Something other than her father's bandoleer and urine-stained sash.

Lastly, she would ask Toño what in the name of every spirit had compelled him to surrender his fort to a foreign power without a fight? What unthinkable threats had Jackson brandished to get his scorpion claws into San Marcos? Or had Toño simply donned a set of milk-cow teats and rolled over with the first blow?

She abhorred thinking of her tío in such mean terms, and yet, she turned the teacup between her hands and considered how sweet porcelain would sound shattering against a wall.

Brisk and urgent, a series of raps sounded from the direction of the front door. Barkton snapped awake, his soldierly instincts honed, it would seem, to door knocking over clock chiming.

From the front of the house, hinges groaned, and a servant recited a Spanish greeting. Next came a rush of fluid Muskogee, familiar in its pushy, feminine tones.

Melon.

Then, a troop of earnest footfalls.

Pretty Wolf's lungs emptied in a drawn-out collapse. Relief wafted from her like pollen clouds off pines, thick and stinging to the eyes. She gathered her aching joints and heaved up from the chair, turning as Melon, trailed by Winter Hawk, scurried into the room.

Sweat dampened her collar, and her bosom worked like a bellows—evidence she'd wasted no time coming to Pretty Wolf's aid. But not two paces in, Melon stopped to blink owl eyes up and down her. "What has been done to you?"

Winter Hawk, appearing quite grown beside Melon's stunted frame, cast a bemused look down on her. "Did I not say you'd find her unsightly?" He skirted Melon and came to Pretty Wolf, his gaze swinging to Barkton and whetting to a brash glare, but the only part of the sergeant that was still at attention was the red plume of his hat.

Pretty Wolf swatted his arm. "What did you bring me?"

Chuffing, he set a fraying satchel on the table. "Runs Like Deer sends two sets of clothes. She says you will know best which to wear and when."

The mention of her sister and all the love of home threatened to undo Pretty Wolf, but she buried the urge and shored up her armor. She was miccohokti now.

Before she could ask after her sister, Winter Hawk blurted, "Stop your worrying. Your sister grieves, but she is not the fragile weed you think her to be." He wrinkled his nose and leaned away from her. "You smell like a butchering table."

"Winter Hawk!" Melon chided, but Pretty Wolf blocked a little laugh that felt too good to be appropriate for the evening of her father's brutal death. "Shoo." Melon bustled Winter Hawk out of the way, yanked out a chair, and dropped heavily into it. Pinching the fabric at her chest, she fanned herself with her blouse. "Report to her, boy. While I catch my breath."

Pretty Wolf retook her seat, which prompted Barkton to do the same. Cracking an impressive yawn, he clasped his hands at the base of his skull and let his eyelids come down. The man might be a Bluecoat, and he might speak little more than a dialect of grunts and whisker twitches, but he was a likable sort.

Pleased with his neglect, she urged Winter Hawk on. "Ehi, give me all you know."

The brave drew himself to his full gangly height. "The wounded are few and stable. None in threat of death. And the warriors have done as you said, gone home to reassure their women and plan for a possible migration."

Finding Pretty Wolf

Pretty Wolf sank back into her chair, having been clueless how deep that particular fear ran until its weight was lifted from her.

Melon used her sleeve to dab at her sweaty neck. When she spoke, her voice had a bitterly dreary hue. "Your mother is inconsolable. The rest are as frightened as one would expect of a conquered people. The fear of slaughter is past us, but tomorrow's sun is dark, Pretty Wolf. Wakulla's end is the whispered dread."

Dread that Pretty Wolf shared. She could little ponder how to face it, how to guide the People through. And she wasn't quite as confident they'd ducked all the arrows launched their way.

Winter Hawk's lips sank with censure, he turned to Melon. "Such dour talk. Pretty Wolf will rally their hope with her fox-smart tongue." His eyes shifted to her, sharp with high regard. "A rousing speech you gave, Miccohokti. The micco would have been proud. I was proud."

The praise struck her like a dart. She didn't want the task, the role. Much less the glory. It came at far too great a price. And yet, she'd paid it.

With no little effort, she kept her tone neutral as she thanked him. "Did Birdie make her escape?"

Mischief sprang up with Winter Hawk's wicked grin. "Sunflower sent her running for the old lodge by the warm springs."

The warm springs. Of course. As Pretty Wolf thought on who else might be cached in that hideaway, her blood began a slow boil. "Which is where I would imagine Kills Many, the scourge, has carried himself, as well."

A growling sound of menace left Melon's throat, the manifestation of Pretty Wolf's own sentiment on the matter. "Sunflower renounces him. Swears she will tie him to the skinning frame herself for his ill-timed, cow-hearted vengeance. He dares not show a hair of his scalp in the talwa."

Despite the clan mother's backing of Pretty Wolf's own position on his fate, the entirety of This World seemed suddenly to perch on her shoulders. Poor, sweet Runs Like Deer. Fragile weed or not, she would splinter under her husband's disgrace. If the baby came to harm because of it… That fear alone was enough to earn Pretty Wolf's forge-hot ire. But if his actions brought down wrath on the People, her own fingernails would peel the hide from his back.

Whatever it took to keep her people safe. To spare slaughter and further suffering.

Whatever it takes. A vow that buoyed her enough to voice the question cowering at the base of her throat. "What do you know of Iron Wood's arrest?" Melon's eyes darted away, and Pretty Wolf began to tremble. She clasped her hands tightly together and steeled herself for the worst. "Tell me."

Blinking away a rare showing of tears, Melon cleared her throat and did as asked.

The Bluecoats came like a flood up the river, she recounted, so swiftly that those at the store could only fall to their knees in surrender. At that point, Iron Wood had not arrived, so they laid in wait for him. Which meant they had everything. Every ledger, every condemning sheet of correspondence. The only good news—they showed no interest in any save him. Not Korsan or Shem or even Rox in his tattered red coat. Once they had her betrothed in their iron cuffs, Melon and the others were driven away from the trade grounds, which immediately became Bluecoat property. The compound, the store, its contents.

"They are thieves," Pretty Wolf ground out, fury like thunder rumbling in her chest. "They cannot have his place, his things. They cannot have *him*." Her nails scored deep into her palms, but she relished the ache. What misery must Iron Wood be enduring that very moment? What sorrows did tomorrow conceal?

Melon laid a gentle hand over Pretty Wolf's knot of fingers and straining joints. "We will get our Iron Wood back."

We. Our. Comforting, empowering words.

Saving Iron Wood was not a task for her alone, but for them all. Hers was not the only life he'd touched; hers not the only heart devoted to him.

Melon, he'd saved from adultery and a **nose-cropping**. Shem from starvation and slavery. Korsan, a pirate's noose and a priest's inquisition. Rox he'd sheltered from abandonment and his own wounded mind.

And Pretty Wolf...

Through long-suffering, unconditional love, he'd clung to Pretty Wolf even as she spiraled into the blackest pit of guilt and grief. Never once had he lost his grip, never given her up for lost.

She raised a tremulous smile and gripped Melon's hand. "Ehi. We will."

Whatever it takes.

"They made Rox leave behind his bag of stones," Winter Hawk said, grave as a death song.

Finding Pretty Wolf

Rox would be despondent until the bag was returned to him, and none but Pretty Wolf would have the power to make that happen. The troubles and tasks piled up around her. Sighing, she rubbed her face. "Where is he?"

Winter Hawk replied. "We are all of us—myself, Korsan, Rox, and Melon—in my clan's guest house."

Pretty Wolf looked to Melon. "Turtle Clan would not house you?" Of the four, only Melon had clan.

"Turtle is generous to welcome me, but the trade-house men are my clan now. I will not leave them, and Turtle hasn't provisions enough for us all. Shem alone eats enough for three." Melon formed a smile that, despite its minute size, was as soothing to the soul as a healing chant.

Rotating in her chair, Pretty Wolf reached for Winter Hawk's hand. A little startled at the contact, he tried to withdraw, but she held fast. Pretty Wolf would be setting the rules now. Offering him a reassuring smile, she squeezed his fingers, same to Melon's. "My heart quaked for you all. That you are well is a relief I cannot express." All except Iron Wood, but they would soon remedy that. "You will sleep here, both of you. In the morning, you will save Korsan from Rox," she said, smirking, "and I will learn what can be done to free our Iron Wood."

For tonight, she would bathe and rest because Iron Wood deserved better from her than a muddled brain and bags under her eyes. Facing off with Jackson again would require both her thoughts and her vision to be spring-water clear.

Yawning, she rose.

"Wait." Melon's clipped voice sank her back down. "Korsan sends this." She glanced to Winter Hawk, who handed over the folder. Leather creaked as she opened it onto the table in front of Pretty Wolf.

In its center crease, a writing feather, and in its pocket, a single, much-abused document. Lines of Iron Wood's beautiful, orderly script gazed up at her. "I don't understand." Heart clenching, she skimmed a fingertip across his signature, adroitly avoiding even a glimpse of the blank space beside it.

Melon set a bottle of ink next to Pretty Wolf's elbow. "Ehi, you do."

Ehi, she did. For whatever reason, Korsan believed this to be important, and Pretty Wolf believed it was well past time. Nodding, she uncorked the bottle, dipped the quill, and scrawled her name beside her betrothed's.

No, my husband's.

She'd learned enough about the English to understand that putting one's name on a paper did not create a union in the eyes of their law. For that, they would require a ceremony conducted by a "man of the cloth," but in *her* eyes, they were salt and sugar. Mixed. Inseparable.

The clamp on her heart released, and a smile touched her lips as she envisioned Iron Wood's expression when she told him.

Ehi, well past time.

Melon blew on the wet ink. "Korsan says to have the Spanish commander sign as witness."

Smart thinker, that pirate.

"I will." The master of the house had yet to return, but sleep would no longer be put off. So, Pretty Wolf bid her friends goodnight and followed the Spanish serving girl up the stairs and into the bathing chamber. She would have to catch Toño in the morning. Probably at his desk in the fort. Unless Old Sharp Knife had relegated him to the broom closet.

With help from the young señorita, she made smart work of scrubbing off the gore and drying her hair. While she wriggled into a sleeping shirt, the girl moved to the adjoining room, saying she would prepare the bed. By the time Pretty Wolf entered, she had already slipped out, but not before arranging two outfits on hangers and hooking them on the dressing screen.

On the left, the crimson, ruffle-sleeved blouse and beribboned skirt she'd sewn for the **Frost Moon dance**. Sturdy cotton. Bright, unfaded dye. Neat stitching and unfrayed tassel-ties. Acceptable attire for any serious occasion, and if ever there was a season for Native pride, it was now.

On the right, the white muslin gown with short-waisted jacket her father brought home from England, the same gown she'd arrayed herself in for Buck's celebratory dinner at the hacienda. A light, almost sheer cotton, the garment was hardly fitting attire for winter, and its lines and adornments were plain by white standards.

But that night, when she'd met Iron Wood on the path, her skirt fluttered like butterfly wings and glowed like the moon above. The wind outlined the form of her legs, and Iron Wood looked upon her as though she were a lone pearl in a sea of barnacles.

Fingertips trailing the jacket's crisp yellow taffeta, Pretty Wolf shed a sigh, then unbuckled her sister's satchel, refolded the stomp dance attire, and tucked it away.

Chapter 37

The fort's short drawbridge vibrated under Sergeant Barkton's bullish tread and Pretty Wolf's own booted feet. She winced at the pinch of her toes inside the unforgiving leather, trivial pain compared to the rusty nail of grief impaling her heart. She glowered up at the portcullis' iron teeth as she hurried through the gate's grinning maw.

Her increased pace hugged her gauzy skirt to her legs and bumped her satchel against her calf. Tonight, she would lay her head on her own couch in her mother's lodge. Wolf needed her. Wakulla needed her. Even if all she could offer them was her presence.

The fort's courtyard, roughly half a stickball field in size, opened before her. Towering battlements skewered the violet dawn, the structure's whitewash now a pale blue. On the wall-walk and in the yard, Spanish uniforms intermingled with American. At present, the only one she could partly stomach strode toward her, paces long and brittle.

Captain Marcus Buck took a benign, appreciative look over her white-lady attire but, thankfully, offered no flattery. Heels clicking, he bent stiffly in greeting. "Miss Francis. Straight to business. As I believe you'd prefer."

She offered a brisk nod.

A sweep of his arm invited her to walk with him. He angled their trajectory toward the row of doors along the east wall. "General Jackson orders a visit to your village this morning. He wishes you to report on the overall mood. You will also relay his intentions for you and your people, the details of which will be conveyed at some point before you leave." As warned, the declaration was efficient and distilled in tone, but the valley carving deep into the flesh above Buck's nose betrayed his true feelings.

Pretty Wolf spat an exasperated sound. Wakulla weighed heavily on her mind, certainly, but Iron Wood ranked a great deal higher. A fact Old Sharp Knife well knew. If he intended to broom her away like stray kernels in the corn keep, he would soon find himself disappointed. Balada's swift hooves could have Pretty Wolf to Wakulla and back before the sun topped the sky—the hour designated for the trial.

"Very well," she said, with a languid, favor-granting wave of the hand. "But first, I will meet with the general." She might not have had sway in the outcome of a highly sought-after Red Stick micco, but the general *would* hear her in the matters of the British lord and the White Stick ally he'd so blithely clamped in chains.

Buck's stride hitched. "Unfortunately, he's preemptively refused all audiences, including yours. Denying you brings me no joy, Miss Francis, and I am truly sorry for it." Sincere regret dipped his volume as well as his head.

The gestures were useless against the rage threatening to burst through her skin. She clenched her teeth to refrain from snapping at him. She was Wolf, canines sharp and bared, not a milk cow to be pastured for Old Sharp Knife's amusement. And neither was her Iron Wood.

"Here we are." Buck stopped before the council room, where she'd met with the general the previous day. He palmed the door handle, then stilled and looked at her. "In a completely selfish attempt to curry your forgiveness, I approved a private meeting with Mr. Bellamy and…someone else." Mischief glinted in his flash of a smile before he swung the door open.

On sight of the two inside, Pretty Wolf's anger became powder in the wind. Her foot had no sooner crossed the threshold than Iron Wood cleared the gap between them, bundled her into his arms, and swung her the rest of the way into the room.

"Polly," he groaned into her neck and shivered out a massive exhale. Prison stench adhered to his clothing, and his hair was mussed and oily, but she could still scent traces of his lavender and mint. And she couldn't recall the last time he'd felt so wonderful against her.

"It's done," she whispered. "I signed." The sparest of statements, but it didn't boggle him for an instant. As evidenced by the catch in his breath and the tightened embrace.

"You honor me." His words came to her gruff with feeling. "I am a man most blessed."

Imprisoned and facing the loss of everything, yet honored. Blessed. Because *she*, the woman who'd walked astraddle with courtship and fear, had scratched her name onto a paper.

There could not exist a less worthy spouse than herself. In small part for her many flaws but chiefly for his great goodness. Down to his core, Iron Wood was burnished gold. And he was hers. Deserved or otherwise.

Ribs grunting, she clung to him, one hand bracing the back of his head to arrest him there. But it was the other face in the room who suddenly captured her attention.

Complexion canting toward gray, lips toward pale, Strong Bear struggled to hold her gaze. The entire state of him—feet restless on the plank flooring, fingers fidgeting at his belt—filled her with dreadful unease.

Intending to question him on it, she pulled back from Iron Wood, only to be caught in a soft, mouth-covering kiss. Startled frozen, she waited for the usual anxiety to grip her lungs. When it didn't come, her shoulders eased down, and her lips eased open. Her last vision, right before her lashes drifted closed, was of Strong Bear wrenching around.

An odd prickle fingered up her spine. A misplaced sensation, it wormed uncomfortably inside her. It wasn't until Iron Wood was gently breaking away that she identified it—the sting of guilt. Though what she might have to feel guilty about eluded her.

Breaths coming light and swift, she gazed at Iron Wood, confusion and astonishment a two-pronged pin on her tongue.

Iron Wood compensated for her mute daze by setting her at arm's length and drinking her in, bun to ankle boots. "Polly, dear heart, you are positively stunning."

The compliment brought her back to him, if shakily. She worked up a small, tight laugh. "I would call you a liar, but compared to your last look of me, what you say can only be true."

He, too, stunned the mind. Grime smeared his temple, and dust clung to the dark carpet of stubble on his jaw. Frock coat wrinkled, cravat twisted, breeches stained, he had the appearance of being wadded up and buried in the manure wagon.

The indignity of it, of him, an English nobleman humiliated to this degree made her quake. Bones, pulse, innards—a silent rumble of anger, like Earth Mother muttering her warnings before bringing This World to its knees. Pretty Wolf had never felt more attuned to Mother than just then, but it wouldn't do to shake the foundations quite yet. For Iron Wood, she would contain her wrath.

Using the cuff of her sleeve, she polished a silver button on his frock coat. "I trust you stand strong." She thumped his chest to indicate where.

Uncertainty streaked across him—a blink and it vanished—before he combed tidying fingers through his mane and lengthened his posture.

"Presenting somewhat rough of a picture, to be sure, but really, I'm marvelous now you've come." He tucked a lock behind her ear and took occasion to glide a touch down her neck. "You slept?"

"A little, yes," she said distractedly, gaze pulled across the room.

Arms extended, Strong Bear leaned ponderously into the sideboard and glared at a rum bottle as if it were singularly responsible for all the world's wrongs.

Spitting on her cuff, she targeted the next button and nudged her chin toward Strong Bear. "What troubles him?" Aside from incarceration, threat of hanging, and Buck's useless aid. "Whatever the ill tidings," she said, timbre muted and weary, "tell me now."

Iron Wood *tsk*ed and encircled her wrists to cease her nervous activity. "I haven't the foggiest notion, my dear. Your lad there has been sullen since he added himself to the guest list." He thumb-rubbed the dirty spots her cleaning had created on her yellow sleeves, the flashy color probably the only speck of cheer within three sights—not counting Jackson, who'd likely been dancing a jig since the stool was kicked from under her father.

Clucking peevishly at the stain, Iron Wood said, "I am merely disgruntled that our *private* tete-a-tete has accrued yet more audience. As to any ill tidings, you'll have to ask him."

"I will." She pulled free, pecked his cheek, and crossed to Strong Bear. At his side, she frowned at his scuffed knuckles. Her name might as well be tattooed into every bruise and scratch; if not for her, he would not be in this predicament.

Again, that prickle.

She quenched it, for she knew Strong Bear well enough—he would rather wear bruises and consequences fighting *for* her than feathers and honors fighting against. He'd always been broken that way. Beautifully, faithfully broken. Perhaps his fits of reckless, sacrificial behavior could be excused by their peculiar brand of love. A love that, for her part, grew every time some part of him was broken for her.

Sight fixed to his knobby nose, she let her affection swell however it willed and barely refrained from slipping an arm about his waist. If she could, she'd squeeze her love and gratitude into him, as they'd always done. Before he was a slave and…something other than a boy.

Since that was out of the question, she pressed on his shoulder until he straightened and turned his agonized expression on her. He wore the look of the doomed.

Oh, Kit.

Didn't he know she'd fight for him as passionately and he did for her?

His black hair had lost its gleam, and his white shirt was smudged. But apart from that—and his troubled mood—he looked himself. Of course, she was accustomed to seeing him in all manner of states. Unlike her perpetually prim Englishman.

A clearing throat brought attention to how long she'd been perusing her friend. Because Iron Wood preferred it, she stayed in English. "You wanted to speak with me?"

The column of Strong Bear's throat bobbed, and his upper lashes swept down. "I do." His voice was a millstone rolling over gravel and carried the faint aroma of pine. "Since I arrived in Wakulla, I have."

So long? A trickle of foreboding slinked through her center, but she covered it with an intrepid smile. "Then we will talk." She led the way to the table and chose a seat, but when he dragged out a chair, he only spread a palm toward it, sight lifting to Iron Wood. "Sit. Please."

A question on his brow, Iron Wood met her gaze, but all she had to offer was a clueless shrug. Striding forward, he accepted the seat with an outward flip of his coattails. To clear his view of her, he shoved aside a bowl heaped with oranges and, back a ramrod, gave Strong Bear a smile that didn't reach his eyes. "Shall we get on with it? Whatever *it* is."

More abashed than she'd ever seen him, Strong Bear nodded into a chin-tuck that he angled slightly for a surreptitious glimpse of his medicine maker friend.

Buck had placed himself before the door, one eyebrow swinging up. A hand draped over his sword as he blatantly guarded, flagrantly watched. Beside him stood Barkton with his arms crossed and his mustache hanging in a scowl.

"I don't suppose," Iron Wood said through a broad, clamp-toothed smile, "we'll get any more privacy than this?"

Buck's mouth swooped to one side. "Not on your life, sailor. Strong Bear,"—the edge fell from his voice—"we haven't much time here. Best hurry it along."

A sheen of perspiration broke out on Strong Bear's forehead, and Pretty Wolf's niggling concern morphed into tummy-churning worry. "Strong Bear?" She reached both hands to him, and he grabbed them up, sinking to a knee before her.

He trembled. The fingers wrapped about hers. The pulse at his throat. The scant climb of his mouth that gradually surmounted his anxiety. "Before I begin, you must know that Sunflower forbade me from speaking of this until the cow pens contract was complete." He blew an indignant huff.

"From speaking *what*, Kit?" What could be so bad that Sunflower would put a seal on his mouth?

"Spit it out, man." Iron Wood flung out an arm and bumped the fruit bowl. An orange toppled off the mound and tumbled over the table's edge.

Strong Bear caught it, his gaze never unlinking from hers. He set the orange in her lap and simply, quietly, almost reverently said, "Flint."

"Flint?" Her mind whirred to connect the term— No, the *name* with Strong Bear. When it clicked, her imagination leaped to conjure little brown arms wrapped about his neck. At the sweet visual, her lips bowed up. "The boy you've made a nephew. He watches for your return from atop the hill."

Life, full and bright, washed over Strong Bear, pushing back his thick lids to better brandish the glow in his earth-steady eyes. "*Our* return, Pretty Wolf." He leaned into her knees and gripped her fingers so ferociously her joints protested. "Flint watches for *us*."

Us. Understanding bloomed, and sorrow for him sank through her.

Strong Bear had never made a secret of his dream for them to rebuild Alabama Town together, but at this point, he should have long abandoned that aspiration. Apparently, by the gleam of him, the hope persisted. But while he languished in a cage, she could not bring herself to upset him.

"All right..." She lowered her chin to show she listened.

For a beat, he said nothing. Merely squinted, studying her, then eased back. "You have not seen it."

"Seen what?"

He indicated the pouch sitting on her hip. His pouch. "May I?"

The timepiece? She jounced a shoulder. "It is yours." To loosen its mouth, she yanked at the drawstring. She cleared her hand so he could shove three big fingers inside. Her jaw clicked shut when he withdrew, not the timepiece, but the folded parchment. "The Ancient Words?" That beat the timepiece for bafflement.

In place of answering, he opened the paper, gazed fondly upon it, then deliberately turned it so she could see.

Tiny but powerful, a jolt rocked her. She sucked a curt breath.

The surprise wasn't so much from the absence of ink and lines of words, or from the expertly penciled face that grinned back at her, but from the profound familiarity in the young features.

She knew that darling face. Plump cheeks, dimpled chin. Big, pale eyes rimmed with the thickest, blackest fringe. Dazzling, those eyes. A beautiful child who became a beautiful man.

But how had the image gotten into Strong Bear's pouch?

Her sight flew to Iron Wood, whose clueless expression helped not at all, and cut back to Strong Bear. "I've not seen this one before." Perplexity began a slow, uncomfortable stir in her belly. She pressed back into her chair, away from the paper, and looked again at Iron Wood. "Why would you give him this?" A brittle shard invaded her tone, and she couldn't pinpoint why.

Neither could Iron Wood, as his face opened wide with surprise. "Give him what, darling?" Half-rising, he levered himself against the table and leaned in for a glimpse of the sketch. Both brows shot to a peak, then crashed into a slant-eyed accusation that he hurled at Strong Bear. "You scoundrel, you've been rummaging through my trunk!"

"I haven't." Though Strong Bear gave his head a vigorous shake, his voice remained firm, undaunted. "This was drawn in the Blackberry Month. In Kossati, where we now live. My good friend, Phillip Bailey, sketched the boy at Willow Woman's request. She gave it to me as a gift."

"The boy?" Pretty Wolf discharged an incredulous laugh. "Are you saying this is your Flint?"

"No." Strong Bear crammed the parchment into her hand and mashed both to her chest. "This is *your* Flint, Pretty Wolf. Yours." In afterthought, he flitted a glance to Iron Wood. As if to imply... As if to say...

Heart, lungs, chest, they seized up. She felt hewn from stone. Even her brain refused to grasp the insinuation.

The room faded—Strong Bear into a blur of browns and blacks. Her smirk slid into a flat line, and every pinging thought converged into *one*. A thought so achingly sweet, so terrifyingly beautiful, she dashed it out, suffocated it with an inferno of fury.

"No," she gritted out, hardening every muscle to keep from slapping him for his cruelty.

"He is," Strong Bear insisted, no give at all in his tone. "Flint is yours. He was saved alive."

A crinkling sound tugged her gaze to her lap where the sketch crumpled inside her fist. In the other hand, her nails bore into the orange. Fingers springing open, she released the wad of paper to the floor, and her memory to that riverside horror. Her son had once lain between these hands, cold and blue and not breathing. To say otherwise, to even hint at it, would mean she...she had...

"No!" On an enraged growl, she shot upright, knocking Strong Bear on his rear, and flung the orange across the room. It broke open and bled all over the wall. Landed with a splat, juices spreading as air whizzed in and out of her nostrils.

The destruction of wholesome things—Pretty's Wolf's defining talent.

She sank back down, the fight draining out of her right a chair crashed.

Iron Wood lurched to his feet, coming fully erect, combat blazing from his eyes.

Pretty Wolf's gaze slogged to Strong Bear as he heaved himself up and faced him, hands up. "Hear me first, Bellamy!"

Somewhere on the outskirts of her awareness, Barkton rammed his musket stock into his shoulder. Muzzle swinging between the men.

The shouting became a background buzz as her focus retreated to the juices that dripped and puddled at the wall's base. The bold zing of citrus climbed her nose and ushered in memories. Simple, sweet, childhood memories of harvesting with her sister.

Runs Like Deer would like an orange, perhaps. Pretty Wolf reached for one.

"Enough!"

She jumped from her skin with Buck's holler and blinked to clear her head in the pandemonium.

He darted in as Iron Wood got a fistful of Strong Bear's shirtfront.

Barkton cursed and swiveled the musket away.

Sounds pummeled her ears. The rip of fabric, the scuffle and scrape of boots. Labored breaths—her own. The river's bellow, and an infant's faint cry.

"What sort of game are you playing, boy!" Iron Wood's cheeks splotched a fiery red. "Look what you've done to her!"

Finding Pretty Wolf

On a snarl, Buck shoved him back and pursued him two steps to stab a finger against his chest. "Back down, Bellamy! Or you're done here."

Protective instincts screamed at Pretty Wolf to leap up and shout Buck back into his corner, but she sat. Heavy-limbed. Lips flaccid. Room spinning and mind catapulting.

It can't be.

Please, please, please.

Impossible! He's mistaken. Do not dare believe it.

Spirits, please, may it be so. Or wake me from this dream!

Strong Bear would not deceive me.

Buck was still hollering. "Just shut up and hear him out, man!"

Arms loose and low, Strong Bear kept such self-assurance in his bearing that Pretty Wolf couldn't deny he believed the story he told, as hard as it was to comprehend.

With deliberate movements, he positioned his body as though to shield her from Iron Wood's assault. "Where Pretty Wolf steps, I follow. If she stumbles, I break her fall," he recited, speech clipped and growing fiercer, faster by the word. "If another strikes at her, I take the blow. Her safety is all things to me. *She* is all things to me." Going slightly hoarse, he jabbed a finger at his chin. "And I would first cut the tongue from my head before playing with her wounded heart! Hate me if you must, Bellamy, but I love her as my own flesh, and though it is hard to understand, I speak nothing but *truth*. Flint is—"

His chest abruptly refilled, a painful, wheezing sound. As he struggled to replenish his air, his jaw trembled. At last, he regrouped enough to rasp, "He is your son."

For three great surges of breath, her two men stared the other down.

Iron Wood and Strong Bear.

As opposite as fire and rain—white and red, learned of books and learned of blows, soldier of fortune and warrior of fate. In one aspect, however, the males were alike. Twin shields, they would each, without a tick of indecision, willingly take a dose of steel for her. They seemed ready to do it now. In some absurd notion to spare her from further breakage.

And all Pretty Wolf wanted to know was, "H-how?"

Strong Bear broke off staring and, in one long stride, eliminated the distance to her. Taking her by the arms, he darted his eyes over every part of her face. If he was checking for damage, he couldn't miss the cracks spreading across her like splintering ice. He stroked stray hair back off her forehead. "It is impossible, I know. I *know*. But Path Maker is merciful. He plucked your boy from Water's grasp and put him into another woman's. Until he could be returned."

Water rimmed his lower lids and overflowed, but he radiated joy as though the mighty Creator himself lived under his skin. Unashamed of his display, Strong Bear let the tears tumble unimpeded to his shirt. "He lives, Pretty Wolf! He is perfect, and he is waiting."

Lives...perfect. Waiting. For us. For us.

The heel of her boot caught in the rear hem of her gown. She looked down and discovered she was standing. And backing away. Her body coming to the rescue of her spinning head.

It was *not* possible.

She'd rubbed her baby's cold, unmoving chest for what seemed an eternity. Breathed into his mouth. Flicked his soles, swatted his backside, wept tears onto his limp body, and begged every spirit to spare him.

Had one heard, acted? Creator Path Maker, as Strong Bear said?

If so, if her son truly lived, if she'd sent their *living* son down the river... Her heart pounded relentlessly, brutally. So hard she bowed inward with the agony of it, with the horrible knowing that of all the things she'd done, this might be the one Iron Wood could not forgive.

Panic tore at her chest. "He, he was dead, Iron Wood! I swear this to you. Blue and very dead!"

But Iron Wood wasn't listening. On the table's opposite side, he stared at the rumpled sketch clutched between his trembling hands and wagged his head. "You said you put him on a raft. Gave him a sort of...water burial."

Roaring waters flooded her ears and drowned her own voice. "I did. We did!" A pain knifed her temple as she fought to comprehend. "Explain, Strong Bear!"

Eagerness brightened the landscape of his face. "The crying you heard. In the water?"

That phantom infant's wail, a single faint bleat, pierced her once again, and she flinched.

"Your ears did not deceive you, Pretty Wolf. He was not dead."

Not dead. Not her imagination. Not the conjuring of soul-deep yearnings. But a plaintive cry for help.

And what had she done? Come instantly alert. Asked True Seeker if he'd heard. But the river was shouting, and her companion was gazing at her so piteously. He'd heard nothing, he said, so she'd reminded herself of the ashen hue of her baby's skin.

Then stood there.

With the river rushing about her, pressing insistently against the back of her broken legs, she'd watched her son be bobbed on the currents until he became a speck rounding the bend. And she'd done nothing. Nothing!

A dozen blades ripping her down the front could not hurt worse than the agony of that knowledge. She felt herself spilling out, her guilty blood washing the floorboards red, never to be gathered up again. How did one recover from such a grievous wrong? How did one *forgive* it?

Strong Bear's voice rumbled on. "He survived. Your mother's heart knew it all along."

There, on that word, her hearing cut out. *Mother. I am a mother.* Not of a stillborn but of a living boy named Flint who knew her name and stood watch on a hill. An urge, monstrous and overwhelming, came over her. To kick off her boots, face north, and run.

How correct Sunflower had been!

Molars clamped, Pretty Wolf clung to the back of the nearest chair and negotiated with her legs. If they would hold her through the trial, through whatever sentencing Old Sharp Knife meted out, she would free them to fly.

"Someone heard him crying." Iron Wood's dull voice sliced into her fantasy. He remained in the same spot, fixed on their son's likeness.

"Yes!" Strong Bear affirmed. "The little craft became lodged in the cane. Near Ockchoy village. Willow Woman followed his cries." He ran a thumb along Pretty Wolf's jaw, and it occurred to her that Iron Wood should be biting his hand off for cradling her so. "You remember me speaking of her?"

Pretty Wolf rubbed at her forehead as she slogged through past conversations. "Your clan sister?" The woman had shown up in his life... Had he said when? Ehi. "Willow Woman moved to Alabama Town shortly after, after..." *After I left.* After she'd abandoned True Seeker to himself, so she could act the little girl and run for her mother.

But if she had stayed even one moon more. If she had only stayed!

Iron Wood raised his head and slew her with his pallid complexion and haunted eyes. What was going through his mind? Thoughts of how much he hated her? How much of his son he'd missed. How much more he might be denied.

Her stomach twisted. Savagely. She hunched and dug her fingers into her belly. Bile sloshed a burning trail to the base of her tongue. She gagged and forced it back to the maelstrom of her stomach. "I'm sorry, Iron Wood. If I had not left! I am so—" A fiery flood rushed her throat. Strangling, she slapped a hand over her mouth. But there was no holding it back.

Strong Bear jumped for the fruit bowl and flung the oranges from it. He thrust it onto the table and under her face just as her stomach surged.

Vomit erupted. Waves and heaves, violent and painful.

Buck was suddenly beside her. Commanding this and that. She processed none of it.

Determined to empty itself of remorse, her stomach torqued and throttled and wrung itself out. She was on fire. Her throat, her nose, her heart. Tears poured. From the guilt or the force of expulsion.

She couldn't see, couldn't breathe. Could barely hear through her own commotion and the suffocating, purging floodwaters.

Close at her ear, a voice coaxed and soothed, assurances that gradually began to penetrate. Iron Wood? He stood so near he warmed her quaking elbow.

On her opposite side, hands consoled, patted and stroked, wiped snot and drool. The medicine maker. He set down a cloth to accept a glass of water that Strong Bear held out, concern scoring ridges in his brow.

It was beyond her to console his worry. She could only manage an open-mouthed pant as, palms flat to the table on either side of the bowl, she fought her stomach for control.

Iron Wood spoke, but a high-pitched ringing in her ears muted him.

Still hovering over the dish, she lifted a blurry gaze to him and found nothing but love radiating from the sweeping curve of his mouth. His tongue moved again, repeating the words he'd been saying over and over but that only now registered. "Our son is alive."

Her breathing pinched off. That was all he had to say? Where was the tirade, the blame? Creator knew she deserved it.

We have a, a—

Her eyelids batted lethargically, weighted with clinging tears. The movement spilled another down her cheek.

Iron Wood caught it with his thumb and, eyes lively with pride, laid the parchment on the tabletop in her direct eyeline. Laughing up at her was the penciled face of the boy who could be Robert Bellamy thirty winters prior but in reality was... "Our son," she croaked. And with that admission, with Iron Wood's adoring—dare she say *forgiving*?—smile shedding down on her, her stomach relented.

The knot unwound, and she gulped a ragged inhale.

"That's it, Miss Francis," Buck hummed. "All finished now." One last wipe of her chin before he pressed a water glass into her shaking hand. "Swish and spit."

She obeyed, then downed half the contents to alleviate her raw esophagus.

"Sergeant," Buck said, "escort Strong Bear back to his cell. And dump this, will you? I do believe she's done." The bowl slid out from before her.

Strong Bear came around to skim a touch across her hair before quietly stepping out with Barkton. Buck left right behind them, warning he could give Pretty Wolf no more than five minutes.

Iron Wood drew her around, took up the fresh cloth Buck left behind, and began mopping sweat from her neck and brow.

Spontaneous shudders still racked her body, but her pulse was regulating—even if her emotions were not. They bounced from disbelief to remorse and back so swiftly her head felt like a stickball field, hurling thoughts from one side to the other. Perhaps if she repeated it. "Our son is alive."

"So he is." Iron Wood cradled her jaw between his hands, and all else dissolved away. "And that, Polly dear, is the only thing in the world that matters. Only that."

If only it were true. Eyes sliding closed, she shook her head. "But, your trial."

"What of it? Buck here will speak to my excellent character. Then they'll deport me, and you'll follow with Flint."

Ehi, she would. Without a moment's hesitation. She would crawl to Kossati on her knees, row to England in a dugout. If that was what it took to undo her wrongs against this good man and unite him with his son. She straightened his coat lapels, a smile nascent on her lips. "And we will be a family."

"As we were always meant to be. Nothing to it." Enfolding her hands in his, he trapped them against his chest. "Have hope, darling. For Flint. Look,

look at his little face." He gazed tenderly at the sketch still laid out. "Is he not the most handsome fellow?"

"He is yours, after all."

"Quite true," he gloated, luring a chuckle from her. "He certainly has my eyes."

"And your loyal heart, if Strong Bear's stories are even half true."

"Hmm. By the set of his chin, he received your mischief and stubborn nature."

"I'll own it," she said on sob-laugh.

Iron Wood drew her close and picked up the paper for a proper look. "Hello, young sir. Master Flint," he mused, trying out the name with a tiny wince.

Pretty Wolf rather agreed. A particular element was missing. "Master Flint Maxwell Bellamy, Wolf Clan." The blood of a lord might travel their son's veins, but a wolf lived there too. Didn't he already sit on his hilltop, watchful?

Iron Wood's teeth flashed wide. "Better."

Twin tendrils of hope and happiness began a cautious unfurling within her. They slinked toward her heart and tweaked the edges of her lips. "He'll grow to be a wise and noble man, handsome and courageous, same as his father." And such a fine father he would be. Father, husband. The finest. How had she been so blessed?

She clasped a flat palm to his face and pressed her lips to his scratchy cheek. "Do you truly forgive me, Iron Wood?"

When she pulled back, tears sparkled in his eyes, enlarging and brightening them to the palest, most beautiful blue. "Dear heart, nothing will ever change the strength of my love for you. Not a mistaken burial. Not a trial or deportation." She stood still for him as he trailed kisses across her jaw, landing the tenderest at one corner of her mouth.

"You are the spark to my soul, Polly," he said, her old name never sweeter. "My very soul."

Chapter 38

Noonday's pine-pole cabin had never felt oppressive. But Pretty Wolf supposed that armed Bluecoats stationed by the fireplace, under the loft, and in the doorway of the sleeping quarters could make any place feel like a sweat lodge. Or maybe it was the brisk trip in from San Marcos.

Apparently, two horses could not be found for Pretty Wolf and Sergeant Barkton anywhere in the villa. Balada had mysteriously—and suspiciously—disappeared from the stables. Pretty Wolf mulishly contended with the stablemaster for substitute mounts, but she'd lost. Which left her with blisters on her booted heels and her guard with sweat stains on his collar.

Perspiration gracing her forehead, Pretty Wolf slowly exhaled the last of the calumet smoke and considered the hastily assembled group. Seated on the split-log benches, they rimmed her mother's long trestle table.

The previous leadership of Wakulla's small council had been all but wiped out: Crazy Medicine, dead. Sun Bird, vanished. Kills Many, in hiding. Water Moccasin, Tall Bull, Mink—exiled for their beliefs, her mother had said.

That left a dappled band of new and old members with Pretty Wolf as, perhaps, the most colorful and peculiar. Figuratively and literally. Her yellow jacket shone sun-bright where she sat in her father's spot, its cheery tone forced and awkward in the gathering's gloom. The only other element of imitation cheer in the lodge was the incessant rattling coming off Screaming Buttons.

Pretty Wolf passed the sacred pipe to him in the Second's position on her left, then folded her hands on the rough-hewn wood and watched the ceremony proceed in silence. The instrument of peace went next to Big Voice, who sat as acting yatika at her opposite elbow. From there, according to rank, each of the ten puffed and prayed. Two elders, four warriors of middling rank, and Winter Hawk, who sat at the far end and squirmed in a squeaky chair.

His hair proudly sported its first feather—an emblem of necessity rather than accomplishment, she suspected. Traditionally, he would not be eligible for a council seat for many winters, but with Pretty Wolf's appointment to miccohokti, tradition was well and truly overturned. The People's histories included tales of female chieftains, but they were not common.

Neither was assigning a one-feather warrior as representative of the talwa's contingent of braves. But strength, Mink had taught her, came in all sizes, genders, and ages. Wakulla was in no position to scorn any variety of it.

Kicking Knife extended the pipe to Winter Hawk. Fighting a grin, the young warrior took it and inhaled his cheeks concave. An instant later, he coughed, smoke billowing over his thrust-out tongue. He pounded his chest, squinting watery eyes. "That is terrible!"

Chuckles rumbled through warrior and soldier alike, bringing a much-needed break in tension. Even Barkton, accepting a steaming mug from Noonday, paused for a mustache wiggle.

Pretty Wolf found a half-smile for the brave. "On behalf of Wakulla, we welcome Winter Hawk to our body of warriors. May Creator make your path straight and honorable, and may your fields be green and your waters still."

Big Voice crinkled his nose and grumbled something about soft-bellied miccohoktis, but Elder Mad Duck christened the blessing with an intoned, "A'ho." *It is so.*

Not long ago, Pretty Wolf might have prayed the bear's strength over him, the mink's ferocity in battle, and the wolf's courage in the hunt.

Times had changed.

Peace was now her greatest aim. For the People, for their tomorrow. Iron Wood's. Their son's.

Flint. My son.

A swarm of butterflies lifted off in her heart and coaxed her lips into a more robust smile.

Son, son.

Repeating the word might eventually make it seem more than a happy dream conjured by grief and desperation. Granted, scarcely a morning had passed since she'd learned of him, but she had yet to fully process that she had a boy in Muscogee country, a child of her own womb. *The* child of her womb.

A male child, a future provider and warrior for Wolf Clan.

Pretty Wolf suppressed a grimace. In her urgency to cobble together a council, she'd set aside telling her clan of him. Now, she tracked her widowed mother and scolded herself for putting it off.

Complexion ashen and stony, Noonday mechanically leaned over Rains Long to set a mug before him. At the opposite corner, Runs Like Deer served corn fritters and dried berries to Winter Hawk, who gaped at the boulder of her belly.

Pretty Wolf's arm dropped below the table where she laid a palm over the pregnancy scars that would have given her away, the price she'd paid for her boy. The child who now had a name and a story and the darling face of an almost three-year-old. The little wolf who had hopes and dreams, a loving pack, and Creator's keen regard.

She brought Flint's pale eyes up before her and left them there to serve as guiding beacons as she made herself tall in her chair and put muscle and bone into her voice. "Elders, brothers, let us begin. On the fourth dawn from tomorrow, we leave Wakulla for the fort named Gadsden. Sergeant Barkton"—she nodded to him; he stepped forward—"will be our guide."

The announcement fell over the room like an edict of silence. No one moved. No one spoke, save for the translator who murmured at Barkton's ear. Casual English floated through the open door—the outside guards having a chat. A hen clucked and wandered inside, head strutting, to peck around Noonday's feet.

They'd known forced migration to be a strong possibility. That didn't make hearing it any less soul-crushing. And voicing it stripped Pretty Wolf's spirit bare. All the battles and lives sacrificed, the bloody soles and wind-split lips, the teeth clean with hunger—to what end? To be spun on their heels and prodded with bayonets back to Muscogee country.

And what would they take with them? She quelled an indignant snarl and braced for the inevitable backlash. "For the journey home, we are allowed to take only what—"

"Home," Eats the Heart sneered.

Grumbles erupted, but she stomped them out with a few sharp looks. "Shift your thinking, and shift it quickly! Wakulla is no longer our home. We must let it go, set our sights north to the land of our ancestors, the land we once held sacred."

"*Still* hold sacred," intoned Mad Duck, his voice marred by age and keen with longing.

Pretty Wolf clearly wasn't the only one eager to put Wakulla and the Point in her memories. The ends of her mouth lifted. "Ehi, *still*. And always. One head," she began the old chant, warming inside when they joined her in resounding accord.

"One mouth, one heart. A'ho."

Pretty Wolf raised her mug to her chin and, nostrils constricting, drew in its calming steam. A tangy sip of the assee wet her parched tongue and fortified her for the rest of the mandate. She flung it out as one did manure from a shovel. All at once to be rid of it. "We are allowed only what we can carry on our backs. No carts. Those with horses may loan them to the elderly and infirm for riding. From the Gadsden fort, we take the Apalachicola by flatboat. The vessels are small, and there will be no room for travois or animals. Horses and dogs will be left to their own fates."

Heated murmurings flared again—disbelief, questions, demands—but Pretty Wolf was riveted to her sister.

One hand occupied with a wooden bowl, Runs Like Deer wrapped an arm around her swollen abdomen and lobbed Sergeant Barkton an accusatory sidelong glare. As though he were personally responsible for thrusting her unborn child into harm's way.

Pretty Wolf sympathized with those violently protective instincts. She'd felt them before, felt them now. For that reason, she would defy every mandate; she would starve herself to bones—if doing so meant Runs Like Deer and her baby made it home alive and healthy. It mattered little how Pretty Wolf herself arrived, so long as Flint stood sentinel on that hill at trail's end.

When the protestations began in earnest, she lifted a quieting hand. "I understand your upsets and your worries, and I share them. But the winter roads will be harsh and wet, the rains coming cold and often. The longer the trail, the louder our hunger. Bodies will weaken. Spirits will crack. The children will cry, and the elderly will falter. We *must* move swiftly. A thing we cannot do if our feet and our carts' wheels are sunk into the mud by the weight of corn sacks and iron kettles."

By the resignation rounding the council's shoulders, it became apparent they would not be arguing. Even so, she left no room for commentary.

"The general has promised provisions at intervals, escorts for protection, and the service of the medicine maker, Marcus Buck. Buck was a recent guest of Antonio Luengo and has been returned to our region for this purpose, to ensure all arrive in Muscogee country in good health."

A laughable impossibility. Buck's presence was due diligence. Nothing more.

Big Voice snorted derisively, but Pretty Wolf scowled him down so fiercely that a hush settled about the table. "So far, Buck's white heart has shown itself to be good." Hadn't he remained for the duration of the execution vigil? Coaxed Noonday into rest and followed through on his promise of a respectable burial? "We are blessed to have the man caring for our weak and injured. And our expectant women."

Her eyes found her sister's for a bolstering smile, and she cursed herself for the weakness of it. Part for worry over a trail-side birth, and part for dread at unveiling her next bit of news.

She sat forward, forearms planted squarely on the table, fingers threaded loosely together in a show of confidence. "Tomorrow's noon sun will see every Wakulla male aged thirteen winters and above at the Spanish fort for a formal surrender."

Several hisses filled the air. Others adjusted in their seats. Rains Long went so far as to cast a poisonous glance at the soldiers. The Bluecoats came alert, bodies going rigid. Hands locking down on their weapons, they darted unspoken warnings between themselves. Pretty Wolf read them as easily as she did her mare's pinned-back ears—they would strike first, question later.

A distraction was in order.

"There is more." All eyes snapped to her, and like a horse plunging headlong into battle, she barreled on. "I received news this morning. From Kossati."

Noonday and Runs Like Deer ceased their piddling at the hearth and turned to listen, Noonday's cropped hair a shock every time Pretty Wolf glimpsed it.

"Speak on, Miccohokti," Mad Duck urged.

Sweat instantly dampened Pretty Wolf's armpits. She should have thought this through. Hadn't considered her mother's feelings at all. Too late now. There was only forward. No, first, she would have to go *back*. To the beginning, she realized with no small chagrin. It would make no sense otherwise. Her tongue swiped out with moisture. "During my long away, I bore a son to Wolf Clan."

Utter silence.

Only Screaming Buttons reacted, his inhale acute, a cog slotting into place.

Runs Like Deer edged forward. "Sister?" Her voice was small with disbelief.

"It's true."

Noonday gripped her chest, heart-struck, as tidbits of evidence combined with motherly intuition began scrolling across her face. "Begin talking, Daughter." She slanted Pretty Wolf a wounded look—wholly justified—but she would change her manner once her lap was filled up with not one, but two little wolf pups.

"At Horse's Flat Foot I suspected I carried Iron Wood's child. But I could not yet be certain." Pretty Wolf's voice wobbled as she set out on her tale. "With battle days off, Iron Wood would have only worried for my safety. So, I chose to spare him. I…regret my silence. Along with many other poor choices I have made since." Her gaze hung, weighted with shame.

She startled when a large hand curled around her forearm.

Screaming Buttons. No one rebuked him the touch, and Pretty Wolf inwardly cheered Winter Hawk for spreading word of the Rule's death. Buttons met her eyes, his hickory orbs as caring as his touch, a gesture that beamed compassion and support, seeped warmly into her skin, and alleviated like a **healing song**.

"Go on." Big Voice nodded. "None here judge." *Or else*, implied the warning in his low pitch.

"Maddo, friends," she said under her breath and resumed a little steadier, making sure to touch on every councilman's eye. "For eight moons, the child grew within me. But before my time had come, I stumbled on river rocks. The shock of the fall set off my labor." Such a simplistic, detached recounting. A drastic curtailing of events, distilled of the childish fears that prompted the crossing, bled of the horror at what it had caused. There was shame enough in Strong Bear knowing she'd foolishly run off to find her mother—the woman who now hunched against her eldest and cried quietly into her palms.

"My companion, True Seeker, guided me through the delivery," Pretty Wolf blurted in a rush, the quicker off her tongue and out of this lodge, the better. "But the baby had no life in him. No breath. True Seeker feared I'd bled too much and would not survive long in the frigid elements, so we chose a water burial. He covered the boy in mud and laid him on a raft of pine boughs. We gave him into Water Spirit's keeping. Only this morning, I learned she gave him back."

Noonday's hands fell away, her face lifting, bewilderment twisting her age lines. She sniffed. "What do you mean, Daughter? How?"

Finding Pretty Wolf

What *did* Pretty Wolf mean? Now the words were out, she wondered how true they could be. "Path Maker," she murmured, thoughtful of the fitting name.

"Who?" Pushing past the seated elders, Noonday bustled over, swiping at her dripping nose, and stationed herself behind Big Voice. "Speak up, girl."

Pretty Wolf lifted her chin and took possession of Strong Bear's claim. "Path Maker is another name for Creator." Because the Ancient Words stated that the Spirit above all spirits hewed a path for every man and woman, one He personally oversaw. "He used a mother from Ochckoy. She heard a cry and followed it to the canebrake where she found my child. Some moons later, after I'd left to find you all, her life crossed with True Seeker's, and the truth was known. Since that day, he has been a father to my son, loved him as his own."

The council members turned to each other, silent wonder on their faces, but Pretty Wolf let their presence fade into the background. Enormous and glistening, Noonday's eyes clung to Pretty Wolf as disbelief and wonder, mixed with flickers of fragile hope, vied for dominance of her features. "Strong Bear did this?"

A prick of pain niggled her conscience. *She* should have been the one. But in her absence, she would have chosen Strong Bear every time. Over Tall Bull, over her father. Over, perhaps, even her paleface betrothed who would have clothed him in ruffled collars and linen dresses and foregone taking him to water at sun's rise. She needn't ask to know Strong Bear had raised her son in the old ways.

Love—pure and simple and strong as the rivers—flooded Pretty Wolf's chest, filled her up until it graced her mouth, lifting its folds in a slow arch. "He did, Mother, and to find me, he joined McIntosh's White Sticks. He battled his way south, always looking for me. The path was opened with his captivity and slavery." Which, she was quite certain, he never once feared or regretted. "Outside of death, is there any greater sacrifice?"

If the look of awe on her mother's face was anything to go by, her answer was no. Eyes swimming again with tears, she tremulously asked, "Our boy's name?"

"My son is called Flint." Only the strongest name for a baby who'd fought the cold, the river, and a witless mother. And won. She beamed proudly. "His eyes are his father's, blue as the sky. Every dawn he watches for my coming. He awaits. *Life* awaits." Her words turned deliberate, handed out with a challenging glance at each man. "For us all. Wherever your tribal talwa may be."

She pushed her chair back, rose to her significant height, and showed them her unbending spine. "So then, brothers. Put hope in your voice when you talk to those under your care. Go. Fill your pouches with corn and your bones with resilience and prepare for the migration home."

Chapter 39

At some point in the morning, Balada leaped the San Marcos corral and scent-tracked Pretty Wolf to Wakulla. The creature never appreciated being left behind, and Pretty Wolf never appreciated her loyalty more than during the ride back to her men. Exhausted in every way describable, she let her legs dangle and her mare do the sweating.

After he stopped in at Snake Clan, Screaming Buttons would follow her to San Marcos. Only Sergeant Barkton was with her now on the outer edges of the villa. In lockstep with Balada, he kept his eyes forward and his mouth shut for the whole three-sight journey. Nothing unusual there, but the closer they came to the villa, the tighter his muscles wound, the one over his jaw bunched and ticking. Once inside San Marcos, his pace began to lag, and Pretty Wolf's seat on the mare tightened.

Senses sharpening, she elongated her neck and panned the villa. Since they'd left, it had come alive, its people abuzz, scurrying down the main thoroughfare. All in one direction: the fort.

Was Iron Wood's trial open for mass viewing? To be held under the sky?

She noted the sun's position to confirm the proceedings would not start for at least a hand of time. Unless this had nothing to do with Iron Wood but with something else entirely, such as—

The muscle of her heart convulsed. Her fingers seized around mane, and Balada skipped sideways. Pretty Wolf let her prance it out as she swiveled to Barkton. "Where are they going?" Command shook her voice. "What do you know, Barkton?"

Do not say it, do not say his name! she silently ordered, while her own head blatantly disobeyed. *Strong Bear, Strong Bear, Strong Bear.*

If Jackson had no qualms hanging a micco without trial, he would string up a three-feather nobody during coffee and biscuits.

An iron clamp, fear fastened hard about her. "Sergeant," she snapped.

The long ends of Barkton's mustache pulled down. An expression she'd learned to mean stubborn refusal.

"Speak!"

Balada's head bobbed up, one ear swiveling back.

"Easy, Miss." The man wouldn't look at her. Didn't need to since it was the horse's halter his hand shot for.

Pretty Wolf snarled and rammed her heels into Balada's ribs. "Eyah!"

The animal burst into action, disposing of their now-hollering escort. Hooves high, she thundered down the middle of the lengthy lane, every pounding thud a double of Pretty Wolf's pulse.

Tragedy was breeding behind those walls. She felt it in every straining fiber.

Ahead, villagers congregated thickly in the street outside the fort's lowered bridge. They craned for a peek inside. Oddly, calm ruled the lot. *Too calm.* Near reverence charged the hush.

From her higher vantage, she saw over their heads to a line of soldiers at the open gate, rifles held crosswise over their chests and used to shove back an occasional overeager spectator.

Spectator to what!

Not a hanging. At least not from the raised portcullis.

The fort loomed now, blinding white in the afternoon sun. From its interior floated the faint sound of barked English. Soldierly. Drilled orders.

Dread swarmed like biting ants under Pretty Wolf's skin. She kicked Balada's flanks. "Forward, girl!" With a gleeful whicker, the mare forged into the cluster of humanity. *"Dejen paso,"* she called out, demanding passage.

The villagers parted with grumbles and startled cries, opening a path to the moat, but those on the bridge had nowhere to go, and Balada didn't care. She whinnied, hooves reporting against the wood as she barreled ahead, bowling people aside and off into the swampy ditch below.

Growling out her frustration, Pretty Wolf threw herself off the mare and speared through the pack at the bridge's end. She thundered up to the line of solid blue stretched across the base of the stone arch. Fists balled hard, she prepared to fire off demands for entry, but as her mouth parted, the center fellow stepped back and away.

"Princess Pretty Wolf," he said, along with a good many other words. None of which she heard.

Her sight had gone long, drawn across the eerily vacant square to the sole spot of activity in the back-left corner. The angle was terrible, too narrow for a proper view. But it was enough to stop the heart in Pretty Wolf's chest.

Eight armed Bluecoats made an orderly row. Nothing stood between them and the white north wall, save for a pole.

And Iron Wood.

Blindfolded. Arms locked behind him. Stance broad and unwavering, he faced the soldiers with his chin at a proud tilt.

A hot poker of horror thrust into her chest. A scream dropped her jaw, but panic fisted her throat. Cut her sound to a strangled bleat. Compensating, her legs burst into a sprint.

A salvo of shouts pursued. Someone snatched at her back. Missed. Grabbed skirt. She stumbled, but the material tore, freeing her. Feet back in use, she clambered forward, boots flying across the open compound, Iron Wood too far, too far! Wind lashed at her clothes and eyes. It crammed dust into her mouth and dried her waste of a tongue.

Off to the side of the firing line, movement. Another Bluecoat raising his arm. He held it aloft. Signaled, "Ready!"

No, no!

As one, eight rifles lifted, locked into aim.

Stop it, stop! Her throat refused the shout.

These men could not do this. They did *not* have this authority!

Behind her, footfalls pounded. Willing power into her legs, she begged swiftness of the spirits. Speed, wisdom. Mercy!

At the slave pole, her body had stopped a killing blade. It would stall these rifles, too. It would! If she could just *get* there.

Fingers splayed, she reached for Iron Wood. Her throat spasmed, choking on words that would not come. *I'm here! Look!*

His necked turned. His posture stiffened. Could he see through the blindfold? He began shaking his head. Small, jerky motions.

He saw her, he did!

Arms lassoed vice-like around her middle, yanking her to a gutting halt just outside the line. Breath blasted from her lungs. With it, finally, a wordless, throat-peeling screech.

Arm stretched, the commanding officer looked at her; looked at Iron Wood, blindfold pointed her way. And chopped the air. "Fire!"

A deafening boom rattled Pretty Wolf's brain. A physical pummel, she lurched.

And Iron Wood convulsed. Lead riddling his torso. The fabric of his white shirt exploded with crimson. A backward snap of his head, and blood ruptured on his brow. His knees snapped like twigs.

Through the gray haze of gunpowder, she watched his outline soundlessly slouch down the pole, his head swinging limply on his neck. A bright scarlet stream poured from between his eyes.

Pretty Wolf panted, frozen inside a cage of arms, her sight welded to Iron Wood's body. Not a man of the eight shifted more than to lower their weapons. Drifting clouds reeking of burned powder stung her nose as the officer marched to the pole and cut Iron Wood loose.

Rope fell from his wrists. He rolled forward and landed in an ungainly heap, face in the dirt.

The heat of Pretty Wolf's skin spiked to fever levels. Lungs pumping in great surges, she gnashed down on bared teeth and let molten rage billow through her. Billow and roil and heave until, in an eruption of spit and limbs, it jetted from every pore.

She left herself then. Like a ghost lifting from a body, she abandoned reason. Unaware, uncaring, she let her fury and anguish do as they pleased with her.

The band of arms about her waist constricted, pinched her skin, and bit into her ribs. She felt nothing, all pain smothered by the fire razing her from the inside out.

Voices shouted. Made demands. In her ear. Before her face.

She heard only the product of her rampaging throat.

Saw only red. Pouring, puddling. Collecting in great pools and squishing between her toes. Exploding from her shoulder, dripping from Strong Bear's nose, seeping from the torn flesh of her father's neck.

A palm landed against her cheek, swift and cutting.

The force audibly cracked her neck. Pain, kindling for the kiln.

Anger, agony. They merged in an uncontainable beast not quite rabid enough to be confused about what it wanted to shred between its teeth.

Who it wanted.

With that targeted thought, she slammed back into herself. Body canting acutely forward, she strained for freedom. Pain burned her shoulders where they were coerced severely back. Unforgiving fingers bit into her upper arms, and clumps of loosened hair dangled over her face, lifting and falling with the massive draughts hissing through her teeth. The world reeled around her in a nauseating medley of sounds and smells, but her vision remained steadfast on a singular point.

High on the wall-walk, Old Sharp Knife peered down, coolly observing her savagery.

How safely he stood far above the dirt and blood. Above those who slapped women and battered good men with lead. At *his* orders.

The scar in her shoulder throbbed in time with her drumming heartbeat. "Coward! Wretched coward!" Ruined from shrieking, her voice had reduced to a croaky squall. "Come down and stand before me! Face the woman whose heart you have ripped out twice over!"

Jackson's gray head tipped sideways as if pondering a curious insect.

She jerked against the restraints and imagined stringing him up from the portcullis and burying a dagger in his eye socket.

Someone planted himself before her and sprawled his hands over the sides of her face. His visage swam out of her vision as her eyes darted back to the maggot above and behind him.

"Miss Francis, please! *Stop!*"

Buck?

Air left her nostrils in a rush, and her muscles began a slow uncoil. Her lashes batted briskly, but just as the red began fading to pink, Jackson turned his back and strolled from sight.

She was nothing. A bit of lint. A smudge on the ground. A fly buzzing around his otherwise perfect conquest.

With another roar, she broke an arm free and rammed it back. Her elbow connected with bone and elicited a pained exclamation.

Spitting a coarse word, Buck charged at her with a cloth. It mashed her lip into her teeth, and bitterness coated her tongue. White fabric occluded her vision, and with her next inhale, she dragged into her lungs a sickly sweet odor. It stopped her short. All her focus directed into shucking him off.

But he was too strong, too determined. "Just breathe, Miss Francis," he said all too serenely. "Calm down and breathe."

Breathe? She was drowning! Choking on that awful smell. What was he doing to her? She would scratch the skin from his face if her limbs weren't flopping, strength bleeding out of them like water from a busted gourd.

Woozy, she gave her head another disorienting shake. What was this? Would Buck poison her? She might ponder his betrayal if she could order her dissolving thoughts beyond, "Wwwhy?" Muffled, slurred, the question was more mewl than word.

"Forgive me, Miss, but you force my hand."

Her eyes rolled, her thoughts lulled, and the sun went out.

Something had surely died and rotted on Pretty Wolf's tongue. Grimacing, she swallowed the putrid taste and creaked her eyes open to a familiar view—the dreary holding chamber she'd first been brought to with her select men. This time, instead of Big Voice and Screaming Buttons as companions, she had Toño and an unlit chimenea.

Slumped over the table, Toño reclined his head on his twined arms and snored to rouse the spirits. A pewter pitcher and mug sat at his elbow, and his dusty hat lay next to his unpolished boots.

Where had he been keeping himself? Or had he been *kept*?

Despite all, it was good to see him, her tío. Pretty Wolf wanted to hate the man, cast stones, and scream his blame. But who could stand against Old Sharp Knife and live?

You did, her father whispered from somewhere along his spirit journey. *You, my fearless wolf.*

She had. By the breadth of a spider thread.

Regardless, it would seem she'd been called to do it again. To stand for the People and fight for their survival. Unless she bartered and begged, a forced journey through winter forest and swamps would come at a high cost. Reason enough to disregard the lethargy weighing her limbs and face the day.

Pushing up, she dragged her feet over the bed's edge. Needles of pain bore into her eyes, and her stomach gave a sick turn. Buck's poison cloth. Better than a club to the skull.

Thick and dry, her tongue begged a sip of whatever occupied that pitcher. Then there was the insistent ache at the base of her ribs. Bruises, most likely, and something more. Something dark and seething. A pit of writhing vipers so frightening she crammed her eyelids closed and went in frantic search of her misplaced armor. She'd scarcely begun the numbing process when quiet scraping noises lifted her lashes.

Awake and upright, Toño gazed at her piteously. Though, really, he deserved the same. Bags hung under his eyes, and his oiled black hair stood up on his head like wildfire. "Lobita." Empathy tinged his melodic Spanish cant. "How do you feel?"

How did she feel? How did one feel when a terrible cavern yawned within her, deep and endlessly wide? When its jagged edges pierced her all at once? When, between them, anger like molten rock slowly oozed and simmered?

Vengeful, she wanted to answer, but she'd already made that abundantly clear in the courtyard when she'd earned herself a slap from one man and a lungful of sleeping poison from another.

She massaged her temple. "My head aches." The words were a scratching stick against her throat. A brutal reminder of her delicious insanity. As foolhardy as it had been.

Hissing filled her head. The vipers. Coiled to strike. She petted them down with promises of *Soon, soon*.

"The ether probably." Toño's smile curved slight and pained.

"How long did I sleep?"

"Less than an hour." He hefted himself up. "The *medico* will wish to know you have woken." After relaying a message to whoever stood outside, he hustled over to wring his hands before her. "You spoke to Señor Bellamy? On Sunday?"

She stared at the war metals hanging cockeyed on his uniform breast. "Sí. And again today." Thanks spirits she had. "We found our peace before…"

Before what? What *was* that?

Moaning, she tipped forward to rest her head on the heels of her palms. Hair tumbled about her face and summoned flashes of the courtyard. Of Iron Wood. Shattered by rifle fire. Nose smashed in the dirt.

"What happened, Tío?" The squeak of her voice made her out to be eggshell rather than iron. Little wonder since her armor still lay mostly in pieces around her.

Toño, hearing her weakness, peppered the air with expletives and didn't bother with his usual apologies. He released his bulk to the bed and gathered her into his side. "The trial was short. All in English. I was given no translator."

Throat vibrating with frustration, she leaned stiffly against Toño and savored the burn of the fire tearing through her gut. Her cavern bubbled with it now, filled to the brim.

Toño rubbed her arm. "Ala! Never have I seen such bravery."

Unbidden, an image of Iron Wood hurdled in—him standing regally before his death—and a proud, joyless smile crept up her lips. "He never feared his end. Only mine."

Though why he'd been *ended* had yet to be explained.

Why, why, why. The word cycloned through her head in another destructive, disorienting round. Why did the trial start early? Why had they condemned him? Why did they not wait for her? Why did the spirits hate her so? Why did Jackson! Had he remembered her and her dagger? Was this punishment?

Toño nodded somberly. "Bellamy went nobly to his death, and he did not flinch." Until he saw her. "But I meant you, Lobita. Shouting at the general as you did, shaming him before his men, daring him to face you. To answer for what he had done."

She drew back to look at him. "You understood that?"

"It was Spanish you spoke."

"Oh." She drooped, realizing how severely she had been lost to herself. "You confuse bravery with madness, my love-blind tío."

His chest shook with quiet laughter. "Perhaps so, *bonita*. But take comfort. You are not the only one touched by madness today. I hear your friend, the bear, is in uproar in his cell."

That jerked her head off his shoulder. The vipers reared up. She riled them with urgings of *On my signal*.

Toño grinned sagely as if he'd known precisely the response he would get. "Will you let General Jackson have him, too?"

She sat bolt upright, the lava jetting now through her bloodstream. Jackson would *not* take one more person from her. He would not have her sweet Kit. No, Strong Bear would be out of that cage before dusk. Pretty Wolf would make it so. As soon as the room ceased its tilt-and-whirl.

Agh, that crippling poison!

A knock sounded, the door handle jangled, and the culprit himself appeared. Marcus Buck entered and made a dismissing motion toward the outdoors. "Commander Luengo, if you please."

"Ordered about in my own home," Toño grumbled while heaving his mass up and running a hand down his taxed buttons. "Lobita, I brought your bag from Los Robles. It is here." He tapped his toe against something under the bed. "And before you ask, I received your message and signed the document."

"Gracias." She would be glad to be out of her wrinkled, sweaty gown, though she couldn't quite remember the importance of the signature. Looking up at him, she tried for a smile but gave up.

"Ay, chica." The awkward pats to the top of her head brought strange comfort. "Do not lose yourself to despair. The Santa Biblia tells us the faithful love of God never ends, that his mercies begin afresh each morning. Hope in him," he said, finger pointed high, "and look to the dawn!" A true commander's charge.

The failed smile became a tiny bud. "I will try." She squeezed his fleshy hand. "Will I see you again, Tío?" Later that day? The next? Ever?

The loss of him would be no simple pluck and toss. She would feel it to the roots of her spirit. The tightening in her chest, a discomforting precursor.

"*Luego*, princesa." He deposited a kiss on her crown. "Later, sí?"

She nodded as if she had any choice, any power. In reality, she had nothing and less every hour. Even her right to lunacy had been deprived her.

As Toño left, giving way to the medicine maker, resentment and gratitude cycled within her. She really did hate Buck for who and what he represented. And for the tomahawk hacking at her brain. But if he hadn't subdued her, saved her from herself, who knew how long Jackson would have put up with her insolence? Then there were her bittersweet last moments with Iron Wood. Buck's doing.

With much aggravation and a goodly sum of humiliation, she extended her hand as he crossed to her. "Marcus Buck, I owe you much."

His bloodshot eyes stared at her overture of thanks before he gently pushed her hand down. "No, Miss Francis. You don't." He offered no further explanation, but there was much to be learned from his wan complexion. Apology. Distress. They did terrible things to his handsome features. Sank his cheeks, carved ravines into his brow, painted smudges beneath his eyes.

Touched by his humanity, her soul reached out with the thinnest of threads and knit to him. This compassion from her enemy was almost more than her resilience could bear. Fresh tears rose, but she beat them off. There would be time later for weeping. Right now, Strong Bear required her strength.

Buck retraced his steps to grab a chair and place it before her. He installed himself in it, and from the black bag on his lap, he withdrew a folded blood-spattered parchment. "Lord Bellamy was holding this. Until the end." He pressed it into her palm.

She clutched their boy to her breast, lower lip wobbling. She firmed it. "Where is he?" Nothing to be done for the hoarse whisper. With the stone obstructing her throat, she was fortunate to manage that.

"Laid to rest beside your father." Buck wore shame in his aspect, and well he should.

The Bluecoats had killed her man without the least consideration of her love or position. Buried him while she'd been knocked out from sleeping tincture. Who would they take next?

Not Strong Bear. Her nails gouged her palm. *Not. Strong Bear.*

She hoisted herself off the bed. Teetered. Swatted off Buck's assistance.

Frowning, he remained standing by the bed but kept a hawkish eye on her as she began pacing. To the chimenea and back. Flexing and coiling her hands as, panel by panel, she slapped her defenses back into place, imbuing them with all the repelling properties of the most tenacious metal.

Fear would not reach her. Grief would not pierce her. Anger would not control her. To her marrow, she was iron itself. Rigid. Unfeeling. Cold as the grave Iron Wood occupied.

"Why?" she gritted out.

She could have been asking anything, any one of the questions tormenting her, but Buck seemed to intuit which answer she most wanted.

"Lord Bellamy," he voiced her husband's name slowly, solemnly, with something nigh to respect marking his tone, "was found guilty of aiding, abetting, and comforting an enemy of the United States, as well as instigating Indian warriors in their movements against us. As a citizen and former officer of Great Britain, his actions peg him a British agent to the Red Sticks. The powder and lead found in the trade house were highly suggestive of an armory, but the item that solidified his ill-advised allegiance was the letter that I— That was discovered in Fowltown."

Her stride arrested. She gave her head a puzzled shake. "Letter?"

A pop of color mantled Buck's cheeks, but when he spoke, his voice betrayed no lack of confidence. "Yes, it was found among Fat Warrior's possessions. Correspondence addressed to a Colonel Terrell. Bellamy wrote it on behalf of Fat Warrior's second in command, a certain Stout Feather. In it, he asked for the release of his captured brother. The document was presented as proof Bellamy had cast his lot with the Red Sticks."

War chief. Fowltown. Stout Feather. The thoughts riddled her. Rapid-fire. Each clicking into a memory slot. *That questionable letter.* Not so questionable anymore.

Arms locked straight at her sides, she let loose a furious growl. "There is no crime in letter-writing!"

Buck's boots shuffled where he stood. His lashes lowered. "I sympathize with your grievance, Miss Francis, I do. But Mr. Bellamy included a postscript with a personal plea and his own signature. It was, regrettably, quite condemning."

Pretty Wolf whirled away from him, jaw aching from its grind. Clenched and bloodless, her hands quaked violently, desperate for something to toss. To destroy. The table, the chimenea, the entire room would do for a start.

Iron Wood had put his mark on that accursed paper after all. She'd asked and asked if he had, and every time, he'd refused a reply. Because he knew the magnificent folly of such an action.

She gazed into the chimenea's dark belly and hurled insults. *Careless! Heedless. Stupid, stupid man!* But he simply could not help himself. When presented with a broken spirit, he'd always been deaf and blind to all but *rescue*. Penning someone else's words was safe enough. But affixing one's own arguments and name… He'd as good as signed his own death sentence.

Out of nowhere, the need for Strong Bear tugged at her hard. She rubbed her hip bone and contemplated the chamber's unlocked door. Then let herself drown in visions of charging through the fort until she found Jackson. She would pound her fists against his cold-as-marble heart until he relented and set her Kit free.

"The prosecution painted a truly unsavory image of him." Buck yanked her from her imaginings. "So objectionable, in fact, that my backing of his character made almost no impression. I even included a detailed recount of his part in Lillian's escape to the States. Unfortunately, my wife's dubious standing with her own country cast a shadow over my witness." Expression pinched, he scrubbed a hand across his forehead. "Combined, these charges were too many to produce any outcome other than guilty."

As much as she hated it, disagreed with it, Buck's explanation did follow reason—Iron Wood had purposefully been striving against the United States, a clear violation of the treaty. But he was no common, forgettable ruffian. "He was a British *lord*," she exploded, arms flung wide. "That alone should have spared him death!"

"You're right, Miss. And it did…at first. The officials sentenced him to incarceration and prompt deportation." Like fishing line tangled in pond sludge, the words dragged out of him. Slow and arduous. Pained. "But…General Jackson overturned it and ordered immediate execution."

The words hit her in the lungs like a grievous blow. She stumbled to the nearest wall and bumped into it shoulder-first, letting it take on her slumping weight. But there was no wall strong enough to hold up a mountain-sized realization—it had all been a sham. The trial, the hope of decency and reasonability. All of it, a mockery of justice, of the Defiance and everything they stood for.

As despicably as they valued her father, Iron Wood's treatment ranked leagues more degrading. More wounding. For it had all been a mere performance of legalities and political maneuverings, a rite for Jackson to shield himself with once England's king reared up and cried foul play. As she desperately hoped he would. Desperately prayed the Great Father in Washington would strike his general down, rip the gold tassels from his uniform and cram them down his gullet.

Maybe she would beat him to it. Deliciously pleasant, that thought. She was luxuriating in it when Buck settled a gentle touch on her elbow.

"You should eat. It'll help balance out the effects of the ether."

She shucked him off. Eat! She'd rather spew all the words she'd been denied during Iron Wood's hearing. Which brought her to another of her whys. "Did the trial begin early?" Barely restrained emotion crimped her voice.

"It began precisely when scheduled."

"The general sent me away?"

"Not the general."

Air whistled through her throat in its rapid inward draw. "Iron Wood." That man and his infuriatingly protective measures!

"He arranged it to spare you, Miss, and I can't fault him. Neither did the general. He approved the request at once."

She whipped him with livid eyes. "A request you filled."

"An *order* I carried out." Not a shade of apology mellowed the statement or softened his eyes, and she liked him a little better for it. Liked that he didn't pet her head or give her pity-eyes but appreciated her resilience. She even grudgingly liked his dogged refusal to disparage the general. Despite the shadows of disapproval occasionally flickering over him.

Arranged it, Buck had said.

Wilting where she stood, she ached to think Iron Wood had preferred her gone, had bundled her off to Wakulla, as if she were a nervous milk cow to be distracted with grain. What's more, he'd sent her on foot to use up more time. If Balada hadn't escaped her handlers, Pretty Wolf would have missed the whole thing. Should she bless the mare? Hate her?

Iron Wood would indeed not thank the animal, or Pretty Wolf, for spoiling his dignified end. And Pretty Wolf would not thank *him* for dignifying his unjust end with order and planning. The last almost meant…

He knew. There'd been no way out of Jackson's clutches. Not alive. And Iron Wood had known it. He'd embraced her and kissed her and dream-talked a future with Flint and *known.*

Pain trundled up her core.

"Bellamy loved you fiercely," Buck soothed, at last replacing the sword-wielding captain with the kind-mannered doctor. "And every man has his pride."

So, which was it? Did Iron Wood wish to spare *her* or himself? A soft, sad laugh huffed from her nose. Either way, she'd ruined it, his final wish. Invaded his execution and turned his last respectable moments into a horror of female shrieks.

"If I may presume to offer counsel, Miss Francis?" Buck didn't wait for consent. "Honor him by remembering him at his strongest."

She huffed again. This time in annoyance. Iron Wood had never been anything less than at his strongest. Even in his last hours as he stood alone and faced his accusers.

Remember him? Absolutely.

In a little while.

Iron Wood was gone, and that cavern within her was yawning wider, the anger burning hotter, morphing into something else entirely.

A sudden, exquisite urge drove her across the room to the cold chimenea. She thrust both hands into its opening and buried them in ash. Withdrawing, she patted them together to remove the excess, then methodically smeared the gray powder over her forehead and down until it covered her face with the acrid stench of destruction.

Finished, she turned to Buck.

His eyes bulged before he straightened his expression into one of careful understanding. "I didn't realize the Creeks wore mourning masks."

Pretty Wolf spread her lips in a wolfish display of teeth. "Not of mourning, my paleface friend. But of battle."

Chapter 40

When Old Sharp Knife sauntered into the study and laid eyes on Pretty Wolf seated behind the desk, his blinking stupefaction was a great deal more rewarding than Buck's had been.

As it shifted to dawning awareness, she flat out laughed, harsh and mocking. Elbows propped on the cushioned arms of the throne-like chair, Pretty Wolf leaned back, laced her fingers under her bosom, and skewered him with a smirk.

He matched it with those ice-chip orbs. "You, dear lady, are in my place." His gaze cut purposely to the much smaller, much less comfortable chair stationed before the desk—the spindly thing she'd been directed to upon admittance.

"Wrong, *dear sir*. I am in Commander Luengo's place. He has no quarrel with my use of it. On the other hand, *you*"—from the tops of her eyes, she shot him a stream of disdain, then bowed her lips up—"have much to answer for."

The man was a born destroyer, an infestation. A plague of corn worms, crawling from the dirt to devour all life.

"You may sit." She flapped a careless gesture at the reject. "Your apologies might drag long."

One eyebrow winging up, he looked at the chair, looked at her. Then he plucked the bicorn from his wind-blown head, tossed it to the soldier who was just entering behind him, and strode in to perch a hip on the desk's front edge. Long, groomed fingers folding together atop his thigh, he peered down at her. "How relieving to see you have your hysterics in hand. Pray tell, Miss Francis, will you be swooning next?"

Outrage bubbled up. In part, she deserved his scorn. She also deserved the respect due her gender and position.

She opened the center-front drawer, her fingers landing straightaway on Toño's letter opener, a miniature sword. Holding it upright, she spun it in the light streaming through the window at her back and formed a twisted smile. "If I swoon," she purred, "it will be at the ghastly sight of your gray hairs tied to my sash."

The general belted out a laugh. "And I thought my day had seen its fill of surprises."

Pretty Wolf clenched a fist around the sword's handle and levied a death-dealing glare, but Jackson missed it, having turned to address his lieutenant.

"The cedar box, Doyle. Bring it. And figure out where that slouch Barkdale has absconded to."

"Barkton," she muttered through her teeth but didn't bother to inform them her guard was off collecting Balada from the stable. Despite her earlier gibe, Pretty Wolf did not intend this meeting to go long, and she had much to accomplish in Wakulla before she could unbuckle her armor for the night.

Doyle saluted the general and left the door open in his wake.

On a vocalized hum of a sigh, Jackson picked at the fringe of his epaulet, neatening it. "Get on with it, Miss Francis. What are your intentions here?"

"To negotiate with the United States Army." Ignoring the gleam of intrigue cocking his head as well as his slow rise, she set the letter opener flat on the desk and set it on a lazy spin. "For that, I require honor and fairness. Captain Buck has exhibited both qualities. Perhaps he should be summoned?" Timbre light and amiable, she glanced up at him through her lashes.

For a three-count, their gazes battled, blades clashing in a silent duel. "That will not be necessary." At last, he moved to settle himself into the bony chair. When he crossed his legs at the knee, the seat wobbled noisily, and his nostrils blew wide. "What, *Princess*, are you bartering for?"

She let his sarcasm roll over her. "The warrior named Strong Bear. You have him in irons, accused of violence to a white man."

"Ah, yes. The White Stick who forgot the color of his stick. Some might call that treason."

"Others would call it self-defense," she fired back. "Your overeager, rather ignorant soldiers gave no ear to his claims of friendship or to the proof of it in his *white* feather."

He tipped his head back and observed her coolly with his shrewd blue eyes. "Hmm. You put forth a reasonable grievance. Immediate measures will be taken to better educate my men on the idiosyncrasies of the different Creek factions. But I'm curious, Miss Francis," he said, taking on a conversational tone. "Who is this Strong Bear to you?"

Not an entirely unexpected question. For the last while, she'd debated whether the truth of their relationship would help his cause or hinder it. With Old Sharp Knife, there was no predicting. Of course, to tell the truth, she would have to determine what, exactly, that was: faithful companion, friend, protector, slave. Husband? The list of possible answers was quite extensive.

She answered promptly. Simply. Truthfully. "He is dear to me."

Jackson sat forward, keen interest sharpening his attention.

"So dear that if you take him from me," she said languidly, yet full of meaning, "I will not rest until I've buried this little blade in your brain." Only great effort of will kept the miniature sword circling lackadaisically on the desk.

"I do believe you would," he replied on a mild chuckle, sitting back again. He steepled his fingers under his chin. "However, as a White Stick under the army's command, your dear Strong Bear is no doubt fully informed of the repercussions of striking a white man, especially one wearing army blue. And yet…he struck anyway."

Abruptly, the sword ceased its spin.

The seams of Jackson's mouth stretched, a window clear to the light-sucking black of his soul. He wanted Strong Bear dead. Or at least, he wanted her to *think* he did. Wanted her to tremble and beg before him. Or perhaps screech a war cry and make good on her promise of attack.

In fearful fury, Pretty Wolf's heart thrashed against its cage, and she worked up a sweat keeping her tone moderate. "Since we cannot come to an agreement on his innocence, we will trade."

He buffed his nails on the knee of his breeches. "And what have *you* of value that might tempt me?"

The emphasis was not lost on her, a rebel chief's daughter with illusions of command. Defeated of everything. Princess of nothing.

Riveted to Jackson, she pressed the point of the small blade into the tip of her finger until the pain peaked and the skin gave way. The tiny *plop* of landing liquid jerked his gaze to the desktop then back up in time to catch the sleek smile she brought to her lips. "What do I have? Only the man who shed Captain Telly's blood."

At the offer, Pretty Wolf's stomach roiled. She lectured it into submission. More than Strong Bear's life was at stake. The entire talwa could suffer if she did not surrender her sister's husband to the palefaces. And the man had to have known his unsanctioned blood revenge would come at a steep price.

Jackson became a stone—all but his eyes, which became blue tongues of flaming ire.

"You will give him to me, regardless."

"I will not."

Relaxing into a smug expression, he said, "So then, the vengeance you swore was a lie."

"It was a vow given to *him*, not his general." Another bead of blood reformed on her fingertip. She smeared it about with her thumb. "Do you wish to put your hands on the guilty, or do you not?"

Snappy steps brought Lieutenant Doyle back in with what looked to be a tobacco box. He waited quietly off the side and within Jackson's eyeline.

The general, sparing his man not a glimpse, reached inside his coat and withdrew a folded square of cloth. Setting it on the desk, he slid it to her. "Your conditions, Princess?"

Lips recoiling at the kerchief, she considered spurning the courtesy, then struck upon a happier idea. Leaving the cloth where it was, she dabbed her dripping finger on the letters embroidered in the corner.

The day's lesson: A for Andrew. J for Jackson. Bloody Andrew Jackson.

An honest smile splayed across her mouth. "My conditions, General." She raised two fingers then, on a wild hair, lifted a third. To begin the count-off, she lowered her stickiest digit. "First, my slave Strong Bear will be forgiven his *crime* and released to me at once. You will also swear to free my warriors. All of them. Tomorrow morning when my council arrives for formal surrender." The third finger curled away. "And finally, before I leave this room, you will promise to abandon your chase of Chief Tall Bull."

Jackson reared back, but she tossed up a don't-speak-yet gesture. "My uncle has gone deep into Florida to begin a new life. He has put aside the **red club of war** and is no longer a threat to you. This you will do as apology for denying me a proper farewell with my beloved."

Lips pursed to a ball of wrinkles, Jackson said nothing.

She pressed on. "As for the blood-shedder, Strong Bear and I, together with Sergeant Barkton, will ride to Wakulla this hour to retrieve him for you. With Lieutenant Doyle as witness, do we have an agreement?"

His posture straightened. "Indeed, Miss Francis, we do."

"As I expected." She tucked the letter opener away and achieved her feet with perfect ladylike form. Jackson's white-man manners lifted him at once from the rickety seat, and her Indian's caution immediately plotted the safest path as she circled to the desk's front. "The warrior will be brought to you before sunset."

"I look forward to it. Before you go, one last detail." He flipped a palm up at his lieutenant.

Doyle stepped forward with the box, opening it as he came.

"I do believe"—turned from her, Jackson reached in—"this belongs to you." When he rounded back, it was with two things: a strange glow of esteem and a weapon laid between his upturned hands.

Silver. Glassy polish. Antler handle.

And stamped on the dagger's finely etched crossguard, her father's mark.

Chapter 41

Cheekbone touching the cold bars of his cell, Strong Bear swallowed thickly at the sight of Bellamy's silhouette filling the corridor's doorway.

Wrists unbound, the Englishman squinted into the gloom. "Strong Bear?" Behind him, sunlight streamed through the window and outlined his tense form in a thin white glow.

The slant of the rays declared the time. One hour to high sun.

News of the execution orders had swirled into the jail with the force of a gale an hour earlier, and Strong Bear's stomach hadn't stopped pitching since. Bellamy's arrival now sent acid to the back of his throat. It tasted of a bitter knowing—the reason he'd been included in Bellamy's death walk.

He reached through the bars and pushed the man's name through his constricted voice box. "I am here."

Against the guard's growled orders, Bellamy forged inside and gripped Strong Bear's arm. "Polly," he said on a croak.

"Yes." Polly. Pretty Wolf. The mighty love of their lives.

Bellamy's head hung, his composure slipping. "Tell her—" He choked up. Stuttering breaths left his nostrils, and the vise on Strong Bear's arm tightened.

"That you love her."

The Englishman's nods came abrupt and emphatic, and when his chin lifted, unshed tears reflected the faint light in his blue orbs. "With my very soul. And I'm sorry, I am so sorry." The man trembled, sweat glistening across his pallid features, words slurring from his mouth like a mudslide. "And tell my son..." His throat lurched hard. "Tell him to make his mother proud and that he was with me until the last." He raised his fist, and the sketch crinkled in his tight grasp.

Raw emotion squeezed Strong Bear's windpipe and reduced him to a jerky nod.

"She is yours now." Bellamy's voice was almost unrecognizable in its garbled thickness.

Agony swelled in the cleft between Strong Bear's collarbones. This was not how it was supposed to be, not how Strong Bear should win the woman.

For it was no fight at all. Only slaughter. Ruthlessly overpowered, the man had been stripped of every defense. His days cut short, his woman passed to another man. His child never to know him.

Guilty or innocent, Robert Bellamy did not deserve this treatment.

Guards moved in. "You've had your minute. Move it along." They pulled at Bellamy, and panic entered his eyes, made scrabbling talons of his digits.

Strong Bear hung on. "Courage, brother."

"Love her for me!"

Their fingers snapped apart.

Bellamy struggled as they dragged him down the corridor. "Love her without reserve. Love her hard. Love them both for me!"

The shout trailed him out the door, leaving Strong Bear to scrape out his answer alone. "I will. I swear it."

The scene replayed over and over behind Strong Bear's squeezed-shut lids, the seal of his vow still burning hot on his tongue. It was the second such vow he'd made to Bellamy, but the first that made him ill.

Strong Bear dug clawing fingers into the flesh of his chest, the man's anguish still a physical pain behind his ribs.

And where was Pretty Wolf?

Where?

"Someone must have rendered her unconscious," a fellow chimed from two cells down, verbalizing what Strong Bear had been refusing to contemplate.

The speculation in the jailhouse had been ongoing for hours—since the rifles reported Robert Bellamy's death and Pretty Wolf's screams sent Strong Bear's fists into the stone wall. Over and over.

An eager gossip, their English-speaking Spanish guard had trickled information to Strong Bear as he received it. First, the trial in which Pretty Wolf was conspicuously absent and Bellamy was awarded death by shooting. Then her untimely appearance and raging shrieks in the square. Which they'd all been privy to thanks to the guard opening the external doors on the pretext of airing out the cells.

The updates ended there. No explanation of why she'd screamed or why she'd so abruptly stopped.

"It is the only explanation," another agreed, grave as the slave pole. "Our she-wolf *miccohokti* wouldn't have quieted so quickly otherwise."

There followed a few concurring grunts, and Strong Bear could not deny the truth of it—in such a state, physical force alone would have shut her up. He groaned, and it had nothing to do with the bloody pulp of his knuckles or the throb of bruised bones forced into a tight wrap around the bars. Propped against the front of his cell, Strong Bear hung his head between his arms, locked in place to keep his sharply bent torso aloft.

Perhaps, he should let go. Fall flat. Mash his ugly nose flat and sprawl in the dirt. The perfect epitome of his uselessness. Little hurt worse than knowing Pretty Wolf's enemy surrounded her on every side, and he could do nothing about it.

And the sound of her agony…

Strong Bear's shoulders rippled with a shudder, and his eyes dripped. Created a little map of craters in the dirt below.

Pretty Wolf loved Strong Bear. With the entirety of her beautiful soul. This he knew as intimately as he did the backs of his teeth.

But could a woman love two men to such a degree? Perhaps only an ignorant would put limits on love's capacity, but every interaction between Pretty Wolf and her betrothed—besides the kiss he wished he could unsee—had been negative. For that reason, Strong Bear had convinced himself she'd doled out only the dregs of her affections to Iron Wood—after giving the wolf's share to *him*.

He'd been wrong. Because that sound, the scream that had shaken every man there, was the noise a blade makes when it severs a soul from its mate. A cry of pure anguish. And a portent of revenge.

As surely as the sun trekked westward, she had wanted to rip the general's head from his neck. Strong Bear would have held the man still for her, had he been given the chance. As it was, he wept in a cage, reeking of unwashed flesh, deprived of weapons and even his cross.

He touched his bare throat and prayed. Tried to block out the other mens' conjectures. Failing that, he clamped his tongue between his teeth to keep his snippy remarks to himself.

"Perhaps she found a weapon," one said. "Took another shot at Old Sharp Knife."

"Hmm, it is possible."

It was. Terrifyingly.

"At least the whites do not kill women."

"No, but there are other forms of punishment. Lashings, the pillory."

"For women?"

"The Spanish whipped the paleface Bitter Eyes of Beaver Clan."

Strong Bear's head lifted. Lillian McGirth was beaten?

"Pretty Wolf is light of skin and eyes, but she is still the daughter of Crazy Medicine. Still Indian. If she struck a Bluecoat, they would certainly not forgive it."

"She has acted rashly."

A noise of disdain. "Without a thought to us moldering in here."

Strong Bear's blood rushed faster.

"If she is dead, what will we do!"

"Shut your mouths!" Strong Bear reared up, his tongue slipping its leash. "Pretty Wolf is your miccohokti, and she is *not* dead. Your theorizing of her failures makes you nattering women! Where is your loyalty, your *trust*?"

The corridor fell silent. Good. Let the defeatists ponder their bad faith.

"Very well," someone said at last. One of the older, more balanced voices of the lot. "What do *you* think has become of your woman?"

His woman? True enough by his own accounting. But by everyone else's, it was a somewhat backward approach to the title of pucase.

While he ruminated on this, another prompted, "Ehi. What does the legendary, wise-to-her-ways True Seeker predict?" The question was put to him without irony.

So Strong Bear would answer in equal measure. With candor, his heart exposed. He straightened and looked down the aisle to the sliver of nose and chin visible to him. "A woman is allowed her mourning wail. Even the Bluecoats accept this. She has had her cry, and now she plots to liberate us." *Creator Jesus, make it so.* "Give her time. She will not disappoint."

"How can you be so certain she was not cut down?"

Molars latched, Strong Bear paced his reply to an irritated grind. "Because she has a strong motivation to live."

Another man piped up. "Us. She lives for us."

"No, fool." There came a thump and a grunt. "For Strong Bear himself."

"You are both correct," said a pretty voice. The prettiest.

Strong Bear whirled, pulse leaping, face split into a grin before he'd even sighted her.

Pretty Wolf glided into the corridor, bare feet swift and silent. Outfitted in her usual work attire with hair neatly braided into a single rope that draped her front, she appeared her usual self but with a few additions. A woolen matchcoat fastened with a wooden pin at her chest. A sheathed dagger in her fist. And a war mask blackening her face.

If she'd received a disabling blow, she showed no sign of it. In fact, she was stunning, a remake of the woman from Tohopeka. The beauty who'd snatched the smart from his tongue, then the heart from his chest. In all these winters, she'd never given it back. Even so, at the vision of her—hazel eyes bright inside her black mask and grit setting her delicate jaw at a commanding angle—Strong Bear fell in love all over again.

His tongue just as stupid now as then, it sat in his mouth, drying out from the breath whizzing through his loose lips. His arm, though, seemed to know what it was doing. It had found its way through the bars and was following her passage as a sunflower does the sun.

On her way past, she skimmed fingers over his as she said, *"Libera a éste, Luis,"* and strode straight to the back.

"A sus órdenes, Princesa." Keyring swinging from one hooked finger, the guard advanced to the keyhole on Strong Bear's cell.

A twist, a click. He was free.

And she was well.

That assurance allowed his mind to make way for other, more selfish worries. Did she blame him for withholding knowledge of Flint? Would it put a wedge between them? Creator help the man who stood between a mother and her child, and Pretty Wolf was no mere mother.

He propped a shoulder against the outside of his prison and ate up the sight of her going from cell to cell, consoling her men, murmuring reassurances: she was well, and they would be too. They wouldn't, however, be freed that day. The next, she told them. At the official surrender where they would stand in peaceful representation of the talwa as she and her select men put their marks on the paper.

To a man, they promised compliance.

When she arrived back at Strong Bear and their eyes joined, hers faltered, crumpled around the edges. An instant only. There, then gone. Overtaken by the rigid mantle of miccohokti.

Small and bleak though it was, he slid on a smile and beat the stupid from his tongue. "Does our Wolf come from battle, or does she go to meet it?"

The folds of her mouth played with the notion of humor. "Both," she said, voice roughened from overuse. "I've haggled for your life. So now, you are mine."

"As I have always been, Pucase."

Her eyes settled on his lumpy nose. "So you have, Kit. So you have." There it was, that ferocious love of hers softening the contours of her face.

No wedge in sight. No resentful, snarling wolf. Only the fiercest of devotion.

Before her hand dropped away, he raised his chin so that her fingertip grazed over his mouth. Circling her thin wrist, he held her finger there for a kiss, then pulled it down to grasp firmly between them. "Woman, you are a wonder to rival the tides."

If Pretty Wolf could dodge execution after hurling a dagger at a general, Strong Bear's fist hurled at a private would be no great challenge. The woman was a dazzling force few men were equipped to resist.

And General Andrew Jackson was only that. A man. An immensely powerful man. But same as any other, flesh covered his bones. Blood ran the paths of his veins. Secret vulnerabilities pestered him. Strong Bear should have known Pretty Wolf would find one to exploit.

Pleased at the thought, he gave a dark inward chuckle. He might be resigned to the treaty, but he nurtured no love for the land-hungry, Indian-razing Old Sharp Knife. Inner, metaphorical hands rubbed joyfully together at the thought of him being brought low by the daughter of his enemy, a Native woman.

She drew closer to speak in a shaky hush. "We have much unpleasant work ahead of us, dear friend. Are you with me?"

As Strong Bear gazed at the blue flecks of her eyes, studied their changing hues, and read in them everything she could not reveal to those around them—fear, doubt, crippling grief—she did not ask for his presence but for his unquestioned backing. Of whatever lay ahead. Whatever *work* was assigned her.

Within the folds of her skirt, he squeezed her fingers. "Lead the way, Wolf, and I will show you."

Her thumb brushed over his mashed knuckles, and a little wrinkle formed between her brows. She retreated a step to inspect the injury and torqued her lips at him. "On our way out, try not to hit any Bluecoats."

He reflected her smirk. "So long as they keep their hands off you."

"Careful, White Stick. I have nothing left to bargain with for your life." On her spin away from him, she slowed to dispense a low-lashed side-eye of warning. Behind her, the exterior's glow outlined the perfection of her profile and glossy lips.

No sane male could interpret the look as sultry, not while understanding Pretty Wolf, not while knowing that hours earlier, her betrothed was slain. Just the same, Strong Bear's pulse tripped its way through his heart and reached his brain, promising it would follow the woman anywhere.

It was a tossup which stirred him more: her shared hints of vulnerability or her power to tramp it down. Her beauty—a mere bonus.

She jerked her chin toward the exit, ushering him along, and Strong Bear launched after her.

Outside, he expanded his chest with sweet, fresh air and thanked Creator for freedom, for life. For the Son who'd given His and for the woman who risked hers. Every encounter with the Old Sharp Knife was a flirt with fire, and Strong Bear couldn't seem to manage the simple task of standing as a firebreak.

That changes now, he determined, hooking a hand around her upper arm. Between that moment and the one in which they crossed the threshold of their Kossati lodge, Strong Bear would not be parted from her. For any reason.

Screaming Buttons greeted him with a slap on the shoulder, and Pretty Wolf, strapping the knife sheath to her belt, pointed out her assigned guard, a Bluecoat who led Balada and two other horses toward them. "Sergeant Barkton. He's a quiet, decent paleface." Voice drab, she added, "Don't punch him."

They mounted up, and he and Screaming Buttons fell into flanking positions with Barkton riding point. They kept silent on the trail to Wakulla, Pretty Wolf's closed, increasingly hard expression signaling she was in no mood for chatter or interrogations. The journey passed as swiftly as Strong Bear's curiosity grew, but he trusted her, and clearly, she had the general's favor in this mystery endeavor.

Their canter didn't slow until they reached the entry to Beaver compound, where she informed Barkton he would not be continuing with them. "The man we seek will run at the sight of you," she explained, then invited him to help himself to the pot hanging over the courtyard fire.

Strong Bear scowled, concern setting in. The man they sought? He touched the empty sheath at his waist. Unarmed, he could not properly fight or protect. A glance at Buttons revealed a turned mouth and shared worries.

Sunflower emerged from the storehouse carrying an empty corn sack, her chin jutted from the clamp of her toothless jaw. "Pretty Wolf, my child, who do you bring me?"

Balada carried her mistress toward Sunflower. "This Bluecoat is called Barkton." Pretty Wolf indicated the soldier. "He will give you no trouble."

"If you trust the man, he is welcome to my fire." Sunflower hobbled close. "Pretty Wolf," the elder began in her creaky voice.

"Did Alligator give their blessing?" Pretty Wolf cut in, just this side of rude.

Sunflower gave her flabby lips a censorious waggle before replying. "Ehi, child. You have it." Bending her stooped back, she scraped up a fistful of dirt and placed it in Pretty Wolf's hand. "May Earth guide and comfort you. And may your man, Strong Bear, save you from harm." Watery and weak though they were, the elder's milky eyes packed him a considerable blow of warning.

"Maddo, beloved. We will not be long away." Pretty Wolf clicked her tongue and heeled the mare around. Once beyond the compound's borders, she dumped the soil, grabbed the horse's mane in both fists, and urged her into a gallop.

They rode hard, climbing gradually until they broke into the obscurity of a thick palm forest. She slowed to leave the trail and picked a silent path through wiregrass and leaf litter. At the edge of a clearing, she halted and visually read their surroundings—a rocky ridge that sloped away to a grassy plane and crystalline lake beyond.

"We've come for Kills Many," she announced dimly yet with no give.

"The man got his vengeance at last, I take it." And Strong Bear would get his. No man drew his wolf's blood and walked away to boast of it.

Screaming Buttons hawked crudely and spat a wad into the sand. "He put an arrow into the neck of a Bluecoat officer."

"After signs of peace were made. Captain Telly died in my arms." Her eyes untethered from this plane to revisit an event unknown to Strong Bear.

Remembering her bloody clothes, he swallowed back a growl of frustration. How much more had she endured while they'd been apart? What new tragedy would she reveal next?

"I swore to Captain Telly I would avenge his death. As it turned out, that vengeance also earned your freedom, Strong Bear. Or will." Pretty Wolf's gaze slanted toward the outcropping, her voice still painfully graveled. "I believe Kills Many to be holed up in the old lodge with Birdie. At the base of the ridge there." She lifted her chin in the appropriate direction. "Strong Bear, with me. Come up behind and restrain him at once. We ask no questions. I want him conscious and able to answer for his deed. Buttons, you'll bring the horses down the slope there." She indicated where stone relented to soft, sloping earth. "Don't delay. Strong Bear is muscle aplenty, but I'll feel better knowing you're a moment away."

"I understand, Miccohokti." Screaming Buttons reached for Balada's halter to steady her for Pretty Wolf's dismount.

Strong Bear slid off his own horse, tossed the reins to Buttons, and loped after Pretty Wolf. The woman was already descending, hopping from slab to slab, her matchcoat flaring out around her.

A beat behind, he placed his steps in hers. Her toe caught on the uneven surface, but he was close enough to snatch her before her stumble became a fall. Righted again, she stalled there, head lowered, surges of air working her ribcage. As though releasing a burden, she turned into him and dropped her forehead against his breastbone. On her next breath, she slumped against him.

He wrapped his arms about her and sighed. "I loathe I wasn't there for you. For any of it." Hands sliding up to burrow into her hair, he continued, desperate for her to grasp this. "Our paths are merged. From here on, we go together. To Kills Many, to Muscogee country, to Flint. Do you take my meaning, Wolf?"

Head tipping back, she showed him eyes big with unnatural submission. "Ehi, Kit. Together."

Close enough. For now.

With reluctance, he unwound from her and stepped back, watching in pride as she donned steel-spined authority and took herself down the hill.

Below, in the patch of dead grass rimming a vine-eaten lodge, events unfolded in snappy procession.

Strong Bear slipped into the lodge's shadows as Pretty Wolf stationed herself at its door.

"Kills Many! Come stand before your miccohokti!" Pretty Wolf hailed.

The male swaggered out, speaking some condescending war-mask nonsense that fueled Strong Bear's soundless stalk from behind.

"But now the lost little daughter has come to—"

Strong Bear struck—a swift, brutal chokehold that shut the man up, incapacitated him in moments. An overturned beetle, he flailed uselessly against Strong Bear's strength. Heels scoring groves into the dirt, he shoved back into the hold but could not budge Strong Bear's wide-legged stance.

"Be still!" Strong Bear snapped, pulling yet harder on his own wrist to tighten the clamp.

He fought on, a spitting, frothing madman, every scratch of his nails across Strong Bear's arms managing only to swell them farther. Then, Pretty Wolf removed the pin from her matchcoat and tossed the garment aside to reveal her violently stained blouse. Bluecoat blood. Kills Many's doing.

As well as his downfall. A thing he instantly recognized, judging from his splutters. Hissing from his throat were pathetic justifications that Pretty Wolf wholly ignored.

"Birdie," she called. "Are you in there?"

The black woman appeared in the darkened doorway and glanced nervously about, only the edge of her bright yellow skirt peeking into the sunlight.

Pretty Wolf asked, "Has he spoken to you of the killing in the square?"

Birdie's eyes traveled a cautious path to Kills Many and bounced right back off to find safety in Pretty Wolf. "He...said he drew the bow." Muscogee came off her tongue mildly accented.

Kills Many wheezed, knees wobbling, so Strong Bear released his neck and seized him by the elbows instead, wrangling them harshly until his shoulder blades jammed together.

Narrowly eyeing the warrior's panted struggles, Birdie elaborated. "He said he put an arrow in the Bluecoat's neck. And he boasted about the distance of the shot."

"Sounds right," Pretty Wolf drawled. "You will give testimony of this?"

"If I must. But you have his own word for it. There." She flicked a finger. "On his arm."

Honing to a blood-spotted sleeve, Pretty Wolf maneuvered around Strong Bear's hold to wrench up the sleeve of Kills Many's deerskin shirt. A neat, if swollen, slice topped a laddered row of ink that had the look of kill tallies.

Wrinkling her nose, Pretty Wolf yanked the sleeve down. "Could you not wait for tattooing implements? Were you so thirsty to have the slaying recognized? Or do you so little value your life you would inscribe your crime into your own flesh?"

Derision jetted from his nostrils. "You will not surrender me to the Bluecoats, daughter of Crazy Medicine."

"True enough," she returned, stepping back and realigning their gazes, hers deceptively mellow and supported by a bob of the shoulder. "I could never betray a fellow tribesman by giving him to the Bluecoats. Even if he acted with malice of soul."

Neck to legs, Kills Many relaxed, souring the air with a haughty chuckle. "So then, call off your beast."

"Maddo, Birdie. That is all." She nodded to the woman and waited for her to vanish into the shadows before turning back to Kills Many. A miccohokti's mien of judgment transformed her features to stone. "Kills Many of Wakulla's clan Alligator, you are accused of slaying a low-ranking chief of the Bluecoats in time of peace."

Kills Many tensed again. "What is this?"

"What do you say of this accusation?"

"Blood law demanded it!"

"White law demands your life in return. As do I. What have you to say?"

"I say," he growled, teeth bared, "if you had let me finish with that potbellied paleface traitor, this would never have—"

Strong Bear had never fully appreciated Pretty Wolf's snake-strike speed. One moment, both arms hung at her sides. The next, her dagger was in her fist, gleaming crimson. One moment, Strong Bear was glancing sideways at Screaming Buttons' approach. The next, Kills Many was convulsing, gurgling on the blood fleeing his slit gullet.

His turban tumbled off. His choker rained beads down his chest. His legs wobbled.

Under the lowered dagger, droplets peppered the dirt, but they were nothing to the spray soaking Pretty Wolf's front.

Expressionless, she stood before her sister's husband and did not flinch from his bulging gaze while he drained onto her. Her unblinking lashes collected runoff and spilled red tears. A thin stream accumulated in the seam of her sealed-flat lips. Not a muscle twitched on her red-and-black streaked face.

Frightened—for her and the tiniest bit *of* her—Strong Bear spun Kills Many away. He released the man to his knees and his frantic scrabbling, then skipped back.

Life left him at speed, pooled beneath his bowing frame, and abandoned him to a humiliating rump-in-the-air posture. Fitting, as he'd been a pain in the backside since Strong Bear's arrival in Wakulla. Enduring season after season of it had to have been exhausting, and Strong Bear wondered whether the man would be missed at all. Or whether the talwa would take a collective sigh of relief. Somewhere, a mother might grieve him. Perhaps his wife.

Clearly, not Pretty Wolf, who hadn't changed posture since her strike, and who still wept blood from her chin.

Strong Bear snatched up the stray turban and gave it a little shake to unwind it. His guarded advance allowed Pretty Wolf to drag her gaze from the corpse and register the long band of yellow cotton he lifted. While she stared through Strong Bear, he proceeded with careful, cloth-soaking dabs of her mouth and eyes.

He saw what she was doing. Cladding herself with indomitability, hiding behind a mirage of strength. A mirage that could not hold forever, and when it dissolved…

When it burst apart, he would be there.

"Why did you do it?" Complexion sallow and lax with shock, Screaming Buttons stood peering down at the deceased. Was he, too, struggling with his perception of Pretty Wolf?

Riled to her defense, Strong Bear said, "His actions endangered all of Wakulla."

"But why like this?"

The exchange roused her into a deep refuel of breath, and Strong Bear exhaled. She brushed off his ministrations. "To deny Old Sharp Knife the pleasure and *him* the humiliation of a rope." She pointed her dagger at the body.

Screaming Buttons' jaw firmed, his eyes traveling from Pretty Wolf to the corpse and back again as if weighing the explanation. "The People's adversary and…a bleeding head," he mumbled, deep in thought.

A quote from the prophecy.

Lost in her own head, Pretty Wolf seemed not to hear. She dropped her arm, and the motion brought the stained blade to her attention. Raising the weapon to eye level, she frowned.

Her reasoning rang true, almost merciful. But her voice sounded as dead as the man at her feet, and her body behaved as though slogging through knee-deep ash. In Strong Bear's estimation, the cost of sparing the scoundrel some part in his well-deserved reckoning was too high. But truly, any price would be if Pretty Wolf had to pay it. What other consequences might come of this slaying?

Strong Bear hardened his legs to prevent a spiteful kick to the man's hip. "Is his clan mother a reasonable woman?" A micco's power extended to punishments when the offense went against the entire talwa, but clans could be volatile. Especially in times of grief. Especially toward makeshift leadership…

Taking the dangling end of the turban, Pretty Wolf wiped the dagger clean. "Alligator approved the killing."

"But…" Screaming Buttons waved confused hands over the crumpled body. "He is your sister's husband."

Unmoved, her funereal eyes watched this behavior before she slid the dagger home. "Was," she stated and turned for the lake.

While Strong Bear and Screaming Buttons secured the body on the largest of their horses, they were vigilant of Pretty Wolf and Birdie's care of her. The woman had scurried out with a bundle of fabric and, with some difficulty, persuaded Pretty Wolf out of her soiled things and into clean replacements.

Now, she sat on the limestone bank, Birdie beside her. Their legs hung out of sight over the edge and created random ripples across the otherwise placid surface. If they exchanged words, they were too soft to carry across the lot.

"She isn't right," Buttons observed, holding the horse by the bit as Strong Bear tied the last knot over Kills Many's arched back.

He yanked the rope harder than necessary, and his bruised knuckles protested. "Who would be?"

"Not myself."

"Not a soul on This World, I wager." Who could possibly be equipped to stand under the cannon shot blown her way over the last days? Without the comfort of Creator Jesus, all the more difficult.

"Quiet now, she comes," Buttons shushed. He rounded the horse to grip Strong Bear's arm and lean close. "Heal her, Strong Bear. Make her well."

"I will, brother." For there was no other option but to guide and sustain her through it. And none but Strong Bear would do.

They tracked Pretty Wolf's shuffling return. Face semi-clean and wholly blank, she appeared unaware of her feet, of the sag of her jaw, or of Birdie trotting alongside trying to wrap the matchcoat about her.

Doubt encased Strong Bear's spine. A prayer chased it away. He clapped his old friend on the back of the neck and squeezed, faith imbuing his spirit. "Jesus help me, I will."

Back in Sunflower's compound, the Barkton Bluecoat reacted hardly at all when it clicked that they'd returned with a dead prisoner instead of a living one. He merely grunted a shrug, clasped Pretty Wolf about the waist, and swung her down. That she did not protest the assistance but patted the paleface in thanks was testament to her mental absence.

Despite the soldier's rumbled warnings, she refused to retrace her steps to the fort that night. In turn, the soldier refused to leave her side. So, he recruited another to escort the body to the general and thus satisfy the agreement.

Runs Like Deer, belly going before her, exited the lodge and went straightaway to her sister. Without a sound, she laid her head against Pretty Wolf's shoulder. Pretty Wolf stroked her hair and uttered words stolen by the passing wind. Runs Like Deer nodded and straightened to press her drenched cheek to Pretty Wolf's in a gesture of love and acceptance so beautiful Strong Bear had to clear a clog from his throat.

The sister shuffled off to her dead husband, and on the last of her reserves, Pretty Wolf mumbled instructions for Screaming Buttons to meet her in Wolf compound at dawn. With an "ehi, miccohokti" and a concerned look for Strong Bear, Buttons left them. Pretty Wolf then shunned Sunflower's invitation to bunk in her lodge, mounted Balada, and set off toward the talwa.

Villagers lined the lanes to watch her pass, grief streaking their faces. Few approached or spoke, but when they did, it was with reverence and gratitude. Barkton received several juicy wads of spittle, but each time, Pretty Wolf snapped at the culprit with accusations of stupidity.

She rode at the head, rigidly but with an almost imperceptible tremble, as though barely holding upright. The mirage was collapsing, her nostrils quivering with a warning of fast-approaching tears.

Strong Bear nudged his horse toward a sidling position, determined to whisk her onto his lap. Just then, they emerged on the square's opposite side, and Rabbit's compound took shape in the fast-falling gloom. A moment more and the guest house came in sight.

The scene opened before them: the pirate, Korsan, and his woman, Melon, shared a massive cedar log before a lazy fire, her head reclined on his shoulder. Shem lay on his stomach, humming and adding sticks to a miniature fort, and the red-coated simpleton squatted in a fetal position, rocking on his heels, both fists repeatedly knocking his head.

Rox was the first to spot them. He tottered upright, already wailing. "Paw-ee! Paw-ee!"

Fingers flying to her mouth, Pretty Wolf drew a hissing breath. A second later, her shaking began in earnest. Big body quakes that sent Balada into a fit of head tossing.

Strong Bear had his hands about her hips before he'd decided to leap from his horse. But there he was, suddenly hauling her off the unsteady mare and hurriedly untucking her skirts to cover her legs while she twisted in his arms for a view of Rox.

The man galumphed toward them in an awkward hop-run, tattered coat flapping, hollering his incomprehensible words and carrying on like a braying mule.

"I am here, Rox," she cried, breaking free.

His heaving boohoos twisted Strong Bear's heart into a painful knot in his breast. Still coming, Rox wagged his head pitifully. "Bag gone, Bemy gone. Pah-ee, Bemy *gone*!"

A strangled sound left Pretty Wolf's throat. The two strides she'd managed were her only and last. Face crumpling, she gouged fingernails into her matchcoat and, ripping at it, released a long, loud wail. A horrifying sound, it could only originate from the bleakest pit of the soul.

She crumbled. Knees giving out. Straight down into Strong Bear's scooping arms.

He swung her up and against him and directed his sure strides at the guest lodge. Nestling her wet face in the crook of his throat, he murmured, "That's right, Wolf. Give it to me. All of it. Cry for them. As hard as you wish."

Obediently, she clawed as the back of his neck and let sobs wrack her. She curled in, her free arm clutching her middle. As though Bellamy were a kidney incised from her body, her father a lung. And if should she let go, the rest of her would come spilling out.

Rox came alongside, hobbling, barely able to keep up. "Pah-ee?" he ventured, brow furrowed. His big paw clumsily petted her hair as he talked to her in his strange way.

She cried on. Unloaded a nightmare's worth of horror into Strong Bear's neck.

Korsan and Shem stayed back a safe distance, but Melon rushed ahead to hold the door flap.

Turning sideways to fit, Strong Bear ducked into the familiar, slightly altered interior. In the days since he'd shared this space with Pretty Wolf and Hambly, someone had cleared out the odds and ends cluttering the bunks and had cushioned them with straw and blankets. Melon indicated the lower one.

Strong Bear made tracks for it, no thought of releasing Pretty Wolf to anyone or anything. He lowered to sit on the couch's edge, hunched his large frame, and scooted back until he could pivot and swing his legs up.

Unconcerned with all but her heartache, Pretty Wolf blinked sopping eyes and let him do with her as he pleased, laying her down to arrange himself, then pulling her back in. Tense and shaking, she buried her face in his chest and flooded his shirt.

Clucking inane sympathies, Melon covered them with a blanket. She wedged a rolled animal hide under his head before backing out and leaving them to the dark lodge and even darker emotions.

This is good, this is right, Strong Bear rehearsed while stroking her hair and intermittently muttering prayers over her, begging Creator's peace and comfort. His green pastures and gentle waters. His protection and provision on the journey. Safety for Flint. Redemption for Pretty Wolf.

Words that were just words without unshakable faith behind them. And Strong Bear was shaken. Not in Creator. But in the lengths Creator was going to reach her. For years, he'd pleaded for her soul, but he could not have foreseen, could never have prepared for the series of blows levied against her.

"Bemy gone, Bemy gone!" The echo of Rox's cries were as poignant as when they'd barreled from his mouth.

Bellamy gone. Gone. Just like that.

And Pretty Wolf here. Flint on his hill. Strong Bear the link between them.

Perhaps he should be heaped with guilt. Or maybe he should recognize Creator's great hand in forging this path. And be grateful.

The second. He would choose the second.

Then, he rubbed Pretty Wolf's back until she was shivering and hiccupping in her sleep.

Eventually, the others stole in, each bedding down with no more than a tender glance their direction.

The night plodded along interminable and sleepless, the slats of the couch seeming to embed permanently into his hip. But when Pretty Wolf woke at the moon's height, calm and dry-eyed, and raised warm lips on his chin, the discomfort frittered into a distant thought.

She turned over and pulled his arm around her. No further prompting required, Strong Bear positioned her against him in their old way. Although it wasn't *quite* the same, there being a notable size difference, but it was as it should be.

He nestled her head in the crook of his arm and folded himself around her. Legs twined, he nuzzled into her hair.

Old habits, he thought wryly, affectionately, then admonished himself about getting too eager to create new ones.

Pretty Wolf's ribs deflated, and soon, sweet sleepy noises were rumbling past her lips.

He settled in, intent on keeping wakeful vigil, but her power to unwind him proved too much, and before long, he was following her into the realm of dreams.

Chapter 42

To Pretty Wolf, early morning lodge noises always had a unique, soothing flavor—the last wee crackle of coals, the groan of couch reeds. The whisper of wind through the gaps of the entry's hide covering and the erratic *tap-tap* of its leather against the doorpost. Then there was Strong Bear's quiet *shish-shish* breaths caressing the back of her ear—the sound of his lightest sleep.

Eyes still heavy with slumber, she lay perfectly immobile to not wake him and spent the next long while basking in his warmth. In the mass of his body tangled around her like the roots of a tree, in the support of the relaxed arm muscle beneath her head. And in the knowledge that if she released so much as a distressed breath, he would snap awake and make everything well again. Or burn himself down to ash trying.

He'd stayed the night with her, never once letting go while she broke to pieces all over him. Had he gotten much sleep? She imagined not. Even now, he sniffed and shifted in discomfort. The likely culprit, a numb appendage or two.

His prayers though… They were yet alive and full of feeling, moving within her even now, stroking her spirit. She'd never heard anyone pray in such a manner, as though the Great Spirit sat at the end of the couch, leaning a sympathetic ear their way. As an intimate friend might do. It had been—still was—oddly calming. Or perhaps that was the prayer taking effect. Strong Bear had, after all, requested it of his Creator Jesus.

Exhaling, she released more of her weight into Strong Bear, more thankful than her mind could process that he was there, at her back, to take it on. What would she have done the previous night if he hadn't been? She didn't care to think on it. Didn't have to. Because he would not leave her—a truth as certain as Grandmother Sun climbing toward break of day.

"From here on, we go together… Do you take my meaning, Wolf?"

She did. Together: with each other always.

But where it pertained to Pretty Wolf and Strong Bear, the talwa had its own understanding of the word. And Strong Bear's did not match up.

"You'd best pray Sunflower doesn't latch onto your mother's ridiculous notions and force the matter. I'll not do it."

He could not have been clearer, more belligerent in his opinion on the matter. At the time, his nostril-twitching repulsion made Pretty Wolf laugh. But if he reacted so again, when he learned they'd been publicly declared wed, she would not be heard laughing.

Pleading, more like. She wanted to keep the ruse going until the People split for their various tribal talwas. One less blunder to air and own. She couldn't imagine Strong Bear would appreciate being forced into marriage any more than he had at being reduced to seed stock for Wolf Clan, but nostril tic or not, he would eventually agree to play along.

Regardless of titles and charades, he would not be going anywhere. Not of his own volition. That, however, didn't mean something or some*one* could not take him from her.

The logical fraction of her mind rejected the idea at once—Jackson had bartered, promised; Pretty Wolf had fulfilled—but she would never have predicted both her father and her husband could be violently wrenched away within the span of a day. And that made it difficult to believe destruction would not touch Strong Bear, too.

The thought turned logic to fear, fear to panic. Her heart fluttered pathetically against her ribs, and blood pounded in her temples with a cruel reminder she'd cried herself sick.

Strong Bear tightened reflexively around her, tuned to her even in slumber.

As always. Through every grisly dream and sleepless night, True Seeker had remained at her side, caring for her. Never questioning her right to grieve as she saw fit. Over the seasons, True Seeker had become Strong Bear, tall and thick with muscle and a touch cocky. The little rabbit was not so *little* anymore, but how grateful she was he had not really changed.

She was tempted to flip over and adhere herself to him like a baby opossum. Bathe in his strength until it soaked through to her bones. But Pretty Wolf *had* changed. Much for the worse. Some for the better. Most prominently, she was no longer the lost daughter.

She was *miccohokti*.

And the talwa faced an emotionally trying day and a physically trying journey. Those facts steadied her pulse and urged her to unwind from her safe cocoon. She wrangled open her crusty eyelids and found Sergeant Barkton stretched out on his back beside her couch. Beneath the arm slung over his eyes, the whiskers of his upper lip shivered over his lumbering exhales. On the other side of the fire, Shem slept belly down, knees tucked, rump high. Beyond him, Rox occupied the lower of the bunks. Melon, the upper. The only one missing of the trade post clan was Korsan.

And Iron Wood.

With the swift rise of pain, Pretty Wolf scrapped the direction of that thought. The cavern within her had grown broader, more jagged, impossibly large and dark, but she did not stand on the brink alone. These here stood with her.

Carried by that buoying knowledge, she slipped out from under Strong Bear's arm, tiptoed over Barkton, and exited into the dark morning.

By the blazing courtyard fire, Korsan knelt on his mat, facing the sun's imminent appearance. She left him to his prayers and padded to the river. Stripped to her skin, she spread her arms wide, closed her eyes, and let her head fall back. Let all This World see her marked stomach, victory tallies from the war with childbirth.

Mother. I am a mother.

Would she be a good one? Good enough for Flint to love and accept her? He already had a mother figure in his life.

Pretty Wolf lowered her arms, then toed the water's rushing edge and visualized the current carrying her baby into another woman's arms. Willow Woman—the mother who'd plucked Pretty Wolf's whimpering child from the spirit trail and literally nursed him into health.

What would this Willow think of Pretty Wolf showing up to steal the boy she'd raised? How would she react? As for Pretty Wolf, she was determined to clobber the woman in a hug, then sit her down for a full accounting of everything she'd missed. Every developmental waypost—words, teeth, steps. That, of course, after she swept her baby boy off his hill and bathed him in tears of joy.

Flint *would* be happy to see her...wouldn't he? Strong Bear seemed adamant he would. *"Our return, Pretty Wolf. Flint watches for us."*

A flood of gratitude washed over Pretty Wolf in a swarm of goosebumps. Or perhaps that was the freezing water she was splashing into, feet high and tramping, as though Flint were even now swifting past and she must catch him.

If only he were that close. She pondered that for a moment before dismissing it. She had much to do first, and Flint was in a decidedly safer place than Wakulla with a stand-in clan and a temporary mother.

Thought of the tasks ahead dunked Pretty Wolf under the icy flow for a hurried scrubbing. Teeth chattering with cold, she buffed herself with sand, taking no notice of the blood she removed from beneath her nails. Telly's death was avenged, and Runs Like Deer was still her dearest sister. Nothing else mattered—apart from getting back to Strong Bear. And sticking to him like sap on bark.

Might he have gone somewhere while she went to water? Wolf Clan? San Marcos? The cow pens to see about their abandoned contract? He was a free man now. He could go wherever he pleased. There was also the cold reality a soldier could take him away again without so much as a *because*. On that terrifying notion, she scrambled into her clothes and sprinted—dripping and shivering, watch pouch thumping her hip—back to the guest lodge.

Deep in pre-dawn shadows, Barkton leaned against its western wall. A tiny red glow, as of a pipe, marked the location of his whiskered mouth. He lifted the pipe in greeting. Thinking a blind dog could guard her better, Pretty Wolf repaid him a distracted wave.

She scurried toward Korsan who perched on the sitting log, his back board-straight, his ankles crossed, and his legs relaxed in a splayed posture. She called ahead. "Has Strong Bear come out?" With any luck, he would attribute the tremble in her voice to the cold.

Steam from Korsan's beverage fogged the lenses of his spectacles as he took his time sipping. "Calm yourself, child," he said in his peculiarly accented English. "Your *dearest friend in all three worlds* is perfectly well."

Breath jetted hard from her nose. "That was not the question." Though it *was* the answer.

And the pirate knew it, if she was correctly translating the smirk walking the weathered skin up one side of his face. He waved his mug in the direction of the lodge. "Your lazy *husband* is still abed."

The familiarity of his playful disdain passed a solacing calm over her spirit. Clearly, he hadn't swallowed the second-husband tale.

"That *lazy husband*," she rejoined with a pop of attitude, "traveled many difficult miles from our home country to bring me important news."

Eyes softening, Korsan bowed his turbaned head. "Allah be praised for the life of my master's son."

So, he'd heard. Good. She had no wish to retell the story. As joyous as the news was, it cast a condemning light over her error—the gravest, most heinous error a mother could make.

Korsan could surely not have overlooked such a detail. Yet, as she waited for him to grow red in the face, to spit chastisement over the offense to his master, to upbraid her for her copious flaws or general unworthiness, he merely put his mug to his mouth for another dainty slurp.

"Yes…" She gazed at the brand on his wrist, giving the pirate ample opportunity to sling rebuke, but it seemed the controlled accountant was at the helm. Or possibly the sentimental father-figure he pretended not to be.

As an ache moved down her throat, she glided in to plant a smacking kiss to his brown cheek.

He reeled back, his mien imperial. "What infringement upon my great person! What—"

"Oh, quit." With a flick of her wrist, she batted his turban down his forehead. Its front edge mashed against the bridge of his gourd nose. "You love it. And you will love it more when it is your master's son spreading kisses across your cheek. Here. I will show you his likeness."

Korsan harrumphed and righted his crown of fabric as she retrieved the parchment from its nest behind the timepiece. "Look at him, Korsan, and dare tell me he is not the most handsome child."

While his shrewd chicory eyes examined her son, she wrung water from her hair with shaking, excited hands and held her breath for his judgement. A thing he was too long in giving as he tilted the creased, red-spattered page toward the firelight. He gazed into Flint's pale eyes, while through his own dark ones, tender affection flickered brightly.

At last, lips pursed, he returned it. "The son of my most gracious master is indeed extraordinary."

Mouth twitching with mischief, she took in each of her boy's perfectly chubby features. "It is quite fortunate for little Flint he did not receive any of his mother's monkey flaws."

"Quite, quite."

The slight crack of Korsan's voice invited her to explore the wizened pirate more carefully—the bloodshot eyes, the bags and smudges under them. It was no exaggeration to say the man had dearly loved Iron Wood.

With great reluctance, she re-folded the sketch to store it safely away, then tapped her chin and hummed a little note of curiosity. "And quite fortunate for *you* that Strong Bear and I drove you from your bunk. And that Melon's short frame leaves so much space in hers…" An easy assumption—the most fastidious pirate in all the seas would never deign to sleep on dirt.

He sniffed haughtily. "A man of my superior breeding requires no *driving out* to procure a woman's bed." Face at an imperious tilt, Korsan narrowed his eyes and raised the mug one second too late to hide his satisfied smile.

"Then we will thank the groomed eyebrows."

"We most certainly will not." An indelicate snort vibrated his nostrils. "If anyone is to give thanks, it is her, for the honor of my attentions. For she is most eager to please me."

This second hum of hers was the dubious sort. "I would like to see this eagerness for myself."

"In due time, you shall, you shall."

"Korsan," Melon barked from the lodge door.

His shoulders jounced, and his tea sloshed out. With a snap of the knees, he shot upright.

"Did you fall into the kettle?" The woman chirped. "Where is my tea?"

While he hustled to the fire, bloomers billowing, Melon grinned cheekily at Pretty Wolf and ducked back inside.

"Mm, you were correct," Pretty Wolf drew out, making a long, impressed nod. "Quite eager indeed."

Mouth arranged in a sour line, he turned and gave her his backside as he bent to collect the kettle from its seat on the coals. "With the bloody head of Kills Many fresh in the grave, let us consider the prophecy fulfilled."

She blinked. "What?"

He refilled his cup, all jest and contrived arrogance wiped from his tone. Replaced by ironfisted command. "You will not provoke the White Devil again." He touched the evil-warding amulet at his throat as he leveled her a meaningful look, eyes on the dagger at her waist.

She touched it, polished antler coasting under her fingertips. Prophecy? A nebulous memory scratched at the back of her mind. Screaming Buttons standing over Kills Many and making a similar connection.

Polly's warbled voice revisited her. *"What exactly did Water Spirit show you?"*

Her father's eyes struck her where she stood. "The People's adversary, a bleeding head, and you."

As it did then, Pretty Wolf's brain seized. Her vision focused downward on the dagger handle near her hip.

Our adversary's head. By my hand.

Kills Many—whose crime had imperiled all the People and whose head received a bloody half-severing as a thank you—met every qualification.

And with that revelation came beautiful release. Of spirit. Of knees. As fate had it, she was still standing before the log when her legs gave out.

By the time she collected her composure and lifted her head to reply, Korsan was peering down at her threw his seeing glasses, issuing further orders. "...must tend my woman's needs now, but do not think to leave for the surrender parley before you have come to me again. I have found something of grave interest, and it must be discussed."

Ruffled at the command, she took his hand and bowed over it, lips grazing his knuckles. "As you wish, your greatness, so shall it be."

"Mock me if it amuses your monkey heart, but I know my worth." He surprised her by lifting her chin with a crooked finger. "As you, dear child, should know yours."

"Do I not know it?" Through her father's eyes, and the People's, she felt she did.

He tutted. "If it is the truth of yourself that you seek vision of, *that*"—he nodded toward Strong Bear just appearing in the doorway—"is the better reflecting glass to gaze into."

"Korsan!" Melon summoned, moving him at speed across the lot, steam trailing in the frigid morning air.

Strong Bear skipped out of his path, then stood there before the lodge, puff-eyed and sleep-clumsy as he yawned and rubbed his disheveled head. Shirt twisted and hanging open, he was rumpled and adorable.

Love for him welled up from Pretty Wolf's depths, and her dark caverns suddenly didn't feel quite so fathomless.

He gave her a torpid smile and plodded over. When he stopped, his knee pressed warm into her thigh. "Wolf." The scent of forest wafted from him.

She breathed it in. "Kit."

Knuckles grazing her profile, he penetrated her with a searching look. "You are well."

On the lift of a shoulder, she said, "You are here."

"Ehi." His fingers curled around her nape, and he pressed a lingering kiss to her forehead before settling beside her. "My brave wolf."

My? More than he knew. But she *really* didn't want to pop the cork from that keg just yet. Didn't have the emotional energy to expend on it, especially considering the looming confrontation with the Sharp Knife.

As Strong Bear settled next to her, Shem bounded out of the lodge and made feverish tracks around the back, shouting, "I gotta go, I gotta go!"

Rox emerged next and shuffled hesitantly toward them. Afraid, no doubt, she would combust again in a deluge of tears.

"Lieutenant Roxworth," she greeted with her most reassuring smile.

A lopsided grin broke out across his face and drool spilled out.

"Come sit?" She tapped the log on her free side, and he accepted, tilting his weight into her once he was seated.

"Pah-ee aw'ight?"

"I'm all right." Apart from the constant battle to push back thoughts of Iron Wood. And the sudden watering of her eyes from Rox's mighty stench.

"Pretty Wolf," Melon hollered from inside the lodge. "Keep that man from wandering off. He'll go after that cursed satchel if you let him!"

"'Ocks," he moaned despondently, as if he understood Muskogee. Maybe he did and had been playing them for fools all along.

"I know, good friend, and I am sorry those mean soldiers took them." Pretty Wolf patted his knee. "But I have a plan."

"Uh?" The man rested big, listening eyes on her.

"If you wash—with soap—and let Melon scrub your clothes—*all* of them, even your underthings—I will go to the store and talk sweet to the soldiers until they return your bag to me."

Rox grunted and leaned harder into her. She would take that as *bargain struck*.

For the next short while, they sat just so. Unspeaking. Rox on one side, Strong Bear on the other. Until the sun crested the horizon, and the time arrived to surrender.

No, she thought, fingers curling around Strong Bear's hand, *to win*.

Chapter 43

With a silent prayer for Pretty Wolf burning through his bones, Strong Bear fixed his gaze to her seated at the ceremonial table at the quadrangle's center.

"How long are you going to let this go on?" Buck hummed the question so close that the hilt of his sheathed sword bumped Strong Bear's thigh.

Balada's shrill whinny, filtering over the fort's walls, seemed an endorsement of Buck's impatience for action.

After the last days, last *night*, Strong Bear desperately yearned to make justice his bow and fury his arrow and take them all down in a bloody shower of vengeance. But one look at the woman's relaxed command of the field said she did not need him.

Strong Bear tipped his mouth toward his old friend. "As long as she wants." He repeated it in hushed Muskogee for his other companions.

They stood in a line off to the side, himself and Buck, Screaming Buttons and Big Voice, Barkton a few paces nearer his charge. Close enough to catch the terse dialogue exchanged over the long table. Luengo, the Spanish commander, along with his muttering Bluecoat translator, had assumed a stance beside the table.

"Unless she signals," Strong Bear added, "no one moves."

Big Voice's irreverent grunt sounded from the other side of Buttons. "If the signal is staring unendingly at a paper, she has been giving it a while now."

Strong Bear bent to peer down the row and droop his eyelids in censure. Though, true enough, she struggled. Or deliberately dallied, politely making a nuisance of herself. A little of both? Either way, he felt the heart in him explode with pride.

Just as a child might perceive grains of gunpowder to be harmless sand, Pretty Wolf might be confused as weak opposite her string of adversaries. On one side: General Jackson, flanked by four officers, every uniform pristine and glittering with power. On the other: Pretty Wolf, skin golden and radiant in the post-noon sun.

Brilliant sunlight created a contrast of deep purple shadows that outlined her features in a fine white glow. An obliterative weapon, her beauty transfixed every male at the table. Wholly disarmed, they found it no chore to gaze while they waited. And while they waited, Strong Bear fumed.

He needn't have the training of a war strategist to see that her seat had been placed in the direct eyeline of the blood-spattered execution wall. For that alone—never mind the ill-mannered gawking—flashes of anger patrolled Strong Bear's system.

In contrast, Pretty Wolf carried on reading-dallying, no trace of irritation or nerves. Backbone tall yet pliant, shoulders sloped at a relaxed angle, she gave no indication she'd spent the night racked with sobs, trembling and almost catatonic with exhaustion. He'd have to commend her later for her exemplary acting. As well as her choice of clothing.

She'd bedecked herself in a proud illustration of Muscogee tradition. Pleated and ribboned skirt. Vivid indigo. Full, ruffled blouse. Battle red. Tasseled waist-sash. Bright yellow. And crowning her head, a braided leather thong from which hung a tasteful display of ribbons and feathers. Hummingbird for beauty, owl for wisdom, wren for protection.

Lashes low, she studied the document before her, one finger gliding across the surface. A snail slowly eating its way across a leaf. Left to right and back again.

The Instrument of Unconditional Surrender, as it had been called, had been read aloud in full by one of the general's underlings. When he'd finished, Pretty Wolf declared she would not touch quill to paper until her own eyes had passed over every word. A process that had grown so tediously long, idle chatter had sprung up among the soldiers, Spanish and Bluecoat alike. Silence still reigned in the ranks of warriors lined up straight like picket rails, Winter Hawk morose among them.

They were one hundred fifty-seven warriors in all, every Muscogee male above thirteen winters, as demanded. To General Jackson's combined two thousand, they were a swarm of vexatious gnats biting the ear of a fighting bull. How Crazy Medicine had ever thought to defy such a foe, Strong Bear could not fathom.

A nebulous figure hung back in the corner shadows, the soft gut and disheveled head of hair naming him William Hambly. Rumor said Mortar had already dashed off home to Muscogee country. Happy endings for all three in their captive band.

Not so for his Wolf—even though she'd laid her life over her enemy's, bowed her head to blood vengeance, exposed her back to death.

White fluttered in Strong Bear's periphery, and he clenched his hand hard to keep from ripping the feather from his locks. The Bluecoats were not his enemy. They *could not be*. Because while he tore away his feather, they could tear away his land, Flint's future. Her life. So, Strong Bear would check his anger through this meeting, then he was through with the Bluecoats. They'd served their purpose.

He had his Wolf.

"I abandoned the cow pens." Buttons' dreary murmur cut into Strong Bear's musings.

The confession reared Strong Bear's chin back. He stared as Buttons shook his hanging head, absorbed the familiar hiss of his many snake rattles, and felt touched by compassion. "At day's end," he reassured, "you would have been sent away regardless. It is none of your doing that the contract is taken from us." Taken. Voided. Payment rescinded.

"Our doing, their doing." Buttons twitched a shoulder. "It is the same result. Failed duty."

"If you are determined to be guilty, then make it up to her."

Buttons said no more but contracted his mouth in a considering look.

Another bump against his hip signaled Buck's increasing fidgets.

"Who do you plan to cut down with that?" Strong Bear sliced his gaze to the stranglehold Buck had on his sword, the one he called Justice. Its name being perhaps the only evidence of *that* within a three-mile circle.

Buck released the pommel to run a crooked finger along the inside of his collar. "Your calm is absolutely unnatural. I'm sweating through my clothes on her behalf."

Calm was a long stretch, but at least he was doing a decent enough job of portraying it. "I worry more for her Ottoman friend." He ticked his chin toward Korsan.

The man should be stashed away in Wakulla, praying to be forgotten. Yet there he stood a few paces off the table's far side, boasting full Ottoman garb. A belt of patterned fabric topped full-bodied trousers that cinched at the ankles. Over a blue tunic, he wore a voluminous red robe, and a green turban towered above his head—the same head that could be separated from his body should his long, gaping sleeves fall back to betray his branded flesh.

Strong Bear scowled at his strong-nosed profile, more than a little disgruntled the man would put his life in danger, risking one more loss for Pretty Wolf to bear. And what was that thing the accountant had under his arm? Some sort of book. No, a carrier. Thin. Leather. For papers?

"You expect trouble?" Buck murmured, fingers falling again to Justice.

"Not from him, but possibly, yes. Pretty Wolf must have a plan if she supports his presence here."

Buck rapped a fingernail against the sword's guard. "I am thoroughly intrigued."

"She is an intriguing woman."

"That she is, my man. And, quite frankly,"—Buck affected a shiver—"a little intimidating."

Strong Bear rolled his lips inward to contain a grin. "Most here would agree with you."

"Yourself not included."

"Wrong. Every part of that woman terrifies me." Her unpredictable, self-hazarding impulses. Her sharp intelligence. Her petrifying beauty.

Buck shook with silent amusement. "Poor is the fellow who isn't properly knock-kneed around his lady."

If that was true, then Strong Bear was rich indeed.

General Jackson, seeming to have spent his patience, heaved a great breath. "It is all in order, Princess Pretty Wolf, I assure you."

At his first words, the rumble of conversation cut off.

She raised her lashes and bowed the ends of her mouth into a sweet smile. "Says he who invades foreign territories and executes foreign lords."

A strangled cough erupted from some quarter.

The general's skin mottled. "Are you quite finished?"

"Shortly." The tiniest of smirks rested at one fold of her mouth. "I shall also have it read by my White Stick liaison and my man of accounts." Her gaze flashed to Strong Bear.

Relief emptied his lungs. He advanced to her side, tension bleeding from him with each stride. With supreme difficulty, he resisted touching her in some way, if even small, and settled for the warm bend of her lips offered solely to him.

"Kit," she greeted low in Muskogee as she pointed the parchment toward him. "Please."

Strong Bear bent to read the scrawl of accusations and stipulations.

Whereas an unprovoked and inhuman war, waged by the hostile Creeks against the United States, hath been repelled in conformity with principles of national justice and honorable warfare— A snort erupted from him.

"What is it?"

Finding Pretty Wolf

He flapped a hand at Pretty Wolf and, from there, secured his emotions and simply skimmed for anything that might leap out as different from the recitation.

...in testimony whereof, they have set their hands and affixed their seals.

Blank space stretched below that final line, marred only by the general's mark—a bold, looping rendition of his full name. Beside it, a seal-pressed circle of red wax.

Strong Bear slid the page back to her. "All in order."

Save for Pretty Wolf's heart and pride. Those would require a great deal of mending and care. Two tasks Strong Bear would diligently carry out.

Leaned back in his chair, General Jackson spread long, genteel fingers in a gesture of *see?*

"Thank you, Strong Bear. And now, my bookkeeper." Pretty Wolf made to rise.

Every man darted to his feet, and Strong Bear remembered how McGirth honored the women of his lodge. He rushed to attend her chair. They would chortle over it later—her royal airs, his white man's manners—but at present, she had a role to play, and he had a driving instinct to meet her every need.

As if on cue, Korsan ghosted over on leather slippers. The oil of his mustache and chin beard caused the trimmed black hairs to gleam, the smile between them, equally oiled. Stopped before Pretty Wolf, he cocked an arm at his middle and bowed over it. "*Salaam aleikom*, beloved of my master."

"And peace to you, my friend." She dropped a curtsy. "Our host, Major General Andrew Jackson." At Korsan's perfunctory nod, she turned. "General, I present Prince Korsan, sixth son to Sultan Mehmed the third, ruler of the Ottoman provinces of Karaman and Konya." Deep lines began stacking on General Jackson's brow while Strong Bear quelled the urge to guffaw.

Pretty Wolf finished the introduction. "Prince Korsan was friend and bookkeeper to Lord Bellamy and is now the same to me. He is known as Korsan the Silent, and it pleases him to join us on the journey north."

Murmurs crowded the square. To the drone of it, Jackson executed a shallow obeisance. "An honor, Prince Korsan, I assure you." That assurance did nothing to dispel the skepticism rippling over his narrow face. Savvy of him to doubt, but then, he was not called Old Dull Knife.

Korsan raised his chin in the barest of acknowledgments and kept it elevated, his dark eyes hidden behind the glare on his smudged spectacles. He sniffed and wordlessly deposited the leather carrier onto the table.

With the grace of a lake swan, Pretty Wolf floated back down to reseat herself, and Strong Bear played assistant. Precisely as he'd seen McGirth do.

As one, the Bluecoats followed.

"A chair for our guest." General Jackson snapped his fingers at no one. Three someones hopped to obey. Ramping a tight smile for Korsan, the general said, "Am I to learn how it is you came to be on our humble shores?"

Korsan settled calm, unflinching eyes on him. "I believe you have lost your way, General. These humble shores belong to Spain." Gathering his robes about him, he lowered himself and posed stiffly. "As to your question, perhaps later I will indulge your request for stories." Accompanied by a swirl of his ringed hand, he declared, "I begin."

After an exacting adjustment of his glasses, he peered down at the sheet, paying no mind to the color flaring high on Jackson's neck. Or to the order he clipped at his lieutenant for rum.

Calm as a sun-drunk cat, Korsan completed his reading and added his approval to Strong Bear's. He dipped the quill into the ink bottle and handed it to Pretty Wolf.

In the next moment, she'd inscribed her name beneath the general's then called her Second. A-rattle with nerves, Buttons fumbled the feather before grasping it awkwardly in his big hand and scratching two letters onto the paper—the S.B. they'd practiced in the dirt. Big Voice, not caring much for letters, followed with a simple V, but the quill caught on the final stroke, and ink spat across the page. Flustered, he dabbed it with his sleeve and backed away.

If the general's aim was to humiliate them, he'd succeeded.

He stood then and, in a loud voice, asked after the female captive taken during the transport massacre on the Apalachicola. A Mrs. Lane. Strong Bear himself had found the woman's companion—throat slit—but the Lane woman had melted into the rivercane with the attacking party. None in Wakulla recognized the name, much to Jackson's scowling disgruntlement. However, he soon put away the emotion to spout a few concluding words, too formal and flowery to bear hearing.

The entirety of Strong Bear's focus belonged to Pretty Wolf sitting so primly, so...*white*. With her finely hewn features: small nostrils, cheekbones high and light. And with her skin the dark beige of a tanned settler and her hazel eyes speckled with that stunning blue. Her attire and noble bearing, though, spoke ardent Muscogee.

Strong and beautiful in whatever role she took up, the woman would always hold the chain to his shackles. The most willing bondage a man ever served.

"Leaving, General?" she chirped, halting him mid-rise, his shoulder tassels suspended in a forward dangle. "I have yet to present my grievances and demands."

"I beg your pardon? Demands?" The glacial chips of his eyes bore into her but didn't chill her saccharine demeanor.

"Indeed." Lashes performing a double-flutter, she pointed to his chair. "Shall we begin?"

Airy amusement burst from his mouth, but he accepted her invitation to retake his seat. "We are all quite intrigued, I'm sure."

Strong Bear darted a glance over his shoulder and caught Buck's eye as well as the grin he wrestled.

Several officers bobbed their chins, their chuckles free and flagrant, but Strong Bear couldn't fault those whose eagerness sat them forward. Call him slavishly addicted, but he, too, stopped his breath for whatever she and Korsan had concocted that morning while he'd gone to water.

She didn't make them wait long. "General, I must insist your soldiers leave the trade store's property at once and that all removed items be given back without delay. Coin payment will be accepted for the vastly consumed sugar, coffee, and smoked meats."

Across the table, incredulity flashed across every brow. Save Jackson's. His gave way to nothing, but when he spoke, it was condescension he indulged. "My dear child, allow me to explain prizes of war. Robert Bellamy was proven an unauthorized agent of Great Britain and, thus, a willing enemy of the United States. Therefore, his illegal store and all his belongings fall into ownership of the United States government."

Pretty Wolf canted toward the general in a manner one might call threatening but for the sweetened turn of her lips. "When you say *prize of war*, I believe you mean *loot* of war. As in theft. General, as Prince Korsan has kindly reminded, this is not the United States. You are a questionably welcome guest in an alien nation. To remove anything from it would be considered theft."

There, she inserted a nervy pause. Time enough to appreciate the tick at the hinge of Jackson's jaw. "Since the spirit road cannot be traveled backward," she continued, voice going from conversational to categorical. "I choose to no longer argue whether Lord Bellamy's life was yours to take, but I *will* fight you for my husband's possessions. Of that, you can be quite certain."

Jackson's mouth opened. Shut. "Your…husband?" he finally managed.

Boldly maintaining his doubting gaze, she said, "Korsan, if you please."

The accountant opened the binder, extracted its sole occupant—a piece of parchment that Strong Bear recognized, shock parting his own mouth—and set it before her.

Spinning the paper, she slid it closer to the general but did not remove the tips of her fingers from its edge. "Here, you see my marriage contract to Lord Robert Bellamy. Signed and legitimized on the twelfth day of October 1813. As witnessed by Commander Antonio Luengo."

Signed by whom? Last Strong Bear had seen it, there'd been a gaping blank spot. He lifted slightly on his toes but saw no better than black squiggles.

During his cursory perusal of it, Jackson's age lines shifted into a chart of dislike. "Commander Luengo, do confirm this is your signature."

The Spaniard bustled over and gave the document an obligatory glimpse before pushing his round cheeks up with a grin. Through his translator, he admitted ownership of the mark.

Once Luengo resumed his station, the general exhaled through the slit of his tight lips. "Am I to believe you were wed to Lord Bellamy while responding to the name Miss Francis?"

She jostled a shoulder. "Creek women do not take on the names or titles of their husbands." A flick of her fingers snatched the document back to herself. "Also, my relationship with Lord Bellamy did not merit your involvement, but it has been openly acknowledged among the People. I am no maiden. Neither am I a pampered Indian princess too fearful of a blue coat to fight for what is mine."

"No…" Jackson mused, watching her through half-lidded eyes. "I suspect you are much more."

"Perhaps, sir, there can be found in you a bit of wisdom after all." On that frighteningly brazen note, she laughed, the sound of it so breezy and lovely, her only punishment was to be subjected to the general's snake-in-the-corn smile.

"What of him?" He cocked an eyebrow at…Strong Bear?

Ehi, what of *me?* Heartrate picking up, he battled for a neutral demeanor. Strong Bear expected a similar reaction from Pretty Wolf. Instead, what came out of her mouth was a dismissive, "One man has nothing to do with the other."

Precisely so. Then why did Jackson bring Strong Bear into it? What tale had she concocted to get Strong Bear out of that cell? It could have been anything. But he had his suspicions.

A terribly timed chortle wrenched his abdomen. He caught it in his nose, then cleared his throat and spread his shoulders. He'd be whatever, whoever his Wolf needed him to be.

"All that concerns you," she was saying, "is my legal marriage to Lord Bellamy."

General Jackson sighed dramatically but said no more.

"So, we are agreed." After skimming a loving touch across the contract's surface, she passed it to Korsan, who promptly stored it away. "I am widow to Robert Bellamy. Commander Luengo?" She looked to him. "What then, according to English law, becomes of my husband's belongings?"

Luengo leaned into his translator. Several moments expired as the man conveyed the question then the answer. "An Englishman's estate transfers to his legally wedded spouse."

"As I thought. Good then. The store, the land, and all its contents are mine to do with as I wish."

A victory whoop barreled up Strong Bear's throat and slammed into the back of his mashed lips. If the meeting didn't conclude soon, he might end up in the cell again. For disorderly conduct.

Bodies shuffled in seats as the officers awaited their superior's reaction.

Apart from the tinge of pink rising to his pale cheeks, the general remained unruffled. "Do you forget, Miss— Pardon, *Mrs*. Bellamy, you will be marched north in three days? The trade store might be a little unwieldy on your back."

"The splinters *would* be a bother." Half her mouth moved sideways, her tone becoming slow and deliberate, patterned for a child. "No, I will sell it. Naturally. Prince Korsan brings a list of all items and their fair values. He will negotiate and finalize all sales with Commander Luenago and your own quartermaster if you wish. Your powder horns will require refilling before long, will they not, General?"

Though he couldn't possibly be glad to been undermined so neatly by a woman and his enemy, General Jackson spread his mouth until his eyeteeth showed. "I trust you will part with these products for a reasonable price?"

"Our dear prince has been known to be reasonable. On occasion."

Jackson's chest jerked with a hoot that had his subordinates gazing at one another confusedly. But Strong Bear understood better than any the power of her charm, and the woman had it out in force. Aimed directly at the white chief. Old and sharp he might have been, but against Wakulla's she-wolf, he became happy prey. By the look of him, eyes shimmering like shards of ice, he knew it. And didn't care.

After begging her pardon, he turned to converse privately with a scraggle-bearded sergeant who'd come up behind him. That finished—the fellow sent off to whatever task—Jackson faced front again, delight cavorting about his features, as though he were returning to a robust game of cards. "Do continue, Princess. Your second grievance?"

"It is to do with the labor accord between my people and the Spaniard, Don Diego Lopez, owner of La Conchita and lands. He agreed to award Wakulla two bulls in exchange for three months of work at the arena stables and cow pens. The contract was in good standing. Until your army arrived. Sir." Chin pulled in, she levied censure through her top lashes. "Today, the overseer says we broke our word and failed our duty, and he refuses to pay even our part-labor. All here present are aware that myself and my men would be there now if not for your…intrusion. How will you correct this injury?"

"On behalf of the American army," Jackson intoned, a hand coming to rest atop the gleaming buttons on his frock, "I offer my regrets that our penalization of crimes has been such inconvenience on you. It is against my policy to assist in matters not pertaining to me, but because you've had trying few days, I'll toss you a bone, so to speak."

"How gracious of you."

"Yes." His lips pulled to the side. "You see, neither Lopez's overseer nor I has the authority to make such a determination. That would belong to the estate's agent. Happily, that very fellow is in company." He swung a lifted finger Strong Bear's direction. No, a shade to the left. "Captain Marcus Buck."

Incredulous laughter trilled out of Pretty Wolf. She swiveled at the hips in her seat. "Captain Buck, is this so? I cannot name the general a liar, but…agent to La Conchita? Truly?"

Buck drifted forward, giving Strong Bear's arm a comradely bump in passing. "Really. Strange as it seems."

"How, when?"

"When the don was duly deprived of life," he deadpanned, a tad smug, "and I became the lucky gent to marry the heiress's mother."

"The mother of—?" Her words spiked and spluttered. "You have wed the Bitter Eyes?"

Brows slashing down, Buck clicked his tongue. "If you mean Miss Lillian McGirth, who will no longer reply to that abominable Bitter Eyes moniker, then yes."

Pinkened at the reproach, Pretty Wolf offered apologies and listened raptly as Buck explained. Mrs. Buck had provided him full legal control of the property. While in the country, he was to shut up the greater part of the estate to await the heiress's coming of age.

On the heels of a gooey-eyed mention of his new, little daughter, Mari, he swore to honor the completed portion of the contract. He added that, since Mari and her mother stuck to Beaver, he was certain Mrs. Buck wouldn't conceive of sending her people off without lending assistance. From his own experience, Strong Bear had high doubts such a claim could be remotely valid, but it was an *amusing* story for the general's sake.

Facts recounted, promise of payment made, Pretty Wolf called the meeting closed, stood, and presented her hand to General Jackson. Then did the same to every man at the table, each of whom bowed over it and offered such phrases as "honored" and "dear lady" and "your highness"; more fodder for the next day's laughter.

"A remarkable woman you have there."

Strong Bear started at the voice, not having heard the general slip in beside him. Heat swamped his gut. Some of it born of startlement, the remainder of sudden discomfort. He was no silver-tongued Pretty Wolf, as the sweat at his temples and the silence on his tongue attested.

Jackson filled the awkward gap, a thoughtful hum in his timbre. "I deeply admire her, you know. Her father was a truly formidable enemy, but he had nothing on his daughter." He uttered a quiet laugh.

They both observed her latest conquest, a clean-cheeked lieutenant who grasped her hands and called her "a genuine Pocahontas." Strong Bear was pondering the significance of the strange name when Jackson spoke again.

"If women could do battle, I might have been in trouble."

Strong Bear looked at him, brows lowered, and began rethinking the man's intelligence. "Forgive me, General, but I do not agree. Women *do* battle." He indicated the table. Never mind the hatchet-throwing Minks of the world who, up to the teeth in blood, could mow down a yard of White Sticks and spare time after to shove one in a closet.

"Yes, I suppose they do. Slave." Jackson vested him a knowing look. "Or...are you the husband on the side not terribly disheartened to have the Englishman out of your way?"

Strong Bear's suspicion was true then—they were to feign marriage. Doable. But he could *not* do the general's incivility. He ground down on his teeth. Turning to him, he challenged a square meeting of the eyes and moved his jaw aslant to relax its clench. "I am the man who will willingly waste himself rebuilding the pieces of her you destroyed."

Jackson stilled, the blink of his pale lashes not swift enough to cover a glimmer of what might have been contrition.

Unmoved, Strong Bear leaned in, pushing his boldness into foolishness. "And I have never, from the first day, been on the side." Not bothering with a dismissal or polite parting or even a notice of resignation from army service, Strong Bear stepped back and left him.

Chapter 44

Outside the fort, the villa had come to a standstill. Eyes large with curiosity, the villagers observed as the last of Wakulla's warriors crossed the drawbridge. Ahead, the long train of them streamed down the central lane, their feet rising higher, landing firmer than when they'd trudged in. At their tail walked Pretty Wolf, Strong Bear beside her, Barkton three steps to their rear. She might be surprised at their turn of mood if she weren't feeling the lightness of triumph herself.

A mite-sized triumph, no doubt, but the most sizeable they'd had since the start of this blue-coated nightmare. Probably the only one they'd have. And the People were battle-wise enough to know when to dance a victory stomp. If only in their souls.

Palm clasped inside Strong Bear's larger one, she expanded her lungs and depleted them in a gust, gaze lifting to the cobalt blue of tomorrow's northern sky. She inhaled the scent of saffron and seafood wafting from some nearby lodge, her ear picking up the soft pluck of a guitar's expressive strains. She would miss San Marcos, its lovable commander, and its vibrant, chatter-prone people. Even its testy cows and cocky vaqueros. But to have her Kit and her Flint, she'd happily make the villa a cherished memory.

Flint...

With the surrender at their backs, Pretty Wolf's mind flew wide open with room for her son to twirl and play, to grab her hands and spin through autumn leaves. Soon, the child would become more than a nebulous image flitting through her imagination. He'd take on bone and flesh, scent and voice. And with those, he would cling to her neck and babble little-boy love into her ear.

Strong Bear gave her fingers a gentle squeeze, tenderness molding his features. His hair, the glossy black of a raven's wing, rippled in the wind and wrapped choker-like around his neck. "It does my heart good to see you smile."

Had she been smiling? *Ehi,* a small curve sat on her mouth. She broadened it some. "We have reason to smile a little."

"You were a beautiful gale in there, Pretty Wolf." His rumbly tones matched the rattling bridge slats beneath their tread. "It might have been your quill that signed surrender, but it was Old Sharp Knife who was defeated." The adoring—and adorable—crinkle around his eyes reached into her heart and brushed away any residual strain.

As it sloughed off, she reciprocated his finger-squeeze. "Half the praise is owed to Korsan."

"The man cuts a believable prince. With that nose always in the air."

She shot him a sidelong look. "Who's to say he is not one?" When a question spiked his brows, Pretty Wolf pulled him to the side of the bridge and leaned in conspiratorially. "The story he told me this morning is that he was captured by pirates. Held for ransom. But being the sixth in a line of heirs—practically worthless to the sultanate—his father kept his coin and lost his son. So, in mockery, the pirates branded him P for prince. They enslaved him at the riggings. In protest, he refused to speak a word. Thus, he became Korsan the Silent. It was a shipwreck that gave him freedom." But Iron Wood who preserved it. Beautiful man.

"Good story." Strong Bear's eyebrows tugged in, seemingly prompted by her reticence. "That's what it is…right?"

In all honesty, she wasn't certain. During the telling, Korsan's gaze had gone distant as though recalling long-suppressed memories. Or concocting an elaborate tale. Fearful it was the first, she hadn't pried.

Pretty Wolf shrugged, her smirk softening to a wistful smile. "Does it matter? Pirate, prince. Red, white. Love does not care. It binds us anyway." When her gaze began drifting toward the fort's courtyard, Strong Bear draped an arm across her shoulders and pulled her snug into his side.

"Come. Look away."

She dragged her sight back to find his expression weighted with shared pain. "What would I be without you, Kit?" Without his bear's strength and rabbit's gentleness?

"You never need find out." Lips bunched with unnamed feeling, he looked at her from shining bear-brown eyes and let her soak up her fill of his devotion. Somehow, she suspected she could look and soak from then until her winter years and never top off.

Tell him now, her conscience nudged.

And spoil this sweet moment? her logic rebutted. *Besides, he practically knows already.*

No simpleton, he'd have heard between the few words she'd exchanged with Jackson and understood an essential role had been created. And still, his adamant declaration came back for another disturbing murmur. *"...your mother's ridiculous notions... I'll not do it."*

He would never leave her, sure, but he might be at her side surly-faced, and rightly so. For being used in such a manner. One he'd plainly, adamantly rejected. Fine repayment for all he'd done for her.

Guilt clotted in her stomach.

Another time. They would speak of it later.

"Never happier to hear it." Patting his chest, she tipped a weak smile up at him and resumed their walk. Strides in sync, they stepped off the dusty bridge and came to an abrupt halt.

Balada stood to her haunches in the canal's murky water, her front hooves walking her along the steeply sloped banked. Head buried in grasses, she tore at the succulent offerings.

On a half-laugh, Pretty Wolf cried, "Get out of there, you filthy beast." Fists propped on her hips, she made her way to the bank.

The mare's head popped up, a thatch of green shoots poking out from both sides of her muzzle. She stretched her neck toward Pretty Wolf and, pink lips unrolling to reveal her big teeth, loosed a fractious whinny. She tossed her head, and the dangling lead rope whipped about.

Strong Bear laughed. "Your horse just sassed you."

"She's worse than a child, that one." Pretty Wolf crossed her arms and lifted her voice to the animal. "It isn't my fault the mean soldiers would not let you in."

Munching, Balada gave her an insolent blue eye. She raised a hoof and stomped forcefully in place. Mud squelched and grass cowered away from her pique.

Pretty Wolf rolled her eyes and threw up her hands. "All right now, come along. Out of that water before an alligator leaves you with half a tail." She began walking off and was rewarded with the sounds of Balada clopping up the shelf and prancing along behind her. The mare passed them, head high, her beautiful cream coat spattered with mire. Stopping suddenly, she gave her body a good shaking.

No stranger to her ways, Pretty Wolf saw it coming and ducked behind Strong Bear right as the droplets began to fly.

"Agh!" Arms raised, he shielded his face.

During the onslaught, she fastened to his clothes, face crammed between his shoulder blades, the scratchy wool of his vest better punishment than muddy rain.

Strong Bear vibrated with a lighthearted growl and brushed at his sleeves only to shake out dirty hands in exasperation. "You rotten females."

Behind her, Barkton grunted what might have passed for humor, while Strong Bear reached back and pretended to search about. "Where did my fearless Wolf go? Ah, there she is." He snatched her from behind him, locked her under his arm, and smeared a wet finger down the bridge of her nose.

A squeal ripped from her. She shoved off him and swiped at whatever nastiness he'd slathered on her. "Aren't you meant to protect me? I was only letting you do your duty."

"I am ever your willing spatter shield," he grumbled, around the smile flirting with the edges of his mouth. Shuffling onward, he adjusted the quiver on his back and finished off with another lackluster growl that had her giggling. A noise she hadn't thought to make again. Ever.

He stopped and gazed down on her with soft-eyed wonder, perhaps as stunned as she. But how could she *not* laugh, with Strong Bear looking the part of grumpy, wet feline? With the store and all its contents belonging to Wolf? With the Sharp Knife forced to cede his will to her cunning?

Grinning, she side-bumped Strong Bear, then twined her arm through his and inclined her head on his shoulder as they strolled on. Beneath her cheek and clasping fingers, his muscles roped and bunched as he busily picked brown specks from his white feather.

It was this strength at her side that kept her spine straight and her voice steady during the standoff with Old Sharp Knife. This strength that cradled her at night, and this strength that would carry her home, supporting her through all the stops between. Beginning immediately with a painful farewell.

She squeezed his flexing muscle, which stilled it. Then stilled him. Once she had his complete attention—eyes large and close and keen—she whispered, "Go to the burial place with me?" They would not desecrate it by entering. Only stand afar and whisper final words of love to the two dark mounds of fresh-turned dirt. "And after, to the trade store to—" Her throat clamped, words choking off.

Strong Bear's lips lowered to skim against the tip of her nose. "I go where you go, Miccohokti."

She battled tears by plying him with a light smack. "The surrender paper is signed, White Stick. I am through with all that micco business."

A short groove formed between his sobering eyes. Mouth pinched, he shook his head. "Until your feet touch Creek soil, you are not through. The many sights between here and there are yours to command, woman. The People look to you. Show them no sign of doubt, for you are miccohokti until the trail's end." On his next exhale, the zing of pine tickled her nose. With the clasp of his warm palm to her cheek, his fingers splaying into the hair at her temple, her heart took a curious dip.

Right to the depths of her belly where it floundered out of rhythm.

At the unexpected sensation, her breath hitched. In the way of dreams, she blinked at him almost hazily, staring, as if confronted with a bead belt encoded with baffling symbols.

Strong Bear chuckled, a secret, knowing smile crooking his mouth and making her wonder what exactly it was he knew that she did not. Before she could find her tongue, he gestured grandly down the road. "Lead on, Wolf."

While its friendlier scents remained, the trade store possessed an unnatural, almost lethal hush. As though, were Pretty Wolf to move too quickly or in the wrong direction, death might attack from behind the barrels. Or down the chimney. Or from one of the Bluecoats stoically patrolling the grounds. Death did seem to be in the attacking mood of late.

Seams in the floor slats drilled into Pretty Wolf's knees as she knelt before Iron Wood's trunk, her hands quivering shamefully as she rested them on its battered leather-wrapped corners. In this curtained haven, they had shared endless intimacies, she and Iron Wood. Weeping and worry over the tragic and the mundane, mutual frustrations and fears, merrymaking and laughter. All but that having to do with the bed they'd shared yet hadn't.

Those memories and more held a terrible power over her, making her breath come hard and strident against her ears.

Strong Bear cupped the back of her head. "Do I stay? Or give you time alone with him?"

Alone with him...

Never again. Except in the painful corridors of her mind.

Her throat ached, but in the night, she had poured out her tears like water, and now she found herself empty. Empty of all but Strong Bear's unflinching presence. She worked a swallow around the knot but still did not clear the rasp from her voice. "Can you…bring the bedside table near? And light a candle."

He did so. Then went down on one knee beside her like a knight vowing fealty in Iron Wood's tales. Or a slave far too enamored of his bondage. He rested fervent, *command-me* eyes on her, and she didn't fight the smile, tiny and wistful though it was.

Thanking Creator once again for merging their paths, she laid a palm along his freshly plucked cheek. "Have a look about his desk, will you? For anything of value." Anything, that is, the Bluecoats hadn't already purloined for their worthless trial. "Something, perhaps, Flint might appreciate."

"Flint. Ehi. Wise thinking, little Wolf mother." With a swift down-stroke along her hair, he pushed up and footed purposefully from the living space.

In the new solitude, the soft release of the trunk's latch came as a startling boom. She breathed a faltering laugh at herself, then honed to Strong Bear's rummaging sounds as she dove into her own task.

Kit is here, he is alive, you are not alone.

On that reassurance, she hefted the trunk's lid and set to work.

Decisions. What to take? What to sell? What to abandon to the Bluecoats' whims?

So little had been allotted them for the journey, and her back was only so strong. But she would snap it in two if it meant preserving a memento for Flint.

As she sorted and debated, the store clock chimed seven, then seven-thirty. In those minutes, she had chosen a medal from Iron Wood's army uniform, a journal, his feathered tricorne. And from the trunk's depths, a yellowed copy of what could only be the Ancient Words, a treasure she hadn't realized he possessed. Or *had* but hadn't recognized its value enough to remember it.

She recognized it now.

Stroking its cracked cover, she hugged it to her heart as Rox did his stones and imagined countless afternoons reading from it with Strong Bear. Smiling, she placed the book reverently beside her other excellent find—Rox's beat up rock satchel.

The thing lay crumpled. Dusty. Hollow. Her heart twisted with disgust at whoever had so callously dumped it out, and with hurt for Rox, whose confusion and grief over the loss would rattle them all.

When she pulled the last item from the trunk—a star-patterned quilt— an oval portrait fells from its folds. Its gilded, palm-sized frame clacked against the trunk's paneled floor and landed glass-up.

Retrieving it, she held it toward the candle. Finely cracked and faded, the painted image trapped the breath in her throat. This might not have been her first viewing of the two little faces, but it was the first since Flint.

The image showed Iron Wood as a boy of possibly four years, manning a wooden horse. Poised beside him, an older child. His sister. Gone the way of spirits at too young an age, she had always been, Pretty Wolf suspected, the cause of Iron Wood's smotheringly protective nature. She had been a beautiful girl with her gem-eyes and shoulder-length ringlets, and Iron Wood…

Her vision clung to him. He was, in a word, "Striking," she murmured, one finger trailing over his likeness. Even in his miniature years, he'd been a work of sheer beauty.

"No mistaking Flint's father," Strong Bear said, coming to crouch at her side. "Those eyes…" He looked off, seeing something, or some*one*, not in the room. Or in the country. "They are a pale winter-blue sky. As cold in color as they are warm in spirit. They see straight through to the heart of you. They burrow *into* you." He chuckled. "The boy puts a porcupine quill to shame—there's no getting him out without destroying you."

An apt description of her betrothed who, it would seem, lived on in his son. "Ehi, as you say. Like his father." Her fingers tightened convulsively around the frame, the tips going white. Not from pain but from a sudden bubbling well of excitement. "On the journey, you will tell me everything, Kit. From the first moment to the last. The color of his hair, the sound of his voice, the naughty things he's done. I want it all."

"Then you shall have it, Pucase."

"Miccohokti, pucase," she drawled, gaze cast to the rafters. "You've convinced me of the need for leadership, but enough with that ridiculous slave ruse. I free you."

"You are master of the impossible now?" He clicked his tongue, haughty airs tipping his chin. "I am the ink under your skin, don't forget."

As if she could. Much like with Flint, she'd have to mutilate herself to be rid of Strong Bear. As if she'd ever want to. "And don't *you* forget that goes both ways."

Using his shoulder for leverage, she brought herself up.

Before she could step away, he roped her about the thighs and drew her close. And somehow—though years had passed and though several layers of fabric served as cover—Strong Bear rested his temple on the exact right spot.

The tiny inked rabbit leaping over her hip bone.

Together. Always.

As she stroked his obsidian locks, a need gripped her as fierce as the next throb of her heart. A need to hear it spoken, the endurance of his vow. "Kit?"

"Mm?"

"Where I step…"

A beat of stillness. A tightening of his fingers on her leg. Then a resonating, "I follow."

Chapter 45

Since Melon and Korsan had both disappeared—curiously at the same time—and Pretty Wolf had gone into the courtyard with Barkton to "see about a friend," Strong Bear had assigned himself Rox duty. "Chew this," he said, tapping a three-needle pine bundle at the man's noxious mouth, "and please, I beg you, give me your arm so we can put you into this jacket." If the tattered fabric could even be called a jacket anymore.

However the thing was defined, it was sacred to the man, rarely leaving his back, to be peeled off only at the steepest of bargainings. At least, that was what Strong Bear had been told.

Lies. The man wanted nothing to do with the faded scrap.

Standing before his bunk in the guest house, Rox screwed his lips shut and glared at Strong Bear through eyes puffy from crying. An hour's worth of it. Muffled by Pretty Wolf's lap.

As expected, he'd been despondent over the empty satchel, but partway in, Strong Bear speculated Rox was cooking up most of those tears. Seasoning them with heaved sighs. Serving them on dramatic shudders and wails.

All rewarded with coos and pets of his hair.

Dimwit, the man was not. Just eternally stubborn.

Bawling in his peculiar flavor of speech, Rox twisted away, satchel hugged tightly to his chest. At his clear-as-a-conch-blast "no!" Shem threw himself out flat on his pallet and belly laughed—much the way he'd done the last quarter-turn of Strong Bear's timepiece.

Which was the same amount of time Pretty Wolf had been gone. He'd been counting, counseling himself not to hunt her down for the simple pleasure of her lovely company. Lovely, easy company. For certain, easier than an obstinate soldier and a giggling boy.

How was it Strong Bear could rear a baby to age three but could not get one garment onto a grown man?

Swallowing a growl, he shoved the pine needles between his own molars and took his frustration out on the tuft. The zesty taste burst across his tongue and cooled the hottest of his blood. At least enough to gentle his tone to a sweetened wheedle. "See? Melon cleaned it nice." He raised the red coat to eye level and shook it in what he hoped was an enticing manner. "Don't you want to wear it to bed? Without it, your fingers will turn blue with cold. And fall off."

Apparently, he'd reduced himself to absurd threats. But nobody was around to slap his wrist. Only Shem, who howled uproariously, and Rox, who glowered and huffed.

It *was* partly true. In the hours since their return from the store, bracing winds had swept in from the north. A frigid reminder they were two moons deep into winter. It had been folly to hope their temperate weather would hold for the march. Even in the cozy warmth of the lodge, Strong Bear's skin was alive with gooseflesh. That could also have to do with his bared skin. His cleaned vest and shirt were stretched across a chairback and trying nobly to dry near a tiny struggling fire.

Rox issued a jumbled string of words, but Strong Bear needed only a glimpse of the snarl torquing the healthy side of the man's face to receive the message: to the Under World with that jacket.

Strong Bear's arms fell to his sides. "Help a brother, Shem."

"Which one?" The boy tittered.

Strong Bear showed him flat, unimpressed eyes.

"Aw right," Shem dragged out, pushing himself up on his elbows. "He think you gonna thieve his rock bag."

"Me! I am not the pirate among us."

"Korsan ain't no pirate! And he ain't no thief."

The no-pirate part was strongly debatable, but clearly, Shem had sunk his teeth into the tale of the Persian prince. "He thieved Melon away well enough," Strong Bear grumbled with a longing glance at the sealed door flap. Against the wind's fervor, it vibrated like a struck drum.

Beyond it, day had given way to the black of a slivered-moon night. He prayed Pretty Wolf was safe, Barkton's guarding abilities still in question.

Rallying for another round, this one at least more educated, Strong Bear turned back to Rox and drew an entrenching breath. "I do not want your bag, Rox. Who do you think had the idea to collect a rock from every special place? And from every stop on the path home?"

"Pah-ee!" Rox sprayed.

Visualizing Pretty Wolf's selfless patience, Strong Bear swiped a forearm across the spittle dotting his chin. "No, it was mine. And it was me who picked the rock from the trade post. Because the crooked white stripe across the middle looked to me like the store's roofline." Putting on his most winning smile, he clasped a hand to Rox's shoulder and felt it gradually lower from its position up by his ears. "I am a White Stick, yes, but I am also your friend, Rox. I want to help fill the bag, not take it away. And do we not both worship the same Jesus?" A slightly irreverent manipulation tactic.

As though dumped on with sand, the fire went out of Rox's eyes. They softened and sank to Strong Bear's choker, repaired by Noonday and returned via Melon.

Strong Bear stroked the sleek silver cross and watched Rox's expression turn fond—as it had every time he'd become fixated on the pendant. Oh, for the day Pretty Wolf's did too. For now, Rox's smoothed feathers would have to suffice.

It took some doing, yanking and grunting and tugging, but at last, Rox was clothed and bundled under his blanket, lumpy satchel pillowing his head like an instrument of torture.

When he began babbling, Strong Bear cut him off. "Go to sleep, soldier." He pointed at Shem. "You too, young brave."

This elicited more giggles from Shem and from Strong Bear, a pleading glance skyward. He snatched up his blanket and flung it around him, intent on finding his Wolf. "Any more trouble from you two, and it's horse feed for breakfast."

Shem's responding shriek of a neigh soon became a duet with Rox's contribution coming out closer to a mule's bray.

Face scrunching up with a contained smile, Strong Bear fed the fire, then unhooked the door covering and slipped into the night. The yard stretched before him, dark and desolate.

A scraping sound to the left called his gaze to Sergeant Barkton. The soldier leaning against the lodge, one boot propped on the wall, the narrow brim of his conical hat sitting cockeyed on his brow. A pipe bowl glowed in his hand. With a flit of a glance at Strong Bear, he shoved the stem under his bushy mustache. In the stillness, it clicked against his teeth.

Irritation plucked at Strong Bear's nostril. "Where is she?" He hadn't meant for his voice to come out a grating threat but concluded it had a fitting ring to it.

Using the pipe as a pointer, Barkton gesticulated broadly toward the storehouse. "Can't report to the general what I don't see."

With a harrumph, Strong Bear decided to forgive the guard. This time.

413

And to trust the night with Pretty Wolf. For another three minutes.

It rubbed him all manner of wrong that Bluecoats roved the talwa and that Pretty Wolf was probably the loveliest thing to cross their vision in a too-long while.

Clouds cluttered the dim moonscape, and wind knifed through Strong Bear's blanket. Tugging it tight, he considered how it would be to sleep in these elements, then pondered how full—or empty—his stomach would be while doing it.

Strong Bear looked Barkton's way. "How much provender does the general send with us?"

The sergeant snorted harshly.

"Whatever you know, speak it," Strong Bear said at a near growl.

Taking his dear time—to find his seldom-used tongue, no doubt—Barkton drew another puff on his pipe, held in the smoke, and released it in a billow that was swept away in an instant. "Enough to get us to Fort Gadsden."

Gadsden? Not even so far as the Scott fort upriver? Gadsden resided a mere eight days to the west. After that, they'd have another forty to go. At least. And only barring an overturned boat or another such catastrophe.

"Then what?" Strong Bear sounded more *bear* with every phrase.

"Supposed to resupply there."

"Supposed to?"

"Food's scarce. Takes weeks to scrounge up. Months." Barkton's shoulder lifted and dropped. "Won't be enough time for it." At that, the black beads of his eyes cut to Strong Bear. "If you haven't seen your ribs before, you might now."

Unfortunately, Strong Bear and his ribs were rather well acquainted. Pretty Wolf's, too, were no stranger. The severe want would be a trial, ehi, but they'd manage. The elderly, though. The children. Runs Like Deer...

Deep concern scoured Strong Bear across the ribs, constricting his heart until the sight of Pretty Wolf released it to bounce back. Then frolic about his chest like a fool colt.

Her lithe silhouette crossed the yard at a float, so sinuous was her gait. Strong Bear's muscles released all at once. On an outbreath, a grin slipped free and completely undermined the bear impression.

Chuckling, Barkton smacked his pipe against his palm to extinguish it before disrupting Strong Bear's sightline by passing before him. When he entered the lodge interior, light sliced into the darkness and flickered against the wet streaking Pretty Wolf's saddened face.

The grin tumbled off him. Strong Bear shoved from the wall and strode toward her with purpose. He opened his blanket wide, and her pace picked up, then became a tempo that jostled her one tiny sob.

She flung herself against him, and he wrapped her up tight. All but the top of her head disappeared inside his protective cocoon, but he felt her everywhere. The breath puffing hot against his skin. The delicious crush of her arms. The burn of her chilled finger pads on his back.

Focus!

The places her hip bones bore into him.

Grr! Not on that.

The woman, the practically *widowed* woman, was crying.

She nestled into him, and at the cool wet against the bare skin of his chest, he felt a sting of anger.

"Who shall I slay for making you cry?" The snarling bear was back.

Her body shook with laughter muted by the cocoon. "Water Moccasin. He sneaked past the patrol to get Birdie. And to say goodbye to me." Arms still clasped firmly at his waist, she canted back to show him her watery smile. "They will be much missed, but I am glad to have seen him one last time. I sent my love to Tall Bull. And to Mink, I sent the paper of Ancient Words. She will be glad for them, don't you think?" She sniffled and rushed on. "I hope that was all right?"

"You did well. We have the whole book now."

"I thought the same." Nodding, she released a hand to brush away her tears, then loosed him altogether and stepped out of his embrace.

A cold, hollow place opened behind his breastbone. The loss of her was so acute he would have reeled her back in amid fierce protest had she not bowed her head, looking suddenly, uncharacteristically shy. And…was she twisting her ring? Old Sharp Knife had not elicited such nervousness in her. Yet Strong Bear did?

The sight stirred up a nasty pot of nausea. Whatever this was, as clear as a torch in the night, it was about *them*. He knew it in the pit of his gut where the acid roiled hottest.

Like pushing into a cane thicket, his mind slogged through every horrid possibility. She would put a stop to their recently increased clinginess or to their shared couch. Or worse, she would declare widowhood and relegate *them* to four years into the future. Or the most unthinkable, she would relegate them to never. If she did that, it would split his bones apart.

He locked his elbows at his sides to keep from rolling her in his blanket and tossing her over his shoulder again. To keep from carting her off much the way her Water Moccasin friend intended with his Birdie. Albeit, with a smidge more coercion.

Feet shuffling, she twisted his innards in time with her ring, and he waited, bile making a slow crawl up his throat.

"In the square," she began at last, "when all the people were gathered, Kills Many questioned my leadership. Because of my youth and unwed status."

When she glanced up, eyes wide and shining like twin black moons, he heard himself—the low growl rumbling his voice box. He severed it with an abrupt swallow.

"My mother put him in his place by saying I was married to you. I…didn't correct her."

Didn't…what? What was she saying? With the way she'd wiped herself of all emotion, it was impossible to know what she meant, what she wanted. And didn't want. Such as a particular response from him.

Which response was soon made clear. "Are you cross with me?"

His head jutted back. Why would he be cross? He opened his mouth for a firm negative, but all that emerged was "I—" before it hit him. The implications. The effects of such a public statement. And lack of rebuttal.

His voice, his mouth dried up. His lips stuck to his teeth.

It wasn't only Jackson who believed them bound in marriage, but Noonday and Sunflower and Winter Hawk and—another swallow undulated his throat—all of Wakulla.

Strong Bear's heart was a cane cutter rabbit, springing up in joy, then crashing back down with a sad realization: he *had* been relegated. To a voiceless slave. To a man denied the power of choice. Same as Pretty Wolf, really, since she'd been tossed into his couch on the ridiculous notion it would somehow give credence to her authority. Yet another sacrifice for her People.

That word—sacrifice—dropped his heart to his feet. For he knew the arrangement could not be ended. He saw it in the worry lines bracketing her mouth and in the simple logic of it.

Sacrifice. Arrangement. Logic.

What of love? What of *them*? The true them. The *them* that was promised him in that solid, Creator-instilled knowing that had driven him south.

Would he have chosen her anyway? A thousand times, ehi.

But would *she* have chosen *him*?

Did she approve of the joining, even on a fabricated level? Which begged the question, were they even legitimately bound? In the world of captives and slaves, most definitely.

So, what was Strong Bear to Pretty Wolf?

His belly was full of questions, but being too much the coward for the answers, he eased his mouth closed and gave his head a slow shake. "Not cross."

Not exactly pleased, but cross over the excuse to claim her as his? Never.

"I'm glad, Kit." Relief flooded her voice and sagged her shoulders.

If nothing else, she valued his blessing.

"What now?" he finally croaked. Then the questions poured out. "How should we behave together? What do you expect of me? Should we set boundaries?" *Where will we sleep?* The last lodged in his cowardly throat.

"What questions!" she teased with a light smack to his arm. "You already know our boundaries. Nothing must change."

That was what he was afraid of. And so very thankful for. If things changed, *when* they changed, it would be by choice because she could not live without him.

"The night grows short. To bed, *husband*." She struck out ahead of him, laughing as though considering him in such a way was nothing but comical.

His hope gave a death scream and flung its arms around Path Maker. *Why*, he prayed, *is my path to her blocked by briars at every turn?*

For a few shuddered breaths, Strong Bear watched her go, knowing if he set out, his feet would trample his sunken heart. Helpless to stop himself, he followed her anyway.

In the now-toasty lodge, every eye was open, Barkton's the narrowest as he looked three breaths from sliding into sleep, Shem's the biggest and brightest. Their dark brown swirled with gold from the firelight's touch. "We wantin' a story."

"Coor woo," Rox predictably suggested.

"Aww, that one *again*?" Shem wailed. "I cain't."

"Coor woo!" was the barked reply.

Barkton's lashes flew up. He grunted and turned over.

"Shh, boys." Pretty Wolf hung her matchcoat on a peg. "Shem, our friend lost his special rocks today. We will give him the choice of story."

"Coor woo!" This time in high-pitched glee.

Groaning, Shem flopped his arms over his head as if the myth had killed him dead before the first word was spoken. "But what about me?"

"Tomorrow's story is yours."

He keened an exhale.

Chuckling at him, Pretty Wolf took up a seat on Rox's bunk. Cleverly, she switched out his bag-pillow for her lap and began a gentle finger-comb of his clean hair. "Corn Woman is the offspring of Earth Mother," she began, tones low and melodic.

At once, Rox's lashed drifted down, but Shem sat up to full attention, objections long forgotten.

Pretty Wolf didn't correct the boy, so Strong Bear let him be. He wound his way around Barkton and sat on his couch to remove his moccasins and leggings. Reduced to his breechcloth, he arranged himself on the far side of the couch. There was no telling how his *wife* would choose to sleep now, but he wanted it starlight clear she was welcome in his bed.

Warm under the blanket and with Pretty Wolf's hypnotic intonations lulling his ears, Strong Bear's eyelids began to droop. He dipped in and out of sleep, a snort from Barkton jolting him awake for the last of the tale. Keeping his eyes closed, Strong Bear listened for the end because the end meant Pretty Wolf would choose where to lay down.

"Corn Woman wept and said,"—Pretty Wolf made her voice old and creaky—"'I will make food to fill your hungry little bellies.'"

Strong Bear cracked an eye and smiled. At Pretty Wolf's comical acting. At Shem's scrunched-up shoulders and girlish titter. At Rox's babbled rebuke to silence. Even at Barkton's obnoxious snoring because it meant freedom to be; they could have been given a guard who lorded his power over them instead of one who looked the other way.

While Strong Bear prayed his thanks and vowed to be more gracious with the Bluecoat, Pretty Wolf's story wound down. "Then Corn Woman instructed the children to lock her in the corncrib for four days. At the end of those days, they opened the crib to find it filled with corn. They ate of it and saved kernels aside to put into the earth. They did this every seven moons. In this way, her flesh and spirit fed them. And so, the children lived through Corn Woman.

"Now, we tell our children to take good care of Corn Woman's flesh because it is her goodness become substance. Whenever you eat it, remember her because she has given her life that you might live. Yet she is not truly dead." She paused, then resumed with Shem reciting with her. "She lives on, and in undying love, she renews herself time and again."

So many echoes of Christ in that story. Might she be open to the comparison? Strong Bear would have to think on how best to phrase it so that he'd be ready at the next recitation.

Another split of his lids revealed a quite dead-to-all Rox drooling on Pretty Wolf's thigh. Painstakingly, she lifted his head and sneaked out from under him.

Strong Bear's heart quickened its beat. She would be coming to him now.

Once she'd arranged Rox's blanket, she moved to bend over Shem for a kiss to the top of his tight curls. "Sleep well, my boy."

A frown stiffened Strong Bear's face as the thought streaked through him that Shem was not *her boy*. Flint was. With a twinge of guilt, he recognized it as untruth and squelched it. Every male in this lodge was *her boy*. Korsan included, though he'd probably rather burn his tower of ledgers than admit it.

Ehi, Strong Bear decided, they were all hers.

Pretty Wolf, however, belonged to no one but herself. Talwa chatter would agree, would say Strong Bear belonged to their miccohokti, not the other way around. Would she soon change their thinking on that?

She will, assured the Maker of his path. *As promised, she will be yours.*

Strong Bear's hope rekindled and made him burn like a forge, a delectable heat he'd like to share with her. If only she'd come to bed.

But no, he sighed, she'd lent her ear to Shem. For an important matter, it would seem. Instead of his usual inane chatter, the boy's poor excuse of a whisper carried serious tones. "...because Corn Woman be like Jesus."

Strong Bear's ears stood rabbit-tall.

Seemed he and the boy shared the same Jesus, too. As well as a fire in the belly for Pretty Wolf to know Him. What they did not share: caution, fear of misspeaking. No, that was all Strong Bear's.

Pretty Wolf's head cocked to one side. "How so, Shem?"

"'Cause He be God who come to the world like a person, just like Corn Woman be Earth Mother who come to the world like a person. And He died to help His children. Except he ain't really dead. He be living, savin' sinners every day."

Up to that point, Pretty Wolf had nodded along, but at the last phrase, she'd gone possum still. "Like Corn Woman. Much life from death..." With those mutterings, her gaze went from distant to sharply focused. On Strong

Bear. "Life of the spirit. Upon our deaths."

A quote of Strong Bear's own words. His pulse quickened with the Spirit's moving.

"Ya see?" Shem rasped, eyes shinier and more eager than any boy's should be at that hour of the night.

Ehi, Wolf, do you see it? Strong Bear gathered his breath and held it close in anticipation of her response.

"I see…" Fingertips to his shoulders, Pretty Wolf nudged Shem down to his back. "…how very smart a boy you are. On the journey, you can tell me more. But now, you sleep."

The air rushed out of Strong Bear through the curve of a smile. *On the journey.* They would speak. They would read the Writings. She would ask her questions, Creator would whisper to Strong Bear the answers, and she would believe.

Please, Jesus.

She collected her nightclothes from the foot of their couch and twirled her finger at Shem. He flipped onto his belly and thrust his rump in the air, face turned away. She never looked Strong Bear's direction, but he draped an arm over his eyes anyway and tried not to imagine what she was doing.

He didn't move until the rustling stopped and his, *their* blanket shifted. Then he raised his arm, kept it aloft. And waited. He watched her in her pale-yellow sleep shirt lay down beside him, worm her way under the covers, worm some more, back, back, until the soft curves of her body contoured to his.

Lips parting, he loosed a batch of breath he hadn't known he'd trapped. With that exhale, his arm fell across her for the most pleasant snare. One she did not challenge.

No, she laid her head on the bulge of his arm, her sigh one of such perfect contentment it triggered his muscles to contract and rope her in closer.

Hair tickled his nose, so he caressed it down flat, then kept stroking. "You did well with Rox," he murmured and planted a kiss on her crown.

"He's an easy one to love."

"But what about me?" he whined in crude imitation of Shem.

She snickered through her nose and quietly sing-songed, "Someone is jealous."

"I have the right. I'm your *husband*." If she could tease with the name—whatever actual weight it carried—so could he.

"Ah, that is true." A yawn garbled the acknowledgment. "You are too quick for my muddled head."

No doubt. With all her heartbreak, she'd not gotten much more sleep than he the previous night. The difference between this sleep and that one was so unthinkable Strong Bear could only attribute it to Creator's almighty peace.

"Then close your eyes, woman, and hunt a few dreams."

"Good night, Kit." She tipped her head and kissed the delicate skin on the underside of his arm.

At the brush of her lips, tingles shot to the ends of his extremities. His tongue pasted to the roof of his mouth, and his thoughts scattered like wheat seed in a field.

Pretty Wolf was everywhere again, overwhelming his senses. Her silky hair rubbing against his throat. Her soft feminine scent: river and cedar berry soap threaded with a hint of the pine needles he'd shared earlier. Her softer curves: the dip of her waist cradling his arm, the mound of her hip, and the—

Focus!

On what? There was only her.

Anything!

Anything but how his blood and his bones sang with want.

Anything. Such as... Such as how greatly he'd been blessed. Ehi. Undeservedly blessed. Over the last days, so many others had received devastation or death, but Strong Bear...

Strong Bear had received a promise.

She will be yours.

Two mornings later, Grandmother Sun's bright orange head peeked past the door covering. Strong Bear snoozed on, but Pretty Wolf screwed her eyelids shut against it and resisted squirming under the covers. What had been a perfect nest of comfort when she'd first woken now felt like a trap. No blame to Strong Bear's embrace. Only to her eagerness and impatience.

The People would march from Wakulla that day, and none in the lodge but her seemed eager to shove this place of hunger and grief behind them. It didn't help that, long into the dark hours of the previous night, they'd danced and feasted away the food they couldn't take with them. Only Barkton had risen so far, but then, he had a march to orchestrate.

Jackson had given his leave to set out. All affairs at the store were settled, and the collar of Toño's shirt had been appropriately watered with her adios. All that remained was to strap on their packs and send Old Sharp Knife one final message.

Then Flint.

Pretty Wolf's patience snapped. If she let them, the rest would laze about until the Bluecoats arrived with their obnoxious bugle. She began lifting Strong Bear's arm off her middle.

He jerked it back down with a grunted, "mmm."

"Kit."

"Chh. Not yet," he slurred, arm an immovable bar.

"Ehi." She wriggled in place to turn over.

He allowed it, allowed her to push him to his back, although rows of frown wrinkles showed prominently on his forehead as he peered at her through cracked eyelids.

"Wake up," she quietly sing-songed, while running a finger from his hairline to his nose-bump to erase the grumpy from his face.

It worked, but drunk on fatigue, his lashes fell and struggled to rise, then gave up and stayed down.

It was then she noticed the slow beat of his heart thumping the bottom of her splayed hand. As well as the broad canvas of ocher flesh and firm muscle between them. Indigo rabbit ears peered from between her fingers, and directly beneath her palm...

Many seasons had passed since she'd laid eyes on what her hand concealed, but she saw it as clearly as if she'd pricked it into his skin mere sleeps ago. She dragged her hand down, and the rabbit's full form emerged, its long body stretched in a mighty leap over his heart. And *on* his heart, a perpetual reminder of what they were, he and Pretty Wolf, of what they'd endured.

The rabbit. And the wolf.

In profile, the inked she-wolf looked up to the rabbit as he covered her with his airborne body. The perfect image of them—the little rabbit protecting the fierce wolf. It had been meant to replace her as she ran off to other peoples and lands.

Clearly, he hadn't approved of the substitute. The current twining of their legs as evidence.

Ah, Kit. She did love him so. Perhaps *more* because even though he'd grown and left childhood behind, he hadn't left *her* behind. Not for a moment. No apologies required, he loved her with all her snarls and flaws, asking nothing of her but to stay at his side.

What if? came the inner whisper, so suddenly it startled her pulse into a trot. *What if you made it real? What if one day you were to offer more?*

More than *with each other always*. More than twined legs.

Gazing down at him, at the solid largeness of his presence, her brain pondered the notion of that *what if* and found it sensible. Strong Bear would make an excellent partner in life.

Then, her woman's eyes stepped in, watched the metered breaths exiting in little puffs from his parted lips, and imagined what it might be like to lean in, brush her mouth against that little divot at the crest of his lips, and linger. Instead, ever so carefully, she lowered to press a kiss to the indigo rabbit ears, then eased up.

Her lashes lifted. And found his eyes dark and keen on her.

She jumped.

The slow sideways push of his mouth said he found her guilty but didn't exactly mind. "Perhaps," he graveled lowly, "we should get everyone out before we start the fire."

Though her cheeks flamed, she grinned back, mischief squinting her eyes. "Let's do it, Kit. Let's burn the place down."

A man should begin each day with a female's lips on his body. How Strong Bear had survived every morning of his life without it was certainly fodder for puzzlement.

It was good she'd darted off at once, crowing like a crazed rooster for everyone to get their lazy carcasses up and out. Or risk burning to rubble. He'd laughed and almost pulled her back to bed to test her lips in another place a little farther north. Alas, she'd escaped him and flitted out the door. He knew it to be there, but despite his close study, he could find no sign of mourning in the heart-stopping smile that brightened her cheeks.

Only Flint.

Now, an hour later, he stood in line with the Wolf Clan women a safe distance from their lodge. Arm looped around Pretty Wolf's waist, Strong Bear got the eerie sensation of having been there before, in that moment. Only, this time, Noonday's home was roaring with flame instead of lying in ash. And he looked *down* on Pretty Wolf instead of *up* at Polly. There was also the small fact, they had set the fire instead of the enemy.

As was Muskogee custom, all broken or useless things must be put to fire. That the People had no desire to see any part of their possessions fall into

Bluecoat hands had nothing to do with it. Of course.

And so, much to the soldiers' consternation, Wakulla blazed.

Heat scorched Strong Bear's face, and smoke stung his eyes. A snap and *whoosh*, and the thatching caved into the lodge's center.

The end of one lodge. The beginning of another. Except the "other" was already standing.

A smile birthed slowly, stretching Strong Bear's lips.

Pretty Wolf's slender fingers wiggled at his ribs. "What wicked thought has you grinning?"

"Not wicked." He extended his foot and began dragging the tip of his moccasin through the dirt.

A circle for a head, a line for a body. Beside it, another circle, another line, and a triangle for a skirt. Slightly smaller.

Pretty Wolf's tiny gasp told Strong Bear he'd snagged her memory from that first day in Alabama Town. Her quick swipe at her face might've been to brush off floating ash.

When he began on the tiniest figure yet, she spun into him, arms flung around his midsection and beamed him a smile. Tears glimmering, she said, "Take me home, Kit."

Chapter 46

The prancing tromp of Balada's unshod hooves greeted Pretty Wolf's hearing with a *wait for me* demand.

Strong Bear glanced behind them and shook his head. "Your horse thinks she's a dog." Fondness sang through his deep timbre.

Bent toward a bush, Pretty Wolf spat out the crushed pine needles she'd munched. She wiped her mouth and sucked air through her teeth. It passed cool over her zinging tongue. "She certainly has the nose of one."

But the mare wasn't exactly *hers* anymore, was she? Balada belonged only to herself now, to the wilds. Last they'd seen her, she'd been on the far side of camp, rolling, hooves up, in a meadow of cat grass. Now, here she was, having sniffed them out, even in the thickets of an odorous swampland. The animal would be wagging her tail next.

Imagining it brought on a smile. Of all the beautiful things the Floridas had to boast—mild winters, crystalline warm springs, dazzling beaches—Balada would be the most painful to leave behind.

They'd reached the point in their journey where Pretty Wolf said goodbye to her beloved mare. As much as she dreaded it, she wanted it over. And it would be—as soon they quit stewing in mud and boarded those flatboats.

Ten sleeps into the march, high waters had bogged Wakulla down on the river's eastern bank. The People camped well inside the tree line, but no amount of dense foliage could muffle the Apalachicola's tirade. Gadsden Fort reigned over the opposite shore, but like a glistening honeycomb just out of reach of a bear's swiping paw, there was no having it. Not until the waters receded.

And there would be no having Flint until they put this bitter journey at their backs. A thing they couldn't do unless they were placing one foot in front of the other. Yet here they sat.

Rox had collected his third stone from this place, one for every sleep, and Pretty Wolf and Strong Bear had worn a meandering trail through the camp. Up and back again, they listened to troubles, solved them, sometimes created them when their attention inadvertently tipped toward unbalanced between the clans.

But really, the complaints could always be tracked to the same cause. Hunger: the one trouble they could not fix. And the greater the hunger, the surlier the people, the more exhausting the role of miccohokti.

Every sundown, Strong Bear took her apart to some isolated nook in the woods, clasped her hands to his chest, and whispered prayers like blessings down on her head. He ushered each prayer to his Jesus Creator, and despite the unfamiliarity of the Being, Pretty Wolf sometimes joined in. For the hope and strength she drew from it.

As promised, Marcus Buck had negotiated with Korsan for cow pens labor pay, but it hadn't resulted as she'd hoped. Because Buck was responsible for feeding the estate's considerable workers through winter, he'd had no recourse but to offer silver and salt. A coin and a fist's worth of the seasoning per individual was respectable payment, but it didn't satisfy the hunger.

And relief sat *right* there, across a span of turbulent water. They could see it, practically smell it—and sometimes they actually did, the cruel aroma of roasting meat forging the river where they could not. Frustrations mounted, and sicknesses multiplied. Children begged, mothers worried, elders weakened. Warriors chaffed, clan leaders squabbled, Pretty Wolf mediated and delegated and wanted.

Flint. Only Flint.

And Strong Bear? He held her. When she cried, when she slept. Over creeks that chilled the bones and over trails that made her feet stumble and her back ache. His hand wrapped softly about hers even now as they padded the last stretch of ground leading to Runs Like Deer. She'd camped downriver with the bleeding women since her birthing time was so near.

In truth, Strong Bear should not be entering the moon-time camp. A woman's power was most potent during menstruation and childbirth and could weaken a warrior's medicine, but Strong Bear waved off the fear, saying such a trifle concern could not separate him from his Wolf.

White influence. Pretty Wolf was certain. He'd had plenty of it over the last many seasons they'd been apart. Since she benefited from the stance, she would not complain.

"Ready?" Without breaking their synced strides, Strong Bear's arm dipped around her waist. "And…jump." He hauled her with him into his leap to get her across the stream on dry feet.

They'd mastered this crossing, though it became easier by the day, the narrow waterway steadily shrinking. Thank Creator for that.

On landing, they simultaneously skipped the next stride. Quiet laughter worked its way out of her, though it petered out on a bleak, guilty note.

The dismal sound ticked Strong Bear's head at her.

"It feels wrong to enjoy my time you," she explained. "Disrespectful somehow. Selfish."

Understanding layered the gentle brown of eyes as his pace slowed to a standstill. "I know. And sometimes I struggle with the same. Right now, though, all I hear, all I feel is...*enjoy you*." He gazed down at her, his tooth-cleaning stick nestled in the corner of his mouth, motionless and forgotten.

She removed it, and his tongue shot out to swipe at the spot. Like a contagious yawn, her own tongue replicated the move.

His attention darted there. Settled and warmed. Then lingered and heated.

Prickles blew across the back of her neck as she eked out, "Enjoy...you?" Time, she'd said. Enjoy time with him.

"Ehi. As I enjoy *you*. A lot. And yet,"—he edged closer—"not as much as I would like."

The stick slipped from her grasp.

This forwardness wasn't new. And it wasn't infrequent. Pretty Wolf first experienced it on the third day of their journey north. She'd twined their fingers as she often did, this time tickling his palm to provoke a smile. Instead, he'd abruptly halted, turned to her, and dropped a veil she hadn't realized he'd been wearing.

Or perhaps it had never been there to begin with, and she was simply letting herself see it, define it. Recognize that while she'd been enjoying their connection of souls, he'd been wishing for a connection of...more.

More intimacies, more tomorrows, more forevers.

From then, he'd made no pains to hide his desire, and he never once made apology for it. *You are what I want*, he declared with every look, in every touch. Sometimes, like now, in a single word. *You. Every hidden part of you.*

It made her heart a hunted rabbit.

Would she be willing to share her life with him? Without a doubt. They had experience in this already, and they'd proven an exceptional pair.

Share her children? She already did. He was loving, dedicated, fun—the makings of a good father. From the stories, Flint already considered him one.

Her couch? There, her thoughts tripped.

To share her couch with Strong Bear was to view him as something other than a boy and a brother. The former, she'd already laid aside. Strong Bear was all man. The latter…

Well, a woman didn't sleep legs-twined with her brother. Or find herself toe-to-toe with him in the woods, staring at his mouth, wondering how his lips might move against hers.

With the way his weight shifted forward and his breaths came in soft, ragged pants, Strong Bear was considering it too. More than considering. His body bent near, hair falling forward and breath washing over her parted lips.

Blue eyes popped into her thinking. Her chest jolted with a snatched inhale.

Strong Bear's lashes batted, and the cloud cleared from his gaze. Pulling away, he sloped his mouth up on one side, then leaned back in to trace his nose across her forehead. Leaving gooseflesh in his wake, he trailed languidly down the side of her face. To the curve of her jaw and back. At her temple, he hovered and teased his lips over her skin.

"Take your time," he murmured, "but do not fool yourself, Pretty Wolf. We both know I am yours."

Her heart punched her ribs. "We do." Was that *her* breathy voice sounding more statement than question? Her nails digging into his vest? To hold him off, to hold him in place—the options tugged her in two. Decision made, her arms went around him, the fingers of one hand spreading into his hair.

Strong Bear groaned and clutched her close with a hard, possessive grip. Nose buried in the crook of her neck, he made her feel him—the resounding bang of his heart and the harried state of his lungs. The warmth pouring off him and the assurance of love and safety.

How nicely their bodies aligned. How good it felt. *He* felt.

Heat flooded from her core, but just as she began melting, he withdrew and set her on her feet. Gripping her by the waist, he descended into a crouch. Mouth planted in a chaste kiss above her hipbone, he claimed the place that belonged to him. Only him.

From that position, he looked up at her, eyes bathed in devotion, and said no more.

And why should he? That single touch was message enough: *I am the ink beneath your skin. You will never get me out.* Everything else had been said already. Many times over. *I love you. I will stay at your side.*

The only question was, should she? Now? With Iron Wood's spirit journey so newly begun?

Mischief passed over Strong Bear's features, but before she could get defenses in place, a massive, furred head poked over her shoulder. A squeak startled out of her. "Balada!" she laughed, relieved at the interruption of her deep thoughts.

"Got you." Strong Bear bared his handsome teeth in a frisky grin. That she'd not heard the animal's approach was a testament to how thoroughly Strong Bear had rattled her. By his smug expression, he was fully aware.

Balada hung her head lower and emptied her lungs in a massive blow all over his face. "Agh!" His grin twisted sour as he pushed the mare away and staggered upright. "Ornery beast," he grumbled, scrubbing his face in the crook of his elbow.

"Good girl." Pretty Wolf planted a kiss on Balada's velvety muzzle.

"Really, Wolf." Still scrubbing, Strong Bear took off down the trail. "Make sure to wash those lips before I have my turn."

That friendly heat stormed back for another full-body rush. She stuttered a laugh. "And when, dear husband, is that going to be?"

Casting a smirk back at her, he merely winked.

Pretty Wolf was still no expert in the wink, but she was almost sure that particular use signaled good things to come.

Entering the women's camp, Pretty Wolf's gaze went directly to her sister reclined on a bed of pine boughs and blankets, her huge belly jutting up. As much as the days of inactivity galled, they'd been good medicine for the elderly and the ill, and for Runs Like Deer whose impossibly large womb appeared as ripe as they came.

My, but Pretty Wolf remembered those days. Flint had punched her bladder like his personal war drum, and he'd come early. Pretty Wolf had never ballooned quite this large, looked quite this pitiful.

Concern opened Pretty Wolf's stride, carrying her hurriedly to her sister's pallet. "Sister," she chimed to hide a grimace of sympathy.

"Sister." Runs Like Deer smiled up at her. Flushed and bloated, Runs Like Deer could not look more uncomfortable, but even the trials of pregnancy were no match for her affable disposition.

No matter. Pretty Wolf grumbled for her. Always out of hearing, of course, but Strong Bear could attest to her vehemence on the subject. Runs Like Deer should be in a moon lodge with heated stones warming her feet and partridgeberry tea steeping over the fire.

"How is the little beetle in there?" Pretty Wolf lowered to her haunches and noisily pecked the mound of baby. She offered a nod to Noonday, who glanced over from where she dished up their evening rations.

"He's grown another elbow and two extra feet." Runs Like Deer moaned for effect but continued to rub loving circles into her belly.

"Is that six feet, now, or eight?" Strong Bear piped in from his place at Pretty Wolf's back; his shin lined up with her spine for support.

"Twenty-eight. Has to be." Runs Like Deer floundered an attempt to sit up.

Pretty Wolf rescued her, keeping a fist at her lower back to knead the tight muscles there. As Strong Bear once did for her.

To the rhythm of the massage, a delirious sigh wobbled out of Runs Like Deer. "Sister, you are my very favorite person."

The day before, they'd spoken further of Kills Many and all that involved him. Runs Like Deer reassured her that she hadn't for one moment held it against her. Better than any, she knew her husband, the sort of man he was. Knew he'd one day go too far. Mournfully, Runs Like Deer admitted she'd seen it coming, his violent death. She only wished she'd been able to spare Pretty Wolf his blood on her knife.

"And you are mine, Sister," she replied with a conspiratorial twinkle for Runs Like Deer.

"What of me," Strong Bear whined, causing Runs Like Deer to giggle.

"Except for your Kit, naturally," she said.

"Ehi." Pretty Wolf nodded sagely at her sister and added in a mock whisper, "At least, we will let him think so."

"Ey!" He swatted her cheek with the end of her own braid, and she pinched his calf so that he skipped away with a "yow!"

"Here, Strong Bear." Her mother shoved a bowl at him. "I saved this for you."

Backing off, he held up his hands. "I cannot accept your ration, Noonday."

Thin by nature, her frame was already showing bone where it shouldn't.

"Your strength is my daughter's. If you fall, who will hold her up?" Noonday waggled the dish at him.

The urge hit to bristle at the insinuation of weakness, but it was sadly true. Without Strong Bear, Pretty Wolf might park herself on the side of the trail and stare down the spirit journey until it took notice and sent Death to collect her.

When Strong Bear persisted in refusal, Noonday narrowed her eyes to slits. "Perhaps eating too little has left you without the stamina to put my third grandchild in your wife, hmm?"

Pretty Wolf whirled around and up. "Mother!"

Jaw falling loose, Strong Bear stared at Pretty Wolf as if for rescue, his eyes taking up the whole of his face.

"Mother, he isn't a stud bull. You mustn't speak so…barnyard."

"Why not?" Noonday shrugged. "*Someone* must move these things forward."

"You push too hard! Strong Bear is already disturbed that you forced him to—"

"Untrue." Strong Bear grabbed the bowl and raised it like a toast. "For the sake of manly…strength. And peace with my wife's mother." Wrangling a smile into a flat line, he lowered to roost on his calves and began shoveling the acorn mush.

Pretty Wolf gladly observed as he devoured it in three massive spoonfuls before swiping two fingers along the insides to collect the remnants. Fingers licked clean, he bent for Noonday's two water gourds and gave them a shake test. Hearing their low slosh, he tromped off toward the creek. They watched him go, his broad shoulders set firm above a rolling, muscular stride that was all male, all man.

Warmth rose high on Pretty Wolf's cheeks.

"If Kills Many had loved me half as much," Runs Like Deer murmured dolefully, "I might have grieved his death."

As she did at every mention of her dead son-by-marriage, Noonday spat on the ground. "Kills Many was the scum at the bottom of my swill bucket. Strong Bear is the succulent hog who feeds from it."

A brief, vagrant laugh cut from Pretty Wolf. "Will you gut him and spit him for our supper?"

"Not today. Tomorrow, I might be hungry enough." Noonday snapped her teeth inside a grin, and Runs Like Deer scoffed playfully.

"If anyone nibbles on that man, it won't be you." Her gaze slithered none too sneakily to Pretty Wolf, who flushed harder.

Her sister had gotten as bad as her mother, but at least she waited until Strong Bear was out of hearing. "It is…too soon," was the only objection Pretty Wolf could stammer.

Noonday gathered her under her arm and jabbed her chin toward the figure of Strong Bear sifting through the underbrush. "Look at him. Even with his white man's cross, he is respectable. Good on the heart, good for the eyes," she said with a suggestive hip bump that made Pretty Wolf cringe. "He is already Flint's beloved father. May as well accept him into your couch too."

Pretty Wolf rested a palm against her tacky forehead and closed her eyes, exasperated.

"No! No more denials, Daughter. Life is too short, too precious. Do not use so much of it on grief over a dead man you loved half as much as the living one at your side." With a parting finger jab to Pretty Wolf's arm, she broke away to go about her business, leaving Pretty Wolf to juggle that unwieldy package of advice.

Half as much? Did she? Even as a rebuttal rose to her tongue, she was conceding to the truth of it. If love could be measured, the scale would dip low under Iron Wood's considerable weight. Until Strong Bear was placed in the counter pan. Then, there would be no dipping, only crashing and breaking.

Where did that leave her? The answer plowed into her like a charging bull. Then it emerged from the palm forest, carrying dripping water gourds and making a direct line her way.

Pretty Wolf's legs jolted into motion and didn't stop churning until they'd bounded straight up and locked around Strong Bear's waist.

Thump, thump. The gourds landing.

Releasing an *oof!* he caught under her seat, using his forearms as a shelf. Brow quirked, he bowed his spine back to get the entire view of her cheek-burning grin. "Wolf," he drawled, suspicious. "What have you done?"

"I lied."

The eyebrow inched higher. "About?"

"My very favorite person."

"Ah," he drew out. "And?"

Clasping both sides of his face, she peered deep into his *I-know-the-answer* eyes. He'd hear it anyway. "You." She laid a tender kiss on his broad forehead. As his lashes fanned down, she swept over their surface with a repeated, "You."

Air whistled through his teeth, his ribs expanding and stilling at peak. Lifting his face, he nudged her mouth with his nose in a seeking manner, so she dispensed another touch of the lips to that darling knot.

"You," she breathed, lavishing him with another kiss, this one slow and speaking and placed precisely on the bow of his plush upper lip.

That he had not been expecting. Otherwise, he might've reciprocated instead of freezing like a bear in winter. By the time his lungs regrouped and his eyes fluttered open, company was bearing down on them.

Sergeant Barkton powered along the path from the main camp. Since arrival at Gadsden, he'd given her some distance, seeming to recognize that his presence during her rounds put the People on edge. She'd found herself almost missing the quiet, perceptive man. This moment excluded.

Strong Bear slung a netting arm around her back and made a pouty face. "Don't go. Your very favorite person is asking."

A chuckle rasped her throat. She wiggle-slid down his front, then stretched up to peck his frown. "That will have to hold you over to later."

The frown slinked sideways. "Then *later* I will hold you to more."

"See that you do." Convinced the situation called for it, she squinched an eye for a wink but ended up blinking. Why was everything *wink* so complicated?

He snorted a laugh, and she huffed and whirled toward Barkton, disappointed when her braid didn't gain enough air to wallop some part of Strong Bear. "What is it, Sergeant?"

Her Bluecoat guard pulled up before her, the mass of his chest surging for air. "River's passable," he said, out of breath. The shift of his mustache suggested a smile. "Made the trip myself. To the fort and back. The colonel in tow. He's waiting, ma'am."

A swell of relief weakened Pretty Wolf's muscles like the sudden lifting of Rox's bag of stones. Tempting as it was to plop down on the leaf litter and relish the sensation, she rallied her joints. Sharing an intimate gleeful look with Strong Bear, she pointed her muck-crusted toes toward the man with the power to further them along toward home.

When they breached the tree line and began through the main camp, their path merged with others hurrying in from various points: Marcus Buck, who was buttoning and straightening his black frockcoat. Screaming Buttons, whose rattling could be heard ten rods off. Big Voice, who looked oddly incomplete without his petulant nose wrinkle. And an unfamiliar soldier, whose shaven cheek sported a nick and whose tan coat hung clumsily off his frame.

"The colonel's steward. " Buck supplied before she could ask.

The youth's scanning eyes snagged on her and grew with excitement. He came bounding up, blonde curls flopping over his ears, cheeks plump and flushed. "Miss Francis?"

"Yes?"

Palm to her lower back, Strong Bear ushered her through the drag in her stride.

"It's a pleasure, Miss." Though his scrawny stature had room for a wealth of maturity, he tried to push between her select men to reach her.

Barkton affected his boar's grunt. "Move aside, kid. Colonel's waiting."

Seemed he also lacked wisdom, as the steward showed a bewildering lack of concern for the demand or the colonel. His gaze, as puppy as gazes could get, was locked earnestly on Pretty Wolf.

Unable to come alongside her—Strong Bear bodily blocked the path, and Barkton scowled voraciously from the other side—the boy walked backward to keep pace with them. "Just wanted to say you's a genuine Christian, Miss Francis. And as perty as they warned, too!"

This time, her stride successfully hitched. Along with her brain. She'd understood only half the words from his grinning mouth.

"All right, young man." Marcus Buck made a shooing motion at him. "That's enough flattery for now. Step back so the lady can be along."

"But…" He wilted as he fell behind a newly wrinkled Big Voice. "I'm honored," the steward called, not to be dismissed. "Real honored!"

"Th-thank you," Pretty Wolf returned, having no trouble understanding that last bit. The words, at any rate.

"What is he talking about?" Strong Bear interjected. The very question on her own tongue-tip.

"Likely to do with this." Sergeant Barkton tugged a folded sheet from inside his coat and passed it to Buck. "Found it nailed to a post in the mess hall."

The glimpse she got of it showed a handwritten leaflet.

Not sparing their pace, Buck began reading in resounding volume. "Among our guests is the youngest and most beautiful daughter of…" Buck slowed to a stop and took up skimming the page's length.

They halted with him, and she and the others drew in to form a ring, with Big Voice and Screaming Buttons edging out the spluttering steward. From behind, Strong Bear hugged her close, his chin coming to rest lightly on her crown.

The ends of Buck's mouth bent with pleasure, but it was an apologetic glance he lifted her before clearing his throat. "'Among our guests is the youngest and most beautiful daughter of the deceased hostile Josiah Francis." Strong Bear's arms tightened about her. "She is lauded for having saved the life of a Georgia planter, whom her countrymen had taken prisoner and were about to put to death. This modern-era Pocahontas, finding her entreaties vain, declared her determination to save his life or perish with him. She was successful, and the man was preserved.'"

Eyes glinting at her merrily, Buck lowered the page. "It goes on, but I don't expect you're interested in decreased rum rations for the lower ranks."

Rocking her back and forth, Strong Bear hummed, "They adore you."

"What does the writing say?" Screaming Buttons asked.

Strong Bear began to roughly translate, but Pretty Wolf let her sight wander off to the river's choppy surface as she absorbed the narrative. None of the contents was false or even embellished—except perhaps the Pocahontas bit, though her own ignorance could be at fault there. But why post it at all?

"Is it how they said, Ms. Pretty Wolf?" The youth bounced to see around Big Voice. "Did you throw yourself over him?"

Brow rumpling, she lifted a confused shoulder. "I did only what was honorable. Do you see so little goodness among your soldiers? Or is it that you do not expect to find it in an Indian?" By the end of her questioning, bitterness edged her words, but the steward shook his head, oblivious.

"Aw, that ain't true. There's hardly any Indian in you at all."

Strong Bear snarled something crude under his breath, but Barkton flat out swore.

"Hold your tongue, young man," Buck snapped.

Picking up on the tension, Screaming Buttons rounded on the boy and loomed, chest-bumping to herd him off.

"I heartily second that," announced a new, commanding voice, winter leaves crunching beneath his boots. "Get on back, Tommy."

The boy darted off like a sand lizard as Buck and Big Voice split apart to allow a crisply pressed officer into their midst.

Heart jerking its tethers, Pretty Wolf stepped out of Strong Bear's hold.

Buck and Barkton snapped to attention and saluted in tandem.

"Captain. Sergeant." Battle hardness rode the man's eyes as he swept the circle, skipping her men and landing softly on her. "Ma'am. Please, pardon the boy. It's been some months since he's been in the presence of the gentler sex, especially one as lovely and acclaimed as yourself."

She wrenched her shoulder blades together. "I am not gentle, Colonel...Colonel..."

"Stoneham, commander of this wilderness rabble." When he bent at the waist, streaks of pale scalp showed through his dark, starkly parted hair. A set of woolly eyebrows and a length of thick brown beard more than made up for the lack. "Fort Gadsden welcomes you as our honored guest."

Her. Not her men. Even less, her people, she suspected. Biting back a smart retort, she fashioned a polite countenance and genuflected neatly. "Thank you for coming."

Stoneham lowered a gracious nod and turned. "Captain Buck, we meet again and so soon. Congratulations on a successful mission. Your new bride will be delighted to hear her intelligence brought the United States a resounding victory."

"I...er..." Paling, Buck flicked a glance at Pretty Wolf.

Puzzled, she frowned at him, at a loss for what he sought. Or for what the Bitter Eyes—rather, Lillian Buck—had to do with the recent conflict. Just as uneasiness was settling in, Buck recuperated. Color refilled his cheeks with a liberal red. "Mrs. Buck would never rejoice in the death of any man."

"Not even that of a savage?"

Pretty Wolf's jaw was falling open to rail at him when Strong Bear took one menacing step forward.

"By savage," he gritted out, contempt turning his tongue to acid, "do you mean the father of your *honored guest*. Or perhaps you refer to Lord Maxwell Bellamy, her cruelly executed husband?" Boldly, recklessly, he cast a thorny glare at the white man, the setting sun's rays glinting in his irises like flame. "There was also the warrior whose throat Pretty Wolf herself slit open. Swift vengeance for having slain one your own, a Captain Justin Telly."

Stoneham's eyes tightened on Strong Bear, then shot to the dagger sheathed at her waist. "Not gentle, indeed," he murmured. "Clearly, the general's runner did not have the full story." He then shocked her jaw shut by offering Strong Bear the barest of nods. "Assuredly not, young warrior. I referred to Antonio Lopez, that snake of a Spanish nobleman. He removed a babe from her mother, an American citizen no less. Captain Buck's new wife." His lip curled up in a snarl. "Detestable man, Lopez. Dead now, devil take him."

"Detestable is putting it mildly." The medicine maker audibly breathed out, as did Pretty Wolf.

"Let's dine," Stoneham boomed and clapped his hands. "I've brought over a generous spread to enjoy with Ms. Pretty Wolf and company. A decent red wine, too. We'll need it to cheer ourselves after my less-than-pleasant news."

Smiling as though he'd announced a Bluecoat retreat from Creek lands, he offered her his elbow. "Shall we?"

Chapter 47

"Go on to bed." With his knuckles. Strong Bear caressed Pretty Wolf's jaw. "I'll be right behind."

Her subdued nod withered his stomach, and when she linked her hand to Barkton's tendered arm, Strong Bear had his confirmation—she was not herself. What miccohokti *would* be after feeling Stoneham's devastating blow? To say the meal had been a disappointment was to say fire was warm. Strong Bear had risen from the table almost physically sore, as if he'd supped on a punch to the stomach instead of the pork he'd barely worked down.

How could he dine so blithely when the People would not?

Insufficient rations, Stoneham announced as he knifed into his juicy chop.

Strong Bear could not fathom Pretty Wolf's state of mind. During the meal, she'd eaten but morsels and wrapped the rest in a cloth. For Runs Like Deer or Winter Hawk was his guess. For herself, she probably intended only tears for food. Having such love and heart for the People could be a spirit-crushing burden. One he couldn't touch, much less lift. And it burned him up inside.

Worry its own weight, he watched Pretty Wolf wend her way through the shrubs and pines interspersed throughout Snake Clan's ring of pallets. He shook his head to redirect his thoughts and jogged after his medicine maker friend. He followed until the man reached the outer edges of the camp, half of his form eaten up in nighttime shadows. Flickers of yellow dotted the other half, the sacred fire—brought from Wakulla—a stone's toss off.

Before Buck could slip away to his next needy patient, Strong Bear dissolved the distance and caught him by the arm. Ignoring Buck's startle, Strong Bear pulled him in for a discreet yet unequivocal, "You owe me a talk, brother."

Resignation dumped from Buck on a prolonged exhalation. "Yeah. Yeah I do." Defeat blotched his tone, and weariness hung from his shoulders at a sharper slope than Strong Bear ever recalled.

As much as he loved his friend, neither defeat nor weariness would halt what needed saying. Legs rooted wide, Strong Bear knotted his arms over his chest. "Which one did the Bitter Eyes betray? My woman's father or her betrothed?"

Fatigue gone in an instant, fire spat from Buck's eyes. "Lillian," he gritted through a stiff jaw. "Her *name* is Lillian."

Unshaken by the display, Strong Bear threaded a barb through his tone. "Pardon, Buck. My throat still burns from her rope and must have misspoke. Which one did *Lillian* betray?"

Buck went still, the iron seeping out of his jaw and fists. "You never said anything about a...rope."

"I never figured you would wed her."

Nodding, Buck scrubbed a hand back and forth through his untended hair. "Do I want to know?"

A casual upward bump of the shoulders belied the venom he put into his words. "It was only a little lesson she taught a half-starved Creek boy." Intentionally hurting a brother never tasted better than skin-peeling acid. This instance was no exception. At the shock and disappointment traveling across Buck's features, remorse coated Strong Bear's tongue in a bitter wash. It wasn't Buck's fault he'd fallen in love with a heartless, Indian-hating witch.

"In her defense," Strong Bear begrudged, "I'd been caught thieving."

Buck's mouth opened for a bark of dry laughter. "Sounds like a story I definitely do *not* want to hear."

"About as much as I want to hear yours." Posture softening, Strong Bear rolled his hand in an urging motion. "And yet, start talking."

Buck pinched the bridge of his nose and scrunched his face as though pained. "Promise you won't tell Pretty Wolf. She seemed to buy the major's neat deflection."

A deflection. As Strong Bear suspected. That his sharp-thinking Wolf missed it meant she was back to practicing her skills of denial.

He offered a curt not. "You have my word." The muscles of his crossed arms hardened in readiness for impact.

Cricket song, sluggish in the cold, serenaded the silence as Buck walked off a few paces and began swinging his arms like ticking clock hands. Big, deliberate rotations that loosened up the mat of scars on his back. The affliction, Buck once explained, worsened with anxiety.

Strong Bear inured his heart to it and manned his patch of ground with a stubborn stance that sank his moccasins into the trampled grass.

When Buck returned, he revealed a care-worn face glowing pale in the starshine. "Lillian heard through the don that Chief Francis was watching for a British vessel bringing aid."

Eyes, ears, fists, they all slid closed and clamped down hard. With that one admission, Strong Bear could piece together the brilliantly ugly plan: throw on a few red coats, fly a British flag from the mainmast, slip secretively into a cove, and *snap!* the snare catches an unsuspecting Crazy Medicine. Easy as shooting a boar upwind.

Opening hard eyes, Strong Bear saw red as he bit out, "Why?" He badly required a leakproof explanation for why Buck's woman would so woefully wound Strong Bear's.

Buck's slick, flat-eyed retort: "In exchange for her life."

Well. Reasons didn't come any more ironclad than that. Strong Bear's muscles began a gradual unwind.

Then Buck clinched it with, "Turning over that information was the proof of loyalty Major Ainsworth demanded."

Head bobbing in slow surrender, Strong Bear admitted to himself this Ainsworth fellow had backed the Bitter Eyes into a corner. And she couldn't have known Strong Bear loved Pretty Wolf or that their connections were so intricately tied.

"And Bellamy?" He had to know. "What about him did she *exchange*?" Blast that tinge of vinegar in his tone, but he couldn't see letting it go. He might forgive the witch her abuse of his neck, but where it concerned Pretty Wolf, he could be as insensibly protective as any threatened bear.

"Bellamy was a different case. He and Lillian boasted a healthy friendship." Though distaste gathered Buck's eyebrows into one, his recounting was a masterpiece of calm articulation. "But while investigating Lopez's books, she came across a ledger, a highly condemning ledger. Accountings of Bellamy's trades. Despite his treachery, she couldn't bring herself to ruin him, and I couldn't bring myself to ruin *her* by insisting." Buck glanced about, then stepped nearer and lowered his voice. "We destroyed the ledger. Turns out, no true evidence was required to send Bellamy to the firing squad."

Strong Bear gaped at his friend, then executed his own shifty-eyed survey of their environs. "That is…treason."

"Ah." Buck elongated the syllable, spreading his hands, "the things a man will do for the woman he loves." None too disturbed by his illicit deed, he tilted a sardonic smile. "Such as rear a child not one's own. Traverse perilous lands in an unpromising hunt. Let oneself be taken captive."

Strong Bear snorted. "There was no *letting*. Tall Bull beat me fair." Rubbing his throat, he bucked his chin in an exaggerated swallow. To Buck's blurt of laughter, Strong Bear grinned unabashedly. "The rest is true enough. I love her."

Eyes rolling, Buck shook his head. "As if there isn't a man, woman, or beast in this camp who isn't aware. Except perhaps the woman herself."

"Chh. She knows." At the surprise rewriting Buck's features, Strong Bear stated, "She's always known."

Even if she hadn't always understood. But no more. Knowledge and understanding had, at last, neatly braided together with action.

"Later, I will hold you to more."

"See that you do."

Oh, he would. Because *later* was now, and it jetted hot blood through his core. His rapidly warming chest radiated heat through limbs already moving her way. "Only now," he tossed back, "I can show her how much."

Buck's coarse laughter rode the chilly breezes. "Just keep it down, lover boy. Some of us want to sleep!"

Buried under her blanket and curled like a woodlouse, Pretty Wolf pretended she was trapping warmth instead of muffling the war she waged against a chest-ripping sob. She would surrender to it if her bedroll weren't positioned so near one of Rabbit Clan's fires. Sometimes, a woman just needed her cleansing tears. A miccohokti, however, couldn't indulge. Especially not when accompanied by the announcement she'd be giving in the morning.

No corn. The words were on constant march up and down her insides. A tramping, spirit-kicking march. *No flour, no beans.* Of dried meat, only a little. Each clan would be allotted one pound. Hardly more than a mouthful per person, and unless their hunters' success improved, it would be all they had to hold them over to Fort Scott. Where, should Stoneham's word not prove to be mere placation, Major Cooley would supply them from his newly stocked cellars.

Teeth of dread clamped onto Pretty Wolf's backbone—this was not a matter of short supply, but of revenge. A disease she feared would spread upriver to the second fort on their journey. The exact route the condemned flatboat had traveled before her father ambushed it and slaughtered all aboard, soldiers and women alike.

All save Marcus Buck, his new wife, and the Mrs. Lane that Jackson asked after. When Strong Bear recounted the details, Pretty Wolf had wept. With grief. With relief for the Bluecoat medicine maker she'd come to respect.

But tears or not, the deed was done, and now, her people would front the cost. Her ancient ones and toddling ones. Her peaceful warriors and pregnant mothers.

She'd never been more grateful Flint was far away in Muscogee country, satisfying his little belly with more than empty swallows. Instead of here, suffering the consequences of his grandfather's violence.

A hand settled on her hip, and she jolted.

"Easy, Wolf," came Strong Bear's voice as she yanked the cover down.

Cold air slapped her overheated, hair-strewn face. Through the strands, she blinked up at him.

Strong Bear had already lowered to knees beside her. "Are you all right?" He rolled her onto her back and re-tucked her, arms and all, under the blanket.

Sniffing, she made sure there was no sign of leakage. "I will be."

"You don't sound—"

"I don't want to talk about it right now." What she *did* want shimmied beneath her skin, an unknown urge she couldn't put a name to. When Strong Bear's mouth went down at the corners, she asked, "How was your talk?"

"Fine."

"Really? Buck seemed—"

"I don't want to talk about him right now." A deft move slung him overtop her, one heavy thigh laid across her hips, one elbow propped on either side of her shoulders, both large hands wrapped around her head.

"What are you doing?" Her testing squirm only made his muscles clench. He'd caged her. Trapped her immobile under the blanket. As if holding her ransom for—

Ah. *Later* had come.

Stormed by unexpected delight, her heart bleated and kicked against its own bars, as if to break free and throw itself at him. Could he hear its cry from under the blanket, see its effects thrashing the vein at her neck?

Likely not, since his smoldering focus had scattered all across her. Firelight danced over his face, the spark of its heat counterpart to that of his eyes. Bright as starlets, they roamed her—forehead, mouth, neck—as if deciding where to begin calling in her debt.

Pretty Wolf's chest inflated starkly, and she became immensely glad she'd not given way to pity. What a mood dampener wet cheeks would have been.

No, *this* was a better way to end the night. To begin *them*.

The thrust of her exhale fluttered the wisps crisscrossing her parted mouth. Callous-roughened thumbs brushed it clear, then his decision was made, and he was diving. Pressing his mouth to the nook under her jaw, he seared her flesh. Her spine arched, straining against the blanket's clamp. Then his teeth were scraping gently across the same sensitive skin, and her lungs gulped at the air.

His rumbling chuckle vibrated through her, and a head-lightening rake of shivers coursed over her body. When the sensation against her neck shifted to the slightest biting pressure, her vision went white behind her closed lids, and she wondered for an instant which of them was rabbit and which was wolf. And whether she minded being prey to Strong Bear.

No, she promptly decided, *not even a little.*

She told him so with the tilt of her head, granting more access. Instead of taking it, his tongue laved soothing strokes across the heady sting before he drew away.

Too love-tipsy to entertain embarrassment, she let a mewl of protest eke from her throat. He smothered it with his mouth. Then embarked on a slow, shivery kiss that stunned her motionless.

What woman has he been practicing on? was her first irrational and irrationally jealous thought. His mastery obliterated her mind, reeled it like a spindle. She hadn't known, hadn't considered he could…that he might…

Embracing her upper lip, he infused her with his taste of pine, then tipped her head to put her at the precise angle he wished. His access deepened, and he took full advantage, melting her into the pallet.

Sweet corn in the summer, the man could kiss. Then again, the kiss without the man, *this* man, would be only a rubbing of skin. But Pretty Wolf felt keenly that the lock of Strong Bear's mouth on hers was the last missing element of her timepiece, a cog slotting into place. Winding her up.

Her soul ticked with life, and her body whirred as she lay there, dazed silly, allowing him free roam. Subject to his whims and snatching breaths in the breaks. Inwardly, she bemoaned her captivity and lack of freedom to reciprocate touch. But such was the fate of prey. To be pinned and devoured. She sighed, a drunken, whining sound that made his fingers bear down in her hair. They curled in around the strands as if anchoring him for the long haul, lest she think to quit.

Time fizzled, counted out in pants and kisses until he abruptly curbed himself and drew back. His gaze ransacked her, his mouth glossy and swollen and shifting into a look of supreme pleasure at his handiwork. Sheets of hair framed his face in midnight black as he ran a thumb over her bottom lip. "You taste…better than I imagined."

Imagined? Of course, he would. Just because Pretty Wolf hadn't opened her mind to it until recently didn't mean he hadn't been pondering it for some while.

This time, when she wriggled, he lifted an elbow and set one of her arms loose. She used it to tuck thick locks behind his ear. "How long have you imagined it?"

"How long has it been since Flat Foot?"

Her eyes widened. That long? Since…the beginning? But they'd been in battle! And he'd been a boy. Scrawny and gangly and standing a long finger's length beneath her.

Bowled over by the revelation, she turned her head and stared into the fire, trying to fathom what he was implying. And remembering… The daily touches, the nighttime embraces. From them, she'd gleaned comfort and companionship, while he… He'd wanted to kiss her.

The notion seemed impossible, kept slipping from her grasp. She couldn't hold it in her head. The whole time, she'd been focused on her pregnancy, her desire to run home, her probably-dead betrothed, while he… He'd wanted to kiss her.

Heat splashed up her neck. Shame at having never noticed, at having been so self-absorbed she'd not *seen* him. Not truly. Tears pushed a stinging path across the rim of her lashes.

"Ey. None of that." The crooked finger at her chin tugged her face around for a devasting view of worry tangling his brow. "Nothing has changed between us. Except now, you know how far back my love for you stretches."

Nothing has changed.

As that sank in, spread through her, and found good ground for root, he watched her. Carefully. Confidently. Nothing of the boy in his square jaw, earth-solid gaze, or sultry slant of his mouth. "We were inevitable, Wolf."

"Ehi," she said, voice rusty.

She'd been Iron Wood's for a season, but Strong Bear was hers for a lifetime.

When his lips climbed higher into a smile, she realized she'd been affixed to them. While licking her own.

"*There's* a look I wouldn't mind seeing more often." Chuckling, Strong Bear slinked a hand under her back and took a cradle-hold of her head. "As much as I'd like you to do with me whatever you will, Pucase," he added with a teasing flare of his eyes, "I'm going to make you wait."

Wait for…? Oh.

A shock of disappointment sifted through her. "How long?"

"I can't be sure."

How could he not be sure? The disappointment bloomed into irritation. "Is this punishment?" She gave his chest a little push. "For the forced marriage?"

He seized her wrist and nibbled at the underside. "You see it as punishment? Good." At her gasp of indignation, he grinned. "I feared you would be relieved."

Deflating, she shook her head. "Not relieved. Curious though. You are the one who's waited. Quite long, too."

Desire became a living fire on his face, and yet he said, "For my Wolf, there's no amount of *long* I cannot take."

"Then, why?"

Clasping her hand to his jaw, he lowered until she could pick out the varying shades of earth in his irises. "I want a binding. A true ceremony. With Flint at our side and our loved ones in attendance." A slow build, water accumulated across his lower lashes. "I want to speak vows to you before Creator and creation. I want to seal them in with a kiss that will make Flint hide in your skirts and Totka bark his wolf call. A kiss that will make your toes curl into the dirt and your pretty ears glow red." He grinned cheekily, prompting a snicker from her.

The stuffy sound brought attention to her own tears cooling her face. Adrift with him in his dream, she let them fall unimpeded. "What else do you want, Kit?"

Eagerly, he obliged, whispering the answer against her mouth. "After, I want to carry my beautiful she-wolf to her lodge, then test the resilience of the couch. Again and again."

Currents shot straight through Pretty Wolf's center. Eyelids sliding closed, she opened to his kisses and gladly lost herself.

Until a voice raspy with sleep dispersed their little cloud of bliss. "Spirits help me." Winter Hawk. Grumbling from his place on the far side of the fire. "I thought you were—"

"Shall I scalp him?" Strong Bear mumbled between pecks.

"—finally done with all that kissing," the brave finished.

"Mmm." She locked Strong Bear in place at her mouth. "Leave him."

"I am happy for you both. Truly," Winter Hawk went on, a dry lilt to his tone.

A threatening growl resonated against her smiling lips.

"But," he continued, unhearing, "when you are finished giggling and kissing in *full light of the fire* and reminding a brave of his wretched loneliness, you might consider—"

"Rip out his tongue then?" Strong Bear suggested, and she nipped lightly at his chin.

"—why it is *that* person is standing over you."

Pretty Wolf cracked her heavy lids.

Fists on her narrow hips, Noonday scowled down at them.

Pretty Wolf squeaked, trying to push Strong Bear off her. "It's Mother."

He didn't budge. Merely shifted interest to her jaw, where he set to grazing.

"Great horned snake in the river, Strong Bear," Noonday clipped, shockingly peeved. "Eleven days, I wait for you to lay your snare, and you choose now?" She let out a huff and flung an arm in the air. "Let her up. The making of my third grandchild will have to wait for the birth of the second."

At that, his head jerked up.

"What?" Pretty Wolf began batting at his great, trapping weight. "What's happening, Mother?"

The greasy clumps of hair that bracketed Noonday's face couldn't dim its glow. "Your sister labors hard. Already pushing. She asks for you." The beads on the hem of her skirt glinted as she spun. "Strong Bear, bring me Sunflower. Up, Daughter! Both of you hurry."

The forest crawled past Strong Bear at a maddeningly slow pace. At Sunflower's speed, they might make it to the women's camp by dawn.

Like river waters rushing to fade into the seas, Pretty Wolf's labor cries were long since screamed and spent. Why, then, were they suddenly reverberating again between his ears?

"Breathe, my boy. She will survive this birthing," Sunflower admonished. Did she mean the pregnant sister? She should, but Strong Bear sensed otherwise.

The elder's jagged nails pinched the flesh of Strong Bear's forearm as she clung to him for support. The trail to the women's camp was dark and treacherous, and her bones could snap as easily as dry kindling. Urgency shoved aside, he minced his steps to accommodate the elder. She'd ridden a mule most of the trail to Fort Gadsen and hated every lurching sway. Tonight, she insisted on walking.

Strong Bear's sight strained through the vegetation to make out the fires ahead, his heart aching for Pretty Wolf and what this birth signified. If it was transporting *him* back to that awful riverside day, what must it be doing to her?

He should be at her side. *Needed* to be.

Nerves jangled through his middle, and it was all he could do not to swing the old woman up into his arms and tromp the rest of the way to his Wolf.

"Talk to me, Strong Bear." The mar of age couldn't weaken Sunflower's command. "Of this child of yours."

"Flint?" Was it ironic that the beloved woman wished to speak of him just then, of all times? Or intentional? Either way, talk of Flint was never a bother.

"Hmm, that one. Have you made a White Stick of him?"

Strong Bear huffed a dry laugh, half exasperation, half pride. "No one makes anything of that boy but himself."

Moonlight streaked through the rustling palms and reflected off her white head as she nodded sagely. "A fine Wolf he will be one day. Pretty Wolf to the marrow."

Not in the habit of contradicting his elders, Strong Bear faltered before giving way to candor. "He is Bellamy through and through, Grandmother. An adventurer, a haggler. A blue-eyed protector of the weak." A fact that, strangely, pleased Strong Bear no end.

"Is he?" Sunflower's voice crackled as with thirst, sleep, age. Any would do.

The creek babbled directly ahead, calming his anxiety and slowing his heart rate. "He keeps a collection of broken arrow shafts, fearful someone will feed them to the fire, certain there is use in them yet."

Thoughtful humming rose from beside him. "Bellamy reborn."

"Once, he toddled far off in the night. To learn where Grandmother Sun makes her couch. I found him on a hillock, searching. We sat, and he slept in my arms until it was time for her to rise and show us."

They came upon the stream, and Strong Bear carefully lifted and carried

Sunflower over. Before he set her down, she patted his cheek. "You make a good father, Strong Bear. No fault in you."

Warmed by her approval, he nevertheless lowered his shaking head. "There was only ever one flawless Father, and He is not me."

"Was he hung on this?" A gnarled finger rose to tap at his silver cross. "Left to die?"

"Ehi." His sharply tilted pitch conveyed his wonder. "His Son, but ehi."

"Put your eyebrows down, boy. These old ears were around many moons before Crazy Medicine banished talk of White myths."

"Jesus is no myth, beloved."

A stint of silence passed as they scooted along, their pace suddenly not so agonizing.

Finally, Sunflower ventured back into dialogue. "Then I would ask to know more about this perfect father sometime."

"And I would tell you." Flushed with gladness, Strong Bear snaked an arm around her bony shoulders and planted his smacking lips on the side of her head.

"Bah! Such exuberance in today's youth." Though she swatted him off her, her body shook with a quiet giggle.

The faint sound of a squalling newborn cut through the trees, and Strong Bear fisted the air and pealed a warbling cry from his throat.

"What did I say? Exuberance!" Sunflower cackled and elbowed his ribs. "Ack, pick me up and get us there already."

He did and moved with careful speed until Runs Like Deer, propped up on a mound of blankets, came into view. Matted hanks of hair clung to her pale face. Arms limp at her sides, she smiled with the brilliance of ten suns. Noonday studiously wiped blood off her legs, not too preoccupied to coo praise at her eldest.

With a single sweep of his eyes, Strong Bear took all this in, then settled his attention on Pretty Wolf. Beside her sister, she sat on her calves and laughed. Wet shone on her cheeks as she gazed adoringly at the squirming bundle in her arms.

Strong Bear demolished the ground between them and was putting Sunflower back on her feet when Pretty Wolf looked up.

Joy lit her face. "Strong Bear." She breathed his name as though it were sacred, as though he were the shade of a cloud moving in to cool her from oppressive heat. "Draw in. Have a peek at our boy's baby cousin."

Our boy. His throat plugged with a messy clump of emotion, and roots seemed to snake through his feet and pin him down.

"Go on." Sunflower's caved mouth shifted into a gummy smile as she nudged him forward. "He won't bite."

Stuck in a vision of their own future, Strong Bear pattered softly to stand over Pretty Wolf.

"She." Runs Like Deer yawned, smearing her words. "A girl for Wolf. Isn't she the most beautiful of all treasures?"

He peered down at the baby's slimy, scrunched face. "Eh…a treasure, ehi, certainly." He would not lie. No female, especially the wrinkled newborn sort, compared to his own treasure's beauty.

Behind him, Sunflower snickered. Thankfully, Pretty Wolf was too entranced to catch his bumbling.

Questionable beauty aside, Wolf Clan had been blessed.

Using a single finger, he lightly stroked the black fuzz plastered damply to her little brow. "Welcome to your life, little one. For you and your cousin, we will make it a better one," he promised, then slid his gaze to Pretty Wolf, not nearly as interested in the baby as in his Wolf's shining—ehi, *most beautiful*—face.

He thumbed a tear trickling down her cheek and bent to meet her mouth in a soft kiss. "Well done, Wolf."

Chapter 48

The thickets along the Apalachicola's eastern bank thinned, allowing Strong Bear to catch a glimpse of the cream-colored fury tearing through the dense tangles of frost-dulled green. "There." He thrust a pointer toward the gap, and the instant Pretty Wolf spotted her mad-as-a-bat mare, he felt it.

Her body went lax against him, and he sighed with gratification. He'd done that. Brought her peace of mind. Putting corn or meat into her moaning stomach might be beyond him, but with one word, he'd made her release her pent-up breath. As well as an hour of accumulated anxiety. And to whom had she released these things?

Him.

The man she'd accepted into her couch and unraveled with her soft, scarlet-ribbon lips. Then, babe in arms, rebuilt with a fetching foreshadow of their life together. One that drew closer by the sleep.

In a few hours, they'd dock at a place called Spanish Bluff. Another day more of river passage and they'd reach the Scott stronghold. From there, many days' travel on foot, many nights' sleep on frozen, ruthless ground—twenty if Path Maker leveled the way before them. If litters needn't be constructed or graves dug.

At least Runs Like Deer was safely and swiftly delivered of her child, the girl a fat bundle of baby with a mighty set of squallers. These were among the blessings he recited before Path Maker at dawn and at dusk, thanksgiving always rapid to his tongue.

Replicating his sigh, Pretty Wolf tipped her head back against him. "I was certain she'd lost us that time."

"That horse has the nose of a hunting hound and the determination of a mule. Not to mention the loyalty of a hairy wart. You'll never be rid of her."

"Perfect." She hummed a serene sort of sound and relaxed impossibly more, melting into him.

Strong Bear approved.

In search of privacy, they'd walked the upper edge of the flatboat's side and seated themselves against the outside wall of the captain's house. Their ledge stretched narrow, but Strong Bear wouldn't hear of her anywhere other than nestled in his crisscrossed legs. What was the point of seclusion if she couldn't enjoy the heat of him wrapped around her?

He was hers, after all. To do with as she pleased. So, her options were either sit in his lap straight-ways or sit in his lap crossways. A flexible, reasonable man, he'd also proposed laying her out flat beneath him and testing their balance against the boat's gentle dips and swells. She'd blushed to her roots as demure as any unspoiled maiden. Fuel for his manly pride, the pink of her tongue had emerged to trail slowly between her lips.

Evidently, Strong Bear wasn't alone in reliving the previous night's intimacies. Countless relivings. Some of which he reenacted. Such as the one grazing his watering mouth over the irresistible flesh where her ear met her throat.

"So then," she said languidly, pensively, "if you follow this Jesus, who died so his children might live…"

The questions wrenched his eyes open. She wanted to talk about spiritual matters *now*? His thoughts churned through a haze of lust to meet her there because the wrenching was good. The questions were better than good. And to be fair, it might be another year of seasons before Strong Bear found his own way out of the fog.

He drew back and made a worthy effort to concentrate.

Words, serious and deep, continued to flow from her as she toyed with the holy book's bent leather corner. "…where are your green pastures, Kit, and your still waters? You've lost as many loved ones as I, endured as many adversities. The king named David promised rest in the valley of death, but where is it?"

"In the soul," he replied, voice tellingly hoarse.

His eyes flickered down toward her breast, the seat of her soul, but he wrestled them back. Strong Bear might be Pretty Wolf's, but Pretty Wolf was not his. Only once they'd spoken willing vows before Creator and clan, only once he'd led her to the lodge built by his sweat, every spadeful of daub laid with a prayer for her.

Only then.

Then he'd free his eyes to roam, to explore every part of her, hidden and—

Focus!

She was reading again. Urgently, he might say.

Bellamy's Bible lay open on her knees. Impervious to the cold, she wiggled her bare toes in the spray of water coursing beneath them as her tongue tripped along her favorite passage. So poor was her skill that Strong Bear suspected she'd been silently cursing the Instrument of Unconditional Surrender instead of scrutinizing it for sly wording.

"Mack-et...?" she tried.

"Not *mack*. Break the word up. Look first at the beginning four letters and remember the two-vowel rule, how it—"

"*Make*." Her triumphant hoot was a replica of Flint's. It made him laugh and swiveled the long neck of a wading blue heron. She brandished an arm at it. "M for make, bird. Ha!"

He grinned, fulfilled to his bones that he could provide for her even in this minor way. "The T and H at the end make a sort of hissing sound when placed together."

They went on in that manner until her reading cut out. "Here it is. *This* one. This is what you mean?" She rapped at the clause, *He restoreth my soul*, and Strong Bear beamed at her perceptiveness.

"That is precisely what I mean."

"Are you saying your soul is restored?"

"Ehi. It is. Purified, balanced, fully restored."

She was nodding, listening, absorbing.

An air of calm fought his control, but he ordered his words to leave his tongue at a precise, steady tempo. "From the day I believed, I have been at rest in Creator's promises, in the peace found in His spirit-made-flesh, His son Jesus."

"Like Corn Woman."

He gave a concurring hum, internally thanking Shem for introducing the rough comparison. Whatever helped bridge their beliefs, whatever path Creator chose to accomplish it, Strong Bear would endorse.

"Jesus and the *still waters* are connected then." Hesitation dimmed her voice. "I see..."

Do you though? he itched to ask. He chose instead to point her to the answers.

"They are connected, ehi. All you can wish to know, as well as the stories of Jesus, of his life and death, are recorded here." He stroked the book's crinkly pages. "For every man and woman of This World to read, to know and believe."

For you *to believe, my beautiful Wolf.*

Could she feel how his lungs had ceased working, how he held them in hopeful expectation?

"Then I will read it all," she stated as if the mass of the Sacred Writings were scarcely longer than the contents of her chalkboard.

Strong Bear wanted to kiss her.

Instead, he freed his lungs on a prayerful sigh of gratitude. "Then we shall. Together."

"Together." Leaning back into the bend of his elbow, she showed him her perked-up mouth. Pointed to it. "Put your lips here, Husband, then tell me how this is done, this purification."

Laughing lightly, Strong Bear obliged but kept it to a single, aching touch. He passed the next moments studying the blue flecks of her eyes and considering how best to explain.

On a silent prayer, he said, "Going to water at dawn purifies the body, prepares it to greet Grandmother Sun. In a similar fashion, the spilled blood of Jesus cleanses the soul, so we may properly greet Creator on the spirit journey, so we may be acceptably presented before Him. Because I live with the promise of forgiveness after death, my life, here,"—he tapped her on the breastbone—"where it matters, is one of peace and rest. Still waters of the soul, so to speak."

Her eyes tightened in consideration before giving way to soft blinks. "I believe that, Kit. You arrived in Wakulla, having grown in more than just stature. I see something beneath the surface. Like an anchor." The cool tips of her fingers traced the planes of his face. "A profound peace. I envy it. I want it."

I want it.

She wanted it.

It. Peace. Him. Jesus. She wanted the cleansing blood.

And Strong Bear wanted to pump his fist and hoot the heron into a startled liftoff. He turned his overflowing eyes into the stinging wind to excuse the surplus moisture but could find no solution for the grin drying his teeth. Nor did he wish to. Letting it burn bright, he subjected her to its blast. "No reason for envy. You can have it freely."

"Oh? Surely, a sacrifice must be made in exchange."

"Only your pride."

Skepticism rumpled her nose. "Traditions?"

"I won't lie. Some do not align and must be put aside. But what you receive in return?" A gliding finger smoothed the ridge of her nose. "Worth every loss. Many times over."

She swung her gaze out over the water. It drifted in the direction of the ducks sunning on a log, then lifted past the palmetto forest and the trotting mare to settle on the purples and reds bleeding across the evening sky.

After a time where Pretty Wolf spun her ring and Strong Bear prayed the Holy Spirit ultimate victory over her father's extremist beliefs, she closed the Book and, hugging it close, turned sideways into him. Her mouth opened on a yawn, and as she snuggled deeper, her shoulder dug into his ribs.

Grunting, he rearranged her more comfortably and skidded fingers down her lashes to lower them. "Hunt a little dream, Wolf. I've got you."

"Mmm, I know. Always." Stretching her neck, she pressed a kiss to the crook of his nose. "Wake me when we're near."

"Ehi, Pucase."

"Strong Bear," she growled playfully and pinched his side.

He bore it with pleasure that rumbled up his throat on a chuckle. "I told you, Wolf. There is no key to my shackles."

"Such a burden having a handsome, willing slave attached to me for life." Her voice had degraded to a groggy slur, her palm plopping down to make a home on his breast.

"For life." In the wake of that ready agreement, he was suffused with keen awareness. Of his loving Path Maker, of promises fulfilled, of an era of blessings on the rise. Like corn shoots through rich soil in time of hunger.

Strong Bear's wide palm sheltered her fingers from the chill air. Could she sense how strongly and rapidly, how passionately his heart thrummed? Did she understand *she* was the cause?

If so, she didn't ponder it long, because in minutes, she went limp and adorably floppy. The previous night's excitement—sensual and maternal—had caught her at last, hauled her deep into slumber. Not even the clap of the square sail billowing above was persuasive enough to rouse her.

As the sun traced down the length of the palm trunks, Strong Bear amused himself by visually tracing her lips, their flaccid shape an exact replica of her son's when sleep gripped him hard. He listened to familiar voices floating over from the open-air passenger hold. Shem's wild giggling. Rox's honking rejoinder. Buck's patient reminder that baby Dawn finally slept. And that Sergeant Barkton wouldn't appreciate being woken either.

The rest—Korsan, Melon, Noonday, Winter Hawk, and the handful of others he'd come to know—were footing the distance from Gadsden. As it turned out, the fort had been in short supply of not only food but transport too. Given the option of travel, Strong Bear decided he'd be a roasting rabbit on a spit before he let Pretty Wolf out of his sight.

The flatboat creaked as the pole men guided it around a bend, and Strong Bear began to feel stalked by a discomfiting awareness. *The landmarks...* That specific arrangement of cypresses at the water's edge. That expanse of grass sloping up into a substantial bluff. And that planked pier—

Strong Bear's heart gave a wild thrash. War shrieks flared to life in his ears, gunpowder a sulfurous stink in his nose.

Ehi, he knew this place.

Why had he not already pieced together the clues? He should have, for how many white establishments could there have been along that desolate stretch of river? For having missed the puzzle altogether, he was a child—or a lust-addled man. Worse yet, he was a terrible friend for not having twigged why Buck passed the day in vicious punishment, swimming in spurts alongside the boat.

To Strong Bear's shame, his medicine maker brother knew what he himself had not—Spanish Bluff to the whites was Medicine Point to the Indians.

And both names referred to the plantation owned by William Hambly.

"Wolf."

The call of her name wrenched her from dreams of a toddling Flint and prompted a crisp indrawn breath. Leather, woodsmoke, and pine. The scents of her future. Pretty Wolf nuzzled her nose into the warm wall of it.

"Wake, now." The firm request tore her from her cozy burrow.

Eyelids fighting her, she lifted her sleep-heavy head. "Eh?"

"You'll wish to see this." Face set in serious lines, Strong Bear indicted.

Coming erect, she blinked the blur from her vision.

Their boat moved sideways against the current and toward a pier cutting into the river. Guiding them in: the splash of poles, the grunt of polemen, and the bark of orders. Animated chatter from her people got her sluggish blood moving and hoisted her off Strong Bear.

She'd only just found her balance when the sight of a paunchy figure, standing sentinel at the crown of a hill, froze her where she stood—toes splayed on the boat's gunwale, fingers hooked to the corner of the captain's house. River-scented wind raced over her teeth.

"William Hambly?" A mixture of nerves and curiosity swarmed her like pestering gnats. "What is *he* doing here?"

Strong Bear groaned like an ancient one as he unfurled his bulk and shoved it vertical. Stealing more than his share of space on the ledge, he grimaced and began shaking out a leg. "Apparently, Spanish Bluff is our Medicine Point. I put it together just now."

She and the paleface settler had shared a kind report, but this was his land. His *violated* land. The place that her own pawa had ravaged. Had invaded in the night and, according to talwa tales, dragged Hambly and his wife from their bed.

Role reversal had never tasted more shameful.

What would Pretty Wolf say to the man? Now that her people dared come to him for aid?

Gaze snagged on Hambly's twilight-darkened silhouette, Pretty Wolf wagged the book at Strong Bear. "Put on your White Stick charm, Kit. We have a tricky host to greet." And a tricky history to confront.

The boat bumped the pier, lurching her in place, and Strong Bear clapped onto her waist. Ropes flying, men leaped out to secure the vessel to the pilings. Before they could move to disembark, an equine roar concussed the air.

On every side, motion stopped. Heads spun toward the racket. Eyes bulged. All but Pretty Wolf's. Hers were rolling in affectionate aggravation. Gratefully, she turned her attention from the uncomfortable task ahead to her beloved mare, then scampered along the gunwale and peered around the cabin.

Tail high and ears pinned, Balada tramped back and forth in the shallows of the opposite bank. Her snorting huffs were audible even over the river's chatter.

"Balada, enough with the tantrums," Pretty Wolf called.

The mare halted, pale head jerking up, front hoof suspended high.

"If you want over, then come on, you goose!"

Balada dropped the hoof in a fitful stamp and loosed a shrill whinny.

"She'll work up the nerve eventually." Strong Bear's warm hand spread across her lower back and ushered her with slight pressure toward Barkton.

The sergeant had stationed himself on the pier, handing women and children across the shifting gap.

With a whoop, Shem barreled past him, shunning the last yards of the jetty in favor of bounding off to the pebbled shore below. On his tail, a slower, less-steady Rox bellowed something unintelligible. Probably akin to "don't pick one without me."

One day, those two would pick treasure stones with her blue-eyed baby. Flint would bring them to her in his grimy palm, and she would coo and crow and call him *very clever indeed*. The imagining had her grinning by the time she and Strong Bear reached Barkton.

Instead of accepting his offer of assistance, she leaned in to kiss his prickly cheek. "Jerome Barkton, you are a jewel among droppings."

The Bluecoats' bushy eyebrows arched high. Then, the edges of his mustache lifted until his mouth could be seen bowing up in liberal approval. The red plume of his hat waggled with his slight bow. No more than a grunt came out of him, but a girl couldn't have it all.

Carrying his smile with her, she traversed the planks with Strong Bear.

The wail of night bugs grew louder, the lap of river quieter as they crossed the winter-scorched grass. At the point's pinnacle, a droopy, low-browed hat concealed any information she might have gleaned from Hambly's expression, the dying ember of the sun no help but to cast him in deep purple shadow.

"Welcome!" boomed down the incline, and tension sprang loose in her chest.

"That, Wolf, is not the sound of a man holding a grudge." Strong Bear's long legs ate up the ground to the top, Pretty Wolf on his heels.

Hambly strode to meet them, and when his hat brim lifted and their eyes connected, every apprehension fell away. His smile was the brightness and warmth of an inviting hearth on a frigid night, and she did feel welcome.

"William Hambly," she said, arm extended, "the sight of you blesses my eyes."

"None of that, girl." He bypassed the handshake for an embrace that expressed a small cough out of her. Belly jiggling on a chuckle, he set her at arm's length. "Let's have a look-see."

While he assessed her, she did the same, wondering at his scraggly mane and unshaven jaw. She'd have thought his woman would have set him to rights, but clearly, Hambly preferred unkempt to groomed. At least he smelled of hard labor instead of stale sweat.

Taking his gruff hands, she beat him to a mannerly reception. "You are most gracious to have us, my white friend. On behalf of the People, I thank you. We are in your debt."

"Hogwash." His smile broadened. "I wouldn't dream of letting my saviors sail on by without offering a place to bunk."

"Saviors?" Hooking an eyebrow, she showed it first to him then to Strong Bear.

Mouth tipping, the latter gave a self-deprecating shrug. Poor disguise for the puff of his posture.

Hambly had no quarrel boasting for him. He fixed his dancing eyes on Pretty Wolf. "Sure enough. Twice, God's spared this pitiful neck of mine. The first is thanks your fearless young buck here." He pounded a flat palm against Strong Bear's muscle-strapped chest. "Oh, you'd have been proud to see him. Flew through my front window like a red-hot cannon ball. Bowled the Hawk fellow over. Knocked him clean out."

"Winter Hawk?" Pretty Wolf felt like she chased the tail of a chain dance and couldn't quite catch up.

"That's the fella." Brows pinched, he scoured the huddles of clans setting up camp on the hill.

"If it's Winter Hawk you seek," Pretty Wolf offered, "he travels the game trail. Look for him tomorrow past high sun."

"Naw, that's not it." Hambly stutter-laughed, nails scraping over his graying scruff. "I don't look for him to come but to *go*." The snap of her shoulders and defensive cock of her head had the man plowing forward in explanation. "Forgive the slight, but I'd be obliged if you keep the brave out of sight. He's a decent enough boy, but the missus will only see war paint and midnight terror."

Having one's home invaded in the night was certain to perturb even the stoutest warrior, but it was hard to imagine baby-faced Winter Hawk rattling anyone to the point of *midnight terror*.

Still, Pretty Wolf relaxed her backbone. "No slight, William Hambly." This distrust was merely the remnants of war-torn spirits. On both sides. She slipped her hand into the crook of his elbow, helping herself to his white manners, and dished up a smile for him. By the time it finished forming, it felt passably genuine. "Is it not true there is nothing we won't do to protect those we love?"

"It is, it is." The skin about his eyes gathered up with renewed contentment. "And there isn't anything I won't do to repay a debt. I owe you a big one, too. Both of you." His voice cracked with emotion. "If you'll come with me?"

They did.

The crest of the hill leveled and stretched out before a dual-floor dwelling, smoke twirling sluggishly from its stone chimney. Dotting the yard around it were three outbuildings of varying sizes. A zagging split-rail fence—that must make deer snicker—ran the perimeter unbroken save for a single wagon-sized gap. Arms linked, she and Hambly passed through, chatting amiably about everything and nothing.

Strong Bear paced quietly at her left, eyes on constant sweep of the terrain, his blue-black hair rippling attractively, distractedly in the breeze. She almost didn't notice when Hambly halted before a covered two-wheel cart and turned to her. He removed his hat and, suddenly, his eyes were flowing.

Startled, she took a step toward him, but he held her off, voice fissured. "Please…" Weighted by great feeling, his head hung. Hands set on his hips, he cleared his throat before lifting his wet gaze and trying again. "The gratitude Mrs. Hambly and I feel for you both, for your humanity and your risk, well… It'll never be rightly expressed. But we pray this here begins to touch it."

He flung back the oiled tarp, and at its contents, Pretty Wolf's breath hissed on its way in.

Six bulging grain sacks filled the cart's deep bed.

Strong Bear grasped her shoulder as if to hold himself upright. "God in heaven," he muttered.

"Exactly so, young man."

Blinking at the abundance, Pretty Wolf dared not hope. "What… William Hambly, what is this?"

"My gift to you." Widespread smile on proud display, he untied the nearest sack.

The sweet aroma of corn cozied up her nose, and a little sob jerked her chest. A steadying arm encased her shoulders, and she leaned into it, her knees little firmer than soft-boiled potatoes.

"After last summer's crops yielded an abundance," Hambly said as he scooped up a handful of the yellow grain, "I asked my Father in Heaven to show me in his time who I could share the extra with. When I heard of your hunger,"—he turned a shameless, sodden grin on her—"I had my answer."

"For us?" On numb feet, she stepped to the side of the cart and combed trembling, unbelieving fingers through the wonder. The cool, hard kernels kissed her skin, and she cried. Great, shoulder-heaving sobs that flung her arms out and bowed her over the offering.

Finding Pretty Wolf

A tentative hand rested on her back, and she spun into Hambly's embrace and proceeded to soak his shirtfront. Repeating copious thanks, she began to feel her spine lighten, her head to clear of its perpetual chant of *feed them, feed them.*

"There, there." He patted her back and, with fatherly patience, suffered her outburst without complaint.

Pretty Wolf might have gone on making a fool of herself but for the rhythmic pound of galloping hooves. She withdrew from Hambly's stained shirt in time to see Balada's pearly form sailing over the fence like a four-footed warrior on a battlefront.

Not missing a beat, the mare landed and charged on.

"Lord help us," was Hambly's trembling cry as he skittered away, but Strong Bear tossed his head back in full-throated laughter.

Joining him, Pretty Wolf raised her arm in a halting gesture. "Ho, girl!"

Balada didn't slow until the last moment when she planted all four hooves and skidded into a dirt-plowing stop. Water sluiced off her mane and tail, and droplets covered her body. She snorted a greeting, then the ornery creature stepped back and shook out her glistening coat.

On a shriek, Pretty Wolf ducked—a useless gesture.

Strong Bear howled so hard that by the time she turned to glower at him—water dripping off her nose—he was relying on the cart to keep himself upright. So distracted was he by his own amusement, he didn't see her coming until she'd pounced.

His eyes flew wide, but he shoved off the cart in time to catch her about the ribs.

She planted her river-water lips on his and, laughing through a closed mouth, gave them a good mashing.

Sobered right up, he reeled her in and took over, kissing her hard, like a man with a message to send.

When she broke for breath, she thumbed at the damp on his lip and tipped her head. "What was that?"

"The love of a husband." Pulling back, he turned them for a better view of the cart. "And that, my beautiful wolf, is the love of Path Maker."

Kossati, Creek Country
Winter's Little Brother Month (January)
Fifty-four days after leaving Wakulla

At the place where Pretty Wolf paused her riverside scamper, the water ran narrow and clamorous. The Coosa. River of her youth, of her long away. Alabama Town, however, was not their destination.

Over the journey, Pretty Wolf had learned her tribal talwa never regained traction. At least, not enough for Strong Bear to make a safe and prosperous home. For that reason—and because he wanted Totka as pawa for Flint—he'd moved to Kossati and settled down in Wolf compound. Just him and Flint. Willow Woman and her boy, Tadpole, now lived in Tensaw with her white kin.

Atop a boulder, Pretty Wolf twisted back to shout at Strong Bear. "I thought you said around the next bend!"

He trailed her leaping path across the slabs, his hair frantic and his shirt dark with exertion despite the low temperatures. A raised arm signaled her on. "I said *Kossati* was around the next bend." With a grunt of effort and a legspan she could never match, he shot past her and bounded off a ledge onto a sandy bank.

His drop was precise. Well-practiced. And it struck her that he was home. The thought sent her sailing.

Spinning on his heel, he caught her midair.

Her lungs ejected their contents and sucked hard to refill, but as soon as he eased her down, she gripped the stitch in her side and pressed on. Soles ruined from the thirty-four-day hike, she felt every pebble pushing up between her toes as she stamped prints down the length of the talwa's full dugout bay. With Grandmother Sun still abed, the vessels appeared as blackened logs laid down as neat obstacles to her progress.

Quicker over than around. She was bunching her muscles to jump onto the underside of the first when a manacle clapped onto her wrist. She scowled. "What are you doing?"

"Ho, there, firebolt. Catch your breath." Strong Bear held fast to her combative arm. "And what about this?" The drag of one roughened finger over her temple put out her fire. He held it aloft, and starlight glistened off its wet surface.

"Then there's this." He plucked up the tail of her bound hair and wagged it before her. More frayed rope than braid, runaway strands tickled her nose.

She snorted and swatted it away. "Very well. I'll bathe." Though it would kill her to delay even those few minutes more.

Two days before, those settling in Kossati split from the main party of migrators. *Main party* being a loose term since, over the sights, it had steadily dwindled until even the Bluecoats turned back. Barkton, too, departed, carting off a fragment of her heart as he did. An unexpected pang.

Only Marcus Buck remained. Loyal to his own destructive fatigue, the medicine maker had determined to see the march through, to see baby Dawn and Sunflower into their new homes, to see Strong Bear complete his mission to its end. Although, this morning, Buck would be seeing nothing but the camp he'd pitched with them three sights south of Kossati.

Unable to sleep, Pretty Wolf and Strong Bear had risen at Moon's height and woken Melon. They'd enlisted her to distract Balada with corn while, makeshift torch lighting the way, they invaded the midnight woodland alone.

Rather, together.

Together in demolishing the last long sights. Together in jogging and sweating. Together in stripping to their shirts, in splashing into the freezing current, in squealing and dunking.

Floodwaters wholly absent.

Pretty Wolf exploded from her dip. Every muscle seized painfully with cold, skin pinched up in desperation. She hadn't cleared the drops from her waterlogged lashes before her sense of smell was inundated with mint and lavender. Her lids flashed open.

Strong Bear stood close. Concentrated shadows obscured his features, but moonlight caught on the rivulets streaming down his clumped hair. An object bumped the underside of her nose. She crossed her eyes to find he was waving that delicious scent before her.

She gasped. "Soap!" With a greedy snatch, she clutched the flawlessly round cake protectively to her shivering chest. "Where did you get this?"

In broad pleasure, he bared white teeth. "Korsan slipped it to me, and I've been saving it for a special occasion." Toes overlapping in the swirling sand, he blew warm breath over her neck when he said, "Shall I scrub your back, Wolf?"

If he knew the scent was Iron Wood's he wouldn't be offering, but the awkwardness was for her alone, and it was hardly that. The morning's joy overwhelmed every other emotion.

A chuckle stuttered up her throat, wrung from her on a shiver that was part cold, part nerves. "That will take too long. But you may scrub my chicken-wing pits." She hiked an arm, elbow bent like a wing, and screeched like a mad hen."

Chin tipping up, Strong Bear blared a laugh. "All right, Flint. Pits it is." He then proceeded to tickle-scrub her underarms. An annoyance she endured exactly as long as it took to flounder back to the shore, her Kit's clawing fingers in keen pursuit.

Panting and giggling, she trudged up the bank and commanded her cold-deadened fingers to wring the river from her locks. "Remind me what Totka said to him after."

The paling sky highlighted the prominent points of Strong Bear's muscular frame as he began a comical stiff-armed stalk—presumably meant to imitate a surly Totka. He stopped and, fists braced on his hips, bent as if looming over a much smaller person. "Is that how a brave speaks to his pawa? I was the talwa's top stickball shooter, I will have you know. And these,"—he jabbed at the meatiest part of his upper limb—"are *not* chicken wings." Strong Bear dropped the pose and spiked his voice to a childlike pitch. "Then why Copper Woman say you squawking and *booding* like a mama chicken?"

"Squawking and-and...*brooding*!" Though she'd heard it before, Pretty Wolf bent double with laughter, slapping her chest a few times before dissolving into tears and wailing, "I love him so much!"

"Aw, Wolf, don't cry." Strong Bear gathered her in, chest vibrating with sympathetic mirth. Their wet clothes made sloppy suctioning noises as he patted her back and rumbled deep, assuaging coos.

Despite the warmth and strength radiating off him, her body continued to judder. The tide of anticipation and anxiety washed over her too powerfully to control. "Will he love me?"

"He *will*." Strong Bear had told her this a thousand times. "He already does. And he is right there. Through the trees and across the clearing." From nowhere, he produced a blanket and began buffing her dry. Every few rubs, he swiped at the cascade she couldn't rein in.

Right there, Flint is right there.

So close? What if he happened by? While she, his miccohokti mother, blubbered like a child with a scraped knee.

That thought wicked her eyes waterless. Ratcheted her spine into a dowel and scrubbed her forearm under her drippy nose. She whipped the blanket from Strong Bear. "Turn around, Kit. I'm getting dressed."

The last of the trek passed in a blur of pine trunks, cumbersome treefall, and skirt-grabbing shrubs. Every determined stride taken with Strong Bear's palm clasped firmly to hers, their harsh, white-fog breaths left behind to vanish into the dawn.

And then they were free of it, free of the forest and the murk, free of the march home that would never end. Before them stretched a canopy of pinkened clouds and a pasture thirty rods long, its summer stalks brown and broken. But beyond…

Beyond, a stony ridge climbed bluntly from the field. And on its peak…

On its peak, a tiny form. An outline only, dark purple against the sun showing the top of her glowing orange head.

Pretty Wolf's jaw trembled; her voice gave out. Neither discouraged her lips from forming, "Flint."

As if he'd heard the single scraped syllable of his name, the figure perked, leaped up.

"He sees us," Strong Bear croaked out, first tugging her, then dragging. "He sees us!"

Pretty Wolf's heart sprang to her throat, tears right behind it. Madly, she blinked to vanquish them. To not miss a moment, a single movement. It was no use. Her baby blurred, his various parts smearing into an indistinguishable blob. A growl of frustration coiled up from her gut.

This would not do.

She released Strong Bear's grasp and snatched up her skirt in both fists. Knees high, she ran. A powerful maternal force swifted her across the distance, her sight utterly useless.

Her ears, though. They worked faultlessly. Picking up the sweet arching trill of a child's victory whoop, they told her everything her heart wished to hear.

She was wanted. She was loved.

Muscogee country was her flesh, the Coosa her blood. Strong Bear was the ink beneath her skin, and Flint…

Flint was theirs: Iron Wood's. Strong Bear's. Path Maker's.

Hers.

The child of her womb, and the boy scampering down the path toward her waiting arms.

Epilogue

Kossati, Creek Country
Windy Month (February) 1818
One month later

A bead of sweat ran a tickling trail down Strong Bear's breastbone. Another dropped from the tip of his nose onto the tongs he was rubbing with a greased cloth. Behind him, the forge fire stung the skin of his bare back, though he'd banked it a quarter-hour ago. Such was the heat of his profession.

Satisfying labor. He'd not trade it for any other. And it would be even better once his partner, who'd returned from Tensaw just yesterday, rejoined him. Hence, the banked fire at high sun instead of sunset.

He hung the tongs on their nail in the post of the open-sided shed, stealing a glance at Flint in his play forge. Last summer, Strong Bear erected a tiny shack a stone's throw from his workplace, complete with red-painted "fire" and tree-stump "anvil." The miniature hammer was real enough, though, fashioned by Strong Bear's own hands. Currently, Flint banged away on a pile of nuts Pretty Wolf had tasked him with. Last season's moldy ones. Fortunately.

As Strong Bear watched, grimacing at the heap of shell bits and mashed nutmeat, Flint's blue eyes focused somewhere behind Strong Bear and flared wide and bright. The clip of Balada's sprightly hooves registered an instant before Flint's hammer dropped, missing his bare toes by inches and landing in the nut bowl. The contents spilled, but the oblivious boy was already bounding off, squealing like a piglet.

Strong Bear shook his head, chuckling, and filled up with contentment. Only one person could provoke such a reaction in the child. He tossed the greasing rag onto the counter and returned a hinge mold to its place, turning in time to see Flint leap into his mother's arms.

Her beautiful laughter perfumed the air, and Strong Bear felt the heart in him expand with a delicious ache. He needed that woman under him in his couch. This time, with nothing between them but their vows to Creator.

Only a few hours more, he consoled himself, wrestling a glower at all that must come first. The feast held appeal, as did the ceremony, of course, but he was already put out over the line of neighborly greetings expected of him.

At least, for this moment, he had a captivating view. Crossing his arms, he supported his backside against the counter and settled in to enjoy it.

Pretty Wolf faked strangulation as Flint hugged her neck, then pulled back to receive a noisy kiss on the lips. She ambled toward the forge, Flint's rump shelved on her clasped arms. Her eyes grew big and impressed as she listened raptly to his chatter, a mangled recounting of all the mundane things they'd done that morning, he and "Bear."

As they approached, Strong Bear tuned out the dialogue and listened to what wasn't spoken yet was so loud, he almost could not hear his own thoughts over it.

I watched for you. Lived for you. You are my mother. You are my world.

And mingled with it, Creator's voice resonating deep within Strong Bear's soul: *My love for you is vast. My faithfulness unending.*

"Kit." By the force of the word, it had been voiced more than once. Pretty Wolf entered the forge and stood before him, her braid hanging down her front and wisps of hair blowing about her face. Perspiration was already breaking out on the warm-beige skin of her neck, and Strong Bear imagined it accumulating and slipping down to—

Focus! Her mouth is moving again. Thank Creator, the pertinent parts of her sentence were at the end.

"...remember your ear protection today?" she finished, having swung Flint to one jutted hip for the purpose of jamming a fist against the other one.

Guilt flipped through his chest as his gaze shot to the forgotten stack of cotton scraps. Pretty Wolf rode him relentlessly about shoving bits of fabric into his ears while he worked, but more often than not, Strong Bear arrived at the forge and let enthusiasm over his projects wipe his brain clean of all but heat, mold, and bang, bang, bang.

"Er..." he said, stupidly, and Flint buried a snicker behind dirty fingers.

Brows slashing down, Pretty Wolf swatted his arm. "Do you *want* to be a deaf old man?"

To salvage his dignity, he transitioned smoothly to a smirk. "Ehi. It is every man's greatest desire for his winter years." He scrunched up his face and sucked in his lips to imitate no teeth. "Eh?" he drew out in a creaky voice, presenting her the side of his face. "You said not to eat the pudding? Sorry, wife. Didn't hear." He squinted and rapped at his ear as if to get it working again.

Flint tittered. "You funny, Bear!"

Pretty Wolf crammed her lips together, but a snort of humor burst out anyway. "You! Making me laugh won't get you out of a good lecture." She then proceeded to dispense it, but she was wearing the firebolt expression he loved most—nostrils and eyes contracted, lips puckering—so he lost himself admiring her. "Are you even listening?"

"Mm, something about safety and another something about burning myself crispy."

"Something about? Kit! What is wrong with you?"

Because the true answer did not belong in little ears, he said, "I'm thinking of how we already sound like a long-time married couple."

"Pah! Married. We won't be if you do not wash up and, and..." Her lashes flittered down as her eyes swept over his dripping, unclothed torso. Pink tinged her cheeks, and satisfaction scorched his blood.

"And...?" He edged closer to blow quiet words into the sweet-smelling hair at her temple. "I thought you liked me this way." Gaze lowered, he watched the front her blouse rise and drop dramatically, an alluring sight, topped only by the touch of her cool fingers to the rabbit sprinting over his equally rapid heart.

"You aren't wrong, Kit." She lifted her lashes first, the coy thing, then her chin tipped up in offering, and—Creator give him restraint—her lower lip quivered in anticipation.

"I did not think I was," he murmured and leaned slowly in. At the last second, he veered off to dart his wide-open mouth toward Flint's middle. "Rawr!" he snarled through a mock bite to his tummy. Very bear-like.

"Bear, no! Mama!" The boy shrieked and shoved at Strong Bear's head, and Pretty Wolf spun away, spouting theatrical promises of, "I'll save you, my baby!"

Grinning, Strong Bear held up his hands in sign of surrender. "The mighty bear has no defenses against the beautiful she-wolf."

"Or against entertaining family and friends." She wagged a finger at him. Very Noonday-like. "Time to stop hiding in this sweltering pit."

He groaned, head thrown back. "Too many people." Had it been *his* idea to invite all of Tensaw and Muscogee country into Kossati's Wolf compound? If so, someone really should have talked him out of it.

Over the last week, the compound, which was already at capacity, had exploded with guests, the most recent having arrived last evening. Although, half of those arrivals weren't *guests*.

The sight of Totka entering the courtyard the day before, Copper Woman and her cradleboard at his side, had caused a startling excess of fluid in Strong Bear's eyes. Their manly embrace strangled him, but he hadn't wanted to let go. The sound of Flint cooing over Rose—the "belly baby," who no longer fit the description—had been what finally peeled him off his mentor and compelled him to wipe his nose on his sleeve and greet the others.

He hadn't seen his clanswoman Willow Woman in an age, and her son, Tadpole, had grown so much the name Froglet might better apply. Charlie—Copper Woman's little brother—boasted more bouncing white-blond curls than ever. For a minute, they'd contrasted comically with the angry red of his complexion when Flint slapped at him for daring to touch *his* baby Rose. Wolf to his protective core, Flint then received a stern talking-to from Strong Bear about when and how to guard those in his care.

Chin hiked to his mother's stubborn angle, he'd listened, then fetched his bow and quiver, plopped Bellamy's tricorne on his head, and planted himself beside Rose's cradleboard. Pretty Wolf had sighed the proud sigh of a love-blind mother, but Strong Bear whisked the boy away to bed.

A proper excuse to escape the *other* person in their company. The woman whose name had reportedly been changed to Butterfly. Not that he'd addressed her as such. For that, he'd have to get within talking distance.

Pretty Wolf tossed him a bag of soap nuts. "You cannot avoid her forever, my love."

"Stop reading my mind, woman."

"Your fault for teaching me letters," she quipped. "S for stubborn."

"Stubborn Bear," Flint spouted, and Strong Bear scowled at him.

Tinkling a laugh, Pretty Wolf set Flint on his feet. "Our boy is darling." She slipped him a piece of carrot from one of her pouches and popped him on the rump. "Off with you, little scout."

"Balada, cawot!" he hollered as he scampered off.

The mare left off munching roadside grass and trotted over, nostrils sprawled with curiosity. She lipped the boy's hair into a slobbery peak, eliciting a giggle, before snuffling gently at his fingers.

Strong Bear clicked his tongue. "What a traitor, that horse-dog of yours. Does she even glance your way anymore?"

"A noble attempt, my husband, but you won't distract me." Pretty Wolf poked at his gut, and he snatched it for a kiss to the soft finger pad.

"Worth a shot." He winked, but at her brow-lowering reproach, he heaved an exhale. "Ehi, Wolf most-wise. Today, I shall endeavor to be kind to the witch, I mean, woman."

"See that you do." She retook ownership of her hand and used it to love-pat his jaw. "Now, go bathe, and don't forget to clean your chicken armpits."

Strong Bear dipped to catch her predicable "squawk!" right in his mouth. He took advantage of her parted lips and swept in for a taste that had him warming to iron-smelting levels. He ended the too-brief kiss on a loud smack. At her sound of disappointment, he smirked. "That will have to hold you over to later.

"Mmm," she hummed, licking her lips as if to savor the kiss. Or to drive him out of his mind. "Then, *later*, I will hold you to more."

Half-turned, she looked back, expression toe-curlingly sultry, and winked. With both eyes.

So much for an attempt at seduction.

Veins protruded across Strong Bear's forehead as he strained to contain laughter. Glaring at him, Pretty Wolf missed a nest of stickers until the little beasts were needling into the arch of her foot. Yipping in pain, she hopped and faltered a few sideways strides.

Strong Bear rushed over, mouth still wobbling. "Ack, sorry, Wolf. I've been meaning to burn that patch of burs."

"Wicked, wicked things. Stop laughing!" she accused as she snorted her own amusement and swatted at the stone wall of his chest.

"Hold there, firebolt. I'll fix you." Doing miserable work of concealing his grin, he turned and plucked up her ankle as if he were shoeing a horse. If she had a tail, she'd switch him for snickering at her back.

One pluck. Two. He was quick and gentle, she'd grant him that.

"Promise me," he said, "you'll never take to wearing moccasins."

The request startled a chortle from her. "Why?"

After a last, pain-relieving pluck, he released her foot and levered upright. "So I can always have an excuse to do this," he said, then swept her off the ground.

Squeaking, she hooked to his neck and blasted him with outcries against undignified treatment of one's pucase and miccohokti. He only peck-pecked her mouth between words.

Childish laughter guided Strong Bear to where Flint stood before Balada, a twig seated in the corner of his mouth. "You carrying Mama."

"I am. Because"—Strong Bear grunted as he swung her up to the horse's back—"Mama hurt her foot."

Her little darling sobered like a brave receiving his first feather. Shiny red, his lips pouted in sympathy, making the twig point down.

Her big darling lowered to his haunches and pinched the front of Flint's shirt to draw him close. Removing the stick, he commanded, "Teeth."

Flint bared them broadly, nose wrinkling up, and held the pose until Strong Bear's squinting inspection produced a rumbled, "Clean." He flicked the twig away, face stern. "I must go the river to make myself presentable for the binding ceremony. Will you hold Mama for me on the ride home?"

"Ehi, Bear." He raised his arms to be lifted, and Strong Bear complied and swooped him up.

Once Flint had been plopped down before her, his sweat-sticky body tucked inside her embrace, Strong Bear leaned in, presumably to adjust the boy's seat. The big, warm hand sliding up the back of her calf said his intentions were not quite so innocent. As did the heated look in his eyes. Eyes that were *not* on their child.

Not that she minded, as the delectable chills climbing her skin attested.

She canted in, sights on his mouth, but after a whisper of a kiss, he pulled back, a devilish grin showing off his handsome set of teeth. "It isn't yet *later*."

Lips pooched, she said, "Tease."

"Ehi." Laughing, he tapped the mare's rump. "Home, Balada."

Pulse still a-flutter, Pretty Wolf held his gaze until the mare's path forced her neck around. In a short while, they would have the lodge—the sturdy, chimney-toting one he'd built her—all to themselves. For an entire night. Only the fire as witness to anything they wished to engage in.

Anything. Everything. *All* the things her imagination had spent the last two months first considering, then testing, then delving into with the eagerness of a wolf presented a wide unexplored forest in which to run. No part of her, not one hair of her scalp, felt shy or conflicted over sharing herself with her Kit.

Truth told, there wasn't much these days that conflicted her. Aside from, perhaps, Noonday's disappointment in her choice of Spirit guide, slight though it was. But then, very little—not even the name of Creator Jesus on Pretty Wolf's prayerful lips—could diminish Noonday's bliss over Wolf's newest members. In her eyes, Flint and baby Dawn set the stars to sparkling in her blackest-night sky, and it would take an earth-shake to unseat her gratitude.

Snuggling her boy closer to her chest, Pretty Wolf understood the feeling. The sensation trickled through her like a refreshing spring, down to her toes and back up in a peaceful swell that expanded her ribs and pulled crisp winter air through her nose. It left her in a puff of white breath that carried a prayer to the Jesus of the Ancient Words.

Her Jesus. The one Strong Bear read about every night before they closed their eyes. The one who owned her gratitude, her worship, her soul.

"My Jesus," she approached Him, head bowed over her son, lips pressed to his hair, and Flint stilled his wiggling. "Surely your goodness and mercy have followed us. All the days of our lives. We feel your still waters in our souls, and we thank you. Your goodness fills our cups, and we thank you. You—"

"Mama?" Flint whispered, twining Balada's reddish mane about his fingers.

Her mouth curved as she savored that beautiful word. Though tempted to ignore him so he'd repeat it, she replied, "Ehi, my son?"

"Sofkee in them goodness cups?"

Her mouth bunched tight to quell her amusement. "Our *sofkee* cups overspill with your goodness, Creator Jesus. You give us green fields to lie in and graze from and—"

"Be cows."

She cleared her throat and let out a low *moo*, then a higher bawling version. The mama and the calf.

"That a fighting cow! She go boom! and up and horns go *poke*." With the last word, both of Flints legs stuck straight out, then dropped hard against Balada's sides.

Before Pretty Wolf could react, the horse perked her ears and picked up her hooves. Pretty Wolf locked her thighs to the rippling muscle and her arms about Flint's ribs and let her mare canter down the lane toward home.

Flint squealed and waved at passersby, most of whom returned the gesture with enthusiasm, for he'd endeared them all to him.

A few, however, showed their backs. Not to the mite of a brave or to his half-wild horse but to the daughter of Prophet Francis. No matter. In time, Pretty Wolf would win them over. Her, her Wolf's charm, and her Jesus

Creator's love. It seemed to flow through her like a wide, steady river, no rapids or slippery stones to be found anywhere. Not on the inside. Where it mattered.

When they veered onto Wolf Clan's lane, Pretty Wolf slowed Balada to a walk, dismounted, and turned to catch Flint mid-hurl from his perch. They strolled the remaining distance hand in hand, arms swinging, the compound's hubbub reaching her ears before she had a full view of it.

Laughter: Marcus Buck's booming and Rox's honking. Arguments: Noonday and White Stone, screeching like territorial hens and Phillip Bailey and Totka, heatedly disputing a chunky toss. Shouts: Winter Hawk and Shem and Enoch scrabbling and kicking up dust for whatever purpose boys rolled about in the dirt. Crying: a toddler's angry tantrum—Lillian's Marisol—and a newborn's squall.

Every muscle in Flint's body stiffened. "Dat Rose!" His fingers wrenched from Pretty Wolf, and he was off, his pale brown legs churning in the tottering way of three-year-olds.

"Slow down," she called after him. Little good it did. The boy was a cannon shot, streaking straight toward the courtyard fire. Her heart kicked up. "Flint, you'll fall and— Korsan!"

The Ottoman dropped his armload of firewood and took two leaping steps from the pile. Turban tumbling, he bent quick as an adder and scooped Flint up.

Pretty Wolf's shoulders crashed down as she released an audible exhale.

From his seat on Korsan's hip, her child pointed frantically toward the racket coming from the lodge. Korsan, his groomed black eyebrows set at a serious line, nodded and obeyed at once.

Beaming at his antics, Pretty Wolf shook her head, then startled at the sound of light laughter coming from over her left shoulder.

Willow Woman, a cut of pork in her arms, dropped the bar over the smokehouse door and fell in step with Pretty Wolf. "Boys. They try a mother's heart better than any sprinter's race."

"Truth spoken." Pretty Wolf patted her chest to the rhythm of her pulse. That she had a boy at all was because of this woman. They'd passed the previous night talking by the fire, Pretty Wolf draining Willow of every speck of memory and Willow happily sharing.

"That first night in Alabama Town," Willow Woman had told her, a wistful expression softening her voice, *"True Seeker told me your story, your*

grief. Then he quite boldly declared Flint should be raised believing his true mother would come to him one day. It cracked my heart open because I'd come to see him as my own. But...the knowledge mended it, too. Flint's mother did *want him*, I realized with much relief, and it was only right she should have him."

They'd shed tears, then, and embraced like sisters. Until Strong Bear emerged, scowly and disheveled, and bluntly informed Pretty Wolf he would not forfeit his turn to keep her up the next night simply because she was overly tired. So, she'd best be quick to hunt a dream while she could.

Willow cut into the lush direction of Pretty Wolf's thoughts. "Should you not be getting yourself into that new dress?" A quick lean-in, a sniff. "Horse?" Her face scrunched up. "No, no. This will not do for our Strong Bear. You fetch the water. I'll fetch the soap and gather the women." Skirts swishing, she scuttled off, adding to the cacophony with a hollered, "Copper Woman! Singing Grass!"

Totka's wife stuck her head out of the storehouse, her tresses falling over her shoulder in a beautiful copper curtain. "Is it time?"

Singing Grass stood paused at the table that she'd dragged outdoors and loaded with all manner of foods. A stack of bowls teetered in the crook of her arm, and she wore a hopeful smile.

"The sun begins her descent," Willow announced. "It is time my nephew weds. It is time!"

Time.

Pretty Wolf's feet slowed to a stop beside the storehouse where she panned the bustling courtyard and acknowledged each loved one, new and old. From Dawn to Sunflower, her vision lovingly stroked every face before lowering. Her hand slid into her pocket and over the letter she'd already memorized, even though she'd had it less than a day.

Two years before, she'd had one brief encounter with Totka Hadjo, but yesterday, she'd recognized her clansman at once by his hobble. After tackling Strong Bear in an unending embrace, the fierce warrior came at her with a startling mixture of angst and determination twisting his features. She almost backed up a step, when he thrust out a folded paper and said her name with a crack in his voice.

"This came for us. For me and you. By way of a trader. His tribe, Miccosukee."

To understand Totka's meaning, Pretty Wolf had needed neither the twined snakes crudely sketched beside the broken seal nor the signature below the blocky script inside. With his last work, she'd known who the message was from, for the Miccosukees lived deep in the Point.

As did her pawa. As did his war woman. The same woman who'd learned letters and how to form them.

Mink's simple English returned to Pretty Wolf now.

We live. Tall Bull is mine. Jesus ours.
For Water Moccasin we watch we pray.
My husband puts here his great love for all Wolf. To Totka Hadjo he says brother we will meet again.

Filled to her bones with thanksgiving, Pretty Wolf stooped to collect a fistful of earth in her palm. Eyelids falling shut, she breathed the last of her prayer. "Before me, you prepare a table of blessings. A son whose body and soul are safe in your keeping. A husband whose love faithfully sought me out. Found me. As you have done, Creator Jesus. For this and for many things more, I will dwell in your presence forever. **Emena**."

Laughing, Strong Bear landed a few firm smacks to the yearling calf's brown neck. "Afraid we hadn't gotten our fill of milking, were you?"

"Milking? Bah. Shoveling." The set of wrinkles on Big Voice's noise grooved deep, this time with amusement as he flashed a collection of crooked teeth.

"But she will be a good milker. So the man said." Screaming Buttons' rattler earbobs sang as he nodded at the animal's rear quarter. "And the width of her hips is indication she'll calve easy."

As though in protest, the young beast raised her head and bawled pitifully. Her big ears stuck out from the sides of her head, and thick black lashes framed glossy brown eyes. "Pretty Wolf will be enchanted, I promise you. The animal is a true prize." Heart constricting warmly in his chest, Strong Bear gripped Buttons around the neck in a man's embrace. "Maddo, my friends. Your gift is gratefully received."

"Only the finest for our miccohokti." That from Big Voice, who swatted dust and specks of hay from the yearling's flank before jerking a satisfied nod.

"Every Wakullan agreed. Nothing less than the best." Buttons opened the corral gate and nudged the calf inside. "Almost all contributed in some way.

Bits of coin, the odd silver adornment. What cost we could not cover, Barkton supplied when he bought her on our behalf."

"Barkton had a hand in it?" Strong Bear rested his forearms on the fence rail and watched the calf as she began to explore her new environs, her distended nostrils leading her to the water trough.

"Ehi," Big Voice put in on a scowl, seeming disgruntled over owing the paleface. "Else we might not have gotten a fair price."

That would teach Strong Bear to judge a fellow prematurely. He hummed approval. "Good of him. The man will be missed today." Sadly, the sergeant had been unable to leave his Mobile post to attend the ceremony. Thought of which sent Strong Bear's stomach twirling with anticipation.

"But not too much, eh?" The gate closed behind Buttons as he exited the enclosure, a twinkle in his eye. "Enough cattle talk, brother. What is she doing in there?" He waved vaguely in the direction of Pretty Wolf's lodge. "Weaving the fabric for the binding cord?"

A dramatic heave of impatience preceded Big Voice's grumbled, "We'll all be dust in our graves before she's ready. You should see about your woman, Strong Bear. She has made you wait long enough."

Strong Bear quite agreed. He appreciated Pretty Wolf's desire to dress beautifully for him, but in all truth, he'd rather move it along. The garments were all going to come off in short order anyway. A roguish grin overtook him. "Ehi, and I will *see* that she obeys me."

To the sound of their scoffing laughter, he shoved off the rail and made snappy tracks for her lodge. With any luck, he'd pass through the populous courtyard unseen. Most congregated around the feasting table and fire, though Sunflower snoozed in Copper Woman's rocking chair.

"Strong Bear," White Stone called from her station at the table.

There went the prayer of invisibility. He ducked his head and pressed on, hoping Wolf's clan mother wouldn't insist he attend to her.

"Strong Bear! Have you eaten?"

Quelling a groan, he looked up. Behind White Stone's portly form, Rox none-too-sneakily reached for a bowl. Without looking, the matron stretched back and bopped his wrist with a spoon. "No more! Go play with the boys."

Bawling to beat the calf, Rox shook out his wounded wrist, then clutched his half-filled sack as though it were his only solace and shuffled off.

Strong Bear replied, "Not hungry, White Stone."

"Since when?" she shrieked, fists jammed to her substantial hips.

Phillip Bailey, stepping in to replace Rox, retrieved a corn muffin from the dish and gave it a little upward toss. In English, he chimed, "Oh, he's hungry all right."

None could mistake the comment for anything other than suggestive. The tone—and subsequent thought—were so distracting, Strong Bear tripped over his own feet.

Heat dashing up his neck, he wished for the first time his neighbor hadn't bothered to learn Muskogee. "Ha. Ha," he drolled to cover his blunder. "So comical you are, Phillip Bailey."

Bailey's wife, Milly, backhanded his gut. "Look what you've gone and done to the poor man."

"Poor man nothing," Totka spouted. He sat before the courtyard fire with his baby daughter and young niece, Rain Child. "Today, he weds a daughter of Wolf. He is practically assured to never go *hungry*."

Milly blushed through her grin, but Bailey outright laughed, howled with it as if *he* were the Wolf. Even Rain Child tittered, her thin shoulders bouncing.

Strong Bear's ears scorched to steaming, but he regained his stride, being sure to add a bit of swagger. "Why do you think I crossed half of This World to find her?" Ignoring the men's hoots and actual wolf calls, he set his sights on the hide-door of Pretty Wolf's lodge and the clamor of female voices beyond it. "Woman of mine! Come rescue me from—"

The door flap peeled slightly away, but the one stepping from the shadows was neither Wolf nor Indian.

Gaze downcast, Bitter Eyes slinked through the crack she'd opened.

Strong Bear's feet skidded to a halt five paces out.

Her sight lifted to some point midway up his chest and stopped. "When did you get so big and scary?" A nervous chuckle vibrated out of her, but when Strong Bear only stared at her, she spun and busied herself reattaching the covering.

Dismissing her trembling hands, he tuned his senses to the tight screw of his face and to the hush crashing over the courtyard.

In the next instant, Buck was at his wife's side.

At his arrival, the small, dark-haired woman breathed deeply, the sound of it a disturbing wheeze. Buck bestowed her a tender, reassuring smile until she turned back to face Strong Bear. So *he* could bestow her with a censorious twitch of his nose.

He itched to cross his arms over his freshly cleaned shirt and skewer her with a glare. But with her husband shooting him a dark, just-try-it look over her head and the woman herself rumple-browed and leaking an unnamed emotion from under her lowered lashes, Strong Bear could only stand there, lips pressed into a line, and wait for her to collect her apology.

The one Buck no doubt shoved into her mouth at some point prior to this one.

When she spoke, however, the words did not ring even faintly of contrived regret. "When our lives first crossed," she began, a tremor in her voice, "I was a foolish and, yes, bitter girl. Since my return from San Marcos I've made many apologies to many people, but this is the one I've dreaded most."

A rather dramatic statement for the mock hanging of a thieving Indian. Would she bring up her betrayal of Crazy Medicine? Surely not. Even so, Strong Bear's pulse spiked in worry, his gaze flitting to the quiet behind the covered doorway.

On noiseless feet, Totka sidled near, his sharpened gaze swinging from Strong Bear and settling on Bitter Eyes, the sister who'd once come between him and his woman.

Buck shifted restlessly, and Bitter Eyes sucked another rough inhale, still not braving Strong Bear's stare. "I greatly wronged you that day in the barn. In body and spirit," she said, tiny and meek. "But Christ has made me a new creature, given me a new name. Forgiven me. Do I hope too much by asking the same of you, Strong Bear?"

When her eyelashes came up, his anger balked, for he saw no hint of bitterness in her eyes. Only the thing she'd claimed—remorse, glistening and hopeful. Which left Strong Bear a solitary option: follow Path Maker's example.

Muscles relaxing down, he dipped a slow chin. "Forgiven. Butterfly." The last word blurted out of him almost without his leave, as though Holy Spirit had moved his tongue before his head fully registered the transformed creature he was seeing.

Said creature blinked up at him, then scrunched up her features and burst into lusty tears.

Startled, Strong Bear backstepped, palms raised to ward off Buck's inevitable defense.

Instead, the medicine maker chuckled sympathetically and passed her a kerchief. "There now, Duchess. Didn't I tell you?"

Brow quirked, Strong Bear sought an explanation of Totka, but his mentor merely growled, "Cease your yowling, woman. You embarrass yourself."

That got a snort-laugh out of her, much to Strong Bear's great confusion. To further mystify him, she darted forward and, giggling, rubbed her snotty face all over Totka's shirtfront.

Without a blip of hesitation, the man's arms swept around her, firm and accepting, his mouth lowering far to the top of her head. His gentle kiss made no noise, but his murmur was not quite hushed enough for privacy. "Well done, Sister. Well done, indeed."

Strong Bear could have stood there and gaped for the next rotation of his pocket watch. Might have, too, had the door flap not cracked open to reveal Noonday's wet, jubilant face. "My daughter's womb is ripe *today*. On with it already!"

Strong Bear took it back—now that he had his Wolf before him, every slender finger nestled inside his own, he was pleased she'd taken such effort with her appearance.

Late afternoon rays cast her flawless skin in gold and vivified the blue slivers in her irises. With her pupils constricted by the sun, bright color took up the whole of her smiling eyes. Fascinating layers of pigment that loosened Strong Bear's jaw as effectively as they had at first glimpse. He could spend a day exploring their patterns—if he weren't distracted by other equally scintillating features.

Arranged in a complex braid, her hair wound about her head like a crown, practically demanding to be torn down and stroked. Or dug into and gripped while he worshipped her mouth. His sight hopped to that spot and stuck. Berry stain made its rosy hue deeper, more tempting than usual.

If he made it through the ceremony without jumping to the end, it would be thanks only to the thirty-some witnesses surrounding them in a ring. As well as the small feet standing on his, the chubby fingers gripping his leggings, and the wide-open face tipped back for a unique view of the proceedings.

To Strong Bear's right, Marcus Buck was speaking, the Sacred Writings held before him, imparting marital wisdom that Strong Bear really should be absorbing. Instead, all he heard was Flint's occasional whispers of *when?* and *now?* and Pretty Wolf's nosey sounds as she tried to contain humor. All he could see was the purse of her plump mouth and the love and life making her countenance shine.

Finding Pretty Wolf

Stunning didn't begin to describe the woman, and that without dipping below the collar. Best he not go there. Yet. He couldn't afford an incapacitated brain, seeing he'd need it momentarily to speak his vows.

The short of it was that no woman in their company could approach Pretty Wolf's radiance, and he'd challenge any who contradicted the fact.

Masculine pride and a brutish internal *mine* created a stew in his chest that puffed it fat.

A sharp tug on his legging. "When, Bear, when?" Flint's whisper-shout released the plug on Pretty Wolf's snort.

She covered it with a blurted, "Soon," but too late, for snickers were erupting from their audience, and Buck's English monologue was cut off for his own cough-laugh.

"Patience, my life," Noonday crooned, wagging a quieting hand down at the boy. She stood at Strong Bear's opposite side, facing Buck, the red binding cord laid reverently over her open palm.

"That must be my cue." Crinkles fanned out from Buck's eyes as he chuckled. The holy book gave a snappy report as it closed. He gripped it under his arm while he added his hands to their set and prayed Jesus's blessing over their union. When he'd finished, Noonday was swift to step up, Winter Hawk also breaking out from the onlookers.

Formalities with Rabbit Clan had been completed days ago, but by special request, Winter Hawk stood in as representative, approving of the binding with his presence. He caught Strong Bear's eye and pointed over his own shoulder. At his love-hopeful, the maiden Plump Dove. Grinning, he contorted half his face in a wink. On an inward wince, Strong Bear resigned himself to adding the young warrior to Pretty Wolf's winking lessons. Outwardly, he waggled approving eyebrows.

Flint popped out from between his and Pretty Wolf's legs and showed Noonday his grabby fingers. "I ready!"

"Ehi. So you are." The matron giggled, utterly, helplessly charmed. "Tut, but where should you be?"

"Stand where I showed you, little scout," Pretty Wolf instructed. They waited while Flint wiggled into position—where Buck had been. "There, ehi. Just so. Listen carefully, now, to the oaths we make, your father and I." The last bit came out with glimmering affection directed at Strong Bear, earning her an overtly heated look.

Fortunately, all attention was on Flint, for in a flash, he'd donned his soberest mien of concentration. Which also happened to be the face he used in the privy: brow low and wrinkled, mouth crushed into a frown.

Strong Bear cleared his throat to mask a chortle. At an admonishing squeeze to his fingers, he cut his gaze to Pretty Wolf, but her flushed cheeks gave away her own battle. He let a grin abscond with him. Terrible influence that he was, he dragged Pretty Wolf right along with him. She proved to be a willing follower, though, and dazzled him with those purple-red lips in a knee-weakening smile.

Noonday was speaking, binding their joined hands with Flint's eager, albeit clumsy help. But all Strong Bear heard was the ker-thud of his stumbling heart and its chant of *mine, mine, mine*. All he could see was his beautiful Wolf and a lifetime of joys stretching before them.

It was her melodic voice that snapped him back to the ceremony. "To you, Strong Bear of Rabbit, Kit of my soul, slave of my heart, do I bind my loyalty, my body, and my days. Offering each to you without reserve, vowing always to love and cherish you, to feed and clothe you, to provide you a hearth and a couch and every comfort therein." One corner of her lips tweaked up, and he could almost feel the approaching tread of *later*.

"With you," she continued, reverential once more, the soul of her expressed in every word, "will I walk Path Maker's chosen trail, both in This World and in the next. Worshiping with you, crying with you, rejoicing with you. Always in love and balance before Creator. Always fearless as the Wolf, wholly dedicated to our pack of three."

Her face blurred and washed away, and cold tracked down over Strong Bear's jaw. Emotion enflamed his throat, and he clung to her fiercely as he gave a harsh swallow. Then another. Despite his efforts, air whistled through his constricted vocal cords as he drew it in then out for a rasped, "To you, Pretty Wolf of clan Wolf, pucase of my heart, miccohokti of my couch…"

He paused to wait out the crowd's hoots, to appreciate her adorable flush, and to gather much needed composure. Her palms were growing damp, but her eyes, like his, were already flooded and overflowing. Love poured through him, and he decided that as touching and monumental and long-awaited as this ceremony was, the time had come to end it.

"To you, Wolf," he resumed, stronger, "do I bind my loyalty, my body, and my days. Offering each to you without reserve, vowing always to love and cherish you, to provide shelter and protect you, and to give you children. For them and for you, I vow to be as strong as the bear, always standing tall and roaring at adversity. May we walk always in rightness before Creator Jesus and always to—"

"—gether," she finished with him, doing him in.

Careless of their witnesses, he flung off the binding cord and snatched Pretty Wolf about the ribs and off her feet. Crushing her to him, he stole her narrowly opened lips and stamped his love across them.

She squealed shock into his mouth but clawed at his hair to hold him in place.

Howls and cheers and applause swarmed his ears, then faded away while he gentled his caresses and let himself enjoy the taste of her. In the far-off distance, Flint shrilled a piercing cry, and in a cloudy corner of Strong Bear's mind, he registered his failure to embarrass the boy.

No, the pesky thing was squeaking, "More, more!" Then climbing. Like a squirrel. Straight up Strong Bear's body.

Heedless of the leach on his back, Strong Bear dipped and gathered his wife into a cradle hold. Since he refused to lose possession of her mouth, he walked bent and awkward, the crowd parting and guiding him along.

His legs moved, and suddenly, the lodge was before them. Someone released the door flap. Another plucked the protesting passenger off his back. The third gave him a playful shove to the rump.

Not that he needed it—he was already well on his way to the candle-lit couch. Darkness descended, and the noise muffled out. His mind blanked, and somehow, they became sprawled on the couch, her slight form lying soft beneath him.

"Is it later yet?" she gasped on a break for breath.

"If you ask me," Strong Bear said into the curve of her warm neck, "from here out, it is always *later*." Her responding laughter was a husky sound that wrenched a groan out of him. Frightened of his own desire, he strove to lighten the mood. "But don't be afraid, Wolf. My building skills have improved since Alabama Town. The couch will hold."

"Afraid," she scoffed as she drew him up two-handed by the jaw and slid into a cocky smile. "I am fearless." Gaze going tender, she skimmed her berry-kissed lips across his forehead. "And found." A second sweet touch to the crook of his nose. "And yours."

Warmth suffused Strong Bear, and he shuddered.

Mine.

She was his. He was hers.

And Flint was theirs, the child of her body and of his heart.
Muscogee country was their flesh, the Coosa their blood.
And Path Maker…
He was their salvation. Their faithful Word. And the prayer of thanks in Strong Bear's spirit as he delved fingers into Pretty's Wolf's crowning braid, tipped her head, and claimed his promise.

The End

Meet Totka and his Copper Woman in
Beneath the Blackberry Moon

April W Gardner

APRIL W GARDNER is an award-winning author who proudly waves an indie flag. Her great passion is historical romance with themes of Native American and Southeastern U.S. culture. Copyeditor, military wife, and mother of two, she lives in Texas. In no particular order, April dreams of owning a horse, learning a third language, and visiting all the national parks.

Enjoy these other books by April

NATIVE AMERICAN HISTORICAL ROMANCE

Beneath the Blackberry Moon:
The Red Feather
The Sacred Writings
The Ebony Cloak
The Untold Stories (supplemental reading, e-book only)
Drawn by the Frost Moon:
Bitter Eyes No More
Love the War Woman
Finding Pretty Wolf

STAND-ALONE HISTORICAL ROMANCE

Beautiful in His Sight

CO-AUTHORED

Better than Fiction (women's fic/historical rom)

WRITER RESOURCE

Body Beats to Build On

Facebook: AprilGardnerBooks
Website: AprilGardner.com
Email: aprilgardnerwrites@gmail.com

Author's Notes

A heartfelt *maddo* to you, my darling reader, for your patience as you waited for the last in this series. Maybe I'm an odd duck, but a scene needs to live and breathe inside me before I can write the first word. And for the longest time, Pretty Wolf planted her bare feet and refused to come to me.

Part of the trouble can be blamed on the difficulty in braiding together three plots (books 4-6 of the series) without messing up the timeline. But most of it was probably my reluctance to write Miss Francis's story. After I'd finished researching her life, I was literally sick to my stomach. For days, I lived in a surreal sort of grief. My heart broke for the Native girl with so much resilience and bravery that her name reached Congress.

Several times, I came close to throwing in the towel, unsure how I'd ever write a love story around so much grief. In the end (more than a year later!), I got over myself and buckled down to figure it out. This woman's story *had* to be told.

Pretty Wolf and her fictional plot were inspired by the life and heroism of Milly Francis (1802-1848) and by the events of the First Seminole War (1816-1819). Here are historical characters and events as they lived and happened in 1817-1818…

Milly Francis
According to all who knew her and wrote of her, the real Milly was every bit as beautiful as depicted here. She is described as "exquisitely handsome" and "most beautiful." Lithe and athletic, she excelled at horsemanship and was able to leap onto a horse from flat on the ground. Ambrister (our Bellamy) was known to go riding with her and claimed her favorite gait was a gallop. The Spanish called her "princess," and after saving McCrimmon (our Hambly) from a blood-vengeance killing, she became known among Americans as the Creek Pocahontas.

A couple of author liberties I have to confess: Milly enjoyed a fond friendship and betrothal with Robert Ambrister, but Strong Bear was my invention. When her father was captured, it wasn't Milly who rowed out to the ship but her sister Polly. It isn't known whether Josiah Francis was at the Battle of Horseshoe Bend (Horse's Flat Foot). The experience there was inspired by another chief named Menawa who was wounded by seven balls but escaped by crawling to the river, finding a canoe, and escaping to lead his people through the Creek Trail of Tears and beyond.

William Hambly

Hambly's character is a merging of two historical figures. The first is the actual Hambly, whose influence on the war is accurately portrayed in *Love the War Woman* and *Bitter Eyes No More*. Also in line with history, Hambly was taken captive during the raid on his property and hauled off to Wakulla, but once there, he was ransomed by Captain Luengo and taken to Fort San Marcos for protection. The merging happens with the second figure, a Georgia militiaman named Duncan McCrimmon.

Duncan McCrimmon

Two of Josiah Francis's warriors captured McCrimmon near the construction site of Fort Gadsden and brought him back to Wakulla. It was McCrimmon who Milly rescued after convincing an angry warrior that the youth's death would not bring back his slain sisters. Milly took McCrimmon to Fort San Marcos for safety. While there, a British vessel appeared at the mouth of the bay. Hoping to find sympathy with the British, he and Hambly asked permission to row out to the ship to inquire about their intentions. To their delight, they discovered, the occupants were not British but their own countrymen. Both men were on board when Josiah Francis followed shortly after and got himself captured.

Josiah Francis

Francis's history as described by Pretty Wolf is accurate to historical record, including his temporary blindness and his habit of communing with Water Spirit. There is also an account of Francis literally scribbling a missive to a British contact and claiming the spirits taught him to write.

Francis was captured and hung as described, without trial and with his daughter as witness. When he realized he was to be hung, he said, "What! Like a dog? Too much. Shoot me, shoot me. I will die willingly if you let me see General Jackson." But Jackson was in his encampment and refused to dignify Francis's death with his presence. It's recorded that when they tied his hands for the hanging, a knife fell out of his coat sleeve. He confessed on the spot that he'd intended to kill Jackson if he'd shown up. Enemies to the bitter end.

Robert Ambrister
Robert Ambrister is the real name of the English trader who courted Milly. He "loved her for her beauty and virtue." By his own admission, he touched her only once since he was "never permitted to put his hands on her," a comment that inspired the Rule. Like our Iron Wood, he also taken prisoner, tried without a lawyer, and sentenced to corporeal punishment. General Jackson overturned it and ordered execution. He justified it by stating that corporeal punish had been banned. In the manner portrayed in this book, Milly stumbled upon the firing squad as they were preparing to shoot. Based on Ambrister's reaction to her appearance, some witnesses believed he could see her through the blindfold.

Forced March
In time, Francis's people were forced north back to their old country, taking only what they could carry on their backs. Milly (admired among the soldiers for saving one of their own) and her family stayed on at Fort Gadsden for six months. It's hard to imagine they would want to stay, but the commander provided their food and shelter. Desperate times, desperate measures, and all that.

During those months, McCrimmon returned from leave and proposed to Milly. She turned him down, claiming she'd acted in the name of mercy not to win a husband. Before he left, he gave her a "sum of money" from the people of Milledgeville in gratitude for saving one of their citizens.

The Next Ten Years
Milly's fame spread across the country and began changing opinions about Natives and their "savagery." Soon, girls were being named Milly Francis in her honor. Not long after re-establishing themselves in Creek country, Milly married a Muscogee man named Cochar and had eight children with him.

1836 and Beyond
The last ten years of Milly's life contained little more than misery. In that time, she and her husband suffered the Second Seminole War in which he died

fighting on the side of the Americans, the Creek Trail of Tears, and deep poverty in Indian Territory. I'll spare you the sad details (see links below if you want more) and end on a slightly happier note.

Governmental Recognition
Colonel Ethan Hitchcock came across Milly in 1842 when he was in her area, investigating fraud. Led by curiosity about the famed Milly Francis, he went to her home and asked for an interview. She graciously told her story, which he recorded and took to Congress. There, he appealed on her behalf, describing both her heroism and her destitute state. She was awarded $96 per year and a medal cast in her honor. Because she was a civilian, you won't find her on any official lists, but the fact remains Milly Francis became the first person in U.S. history to receive a Congressional Medal of Honor.

Unfortunately, the stipend and the medal arrived too late to improve her health or extend her life. Milly died two months after receiving the money. Her only living son took subsequent payments on her behalf, and her descendants rightly hold dear both her story and her medal.

For those who want to learn more, I've provided a list of links to webpages that give short bios on Milly's life, including the years I skipped. For a comprehensive lesson, Dale Cox's *Milly Francis: The Life & Times of the Creek Pocahontas* is the book you'll want to pick up. Excellent read. From these sources, you'll be able to pick out the fiction and appreciate the details that are true to Milly's life.

Now, for my short list of trivia:

--Robert Maxwell Bellamy (Iron Wood) is based on the figure Robert Ambrister, also a former member of the Royal Navy who traded with the Red Sticks from a post on the Wakulla River.

--Polly and Josiah Francis had three children: Polly, Milly, and a son named Earle who went to England with his father and stayed to receive an education. It's unknown to me what became of the son. I named my Polly after Milly's mother and sister because my series already has a Milly in *The Ebony Cloak*.

--My talented mother sewed the culturally accurate Muscogee blouse worn by Mariah Henry, my gorgeous cover model. My mom is uh-mazing! As is

Mariah, who happens to be the sister of my sister's husband. :-)

--It is believed the Native woman on the Florida seal/flag is Milly Francis.

Thank you for joining Strong Bear as he finds his Wolf, and Pretty Wolf as she finds her still waters. All praise to Path Maker who always opens the way before me. To be notified of future releases, follow me on Facebook or sign up to my newsletter.

Links:
Alabama Women's Hall of Fame:
http://www.awhf.org/Francis.html
Explore Southern History1:
https://www.exploresouthernhistory.com/millyfrancis.html
Explore Southern History2:
https://www.exploresouthernhistory.com/millyfrancis2.html
Exploring Florida:
https://fcit.usf.edu/florida/photos/military/marcap/marcap18.HTM

April W. Gardner
www.aprilgardner.com

*quotes taken from the eyewitness account of Dr. J.B. Rogers.

Acknowledgements

Write the unexpected. My author goal for 2020.

What I didn't anticipate was for the unexpected to invade my entire life. Mine and everyone else's. The pandemic came on like a speeding semi, and few of us can say we weren't plowed over like the proverbial deer in the headlights.

Quarantine, my son's high school graduation, my husband's retirement from the USAF, introduction to civilian life, returning to college for my degree. It's been a big year all around, and in the middle of it, I've been pecking out the most complex book I've written to date.

Finding Pretty Wolf would still be a nebulous thought in my head if not for a list of very special people.

My writing buddies at CWG were at the frontline of edits until COVID got pushy. Thanks, guys, for your sweet encouragement. I miss you so much!

To my critique partners, Tanya, Rebekah, and Michelle, you are absolutely indispensable. You each contribute something unique, and what you troopers you are, reading these massive books, helping me keep my world and characters straight, and sorting through my wordiness. If there is a crown in heaven for saintly crit partners, you've each earned one! You're all so dear to me.

Michelle, this is the tenth book of mine you've critiqued, and I can honestly say you've never given more. More time, more guidance, more patience, more loving slaps on the wrist and uplifting hurrahs. You read every scene at least three times, getting down in the weeds with me in each one. From word 1 to word 169,936, you were at my side, standing so close that this book feels half yours. There's no one else I'd rather share it with. I love you, girlie.

Beta readers Karen and Therese, you were both johnny on the spot there at the end, and your feedback was just the thing. Thank you both for your patience during the interrogations. Hehe. :-)

Thanks, Mom, for "callousing your needle fingers loving" me. The Muscogee blouse is utter perfection. And Mariah, thank you for the loan of your lovely face. You make a beautiful Pretty Wolf. I appreciated your flexibility and patience.

As always, I'm eager to thank Ghost for his endless Native American and Muscogee knowledge, as well as Edna for her friendship and selfless service. Over the years, you've both faithfully been there for me, and as this series comes to a close, I thank Path Maker yet again for putting you in my life, and for the opportunity He's given me to know you both. Much love and gratitude.

And to Path Maker… My cup runneth over.

Because of Him,

April W Gardner

Glossary

A'ho: commonly used Native American term that roughly means "may it be so" or "blessed be."

Assee: holly (yaupon) leaf tea popular among Southeastern tribes (Muskogee language). It was used recreationally, as their version of black tea or coffee, as well as ceremonially. Also called "black drink" by settlers for its dark color, or "white drink" by the Creeks for its purgative qualities when combined with other herbs for ceremonies.

Beloved Men: old war leaders retired from battle but venerated in council.

Blood Vengeance: among the topmost legal principles of Southeastern Indians of the time. If a person was killed, it was the responsibility of his male clansmen, under guidance of the clan mothers, to retaliate in equal manner. The purpose being to restore balance in the clans.

Bluecoat: suletawa in the United States Army. So named because of their blue wool coatees. For this era, my creation.

Breechcloth: a long rectangular piece of animal hide or cloth that was brought up between the legs and under a belt at the
waist. The ends hung like a flap over the belt in front and behind. Worn as outerwear by men and sometimes as underwear by women.

Che-lo-kee: extinct spelling of Cherokee.

Clan: a category of people who believed themselves to be blood relatives, even if untraceable. Clan permission, authority, and protection were often called upon. The blood law fell on clan shoulders. Clan structure and responsibilities extended across the confederacy so that a member of Deer Clan would expect to be received as a family in any Deer Clan home in any town. Clans were associated with particular animals and natural phenomenon, the care of which they were often responsible. Deer Clan elders, for example, would monitor proper hunting in proper season.

Corn Woman: the being who, according to Muscogee mythology, brought corn to the Creeks. When she scratched one thigh, corn would pour down. The other thigh produced beans.

Couch: used for sitting and sleeping. Couches were arranged along the wall, raised two-three feet off the ground, made of saplings and cane, and covered with split-cane mats and animal skins.

Creek Confederacy: formed by survivors of the devastation wrought by 16th-century Spanish expeditions. The Muscogee were the strongest tribe at the time, and over the course of one hundred plus years, accepted refugee tribes under the umbrella of their protection. At its peak, it was so mighty George Washington treated the confederacy on a level of respect equal to that of France and Britain. The Creek War of 1813-14 began its decline.

Darkening Land: the spirit world; where a soul goes after death; located in the west. Also called Spirit Land, or the Haven of Souls.

Defiance: the group of Red Stick who would not sign Andrew Jackson's treaty at the end of the Creek War but fled to the Floridas for refuge. My creation.

Earth Spirit: female; one of the four law-giving elements. Takes forms such as soil, rock, and Corn Woman who is the embodiment of the spirit and from whose body corn originated. Also called Earth Mother.

Ehi: yes (Muskogee language, pronounced eh-hee)

Emena: amen (Muskogee language)

Fire Spirit: male; assistant to the Sun Spirit.

Four-day Journey: the number of days it was believed to take for a soul to journey to the darkening land.

Four-legged, a: Native American term for any animal with four legs.

Frost Moon Dance: a dance led by four hunters who offer portions of a hunt to the sacred fire in order to bless the upcoming hunting season.

Ghost: according to Muscogee tradition, a person's life spirit. There were two aspects of spiritual beings, the soul and the ghost. The ghost resided in the gut. At death, the soul left the body on a four-day journey into the West, but the ghost stayed near the body. If the body was not properly handled and buried, the ghost could afflict those who come into contact with it. To protect their kind, warriors returning from battle went through ceremonies to rid their bodies of clinging ghosts.

Go to Water: a sunrise ceremony done all year no matter the weather. Its purpose was to renew a birth connection to Mother Earth and to cleanse the spirit in her lifeblood (water).

Great Warrior: the warrior selected led the town in war. He arranged ball games with Great Warriors from other towns and carried out the will of the micco.

Healing Song: a formula chanted or sung over a patient with the intent of engaging his spirit, restoring the correct flow of energy, and returning him to full health.

Horse's Flat Foot: the Muscogee's term for the Battle of Horseshoe Bend (Jan. 8, 1815)

Knower: an individual who "lives between the worlds." He is gifted with spiritual and psychological wisdom and also possessed second sight. A knower could foretell death and interpret dreams, among other things. A knower diagnosed but did not cure illness. Not to be confused with medicine maker.

Kossati: a town of my creation based off of a Muskogean tribe that still exists, the Koasatis. Ancient Koasatis lived in two towns near the location of my fictional Kossati both bearing the name Wetumpka. Big Wetumpka was situated on the site of present-day Wetumpka, Alabama. Koasati Indians were *not* Muscogee but a tribe of the Muskogean linguistic group and part of the confederacy. They were closely related to the Alabama tribe.

Maddo: thank you (Muskogee language, pronounced mah-doh).

Matchcoat: an outer garment consisting of a length of stroud, worn wrapped around the upper body.

Medal Chief: a chief who had received a medal from either Britain or the United States. The medals were worn as a symbol of peace between the nations and as a display of prominence in the tribe.

Medicine: Creeks' equivalent to our terms "magic" or "power." Bad medicine was used by witches. Examples of good medicine were herbal warriors or healing songs. Medicine could also be neither good nor bad. A woman's medicine during menstruation was powerful but not bad, so long as it was properly handled.

Medicine Bundle: small items wrapped in a package and worn by warriors for spiritual protection. Items varied from individual to individual but each held special significance to that warrior.

Medicine Maker: men who were trained in the nature of diseases and healing herbs. Valued for their knowledge, not for any innate power they might have.

Micco: chief (Muskogee language, pronounced mee-koh). There were many levels of micco in both civil and military roles.

Miccohokti: female chief (Muskogee language, pronounced mee-koh-hoke-tee).

Moon Lodge: a place set apart for women, especially for menstruation.

Muscogees: an indigenous people who once dominated the Southeast. They occupied land from the Atlantic coast to central Alabama and were the founders of the Creek Confederacy. Also known as the Creeks.

Muskogee: language spoken by the Creeks and Seminoles.

Nose-cropping: the punishment for adultery. The tip of the nose or the ears (or both) would be cropped off the woman and sometimes, the man too. After, they would be free to be together.

Old Beloved Path: tribal traditions handed down by elders generation after generation.

Old Sharp Knife: the name given to Andrew Jackson by the Muscogees of his day.

Order of Things: natural law that encompasses ecological principles. A way of doing things to promote harmony, show reverence for law-giving elements, and to avoid their displeasure.

Pawa: maternal uncle (Muskogee language, pronounced pah-wah). A pawa oversaw the discipline and training of his sisters' sons. See elder brother. (Muskogee language.)

Red Sticks: 1. one of two social labels available to Creek men (Red Sticks/White Sticks). Red Sticks were known for courage, strength, alertness, physical skills. They held leadership roles in warfare, security, and law enforcement. So called because of the red war club, the symbol of war. **2.** During the Creek War, the term "Red Stick" took on new meaning for the white settlers. For the duration of the war, a Red Stick was a Creek warrior who opposed the Americans; however, many warriors of the White persuasion shared their views and fought alongside them.

Red War Club: symbol of war. Before the musket, it was the preferred hand-to-hand combat weapon. To call men to battle, a red war club was raised in the square.

Roach: a stiff crest of hair running down the middle of the head. Also called a Mohawk.

Sacred Fire: the principle symbol of purity. Sun's representative on earth. Believed to report evil to the Sun who would dispense punishment. Found in each town's square and chokofa.

Sight, a: as far as one could see. Rough equivalent to our mile.

Slave Pole: a pole stationed in the town square to which slaves and captives were tied and often tortured. By the historic period (the story's setting), slave poles were no longer in use. I brought them back into use to serve the story's purpose. However, during the Creek War, suletawa *did* come across Red Stick towns (see Red Sticks definition 2) that featured red poles adorned with scalps.

Sleeps: the marking of days or the passage of time. One sleep equals one day.

Sofkee: a thin gruel made of cornmeal or rice. Cooked with wood-ash lye and often eaten after being left to sour.

Stomp Dance: intertribal celebrations or social events. As with most every Creek event, stomp dances were religious in nature and, through ritual, blended the four law-giving elements in a reverential way.

Tafia: a cheap trade rum, the primary liquor consumed by the Southeastern Indians of the 18th and 19th centuries.

Talwa: a Creek community (Muskogee language, pronounced tahl-wah)

The Floridas: the combination name given the two regions of Florida (West Florida and East Florida) which existed during the setting of this book. In 1813, both were owned by Spain. Also called Las Floridas.

This World: the middle world of the Indian three-world cosmos. The place Indians lived.

Tribal Township: a grouping of independently governed villages that gather periodically for social events or battle.

Under World: the lowest of the Indian three-world cosmos. Existed below the earth and water. Epitomized chaos.

Upper World: the highest of the Indian three-world cosmos. Existed above the sky. Epitomized order.

Warriors' House: the communal lodge where warriors met for council, purification, and to plot warfare.

Water Spirit: female; one of the four law-giving elements. Takes the form of rivers, lakes, rain, mist, streams, and the ocean.

West, Sacred: one of four sacred cardinal directions; associated with the Moon Spirit, souls of the dead, and death.

White Sticks: 1. one of two social labels available to Creek men. White Sticks were known for reasonability, patience, mediation skills, scientific knowledge. Their roles included medicine maker, civil duties, diplomacy, ensuring of peace. **2.** During the Creek War, the term "White Stick" took on new meaning. For the duration of the war a White Stick was a Creek warrior who allied with the Americans; however, many warriors of the Red persuasion shared their views and fought alongside them.

Wind Clan: the most prestigious clan. Specialized in predicting weather.

Wind Spirit: male; one of the four law-giving elements. Also called Master of Breath.

Winter Woman: Native term for an elderly woman, one who is in the final years of her life.

Winters: the span of a year. My creation. The Creek year began in late summer at the Green Corn Festival.

Yahola: war rank (Muskogee language, pronounced yaa-hoo-la). Also a sky deity and the cry given during the black drink ceremony.

Yatika: speaker, orator (Muskogee language, pronounced yah-tee-kah). Every talwa had a yatika who was well-versed in the nuances of the many Muskogean dialects. Typically, a micco did not make public speeches. This job fell to the yatika who knew the micco's mind and used his oratory talents to convey the micco's (and the council's) wishes.

Made in the USA
Monee, IL
24 March 2022